BOND
STREET
BOOKS

DOUBLEDAY
CANADA

CITY ON FIRE

CITY
ON
FIRE

GARTH RISK HALLBERG

BOND
STREET
BOOKS

DOUBLEDAY
CANADA

Bond Street Books and colophon are registered trademarks of Random House of Canada Limited.

This book is a work of fiction. Names, characters, places, events and incidents are either the product of the author's imagination or are used fictitiously. Any resemblance to actual persons, living or dead, is entirely coincidental.

Library and Archives Canada Cataloguing in Publication

Hallberg, Garth Risk, author
City on fire / Garth Risk Hallberg.

Issued in print and electronic formats.
ISBN 978-0-385-68274-9 (bound). ISBN 978-0-385-68275-6 (epub)

I. Title.

PS3608.A445C58 2015   813'.6   C2015-901972-9
C2015-901973-7

Front-of-jacket photograph © Tetra Images / Alamy
Cover design by Chip Kidd
Printed and bound in the USA

Published in Canada by Bond Street Books,
A division of Random House of Canada Limited,
A Penguin Random House Company

www.penguinrandomhouse.ca

10 9 8 7 6 5 4 3 2 1

BOND
STREET
BOOKS | Penguin
                      Random
                      House

For Elise,
who believes

"There is your precious order, that lean, iron lamp, ugly and barren; and there is anarchy, rich, living, reproducing itself—there is anarchy, splendid in green and gold."

"All the same," replied Syme patiently, "just at present you only see the tree by the light of the lamp. I wonder when you would ever see the lamp by the light of the tree."

—G. K. CHESTERTON
The Man Who Was Thursday

CONTENTS

CITY ON FIRE

Prologue

IN NEW YORK, you can get anything delivered. Such, anyway, is the principle I'm operating on. It's the middle of summer, the middle of life. I'm in an otherwise deserted apartment on West Sixteenth Street, listening to the placid hum of the fridge in the next room, and though it contains only a mesozoic half-stick of butter my hosts left behind when they took off for the shore, in forty minutes I can be eating more or less whatever I can imagine wanting. When I was a young man—younger, I should say—you could even order in drugs. Business cards stamped with a 212 number and that lonesome word, *delivery*, or, more usually, some bullshit about therapeutic massage. I can't believe I ever forgot this.

Then again, it's a different city now, or people want different things. The bushes that screened hand-to-hand transactions in Union Square are gone, along with the payphones you'd use to dial your dealer. Yesterday afternoon, when I walked over there for a break, modern dancers were making a slo-mo commotion beneath the revitalized trees. Families sat orderly on blankets, in wine-colored light. I keep seeing this stuff everywhere, public art hard to distinguish from public life, polka-dot cars idling by on Canal, newsstands ribboned like gifts. As if dreams themselves could be laid out like options on the menu of available experience. Oddly, though, what this rationalizing of every last desire tends to do, the muchness of this current city's muchness, is remind you that what you really hunger for is nothing you're going to find *out there*.

What I've personally been hungering for, since I arrived six weeks ago, is for my head to feel a certain way. At the time, I couldn't have put the feeling into words, but now I think it is something like the sense that things might still at any moment change.

I was a native son once—jumper of turnstiles, dumpster diver, crasher on strange roofs downtown—and this feeling was the ground-note of my life. These days, when it comes, it is only in flashes. Still, I've agreed to house-sit this apartment through September, hoping that will be enough. It's shaped like a stackable block from a primitive video game: bedroom and parlor up front, then dining area and master bedroom, the kitchen coming off like a tail. As I wrestle at the dining table with these prefatory remarks, twilight is deepening outside high windows, making the ashtrays and documents heaped before me seem like someone else's.

By far my favorite spot, though, is back past the kitchen and through a side door—a porch, on stilts so high this might as well be Nantucket. Timbers of park-bench green, and below, a carpet of leaves from two spindly gingkos. "Courtyard" is the word I keep wanting to use, though "airshaft" might also work; tall apartment houses wall in the space so no one else can reach it. The white bricks across the way are flaking, and on evenings when I'm ready to give up on my project altogether, I come out instead to watch the light climb and soften as the sun descends another rainless sky. I let my phone tremble in my pocket and watch the shadows of branches reach toward that blue distance across which a contrail, fattening, drifts. The sirens and traffic noises and radios floating over from the avenues are like the memories of sirens and traffic noises and radios. Behind the windows of other apartments, TVs come on, but no one bothers to draw the blinds. And I start to feel once more that the lines that have boxed in my life—between past and present, outside and in—are dissolving. That I may yet myself be delivered.

There's nothing in this courtyard, after all, that wasn't here in 1977; maybe it's not this year but that one, and everything that follows is still to come. Maybe a Molotov cocktail is streaking through the dark, maybe a magazine journalist is racing through a graveyard; maybe the fireworker's daughter remains perched on a snow-covered bench, keeping her lonely vigil. For if the evidence points to anything, it's that there is no one unitary City. Or if there is, it's the sum of thousands of variations, all jockeying for the same spot. This may be wishful thinking, still, I can't help imagining that the points of contact between this place and my own lost city healed incompletely, left the scars I'm feeling for when I send my head up the fire escapes and toward the blue square of freedom beyond. And you out there: Aren't you somehow right here with me? I mean, who doesn't still dream of a world other than this one? Who among us—if it means letting go of the insanity, the mystery, the totally useless beauty of the million once-possible New Yorks—is ready even now to give up hope?

BOOK I

WE HAVE MET THE ENEMY, AND HE IS US

[DECEMBER 1976–JANUARY 1977]

Life in the hive puckered up my night;
the kiss of death, the embrace of life.

—TELEVISION
"Marquee Moon"

1

A CHRISTMAS TREE was coming up Eleventh Avenue. Or rather, was trying to come; having tangled itself in a shopping cart someone had abandoned in the crosswalk, it shuddered and bristled and heaved, on the verge of bursting into flame. Or so it seemed to Mercer Goodman as he struggled to salvage the tree's crown from the battered mesh of the cart. Everything these days was on the verge. Across the street, char-marks marred the loading dock where local bedlamites built fires at night. The hookers who sunned themselves there by day were watching now through dimestore shades, and for a second Mercer was acutely aware of how he must appear: a corduroyed and bespectacled brother doing his best to backpedal, while at the far end of the tree, a bedheaded whiteboy in a motorcycle jacket tried to yank the trunk forward and to hell with the shopping cart. Then the signal switched from *DON'T WALK* to *WALK*, and miraculously, through some combination of push-me and pull-you, they were free again.

"I know you're annoyed," Mercer said, "but could you try not to flounce?"

"Was I flouncing?" William asked.

"You're drawing stares."

As friends or even neighbors, they were an unlikely pair, which may have been why the man who ran the Boy Scout tree lot by the

Lincoln Tunnel on-ramp had been so hesitant to touch their cash. It was also why Mercer could never have invited William home to meet his family—and thus why they were having to celebrate Christmas on their own. You knew it just to look at them, the doughy brown bourgeois, the wiry pale punk: What could possibly have yoked these two together, besides the occult power of sex?

It was William who'd chosen the biggest tree left on the lot. Mercer had urged him to consider the already severe overcrowding of the apartment, not to mention the half-dozen blocks between here and there, but this was William's way of punishing him for wanting a tree in the first place. He'd peeled two tens from the roll he kept in his pocket and announced sardonically, and loud enough for the tree guy to hear, *I'll take bottom*. Now, between fogged breaths, he added, "You know . . . Jesus would've cast us both into the fiery pit. That's in . . . Leviticus somewhere, I think. I don't see the point of a Messiah who sends you to hell." Wrong Testament, Mercer might have objected, besides which we haven't sinned together in weeks, but it was imperative not to take the bait. The Scoutmaster was only a hundred yards back, the end of a trail of needles.

Gradually, the blocks depopulated. Hell's Kitchen at this hour was mostly rubbled lots and burnt-out auto chassis and the occasional drifting squeegee man. It was like a bomb had gone off, leaving only outcasts, which must have been the neighborhood's major selling point for William Hamilton-Sweeney, circa the late '60s. Actually, a bomb *had* gone off, a few years before Mercer moved in. A group with one of those gnarly acronyms he could never remember had blown up a truck outside the last working factory, making way for more rattletrap lofts. Their own building, in a previous life, had manufactured Knickerbocker-brand breathmints. In some ways, little had changed: the conversion from commercial to residential had been slapdash, probably illegal, and had left a powdered industrial residue impacted between the floorboards. No matter how you scrubbed, a hint of cloying peppermint remained.

The freight elevator being broken again, or still, it took half an hour to get the tree up five flights of stairs. Sap got all over William's jacket. His canvases had migrated to his studio up in the Bronx, but somehow the only space for the tree was in front of the living area's window, where its branches blocked the sun. Mercer, anticipating this, had laid in provisions to cheer things up: lights to tack to the wall, a tree skirt, a carton of nonalcoholic eggnog. He set them out on the counter, but William just sulked on the futon, eating gumdrops from a bowl, with his cat, Eartha K., perched smugly on his chest. "At least you didn't buy a crèche," he said. It stung in part because Mercer was at that moment rooting under the sink for the wiseman figurines Mama had enclosed with her care package.

What he found there instead was the mail pile, which he could have sworn he'd left sitting out in plain view on the radiator this morning. Usually, Mercer wouldn't have stood for it—he couldn't walk by one of Eartha's furballs without reaching for the dustpan— but a certain unopened envelope had been festering there for a week among the second and third notices from the Americard Family of Credit Cards, redundancy *sic*, and he'd hoped today might be the day William finally awoke to its presence. He reshuffled the pile again so that the envelope was on top. He dropped it back onto the radiator. But his lover was already getting up to splash 'nog over the clump of green gumdrops, like some futuristic cereal product. "Breakfast of champions," he said.

THE THING WAS, William had a kind of genius for not noticing what he didn't want to notice. Another handy example: today, Christmas Eve 1976, marked the eighteen-month anniversary of Mercer's arrival in New York from the little town of Altana, Georgia. *Oh, I know Atlanta*, people used to assure him, with cheery condescension. *No*, he would correct them—*Al*-tan-*a*—but eventually he stopped bothering. Simplicity was easier than precision. As far as anyone back home knew, he'd gone north to teach sophomore English at the Wenceslas-Mockingbird School for Girls in Greenwich Village. Underneath that, of course, there'd been his searing ambition to write the Great American Novel (still searing now, though for different reasons). And underneath *that* . . . well, the simplest way to put it would have been that he'd met someone.

Love, as Mercer had heretofore understood it, involved huge gravitational fields of duty and disapproval bearing down on the parties involved, turning even small-talk into a ragged struggle for breath. Now here was this person who might not return his calls for weeks without feeling the slightest need to apologize. A Caucasian who waltzed around 125th Street as if he owned the place. A thirty-three-year-old who still slept until three p.m., even after they started living together. William's commitment to doing exactly what he wanted, when he wanted, had at first been a revelation. It was possible, suddenly, to separate love from being *beholden*.

More recently, though, it had started to seem that the price of liberation was a refusal to look back. William would talk in only the vaguest terms about his life pre-Mercer: the period of heroin dependency in the early '70s that had left him with his insatiable sweet tooth; the stacks of paintings he refused to show either to Mercer or to anyone who might have bought them; the imploded rock band whose name, Ex Post Facto, he'd annealed with a wire hanger into the back of the motorcycle jacket. And his family? Total silence. For a long time, Mercer hadn't even put together that William was one of *those* Hamilton-Sweeneys, which was sort of like meeting Frank Tecumseh Sherman and not thinking to inquire about any kinship to the General. William still froze whenever anyone mentioned the Hamilton-Sweeney Company in his presence, as though he'd just found a fingernail in his soup and was trying to remove it without alarming his tablemates. Mercer told himself his feelings wouldn't have changed one jot if William had been a Doe or a Dinkelfelder. Still, it was hard not to be curious.

And that was before the Lower School's Interfaith Holiday Pageant earlier this month, which the Dean of Students had stopped just short of requiring all faculty to attend. Forty minutes in, Mercer had been trying to distract himself with the program's endless cast list when a name had leapt out at him. He ran a finger over the type in the weak auditorium light: Cate Hamilton-Sweeney Lamplighter (Children's Chorus). He generally kept to the Upper School—at twenty-four, he was its youngest teacher, and the only Afro-American to boot, and the littler kids seemed to view him as some kind of well-dressed janitor—but after the curtain calls, he sought out a colleague who taught in the kindergarten. She indicated a cluster of ecumenical sprites near the stage door. This "Cate" was apparently one of them. I.e., one of her own. "And do you happen to know if there's a William in her family?"

"Her brother Will, you mean? He's in fifth or sixth grade, I think, at a school uptown. It's coed, I don't know why they don't send Cate, too." The colleague seemed to catch herself. "Why do you ask?"

"Oh, no reason," he said, turning to go. It was just as he'd thought: a mistake, a coincidence, one he was already doing his best to forget.

But was it Faulkner who said that the past was not even past? Last week, on the last day of the semester, after the last dilatory scholarship girl had handed in the final final exam, a nervous-looking white woman had materialized at the door of his classroom. She had that comely young-mother thing—her skirt probably cost more than Mercer's entire wardrobe—but it was more than that that made her look familiar, though he couldn't quite pin it down. "May I help you?"

She checked the paper she was carrying against his name on the door. "Mr. Goodman?"

"That's me." Or *That's I*? Hard to say. He folded his hands on the desk and tried to look non-threatening, as was his habit when dealing with mothers.

"I don't know how to do this tactfully. Cate Lamplighter's my daughter. Her teacher mentioned you had some questions after the pageant last week?"

"Oh, geez." He blushed. "That was a mix-up. But I apologize for any . . ." Then he saw it: the sharp chin, the startled blue eyes. She could have been a female William, except that her hair was auburn instead of black, and styled in a simple bob. And of course the smart attire.

"You were asking about Cate's uncle, I think, whom we named her brother after. Not that he'd know that, not ever having met him. My brother, I mean. William Hamilton-Sweeney." The hand she held out, in contrast to her voice, was steady. "I'm Regan."

Careful, Mercer thought. Here at Mockingbird, a Y chromosome was already a liability, and no matter what they'd said when they hired him, being black was, too. Steering between the Scylla of too-much and the Charybdis of not-enough, he'd worked hard to project a retiring asexuality. As far as his coworkers knew, he lived with only his books for company. Still, he relished her name in his mouth. "Regan."

"Can I ask what your interest in my brother is? He doesn't owe you money or anything, does he?"

"Goodness, no. Nothing like that. He's a . . . friend. I just didn't realize he had a sister."

"We don't exactly talk. We haven't for years. In fact, I have no idea how to find him. I hate to impose, but maybe I could leave this with you?" She approached to place something on the desk, and as she retreated a little pain rippled through him. Out of the great silent sea that was William's past, a mast had appeared, only to tack back toward the horizon.

Wait, he thought. "I was actually on my way to the lounge for coffee. Can I get you some?"

Disquiet lingered on her face, or sadness, abstract but pervasive. She was really quite striking, if a bit on the thin side. Most adults when they were sad seemed to fold inward and age and become unattractive; perhaps it was some kind of adaptive thing, to gradually breed a master race of emotionally impervious hominids, but if so, the gene had skipped these Hamilton-Sweeneys. "I can't," she said finally. "I've got to get my kids to their dad's." She indicated the envelope. "If you could just, if you see William before New Year's, give him that, and tell him . . . tell him I need him there this year."

"Need him where? Sorry. None of my business, obviously."

"It's been a pleasure meeting you, Mr. Goodman." She paused at the door. "And don't worry about the circumstances. I'm just happy to know he's got someone."

Before he had time to ask her what she was implying, she had withdrawn. He stole out into the hall to watch her go, her heels clicking through the squares of light on the tile. Then he looked down at the sealed envelope in his hands. There was no postmark, just a patch of corrective fluid where the address should have been and the hasty calligraphy that said *William Hamilton-Sweeney III*. He hadn't known there was a Roman numeral.

HE AWOKE CHRISTMAS MORNING feeling guilty. More sleep might have helped, but years of Pavlovian ritual had made this impossible. Mama used to come into their bedrooms when it was still dark and toss stockings engorged with Florida oranges and gewgaws from the five-and-dime onto the feet of his and C.L.'s beds—and then pretend to be surprised when her sons woke up. Now that he was theoretically a grown-up, there were no stockings, and he lay beside his snoring lover for what felt like the longest time, watching light advance across the drywall. William had nailed it up hastily to carve a sleeping nook out of the undivided loft space, and had never gotten around to painting it. Besides the mattress, the only concessions to domesticity were an unfinished self-portrait and a full-length mirror, turned sideways to parallel the bed. Embarrassingly, he sometimes caught William looking at the mirror when they were *in flagrante*, but it was one of those things Mercer knew he wasn't supposed to ask about. Why couldn't he just respect these pockets of reticence? Instead, they pulled him closer and closer, until in order to protect William's secrets he was, perforce, keeping secrets of his own.

But surely the point of Christmas was to no more turn aside and brood. The temperature had been dropping steadily, and the sturdiest outerwear William owned was the Ex Post Facto jacket, and so Mercer had decided to give him a parka, an envelope of warmth that would surround him wherever he went. He'd saved fifty dollars out of each of his last five paychecks, and had gone into Bloomingdale's still wearing what William called his teaching costume—necktie, blazer, elbow patches—but it seemed to make no difference in persuading salespeople that he was a legitimate customer. Indeed, a store detective with a rodential little moustache had trailed him from outerwear to menswear to formalwear. But perhaps this was providence; otherwise Mercer might not have discovered the chesterfield coat. It was gorgeous, tawny, as though spun from the fine fur of kittens. Four buttons and three interior pockets, for brushes and pens and sketchpads. Its collar and belt and body were three different shades of shearling wool. It was flamboyant enough that William might wear it, and hellaciously warm. It was also well beyond Mercer's means, but a kind of enraptured rebellion or rebellious rapture carried him to the register, and thence to the gift-wrapping station, where they swaddled it in paper stamped with swarms of golden *B*'s. For a week and a half now, it had been hiding underneath the futon. Unable to wait any longer, Mercer staged a coughing fit, and soon enough William was up.

After brewing the coffee and plugging in the tree, Mercer set the box on William's lap.

"Jesus, that's heavy."

Mercer brushed away a dust bunny. "Open it."

He watched William closely as the lid made its little puff of air and the tissue paper crinkled back. "A coat." William tried to muster an exclamation point, but stating the name of the gift, everyone knew, was what you did when you were disappointed.

"Try it on."

"Over my robe?"

"You're going to have to sooner or later."

Only then did William begin to say the right things: that he'd needed a coat, that it was beautiful. He disappeared into the sleeping nook and lingered there an inordinate amount of time. Mercer could almost hear him turning in front of the skewed mirror, trying to decide how he felt. Finally, the beaded curtain parted again. "It's great," he said.

It looked great, at least. With the collar turned up, it flattered William's fine features, the natural aristocracy of his cheekbones. "You like it?"

"The Technicolor dreamcoat." William mimed a series of gestures, patting his pockets, turning for the camera. "It's like wearing a Jacuzzi. But now it's your turn, Merce."

Across the room, drugstore bulbs blinked dimly against the noon light. The tree skirt was bare, save for cat hairs and a few needles; Mercer had opened Mama's present the night before, while on the phone with her, and he knew from the way she'd signed their names on the tag that C.L. and Pop had forgotten or declined to send separate gifts. He'd steeled himself for the likelihood that William hadn't gotten him anything, either, but now William squired forth from the sleeping nook a parcel he had wrapped in newspaper, as though drunkenly. "Be gentle," he said, setting it on the floor.

Had Mercer ever been anything but? A gun-oil smell assaulted him as he removed the paper to reveal a grid of orderly white keys: a typewriter.

"It's electric. I found it in a pawnshop downtown, like new. It's supposed to be much faster."

"You shouldn't have," Mercer said.

"Your other one's such a piece of junk. If it was a horse, you'd shoot it."

No, he *really* shouldn't have. Though Mercer had yet to find the gumption to tell William, his slow progress on his work-in-progress—or rather, lack thereof—had nothing to do with his equipment, at least in any conventional sense. To avoid further dissembling, he put his arms around William. The heat of his body penetrated even through the sumptuous coat. Then William must have caught a glimpse of the oven clock. "Shit. You mind if I turn on the TV?"

"Don't tell me there's a game on. It's a holiday."

"I knew you'd understand."

Mercer tried for a few minutes to sit alongside and watch William's beloved sport, but to him televised football was no more interesting, or even narratively intelligible, than a flea circus, so he got up and went to the kitchenette to do the other stations of the Yuletide cross. While the crowd whooshed and advertisers extolled the virtues of double-bladed razors and Velveeta shells and cheese, Mercer glazed the ham and chopped the sweet potatoes and opened the wine to let it breathe. He didn't drink, himself—he'd seen what it had done to C.L.'s brain—but he'd thought Chianti might help put William in the spirit.

Heat built over the two-burner stove. He went to crank open the window, startling some pigeons that had settled outside on his winter-bare geranium box. Well, cinderblock, really. They fled down the canyons of old factories, now lost in the shadows, now exploding into light. When he looked over at William, the chesterfield was back in its box on the floor beside the futon, and the jumbo bag of gumdrops was nearly empty. He could feel himself turning into his mother.

They sat down at halftime, plates balanced on knees. Mercer had assumed that because there was a gap in the action William might turn the television off, but he didn't even turn it down, or look away. "Yams are terrific," he said. Like reggae music and Amateur Night at the Apollo, soul food was one of William's elective affinities with negritude. "I wish you wouldn't stare at me like that."

"Like what?"

"Like I killed your puppy. I'm sorry if today fell short of whatever was in your head."

Mercer hadn't realized he'd been staring. He shifted his gaze to the tree, already desiccating in its aluminum stand. "It's my first Christmas away from home," he said. "If trying to preserve a few traditions makes me a fantasist, I guess I'm a fantasist."

"Does it ever strike you as revealing that you still refer to it as 'home'?" William dabbed a corner of his mouth with his napkin. His table manners, incongruous, beautiful, should have been an early clue. "We're grown men, you know, Merce. We make our own traditions. Christmas could be twelve nights at the disco. We could eat oysters every day for lunch, if we wanted."

Mercer couldn't tell how much of this was sincere, and how much William was merely caught up in winning the argument. "Honestly, William, oysters?"

"Cards on the table, sweetheart. This is about that envelope you keep trying to shove into my field of vision, isn't it?"

"Well, aren't you going to open it?"

"Why would I? There's nothing inside that's going to make me feel better than I already do. God damn it!"

It took him a second to realize that William was talking to the football game, where some unpleasantness announced the start of the third quarter.

"Do you know what I think? I think you already know what's in it." As Mercer did himself, actually. Or at least he had his suspicions.

He went to pick up the envelope and held it toward the TV; a shadow nested tantalizingly within, like the secret at the heart of an X-ray. "I think it's from your family," he said.

"What I want to know is, how did it get here without a postmark?"

"What I want to know is, why is that such a threat?"

"I can't talk to you when you get like this, Mercer."

"Why am I not allowed to want things?"

"You know damn well that's not what I said."

Now it was Mercer's turn to wonder how much he meant the words coming out of his mouth, and how much he just wanted to win. He could see in the margins the cookware, the shelf of alphabetized books, the tree, all physical accommodations William had made to him, it was true. But what about emotionally? Anyway, he'd said too much now to back down. "Here is what you want: your life stays just the same, while I twist myself around you like a vine."

Pale points appeared on William's cheeks, as they always did when the border between his inner and outer lives was breached. There was a second when he might have come flying across the coffeetable. And there was a second when Mercer might have welcomed it. It might have proven he was more important to William than his self-possession, and from grappling in anger, how easy it would have been to fall into that other, sweeter grappling. Instead, William reached for the new coat. "I'm going out."

"It's Christmas."

"This is another thing we're allowed to do, Mercer. We're allowed to have time alone."

But *Solitas radix malorum est*, Mercer would think later, looking back. The door closed, leaving him alone with the barely touched food. His appetite, too, had deserted him. There was something eschatological about the weak afternoon light, made weaker by the tree and the layer of soot that coated the window, and about the chill blown in through the crack he'd left open. Every time a truck passed, the frayed ends of the wine's wicker sleeve trembled like the needles of some exquisite seismometer. Yes, everything, personally, world-historically, was breaking down. He pretended for a while to distract himself with the flux of jerseys onscreen. Really, though, he'd snuck back into his skull with tiny wrenches to make the kinds of adjustments that would allow him to continue living this way, with a boyfriend who would walk out on you on Christmas Day.

2

LATELY CHARLIE WEISBARGER, age seventeen, had been spending a lot of time on appearances. He wasn't vain, he didn't think, nor did he particularly dig his own, but the prospect of seeing Sam again kept sucking him back toward the mirror. Which was funny: love was supposed to carry you out beyond your own borders, but somehow his love for her—like the music he'd discovered that summer, or the purposeful derangement of his senses—had only ended up casting him back on the shores of himself. It was as if the universe was trying to teach him some lesson. The challenge, he guessed, was to refuse to learn.

He took an album from the stack by the stereo and put a penny on the stylus to keep it from skipping. The first Ex Post Facto LP, from '74. Bonus trivia: released only months before the band's breakup, it had also been the last. As power chords ripped through the speakers, he fetched a round black box from the closet shelf to which he'd banished the getups of his childhood. Dust clung to the lid, like skin on cold soup. Instead of clearing off when he blew on it, it swirled up and got all in his mouth, so he wiped the rest off with the nearest thing to hand, an old batting glove scrunched scrotally against the base of his nightstand.

Though he knew what was inside the box, the sight of Grandpa's black fur hat never failed to send a jolt of lonesomeness right through him, like stumbling on a nest from which birds have flown. The Old

Country Hat, Mom had called it—as in, *David, does he have to wear the Old Country Hat again?* But for Charlie, it would always be the Manhattan Hat, the one Grandpa had worn a couple Decembers ago when they'd ridden into the City, just the two of them. Their cover story was a Rangers game, but what he'd made Charlie swear to keep his trap shut about was that they were going to the Radio City Christmas Spectacular instead. Brusque as hell, the old Bialystoker had been, shoving through the crowds. Honestly, Charlie didn't see why all the cloak-and-dagger: no one was going to believe his grandpa would pay to see those shiksa hoofers anyway. Afterward, for an hour, maybe, they'd stood above the rink at Rockefeller Center, watching people skate. Charlie was underdressed for the cold but knew better than to complain. Finally, Grandpa reached over and opened his knobbly fist. Inside, embalmed in wax paper, was a butterscotch candy Charlie had no idea how he'd come by, like the last heirloom smuggled out of a war zone, more precious for having been hidden.

The truth was, Grandpa was feeling sorry for him. Since the miraculous birth of Charlie's twin brothers, no one was supposed to acknowledge the fact that the older son was being shunted aside, but Grandpa meant to atone—a frankness Charlie appreciated. He'd asked to go to Montreal for Hanukkah this year, but Mom and Grandpa still blamed each other for Dad's dying. So it was like two deaths, almost. All Charlie was left with was the hat.

He was surprised to find now that Grandpa's huge head had been no bigger than his own. He posed in his closet-door mirror, three-quarters, right profile. It was hard to tell how he'd look to Sam, because other than the hat, he was wearing only briefs and a tee-shirt, and also because shifting fogs of allure and disgust seemed to interpose themselves between Charlie and the glass. His long white limbs and the goyish down on his cheeks sparked a hormonal flicker, but then these days so could the rumble of a schoolbus seat, the scent of baby oil, certain provocatively shaped items of produce. And his asthma was a problem. His Clamato-red hair was a problem. He tugged the hat down, filled his birdy chest with air. He shifted his stance to conceal the zit sprouting from his right thigh. (Was it even possible to get a zit on your thigh?) He checked himself against the photo on the LP sleeve: three artless men, skinny like himself, and one scary-looking transvestite. He wasn't sure he could picture the hat on any of them, but no matter; he found it beautiful.

Besides, he had picked it specifically for its violation of the canons of taste. In the broad and average middle of broad and average Long Island, 1976 had been the year of après-ski. The idea was to look like you'd tackled a slalom course on the way to school: acrylic sweaters and knit caps and quilted down jackets with lift-passes clipped to the zippers. These passes, gone a poignant off-season yellow, were the only way Charlie knew the names of the resorts; his tribe, as a rule, did not ski. And Grandpa's hat . . . well, he might as well have gone around in a powdered wig. But that was the point of punk, Sam had taught him. To rebel. To *overturn*. Memories of their illicit summer, those dozen-plus trips to the City before Mom had ruined the whole thing, stirred deliciously inside him, as they had last week when he'd picked up the phone to find Sam on the other end. But how quickly pleasure sank back into the customary slurry of feelings: the mix of nerviness and regret, like something he both was and wasn't ready to let go of was about to be taken from him.

He flipped to side two, in case there was a riff he'd somehow missed or some nuance of phrasing he'd failed to memorize. *Brass Tactics*, the record was called. It was Sam's favorite; she'd been gaga over the singer, the small guy in the leather jacket and Mohawk flashing the middle finger from the sleeve. Now it was Charlie's favorite, too. This fall he'd listened to it over and over again, assenting to it as he'd assented to nothing since *Ziggy Stardust*. *Yes*, he too was lonely. *Yes*, he too had known pain. *Yes*, he had lain on his side on the attic floor the afternoon of Dad's funeral and listened to the hot wind in the trees outside and *Yes*, he had heard the leaves turning brown and had wondered, really, if there was any point to anything at all. *Yes*, he had sat that year with one leg out the attic window and watched his skull burst like a waterballoon on the cracked concrete of the drive, but, *Yes*, he'd held himself back for a reason, and maybe this was the reason. He'd discovered Ex Post Facto too late to see them play live, but now the band had reconstituted itself for a New Year's show, with some guy Sam knew replacing Billy Three-Sticks on vocals, she'd said, and some kind of pyrotechnics planned for the finale. This "some guy" rankled, but hadn't she just admitted to needing *him*— meaning *Charlie*?

Snow was collecting on the windowsill as he made a last pass through his dresser. Shivering was unmanly, and he was determined not to be cold. On the other hand, his long johns made him look sexless, and when Sam unzipped his pants tonight—when they found themselves alone in the moonlit room of his imaginings (the same eventuality for which he'd pocketed an aging Trojan, sized magnum) he didn't want to blow it. He decided, as a compromise, to wear pajama bottoms under his jeans. They'd make the jeans look tighter, like he was the fifth Ramone. He took a long pull on his inhaler, turned off the stereo, and shouldered the bag.

Upstairs, his mother was scrubbing dishes. The twins sat on the curling linoleum near her feet, shuttling a toy back and forth. A Matchbox car, Charlie saw, with an action figure rubber-banded like luggage to the roof. "He sick," Izzy volunteered. Abe made a "Woo, woo" ambulance sound. Charlie scowled. Mom had now been alerted to his presence, and he couldn't imagine deceit wouldn't be written all over him when she turned around. Then he noticed the coil of wire stretching from her head to the wall-mounted phone. "Is that you, honey?" she said. And, into the phone: "He's just come in." He would have asked who she was talking to, except he already knew.

"Yeah, I'm off," he said carefully.

She had pinned the receiver between shoulder and chin. Her arms kept up their ablutions over the sink's steaming water. "Did you need a ride?"

"It's just Mickey's house. It's walkable."

"This snow's supposed to get worse before it gets better."

"Mom, I'm fine."

"Guess we'll see you next year, then."

The joke baffled him for a moment, as it did annually, like the first girl to pinch him on St. Patrick's Day. Even after he got it, a bitter liquid seemed to have flooded his throat. What he really wanted was precisely for her to turn and look and try to stop him. But why? He was just sneaking off for the night, and would be back by dawn, and nothing was going to change, because nothing ever changed.

Outside, free from the complex binding charms of the house, his movements came easier. He retrieved his bike from the side of the garage and hid the overnight bag behind the heating unit. It held a decoy wad of dirty laundry harvested from his bedroom floor. The snow was coming thicker now and had begun to stick to the pavement, a textureless sheet of waxed paper. His tires slicked great black arcs behind him. When he passed under a streetlamp, a monster swelled on the earth ahead: spindly at the bottom, huge of shoulder and mane (his lumpy jacket, his furry hat). He rode on, narrowing his eyes against the daggers of snow.

Downtown Flower Hill, despite the Village Council's best efforts, couldn't quite outrun what it was. By day, it counterfeited a down-at-heel urbanity—there was a florist, a bridal parlor, a not-very-good record shop—but at night, the lit-up storefronts blazed the coordinates of the town's real urgencies. Massage. Tattoos. Gun and Pawn. Outside an empty deli, an animatronic Santa pivoted stiffly in time with "Jingle Bells," its legs chained to a fence. Charlie, unable to feel his hands anymore, stopped and went in to bolt some coffee. It was just hitting him ten minutes later, when he stowed his bike under some bushes at the station. He would really have to remember to get a lock.

He found Sam waiting in a cone of light at the far end of the platform. It had been half a year since he'd seen her, but he could tell from the way she gnawed the thumbnail of her cigarette hand that something was eating her. (Or anyway, he *should've* been able to tell, via their telepathic connection. How many nights since his grounding had he stayed awake talking with her in his head? But when you got right down to it, telepathy, gnosis, and all the other superpowers he'd at various times imagined himself to have did not exist. No one in real life could see through walls. No one (he would think later, after what happened happened) would be able to reverse time's arrow.) Amazingly, she didn't see him slip on the snow as he hurried over. Even when he was practically on top of her, she continued to stare up at the lunar face of the station clock and the white flakes vanishing there. He wanted to put an arm around her, but the angle of their bodies being off, he settled for punching her shoulder—which came out weak, not at all the sign of affection it would have been from hands more practiced than his own, so he turned it into a little dance, punching the air, pretending to have only accidentally hit her. *'Ey! 'O! Let's go!* And finally, she turned to him the face that had been withheld for so long: the burning dark eyes, the upturned nose with its hoop of silver, and the mouth made for the movies, slightly too wide, from which her smoke-coarsened voice—her best thing—now came. "Long time no see."

"Yeah, well. I've been keeping busy."

"I thought you were grounded, Charlie."

"That, too."

She reached for the fur hat. Charlie's cheeks burned as she inspected the self-inflicted hair trauma that had led indirectly to his exile. *You look like a mental patient*, his mother had said. It had grown back, mostly. Meantime, Sam had done a thing to her own hair, chopping it boyishly short and dyeing it from amber to black. She was almost as tall as Charlie, and with a dark blazer hiding her curves, she looked like Patti Smith on the cover of *Horses*—their second-favorite album. Though who knew what she listened to now that she'd gone off to college in the City. Asked about dorm life, she said it was a drag. He offered the hat. "You wanna wear it? It's warm."

"It's only been fifteen minutes."

"The road's pretty slick. And I had to stop for coffee. Sorry no car." He never mentioned how terrible her chain-smoking was for his asthma, and she, reciprocally, now pretended not to notice him suck down a chemical lungful from the dorky inhaler. "My mom thinks I'm staying at Mickey Sullivan's, which tells you what planet she's on." But Sam had already turned to where the track curved into darkness. A light glided toward them like a cool white slider homing in on the plate. The 8:33 to Penn Station. In a few hours the ball would drop over Times Square and men and women all over New York would turn to whoever was nearest for an innocent kiss, or a not-so-innocent. He pretended the tightness in his chest as they boarded was just caffeine. "Like I care what Mickey thinks anyway. That jerk won't even like nod at me in the lunchroom anymore." The three of them—Mickey, Charlie, and Samantha—should have been in the same class at the high school. But Sam's terrifying dad, the fireworks genius, had sent her to the nuns for elementary, and then to private school in New York proper. It must have worked; Sam was only six months older, but had been smart enough to skip sixth grade, and was now at NYU. Whereas he and Mickey were C students, and no longer friends. Maybe he should have found someone more willing to serve as tonight's alibi, actually, because if Mom called the Sullivans in the a.m. to thank them (not that she would remember, but *if*), he'd be in big trouble, a ripe steaming mound of it. And what if she found out where he'd gotten the money to cover two round-trips into the City? He'd be locked in his room till like 1980. "You got the tickets?"

"I thought you were buying," she said.

"I mean for Ex Post Facto."

She pulled a crumpled flier from her pocket. "It's Ex *Nihilo* now. Different frontman, different name." For a moment, her mood seemed to darken. "But anyway, this isn't the opera. It's not like a ticketed event."

He followed her down the aisle, under fluttery lights, waiting as long as possible before reminding her that he couldn't sit backward, on account of his stomach. Again, her face grew pinched; he worried for a second he'd already jinxed their (he couldn't help thinking) *date*. But she'd pushed the door open and was leading him toward the next car.

The LIRR belonged to kids that night. Even the grown-ups were kids. There were few enough of them that each little band of revelers could leave several rows of Bicentennial red-and-blue seats on each side as a buffer. They talked much louder than adults would have, and you could tell it was meant to be overheard, as a means of preemption, a way of saying, *I am not afraid of you.* Charlie wondered how many Nassau County moms tonight had no idea where their kids were— how many mothers had simply granted them their freedom. As soon as the conductor had passed through, beers began to circulate. Someone had a transistor radio, but the speaker was cruddy, and at that volume all you could hear was a voice moaning hornily. Probably Led Zeppelin, whose Tolkienish noodlings had been the soundtrack of the carwash where Charlie had worked freshman year, but which he'd renounced last summer after Sam dismissed Robert Plant as a *crypto-misogynist show pony*. She could be like that, sharp and full of fire, and her silence now wrongfooted him. When a kid a few rows away pump-faked tossing a beercan their way, Charlie reached for it, like a jerk. The kid's friends laughed. "Preps," Charlie muttered in what he felt was a withering tone, only not loud enough to be heard, and sank back into the noisy pleather of his forward-facing seat. Sam had turned away again to gaze at the settlements of Queens glimmering beyond the window, or at her fogged breath turning them to ghosts. "Hey, is everything okay?" he said.

"Why?"

"It's a holiday, you know. You seem like you're not, like, real festive. Plus shouldn't you be documenting this stuff for your magazine thingy?" For the last year, she'd been publishing a mimeographed fanzine about the downtown punk scene. It was a big part of who she was, or had been. "Where's your camera?"

She sighed. "I don't know, Charlie. I guess I left it somewhere. But I did bring you this." From the army-surplus bag on her lap came a gummy brown labelless bottle. "It was all I could find in the liquor cabinet. Everything else is water at this point."

He sniffed at the cap. Peach schnapps. He brought it to his lips, hoping there were no germs. "You sure you're okay?"

"Did you know you're the only person who ever asks me that?" Her head came to rest on his shoulder. He still couldn't tell what she was thinking, but the medicinal heat of the booze had reached his innards, and kissing her—*making* her, R. Plant would have put it—again seemed within the realm of possibility. For the rest of the ride, he had to picture the wobble of President Ford's jowls in order not to pop a full-blown bone.

But at Penn Station, Sam's restlessness returned. She hustled through the hot-dog-smelling crowds, faces moving too fast for the eye to distinguish. Charlie, by now well-lubricated, had the impression of a great light beaming from somewhere behind him, setting fire to every dyed-black hair on the back of her head, her several earrings, the funny flattened elfin bits at the top of her ears—as if a film crew was following, lighting her up. Of light not reflecting off things but coming from inside them. Inside *her*.

They hopped a lucky uncrowded Flatbush Avenue–bound number 2 express train, and as they racketed through a local station the train seemed to echo the conductor's garbled syllables: *Flat-bush, Flat-bush*. Sam turned in her seat. Girders on the elongating platform strobed the light into pieces. Charlie noticed for the first time a small tattoo on the back of her neck. It was like a king's crown rendered by a clumsy child, but he didn't want to ask her about it and thus remind her of all the things about her he apparently no longer knew. He let go of the bar he'd been holding and shoved his hands in his pockets and stood trying to absorb the jolts—*Flat-bush, Flat-bush*. It was a game she'd taught him called "subway surfing." First one to lose his footing lost. "Look," he said. When she didn't, he tried again. "Play you."

"Not now." Her voice had none of the maternal indulgence he was used to, and once again he felt the night faltering, like the light of the bypassed station.

"Best three out of five."

"You are such a child sometimes, Charles."

"You know how I feel about that."

"Well, stop acting like a Charles, then."

It shamed him, how loud she said it. Anyone who didn't know better might have thought she didn't even like him. So he threw himself down onto the opposite bench, as if he'd decided on his own that this was where he belonged. At Fourteenth Street, one of the doors jammed, leaving only the narrowest space to exit through. And of course, being a gentleman, he let her go first, not that there was any kind of thank-you. Then it was onto the local for one stop and up at Christopher Street. Before he'd gotten busted, they used to hang out here eating ice cream and 'ludes and drinking her dad's whisky. Half-bombed in the afternoon, he'd goof on the homos passing into the sex shops, as away to the south, buildings rose like kingdoms. The sky that had stretched over them like a great throbbing orange-blue drumhead was now flaking off in little pieces and falling. And he was burning up in his double-layered pants. He told her he had to pee.

"We're on kind of a schedule here, Charlie."

But he ducked into a pizzeria toilet with a **FOR CUSTOMERS ONLY!** sign. With the door locked, he stripped off his pants and pajama bottoms, wadded the bottoms into his jacket pocket, and put the pants back on. The counter guy glared as he made his way back outside.

"You know, if you're going to be like this . . . ," she started.

"Like what?"

"Like this. I can feel you like *beaming* anxiety at me. And would you pay attention? You're blocking the sidewalk."

As indeed, he saw, he was. The crosstown blocks, West Village to East, were jumping with tourists and freaks and other NYU kids. But when had she ever cared about courtesy? "Sam, I feel like you're pissed off at me, and I didn't even do anything."

"What is it you want from me, Charlie?"

"I don't want anything," he said, dangerously close to whining. "You called me, remember? I just want to be buds again."

She thought about this for a second. If there had been some sign he could have given her, one of the recondite handshakes of third graders, spitting in a palm, inscribing a cross, he would have done it. "Okay," she said, "but let's just get where we're going, can we?"

Where they were going was a pigeon-shitted old bank building on an especially run-down stretch of the Bowery, its columned portico swimming with graffiti she would once have insisted on photographing. The line spilled out of a side door, and they took their place at the back, under an erratic streetlight. A safety pin winked at Charlie from the face of a tall guy a dozen spots ahead; he resembled an ogreish friend of Sam's he'd met once, not far from here. Charlie became conscious of his hat. He wanted to take it off before the guy, if it was the guy, could spot them, but the light had cut out. When it buzzed back on, he nudged Sam. "Hey, don't you know him?"

She looked around edgily. "Who?" But the safety pin had been swallowed by the building, and her gaze fell on another man, the size and shape of an industrial refrigerator, who opened and closed the steel fire door without appearing to see the people passing through it. "Oh, that's just Bullet." She seemed almost to collect these obscure connections with older men. This one was heavily tattooed—blades of black ink that extended from his neck all the way out onto his toffee-brown face, like warpaint—and dressed head to toe in leather, with an earring shaped like a shiv. "He's the bouncer."

"I don't have an ID," Charlie hissed.

"What do you need ID for? Just be cool. Follow my lead."

He tugged the fur hat down over his eyes and forced himself to stop slouching. His efforts to look grown-up turned out not to matter; the bouncer was lifting Sam off the ground in a bear-hug, his face splitting into a broad, pink grin. "I thought we weren't going to see you tonight, sugar."

"Places to go, people to see," she said. "You know how it is."

"Who's the beanpole?" He nodded in Charlie's direction without looking at him.

"This is Charles."

"Charles looks like a narc in that hat."

"Charles is cool. Say hello, Charles."

Charlie mumbled something but didn't put his hand out. He was a little scared of black people in general, and in particular of this man who, if he'd taken the notion, could have snapped Charlie over his knee like kindling. If indeed he was black and not super-swarthy, or Turkish or something—the tattoos made it hard to tell.

"Listen," Sam said, leaning in. "Has anybody been asking for me?"

"For you?"

"Yeah, like . . . did someone ask you was I here? Preppy guy? Good-looking? Thirtyish? A little out of place?" She seemed to tremble, glossy with snowmelt, expectant. Charlie did his best to keep his own face blank. Never let them see you bleed, Grandpa had said, before disappearing into a DC-10 a week after the shiva.

Meanwhile, something like pity, a *Where are your parents?* look, had slipped the bouncer's jovial mask. "I don't know, sweetheart. I've been on since eight, and, like I said, I wasn't expecting to see you."

"Charlie," she said, "can you just hang here with Bullet for a sec while I go in and check on something?" So he waited, shifting from foot to foot, trying to edge away from the bouncer. Pigeons brooded on the streetlight's bent neck. A person dressed like a mime, only needing no makeup to chalk her face, blundered out of the door and fell on the icy sidewalk. She laughed and laughed, and Charlie wanted to go to her, but no one else moved. The bouncer shrugged, as if to say, *What are you going to do?*

Which, what *was* he? That Bicentennial summer, the summer of Sam, had arrived like a glass-blue wave, picking up his godforsaken life in one steep rake and thrusting it forward at such an angle he'd had to look up to see the shore. But as all waves must, it had broken, and anyway, he'd always been scared of heights. He'd seen her once afterward, from the passenger's side of the station wagon his mom would no longer let him drive. She was sitting at a bus stop in Manhasset. And maybe she'd seen him, but something in him had held back, and something had held her back, too—the part of her he now saw had stayed out here, riding a redoubled wave, testing the city to see if it was strong enough for her. *Be cool*, he told himself. *Just be cool.*

"Charlie, listen to me," Sam said, when she re-emerged. "If it turned out I had to run uptown, would you be all right on your own for an hour?"

He would have done anything for her, of course. He would have missed Ex Post Facto, if she wanted, or whatever they were calling themselves these days. But what happened when what she wanted was for him to do nothing? "What the fuck, Sam? I thought you wanted to spend New Year's with *me.*"

"I do, but I'm going to feel like absolute shit if you miss the first set, and I just . . . there's a problem here I can't put off any longer." Beyond the baffle of the warehouse wall, a struck drum signaled a shift from recorded music to live. "It's starting. You'll be okay?" She turned to the bouncer. "Bullet, can you look after Charlie here?"

"He can't look after himself? Charlie feeble-minded or something?"

"This is fucked up," Charlie said, to no one in particular.

"Bullet—"

The bouncer reached out and, pincering his massive thumb and forefinger, lifted the brim of Grandpa's hat so Charlie could see his eyes. "You know I'm just playing with you, boss."

Charlie froze him out, focused on Sam. "What happened to 'I need you, Charlie'?"

"I do need you, Charlie. I'm going to need you. Look, if I'm not back by eleven, come and find me. You can meet me at a quarter to twelve on the benches by the 72nd Street IND station. You know where that is?"

"Of course I know where it is." He had no idea where it was.

"Either way, I swear, we'll ring it in together." The flat of her hand between his earflap and cheek was like a cold pool on a hot day. Then she walked away backward, and for the first time since the LIRR platform, she seemed to actually see him. Despite the secrets she was plainly still keeping, he wanted to believe her. He wanted to believe it was possible for this wild free creature to need him. But she was gone. The bouncer, Bullet, swept open the door. Charlie thought of a car with open doors rolling through the parking lot at school, surging out of reach even as voices from within said, *Come on, Weisbarger. Hop in.* But that wasn't real anymore—nor was it real that he'd kissed Sam already, back in the basement of that weird house on East Third Street all those months ago. What was real, in the vacuum she'd left, was the memory of her skin on his skin and the music now blasting from the maw of the club.

3

THERE WAS NOWHERE ON EARTH more desolate than a Gristedes on New Year's Eve. Sprigs of limp parsley clinging to the holes of the grocery baskets; dreary fluorescent bulbs, one of them gone gray, like a dead tooth; the palsied old man at the head of the checkout line, shaking out his coin-purse. It was the last place you wanted to take stock of your life. Indeed, for most of the last decade, Keith Lamplighter had managed to avoid thinking about groceries at all. He marched off to Lamplighter Capital Associates in the morning and returned home around this time, seven or eight, to a replenished fridge—as if heads of lettuce had just sprouted there while the door was closed, Regan had claimed, there at the end. "You don't even know where the store *is*." Which wasn't true; Keith did. It was just that the numbers escaped him: between Sixty-Fifth and Sixty-Fourth? Or Sixty-Fourth and Sixty-Third? He'd walked by it often enough, but it took up no space in his consciousness, as the number of his extension at the office took up no space, because he never had occasion to call it. Now he was getting to know the Gristedes the way you know a person with whom you are really angry: intimately, from the inside, he thought, as a bell shot the cash drawer out from its hiding place.

No, Regan had been right, as usual. Success in America was like Method acting. You were given a single, defined problem to work through, and if you were good enough in your role, you managed to convince yourself of its—the problem's—significance. Meanwhile, actors who hadn't made the cut scurried around backstage, tugging at ropes, making sure that when you turned to address the moon, it would be there. You told yourself you were the only one who ever labored, even as the curtain behind you rippled, as from the swift soft movements of mice. How many times recently had Keith resolved to bear in mind his beaten-down supporting players? To be a better and more Christlike person? But it was as if some allergic reaction to the Gristedes was blocking him. The light had a lurid green in it that made everything it touched seem sickly. Perhaps it was to irradiate the food, to keep microscopic spores from spreading across the surface of Keith's bachelor provisions—pretzels and Sabrett franks and Air-Puft buns—until he'd made it out of the store. If he ever made it out of the store.

The old man at the head of the line having tottered out the door, the only other people around were women. They stared at the colorless flecked-tile floor or the soap-opera stars on the magazine racks. Directly ahead, some wisps had freed themselves from the drab ponytail of a teen mother already pregnant with her next kid—a hairstyle for someone who had no time for a hairstyle. She seemed not to see the daughter tugging at her trailing scarf, begging pretty please for an Almond Joy. For a second, the curtain was about to part, Keith's heart was in motion . . . That could have been his scarf-end, once. That could have been his hand feeling for the quarter he surely would have come up with had this been his little girl. But he'd believed he had better things to do, and the girl seemed to know this; when he flashed her what was meant to be an anodyne smile, she nuzzled into the leg of the mother, who glanced back at him with an expression that pretty clearly said, "Pervert."

It took several more lifetimes to reach the cashier. The *checkout*, the kids would have said. Will had wanted to be *a checkout* when he grew up. This was when he was three or four, and Regan had still been home with him all day, barring some business with the Board. She'd blushed, though Keith hadn't meant to signal disapproval. "That's not what you said yesterday, honey. Tell Daddy what you said yesterday." Keith could feel something welling up inside him. *He wanted to be like his dad!* But when Will didn't respond, Regan said, "Fire truck. He wanted to be a fire truck." Well, of course he did, because how, at four or however old he was, could he have understood what a wealth adviser did? Keith himself didn't understand, it turned out. But it would become one of those moments, one of those little domestic moments he'd let slip behind the curtain while he was busy center-stage, Succeeding. And now, trying hard to meet the eyes of the surly teenager totting up his purchases and to remember that she was as real as he was, he was doing it again. Thinking only of himself, of how to get to where he was going. And of how he would now be late.

IN TRUTH, he'd been looking all along for some excuse to blow off the annual Hamilton-Sweeney gala. Uncle Amory had signed his invitation personally, but even the five-minute *intermezzi* in which he and Regan met to hand off the kids were unbearable, and though it should have been possible in a crowd of several hundred guests to avoid each other, he knew it would never happen. Regan would keep close to him, ostensibly because they were adults and could behave like adults, but really as a kind of self-punishment. He'd lately come to understand that she'd been punishing herself for a long time.

Though now that she'd taken Will and Cate and moved to Brooklyn, he felt as if *he* were being punished, too. He wandered the old apartment like some wraith with no power to alter anything he saw. Absent her half of the books, those remaining had collapsed into decrepit piles on the shelves or fallen to the floor. She'd taken the lamps, too, and her million framed photographs. Sometimes at night, in the dark, he heard phantasmal children sliding down the hallways in their socks. They might have been living here still, had Regan not eventually learned about the time he'd brought his mistress into the apartment. It was the one bit of information he'd left out of his confession, knowing the pain it would cause. (Well, that and her age. And her name.)

He'd sworn never to bring Samantha here again, and, since breaking things off, had refused to take her calls. Then, earlier this week, she'd reached him at work. She'd somehow found the number—the one he didn't know himself. She was coming into the City for New Year's; could they meet? He got a kind of helpless hard-on thinking about her, or the ghost of her, kneeling on the couch in her white cotton panties, elbows on armrest, looking back over her shoulder, like a dare. "We have to talk," she said. "I'm not pregnant, so you know. But it's important." He said his in-laws were expecting him at the gala. It was true, technically, and in case she thought she'd ruined his life, he wanted her to understand that she hadn't. But he might, he added, have a little time earlier in the evening, so long as they met in a public place. "You don't have to worry, Keith," she said. "You're not that irresistible. And I'll be bringing a friend." And so it had been established that they would meet at 9:30, at a nightclub downtown called the Vault.

COOL NIGHT AIR summoned him back out of himself. The avenue lay hushed under the first snow. He stood for a minute, breathing it in, listening to the meticulous tick of flakes hitting the grocery bag propped against his hip. Half a block away, a figure with a shopping trolley had doddered out into the crosswalk. The signal flashed DON'T WALK, staining the snow red. Keith noticed the headlights of a school of taxis farther north, carrying speed downhill. Could the cabbies see, in this weather?

He reached the stranded shopper just in time to hustle him across to the far curb. It was the old man from the store, a little bald fellow in a soiled fisherman's cap. "Jesus. You've got to be more careful," Keith said. The man blinked up at him through thick glasses, his eyes wet and uncomprehending as a farm animal's. He said something in a high-pitched voice that sounded Spanish, but the consonants had all been gummed away. Keith caught himself replying at half-speed, and in an accent, as if that would make his English any more intelligible. Finally, he managed to establish through a ridiculous pantomime, pointing to things and holding up certain digits, that the man lived a few blocks south.

In fact, it was a hell of a lot farther than that. The old man was obviously capable of forward progress, but on Keith's arm, and in deepening snowfall, he locomoted only in tiny, truculent shuffles. It took ten minutes to travel the first hundred yards; crossing Fifty-Ninth was even slower. Keith wondered if in fact he was terrifying the man rather than helping—if the man perhaps understood himself to be being kidnapped. He appealed silently to passersby for help, but they had engagements of their own to get to, and, knowing the obligation he aimed to put them under, they pretended not to see him. Clearly, God meant the old man to be Keith's responsibility.

By the time they reached the no-man's-land east of Grand Central, Keith's bare hands were numb, his waterlogged grocery sack starting to split. He had no idea what time it was; Samantha might already have given up waiting on him. Finally, before a run-down building, the man ceased to move. "This?" Keith said. "This is where you're going?" *Zees where yoor go-ing?* "*Domicilia? La casa?*" Tentatively, he released the sleeve. The man slumped against the bars of the little fence that protected the garbage cans from whatever garbage cans needed protecting from. His hands curled around the bars. "Zay hal-lah ear," he said, it sounded like, and licked spittle from his lips.

Keith shook off a little shiver of déjà vu. "Come on, sir. Let's get you inside."

But the man would not let go. "Day allah here," he insisted. Or was it a question? He looked past Keith's shoulder, eyes widened fearfully. A gypsy cab slipped past on the snow-slick street. Obstinate old thing. Keith detached himself and went to peer into the lobby, hoping to find someone who knew the man and could let him in, assuming this was his building. He saw smoke-damaged carpet, stacks of yellowed phone books along one wall, an elevator light stuck on the fourth floor, but no people. Who left a deranged old man alone like this?

He recalled, out of nowhere, a book of the *Arabian Nights* he'd bought Will for Christmas one year. Or rather, that Regan had bought on his behalf. Laminated covers, watercolor plates, the smell of glue from the binding. Sometimes, when he got home in time, he had to read to Will from it. The story Will asked for, over and over, was about an old man who asked a traveler to carry him across a river. Once he was on the traveler's back, the man refused to let go. Will hadn't seemed perturbed, but Keith found it creepy, especially the illustration: the old man's pale blue skin, his sinewy legs squeezing the air from the chest of his patron, now his slave. An allegory of paternity, maybe, or of romantic love. Nor could he recall how the spell finally got broken, as in stories all maledictions must at some point break. Was this only a feature of stories?

Suddenly a young woman was beside him, precipitated out of the snow. She was full-lipped, Dominican or Borinquen, in a short skirt and fishnets that wouldn't help with the cold. "Isidor," she said. "You bad boy." She coaxed the old man off the iron fence as you might a rose from a trellis. "You're playing your trick on this fine gentleman, aren't you?" The old man's palsy, at this distance, resembled triumphant nodding She turned to Keith. He could see that she was not young at all—she was probably his age—but was so thickly rouged and mascara'd that in the headlights of a passing car, say, she might look like an extra from a porno film. The roll of fat peeking between her waistband and her parka, like excess material left over from her manufacture, only made his feelings toward her more tender. "He does this to people. I don't know why. He walks fine." They watched the old man shuffle pigeon-toed toward the door of the building. A painted nail circled around an ear. "*La locura.*" And then, after sizing Keith up once more, she sashayed off toward the corner.

Watching her go, Keith was struck by the supreme joke: he knew this block. There, on the corner, was the strip club called Lickety Splitz. And just next door was the by-the-hour hotel where he used to bring Samantha, outside of which off-duty go-go girls would mingle with cross-dressed hustlers from over on Third Avenue. He squinted against the snow. Something in him deflated. Downtown, uptown; what was the point of trying to decide anything? He dumped his bag of groceries inside one of the battered ashcans and set out after the stripper. It was as if, he told himself, the decision had been made for him. As if this were not his own brain telling him that every avenue away from his sins led him deeper into them. The sound of the white touching down all around him was like the sound of feet behind an arras, or like tiny, glottal laughter, if not of God the father, then perhaps of one of his angels, archangels, principalities, thrones, dominions, powers, seraphs, he'd known them all by heart as a choirboy in Stamford. What was the last one? A bird arced high above him, rooftop to rooftop. Oh, right, the cherub, the cupid, the little laughing boy.

4

BUT WHAT HAD HE BEEN DOING THERE to begin with? Why that day, at that particular hour? (And behind that, like a faint perpetual wind-chime: Why me, and not nothing at all?) Soon enough, William Hamilton-Sweeney would have cause to revisit these questions. At the time, though, he would have said he'd gone to Grand Central for exactly the reason he'd given Mercer: to be alone. For years, he'd been coming here when he needed to think, or not think, or to act or not act on the things he did or didn't think about. Granted, there was also all the architectural whatnot that used to knock him out in his youth, the arches, the sconces, the vaulting blue zodiac at the center of everything where pigeons roosted among the stars. But grime had long since dulled the color and advertising ruined the lines. What abided was the sense of any one person's life tapering amid the crowds to a meltingly thin slice. Proximity to the forty-story office tower bearing the family name had once raised the possibility of scandal, or pity, but any suburb-bound underling of Daddy's he'd bumped into on his way up from the lower level likely wouldn't even have lowered his eyes from the departure board before rushing on. And if anything, the years had rendered William's anonymity here more vivid and complete. In the circles he now moved in (to the extent that he still moved in circles at all) to cross north of Fourteenth Street, at least east of Eighth Avenue, was to sail right off the edge of the earth.

He stood now near a staircase, waiting to see just how badly the betrayal with the envelope had shaken him. Memories of Mercer's plaintive look threatened to shade into memories of his mother, but then he did the thing a drawing teacher had once taught him of flowing out into the world, of letting his eyes forget what they were supposed to be seeing. *You are what you perceive.* He perceived pantlegs bearing the sooty imprints of escalators. Street-level doors blowing open to admit the ringings of Salvation Army Santas. Goldish particles sifting through slabs of sad late light, paper pulp and cigarette ash and the shed skin of Americans. The crowds were about what you'd expect with the holiday, and even that was an illusory kind of presence. Really, these pitiable consumers hurrying past with their last-minute packages were already up in Westchester, in fuzzy slippers, watching the Yule log burn. Only the rare soul, William was thinking, was ever truly *here*, when out of the archway that led to the 7 train skulked a hulking punk named Solomon Grungy.

He would have been hard to miss even without the safety pins or the blindingly white hockey uniform or the big duffelbag on his shoulder. He was six foot six and seemed paler than usual, his mouth pinched like a rabbit's. It was with some relief that William noticed his eyes were still on the floor. And then, as if sensing danger, they weren't. To pretend not to see him would tax credulity. How much simpler the world would be if people could admit openly to hating each other! On the other hand, this was not that world. And William still believed, questions of utopia aside, in the social graces. "Sol!" he said, straining for warmth.

"Billy."

"Of all the terminals in the world . . ." Sol was already scanning for exits, which meant William had an edge here. Ditto the Rangers-logo jersey; Sol was aggressively punk, shaven-headed, multiply pierced and inked (was that a new tattoo on his neck?), and should have opposed on principle the fascism of team sports. But then William recalled his own clothes, the ridiculous coat that swept the floor when he walked. This would almost certainly be reported back to his ex-nemesis Nicky Chaos, whom Sol served as foot soldier, cupbearer, avatar. The trick was to stay on offense, to keep Sol from noticing. "Late with your shopping?"

"What? Oh." Sol glanced at the duffel as if at some jungle predator that had dropped down on him from a tree. "No, uh . . . hockey practice. The nearest free ice is out in Queens."

"On Christmas Day? I didn't know you even played."

"Well, I do." No one was ever going to accuse Solomon Grungy of repartee.

"I guess you've always had the makings of an enforcer," William said. "Just be sure you take those piercings out when you play." No response. "But how's tricks? How's Nicky?"

Now Sol grew testy; why did everyone always assume he knew how Nicky was?

"It's a pleasantry. I'm just asking, without the band, what you guys have been doing."

"Some people have to work."

"I don't remember Nicky being among them. I heard he was trying to paint now."

"That's just like you, Billy, to act like painting still matters, with the world going to shit all around you." And here, falling back on Nicky's old hobbyhorse about art versus culture, Sol seemed to relax; you could actually see a calculation lope across his face, where on most people's it would have flitted. "But I guess Nicky's been meaning to get in touch. What we've been doing is, we're getting the band back together."

"Like hell you are."

From its inception, Ex Post Facto had been William's baby. Well, his and Venus de Nylon's. They'd dreamed it up that hazy summer of '73. William had scribbled out a manifesto and a few songs, they'd enlisted a couple friends as the rhythm section, Venus had found some old bowling uniforms at a flea market and resewn them to look paramilitary, and they'd worn them down to the nightclub where a Hells Angel who lived in William's building sometimes worked the door. They'd played those early shows as a four-piece. Only after they'd cut a record had Nicky Chaos come along. The sound needed a second guitar, he insisted, though his musicianship made Nastanovich, on bass, look like Charlie fucking Mingus. No, Nicky wanted to play guitar because William played guitar, paint because he painted. Sometimes it seemed as though what Nicky Chaos really wanted was to out-William William, even as William tried his damnedest to become something else. Sol shifted the bag on his shoulder and winced. "It's true. Nicky booked a New Year's show, a comeback."

"Why'd he do that? You've got exactly zero original members of the band."

"We found a real PA for me to run this time."

Probably stolen, knowing Sol. Like the hockey uniform, which was suspiciously pristine, given the mud all over his boots, the black stuff under his nails.

"Plus we've got Big Mike."

Ah. So they'd stolen his drummer, too. And if they had Big Mike, who else was left to stand in their way? Venus had washed her hands, and Nastanovich was no longer in any position to object. All of a sudden, William couldn't remember what he was still trying to hold on to. Still, Nicky's habitual indifference to the fact of other people brought out his inner autocrat. "Well, so long as you guys don't use the handle."

"What?"

"Tell him he can have Big Mike, but the name, Ex Post Facto—that belongs to me."

"But we need the name, man. How do you think we landed a show at the Vault?"

"I'm sure you'll come up with something. Nicky always had a way with words."

For a moment, a helplessness entered in, an appeal to a camaraderie that had never really existed. "You should come see us, you know. You might be surprised."

"I may just do that. But wait a minute ... aren't you missing something?"

"Huh?"

"Your stick." He reached out to touch the place on Sol's wide shoulder where a hockey stick would have rested. His rustling coat must have been charged up with static electricity, because a spark leapt between them, mute amid the terminal noise. And it was strange how time seemed to wind down. How, at the apex of Sol's literal jump, fear gaped from behind his shocked-white face. Then he forced it back into a facsimile of the old Grungy sneer.

"I broke it over some guy's head when he crossed me."

"I bet you did," William said. "Anyway, I'll be seeing you." And after agreeing that he would—maybe New Year's?—Sol hurried off toward the downtown 6.

Fucking holidays, William thought. Occasions to rethink your life, ostensibly, but how were you supposed to do that when other people kept dragging you back toward whoever you used to be? Even now, for example, he knew he wasn't going to be able to ignore his curiosity about what Nicky Chaos was up to—just as he knew that in a few minutes, he'd be back in the basement-level bathrooms, seeking out the various forms of sweet release that waited there. Truth to tell, it was probably why he'd really come here in the first place. But so then, putting aside this hockey nonsense, what was Sol Grungy's excuse?

5

MERCER UNTWINED THE MEAGER SHEAF of manuscript pages, set them face-down on the coffeetable, and rolled a sheet of A4 onto the drum of the new IBM Selectric, whose hum seemed accusatory. For half a year now, he'd let William believe this was a more or less daily ritual. If, when he got home from teaching, William was up in the Bronx attending to his own magnum opus—a diptych called *Evidence I and II*—that was okay; Mercer could use the time to toil in the vineyards of the novel. And if later, over dinner, Mercer refused to discuss the day's progress, it was because it was his policy not to disclose details, rather than because they didn't exist. He really would every so often sit down to the ramshackle Olivetti, as he used to back in Altana. Mostly, though, he lolled on the futon under a spavined volume of Proust. Blocked, he'd thought. But had writer's block stopped old Marcel? Probably it was just a synonym for failure to buckle down, and as soon as he touched these virgin keys, fire would sweep across his cerebellum, flaming letters fly down through his fingers to scorch the page. By the time William returned, a Christmas miracle would be complete—duplicity exorcised for all time, months of inertia transubstantiated into art.

But things didn't happen like they did in novels, and nothing continued to come. The last daylight inched like a cortège across the secondhand furniture, the *Gentlemen Prefer Blondes* poster, the tabby odalisqued on the rabbit-eared Magnavox, the cut-to-fit kitchenette congoleum, the tiny mirror placed above the sink because the bathroom was out in the hall, shared by the whole floor (another quirk from the factory days). The cremains of Christmas dinner, doubled there, were like an exhibit in the museum of his personal failings.

It was a measure of the derivative nature of Mercer's distraction—distraction from distraction—that he didn't hear anyone come upstairs until the doorknob began to rattle. Night having fallen, the person trying to get in was just a silhouette against the pebble-glass, and there was something odd in the way it carried itself. Some wild-eyed addict curled around a blade? A white-ethnic vigilante determined single-handedly to de-integrate the neighborhood? It was William. And when he opened the door and flicked on the overhead light, his lip was split open, his right eye swollen shut. Under the chesterfield draped over his shoulders, some kind of makeshift sling pinned his right arm to his torso. In the dizzy microsecond before he jumped up, Mercer was suspended between present and past, *eros* and *philia*.

"Jesus God, William, what happened to you?"

"It's nothing." His voice came from high up in his chest, a place Mercer hadn't even known existed. He looked away as Mercer examined him up close.

"God! That's not nothing!"

"Don't be dramatic. It's just a sprain. It'll heal."

Mercer was already rifling through his shaving kit for the mercurochrome, which Mama used to swear by when C.L. came in looking like this. Wages of sin. He made William sit on the futon and cocked the swivel-necked lamp. He raised his face to the light and brushed the tangled hair back with a thumb. There was another cut on the forehead, and a fist-sized bruise to match the arm. "I don't suppose you'll tell me what happened."

William was pale. Shaking a little. "Please, Mercer. I just fell down some stairs."

More likely, he'd been jumped for his wallet. William liked to tease Mercer about his "fear of the black man," but the one time Mercer had allowed himself to be dragged north of 110th Street—ribs at Sylvia's, followed by Patti LaBelle at the Apollo—the poverty had made their current living situation seem positively deluxe. Sere-looking vagrants scratching themselves in doorways, eyeing him like some kind of Benedict Arnold. . . . He dabbed gently at the cut with the mercurochrome. William sucked in his breath. "Ow!"

"You deserve it, love, scaring me to death like that. Now hold still."

THAT NIGHT, and indeed that entire last week of 1976, William would refuse to go see a doctor. Typical, Mercer thought. Secretly, though, he had always admired his lover's independence: the grin he kept up even in the midst of the most heated dinner-table arguments with friends, and the Morse code his hand seemed to press into Mercer's thigh beneath the tablecloth's white hem, the air of secret exemption. Living with him was like getting to see the side of the moon that usually hides its face from us. And as he tended to William's injuries—black eye, sore jaw, a sprain self-diagnosed as "mild"—Mercer again began to feel that, if he did everything right, William might eventually come to depend on *him*. He moved the TV to the sleeping nook. He cooked elaborate meals, keeping mum whenever William filled up on candy bars instead. Against his every inclination, he didn't press William any further on what had happened. And when, on New Year's Eve, William finally said he was starting to go stir-crazy, he had to go put in a couple of hours at the studio, Mercer swallowed his objections and shooed him out the door.

As soon as he was alone, Mercer cleared as much of the fold-down counter as was possible and got out the little sawed-off ironing board. From the wardrobe rack by the door, he retrieved William's tuxedo and his own good suit, the one he'd come to the city with and now realized made him look like an insurance salesman. He'd made dinner reservations for nine o'clock at the little deconstructionist bistro downtown William had liked so much last summer. And maybe they could go out afterward, just the two of them. It was true that it had been a long time since they'd been dancing. He methodically attacked wrinkles and then laid the jackets out on the coverlet. They looked like paperdolls, William's white tuxedo jacket, his own tame brown suitcoat, just barely touching at the ends of the sleeves where the hands would have been. But when the phone rang, he knew even before picking it up who it would be. "Where are you?" he couldn't help asking. "It's almost eight."

Change of plans, William said. Had he mentioned he'd run into an old acquaintance, who told him Nicky and the others were premiering their new project tonight? It behooved him, he'd decided, to verify with his own eyes that it was a total disaster. "You should come. It'll be like watching the Hindenburg." There were voices behind him.

"You sound like you're with people already."

"I'm at a payphone, Mercer. A Chinese woman is trying to sell me cigarettes off a panel truck." There was a muffled sound, and he could in fact hear William, at some distance from the mouthpiece, saying, *No. No, thank you.* "But yes, I thought we could meet up with people at the venue. You won't have to pay. Bullet will be working the door."

"Bullet scares me, William."

"I can't not be there. I need to see with my own eyes the extent of the travesty."

"I know, but I thought with your arm still healing . . ."

"It's punk rock, Merce. Come as you are."

There was a spike in background noise. A television or radio seemed to be shilling something, but exactly what got lost in the miles of wire. Distance seeing. Distance hearing. Someone near enough to drown out even the ads laughed or coughed. For the first time he would consciously admit, it occurred to Mercer to wonder if William might be cheating on him. "You know what? I'm feeling a little under the weather."

"What are you talking about?"

"Kind of achy. Fluey." It was too much detail; the secret to lying, he'd learned, was not to appear too eager to persuade. But he wanted William to detect the fib, to come home and confront him. The second that elapsed here was enough for Mercer to know he wouldn't. His voice grew honestly hoarse. "Don't you at least want to change clothes?"

"Why don't you come out, honey? Cut loose a little."

"I told you, I don't feel good. I've got to lie down."

The silence that followed was audible; the wire took it and twisted it into a sound, a faint, cottony buzz. "Well, don't wait up. We'll probably be out late."

"Who's we?"

"Be good to yourself, Merce. Drink fluids. I'll see you next year." And in another eruption of noise—laughter, almost certainly—the call ended, leaving only a dialtone.

Mercer returned to the sleeping nook with its matched jackets.

He had wanted it to strike William as a kind of blissful bower; now that future had been ripped away, and all he could see when he put on his glasses was how young the mirror on the wall made him look. Not sexily, androgynously young, in the style of the age, so much as, frankly, naïve. His soft belly, the dark skin stark against his briefs' white elastic. He'd assumed that the discomfort he sometimes felt about going out in public with William had to do with shame about . . . well, about the way they were. But he wondered now if it wasn't rather that he was afraid it was only this, the blackness, that William saw when he looked at him. Of people thinking he was some kind of trophy. The best times had been right here in this apartment, where they performed for no one but each other: dreams recounted, games of Scrabble played, sporting events enjoyed (William) or tolerated (Mercer). Behind him in the mirror lay the parched Christmas tree. And on the radiator, that goddamned envelope.

He hadn't touched it since Christmas, but now he picked it up: creamy, densely grained, redolent (amid the kitty-litter funk of the loft) of some substance so precious it only existed in books—myrrh, maybe, or mandragora. The iron was still hot enough to steam it open. The card was, as he'd suspected, an invitation. *The richly escutcheoned Goulds,* William had said of his stepmother and -uncle, the one time he'd ever spoken of him, the week Mercer had discovered he was indeed the Hamilton-Sweeney heir, albeit disowned. *A golf club rampant on a field azure.* He copied down the address, sealed it back up. On the wire-spool coffeetable, William had left out a bottle of rye, which for Mercer had always had literary connotations, Robert Burns by way of Salinger connotations. He took an exploratory nip, and then another. He was unable to report any of the rumored sensations of suavity and sophistication. Gradually, though, a garment of grim resolve slipped down over him.

He squeezed himself into his lover's tuxedo and the chesterfield coat William had left behind in favor of his motorcycle jacket— almost as if he'd known. Mercer twisted William's bow tie around his hand, wanting it, somehow, to hurt. He sipped. When the person in the mirror looked suitably remote, he went down in a hurry, lest he change his mind. It was impossible to find a cab in Hell's Kitchen after dark, especially when you were, yourself, dark. But the cold turned everything crisp, so that he could see from two long blocks off the train's half-shattered green globe. The branches of a lone surviving tree, a fruitless Callery pear, were etched in white. Beyond them, through a swirl of snow, the crown of the Empire State Building floated on gossamer light, and Mercer could feel something inside him floating, too—his hopes, he guessed. The year of living passively was over. Tonight, he was taking matters into his own hands, and something big would come of it. Had to come of it. Yes, this year, the Year of Mercer, was going to be different.

6

REGAN HAD BEEN TOO FAR INSIDE what it was to be a Hamilton-Sweeney to see it clearly. To her, the Sutton Place townhouse where she'd grown up had been no different than the homes of her classmates: roomy, sure, but not conspicuously so. Daddy worked long hours, and she and William had the run of the place. By freshman year of high school, she'd known every inch of it, its safest hiding spots and which windows admitted the most sun at which times of day, and it might have gone on this way forever, like a village inside a snowglobe, just the three of them (or four, counting Doonie, their cook and de facto nanny) sealed up in the hermetic clarity her mother's death left, had the Goulds not had different ideas.

She'd come to see them this way, as a package deal—*the Goulds*—even though Felicia had appeared first. One evening the table was set for four, and there she'd been in the foyer: a tiny, birdlike woman whose coat Daddy took himself. He introduced his "friend" to Regan, who watched from the stairs, and she didn't need to be told any more—didn't need Felicia's avid hands skimming chairbacks and tables, already sorting the expensive from the merely sentimental, or Doonie's significant looks, the tight-lipped shake of her head. Then, a few months later, Amory was produced, like a fist from a kid glove. He would be joining the firm, Daddy announced, after several uncharacteristic glasses of wine. William, across the table, hid his irritation under a layer of obsequy. Nor would Felicia's brother let himself be outfawned, and the dinner became a kind of gladiatorial tournament of insincerity unfolding right in front of Daddy, who beamed all the while, as if he were seated at some other table, in some private, pleasant dream.

Soon Daddy had decided, independently, he said, that William's gifts would be better served by boarding school. *You see?* said William, long-distance from Vermont, and then he unveiled a private nickname. *The Ghouls play hardball.* She told herself this was just his persecution complex, but it was true that Amory and Felicia were around more often with William gone. And when Daddy finally proposed to her, Felicia began plotting to move the entire clan to this castle on the Upper West Side.

Or maybe it wasn't a castle, it was hard to say. It perched atop a tall brick building, invisible from the street, so that you only ever saw it from within—like one's own head, it occurred to Regan, standing before it on New Year's Eve. There was no apartment number, and the word "penthouse," thanks to Bob Guccione, would have been beneath the dignity of the family name, which Felicia had of course taken as her own. You said you were "here for the Hamilton-Sweeneys." Those last five syllables had never felt more alien than they did now in Regan's mouth. The concierge and a coworker were watching a small television behind their desk. Regan couldn't imagine Felicia approving, but before the concierge's eyes could detach from the screen, she felt guilty for her condescension. What was his name? Manuel? Miguel? "For the gala," she added.

The way he looked at her made her conscious of parts of her body she'd been ignoring, the bare clavicle under her coat, the sad décolletage she'd tried to hide with a butterfly pin, the wisp of fugitive updo tickling her neck. She must look like a high-schooler tarted up for prom. And why should Miguel recognize her? She avoided this place as much as possible. Only recently, with Daddy's memory crumbling, had she started coming over to get his Hancock on various bits of company business. And besides, she wasn't the same person she'd been a month ago; she was single. "I'm Regan. The daughter."

"Jes. Ms. Regan." He glanced down at his list, as though to double-check she wasn't part of some terrorist cell seeking to infiltrate the apartment. "I take you right up."

The elevator was the old-fashioned kind, with a folding gate and an uncomfortably floaty feeling. Though there was a stool next to the levers, Miguel remained standing. Regan couldn't think of anything to say. Then the gate peeled back to reveal a high-ceilinged entry hall, empty except for the great blue Mark Rothko painting on the wall and, flanking it, two tall, what would you have called them . . . ? Braziers, she supposed, each crowned with a gas-fed flame.

Little about Felicia's New Year's gala had changed in a decade. It was like that game, red light/green light. You turned away for a year, life went on, but when you turned back, everything looked just as you'd left it. The same four hundred people, the same conversation, the same drunken laughter at the same stale jokes. The only differ-ence would be the theme. A theme imposed a degree of discipline on the otherwise unruly social body, Felicia believed. The previous year (God, had so little time really passed?), it had been "Hawaiian Night," meaning that in place of whatever usually topped the end tables had sat vases of birds of paradise and pineapples viscid with glitter-glue. Garlands of real orchids, airlifted from the Pacific, wove precisely through the newels of the staircases. Felicia's grass skirt had nearly swallowed her wee frame. The year before had been something Ibe-rian; Regan could recall only yards of raw velvet and toreador pants. And what did these braziers signify? *Let There Be Light? Let Me Stand Next to Your Fire?* If Keith were here, he would have made it a game to guess, but once inside, mingling, would have easily hidden how frivo-lous he found the whole thing. The thought of facing Daddy and the Goulds without him made her want to retreat to Brooklyn Heights, settle up with the sitter. Half the boxes in the new place remained to be unpacked. But it was too late. Miguel was probably already back at his desk, and here she was, at the threshold, alone. She hung her coat in the front closet, ignoring the coat-check that had been set up in the hallway to her left. Special treatment still made her feel guilty. From several rooms away wafted the drunken noodling of the piano. She took a diver's deep breath and headed toward it.

It always caught her off guard, the swell of sound as she rounded the corner to the great reception hall, the scores of people. The bolts of green fabric that draped the walls made her think of a ballgame her father had taken her to years ago, before they'd torn down the Polo Grounds and she'd converted to the Yankees—of the dim, pigeon-infested concourses, punctuated by squares of bright green beyond which lay summer and humanity and life. Except that, in the glow of a half-dozen more of the indoor torches, this green was hellish, combustible. Chatter collected in the vaults of the ceiling. Below, each guest wore a half-mask, as in the *commedia dell'arte*. Her stomach tightened again; no one had told her to bring a mask. Besides which, she hardly saw the point; did people really not recognize each other because this small swath of features—the cheekbones, the bridge of the nose—was covered? No, the true purpose of the masks was to give the hostess a way to confirm that she'd managed to impose her will on the assembled guests. Vis-à-vis Felicia, there were only two viable positions one could take: escape completely, as William ultimately had, or submit.

Just then, a horripilating Scaramouche appeared at her elbow. The prosthetic nose was long and carbuncled, and seemed to waggle suggestively. "Jesus," she said, placing a hand over her chest. "You scared me."

The voice from beneath the mask was labored, adenoidal. He wasn't much older than her son, she saw, and she couldn't understand what he was saying.

"What?"

"I said, may I offer you one?"

She looked down into the proffered basket, where cheap black plastic Lone Ranger masks were piled. To be polite, she took one and secured its rubber band around the back of her head. Before she could thank the kid, he evaporated.

There was no shortage of servants, though. They seemed to outnumber the guests. Canapés circulated at shoulder height. Behind a wet bar along each wall, a pair of Punchinellos with martini shakers struggled to keep up with demand, like a single, four-armed organism. Regan waited in line. She was in fact more comfortable now that she had a mask of her own. Despite the recognizably willowy figure inside her cocktail dress, none of the guests seemed to know who she was. No one singled her out as a latecomer, or as the firm's new head of PR, or as the presumptive heiress and youngest member of the board, and not a single person asked about Keith or the kids. She could get through an hour like this, easy, and then she could go home. Take off her shoes, humble herself with some Gallo, put on Carly Simon soft enough not to wake Will and Cate, and peek in on their faces, each lit by a stripe of hallway light, before returning to the living room to throw a party of her own, the kind where you could cry if you wanted to; her analyst would be proud.

At the front of the line, she took a glass of champagne and turned around. A gap in the crowd offered her the first glimpse of her father's wife, backlit by a stone fireplace big enough to walk around in. Against the flames, Felicia's body was a smudge, save for her mask, whose red sequins shimmered intelligently. Peacock feathers soared from each temple. Then the party swallowed her once more. Regan couldn't tell if Felicia hadn't seen her or had only been pretending. Either way, it might have been a blessing, but it vexed her that Felicia was the one always holding the cards. The mask had emboldened Regan, or the champagne had, tickling the back of her throat. She took another glass from a passing tray and then, with no memory of having crossed the room, waited for Felicia to reach for the hands of the dignitary or potentate she was talking to. This pressing of your hands in her own was how she let you know that she released you.

When the man left, Regan and her stepmother were face-to-face. Felicia's eyes seemed to retreat into the extraordinary plumage, and only there, safely ensconced, to risk seeing her. For it was always a risk, wasn't it, to see? Regan felt the onset of wisdom, a discovery dammed up inside breaking auratically loose as Felicia reached out.

"Regan, darling, is that you? I hardly recognized you."

"You look terrific yourself. The mask is quite something." Regan couldn't bring herself to take the extended hands.

"Oh, this is just a Carnival thing your father brought back last time from the tropics. Now you'll have to give me your honest opinion on the décor, as I know most people will say whatever keeps them in good graces. Times are tight, but we did put more resources into it than ever before."

More of Daddy's resources, she meant. More of what would have been Regan's resources, if she hadn't long ago renounced her claim to the Hamilton-Sweeney fortune. "You've outdone yourself again," she said. "Speaking of Daddy . . . is he around here somewhere?"

"I told him not to book his return flight for the day of the gala. I said, Bill, you never know. Chicago? The way weather blows up off the lake with no warning? Amory and I were in Buffalo for decades. We know what real winter looks like."

"I thought the clinic was in Minnesota. What is he doing in Chicago?"

"A layover. His assistant called at four to say the runway wouldn't be cleared until after the snow stopped, nine o'clock at the earliest, which was only"—she checked her watch, a slinky gold thing—"an hour ago. And of course I haven't been *near* a phone since then. I think we must be getting the leading edge of that storm now ourselves."

"And you went ahead with the party?"

"Well, of course. It would have been irresponsible not to. These people all depend on us." The eyes seemed to rouse themselves from their sequined foxholes. The rest of the room was melting away. "But where has that husband of yours gotten off to? He always has been such fun, socially."

"Keith won't be coming tonight, I don't think," said Regan quietly.

"Mmm?"

Regan had long since given up trying to peek inside the black box of her father's marriage, and so had no idea whether their private communication surpassed their by now rather etiolated public mutuality; still, it seemed impossible that she herself could be en route to divorce without Felicia having picked something up. Like most authoritarian regimes, the Goulds' depended on intelligence. Indeed, Amory had worked in the Office of Strategic Services as a young man before entering the private sector.

"We've decided to separate. As a trial."

Regan hated all the possible constructions, including this one, as soon as they left her mouth. *Time apart. Get some perspective.* Strange to say, though, the calculated pageant of emotion seemed to suspend itself; Felicia's lips parted, and Regan had the feeling she wanted to put aside the masks. Maybe she really *hadn't* known. Then the moment passed.

"You've informed your father, I presume."

"Of course I have."

"He's always been a sound judge of character."

"Daddy *loved* Keith."

"Well, that's just what I mean. We'll all be sad to lose him. Tell him when you see him next, won't you? Though of course our sympathies are with you and the children."

"The kids are going to be fine. They adjust to these things, as you probably remember. I can't imagine why Daddy wouldn't have mentioned this, even with his condition." The party had snapped back into focus. There had been a distinct thickening, a press of bejacketed arms and shoulders. Somewhere nearby, a platter trailed the scent of roast meat. The piano was being molested again. Was being molested still.

"I'm wondering now if this is why your Uncle Amory has been so grim about the mouth this evening. He's looking for you, you know. He claims it's Board talk, something to do with the firm, about which I'm as you know completely ineducable. Now where has he gotten to?" The little woman rose preposterously on her toes, as though an extra inch of height might allow her to pick her brother out of the crowd. Regan was relieved when she de-levitated, disappointment slathered perhaps too broadly on her visible face. "Well, I don't see him. But I'm sure you'll bump into each other before the night is out. He was adamant about not letting you go until he'd had a chance to confer."

Regan would not reward Felicia by letting her see she felt menaced. "Well, I'm sure you've got many people to confer with yourself, and my drink needs freshening."

"Naturally."

"But as I said, you've really outdone yourself. Is there a theme, by the way, tying all this together?"

"You didn't get the invitation?"

"I must have read it in a hurry."

"'Masque of the Red Death.' A little private joke of my brother's. Plague years and so forth, he says. He has that unusual sense of humor, you know."

"Very droll."

"Fabulous to see you, Regan."

It had been their longest exchange in several years, and certainly their most disconcerting, and so at some point, Regan had let her guard down, at least as regarded hands—and now Felicia pounced. Her palms, closing around Regan's, were like cool, carnivorous plants. The pressure she could generate was enormous. "And Regan, dear, we must keep our chins up. It's our lot in life, as it's the lot of men to be incorrigibly men, and who's to say, in the end, which is harder?"

So they *had* known, Regan thought, less in bitterness than in foreboding, as she returned to the crowd. When she looked back, her stepmother was again a dark mark against the hearth, like a bundle of kindling awaiting the flames.

STEERING CLEAR OF AMORY GOULD had never been easy, and tonight was no exception. The dangers of the reception hall were obvious; the room was getting fuller and drunker the closer it got to twelve, and he could have been lurking behind any number of masks. On the other hand, smaller spaces exposed her, too. She sequestered herself in a bathroom for a while but couldn't stay there forever, and when the scale there beckoned her to check her weight, as Dr. Altschul had forbidden her to do, she removed herself to an adjoining room normally used for music (whence the piano sounds had come). She stood with her back to one wall for support and sipped her third champagne. Tough it out till midnight, she thought. One more hour, and you'll have put in your time. From atop an orange-draped table, a TV stained the gloom. Dick Clark hadn't aged since she'd been in college. A man switched over to the football game. Anybody mind? "Please do," she said.

If you'd suggested fifteen years ago—say, the weekend of what turned out to be her father and Felicia's engagement party, at the Goulds' summer house on Block Island—that she would one day have a measure of power over these people, the men in their gabardine slacks, the kerchiefed wives in their pedal pushers, she wouldn't have believed you. Offstage, she was by and large a wallflower, lacking her brother's loquacity. It was what had drawn her to the theater at Vassar: someone had already written your lines. And yet, on the eve of his wedding, Daddy had asked her to join the Company's Board of Directors. Even before that, he had to have noticed all the weight she'd lost, and sensed her unhappiness (which in their shared theology was like spiritual weakness). "You don't have to do this," she had said. They looked at each other for a long time. Then he told her he believed in her. It was as if he'd been holding this place for William, his male heir, but now could recognize its fitness for her. Besides, she wasn't going to make a career of acting; she was a Hamilton-Sweeney, for God's sake.

She had been quiet but diligent through years of monthly board meetings, and then last summer, just when Dr. Altschul suggested that, with Cate starting school, maybe Regan should find some way to occupy more of her time, the position in the company's troubled Public Relations and Community Affairs department had opened up. She insisted on going through an interview like anyone else, but it was a foregone conclusion that she would get the job. She couldn't imagine a better-qualified candidate; putting the best possible face on things was more or less what she'd been trying to do her entire life.

On the other hand, she couldn't be sure that the previous PR chief's departure hadn't been arranged by Amory, for arranging, above all, was what he did. You never actually saw the arrangements taking place, of course; you simply noticed him darting along the edges of a room, deft as a cuttlefish, darkening the medium around him . . . and then you might infer his intervention from the fact that things had gone his way. The Demon Brother, the junior execs called him. You worked long enough at the firm, you came to feel that he was everywhere and nowhere, like a Deist's conception of God. Though part of his genius, she had come to realize, was that he only actually intervened on occasions when it truly mattered. Just once, that long-ago weekend on Block Island, had she personally felt the power of his arrangements. He had still been youthful then, his face alive with the flicker of torches as he brought her fruity drinks in cups shaped like tiki gods, his hand soft and insistent against her lower back. She hadn't noticed the black stormclouds that had begun to pile up over the darkling blue strip to the west.

In a sense, they'd never gone away. And when she heard his voice now in the hallway a dozen feet off, his unmistakably high, soft voice, calling back to someone that he would "be right in to check the score," she could feel herself shrinking. She pressed the champagne flute to one cheek to regulate her temperature, and the stem got caught in the rubber band of her mask, snapping it free from its staple. The mask fell. One of the wives turned to look at her disapprovingly. Fine, maybe she was tipsy, but whatever happened to solidarity among the sexes? Then the bathroom door was closing in the hall, and she saw her chance to escape. She bolted the last of her drink, put the glass down on the nearest surface, and stole out of the room. Amory was nowhere to be seen. Behind her, the reception hall was a madhouse. In the other direction, the swinging door of the kitchen was outlined in white. She hurried toward it, hoping to be out of sight before Amory emerged from the bathroom. But the guests seemed to be multiplying, surging back toward the party's center. Worse, she was unmasked. They had in years past been content to talk to Keith, with whom one could talk about anything. For Regan, they'd had nary a word. Now that it was imperative that she reach the far end of this hall, however, hands pawed the sleeve of her dress. Regan, you look fabulous, so trim. How's Keith? Where's Keith? By which was meant, she assumed, *Are the rumors true?* Her gift for stonewalling seemed to be failing her. She thought she heard the toilet flush. "Terrible, actually, we're getting divorced," she blurted. And, not waiting for a reaction, reached for the swinging door.

The kitchen was a long, narrow galley that didn't seem to match the rest of the apartment, until one considered that it was the only room not meant to be gawked at by guests. Regan early on had had fantasies of spending afternoons here, commiserating with Doonie, but Felicia had fired her in favor of her own cook, and Regan eventually resigned herself to remaining an outsider, lumped in with the rich folks on the far side of the door. There were now six or eight dark-skinned women working at the various counters, drying dishes, thawing dough that perfumed the air with yeast. Unlike the waiters flitting in and out, they did not wear masks. And at the far end of the room, sitting at a little table crowded with wine-bottles, unnoticed by anyone, was a black man in a white jacket. He had pushed his false face up onto his head, and even in her intoxication it took her only a second to place the real one beneath: round cheeks, unstylish glasses, overbite. "Mr. Goodman! Is that you?"

She had forgotten that black people could blush. He murmured something she didn't quite catch, and then she pulled him to his feet and offered him her cheek to kiss. The nearest cook glanced over disapprovingly. Regan sat down, determined to make it seem that she and William's lover—for that's obviously what he was—were old friends. "I can't believe you got him to come! Where is he?" She looked around.

"William? He, uh . . . doesn't exactly know I'm here."

Her heart sank. "Doesn't exactly?"

"Doesn't. I kind of thought I'd come in his place. It's a long story." He studied one of the bottles. Humidity from all the cooking had begun to curl its label. His apparent chagrin distracted her from her own.

"What are you doing back here, then? You should be rubbing elbows with the beautiful people. You know Norman Mailer's out there." She chucked him on the sleeve of his too-small jacket. Maybe this was overly familiar, as she'd only met him that once, but at least there was *someone* here who owed no loyalty to the Goulds.

"I didn't last ten minutes. One woman handed me this." He pulled from a pocket a crumpled napkin, a tiny bindle of half-eaten food. "I think she thought I was a waiter."

"That dinner jacket can't have helped. Is that William's?"

His smile, even embarrassed, was lovely, she saw. "You think it's too much?"

"At least you get a nice story to tell, when you go back to your other life. Me, I don't get to go back to anything else. This is my other life."

"It seems to agree with you."

"Does it?" She raised her hands to her face. One of them—hands or face—was still hot, but she couldn't have said which for certain. It was generally a warning sign when her body and her head disconnected from each other. "That's just the booze. Speaking of which, we should have a drink." She had taken a wine-bottle from the table between them and was scanning the countertops for an opener.

"Are you sure you need another drink?"

She rummaged through an all-purpose drawer, ignoring the peripheral consternation of the servers. "To celebrate finding each other. It really is a nice surprise."

She couldn't locate a corkscrew, but there, among rubber bands and wire whisks and paintbrushes, the hidden disorder of Felicia's household, was an underweight Swiss Army knife. She flipped out the various appendages. Corkscrew, corkscrew . . . You would have thought the Swiss would have prepared for this contingency, but the best she could find was a long, narrow blade. She plunged it into the cork and began a little manically to prize it out.

"Uh—Regan?" Mercer said, and reached for her. And that was when the knife folded back toward the handle. There was a moment after the cutting edge had already gone through the skin and into the meat of her thumb (but before the alarm signals out in the neurochemical vastness had reached her) when it could have been someone else's finger caught there, or a piece of anatomical wax. *Geez*, she thought. That looks deep. And then there was a nearly audible fizz as the future she'd been projecting for herself—a glass of wine; a toast shared with Mercer Goodman; a flight from the party, undetected by Amory—dissolved, and the thumb became hers. Blood came, a gout, a freshet on the gray-white marble between them. It was shocking that something so thick and red could come from her body. Here she'd been thinking that her life was not her own, and all the while it beat on within her. There was that second of almost giddiness, always, before you felt the pain.

7

C HARLIE'D BEEN TRYING TO ACT like tonight was no big deal—like he went to nightclubs all the time—but in fact he'd been counting on Sam to sherpa him through the country of velvet ropes and mirror balls he imagined waited. Instead, here he was, utterly alone, at the back of a hot black room packed like a subway car. The stage was invisible; all he could see up there were shoulders, necks, heads, and in the spaces between, a nimbus of light, a sporadic microphone stand or fist or spray of—what was that, spit?—rising into the air. The music, too, was murky, and without the deciduous rings of an LP to study, it was hard to tell where one song ended and another began, or whether what he was hearing were actual songs. The best he could do was face the same direction as everyone else, bop up and down in some semblance of rhythm, and hope no one noticed his disappointment. And who was going to notice? The bartender was the only person farther from the stage. Charlie stripped off his jacket and tried to knot its sleeves around his waist the way kids at school did, but it fell to the floor, weighed down by the pajama bottoms in the pocket, and now there was someone watching, a girl, so he had to pretend to have meant to let the jacket fall, that's how passionate he was about the music. He put on his most impressive scowl and tried to imagine what it might look like to be transported.

"Fuck," the girl said, when the band's set finally ended.

Was she talking to him? "What?"

"Groovy, right?" Recorded music now blasted from the PA; a snarl of Christmas lights above the bar had been plugged back in, doubled by those parts of a long mirror not covered in spraypaint, and the crowd was surging toward them, water in a sloshed bowl. The girl was tall—though not as tall as Sam—and plumply curvy beneath an oversized Rangers jersey. Her features were soft and womanly. "But I think you're standing on someone's coat."

"Oh, I . . . that's mine." He stooped to retrieve it from a puddle of what he could only hope was beer. When he stood back up, the girl was exchanging frantic charades with someone across the room. Probably making fun of him; Charlie thought he'd detected the international symbol for drunk—thumb to mouth, pinky lifted like an elephant's trunk. Well, screw her. "I'm going to go stand over here now," he said.

"No, wait." She grabbed the upper part of his sleeve. "I like the way you dance. Like you don't give a shit who sees you. You're not one of these grad-school poseurs just trying to fit in. People are afraid to let themselves go crazy like that anymore."

She must be *on* something, Charlie thought, to make her eyes glassy like that, with the Christmas lights glimmering there like cheap stars; something that made her seem older and cooler than he was. He shrugged. "They're only like one of my favorite bands."

"Get the Fuck Out?"

"Beg pardon?"

"If you like Get the Fuck Out, wait till you hear the headliner."

His mistake embarrassed Charlie. No wonder he hadn't liked it that much. "No, that's what I meant," he said. "Ex Post Facto. Or Nihilo."

"*Nihilo*," she said, with a short *i*.

"Sure. They're the best."

"Really? My boyfriend does their sound. I could probably get you backstage. But you'd have to do something for me in return. Oh, fuck. I love this song. Come dance with me."

"I don't even know your name."

"Call me S.G.," she said over her shoulder as she forced her way past eddies of punks.

"Charlie," he said, or mumbled. Then the record changed. A voice like an old friend's came over the speakers: *Jesus died / for somebody's sins, / but not mine.* In the graffiti'd mirror above the bar, he still looked a mess, but someone apparently thought different, and who cared if she was a little overweight? His only regret was that Sam wasn't around to see him.

They danced near a chest-high two-by-four running along the wall. Charlie might not even have noticed it except for the lemming-like rows of plastic cups crowded there, ice in various colors melting against the sides. He took one of the drinks so S.G. wouldn't see he was underage. It was hard to remember himself that he was only seventeen, a timorous weed sprouting from his combat boots. As the song neared escape velocity, Charlie did, too. Impossible, that this was the same place he'd felt so lonely minutes before. In every direction were people, musky, funky, undulant. And here was this broad soft broad in her oversized jersey, boogieing closer, and when his chest accidentally smooshed against her tits, she just smiled, like there was a TV on the wall behind him and she'd seen something funny. Charlie tipped back the last of his translucent blue goo and with it still numbing the roof of his mouth and luffing the surface of his face away from his skull, he put an arm around her. "I'm glad you decided to talk to me," he yelled. He was just assaying the wisdom or stupidity of explaining how he'd been stood up when she raised a finger to his mouth.

"Wait. This is the best part."

He leaped over the half-second when his feelings might have been hurt and gave himself to the rest of the song, the blissed-out drone in the flashing smoky room with his sweaty hair stuck to his forehead and his jacket in his hand like a pom-pom.

When the record ended, Charlie looked at the Nazgûls circulating around them, any of whom might have been the boyfriend he'd just remembered. He was unsure what he was supposed to do next; his crotch bestirred itself happily when, in the invisible understory below shoulder height, she let the back of her hand rest against it.

"So hey, Charlie, about that favor. Are you holding?"

"Holding?"

"Like more of what you're on. 'Cause whatever it is I definitely want some."

"Um . . . fresh out," he said. Sam had been the one who bought the drugs, when there were drugs. He wouldn't have known who to talk to besides the guys at school who sold Valiums snuck from their moms' medicine chests. And now the girl would pull away, disgusted; her hand had already drifted from between his legs.

"Bummer," she said, tossing her long hair. "I totally would have made it worth your while." She didn't sound especially crushed, though. Maybe she was already too high to care. "But Sol can probably scrounge up something, if you want to come backstage with me. I just need ten bucks."

Sol was the name of that lunkhead Sam knew; it must have been him outside, after all. "Wait. Solomon Grungy is your boyfriend?"

"Yeah, the sound engineer. I thought you said they were your favorite band."

Which was when the lights went out again. The recorded music stopped mid-syllable. People began to surge forward, nearly knocking him down. "Listen up, scuzzballs . . . ," said a voice, and the rest was lost in the roar rising all around Charlie. It swept him forward, and though the crowd grew denser with every step—his advance was checked several yards short of the stage by a wall of spike-studded leather jackets—he was now closer than he had ever been to live music, save for at his bar mitzvah. The sheer monophonic power of this sound blew away any impression those tuxed fucks had left. It was an avalanche, hurtling downhill, snapping trees and houses like tinkertoys, taking up every sound in its path and obliterating it in a white roar. As Charlie felt himself being taken up into it, totally, unable to decide whether it was good or bad—unable, even, to care. On record, in their Ex Post Facto versions, the songs had been taut and angular, with each instrument playing off the others: the spastic drumming, the laconic bass, and Venus de Nylon's summer-bright Farfisa. It was, in particular, the gap between the arch, faux-English talk-singing and the passionate squall of guitar that had drawn Charlie in. It was like the guitar was articulating the pain the frontman, Billy Three-Sticks, couldn't allow himself to name. Now everyone from the record sleeve was gone except the drummer. One guitar was in the hands of a black guy with green hair, and the other was around the thick neck that had just appeared above him. It was the new lead singer, Sam's latest friend. He was buzz-cut, dark-haired, savage, powerfully built. A person who *did* things, she'd said on the phone, ambiguously. His wet white straining face was only a few feet away, leaning out over all of them. He seemed to promise complete freedom, on the condition of complete surrender. And surrender happened to be what Charlie Weisbarger did best. His hands were on the shoulders of strangers. He was launching himself toward the singer to chant back at him the words that had once belonged only to Charlie and Sam: *City on fire, city on fire / One is a gas, two is a match / and we too are a city on fire.*

EVENTUALLY, IT WAS OVER. The lights were up, the room deflating. A disembodied voice was saying the band would be back at midnight for the second set, and Charlie felt himself contracting painfully back to the size of his regular body. By way of medication, he grabbed another half-empty drink from the rail along the wall, but it was mostly ice-melt. Then he spotted S.G. at the side of the stage, talking to another biker-looking guy. It was Charlie's turn to grab her arm. It seemed to take her a minute to remember who he was. "What?" she said.

"We're going to go backstage, aren't we?"

"I thought you'd split."

"I've got a twenty in my wallet. Don't make me beg."

She shrugged and turned back to the biker. "Cool if my friend comes, too?" The guy yawned and unhooked a mangy velvet rope from its bollard.

Backstage turned out to be a labyrinthine subbasement lit by bare bulbs and so crowded with staples and tags and tatters of old fliers that you couldn't see what color the paint had been. They came to a squat room with a drain sunk into its floor. The only concessions to hominess were some votive candles and a snot-green sleeper-sofa, on which the singer was slumped. From the doorway, he appeared fore-shortened, a narrow waist swelling into sturdy legs, legs giving way to massive shit-kicking boots. He had a chin-beard and a chipped front tooth and was covered from the neck down with tattoos. On the front of his sleeveless tee, the words *Please Kill Me* were scrawled in black marker. The sight of S.G. seemed to bring him to life. He patted the cushion beside him. "Hey, you. Get over here." In two steps, she was across the room and landing knee-first on the couch. She put her arm around the singer's shoulders and stared back at the doorway, obscurely victorious. Charlie couldn't remember all of a sudden what people did with hands.

"You guys were righteous. Oh, Nicky Chaos, this is, ah . . ."

"Charlie," Charlie said. Should he say something else? *Great show?* Oh, no, not *Great show*—anything but that! But Nicky Chaos wouldn't have cared anyway. He had put his head close to the girl's to whisper something. Charlie was confused; he'd thought her boyfriend was Sol Grungy. He couldn't leave without showing weakness, but couldn't stay without calling attention to his lack of a reason for doing so. Members of Get the Fuck Out were moving guitars and amps in the hallway behind him. From farther off came the buzz of the crowd, distorted by the cement floor. Then Nicky's eye was on him again. "Are you gonna say something, Charlie, or are you just going to watch?"

"Which do you want me to do?" It just slipped out, really, and was sincerely meant: Charlie was ready to do whatever was expected of him. But it sounded, even to his own ears, like smart-assery. Nicky Chaos became intensely still, as if trying to reach some decision.

"Somebody get this guy a beer," he said finally, "I kind of love this kid"—though the person to whom he was talking appeared to be Charlie.

Someone from out in the hallway set a cold beer on Charlie's shoulder. The green-haired black guy, the guitarist. Charlie tried not to let his hands shake, but the beer rose away from him at exactly the same speed as he reached for it, recalling those kids on the LIRR. Then it stopped. His fingers closed, grateful, around the can.

When he looked back at the couch, S.G. appeared to have conked out with her head on a cushion. The singer looked down at her like she was money someone had dumped in his lap. "So how do you know our friend here, Charlie?"

Charlie blushed. "We just met."

"Well, make sure to wear about three condoms if you plan on touching her," the guitarist said dryly behind him.

"Hey. That's my old lady you're talking about, Tremens," said another voice from the hall. It was an impossibly tall skinhead with safety pins through his eyebrows and both ears and a face like he'd sucked a lemon. Yep: Solomon Grungy, with whom Charlie had had the distinct displeasure that one other time, last Fourth of July. He'd been intimidating then, but seemed now like a watered-down Nicky Chaos. Similarly brawny, but larger and paler and less hairy. And less smart.

"Yeah, well, you'd better keep her away from Charlie here. I think she was about to give him a hummer," Tremens said.

Charlie looked at the wall while Sol inspected him. Sniffed. "I know you. You're Sam's little lapdog, from the summer. You couldn't get head from a cabbage."

Tremens laughed, but Nicky Chaos said, in a steely voice, to leave Charlie alone.

"Yeah, well, tell him to stay away from my girl," Sol said. Then he turned and stalked away, grumbling about the soundboard.

"Sounds like someone's got the property disease again," Nicky told the girl, who had opened her eyes at something someone had said. "It's counterrevolutionary. Preposthuman. You'll have to work on him." Then, to Charlie: "Hey, were you planning to drink that?"

Charlie gulped down half of the beer, aware that at any minute they could tire of him and ask him to leave, and then he'd no longer be fucking *hanging out* with Ex Whatever. The drummer, Big Mike, had now wandered in, along with the new organ player, each nodding at Charlie as if they'd been expecting to find him here. The pop-tops of Rheingolds exhaled contentedly, and another cold one found its way into his hand. He wondered where they were coming from: a fridge, a cooler, some inexhaustible aluminum tree sprouting deep in the warren of wonders that was "backstage."

Listening to them talk about who was in the audience reminded him that this was their first real performance. *That gallery fag Bruno was out there, did you see him? And Bullet's Angels, scary dudes, man, scary dudes. Plus the dissertationists, your Nietzsche Brigade. But has anyone seen Billy? Little bastard is probably too . . . Hey. . . .* All the while, the girl on the sofa, sitting up again, gazed at Charlie. "So you know Sam," she said. "You never told me that."

"Yeah, we're like best friends."

Nicky seemed to grow interested, though Charlie had the feeling he was trying to hide it. "Sam Cicciaro? She here with you?"

"Well, she was, sort of, but she had to run uptown to take care of something. Hey, do you guys know where the 72nd Street IND is? I'm supposed to meet her up there if she doesn't show soon," he said, importantly. "I'd hate to miss the second set, but . . ."

S.G. got to her feet. "Speaking of which, let me go talk Sol down from the ledge before he fucks up your mix. Come on, D.T. You'll be too fucked up to play." Charlie made to follow her and the guitarist until she stopped him. "Sol can get pretty jealous. Probably not the best idea he sees you with me." Laughter throbbed in the close chamber of the room.

"No, I just—" Except she'd left him behind. He wanted to explain to the newcomers, *She was decent to me*, but instead found himself saying, "She was going to give me a . . ."

Nicky Chaos laughed, and this was enough to drown out the little voice of self-hatred. "That's good, man."

Someone else said, "Oh, man. Charlie's just a baby."

"He needs a handle, though."

"A handle?"

"Yeah. Like your lady friend there. How about Backstage Charlie?"

"Charlie Boy, Charlie Baby," Nicky said. "Charlemagne. Don't Squeeze the Charmin."

"Or Charlie Blowjob. Chuck Fellatio."

Charlie couldn't see what was so funny, or whether they were laughing with him, at him, on him . . . Nicky Chaos's hand on his shoulder was reassuring. "Come on, Char-man Mao. I want to show you something."

Pretending not to see him wink, Charlie let himself be led deeper into the bowels of the club. There was no beer tree—just ceilings getting lower and lower, naked bulbs and dangling flypaper. "Watch your step," the singer said. All kinds of crap crunched underfoot: wires, chicken bones, bits of shadowy brick. Charlie was getting nervous again. It was, what was the word, *sepulchral*. Catacomb-y. They stepped over the threshold of a tiled and doorless bathroom. "We've still got to play another set," Nicky Chaos said. "You know what that means?" He drew a bit of plastic from his pocket. "Zoom zoom."

That summer, with Sam, Charlie had had a clear line in his mind, like the line on a strip of litmus paper, separating their dalliances with controlled substances from the hard stuff. Hazel liquids, grayish mushrooms, bright red canisters of unshaken Reddi-wip, milky blue spansules of painkillers that made his mouth water: all fair game (except the thin green confetti of Washington Square ditchweed, which he couldn't smoke on account of his asthma). But they swore off anything white. He'd seen *Panic in Needle Park*; that shit ruined lives. Then again, he'd never imagined himself here, in the sub-subbasement of a former bank, alone with a man who at any minute would ask him to cement their friendship. It was as if that thumb-sized glassine pouch contained not ordinary drugs, but some magic substance, a chalk-white eye of newt or the powdered tusk of a narwhal.

The spell had overtaken Nicky Chaos, too. His expansive gestures turned all business as he wrenched tight the dripping faucet, as he took off his tee-shirt, as he used it to wipe any moisture from the industrial sink. With all those tattoos on his superhero physique, he was like the Visible Man, but he seemed utterly unselfconscious—unaware even that there was anyone with him. Charlie could already see that he would go onstage like this, swept up in the moment, half-naked, and that his disregard for interpersonal niceties would be part of the power he exerted. His face was tight with concentration and yet somehow also vacant as he pinched open the slit of the plastic pocket and used an index finger to tip a little white onto the sink's steel lip. A switchblade came out of his back pocket, and with the dull side he combed the powder into two distinct middens, one large, one small, the brightest things in the room. The knife clattered down into the sink, but was still open and in plain view when he turned to Charlie like a newly rich man showing off his mansion to poor relations. "You done coke before?" The muddy tile amplified Charlie's cough into a small grenade. Music throbbed distantly overhead.

He lied. "Sure, yeah, one time."

"Well, have at, then."

A vision of himself toothless and sleeping in a cardboard box flared within Charlie, but there was also something deeply attractive at work, the glamour of a long slow dive into an empty pool, and the faces of all the people who'd let him down looking on, regretting their powerlessness to stop him. The face of Mom. The face of Sam. "Oh, you can go first."

"Hospitality, *hombre*. Guests before hosts."

Charlie took a breath and bent down to level his head with the sink. He thought you put a finger over each nostril, and then a single sniff did it. But someone else was watching from the doorway behind him.

"Give the kid a break, Nicholas."

It was a smallish man with a motorcycle jacket and a mass of black hair and a record sleeve clasped weirdly under one arm. The right side of his face was puffy, the eye swollen a deep purple, which was why it took Charlie a minute to recognize that this was the great Billy Three-Sticks.

"Jesus, what happened to you?" Nicky said, but he'd straightened up radically, at attention.

"Guy walks into a bar."

"I mean, I knew you were whipped, but not like literally . . . That even apply? Whipped?"

"Nothing was going to stop me from checking out your latest antics."

"You're awful generous with your time," said Nicky, with some heat.

"Pure selfishness. I had to make sure you weren't ruining my good name."

"You wouldn't let us use your good name, remember? But you'll be glad to know the first set was fucking *amazing*. Go on, tell him." Nicky nudged Charlie, but Billy Three-Sticks was unconvinced.

"Who's your friend here, Nicky? Do you really want to play corruptor of youth? Hey, if you know what's good for you, kid, you should keep clear of these fuckups."

"He does this all the time, he says. And you're one to talk."

"Besides," Billy continued, "it seems like you'd want your wits about you, Nicky. From what I hear, you're planning to go out in a real blaze of glory. Crude but effective, right?"

Nicky froze. It was like all the air had been sucked from the space between them. "Who told you that?"

"What do you mean, who told me? The ball drops in half an hour, and Bullet said you got a bunch of fireworks to shoot off at the end of the set. Some kind of big-ass bang."

Even as he relaxed, Nicky's armor seemed dented. "You know, Billy, we could still try to make the band thing work. It's never too late to change."

"Honestly, I'm just relieved to see Ex Nihilo's for real; I had gotten a little suspicious it was some kind of ruse. Which reminds me . . . I brought along a belated Christmas gift." Billy held out the record he'd been carrying. "Think of it as a peace offering of sorts. Deep stuff, but if you listen carefully, there's a message."

Charlie had an obscure impulse to tell Billy Three-Sticks not to give up or over so easily, but he kept his mouth shut, because whatever was being worked out here, it wasn't about him. And Sam would have died if she'd known she was missing this meeting of the minds, Ex Post Facto, Ex Nihilo. Then he remembered: *Quarter to twelve . . . Sam!* He could see her, waiting by the subway exit in the slanting snow, looking left and right, alone. The little snowdrift before him gave a last, potent dazzle, but not even the promise of Nicky's fireworks could match the purity of Charlie's vision, which was the purity of dreams. "I just remembered," he said. "I've got to go." He pushed past the man in the doorway, whom a minute earlier he wouldn't have dared to touch, but who seemed diminished by whatever he'd just ceded to his replacement. Only out in the corridor did Charlie look back, so that the last thing he remembered seeing before forging on through the maze of the basement and up the stairs was the two men, one burly and one small, inclined almost Talmudically over the sink, murmuring over what it contained.

8

THE BENCH HAD ALREADY ALL BUT DISAPPEARED in the first five or ten minutes, its bottle-green slats gone white to match the white drifted underneath. Now, as the wind kicked up, tufts of her hood's lining blew into her mouth, but she hardly noticed them, or the wind, or the snow, or even the fact that Charlie hadn't shown— because he would show eventually, was the beauty and the tragedy of Charlie. Instead, her attention was on the fleecy globes of light out front of the apartment house down the street, and on the schmancy vestibule door. Every time it opened, she leaned forward a little . . . but it would only be some society couple lurching out through the storm, toward a gleaming black towncar that was even then, as if by secret prearrangement, gliding to the curb. Sam finished her cigarette and drew her coat tighter and squinted through a wreath of smoke. She'd made a resolution: tomorrow she would stop smoking, stop waking up with the wheezy pain in her lungs, stop forking over five bucks a week to evil multinationals. One last little cylinder of death remained, though, rolling around in its pack. She wondered how long she had left.

Making resolutions had been something she used to do with her mother. New Year's was the one time of the year when Mom would bypass the bulgur wheat and wheat germ at the store in favor of the sweets Sam craved, and then they'd sit up together on the couch, dunking pizzelle in hot chocolate until sugar shock set in. Sam had been fat then. Mom had most likely been stoned. And what about Dad, where had he been? Work, probably. New Year's was the second-biggest night of the year for fireworkers, and he hadn't yet lost the contract to handle all the city's displays, or settled into beery automythology with the magazine reporter who would become his Boswell. Or Groskoph, as the case may be. The television had been half commercials, but Mom left it on. Every shot of Guy Lombardo with his bow tie and his microphone the size of a seal club brought them closer to the big moment. There was a Timex-sponsored clock in the lower right corner of the screen, and at T-minus thirty minutes, Mom would go get last year's resolutions, which had gradually been forgotten among the florilegia magnetized to the fridge. Sam could still remember how her mom smelled as she returned to the couch, cocoa powder and marshmallow-melt, yes, but also an intricate woodland thing that spoke of California, from which she'd so improbably come.

What you did was, you read your resolutions out loud and put a check by the ones you'd managed to keep. The ones you'd broken became a starting point for your new list. Fifty percent was considered pretty good, unlike at school. As she looked back now, though, several things struck Sam. The first was that Mom had already harbored yearnings she must not have realized were legible there, in the resolutions that had been hanging in plain sight for the last 364 days, if only Dad would have thought to look. The second was the guilty way Mom had glanced at the streaks of powdered sugar on her daughter's Dacron thighs as Sam read aloud her previous vow to lose twenty pounds. And finally—now that she had ten years of data on the two of them and an additional five on her own (for Sam was a manic documentarian, and had squirreled away all the lists)—there was this: how little difference it made. In the end, like every human project, these plans that on December 31 burned so brightly in the forebrain would gutter and come to grief. It was remarkable how many of her own resolutions Sam would forget in the course of the year. They would return to her at its end like sealed messages, bottles set adrift by some other self on the far shore of a wide sea.

For example, after swearing not to see Keith again (it was at the very top of her '77 list) she found herself waiting for him. The glass door was like the shutter of a Coleman lantern: the square of yellow light on the sidewalk shone brighter when it was open, but this time it was only a doorman in a long coat and epaulets, ducking out for a smoke. As if in sympathy, and before she could stop herself, she lit her own last cigarette and watched the lonely figure, his face the color of a pecan shell, pace back and forth in a cloud of his own breath. Her nose-ring stung her nose. It was hard not to crumple the cigarette pack now that her fingers had lost feeling, but she was not—*was not*—cold. This had been a late addendum to her list: that just for the night, for the sake of feeling brave enough to do what she'd come here to do, she would not worry about the time or the temperature. *The stubbornest person on earth*, her father called her. He didn't know the half. With those she loved—with Charlie, or with Dad himself—she could be, by her own standards, accommodating. She was most implacably stubborn when her opponent was herself. Because how many of her resolutions were really prohibitions? I will not *x*; I shall not *y*. She'd watched her mother closely, in those long-ago times when she'd been too little to know exactly what kinds of things one should promise oneself. She'd copied the syntax of Mom's list, negation for negation, and had felt a surge of closeness every time Mom said, "Hey, that's a good one." Marrying Dad had itself been a kind of negation. The problem with Sam was that, right up to the deadline, midnight or whatever date she'd set for herself to give something up, she would double her indulgence, as if stockpiling. She'd given up sweets for Lent one year, and had made herself sick on Pez the night before Ash Wednesday, and so had missed them all the more. By midday Mass, she was headachey, salivating, and as soon as Easter came she wallowed in Cadbury eggs. The truth was, she didn't in her heart of hearts want to give *anything* up.

When Mom left, she'd collapsed for a year, after which she had to more or less rebuild herself from scratch. This she had done in secret, in the confines of her room, requiring only pictures from magazines, an AM radio, and the binding glue of her need not to be hurt again. The self she'd put together was a kind of Minerva of suburbia: fierce, cosmopolitan, dependent on no one. Her body was changing—she helped it along by living on Marlboros for six months, blowing smoke out through the window fan—and when she emerged, her mother hardly would have recognized her. She rid herself of her virginity at fourteen, her first year at the new private school in the City, to a junior, the leading scorer on the lacrosse team and second-richest boy in his class. His parents were never home, and there was something thrilling and dangerous about the empty seventeenth-floor apartment where they could do whatever they wanted. For a month, they hung out there after school, getting high, looking at his dad's skin magazines, which she pronounced "gross," and fucking. He knew what he was doing, she'd thought then. At any rate, she'd learned a lot. She'd learned to carry herself, sexually, like someone who knew what *she* was doing.

And she had learned that you couldn't stockpile anything that mattered, really. Feelings, people, songs, sex, fireworks: they existed only in time, and when it was over, so were they. Right now the stripped branches of the trees above her were like knuckles, like a child's knuckly cursive on the soft purple vellum of the sky, and there was snow soaking through her jeans and the water in the corners of her eyes was stuck there, freezing, refusing to fall, and the little man was pacing in front of the limestone redoubt, but the second this interminable wait ended, it would all start to fall away into the past, to become unreal. Her need to tell Keith was a physical thing now, like the cells of her body crying out in alarm, even though she'd opened the door inside herself only the tiniest crack. But she would hold out another minute, and another, because she could.

IN SOME SENSE, SURE, she had already known what was coming six weeks ago, waiting for him in the park near his office. He was staging this in public so that she would have to maintain her fragile (he assumed) composure. Part of what had attracted her to him in the first place was the way he could be completely transparent to her while remaining to himself opaque. She loved the things he wanted to believe about himself, the way you love a little kid when he lies about who broke the flower vase. He wanted to believe, for example, that he'd been moving toward her these last few months, when really it was what he was running away from that mattered. As he climbed the steps to the park, a neglected oasis elevated one story above the hurly-burly of Midtown, she saw how this running had aged him. There were lines around his mouth she'd never noticed before, and bunchy little pouches under his eyes from lack of sleep. Honestly, they turned her on, an erotic charge that cut through her mood of resignation. She pictured herself kissing them. Straddling him in a curtained room, bending down to lick away the worry. But the most he would give her was a quick peck on the cheek, and even that was like he was doing her some big favor. The park was a semi-proprietary possession of the brick buildings of Tudor City Place, and at midday, it was sparsely occupied. She and Keith circled it like swans on water, a long, slow gyre on the path that might have been laid only for them.

"There's something I've been meaning to discuss with you, Samantha."

"Uh-oh. Sounds serious." He used her name only when he was feeling especially paternal. She plucked a few nuts from the white paper bag he was holding—but how serious could it be, if he'd stopped to buy nuts?—and popped them into her mouth, insouciantly, she hoped. "But we're talking right now."

"I shouldn't have let you come up to the apartment the other day."

Well, of course he shouldn't. They shouldn't have been fucking in the first place, if he wanted to be strictly ethical about it. It was amazing; he seemed to believe that his actions had consequences only as kids believe in the Tooth Fairy: because other people said so, and because when you lifted up your pillow . . . look! A quarter!

"There's a whole other side of my life you don't see, Samantha. It's like I split off from myself somewhere . . . And having you there, it made me feel like that me was watching this one, and I realized that all this has been a huge act of personal recklessness. I care about you, you know that. But that other me was always the person I meant to be."

They had by this point, what with the charged pauses, made a complete circuit of the park, but the graveled path before them, across which a little boy was chasing an errant spaldeen, seemed to draw him on. Or maybe it was just the faceted perfection of his speech, which he must have turned over in his head for days, like a rock tumbler with a particularly obdurate chunk of rock. He was saying he felt like he needed to take some time and figure some things out, because he felt he may have made some . . . miscalculations somewhere, and however things shook out, his kids were . . . look, they were the most important things in his life. He didn't deserve them. (*Well, obviously,* Sam thought. *Parents never do.*)

His face was chapped now, and he had worked himself up to soulfulness, if not actual tears, and she felt an almost distaste when he said he hoped she didn't think it was anything personal. "Don't patronize me, Keith. Of course it's personal."

"I just need some time."

"Fine. Let's not see each other, then. I'm not a child."

Now he stopped and looked at her. Was *she* breaking things off with *him*? The glister of midlife sentiment was gone from his eyes, and his entire body was tensed at the midpoint between anger and hunger, which is exactly where she liked him best. In the second when she thought he might forcefully kiss her, she could see how hard it was actually going to be, giving him up, this wayward animal she'd learned to make trot or canter. But she forced herself to reach into the translucent little bag he was holding and take what remained and to say, around a mouthful of nuts, "It was getting a little stale anyway."

And with that, it was essentially over, though they'd taken a few more laps around the park: one with him in his impulsive, ardent mode; one minimizing—*poor kid, in over her head, doesn't know what she's saying*—and one, finally, with him back to his impossible, his selfless and selfish, self. He took her hands in his expensive gloves and looked at her, and she could see him willing her not to be permanently fucked up by the last three months. (He, too, was a Catholic, she knew. In the sealed grave of a by-the-hour hotel she'd lain with her head on his chest and twitted with her finger the little silver cross he wore, until he'd told her to stop it.) He wanted her to remember, he said, that he cared about her, and that she deserved better. He would not use the word love, nor would she. It wouldn't have been true, and anyway, she didn't want to give him the satisfaction.

IT MUST HAVE BEEN CLOSE TO MIDNIGHT NOW. Cabs had sublimated off Central Park West to be deposited in other, more populous precincts. (Funny how in the City the money followed the energy, but could never quite keep up.) The lingering warmth of their tires left dark tracks on the road. Otherwise, a white perfection obtained. No feet had marked the sidewalk where Sam sat. No dogs had come out to yellow it. The glow of the traffic signal stretched almost as far as the vestibule, the party, Keith: red, then green. She'd never noticed before that it actually made a small click when it changed. Across the street, in front of the synagogue, a halo of green snow marked the entrance to the B/C station, from which Charlie continued not to emerge, and suddenly, shivering, she was struck by a deep fissure in the fairness of things. The adult who had fucked her and ditched her got to return to the world twenty stories above street level, while she, the seventeen-year-old, got left out in the cold alone. She stubbed out the cigarette, the last one. She made for the door. She'd changed her mind; she would storm the castle, propriety be damned. Charge in among the tailcoats and furs on behalf of every wronged woman since the beginning of time, make a spectacle of herself, as a kind of warning. She would tell him he'd better come hear what she had to say, if he didn't want them both to land in jail, or worse, and everyone he knew and respected, everyone whose opinion he valued, would see the truth about the two of them, even as she discharged her duty.

She got close enough to reach for the curving brass handle. She could see the doorman at his post, and the ghost of her own face floating in front of it. Her indignation made her beautiful, even to herself. She wouldn't know for sure which one the wife was, but that didn't mean the wife wouldn't sense who *she* was, and there would come a moment when their eyes met and Sam would have to see what she'd done to this woman, how she'd hurt her. Then Sam thought of his kids, and particularly his son, five years younger than she was. The scene she would make, the whispers that would find their way back to him, his potential sense of it being, somehow, his fault. She made an awkward shrug at the doorman, the visual equivalent of "Sorry, wrong number." She trudged, cold and smokeless, back toward her bench. It was almost a whiteout now; how would anyone see the ball when it dropped? Possibly it had dropped already, and the fireworks down in the harbor were too far away to hear. But then where was Charlie? She wished he would hurry up and come. She was about to sit down when someone, from the park entrance, said her name. She couldn't quite make out the figure who stood there, a new depth in the shadows, in the snow, but the voice set tumblers falling inside her, in a keyhole that had locked up other things she ought to have known. "Hey," it said. "We've been looking all over for you."

9

"WHAT WAS THAT?"

"What was what?"

"You didn't hear that?" It had been a pop, a metallic flaw in the otherwise immaculate hush of the Park, so small Mercer might have imagined it. He cocked his head, as if to summon it back. Distant revels seeped through layers of stone and glass; over on Columbus, a snowplow mushed wearily past. The only other sound was William's sister coughing beside him. Light through the curtained door striped her ear and jawline, but her face, turned toward the end of the block, was invisible. "Maybe a firework or something," he said.

"Is it next year yet, do you think? Because if it is, you have to kiss me."

"William would love that," he said.

"Just blame it on alcohol." Regan did seem pretty drunk. Also high.

"But he knows I don't drink."

"So what were you doing with that wine when I found you in the kitchen?"

"Wait, was that—? Dag, I thought I heard it again. Must be something wrong with me."

The balcony was outside her bedroom suite. Or rather, *the suite of rooms her father's wife insisted on pretending was hers*, as she'd put it a few minutes ago, while he'd held her injured hand under the faucet (it being his lot in life, apparently, to play nursemaid to the Hamilton-Sweeneys). Water made pink by blood fanned against the porcelain sink and clung in drops, and when a flap of gray skin flipped back in the gush, he could see she was going to have a handsome scar. She was lucky she hadn't hit bone. He searched the medicine cabinet. Not only was there no mercurochrome, there weren't even band-aids. "Don't expect to find anything under the surface," she said airily. The champagne was analgesic. "I haven't slept a night here since college. Felicia just likes it to look inhabited." He'd folded a monogrammed washcloth into thirds and, after blotting her wound dry, wrapped the makeshift bandage around it. She needed to keep the pressure on, he said, until it clotted. But how to secure the tourniquet? "How about that thing?" She nodded toward the mirror. He scoured the reflection—the ivory carpet of the bedroom beyond. Then he saw that she was looking at her own chest, the butterfly brooch pinned there.

"Oh, I don't want to use that. It'll get all bent out of shape."

"It was a Christmas gift from Felicia, I only wore it so Daddy would see me wearing it."

"What's she going to think when she sees you using it as a clothespin?"

"What's she going to think when she sees you clinging to my hand? Because that's pretty much the alternative." She reasoned surprisingly well, for a drunk person.

His left hand keeping pressure on the cut, he had to use his right to undo the pin of the brooch and slide it from her low-cut dress. It was like a game of Operation. His pinky was inches from his lover's sister's breast. "You're not helping anything, staring like that."

"Be patient with me, Mercer. This is the most fun I've had all night."

Finally, the brooch was loose. Once he'd pinned shut the washcloth, he retreated to the outer room to plunk down on the bed. The bedside lamp made the room swim up in stronger light. It was the Platonic ideal of a girl's room, the one he imagined his students returning home to after a hard afternoon of field hockey: flounced bedspread, lacquered dressing table. Regan, now cradling the maimed hand, wobbled toward the French doors.

"Make sure you give that a more thorough cleaning as soon as you get home," he said. "I'd hate for you to get lockjaw."

"Come here. I'll show you something." And she'd led him out onto the little balcony.

The view was godlike, cinematic: the City as he'd dreamed it from his homely hometown seven hundred miles away. Resolving out of the snow, like a picture tuned in on a television, were crenellated apartment buildings, yellow windows punched out of the darkness, powdered sugar shaking down over the layer-cake hotels down on Central Park South. Light pollution seemed to emanate from within the clouds, the byproduct of some hidden organic process, like the warmth made by blood. To the east, the Park was a vast dark quarry. The lintels and pergolas and gargoyles massed above kept the snow off, mostly, but he was surprised that Regan, in her skimpy dress, wasn't ready to turn back inside. Indeed, she seemed to breathe easier out here, in the quiet. "You should see it on a clear day."

"No, it's a hell of a view," he said.

"I mean I don't want you to think I'm in thrall to Felicia or any-thing, but it did seem like a shame not to show you the room's best feature, since you're up here. Also . . ." Fumbling one-handed in her clutch, she'd pulled out a lighter and what looked to be a slightly zaftig toothpick. "I got this from the woman who did my hair. You want?"

Mercer demurred. "I don't do that, either."

She said, "I wouldn't, normally, but I'm in the middle of this divorce, and tonight's been a train wreck, and I figured . . . Would you mind holding that lighter for me?"

He was getting cold himself, but obliged her, and when she'd taken a long pull on the charred-smelling stuff—the heat radiated—he decided he was well wide of his mark for the evening, anyway. With-out asking, he took the doobie from her good hand and copied her, the three-fingered grip, the held breath. "Don't exhale yet. Like that. Slowly."

He coughed. "You really are peas in a pod, aren't you?"

"Who?"

"You and William. He doesn't talk to you, you don't talk to your stepmother . . ."

"Father's wife." Their voices were at odds, but their hands cooper-ated to get the joint back to her. The streets below were like streets on maps, free from people and eye-level disorder, and he could feel the force of mutual appreciation binding them together. "My brother hates her, too. Does he not talk about this?"

"Not as such."

She sighed. "What are you really doing here, Mercer? I mean, what exactly are you and William to each other? It's okay—you can tell me."

It was at this moment that he'd first heard the pop.

"HONESTLY, I DON'T KNOW," Mercer said now, as if her question had just reached him. "I don't know anymore. I mean, like you said, it's good to have someone. But whatever happened between the two of you, it eats at him, like a hole inside him he thinks he has to hide. I suppose the sense of mystery was part of what attracted me. But I didn't come to New York because I wanted to live with a stranger. At some point, I assumed he'd . . . I don't know." He motioned for the joint, but it was now too small to suck on without burning his fingers, so he flicked it, sending it skittering down however many stories, a flare in the dimness.

"Look at that. You're a natural." She tucked the lighter away in the clutch, saying something about her kids finding it, but made no move to return to the party.

"Aren't you freezing?" he asked.

"I just can't quite face having to go back in there yet. There are some people I really don't want to talk to."

He hugged himself and stamped his feet, waiting to feel different. "Anyway, William has a lot more experience at this than me, you know? At relationships."

"Is that what he told you?"

"I thought maybe because I'm a boy, or man, I guess, was why he was keeping me in one compartment and y'all in another. But when you showed up at the school last week—"

"I'm sorry if I put you in a position. I had just moved out of my husband's apartment. I needed so badly to talk to someone, and I thought maybe the divorce meant everything else might change, too. Maybe William would finally be ready to take down his stupid wall."

"And I guess for my part I thought he'd open that invitation and some golden door would just be thrown open, and then we wouldn't have to live anymore the way we've been living. It's not without its charms, sort of, but how can we have a future together if I can't even know these basic things about his past?"

"He's always been secretive, my brother. Since he was a little kid.

He thinks it creates some kind of personal power, to have a double life. I think he read too many comics."

"So maybe I really came here because I knew it would piss him off if he found out. Not that you're not lovely company." And an almost unaccountable smile broke from somewhere within him. It was true. He *liked* Regan. She reminded him of other white girls he'd known, the fellow English majors who'd adopted him at U. Ga. "Can we go inside now, please? I'm bleeping gelid."

She touched his arm with her good hand. "Hey, why don't you come with me?"

"Come with you?"

"I've been summoned by Felicia's brother. I'll introduce you, and you can see what William's up against. And maybe you can protect me."

"Protect you from what?" But she had turned back toward the warmth of the bedroom. He retrieved his mask. "You're sure you didn't hear that sound?" he asked, before he pulled the French door shut. "I'm from the South. We know guns."

She shrugged. "It's Central Park West, Mercer. Probably just a truck backfiring."

Inside, her stride grew more purposeful with every threshold they crossed, as if she were drawing strength from his presence, or from the drug, though he couldn't be sure this wasn't just the swimmy tempo of his own head. The guests seemed denser, too. Out of a jumble of bodies came hands clutching bottles, dentures bared in brays of Republican laughter, teeth freaky in their perfection, like Chiclets. He was the only nonwhite guest—though he hadn't in the strictest sense been invited. And it must have been past midnight. Where was William right now? Leaning back against the wall of some bar's men's room while a blond head worked on him down below? He pushed the image away, let his consciousness become a tide coursing over the Persian rugs. Let Regan lead.

He couldn't have said how many times she got detained, how many whisky kisses she endured from how many middle-aged men, how many compliments on her appearance—you look *good*, a woman said, *healthy*, euphemisms whose referents he couldn't quite pin down— how many frowns about her washclothed hand, nor how many eyes sized him up through slitted card-stock. A servant? Hanger-on? Charity case? Still, it bothered him less than it had in his first hour of the party, which he'd spent hiding behind an enormous potted palm. If he couldn't yet enter the enchanted circle of the Hamilton-Sweeneys, he could at least make a close study of its effects, and maybe someday he would return hand-in-hand with William and none of them would dare say a word. And Regan, who'd looked so down when he'd spotted her in the kitchen—was that really a half-hour ago?—was magnificent, even with no mask. He'd seen this in William, too, the switch that got flipped in a crowd. What Mercer had put down to personal pathology was apparently genetic. She glowed like a holiday bauble while he bobbed along behind, unsure whether he was having a great time or an awful one.

Then, in the midst of a tall room packed with people, he looked up. Ten feet above his head, where the second story would have been, a gallery ran the perimeter, with a doorway leading onto it from each of the room's four sides. And up there, facing them, stood a small, white-haired man who seemed to be smiling directly at Mercer. He wore no costume and no mask. Still, in his black tuxedo he had the air of a duke overlooking his domain. Mercer felt the masked heads receding, the chatter retreating like the sea inside a shell, the heat of the assembled bodies fading. The man unwrapped a hand from the wrought-iron rail, raised it palm-up in the air, snapped it closed.

Then Mercer realized that Uncle Amory—for that's who it had to be—was beckoning Regan, not him. He nudged her, and she excused herself from whatever conversation she'd been in. She slipped her injured arm through Mercer's and steered him toward a spiral staircase. They mounted to the balcony as through a cold, resistant fluid. The man's close-lipped smile never wavered. He must at some point have been nice-looking; not a single fleck of color was still visible on his fastidiously groomed head. "My dear," he said to Regan. "I had so hoped we would find each other tonight."

"Amory Gould," she said. "Allow me to present Mercer Goodman."

Mercer noticed with a sinking feeling that she had not introduced him *as* anything, and that the implication was that he was somehow involved with Regan, rather than with William. Brute facts of his appearance were being used to shock, even to injure. But to dispel the confusion would be to betray her, and he couldn't; her good hand now squeezed his biceps like a blood-pressure cuff. He was aware of the dryness of his mouth, the near-audible thump of his heart. The odd thing was that Uncle Amory had not stopped smiling. It was impossible to say what was anxious-making about him, apart from the hard blue stare. "So, Mr. Goodman," he said. "What's your line?"

Mercer coughed. He probably smelled like Woodstock. "Pardon?"

"What do you do, son?"

He'd learned not to let belittlement or even open insult goad him into a reaction. *You're the only one who has power over you*, Mama had reminded him before he'd left for college, though he wasn't sure he'd ever really believed it. What he was sure of was that Amory Gould didn't. The man was watching him the way a kid watches an ant on whom he's trained the sun via magnifying glass.

"I'm a teacher," he ventured. "I work in the high school at Wenceslas-Mockingbird."

"You must know Ed Buncombe, then, the Dean of Faculty."

"Dr. Runcible is the new man." Later, he would wonder why he hadn't stopped there. But Regan's talons were practically piercing the material of his dinner jacket, and Amory Gould still beamed inscrutably, and as the silence up here on the balcony thickened, Mercer had a sense that people were starting to watch from below. "And I write." He knew instantly that it was a mistake.

"I see. And what do you write, Mr. Goodman?"

"Amory, don't pry, please," Regan said. "Mercer, you don't have to answer that."

"She's right. Quite, quite right," Amory said. "When you reach a certain age, you forget how fragile these things can feel. A puff of breath might knock them over. Would you believe I used to churn out verse myself, as an undergraduate? Dreadful. Eventually, I put it aside, took up a more practical career in government, then business. The three ages of man, you know. But let me ask you this, Mr. Goodman." The head seemed to be swelling now, growing closer. Its eyes were rimmed with pink, like chunks of ice that had torn holes in the hands that handled them. "Your day job, the teaching, do they know about these other proclivities of yours? Because one owes it to them, and to oneself, to be honest."

"Come again?"

"Writing, my boy. Oh! You didn't think I meant . . . How embarrassing."

Proclivities. The innuendo here had little or nothing to do with him personally; he knew it was meant to wound his presumed date. And yet the lightness of Uncle Amory's regard was, in itself, humiliating. Nor did Regan make any effort to defend him. How had he ever kidded himself into thinking he could be part of this world?

Mumbling something about the lateness of the hour, he took his leave. Amory didn't deign to shake hands, or say that it had been nice to meet him; he'd already turned to Regan and was telling her that, if she had a minute, they had *important matters* to cover; and what ever had she done to her finger? When Mercer glanced back, on the off-chance that she, at least, was ruefully watching, the two of them had already been sucked through one of the balcony doors. He wished he could disappear that easily, but the only way out was down the twisting staircase and across the full breadth of the room. His mask was suddenly meaningless. He was distinctly aware of the darkness of his skin against the white dinner jacket, the dryness of his eyes and mouth, the nap of his hair. The women, in their variegated little dominos, looked like savannah birds turning to watch a wounded rhino blunder by. Even the coat-check girl in the foyer seemed to smell weakness on Mercer. She took her time retrieving the Coat of Several Colors, and still he had to leave her a tip, so as not to confirm her worst intuitions. The elevator was obnoxiously slow.

By the time he hit night air, he'd begun to sober up somewhat, his shame cooling to a sort of melancholy. Here he was, expelled from Eden, back down on the street, where a lamppost was once again a lamppost, a parked car exactly the size of a parked car. The spires of Midtown were lost to the snow, and even the balcony from which (however briefly) he'd possessed the glittering life he longed for seemed smudged and blurry, like the memory of a dream. For a minute, the only evidence that he was in a functioning city and not in the ruins of the future was the bench across the street, where a human-sized patch of green amid the snow attested to recent occupancy. Someone waiting, no doubt, for a bus.

Then miraculously, way up Central Park West, at the very edge of what the slackening snowfall permitted him to see, one glimmered into view: two bulbs surmounted by a headband of light. It was always a mug's game, trying to calculate whether surface streets or the subway would get you home faster, but he'd learned by trial and error not to overlook the transportational bird in the hand, especially not after midnight, and there would be something fitting, would there not, about ending this night and this year on a poky and prosaic city bus, amid the alcoholic, the epileptic, and the otherwise damned, in mortuary fluorescence, on a sticky floor, in the seat nearest the driver?

In the time it took these stoned apprehensions to shamble across the stage of his attention and do their little twirl, the traffic signals had gone from yellow to red, pinning the bus into place a dozen blocks off. He leaned against the pole of the bus-stop sign, trying to recover the earlier image of himself as a romantic figure, the loner in the long, brown coat. He whistled a few bars from *La Traviata*. He thought poignantly about himself thinking. He was appreciating the soulful billow of his own breath before him when from behind the stone wall across the street, the darkened Park, came the most upsetting sound he'd ever heard. It was a sob: high, breathless, gurgly, like a dying seal. And then it stopped. It must have been another fantasy, or at the very least none of his business, but even before it came a second time, some animal matrix beneath the skin of his consciousness had been activated. The bus was now only ten blocks away, or fewer, kneeling to discharge a passenger. He willed it to hurry up. He would hop aboard, and the sound, assuming it even was a sound, would be the problem of the person now climbing off. Except the traffic signals had gone red again. *Shit*, he thought. Shit. What was he supposed to do?

The noise did not recur. He thought of all the harmless things it could be. A dying fox; there were foxes in Central Park, weren't there? The wind moaning over a plastic bag caught in a tree. One of those sad, compulsive men who cruised public spaces in search of anonymous rough sex. Whatever it was, it was not his responsibility, and this timely ride home, his reward for all he'd endured tonight, was—

The driver laid on the horn as Mercer darted in front of the oncoming bus, toward the far side of the street and the park entrance. As he plunged under the snow-crazed tangle of limbs and into the bosk, he had to rely on his memory, on an impression of something he hadn't been listening for. It had seemed close to the wall, hadn't it? He cursed his dress shoes, which threatened to slip out from under him on the icy downhill path. A pile of black boulders rose to the left, a screen of bushes to the right. You're a fool, Mercer Goodman, he thought—a clown on the heath, with no Lear. Still, what if it had been a human being? Well, what if? In that case, there was probably more than one human being, an attacker and a victim, and Mercer, with his bow tie and his soft dilettante's hands, would just be fresh meat.

He stepped over the knee-high iron piping that edged the path and forced his way between two bushes. At first the earth running up to the wall was an illegible sheet of snow and shadow. But he must, with that same animal attunement that had marched him here, have sensed breathing, or warmth, because as he stared at the base of the wall, a crumpled mess resolved out of it. He approached. Some birds perching atop the masonry nestled down in their feathers, vigilant. It was just a kid, he saw. A boy. No, a girl, short-haired. Her face was turned upward, toward the plane of light spreading over the wall, her head twisted back uncomfortably on her neck. She was unconscious, maybe dead. Blood from her shoulder had spilled out to color the snow. Mercer was appalled to remember that blood had a smell, a coppery kind of smell. He thought for a second he might vomit.

"Help!" he yelled. His voice boomed off the wall and dissipated in the void behind him. He yelled again. "Help!" The birds resettled themselves. The girl did not stir. You weren't supposed to move a body, and he didn't want to touch it, so he stood for a minute, looking down at the black form he would now forever be involved with. Then he took off, between the bushes, up the path, a ghost burst out of the jaws of hell, shouting as if anyone might save him.

10

REGAN HAD FELT THE EYES before she'd seen them, moving over her like a pawnbroker's fingers. And if she'd imagined having William's gay black boyfriend on her arm might protect her, those eyes made her feel that even this had been choreographed, like the divorce, the storm out in Chicago, the knife with which she'd cut herself. Which was of course somewhere near the heart of Uncle Amory's power: to be in his presence was to come into propinquity with designs far larger and older than oneself, great star-maps wheeling across an empty planetarium dome. As far as she could tell, these designs were the sole basis for his interest in other people. Not curiosity, not sympathy, not even amusement, but underlying the canny simulation of normal personhood, the simple question of what might be in it for him. Whatever it was, in this case, must have been significant, because the last time he'd appraised her so openly had been that long-ago weekend on Block Island, when she'd mistaken it for attraction. And then there was how swiftly he'd dispatched poor Mercer, alighting on his secret in a single swoop. She felt bad about this, but compared to her own, decades-old injury, it was a flesh wound; Mercer would heal. She hurried into the room off the balcony not to abandon him, but to deprive Amory of the chance to steer her.

It was the old conservatory, the one room in the triplex penthouse she'd ever really been able to stand. When he'd bought the place for Felicia, Daddy had done it up as a proper library. Regan liked to think of this as Daddy's oblique apology to her and to William for the impending remarriage. (Of course, by that point, William was off at his second or third school, and anyway, he'd always confused stoicism with not suffering at all.) Her mother's books, with their motley spines, were easy to spot among the uniform leather sets of *gesammelte Schriften* Felicia had bulk-ordered from the Strand. Her first and only summer here, Regan had sequestered herself among the rolling ladders and soft couches, recovering. At sunset, the south-westerly light, unobstructed by any higher building between here and the river, poured through the jewelbox windows. It had made her feel like a passenger on the *Titanic:* the vessel was doomed, but the memory would be extravagant. But what good did it do anyone to recall such things now? The ladders were gone. Where one shelf of Mom's books had been was a sort of television, which she recognized as one of the firm's new electronic stock-price terminals. And in place of the leather couch where she'd reclined, in secret mourning for all she'd lost, was a huge desk taken up mostly by a three-dimensional architectural model. She could tell from the complicated silence that Amory was still watching, so she stiffened herself. Reined her head in. "You've really made yourself at home here."

"This?" He passed around her, trailing a hand over the edge of the desk, and settled himself in the swiveling chair. "This was your father's idea. With him working from home so much these days, he wanted a place where I'd be near at hand. His man Friday, as it were." Sometimes Regan wondered whether her father even existed anymore, or whether he was a mere syllogistic convenience, a floating variable that could be brought in to balance accounts. "Have a seat."

"I've been sitting all night," she fibbed, but she knew the way she stood behind the armchair with her hands on its back probably read as fear.

"Suit yourself." Amory smiled harmlessly. Then he leaned back as if the better to see the model on the desk. It was a stadium of some kind, Regan saw, rising among dozens of spikier buildings next to a flat blue river one nth of its actual size. He read her gaze, rather willfully, as a question. "Has no one shown you the plans yet for Liberty Heights?"

"Don't tell me we're buying a football team."

"Of course not. Just the stadium. Building it, actually. The anchor tenant for eighty acres of redevelopment."

"This is the South Bronx? It's been burning up there for years. Our underwriters would revolt."

"One man's obstacle, Regan, is another's opportunity. You'd be surprised at how swiftly you can have a Blight Zone declared, once a neighborhood gets sufficiently torched. And then it's whole parcels of blocks, resold for pennies. Funds matched. Taxes abated."

"Not exactly the textbook free market."

But it was as if he'd unconsciously slipped into his pitch, and could no longer hear her. "We broke ground on Phase One in November, though only unofficially, once the Blight decree came through. I can't believe this didn't reach you. At any rate, you'll be working on it soon enough, when we formally unveil the project."

Since he'd joined the firm, diversification had been Amory's watchword; Regan had been aware of it largely as a succession of debt-financed acquisitions awaiting the board's approval. She was inclined to vote against them, as were a few others of the old guard, but during intermissions of the board meetings, this still-elegant little man, who had sat almost unnoticeable in his chair halfway down the table, would abscond to empty corners with this or that director. Later, when they reconvened to vote, Amory inevitably won. And Regan had been wrapped up in more domestic problems during those years. It was only when she came on full-time that she saw the scale of the ventures she was being asked to flack: bauxite mines and cigarettes and a major coffee concern in Central America, and now, once again, real estate, on which he'd always been oddly bullish. *Why invest in others, when you can have them invest in you?* He covered the model with a cloth that had been folded behind. The proselytic urge seemed to subside.

"But we're all busy these days, Regan, who can blame us for not staying informed?"

"Informed of what?"

"Well, of the news it gives me no pleasure to break, before it reaches you some other way. A family matter. In a way, it may be a blessing that your father's not here tonight, as it buys us some time to make decisions."

News was a synonym for bad news, and she couldn't keep from leaping to the worst conclusions. The test results were in; the cloud that had battened on Daddy's mind was a brain tumor. Or his plane was in a ditch beside the O'Hare runway, in flames. Both. Still, she would not beg Amory to tell her.

"There is no way to sugarcoat this, I'm afraid," he said, following a too-long pause. "When your father steps off the plane tomorrow he is going to be arrested."

"What?"

"Insider trading, I'm told is the charge. It's all rather convoluted."

"Told by whom? I thought indictments were sealed, or classified, or something."

"I keep an active Rolodex. You know that."

"You're making this up."

Having gotten this out of her, Amory was free to lean forward, to show his eagerness. He was weirdly tan for December, she thought. He must have gone down to the isthmus again to meet with the Café El Bandito people, or his cronies in the junta. "Now why, dear niece, would I want to do that?"

Why indeed, she thought, when upon Daddy's return she would just have found out he was lying? "Fine," she said, "maybe it's true. But we face lawsuits all the time. That's why we have a legal department."

"This is different. There's a mole inside the firm. Your father is the named defendant. There is jail time involved, not to mention the scandal."

"Well, what do you propose we do?"

After swallowing her revulsion, she worked out with him that Daddy would remain in Chicago until Monday, when he'd surrender in person before a judge. This way, they could keep it out of the papers, or at least confined to the business section. Amory was of course confident, he said, having tortured her sufficiently, that there had been no actual wrongdoing. That this would blow over.

BUT WOULD IT? When Regan reached street level a half-hour later, the sirens she'd been hearing in the distance were imminent. Red and blue lights lapped at the elevator gate. The block beyond the front windows was now a horror show of police cars and ambulances and people falling off the sidewalks: people from the party, people from other parties, snowy-haired women from surrounding buildings who had come out in slippers, putatively to walk their tiny dogs one last time before dawn, but really just to gawk. And shame on you, Regan, for pretending you're any purer of heart. Her first instinct, despite the jostle of endorphins and cannabinoids in her bloodstream, was to go ask: Had the police arrived already? Then Miguel had explained, in a chastened voice, that someone had got shot in the park. She wished she could travel back in time and erase the part of herself that had assumed this must be about her father, her problems. "A damn shame," the doorman said. "A kid." And there instantly were her own kids, uncarapaced in their beds, with only three locks and Mrs. Santos the sitter to protect them, and all she wanted was to be in motion toward them.

She teetered over to Amsterdam in her heels and caught a cab. She asked the driver to take the Transverse, to avoid the quagmire around Daddy's. Only after a minute did it occur to her that she'd given the cabbie the address of the old place, out of habit. She leaned forward to request that he take a right when they hit Fifth—they were actually going to Brooklyn. She still thought of it that way, as a *request*, rather than an *instruction*. He could just as easily have adopted some alternate route to run the meter up, or left her for dead in a field near one of the airports, having taken her wallet. She used to have a gift for trusting people who claimed to know the way, but wherever you turned now, these nightmare scenarios seemed to fly at you, like tabloid sheets gusting up from the gutters. Thieves posing as cabbies. Killers posing as cops. And now *Kid Shot in Park*.

Fighting nausea, she pressed her forehead to the window. Through the cold glass and the snow, she could see up to the top of the wall that hemmed in the transverse road. Branches tattooed the sky. A man with a gun moved from tree to tree, tracking her, but not really. When had she become such a fraidy-cat? She had contrived by certain arcane strategies to keep the answer hidden, even from herself. These always involved a man, analysis had helped her to see. There had been Daddy, and then William, and then Keith, each taking over at the point where his predecessor had failed. But now there was no one left to look after her, or to whom anyone who hurt her would have to answer. She herself was the protector, the final line of defense between Will and Cate and the world, and what frightened her she would just have to face down.

The potholes of Fifth Avenue and the cab's jellied suspension sent her stomach floating again. The snow was tapering off beyond the breath-fogged glass. Down the length of a sidestreet, the lights of Times Square were cold and inhuman. Surprising, how quickly it emptied out once the cameras were off. She had a sudden vision of the city surrendering to wilderness. The snow would blow off to reveal vines climbing townhouses, cougars prowling the subway entrance. Not a natural order of things, but chaos: children turning against parents, cars falling through holes in the street. Commercial districts empty, neighborhoods overrun. Indigents hunkered in alleys, looking up raccoonlike into the sweep of light from passing cars, paws pressed together, faces smeared with blood. And underneath it all, an echoing pop—the sound she now realized she'd heard, too, up there on the balcony, of a gunshot. In a just world, she thought, whoever the kid was would still be ambulatory, and Amory would be the one in that ambulance, screaming off downtown.

She couldn't get his voice out of her head. *This will all blow over.* A Blight Zone. Nor could she forget that shot. Bile rose hot in her throat. She made it as far as the expressway, but then had to ask the cabbie to pull over. She hunkered, hands on knees, over a Jersey barrier. She hadn't closed the door behind her, and from it spilled the dome light and the sound of the radio, which the cabbie must have turned up to cover her retching. It was that one call-in host, the primal screamer, Dr. Whosit, with a Z, not actually a doctor. But was it possible his show was already on, at whatever a.m. on a Saturday? And again: could she really be hearing him rant about crooked financiers, so soon after settling with Amory to keep the indictment under wraps? She could feel the telltale spike of her temperature. The alcohol would not let go of her. She would not, would not put her finger down her throat; it had been half a year since she'd last made herself throw up, and what if her kids could see their mother now? Cars whizzed by behind her, a belt of broken lights printing woozy shadows on the concrete. And then it came, and her streak was ended, so that arguably Regan's first official act of 1977 was to puke her guts out on the shoulder of the FDR.

11

FOIL-EMBOSSED FRONTALS uncoupling from diadems, confetti dull with soot, business ends of noisemakers trampled under boots, cracked bottoms of disposable champagne flutes, butts of khaki Luckies and pale Pall Malls, nickelbags like punctured lungs, plus bottles: half-full, empty, broken off at the neck for the commission of crimes or smashed into green and brown explosions the red flash of a peep-show sign makes look romantic, in a sleazoid kind of way. Here is the stuff you don't get on TV. Extraneous footage, B-roll of the aftermath. Broadcast personalities let their Fruit of Islam bundle them into the plush rear cabins of towncars. A union technician in a satin jacket winds cable around his forearm like a hawser; its loose end scrimshaws the snow. By the time the ball, that descended mon-orchid, goes dark above Times Square, the last masses have drained underground. For a second, the city seems to lean forward and make contact with a future self: ruined, de-peopled, and nearly still. In a sealed hangar, forensic economists move around numbered lots with scales and calipers. Believing themselves to have evolved beyond delusion and loneliness, beyond illness and longing and sex, they hum distractedly and wonder what it all meant. To the extent that they're right about themselves, they'll have no way of knowing.

And let us not forget the pigeons, who shouldn't be active this late, but are. They scrabble over hamburger papers that gust up the building fronts, carry their spoils back to the Public Library lions a few long blocks away. Normally they wouldn't range this far, but they are agitated tonight by sirens that sing of time out of joint, of things gone terribly awry. Which may explain why a little band of them has taken refuge in the busted skylight of a precinct-house in the quiescent blocks south of Lincoln Center. They choir around a sag of see-through plastic. Their claws make little ticking sounds when they move.

It will take Mercer Goodman some time to identify the egg-like shadows up there, but then, sitting almost directly below the sloppy hole cut into the drop-ceiling of Interrogation Room 2, what does he have if not time? The acoustic tiles around the hole terminate in discolored edges that look less sawed-off than gnawed. Some water has collected in the sagging underbelly of the plastic sheeting stapled there. Every time the wind kicks up, the seams wheeze asthmatically, letting in the bone-cold air, and then in the silence that follows comes the ticking. Mercer shivers. Just behind his eyes is a stippling pressure like the popping of a thousand champagne corks. Or, more accurately, blood vessels. Mashing his hands to his orbitals brings some relief, but for reasons he's trying not to think about, he doesn't want to close his eyes. He's started to wonder, not quite abstractly, whether the hole in the ceiling is some kind of invitation—whether, by standing on the table in front of him, he might reach it and escape—when it occurs to him that the shadows are not eggs, but birds. Which accounts for the smell in here, like sawdust and the unmucked coops of his childhood. It's as if they've been following him.

And in a way, they're a welcome diversion; this room is in most other aspects an anxious void. At eye level, the white is monolithic: white door, white formica tabletop, white walls to stare at while you wait for a white man to return, the one who brought you here in the back of a car whose doors lacked interior handles. What had the guy's name been? McMahon? McManus? Mercer had been too rattled to pay attention, but he's certain it was McSomething. He'd nudged a Styrofoam cup an inch or two forward, as if to get it exactly halfway between himself and his detainee, white upon the white table. His big body had crowded the doorway. Mercer could see beyond it the open-plan office he'd just been escorted through, the wall of glass blocks like ice unwarmed by sunlight, though Mercer's throat (bitter ash) and eyes (sandpaper-scoured) suggested it had to be near morning. The tubes of light now overhead revealed Detective McSomething's eyeglasses to be subtly tinted. Their lower regions, the same blue as his irises, reduced his eyes to pupil. *Have a seat*, he'd said. *I'll be back in five minutes.*

Of course, with no clock, Mercer had no way of numbering the minutes. There was no way of knowing how long it had been since, in a fever of compassion, he'd knuckled his dime into the NYTel slot uptown. Was it late enough now that William would be home? If so—had he started to wonder?

Not that Mercer was under arrest. Not yet, anyway. Rather, he appeared to be a casualty of some ambiguity in the term "witness," which he'd assumed connoted actually witnessing something happening. What he'd witnessed, instead, was what came after, to which the medics who'd answered his call, or the cops themselves, could just as easily have testified. He could see them still, the first responders, emerging from the park grimmer than when they'd gone in. He could see the stretcher, the grotesque bulge of feet under the white sheet. And the outstretched arm, the bloody snow. It was all burned into his eyelids. Hence his effort to focus only on what was here before him.

His hard institutional chair was bolted to the cement, and there was a hole in the table through which the cuffs, had he been wearing cuffs, would have passed. The coffee cup had a nibble missing from its rim. It all contributed to the room's air of experiment, of elaborate dare. Set into the wall was a mirror that was probably no mirror, and he could imagine three or four cops watching, rumpled, tending to fat. *Five bucks says he tries the skylight. No, five bucks he goes for the cup. Five bucks says five more minutes and this nigger's gonna break down and confess.*

Though perhaps this was lingering paranoia from the marijuana they doubtless knew he'd smoked, or a craving on some level for punishment, or the residue of William's TV shows bleeding through the beaded curtain at night and into his dreams, *Baretta* and *Starsky* and *Barnaby Jones*. Because when the door reopened at last, there was only Detective McSomething again, and the long, low ranks of cubicle walls behind him, dividing the empty cop-shop into offices, nested rectangular hells. "Everything okay in here?" Without waiting for an answer, he dropped his imitation-leather jacket over the back of an empty chair. His revolver's grip jutted from its holster like a hand eager for a shake.

To be honest, everything was not okay—in addition to being half-deranged with uncertainty, Mercer was now freezing his ass off, and could have put that jacket to good use—but he knew better than to be honest; he could already see how this was going to be.

From the pocket of a garish tropical shirt, a flip-top notebook emerged, and after some theatrical patting of pockets—more delay—so did an eraserless half-pencil familiar from miniature golf and the tops of library card catalogues. "I'm going to ask you some questions now, Mr. Freeman."

"Goodman."

"Sure. Goodman." The cop yawned, as if it were more exhausting to sit on that side of the table in judgment than to sit on this one being judged. Then he proceeded to take down the very same information Mercer had volunteered up on Central Park West, maybe testing to see if the answers would change. Mercer gave his date of birth. "So that makes you, what?"

"Twenty-five." Or almost twenty-five, but if the guy couldn't be bothered to do the math . . .

A sneaker from beneath the table found purchase on the empty chair beside him. The detective levered himself back at a lazy angle. His gum cracked like a flatting tire. Was Mercer supposed to think, *Wow, we're just alike, you and me*, or was this simply part of a general lowering of standards, the entropic bent of all things? "I take it you're a transplant?"

"I'm not from around here, no."

There was a little crackle of danger as the cop looked up from his pad to see if he was being mocked. No, for whatever reason, McSomething didn't like him. Paranoia mounted. It was like when you drove past a speed trap and all of a sudden it seemed entirely possible you were carrying a body in your trunk. And did they know this, too? Was the possibility of their knowing one of the scenario's complex parameters?

Asked for an address, he gave an address.

"That permanent, or . . . ?"

"I'm staying with a friend until I get my feet under me." It was a line he'd used on his mother. He couldn't tell anymore whether or not it was a lie, technically speaking.

"Right, this is coming back to me. And remind me, what was the name of the friend?" The man's outer-borough inflections had sharpened, the better to convey the vast and widening difference between them. Mercer had heard it before, this special machismo reserved for suspected inverts. *You'll never turn me, fairy!* As if Mercer could ever be attracted to so unremarkable a face. Take away the glasses, and it was like the average of every Irish-American face in New York: just so many freckles across the bridge of a just-so-upturned nose. But his cheeks did dimple when he smiled. "Oh, wait, I got it. It's Bill something. Billy-boy. Bill Wilson." Mercer had grabbed a surname from a Poe story; if caught, he could claim he'd been misheard. "This is just a roommate deal, right? Just two bosom friends." The Hawaiian shirt seemed to swell to fill the room, and here was Mercer, tiny, defenseless, free-falling past coconut trees and moonlit water and finding nothing to grab on to.

He blew on his hands. "Can I ask you a question, Detective?"

"You just did."

Eighteen years on the lee side of C.L. should have been enough to scare resistance out of him. You kept your fool head down. You *Yes, sirred* and you *No, sirred,* and you did not give them an excuse. But this was 1976, not 1936—or it was 1977, in the capital of the free world, and *he had done nothing wrong.* "If you already know this stuff, why go back over it?"

The quiet that followed did not bode well. But then there came a knock from outside, shave and a haircut, and a gray head, much lower than it made sense for any head to be, poked through the widening gap in the door. "I'm not interrupting anything, am I?"

The detective didn't answer, or even turn around.

"Fantastic." The door opened wider, and a body followed the head into the room. Given the obstruction of McSomething's shoulders, not to mention all the other calculations he was in the middle of, it took Mercer a second to puzzle out what wasn't quite right about the head: it never straightened up. With its bemused eyes, its ruddy billiard-ball cheekbones, its mouth all but vanishing under a thick gunmetal moustache, it appeared to be falling forward, dragging the body after it like an anchor trailing its chain. A metal half-crutch was clipped near the elbow of the newcomer's neat sportcoat; the dull thud of its distal end on the concrete floor made the pigeons resettle themselves in the skylight. *Tick, tick.* The other arm hugged a brown paper bag, which the man deposited on the table. Releasing the crutch, he gripped the table's edge and reached across to Mercer with a grin. "Larry Pulaski."

Mercer took the hand reluctantly. Its knuckles moved in his grip like marbles in a velveteen bag. The man produced three blue deli cups. "You have to go a few blocks to find coffee, this time of night."

"So where did that come from?" Mercer asked, nodding toward the Styrofoam cup on the table. He'd been helpless to hold it in, another little burst of defiance, and now he braced for Detective McSomething's big hand to let go of its notepad and dart like a kiss toward his mouth. (And how would he explain his own split lip to William, without revealing where he'd been?) Instead, he got a contemptuous smirk.

"That's to catch the drip when the skylight leaks. You want to drink pigeon shit, be my guest."

The older man continued to beam. "Some of my younger colleagues, Mr. Goodman, such as Detective McFadden here, make do with that add-water-and-stir stuff."

"I don't see what you've got against Nescafé," McFadden said. "I'm feeling frankly a little what do you call it. Devalued."

"But dinosaurs like me, we're set in our ways."

Pulaski was a detective, too, then, and this must have been part of their patter, their routine. But there was something rusty in it. As the grizzled veteran, Pulaski had too light a touch. And he made McFadden, with his hypnotically Polynesian shirt, seem suddenly less convincing, too. It was as if they'd passed through a wardrobe room on the way here, grabbing whatever was to hand. "So you're the good cop?"

McFadden turned to his partner. "Mr. Goodman here has decided to play smart."

"Am I entitled to a lawyer?"

"You see what I mean, Inspector?" To Mercer, he said, "You're not under arrest, smart guy. No arrest, no lawyer."

"I'm free to go, then?"

Pulaski's smile floated above the table like a croupier's. "I was hoping that with some honest-to-God java we might do this less adversarially, Mr. Goodman. Go ahead, get some kind of statement down, and then get you on your way. I've got one light and sweet, one just milk, and one black." He touched the lid of each of the cups as he named it. "I'm flexible, so I can go either way. Preference, Detective?"

McFadden shrugged. "So long as it's hot."

"So we're flexible, you see. The choice is yours, Mr. Goodman."

If Pop had been here, he would have warned about Pulaski. Men like this had hovered over Mercer's ancestors in cane-fields and cotton plantations; *shtick* was just *stick* with an accent. But you haven't smelled coffee until you've smelled hot, sweet deli coffee at let's say four-thirty in the morning on the night you've seen your first murder. Or attempted murder? "I'll take the one with milk," he said.

The coffees having been distributed, Pulaski pulled out the chair where McFadden's foot had been resting. He kept his jacket on, as if he might be leaving at any moment, but unclipped the crutch from his forearm and leaned it against the table. McFadden slid the notebook toward him. "We were just coming to the end of preliminaries, Inspector. I'm going to continue now. That all right with you?"

There was an edge to it, but Pulaski raised his hand without looking up from the pad, as if to indicate that he, Pulaski, was not worth considering. "Please." So to the extent that he actually was that mythical creature, the good cop, he was going to be completely ineffectual in defending the witness against his hulk of a junior colleague, who now leaned forward on his elbows. Mercer took a long sip of coffee, just to place some object between himself and his interrogator.

"So what you were telling me in the park, you leave a party on Seventy-Second, you go to the bus stop to wait. You weren't wearing just that monkey-suit, were you? I mean, it's cold out."

"It's a tuxedo, Detective. And no, I had an overcoat."

"Right, you seem like a guy who knows from menswear. This would have been, what, a nice shearling overcoat? From somewhere on Fifth Avenue?"

"Bloomingdale's. You must have found it covering the . . ."

"The victim. That's right."

The missing coat, it occurred to him, was another thing it was going to be hard to explain to William. "It probably, I don't know, went into the ambulance or something, or is still there in the park. I don't see how it matters."

"Oh, piece of evidence like that, we wouldn't have left it in the park, I can guarantee you that." McFadden was warming to this, performing, but Pulaski winced, as if having to swallow, for the sake of etiquette, an hors d'oeuvre that wasn't to his taste.

"I think we might dispose of some of these details, get Mr. Goodman home quicker."

"It's funny, though," McFadden said. "Wearing a nice coat like that, but waiting for a bus instead of taking a cab?"

"It's my roommate's, if you must know."

"Ah. Here we are again. The mysterious roommate, William Wilson."

Pulaski looked up. "This reminds me of a person we both know, Detective, when you do this with the details."

"Fine. Let's back up. This party, this very high-toned party you've stated you were at. Were there any controlled substances being consumed at this party, to your knowledge?"

Mercer was doomed. "I don't know what you're talking about. Are you talking about champagne?"

"I'm talking about—you know what I'm talking about, Mr. Goodman. Have you been under the influence of narcotics at any point this evening?"

But again, Pulaski winced, and this time, it was accompanied by a tiny cough.

McFadden looked nearly as frustrated as Mercer. "The thing is, Pulaski, I don't like this story."

"I called you," Mercer said. "*I* called *you*. I could have just left her there, pretended I didn't see anything. I waited around for y'all to show."

"Something doesn't add up. What's your job, Mr. Goodman? Your source of income?"

Mercer could feel his cheeks burning. "I work at the Wenceslas-Mockingbird School. That's a very prestigious school, down on Fourth Avenue."

"Well, do you like answer phones, or mop the floors, or what?"

"Why don't you call them and see?"

"It's four in the morning on a federal holiday, so that's convenient for you. But you can bet I'll be calling as soon as they're open."

McFadden's jaw rippled as Pulaski's hand rose again. "Detective, if I may. Mr. Goodman did call us, and I can see you've got a very thorough set of notes here. If you wanted to go type up the preliminaries, Mr. Goodman and I might be able to clear up some of the remaining confusion."

A look passed between the men, which Mercer was fairly sure he wasn't supposed to see. Two hands gripping the same ineffable baton. To his surprise, Pulaski won.

The minute McFadden left, the bristle of danger dropped right out of the room. What Mercer felt for Pulaski then was akin to gratitude. The little man, who hunched over even when he sat, took an inordinate amount of time wriggling out of his sportcoat and folding it over the back of the chair. "Polio as a kid," he said *sotto voce*, as if he'd noticed Mercer staring but didn't want to embarrass him. "More common"—wriggle wriggle—"than you'd think. Don't worry. I'm not in any pain." He was slightly out of breath as he sat back down. He adjusted his crutch so that it intersected the table's edge at a right angle. He drew his own notebook from a breast pocket, which seemed to be where they kept them, and aligned it orthogonally in front of him. He patted his pants—"Now where did I put that pen?"—and then, with the sly flourish of a magician, brought out a silver one, like a Waterman Mercer had once had. "I have a weakness, my wife says. But my motto has always been, modest needs, lavishly met." When the pen was perfectly parallel to the notebook, Mercer thought he heard a purr of contentment. "I must explain to you, Mr. Goodman . . ."

"You can call me Mercer."

"Mercer, thank you. Detective McF, rough around the edges though he be, is good police. He believes, and it's not been disproven, that people are basically animals, and in order to get them to do anything, you've got to show your whip-hand. Now I"—slight adjustment to the position of the notepad—"I have my own somewhat esoteric idea, evolved over more years than I'd care to count, which is, provided a spirit of mutual cooperation exists, why make things difficult?"

Mercer might have detected an implied threat here, but his body, still humming with the chemicals of relief, refused to care. And in the sudden absence of any tension to keep him alert, he realized he was exhausted. "It's freezing in here."

"Budget cuts."

"It's been a long night."

"I can imagine." Of course Pulaski could imagine. The record of ten thousand nights like this one was tallied in the white hairs sprinkled liberally in his black brush-cut. In the ridges of spine visible through the fabric of his shirt as he bent to his notepad. It was Mercer who couldn't imagine. *Witness is terminally self-involved*, the Waterman would write. "Now Mercer, what I'd like you to do, what would help me, is if you could just start from the beginning, and tell me, as plainly as possible, how you came upon Ms. Cicciaro. That's the victim. And the name is confidential at the present time, her being a minor. I'd ask that you not repeat it."

"Can I ask you something first, Detective?"

"Shoot."

"Is she alive?"

Pulaski looked up, a gaze of infinite pity. "Last I knew, she was in between surgeries."

"What does that mean?"

"Listen, if I were a doctor . . ." It would have been superfluous for him to touch his crutch; at this point, Mercer felt, they understood each other perfectly. This was confirmed when Pulaski retrieved a pack of cigarettes from the pocket of his coat and pushed it into that medial space where the Styrofoam cup still stood. "I picked those up, too." Mercer's hands were shaking, from fatigue or cold or nerves, and he had to concentrate to guide his cigarette to the detective's lighter. The flame danced in a small gold cross. "To be candid, Mercer, whether she lives or dies is out of our hands at this point. We've got to focus on justice, and that means treating this as attempted homicide. Now, anything you can tell me. Anything at all, beginning at the beginning."

He had to struggle not to cough. It had been a long time since C.L. had tried to teach him to smoke, but all his little renunciations seemed to be crumbling tonight. Above him, a brown waterstain in the shape of Florida marred the white foam of the drop-ceiling. A warped tile sagged below the edge of the semiclear tarp, revealing a darkness within which lurked wires, guts, cameras, who knew. In a way, how to begin had been the great problem of Mercer's life. But now, when he closed his eyes, he could feel the memory coming on like a migraine: trigger, then aura, then pain.

THE INTERVIEW MUST HAVE TAKEN another hour, proceeding forward in little steps, prodded by Pulaski. Roommate unable to make it to party. Mercer there instead. Overstuffed rooms, a kitchen, a pink sink, a conversation on a balcony, insubstantial as smoke. He'd thought—Mercer blanched now, in the interrogation room—he'd thought he'd heard two pops, echoing like firecrackers in the night. And then the park, the body. Maybe twenty minutes later. Legs splayed as if to make a snow angel. He saw his hand returning the payphone to its cradle. He'd stood there alone for the longest time, in the sickly light of the booth. Then he'd gone back to check on her. Then back up to meet the sirens, leaning against a police cruiser, trying to explain to whoever wanted to know, the fender cold against his thighs, salt caked onto it. More vehicles frozen at odd angles in the street, beyond which massed party-goers, faces looming and receding in the ambulance lights. The rear compartment of that selfsame cruiser, whose plashing tires, whose dryness and darkness and emphysematic heater, rendered the world beyond the window remote. The light on the dashboard conducting them through inter-sections already empty.

When he'd finally narrated his way back to the little white cube in which they now sat, he and the detective both yawned, so close to simultaneously it was impossible to determine who had influenced whom. Mercer, embarrassed by how far he'd lowered his defenses, wasn't sure what else to say. Pulaski had gone quiet, too. The fluorescent bulbs behind their square of ridged plastic gave a bleached, insistent thrum. Pulaski had taken notes in small block-capitals, and as he flipped back through the pages (how had he managed to write so much so neatly, and in so short a time?) Mercer tried to read them upside down. REGAN, he saw. And BUS: M10? Had he sensed Mercer's conscious omissions? Well, it was none of Pulaski's business whom Mercer chose to sleep with, and though it was in a literal sense his business to know that Mercer was coming down from a marijuana high, it didn't bear on the crime before them. He thought he sensed in the detective's attention other, unintentional lacunae: questions he hadn't thought to ask, shadowy agencies behind the surfaces of things. But perhaps the ticking of the pigeons was driving him crazy. Then the Waterman tapped the pad, and Pulaski looked up, a sum-mary glance. "The tie," he said.

"Excuse me?"

"You had on a tie when you arrived at the party. You said you stopped to retie it before you went in." The butt end of the silver pen indicated the open collar of Mercer's shirt. "You must have removed it at some point."

"Yeah. Yes, sir. When I was waiting for the bus, I think." But all he could remember was having it on. From one end of the night, he looked back at the other, at a boy on a deserted corner. The apartment building across the street had been a great, glass pleasure-ship. If he could just get in the door, all his dreams were going to come true. He'd squatted to brush some snow from a sideview mirror while he untied, retied. Having practiced this a thousand times, he'd needed the mirror only to check that it looked right. He hadn't yet understood that it took more than a bow tie to make things look right. "I must have left it in the pocket of my coat."

Pulaski made a signal with his hand, and the door to the room opened. It was McFadden, carrying William's overcoat. He cast it down in the middle of the table like a fuzzy gauntlet, stared smugly at Mercer, and then turned and walked out. "Any guess where we found that, Mr. Goodman?" Pulaski said.

"I was trying to keep her warm until the ambulance came."

"And any guess what we found in it?" He reached into the pocket with both hands. One emerged and unfolded itself, and a black necktie uncrumpled. When Mercer reached for it, the other hand placed on the table, with fearsome tenderness, an unzipped leather kit the size of a small Bible. Inside were two syringes and a Saran-wrapped bulb of powder.

"See, this is confusing for me, Mercer. I'm a cop. You know what the job is? Evidence. That and paperwork. Handwriting and fingerprints, is what it is. And what I've got here is a coat, linked to you, linked to the girl, and what looks like a gram of street-quality heroin."

"But that's not mine!" He felt like he'd been kicked in the balls—the same dull sickness spreading through him. They were framing him. He wanted a lawyer. Then he knew where he'd seen the kit before: oh. Oh. "It must be someone else's. The person whose coat it is."

"Looks like you and that person need to have a talk, then." They stared at each other for who knows how long. Beneath the brushy moustache, the little cop's face twitched. Mercer was about to put his wrists forward and ask for the cuffs already when Pulaski added, "Meantime, you're going to want to have the coat dry-cleaned. There's some blood on it. We'll be keeping this, of course." He palmed the kit.

"Wait, you're not going to arrest me?"

"Mercer, I tell you, I get myself in trouble this way, but you've got a face I want to trust, and I feel you've been honest with me, to the best of your ability."

"I have. I swear I have."

"So here's going to be our bargain—" and now, from some-where within the mysterious creases of the notepad, a business card emerged. "Should anything else come back to you—I mean the smallest thing—you're going to call me. Otherwise, I know where you live." Mercer reached for the card. For a second, their fingers were in contact. "Now comes the part where you get the heck out of here."

Pulaski let him get up, collect his coat, and move for the door, all the while pretending to be adding to his notes. He was halfway out the door when the guy said, as if to no one in particular, "You realize you may have saved a life tonight." And it was funny, at this specific moment, this was exactly how Mercer felt about the little detective. Or inspector, really. DEPUTY INSPECTOR LAWRENCE J. PULASKI, the card said. And as he stood there, something was already com-ing back to him, something he might have told Pulaski, had he not suspected it would have kept him even longer. He'd thought for a moment someone had been watching in the park. Kneeling there in the snow—stupid as a pigeon, settling the beautiful overcoat over the twisted and now silent body whose smell would never leave him—he'd felt sure, for the briefest second, that he was not alone.

12

WIRES RACING ALONG through chords and triplets, swelling every so often into corroded connections, weird shapes against the sky, triangles and spheres like a coded message trying to tell him something. This morning, the whole mute breadth of Long Island was trying to tell him something: that he was a fucking coward, that he should have been back there with Sam, instead of here on this train, with the pajama bottoms on his unjeaned legs and this hat on his head so he looked like a fucking loon. Power transformers tilted up like weary crucifixes, shot through with rust and ice on the far side of a window he could see through only imperfectly, as he could remember the night only imperfectly. Condensation drew lines on the fogged parts of the glass, and beyond these lines, birds floated in a clearing sky, the gulls of Jamaica. Grasses sprouted from the snow like whiskers on a pale gray face. "Tickets," the conductor said. "Tickets." Under his breath, Charlie began to hum, both to calm himself down and because maybe that way the conductor would take him for an actual loon and pass him by. *Keep your 'lectric eye on me, babe. Press your raygun to my head . . .*

The truth was, he didn't have a ticket. He'd spent the last few hours hiding out in the predawn freak show of Penn Station, trying to find a place far enough from tourists and hustlers and junkies and the odd baby-faced cop to safely crash. But he could feel hungry eyes sizing him up. *I am a human being!* he wanted to shout; *Leave me alone!* And when he did find a patch of floor upstairs in the deserted Amtrak waiting area, between two planters of sickly hostas, the last thing he felt capable of was sleep. The stench of the basement level reached him even here, like hot-dog water mixed with roofing tar and left in an alley to rot, and when he closed his eyes, a high-frequency white flashed against the normal, reassuring pink. That would have been some mixture of beer, schnapps, and panic. Because he had no idea where they'd taken her. How many hospitals were there in the City? With a phone book and a roll of dimes, he could have called them all. But even as every inward cell twitched and fluttered, outwardly he was comatose, curled on his side, with Grandpa's hat cushioning his head and his pajama bottoms picking up stains from the tile and his size 14 combat boots trying to stay drawn up out of sight between the ugly stucco planters. And how dare he feel sorry for himself, when this could have been snow underneath *him*, or a stretcher, or . . .

He was trying to remember how to pray, *Baruch atah*, when he heard a cloud of disco somewhere nearby. He opened his eyes to see an aging black man dragging his custodial cart down the rows and rows of empty seats. They might have been the only two people on the Amtrak level at this hour, and the man affected not to see Charlie as he gathered yesterday's newspapers from chairs and stuffed them into a trashbag. Most significantly, there was a transistor radio hooked to one leg of the cart. It was too early for morning papers to have been delivered to the station's shuttered stands, but there was news every ten minutes at 1010 WINS, if Charlie could somehow get the radio retuned. If AM penetrated down here. With the man almost out of sight, Charlie stole after him. And when the cart vanished behind a column, Charlie hid on the other side. He kept close enough to hear the disco giving way to endless commercials, but the man never got more than ten feet away from the cart, and when he moved downstairs, the signal broke up. Charlie was still waiting for it to return an hour later when the departure board began to ripple with Saturday morning's first trains. And so could he be blamed for having forgotten that his return ticket was back in the pocket of his jeans, in a bush in Central Park, and that he'd given his only money to a chick at a nightclub he shouldn't have been in in the first place?

Nearer now, he heard the click of the conductor's ticket punch, a tiny, elegant noise, like a beak stabbing at a tree. He dug in his jacket pocket and came up with a crumpled glove and a stick of Juicy Fruit gone brittle in its wrapper. And what if the conductor was onto him? What if they were searching all eastbound trains for a boy, 28 waist, 34 length, with missing pants? He didn't want to call attention to himself, so he stopped humming. He had made up his mind—he owed it to Sam—to get home without getting caught.

Maybe it was a good thing, then, that there'd been no news of her yet. Because say she was at Bellevue, say some anchor had come on the radio between Wild Cherry and the Sunshine Band and said, like, *Central Park shooting, trauma center, Bellevue;* could he be certain he wouldn't still be on this train, trying to escape, trying to convince himself that he could be more help to her if he was free, with no one knowing the whole thing was, indirectly, his fault?

He tried again to pray. He wasn't sure for what—to go back in time, do things differently, make her get better?—and he'd thought, back at Penn Station, that this was the problem. But it wasn't. Nor was the problem his nonexistent Hebrew, or the welter of distractions, the little hum of the train's toy engine, the townships rattling past, the other passengers, the clickety-click of the conductor's puncher; it was the silence behind all these, the answering silence. And maybe Charlie Weisbarger got no answer to his prayers because he didn't know whom to address: the G-d of Mom and Dad, who had (though he did his best to forget it) plucked him from an orphanage when he was ten weeks old, or the intercessory Virgin to whom his biological ancestors had turned for help, or the long-haired, easygoing Jesus who was Just All Right with the *Godspell* kids at school . . . ? Before he could arrive at an answer, the conductor was standing over him. "Tickets, please, all tickets."

"I think I got on the wrong train," he heard himself mumble, untruthfully. "Is this the Garden City?"

"This is the Oyster Bay, kid. Do you not listen to announcements?"

"I meant to go to Garden City."

The conductor, a short man, was large of hand, impassive of face—it was a long shift—but wiry like the boy's father had been. Adoptive father, Charlie forced himself to remember, yet the best and only one he'd known. "You'll have to get off at the next stop, go back and transfer."

"What if I just stay on? I could call my mom to pick me up at . . . uh, Glen Cove or something."

"You still need a ticket."

"But I only have enough money for Garden City."

This, too, was a bluff. But maybe some trace of his insanity gambit still clung to him, or maybe the conductor took him for homeless and felt sorry for him, or perhaps he was simply infected by the urge to turn his back on the malice of the previous year, because he just said, "Jesus Christ, kid. Do whatever you've got to do," and moved on.

No, this was definitely a glimmer of divinity. Some force out there wanted him to get home, and was preserving him for a greater purpose. As soon as he knew he was home free, he would scour every newspaper, call every hospital, if necessary, to find out about Sam. By the time the wires slowed again and the train hit Flower Hill, he was already, in his mind, at her bedside, making amends.

13

CURTAIN UP. Or there were no curtains up. Where was she? A large window. Light on a painted wall. Right: the new apartment. The fourteenth floor. Brooklyn. Like almost everything in her life right now, the curtains were in a box somewhere in the great jumble of boxes, likely the very last one she'd think to look in. Regan believed, or believed she believed, that the contents of boxes shifted around when the lids were closed, and even sometimes teleported from box to box, so that whatever you most desired at any given moment was wherever you weren't looking for it. Was this a metaphor for something? Light from the east-facing window smashed into her face like a blunt-force trauma. Was *this* a metaphor for something? And why hadn't she noticed it before? She was usually up earlier, was why. *Someone* was up—she could smell eggs, and the TV was on in the living room—but it wasn't, apparently, her. Why couldn't the TV be in a box instead, and the curtains be up? Chalk dust seemed to cover her mouth and throat. Her thumb throbbed. Pain crept from her temples back into the vault of her skull, where her withered brain now sat, tiny ruler on its outsized throne, nattering to itself instead of doing what it should have been doing, which was sleeping off its hangover. She'd had too much champagne—had thrown it up, she recalled now, on the edge of the FDR, which accounted for the chalky mouth, though she must have brushed her teeth, she wouldn't have gone to bed without brushing, would she? Honestly, who could remember? She felt sure that if she turned over, away from the sunlight, the back of her brain would slosh against her brainpan, and the pain would start to oscillate, but she had to do it or she'd never fall back asleep. Holding shut the curtains of her eyelids, she took a breath and rolled, groaning. Some undercurrent of activity in the next room came to a stop. "Mom?" She should really get up, she wasn't sure how she felt about Will using the stove while she slept, but eggs smelled like death. This was a symptom of her hangovers, she remembered, which, at the time she'd put hangovers behind her, had become baroque profusions of symptoms. Synesthesia. Racing pulse. Auditory oddities. Grandiosity. Self-loathing. Neurosis. An inability, once awakened, to do the only thing that could cure her, which was fall back asleep. She pulled a pillow over her head and peeped cautiously at the nightstand clock. 8:15. How could they already be awake, when on any other morning, getting Will out of bed this early would have been like pulling teeth? Why, in the box of her life, couldn't they still be in bed, dreaming sweetly, pure potential? The pain meant business now, hurrying back toward her cerebellum with dirk and dagger. In her mind, she rehearsed next steps. Sit up. Brush again; drink from the faucet; wash down aspirin. Prepare her face to meet the faces . . . Ugly, but necessary. Because if there was one thing Regan knew about herself it was that she wouldn't be falling back asl

CURTAIN UP. TV still on, though not cartoons anymore; the wall-muffled voices were too adult for that. Also: the shower was running. Flannel pillowcases shrouded her head like a mummy's, but inside there was simply nothing. She couldn't have tied her shoe right now. She was amazed she even had the language left to think with, assuming people thought in language at all. She let the crack of light between the pillows widen. It was almost ten, the clock said. To drowse further would have been an abdication; she'd had her eight hours, more or less. And yet every movement took her further beyond the envelope of warmth her body had hollowed out in the night. She had to try to find her way back to that exact posture. But what had roused her this time? It wasn't the clock, since she hadn't set the alarm, and it wasn't the TV, since that was on already. No, it was the sense of being watched. With heroic effort, she turned onto her back and let her injured hand flop out of the way, and there, just inside the bedroom's open door, were popsicle-stick legs jutting from a nightgown. Hair wild with static. It was Cate.

"Will said not to come, but I said you would want me to."

Each syllable was a miniature hammer tapping at the dam that held back Regan's headache. She peeled the cover off of a warm wedge of bed and patted it. "Come here, sweetie. But be . . . easy, Mommy's head hurts."

It was too late. Any uncertainty had vanished as Cate scampered over and catapulted into the bed. And of course it was a kind of relief, to have this little furnace wriggling in next to one, reminding one that there were other and more important bodies than one's own. A hand crept across her forehead like a small domestic animal, feeling her for fever, as she'd done so many times for Cate. It had become one of her favorite feints, when she didn't want to go to Keith's. *Mommy, I've got a fever, feel my forehead.*

"I'm fine, honey." Lines were forming in the lineless face, cinching it into a moue of displeasure. Realizing how her breath must smell, Regan covered her mouth. "Sorry."

"Mommy! What happened to your hand?" Cate was already examining the bandaged thumb like a fortune-teller, and as much as it hurt, Regan loved this, the thoughtless thoughtfulness, the way Cate, at six, hadn't quite internalized-slash-hallucinated the difference between her own pain and the pain of others.

"It's nothing, sweetie. A scratch."

"Do we still have to go to Dad's?"

"Absolutely." A spasm exploded out of Regan's head as she sat up. "Listen, do you think you could bring Mommy a glass of water and some aspirin?"

"Will won't come out of the bathroom."

"Don't tattle, sweetie. Anyway, it's in *my* bathroom. There should be a first-aid kit on the counter. The bottle says *A, S, P* . . . If it's not there, it's in one of the boxes."

Having a job to do seemed to soak up the anxiety that otherwise swam around Cate. She was her mother's daughter. But it took her a quarter of the time it would have taken Regan to find the aspirin. She watched, satisfied, as her mother shook three pills into her hand, and then monitored to see that she washed them down with water. "You're going to make a great doctor someday, Cate."

"A pony doctor."

"A veterinarian. Now, honey," Regan said, almost whispering, enlisting Cate in a conspiracy. "I need about twenty minutes for these to start working. Do you think you can make sure your brother doesn't come in?"

Cate nodded.

"Twenty minutes, I'll be up, I promise. Now come here." She plastered a kiss on Cate's forehead, and as she lay back against the pillows and let her eyelids drift south, she could hear the girl skipping off to wait outside the kids' bathroom to lord it over Will.

CURTAIN UP, AGAIN. It was nearly noon, the clock said, and the bone-white walls and brilliantined floors around her throbbed with yellow light. There were windows on two sides. The real-estate broker had gone on and on about "southern exposure"—it had seemed to be her rejoinder to every reservation Regan voiced about the apartment, which she'd had to find on short notice. "Oh, but the exposure is magnificent." Regan's disposition toward all of humanity had been pretty mistrustful at that point, and so she couldn't quite credit the enthusiasm of the woman, who was after all trying to sell her something. They'd had southern exposure on East Sixty-Seventh, too, but all it had meant was a nice view of the windows of the nearly identical building across the street. And after a couple of weeks in this new place, she'd forgotten about it, just as she'd forgotten about the other selling points. *Utilities included* meant you were at the landlord's mercy for the temperature and duration of the heat and hot water. *Cozy bedrooms/closets* meant one or the other, take your pick. They'd moved in right in the middle of the lightless part of the year, when the sky warmed at best to the hue of skim milk. By the time she got home from work, the last sun would be bleeding off the horizon beyond the World Trade Center, and just before she pulled the blinds, the canted bowl of the harbor would appear to her as a sheet of lead, broken only by the lights of a slow-moving ferry. Now she understood: here in Brooklyn Heights, there were no obstructions to block the view, and when, as today, the clouds parted, midday light poured off the water like a second sky. It was like trying to sleep on the surface of the sun.

She peeled back the gauze she didn't quite remember putting on her thumb. Against the orange coverlet, the slash looked livid, possibly infected. Besides which, there was that other affliction: her father, sixty-eight and at best halfway senile, was going to be arraigned on Monday. She wished again that her brother were here to help her stay upright. Still, the light on the walls and bedspread and on the gold hair of her arms answered to something deep in her body. And there was the imminent likelihood of coffee, which, with great foresight, she'd bought yesterday. So much for alcoholism. Okay, world. Okay. She was getting up.

SHE SHUFFLED into the big room in slippers and bathrobe, careful not to spill her steaming coffee, or to trip over the boxes piled inside the doorway. The Christmas tree looked lonesome in its corner, with no furniture to surround it. All it took to turn a tannenbaum unlovely, it turned out, was direct sunlight. A few twists of wrapping paper had blown like dust bunnies into the corner. A wreath of dry needles decorated the floor.

"Geez, Mom. You look like Edith Bunker," Will said, and turned back to the TV before she could compose her face into whatever reaction he wanted. The separation seemed to have aged him already. The way he closed down now when around her, became inward and world-weary, was prominent in her ledger of regrets. She sat down on the couch beside him, and he stared and stared at the commercials, as if the answers to life's great questions might at any moment flash across the bottom of the screen. In the old apartment, they'd had a strict limit, five hours of tube per week; he might have exceeded that already today, but of the many elements of the old dispensation that had suddenly evaporated, this one seemed, for now, the least worth haggling over. "Where's your sister?"

He shrugged.

"Well, I appreciate your making her breakfast." She brushed the wet hair back out of his eyes. She knew he thought he was ugly, because he was at that age, but to her, even in pajama bottoms and one of Keith's old stretch-necked tee-shirts—even if he would never forgive her—he was beautiful. "You've been great to her, through all of this. I know it's going to mean a lot to her someday. It means a lot to me."

"Mom—"

"Okay." She offered him her mug, and he took a sip of coffee, try-ing not to let her see him grimace at the taste.

"Cate said you weren't feeling good," he said.

"I'm fine, I'll be fine."

"Did you have a good time, at least? Did you see Grandpa?"

"He and your grandmother loved the Christmas gifts," she said. The kids didn't know about the Mayo Clinic visit, and now wasn't the time.

"Cate's in her room, I think, packing. It's like she's got to choose her five best stuffed animals and all her best picture-books and every single last sweater she might want to wear."

"We could buy you guys dressers for Dad's. You could keep clothes at each house."

"It's not that," he said, and reached for her coffee again. For the moment, at least, he was mostly angry at her for having left them on their own for so long: sixteen, eighteen hours since she'd buzzed in Mrs. Santos and kissed them goodnight. She'd have to do better; the book her analyst had given her warned about the abandonment com-plexes kids could develop. But with a divorce, how could you avoid it? Even as they needed twice as much of your attention and care, you found yourself with half as much to give, because you had to work twice as hard, make twice as much money, and meet your own redoubled needs. "It doesn't seem healthy to me. We're only going for a night."

"Well, I might need you to stay over this Sunday, too."

"Why?"

The noontime news was coming on, and she worried, suddenly: What if she hadn't imagined that scrap of the "Dr." Zig show on the radio last night, but had been betrayed, again, by Amory? What if he had failed to delay the arraignment until Monday morning? What if her son were to look over and see his grandfather and namesake being led from a plane in handcuffs? She had to avoid the temptation, sometimes, to confide in him as if he were the adult he talked like. "Don't ask me why. Just, when you get your stuff together, throw in an extra shirt and underwear. We're meeting Dad in an hour."

"I'm fast."

"I know you are, but why don't you go take care of it now, and then we can both worry about Cate."

With him safely out of the room, Regan could give in to her curiosity. She turned the volume down and stood a few feet from the TV. Sure enough, the third news story featured a reporter in earmuffs, standing against a backdrop of Central Park, now sunny. Her heart was hammering; her headache was making a comeback on the strength of all that blood. She knelt to hear better. It turned out, though, that the reporter was talking about last night's shooting. The victim, a freshman at an area college, was in critical condition. A minor. Possible robbery attempt. Police had several leads, but no comment beyond that. She hated herself for the gratitude she felt: it was as if the shooting had somehow made Daddy's indictment never happen. *Not releasing the name, due to her age,* the guy was saying, when a voice from behind startled Regan. "Mom?"

"What happened to packing?"

"I told you I was fast."

"Well, let me go throw some clothes on, and we can go down to the playground and run around a bit before your father comes."

"I'm twelve years old, Mom. I don't run around."

"I'm thirty-six, and even I need to run around sometimes," she said. What she needed, really, was to get away from reminders. "Come on, it's getting warm out, the weather says. We may not see another day like this for ages."

IT WAS LESS than a hundred steps from the front door of the new building to the wrought-iron gate of the Pierrepont Street playground—so the broker had said, and so Cate had verified the afternoon of the move, making her steps slightly larger than usual, "grown-up sized," she'd explained to Regan as she scrupulously counted them off. It was a decent little park, too, slotted into a space where two or three rowhouses would have been, overlooking the harbor, and today, as most of the snow had already melted, the playground equipment was swarming with the kids Cate dashed off to join. Their little bodies pumped blood so much more efficiently; any minute now, Cate would be rushing back to ask if she could take off her coat. Regan settled on a bench near some women she thought she recognized from the grocery over on the main drag. Doing her best impression of a responsible, non-hung-over mother, she gave a nod, big enough to invite a response, but small enough to be played off as accidental. The nods that came back were too small to interpret as invitations, so she turned back to the kids. Cate, with a native's sense of distances, had protested most vehemently about the move from East Sixty-Seventh, on the grounds that she would be far away from her friends. Now she was with two new ones. They'd peeled off from the throng in the secretive way of girls and were scrabbling with sticks around the base of a tree still footed in white drifts. They would have liked more snow, she thought; it had been the year's first, and they were too young to know they should enjoy the thaw while it lasted. She resisted the urge to call to them to watch out for the birds in the branches above, whose droppings had turned the wet asphalt beneath a greeny gray-white, because whoever said youth was wasted on the young had been dead wrong. It was adulthood that was the waste.

Will, meanwhile, leaned brooding against an empty section of fence, his own overnight bag and his sister's at his feet. It would have been terminally uncool to sit with his mother, an admission of his own difficulty making friends, though the only conceivable reason any kid wouldn't have wanted to be friends with her brilliant and warm and spooky-sensitive child, now stretching his arms out cruciform and wrapping his hands around the bars, would have been jealousy. He looked like an advertisement for boredom. Behind him, the sky, New Jersey, and the water were a parfait of diminishing brightness. He'd been right. He was too old for playgrounds. But she didn't want them making the long subway or cab ride uptown alone—it didn't seem safe—and when Keith, after she'd refused to meet him halfway (why should she?) had agreed to come down here and pick them up, she'd found she couldn't bear the idea of him in the new apartment, or even in the hallway outside it. That was the point of the move, after all, and was maybe why everything was still in boxes—because she couldn't be sure what *she* (the other *she*, whoever that was) had touched. And so, Tuesdays and Saturdays from now until the kids were old enough, they would all come out here and wait for Keith . . . which was what, she realized, she was doing. She had chosen this bench for the view it offered, not of her kids, but of the park entrance. And what would the other women think when he arrived? She crossed her arms.

Then Cate was dragging her brother across to the tree, and the other little girls were screaming and laughing and fleeing before the giant interloper. Will stooped to examine the spot they'd been poking at. He glanced over at Regan, and his look made her understand the thing on the ground differently. "Honey—honeys—don't touch that, please." Some subfrequency of concern made the other women turn toward her, but she was already up and moving toward the mound of feathers they'd uncovered. "It's probably crawling with germs." And now, thrust by minor emergency back into her role as a mother, she knelt on the asphalt, ignoring the wet salt-pebbles digging into her knees, to look at the thing.

It wasn't the kind of bird you ever saw in the city. It was too big by half, the size of a football or lapdog. And too gaudy to blend in with buildings and streets. Its plumage was the blue and orange of jungle flowers, flamestitched in black. She tried to recall anything she'd ever known about birds. A woodpecker, maybe, or some mutant jay? Its head must have been tucked underneath its body. There was a stick in her field of vision, too, its tremulous end only inches from the bird, and she assumed Will was the one holding it, but when she reached for it, she discovered it was attached to a new kid, or not a new kid— her kids were, she supposed, the new ones—but a kid that wasn't hers. He was either Japanese or Korean, halfway between Cate's age and Will's, with hair like black straw sticking out from the back of his Yankees cap and a smooth little face that gave away nothing. In the seconds during which he held her gaze, she felt him to be older than Will. Than herself, really. This had to be a hangover thing, this roaring mysticism or racism or whatever. Then the boy shrugged and let go of the stick.

It shook a little in her hand. She wanted to stop when she felt the soft weight of the bird at the end of it, but (this was absurd) the Japanese kid, from the shadows beneath his brim, seemed to be evaluating her performance, and beyond, in the blurred middle distance, she was sure the mothers whose park this was were watching.

"What are you doing, Mommy?" Cate asked. Will shushed her but looked a little pale as Regan drove the stick farther into the space between the bottom wing and the asphalt. In truth, she didn't know. Was the bird still breathing? Would she have to put it out of its misery? The give of it was nauseating, the sagging articulation of a wing that refused to come loose from the ground. And then, as though a frame of film were missing, the body flopped over and the head, previously hidden, came into light. One eye was missing, or stove in, it was impossible to tell amid the dried brown blood. The blood had matted the feathers—had been what was gluing them to the ground.

But the other eye, intact, no larger than a pea, stared up toward the vacant heavens. It had a tiny lid, she noticed. She imagined the bird blowing off course during the snowstorm, breaking short its migration, straying into the wrong neighborhood, alone but assuming it would stay aloft, everything would continue just as before. She hadn't cried last night, when she'd seen the stretcher, but now she almost—almost—let go. It was the stranger kid who stopped her.

"Are you all right, miss?"

She sniffed. She was fine. She had to be fine. "A cat must have got hold of it."

"If it was a cat there'd be more blood," the kid said, scientifically.

"Well, some predator, anyway. Will, can you find me a bag or box or something, please? We don't want to just leave it here to get stepped on."

When Will had returned with an old newspaper, she scooped the bird up in the sports section. It seemed undignified. She thought of asking the Japanese boy if he knew some special way to fold it, but thought better of it. Instead, she found a nearly full trashcan and laid the little bundle of newspaper inside. On the ground nearby were some dried-out branches with leaves still attached. She reached for one and laid it gently over the top of the newspaper. "Does anyone want to say a few words?" When no one did, she said, "Goodbye, bird."

"Bye, bird," Cate repeated, laying on another branch. Will and the other kid were too old or too male to be this sentimental, but each added a branch, and when they were done, the lines of newsprint carrying tidings of another Knicks defeat were barely visible through the winter-brown pyre of leaves. For a moment, Regan relaxed.

Then something made her turn. Keith was watching all four of them from the park entrance. But mostly, she couldn't help noticing, watching her. From his stubble and a certain squinty quality around his eyes, her guess was that he'd spent his night as she had, drunk—maybe with the other woman, despite his protestations, or with someone else. It hardly seemed fair, the way dissolution made him look even better, the steel-blue shadow tracing the strong line of the jaw, the blue eyes wounded, the off-center cleft on his brow that used to appear only when he was deep in thought. And it hardly seemed fair that he could watch her openly and without rancor, when the separation was his fault. To stop herself from moving toward him, she touched her kids' shoulders. Their rites over the bird had brought them into keen attunement; they looked up from the trashcan in unison, like grazing antelope at a distant sound. Neither ran to their dad, she was relieved to note, and also pained. Nor did Keith come to them. He seemed to recognize the invisible line drawn on the asphalt. This was Regan's place, not his. Will gathered up the bags he'd left along the fence, and together they crossed the melting park.

"Happy New Year," was the first thing Keith said, after Cate had clamped herself around his leg. "I sent the check for spring tuition."

"Already deposited." Regan wasn't sure if they were supposed to shake hands or embrace. She let him kiss her cheek. "I don't know if happy's the right word."

"Or lucky, maybe. Double sevens. It'll be better than last year, anyway."

Having been smart enough to stay away from the party, it occurred to her, he wouldn't have heard about the indictment, or the shooting in the Park, or any of it. She longed, irrationally, to confide in him, but the kids were standing right there, Will already closer to him than to her. "Keith, I need a favor. Something's come up at work, and I may need to go in early Monday morning. Would you mind keeping them until then?"

Behind her almost-ex-husband, brownstone Brooklyn was a blur: ladies with shopping trolleys, people walking dogs, mottles of ice in front of buildings whose owners hadn't sprinkled salt, and all the way up the hill trees dripping in the rare air. He seemed to be trying to read her. "Sure, Regan. No problem."

"I'd really appreciate it. I know it's not your day."

"Don't. Don't do that," he said. "This is hard enough as it is." And then he peeled Cate from his leg and lifted her, and her face was botched with tears. Regan reached for Cate's back.

"Honey, what's the matter?"

"What do you think's the matter?" Will said.

It took Cate a few seconds to steady her breathing enough to speak for herself. "Who will take care of Mommy?" she wailed, and then she buried her face back in the front of Keith's coat.

Keith asked what she was talking about.

Regan blushed. "It's nothing. I was a little under the weather this morning, and Cate was a good helper." But was it really nothing? Because she'd be on her own for the next thirty-six hours, in the empty apartment. She'd managed all right in the old place uptown, when Keith had been sleeping on his friend Greg Tadelis's couch and would come to take the kids ice-skating or to the movies. That apartment understood her. That mirror was the one she'd looked into all fall to remind herself that, no matter how bad things got, she would not stick her finger down her throat. But last night she had thrown up again, and once the kids were gone there was nothing to stop her from going into the bathroom and repeating, and repeating. Nothing but herself.

"I'll be fine, sweetie," she said, and she had to draw closer to Keith to squeeze her daughter's shoulder. She could smell his aftershave. She could feel his eyes on her.

"We should talk some time," he said.

She ignored this. "You can usually find a cab up on Clinton. Make sure these two wash their hands as soon as they get back." She squeezed Cate again. "Give Mommy a kiss, sweetie. I'm going to be fine. You're going to be fine." Cate sniffed and nodded. "Take care of each other," Regan whispered in Will's ear.

"It's just two nights." His embrace was stiff. And then she had to step back, to break contact. Otherwise she would never have let them go.

"Tell your dad I said Happy New Year's," Keith said, pointlessly.

She watched them walk up Pierrepont Street, Keith holding Cate's hand in one of his, the other hand carrying both bags. Will's own hands were in his pockets, his head down, watching the rock-salt he scuffed skitter gutterward. And she was okay with this not because she was a bad person, but because there was no alternative. She could keep herself busy until their return. There were phone calls to make. There were—Lord knew—boxes to unpack. She would be fine. Everything was going to be fine.

14

H AD THE RASP OF THE KEY IN THE LOCK brought William to the
door—or had William been waiting inside on the futon, arms
crossed, in the shiny blue kimono of judgment—and had he then
demanded to know where the hell Mercer had been all night, Mercer
might have been prepared to confront him straightaway about the
heroin. But at 6:15 a.m. on the first day of the year of somebody's lord
1977, the loft was empty, save for the cat. In the grayblue light from
the windows, the lump of sheets on the bed was an actual lump of
sheets. Was it a kind of revenge, then, to return the chesterfield coat
to its box, to slide it back under the futon where it had waited so long?
Or was it, rather, a test, to see if William noticed it was missing? Too
tired to decide anything for certain, Mercer trudged to the sleeping
nook, shooed Eartha from his pillow, crawled half-dressed under the
coverlet, and abandoned himself to troubled dreams.

He woke hours later to the warmth of another body in the bed,
a heavy forearm across his chest, the ebb and swell of breath on the
back of his neck, neutral with toothpaste. The faint catch in William's throat meant that he, too, had begun to dream. Before the
inevitable whimpering could start, Mercer decided to get up.

He put on one of the overdue Puccini albums he'd checked out from
the library. He turned it up loud. He clattered around in the kitchenette, preparing breakfast for one; one way or another, he would

pick a fight. But when William stepped naked through the beaded curtain (for he always slept naked), he looked as innocent as Adam. Finger-shaped bruises had appeared on his arm where it had been hurt a week ago, and he still held it against his chest, instinctively, for protection. Wouldn't there have been needle-tracks? "What are you doing, you ridiculous man? It's New Year's Day, and you're unwell."

"*I'm* unwell?" This was Mercer, still/again full of doubt.

"Your cold." Right. His cold. "Why don't you come back to bed, let me take care of you? God knows you did it for me when I was down."

William moved the Magnavox into the sleeping nook, placed it on a towel on the radiator at the foot of the bed. Mercer watched him work the rabbit ears. He decided to say something. "You have a good time last night?"

"*Comme ci, comme ça.* The Ex-Post revival seems harmless enough, though I'm half-deaf now. I missed you." So maybe everything since their phone conversation had been a confusion, Mercer thought. Or if it hadn't been, he wasn't sure he wanted to know. He laid his head on his lover's chest and let the static and glow of a soap opera sweep him away.

For lunch—or dinner, really—they ordered Chinese. They forked moo shu out of white cartons right there on the bed, a concession to Mercer's ostensible ill health. At any rate, spending all day in bed had been enough to make him *feel* somewhat ill, like a kid playing hooky from school. William parceled out crumbs of information about his ex-bandmates, dressed up as anecdotes—just enough to seem not to be hiding anything. Occasionally, Mercer obliged him with a cough. He couldn't find a way to turn the conversation to the drugs, and then William was asleep again.

Nor was this a new thing, the rhythm of small-talk and deferral, the elegant Noh dance around whatever was really at issue. William had always had a preternatural sense of how much he could get away with, of when to push and when to pull back. Mercer stared through the caul of televisual light at the sleeping face, trying to imagine it as a junkie's. The black eye fit, anyway. And he wanted so badly to tell this face what had happened to him—and to ask it, What happened to *you*? But what if he did? The little kit with its needle and spoon, still vivid against the white of the interrogation room in his mind, seemed tied by invisible threads to all the private pain that predated Mercer, the stuff William didn't ever talk about, the secretive slipping away he, Mercer, had pretended not to see. It was where all the loose ends met. If he started tugging at them, their entire life together might unravel. In the next room, a bell began to ring.

It was genuine dusk now, the bookshelf where the phone sat submerged in shadow. The ringing seemed antique, somehow, prematurely quaint, like the carillon of a village church slated for demolition. Mercer let it continue, to see if William would stir, and when he didn't, gathered breath and reached for the receiver. It being a holiday, this had to be his mother. "I was beginning to think you'd been hit by a bus," was her opener.

He wanted not to sigh, not to be the sort of person who sighed at his mother. "Occam's razor, Mama. Happy New Year's to you, too."

"This is a bad connection. I can't understand what you're saying."

"I'm saying, why hit by a bus? I could have been working, or out on the town, or just decided not to call. I could have been doing any number of things."

"Well, anyway, I'm glad you're safe. What was that?"

"What?"

"Did you say something?"

In the sleeping nook, William had groaned theatrically. Mercer threw a couch cushion, aiming for the beaded curtain, but it missed and hit the window instead. More birds took flight from the cinderblock flowerbox outside: bursts of light loosed in the gloaming. Down in the street, a white van was double-parked, mired in graffiti, but why, in New York in 1977, would you paint a van white to begin with? "Nothing, Mama. Just opening a window."

"Isn't it cold there? The radio this morning said high thirties. You know I always listen for your weather, you and your brother's. I certainly couldn't live like you do, with the cold. And how are things working out with that new roommate of yours? I don't think he's ever once given you a message from me."

She'd picked up the word *roommate* the first time he'd let it drop, and had been wielding it as a shield or weapon ever since. It was a tiny thing, really, and accurate as far as it went, but each repetition on either side, in holiday cards and birthday cards and the thank-you cards he wrote when a check from her appeared out of the blue (for the purpose of eliciting a thank-you) made him feel a little guiltier, until he'd stopped writing home altogether—another failure she'd detected with alacrity. "You must keep busy, Mercer, because when someone does pick up, it's usually what's-his-name." Translation: *Can you really believe you're too busy to speak to your own mother?* She was a kind of Rembrandt of implication.

"Actually, I gave my last exam two weeks ago, I told you that. I've been more or less free since then."

"Well, we missed you at Christmas. C.L. missed you, I know."

"They let him come home again?"

"Your father missed you." And always there was this, the *sfumato* of guilt. Always *your father.* Yet if he'd told her to put the old man on the phone . . . what would either of them have done then? "Maybe you could make it down for Easter."

"Geez, Mama. It's January first. I'll have to look at my teaching schedule."

"They don't let the kids off for Holy Week? What kind of school is it?"

"Not everybody's a Christian, Mama."

"Well. Spring break, at least," she said, even though they both knew he wouldn't be back for that, either. And, no better than she was, he agreed that he would think about it.

After ringing off, he had to lie face-down on the futon with the throw pillow over his head. He could hear William up and dressing on the far side of the beaded curtain. It parted and clacked back together. "Am I to surmise you've been talking to your family again?"

Mercer grunted, powerless not to wallow a little.

"What did we say about this? You've got to just make a little box in your mind, put them in there, seal it up."

But what Mercer wanted wasn't advice; it was commiseration. He flipped over onto his back and let the pillow fall to the floor. William had turned on a lamp, but otherwise, it was night. The blue windows of the warehouse across the street had gone black. "My father is an insane person," Mercer said.

"Don't be dramatic, sweetheart. Everyone's father is an insane person. It's a box they make them check on the hospital form before they let them take you home." But William was back on autopilot; he wasn't looking at Mercer but rummaging through the garment rack that served as their closet. Mercer watched from the futon, as though gathering evidence: the lamplight reaching its fingers across William's neck, his slightly anxious face, his swollen eye. The day in bed, the Chinese feast, was a lie they'd both wanted to believe, but now William was once again distant and away, and things were going to end. Relapse or no relapse, William would eventually leave him. "Have you seen my coat?"

"Which one," Mercer said, though he knew very well which one.

"The one you gave me, honey. The beautiful one."

Here it was at last: an opening. But how was he going to explain why he'd taken the coat, and how he'd discovered drugs in it, without revealing where he'd gone last night? He needed more time to prepare. "Oh, that? I had to take it to the cleaners."

"Why'd you do that? Which cleaners?"

"They'll all be closed now. I lit a candle on the bookshelf there and I knocked into it like an oaf and splashed wax everywhere. I'm really sorry."

"This was yesterday? Well, when did they say it would be ready?"

"I don't know. A week?"

"A week?"

"I didn't realize this would be such a big deal, William. It's not like you were wearing it." He was trying to decide whether William's difficulty staying calm confirmed his fears. Though maybe this need for confirmation was itself a kind of confirmation.

"I guess I'll just take this." William grabbed his motorcycle jacket, his Ex Post Facto jacket, off the floor. "I'll try to be quiet when I come in."

"You're going out?"

"I've been malingering too long, honey. Work to do; I'm weeks behind on the diptych. And I expect you'll be turning in early, with your cold and all." William gave him a quick, cool kiss on the cheek, and with that he was gone, leaving Mercer somehow more alone than he'd been before—as if it were having once not been alone that made the difference.

15

THAT SUNDAY, when Ramona Weisbarger stuck her head into the basement, she would find Charlie lying back on the dandelion shag with clamshell headphones clamped to his ears and his eyes closed and his hands folded over his chest like a pharaoh's. He was sensitive about light, as about everything else, and two years ago, the year of David Bowie, all the lamps in his room had been covered with scarves, so that she began to wonder if he might be homosexual. Now there was only the gray light from the window up near the ceiling, which made him look a little peaked. His color had been bad at dinner last night, too, and he'd barely said a word, but she'd chalked that up to him staying up till all hours New Year's Eve with the Sullivan kids, whom Maimie let run wild. And she hadn't at the time noted his failure to appear for breakfast this morning—there was plenty else to worry about—but when one of the twins complained about weird noises coming from Charlie's room, she'd come down and found him like this. She knew better than to ask if anything was wrong; there was no surer way to start a fight. Instead, she asked what he was doing, and got no response. Her knuckles drummed a tentative solo on the doorframe. "Earth to Charlie."

He opened his eyes, pointed without expression to the headphones. He mouthed the word: *Headphones.*

So take the damned things off, she might have said, back when she'd had a husband to back her up. Since the blowup this summer, though, uneventful little exchanges like the one just passed had come to seem like blessings, and she never thought to wonder whether they weren't worth shattering.

Not that the headphones really obstructed much. The radio had been turned all the way down, she would have noticed if she'd wanted to, and beyond the airless voids around his ears, Charlie could hear her quite clearly, as he now heard the stairs creaking with her retreat and, directly above him, the twins arguing about who got to go fight the monster and who should stay behind. How could she not have noticed the money missing from the babysitting envelope? How could she not have wondered why he'd come home so early Saturday morning? How could she not have noticed the alcohol boiling out of his pores at dinner? When she reached the first floor, he went to shut the door again, which, in some pathetic gesture toward maternal omnipotence, she'd left open. This time, he locked it.

He lowered himself back to the rug, gingerly. Twenty miles away, at Beth Israel Hospital, the best friend he'd ever had was lying in more or less the same posture, and all he wanted to do was go and be with her, watch over and protect her, but he was too late, and now he'd trapped himself here in this wood-paneled prison, where no one knew that the victim, the one whose name the radio said they weren't releasing, was Samantha Cicciaro, or that her friend Charlie Weisbarger had been with her both before and after the shooting, or that any second now, some machine might start making the dreaded beep that meant her heart had stopped. It seemed to him, studying the chaotic stalactites of the sprayed-on ceiling texture, that every person on earth was sealed in his or her own little capsule, unable to reach or help or even understand anyone else. You could only ever make things worse.

The facts supporting this theory he'd spent the weekend dredging up one by one: the graffiti on the tile of the 81st Street station, the exit gate like a barber's jar of combs, the rending sound it had made as he pushed through it. He'd even been humming, he now remembered— humming!—as he'd ridden up to meet her. It was a habit he'd had since he was a kid, something grounded so deep inside his body he couldn't always be sure he wasn't doing it. Or maybe he liked the conceit of not being quite in control of himself, which meant he couldn't be held accountable. Plus when you hummed audibly in public, other people kept their distance. This had become increasingly important over the last year, when he'd been forced to spend more of his life in waiting rooms, in a house teeming with black-clad cousins and people from temple, in the office of Dr. Altschul, the board-certified grief counselor. But there weren't like great throngs of people on that uptown train. It had been either just shy of midnight or just after—not a time anyone wanted to be caught out of range of TVs and friends and girls to whom they were ready to give their virginity. Charlie himself was only here because he'd lost track of time. His dad had left him a watch in the will, but Charlie refused to wear it, at first as part of some general rebellion against the tyranny of clock-time, and later (after Grandpa had pointed out that it was a perfectly good watch, and that David could have left it to his own blood descendants, Abe and Izzy) as a kind of penance. He consequently had no idea how late he was to meet Sam. He had hope, though. That, plus—for real this time—a serious need to pee.

Aboveground, the snow had started falling again. Trees on the lawn of the Natural History museum, which apparently was right here, were ensnared in ceramic bulbs, and in the red and blue and orange balls of light around them he could see it was coming down fat and at an angle. A solitary bus shooshed past as the traffic signals went green. Amazing, how quiet the city could get here, between the high buildings and the wilderness of the park.

She'd said the benches by the subway exit, and Charlie, unable to keep track of the lies he'd told about his Manhattan savvy, had acted like he knew what she was talking about. And now here was a mile of benches stretching away in either direction from Eighty-First Street, along the granite wall that bordered the park, and no sign of Sam, which meant that it could be earlier than midnight and she hadn't come yet, or later, and she'd given up. Or that she'd said Seventy-Second instead of Eighty-First, which—*crap*—she definitely had.

It took him a minute to figure out which way was south. He moved at a trot, peering into the snow for the faintest silhouette up ahead. His boots crunched under him. The park on his left was forbiddingly black, and it was a well-known fact that after dark it belonged to muggers and dope fiends and fags. Stories of the decaying City had reached even unto Long Island. On the other hand, the movement was jostling the contents of his bladder, and if he didn't pee soon, he was going to like rupture. He was coming up on a break in the wall.

With no sign of Sam, he steeled himself and plunged through it, under the trees.

He had stepped off the path and was maybe a second from getting his fly open when a voice made him stop: a single syllable that seemed to come first off the stone wall and then off the path, and then to gallop off uselessly through the underlit underbrush. "Help," is what it said. In the silence that followed, he became aware of his own breath, the wind gusting, the fierce bleat of blood in his ears. Perhaps in his agitation, he'd mistaken one of these sounds, or some mixture of them all, for the vox humana. He stepped farther away from the path. There was a steady ache now in the region just behind his beltbuckle; systems of hydraulic tubes and reservoirs whose names he'd failed to learn in first-period Bio were asserting their demands: if he didn't relieve the pressure *right now* . . . but before he could cross the five or so feet that would have guaranteed his privacy, it came again. "Help!" And now, much dismayed, he found himself back on the path, lurching out of the circle of light, in the direction of what had registered at bone level as a kind of call to arms.

An unlikely respondent, Charlie Weisbarger, battling the winter-bare branches, slipping over slick spots where feet had trod snow into ice. Still, he was helpless not to imagine himself coming to the rescue of this person who had called out. Male, by the sound of it, maybe cornered by a mugger, or maybe, if Charlie was lucky and the incident was already over, needing help only to call the police. He would emerge from the park a hero. Sam, waiting under a streetlight, would throw her arms around his neck.

The pattern of footprints on the gray-white path grew more involved, then less. There was no third cry; he was beginning to think he'd overshot his mark, or imagined the whole thing, when he heard quick steps coming up behind him. He looked back and found the path empty. Except. Except behind the flanking shrubbery, someone was panting. Against his better judgment, he let himself be lured from the path and circled the bushes, waiting for the moment when the branches would thin out enough for him to see clearly.

The ground sloped away. Here, under the trees, the earlier snow was untouched. It made a gray swale against which he spotted a few black shapes, rocks. There was the border wall, taller here, because the ground was a good fifteen feet below street level. And there, beneath it, was a black shape murmuring, kneeling, about ten yards from Charlie and facing away. Or two black shapes. A black man, hunched menacingly, and the body on its back in the snow.

Charlie couldn't go forward, or even breathe: he was afraid a cloud of breath would float across the open space and call attention to him, and then he, too, would become a body stretched out on the snow. But he couldn't just leave, either—not even with his wang starting to actually throb from having to pee so bad—because he realized, was realizing even now as his eyes adjusted, where Sam had been all this time.

Then a siren sounded somewhere, a far-off wail, and the black man glanced up from whatever he was doing. He staggered to his feet and stumbled off, trailing one hand along the wall, as if trying to exit a maze. With the sleeves of his white jacket bunched up, he was even more underdressed than Charlie, and the weird part, Charlie would realize later, was that he seemed to be headed toward the siren, rather than away. As soon as he was out of sight, Charlie was on his knees beside Sam. She looked so small all of a sudden—when the fuck had she gotten so small?—under the thick coat that had been spread over her. That she wasn't shivering scared him. Her mouth was slack, her eyes closed. The coat was a dark spot. The snow around her head was dark, too, and sludgy, the snow he was kneeling in, and when he touched it and brought his fingers to his face, there was a burnt smell like the drill at the dentist's. The solidity of her arm against his leg. The weight of her. "Oh, God," he said. "What did he do to you?"

The hole that had opened in his chest threatened to swallow him. He may have started to pee a little. Above his head, sirens called and answered, a kaddish ramifying down empty streets. *It is happening again. Still.* He nudged her shoulder. "Sam, come on. Wake up." He knew already it wasn't a question of waking. "Sam. It's me. I came to save you." If she'd only stayed by his side. Why hadn't she? And this, too, would pain him in retrospect, because he shouldn't have been thinking about himself at this moment, or imagining it didn't happen however it had happened. He would have to live with the fact that this was how he reacted to other people's suffering—selfishly—and there would be times, he already knew, when he would wish it was him lying there unconscious, instead of awake, having to make choices.

Up where the wall ended, beams of blue and red whirled, cantilevered out over the park. He could hear doors slamming—as now, in his basement room in Flower Hill, he could hear the radiators wheezing, the artless feet of little brothers on the stairs. Even before they knocked on his door, he yelled, "Go away!" With his eyes closed, it felt like he was ripping a tumor out of his chest, and still the sickness remained. He tried once more to summon some foggy, bearded figure who would hear him. *Lord, have mercy on me, a sinner,* but Abe and Izz had retreated, and beyond the headphones all was silence. The bearded figure had likewise run away from him. Or had he, Charlie, been the one to run? Because, when push came to shove, he'd run from Sam, too. He saw himself again kneeling by his friend, literally red-handed. A voice, the voice that had earlier called for help, had been up above the wall, where flashlights poked holes in the night, scattering the birds: "It's this way." Charlie's bladder had released at last, and warmth had trickled down his leg, and he was biting his lip not to cry out loud in shame and misery and terror, and at what seemed the last possible second, on pure instinct, he'd bolted back through the bushes and onto another path and sprinted off deeper into the dark, clutching his groin. He assumed they were on his heels.

By the time he realized that they weren't going to catch him, that no one even knew he'd been there, he'd reached the park's center: a huge, bleak field stretching away to a fringe of black trees. Except for his breathing, the silence was perfect. The purple-gray clouds were still, brittle. The muggers who should have been prowling around were nowhere. In the distance, buildings were lit-up prison towers, no life in them. It was like a nuclear wasteland, with Charlie the only thing alive. His jeans were soaked with urine. And tears and snot were frozen on his face, so he must have been crying. All he wanted was to lie down and close his eyes, but something in him felt that if he did, he wouldn't open them again, and something else, something pusillanimous and unpunk, could not even now consent to that. He stripped off his damp jeans and Fruit of the Looms, wadded them up and pushed them into a bush. Naked from the waist down, he used a handful of snow to try to wash the pee off his leg. He'd heard people stranded in the Arctic buried themselves in snow for warmth, but he was too much of a wuss to keep this up for more than a second. He took the pajama bottoms from his jacket pocket and pulled them on and, leaving behind the rest, broke across the field, aiming for the tower at what seemed to be the corner of the park. His legs were going numb, numb, numb with the wind through the thin cotton, and numbness made things a little better, so he ran even harder, promising himself that soon he would be home in his bed and when he woke in the morning this would all turn out to have been some really crappy dream.

WHEN HE SLIPPED UPSTAIRS late Sunday afternoon, his mother was on the phone with the Asshole again; he could hear from the foyer the murmur of the voice at the other end of the wire. The time when the light available outside the house exceeded the light in the living room had passed, and still Mom wouldn't reach the two feet to pull the lamp chain. She just sat there, like an old person. Then the doorframe was behind Charlie and his fingers were closing on the jacket she hadn't reminded him to wear and lifting it from the hook. It seemed impossible that two nights ago, when this jacket had traveled with him to the City, he'd been so full of hope, he thought. And now the kitchen door clicked shut like his youth behind him.

The held breath of the world at five p.m. in winter. The sky above the haloes of the streetlights, electric air indifferent to anything happening below.

He let gravity pull him downhill toward the little church at the corner of the highway, Our Lady of Lamentable Perpetuity. Aside from the floodlights lighting up the nativity scene out front, the church gave no sign of being open. For a moment, he was sure he'd wasted his time. In the glass case by the church door, white plastic letters had been slotted into the black felt. *MASS A.M., NOON, P.M., FROM HIM NO SECRETS HID.* When he'd tried to explain his feeling sometimes that the whole world was trying to communicate with him, the grief counselor had laced his fingers together over the knee of his crossed leg and had said, "I'm wondering, Charlie, if that makes it easier to believe."

"To believe what?"

"Well, whatever you feel is being communicated."

He checked the bottom of the glass case in case a couple of letters had fallen there, some part of the message he was missing, but there was nothing. He reached for the handle of the church door. It was unlocked. He went in.

It wasn't his first time in a church, or even this church. He'd come here back in middle school to see Mickey Sullivan make his first communion. Then last year at the Catholic hospital, when Mom had asked for a few minutes alone with Dad, he'd parked the outgrown stroller in the gift shop, Abe and Izzy inside, and snuck over to the chapel off the lobby to sit there with his hands in his lap. His brothers never squealed, and this made it worse, somehow, his tropism, his secret apostasy. The hospital must have toned it down a bit, though, because he'd forgotten about the glazed plaster Messiah hanging over this altar, its blue eyes gazing mournfully down among drops of ketchupy blood. Farther forward in the rows of pews sat three old women in black. Like the priest yammering up on the stage, they had their heads bowed, eyes presumably closed. Charlie stole forward and slipped into a seat in the shadows and pretended not to be peeking through his own shut eyes. They did that crossing thing to their chests, too quick for him to follow. Then the priest announced he would read from the book of Daniel. *Was* there even a book of Daniel? Oh, right. He remembered the general outlines from Hebrew school. Israel lay vanquished again. The Gentile king, uneasy, called to him a Jew gifted with prophesy. For the king could not know what the future held, but the Lord knew. The Lord always knew, as surely as if He were seated here right now.

This first reading, disappointingly, was in English, not Latin. Then came a Gospel. And all at once, as the priest read on, Charlie could finally feel Him, displacing the air at the back of his neck—not a benevolent giant, or a figure of plaster, but an athletic man only slightly older than Charlie himself, lightly acne'd beneath his beard, kneeling in the pew right behind, staring through Charlie's shoulderblades and into his busted heart:

Yea, the hour cometh, that whosoever killeth you, will think that he doth a service to God. And these things will they do to you; because they have not known the Father, nor me. But these things I have told you, that when the hour shall come, you may remember that I told you of them. But I told you not these things from the beginning, because I was with you. And now I go to him that sent me, and none of you asketh me: Whither goest thou? But because I have spoken these things to you, sorrow hath filled your heart.

Oh, it had, it had! Sorrow had filled Charlie's heart. It was as if Jesus was speaking to him specifically. Charlie couldn't turn around, though, to verify that he was imagining things, because what if he should see that he was *not* imagining things, that a homeless man had slipped into the pew right behind him? Or that verily this was the Lord Jesus Christ, come to make him surrender?

But when he, the Spirit of truth, is come, he will teach you all truth. For he shall not speak of himself; but what things soever he shall hear, he shall speak; and the things that are to come, he shall shew you. He shall glorify me; because he shall receive of mine, and shall shew it to you. All things whatsoever the Father hath, are mine. A little while, and now you shall not see me; and again a little while, and you shall see me.

Charlie clasped his hands and rocked forward and closed his eyes, but in the velvety dark behind his eyelids, like a curtained theater where the lights have gone out, he still saw the Savior Jesus Christ, with a swimmer's shoulders and an expression like longing. The priest's voice ran on far away. Much closer a voice whispered, *Fear not, Charlie Weisbarger.* He was terrified now, in the darkness of his own closed eyes, utterly alone and nearly in tears. *I have set my mark on you. I will make you the instrument of my strong right hand. You have only to repent.*

I repent, Charlie was helpless not to think, even as he wondered what he was signing up for—what this word, which he'd heard so often, actually meant. And then the vision was gone, leaving only an immense silence that filled the spaces of Charlie's chest, pushing out what had been there before. When he looked, there was no homeless man.

Notwithstanding whatever had just gone down, he could not bring himself to do communion. The next time the widows bowed their heads to pray, he ducked into the side aisle and hurried to the back of the church. The priest was watching, puzzled, but Charlie kept his gait steady, as though redemption was a bowl of broth he might otherwise spill.

Outside the wind was changing, whipping up the wet trees, embattling the birds of Long Island. Armies of them, serried avengers, wheeled against the bruised sky. He slowed on the sidewalk so he wouldn't have to watch his boots, and then, beneath a burnt-out streetlight, stopped. *Be still,* he heard. *Be still and know thou art with God.* Over the white box of the Exxon station darted the shadows of the birds, singly, one after another, as though launched by some catapult on the far side of the roofline. Gulls up there, pigeons, sparrows, jays, and starlings, a congress of birds converging for some reason on Nassau County, every wingèd thing on earth soon to take its place along the barricades.

𝕬nd all the places wherein the children of men, and the beasts of the field do dwell, the reading had said, he hath also given the birds of the air into thy hand.

Not Charlie's hand, of course. Somewhere in his borrowed ancestry stood some patriarch to whom various other things had been entrusted, and look what had happened since. The hands now in his pockets could not be counted on, nor could any other, save the Messiah's. And the Messiah, Charlie knew, was not going to come out of the church across from the gas station until Charlie was no longer here. The Messiah was not ready yet to be seen. But he had come to reclaim the beasts and the fowls and the children of men and Sam, and to save Charlie, personally, from all his sin. His heart was like the beating of wings, and behind it, Charlie heard again the words. 𝕳is kingdom shall not be delivered up to other people, and it shall break in pieces, and shall consume all these kingdoms. 𝕬nd itself shall stand forever. But first the earth had to be prepared. And so, under a storm of birds, armed by heaven against the temptation to turn back, Charlie Weisbarger hurried home to await further instruction.

THE FAMILY BUSINESS

May 14, 1961

How much do you remember, I wonder,
of the old Hamilton place out in Fairfield
County? You can't have been older than
three or four the last time you saw it.
By that point we were paying a caretaker;
the furniture had all been covered with the
cream-colored dropcloths under which you
and your sister spent the afternoon hiding
and seeking, your shouts filling the forsaken
rooms.

   When I was a boy, though, there were
over a dozen of us still living beneath that
great slate roof. Back-country Connecticut
was the opposite of a city then: rolling
meadowland, long lanes and horseshoe drives,
trees at what was almost the horizon blotting
out the lives of other people. Six mornings
a week our driver, Hans, would fetch the
black Packard from the car barn and ease
up the quarter-mile of gravel to the lip
of the front porch. The hand-cranked engine,

even at idle, set the whole house atremble.
And when I think of my grandfather, your
great-grandfather, Roebuck Hamilton, Jr.,
it is this tremor I think of first. As the
breakfast-room chandelier began to shake, a
kind of inward agitation would seize him,
the violence of the cocked hammer. He was
far too disciplined to have leapt straight
up from his chair, but he would already
have sent a hundred little signals regarding
the contingency of his presence among us.
The black bowler hat perched on his knee;
the cane hooked to the edge of the long
table; the pocket watch placed beside his
eggcup and the way his eyes kept darting
to it as he importuned the eggshell with his
spoon ... all of this now slightly aquiver,
as though, standing between him and the
business that awaited, it might as well
explode.

According to your great-aunt Agnes, our
authority on family history, Grandfather had
made his way on foot to West Virginia at age

nineteen, after landing in New York from Manchester. His prospecting yielded nothing for over a year, yet he had persisted, tramping all over those hills, shooting game to smoke over green-wood fires. In five years he would own half the coal under the state.

By custom, the very last thing he did before going out to Hans in the morning was shave. He wanted the skin around his moustache at the very peak of depilation when he arrived at his offices in Manhattan, which to my small self seemed as distant as India or Indian Country. He would lock himself into the bathroom under the stairs, against whose door I sometimes liked to put my ear. Such sounds as I could detect beneath the oceanic thrum of the Packard were different, richer somehow, than the sounds my father made shaving. In particular, Grandfather's razor fascinated me, as what is forbidden will fascinate any child on whom the world has not yet pressed its discipline. I can still see it coming out of its leather kit to be stropped. The monogrammed handle. The blade like honed glass.

One morning, I remember, having excused myself early from breakfast, I stole into the bathroom under the stairs to look at it. The kit was waiting atop a clothes hamper. I unfolded it and extracted the razor carefully, handle-first, from its place between the moustache scissors and the two-tone shaving brush.

Light flashed on the blade, diffused through the frosted window patterned with the gray shadows of the branches outside. When I turned it, reflections danced over my sweater.

Soon, I was waving it about like a pirate in a book, ordering captives to walk the plank. I was often losing track of the real world then; I somehow failed to hear, over the car engine outside, Grandfather's footsteps, the stump of his cane, until they

were nearly at the bathroom door. There
was a voice from farther down the hall, and
he paused for a moment with the doorhandle
held ninety degrees from rest. Only then did
I recognize the scale of my transgression.
I had time to shove the razor back into the
kit, but there was no escaping the bathroom.
There was, however, a large mirrored
bureau opposite the medicine chest, and at
the very last possible instant, I balled
myself up inside and pulled the door shut,
and all was rumble and darkness.

At first, I had only the pounding of
my heart to mark the time. Which way had
the blade been facing when I'd found it?
When I'd put it back? Then there was an
inch-wide strip of light in front of me;
the juddering of the house had dislodged
the door of the bureau. I should have
pulled it shut, but instead moved closer
to the crack. The sight of Grandfather's
nude back led to a ghastly presentiment.
I had caught him in some hermetic ritual

of the kind my cousins whispered about. In fact, it was only the shirt that was missing. With my eye pressed against the gap, I could see it hanging neatly from a hook on the back of the door, could see his braces hanging from the high waist of his pants. Though the skin of his upper body had mottled with age, the muscles beneath were a younger man's, and they seemed to twitch or ripple as he flicked the razor across his soapless skin. And he whistled, I remember, as if to increase the degree of danger, or as if genuinely happy (this man I'd never once seen smile), a tune I barely recognized over the rumble of the car as Schubert's lied about the little trout. Then my forehead again knocked into the door that hid me, swinging it wider, and in the mirror above the sink our eyes met. Next thing I knew, I was being dragged out of the darkness by this looming strange man who lived in my house. The razor floated between us. Well? he demanded.

All I could think to say was: Why don't you use soap?

There came a single laugh. Almost a bark. Child, there is something one learns when one goes out and lives with nothing (a monitory intensity purpling his face as he pronounced this last word). It's not soap that makes for the closeness of the shave; it is the razor itself.

He seized my hand and drew the blade across my forefinger so swiftly I felt nothing. Like the tiniest stroke of a calligrapher's pen, a line of blood appeared, became a drop, two drops. Then he unlocked the door. As I ran off down the hall, I was convinced that he was on my heels, that I could feel his sour hot breath on my neck, but when I looked back, he was still standing half-clothed in the doorway of the bathroom, grinning, blurred by my tears. That was your great-grandfather: a distant and altogether terrifying man.

Peculiarly, it was my own father I

would hold responsible for the scar on my finger. I don't think I ever forgave him for his failure to protect me that day, or for forcing my mother and myself to live in uncomplaining proximity with a person who, it now seemed to me, might kill us while whistling Schubert and then clean his teeth with our bones. Even after we had moved to Upper Fifth Avenue, so that my father could be closer to the offices of the firm (whose day-to-day operations had been ceded to him), I longed to break away from the family altogether.

I wanted to be a playwright; did your mother ever tell you that? One afternoon when I was not much younger than you are now, Aunt Agnes took me to see Desire Under the Elms, by Mr. Eugene O'Neill. The stage was like a solution to a problem I had not yet formulated. Maybe if I went to school somewhere out in the Middle West, I thought, away from my lonely, crowded life, I might discover it. My father, of course, expected me to follow him to the firm. How vividly I recall being summoned to see him in his office there (for if you were to see him between eight in the morning and six at night, it would have to be in his office). We sat, just the two of us, under a slowly spinning fan. We had not been alone together in what felt like a decade. What was this he had been hearing about Chicago? he wanted to know; Yale had been good enough for him.

I forced myself to say what I'd long been thinking. But I'm not like you.

At which he put his hands on his trouser thighs and leaned forward. He had always been something of a ghost to me, my father, an echo of the muffled explosion that had been his father. Part of this may have been the lush moustaches he'd cultivated himself, which hid most of his lower face, and part the pince-nez behind which his eyes now glimmered. Bill, he said mildly. Do you think I'm like me?

I meant, I said, that I was not drawn

to the family business. Or blessed with Grandfather's golden touch.

He took another sip of whisky. Chewed a cube of ice. Had I been talking to Aunt Agnes again?

Grandfather told me himself, I said, how he made all of this. Everything around us.

Since we were speaking man to man, my father said (and no doubt since the object of our discussion had by then been dead for five years), why did I think Grandfather had gone about in such a rage all the time? It was because he knew he'd done no such thing. He had wanted, above all, to be a self-made man, like George Hearst or William A. Clark: sufficient unto himself, listening to the earth, chosen by it to run the world. In truth, the earth had wanted little to do with him.

But what about West Virginia? I asked. What about living with <u>nothing</u>?

Your grandfather lost two toes to frostbite, contracted chronic dysentery, and couldn't keep a mule alive for more than a month, my father said. It was only with Grandmother's capital (the Sweeneys owned breweries in Belfast) that he had been able to buy up half of the Monongahela Valley, and the premium he'd paid for it had been a lifelong sense of failure and the hyphenation of our last name. He sold his stake during the boom of 1890 and limped back to the city with a trunkful of paper money, because that was where his talent lay: not boring and hewing, but buying, selling, holding. Each additional million only made it clearer that he was not one of the great men.

You see, we Hamilton-Sweeneys are not discoverers, my father said, we are investors. We facilitate the greatness of others. And this is what it means to be a man: learning to see the world not as a question of what you want to be, but of what you are …

But it is late, and I feel myself wandering far from what I set out to say.

It is as though in the many years since I last put pen to paper like this, the memories have grown too ripe inside me. Or as if the intervening time were an illusion, and instead of the boxed-up study on Sutton Place in which I now sit, I am back in my first office in the Hamilton-Sweeney Building, under the green-shaded banker's lamp after everyone has gone. It has ever been easier for me to express myself with a pen. One risks less, somehow, of that entire world inside—or risks more slowly.

William, what I have been trying to show you here is that I understand your anger. That I can imagine how arbitrary my life must appear to you. You think that I am distant and passionless, that I do not see what I've sacrificed, that I do not know how to dream of things beyond my control. But you must believe me, as someone who made the same mistakes about his own father, and his father's father, that what you see is not the whole of me.

A month from now, Felicia Gould and I will be married. I am not asking you to see her many fine qualities, to grow to care for her as I have (which is not, I should say, the same way I cared for your mother). I am not asking you to want what I want, or even predicting that your own ambitions, whatever they may be, will prove as mine did beyond reach. But I am asking you to see me clearly before you decide how to respond. To see that if I choose not to spend the rest of my life in mourning—if I am not as strong or as principled as you might be in the same circumstance—I do so consciously. That your father is a man, Son, as you are: this is the impossibility I ask you to imagine.

I do not need to look back over what I've written here to hear the note of self-pity you will no doubt have detected. In fact, I shall probably throw this letter on the fire as soon as I've finished it. Start over, in a greeting card that will bank my confessional mood, and simply ask, in a few brief lines, if you'd serve as my best man at the wedding. But even the flames of our fireplace swallowing these pages, burning the paper to the color of ink, will not erase the fact that I sat here well after midnight tonight, dredging up things I thought I'd never tell you, in the perhaps vain hope that you might receive them without the garbling of intentions, suspicions, grievances that seems to pass down through the blood, father to son, Hamilton-Sweeney to Hamilton-Sweeney.

And so one more memory, if you will indulge me. It is how loudly you bellowed, William, when first I held you. You were afraid, Kathryn said; I must hold you tighter. I looked at her, exhausted in the hospital bed, and she looked at you, and you looked at me looking at her with eyes that had never known anything else, and for a moment there I swear we saw each other with a clarity that nothing can alter, not

time, not heartbreak, not death. And in some
sense, Son, I am still holding you just that
tightly to me, remaining

Passionately, however distantly,
Your father

BOOK II

SCENES FROM PRIVATE LIFE

[1961-1976]

We tried to run the city,
but the city ran away;
and now, Peter Minuit,
we can't continue it . . .

—LORENZ HART
"Give It Back to the Indians"

That Chicago, Philadelphia and Boston are not experiencing the
same trouble suggests a special madness here. . . . Americans do
not much like, admire, respect, trust or believe in this city.

—ROWLAND EVANS AND ROBERT NOVAK
Inside Report

16

KEITH HAD ALWAYS TENDED to see the great events of his life not as things he made happen, but as things that happened *to* him, like weather. And, believing there was nothing he could do to change them, he took them in stride. When his junior-high gym teacher put a football in his hand, for example, he ran with it. When football earned him a scholarship to the state university, he went. When his knee blew out senior year, he continued to turn out for games, wearing his jersey under his blazer, to show the sophomore who'd replaced him in the backfield there were no hard feelings. Regan, then, from the very beginning, had been a kind of departure: She was something to which he had no natural right. Something he had chosen for himself, freely.

Not that he would have been constitutionally capable of framing things this way in the spring of 1961. Instead, there was mostly an oblique thrill in his chest when, masturbating himself to sleep in Mansfield, he thought of her in her sorority house in Poughkeepsie. He'd never seen her room there—suitors were required to wait in the front parlor of the rambling Victorian until their dates were ready—but he pictured it as Spartan, self-denying, its only luxury a mirror like the one that had hung in the hallway back home. Having the attractive person's indifference to his own attractiveness, he'd barely noticed that mirror himself, growing up, but it was for some reason the one that came to mind when he imagined Regan standing nude before a glass, her body almost touching it as she stared into it at something he couldn't yet see.

Perhaps she'd spent a long time standing like this the night she was to drive him down to New York to meet her family for the first time. At any rate, he'd been stranded for upwards of half an hour on the davenport downstairs. Every time he'd said something, the sorority sister perched on its arm, the quote-unquote chaperone, had absentmindedly touched her face, her collar, the pale bare knee she pretended not to notice her skirt riding up. Keith had been all-conference the previous year, and could easily have had her phone number, but he found himself less and less interested these days in what came easy.

Finally, Regan appeared on the house's center staircase, in a long blue cardigan that almost swallowed her. Her red hair, loose, hid the sides of her face. When the sister told her she looked great, she seemed to wince a little, as if that hadn't been her intention. And in fact hadn't there been a certain anxiousness in the invitation to come with her to the City? Hadn't her voice sped up, as if she were trying to get the question out before she could second-guess herself? Keith kissed her on the mouth in full view of the chaperone. "You do look great," he said. "As usual." Then he helped her into her raincoat and opened his umbrella over her and followed her down the damp lawn to her cute white Karmann Ghia.

Rain drummed the ragtop like fingers on a desk. It seemed to mute not only Regan, behind the wheel, but also the lights of other cars along the Thruway. Somewhere north of the Bronx, he found the signal of an AM station he liked, Saturday night pop, the seraphic harmonies of the Everly Brothers. The City should by now have been staining the horizon purple, but it stayed dark out there. The cupped flame of the radio dial lit only Regan's chin and nose, the teeth worrying her soft lower lip. "Nervous?"

"I hate to be a wet blanket," she said, "but is it okay if I just sit here and think?"

It struck him as a loaded question, one of her little tests of his devotion. He turned the music down. "I'm not going to embarrass you, Regan. I promise."

She felt for his arm in the dark, which meant he must have done something right. She wasn't usually physically demonstrative; you might even have called her a little skittish. "It's not you I'm worried about."

"How bad could they be?"

"It's not just William, or even Daddy. His fiancée will be there, too, which means the Demon Brother, and I . . . I just don't want you to feel ambushed, is all."

Hell of a strange way to talk about your own family, he thought, but "ambushed" turned out to capture certain aspects of the experience pretty neatly. The house, for one thing: an actual freestanding brick mansion on Sutton Place, smack in the middle of the east side of Manhattan, aloof to the high-rises that had seemed so impressive on previous visits. He'd known she was rich, obviously—she shared a name with a holding company whose headquarters was one of the tallest buildings in New York—but he had to struggle not to gawk while Regan fumbled with her keys at the side door. Before she could get it open, a severe woman in a nurse-like uniform pulled it inward. "Your father is in the drawing room." Keith had always wondered about this term, about people who could afford a room just to draw in, and it made the bouquet of flowers in his hand seem flaccid, minuscule, even as the woman snatched them from him. "I'll put these in water," she said, in the same tone with which she might have offered to toss them in the trash.

In the flickery, wood-paneled space to which Regan led him, people were already standing like statuary. One of the men was quite tall. The other man and the woman couldn't have been over five foot two. The window casings were lead, the rugs Persian, the fire in the fireplace dying . . . this was all there was time to register before the woman was crossing the room, her hands thrust before her as if she were being tugged along helplessly behind. "You must be Keith. We've heard so awfully much about you." Then Felicia Gould's hands were passing him on to the gray, trim, bland little man she introduced as her brother, Amory. The third man, presumably Regan's father, hung back, as though awaiting permission. He'd started to ask if Keith needed a drink when the fiancée interrupted. "Patience, darling. Lizaveta will be out with the martinis any minute. You look fabulous, by the way, Regan. Have you lost weight?"

Regan was still hovering near the door. "Where's William?"

"Ooh, we can fetch him later. You kids have a seat." Felicia hurled herself onto the end of a long divan and patted the cushion beside her while the father tinkered with the fire and the small man looked on inscrutably. Fortunately, it was in Keith's nature to be charming—particularly after one of the bone-dry martinis had vanished down his gullet and another had materialized in his hand. To answer Felicia Gould's questions, though (about his family and football and wasn't Hartford lovely in the spring), he had to turn toward the fire and away from Regan, seated to his right. He almost had the feeling that Regan had planned it this way, that it was part of the same disappearing act as the cardigan and the drooping bangs. What was it she was afraid of? The stepmother seemed perfectly harmless. Stepmother-to-be, rather; she and Bill were to be married that June, she explained, noticing him noticing her ring.

But by then, a slight, black-haired boy in a logging shirt and dungarees had paused in the doorway. "William!" This time it was Regan who was up and crossing the room. The kid blushed as she embraced him. And though no one else rose, Keith felt he should go introduce himself.

Regan had talked a lot about her brother, usually with concern over his delinquent tendencies. He'd been only seven when their mother died, she said, and had taken it hard (as though there were some more noble way to take a fatal car crash; as though she, at eleven, had been the picture of maturity—which he supposed, comparatively, she was). Last year, while she'd spent a semester in Italy, William had managed to get himself expelled from three consecutive prep schools, a personal best. "I don't know what he's going to do if I don't move back to New York after graduation," she'd said. Keith had told her he was sure William would be fine. It was the only time she'd ever gotten mad at him, so far, and it was like she didn't know how to do it. Her voice just got quiet and choked, the sound of a marble caught in the throat. He'd sensed for a second that perhaps underneath was where she'd been keeping her feelings about her mom.

"No, you don't understand. My brother is . . . sensitive. Maybe even a genius."

Keith found sensitive geniuses annoying on principle. In person, though, he couldn't help liking the kid, both because Keith liked people generally and because William didn't seem to give a fig whether he did or not. "Ghouls behaving themselves?" he asked Regan, pouring himself a martini from the shaker the maid had left on the sideboard. Then the siblings were off, murmuring to each other in their own private language. Keith was starting to get a glimmer of exactly what Regan had meant by "sensitive"—there was something bristling, even feline, in William's self-presentation—when Felicia approached. "William, dear, let's not monopolize our guest. He must be famished, with these muscles of his. Keith, shall we adjourn to the dining room?"

"What do you say, Keith? Shall we?" the kid said. It was impossible to put your finger on just what made this mocking, or even who was being mocked. But Regan, as if fortified by her brother's presence, spoke up—"Yes, let's"—and took Keith's arm.

The dining room was long and narrow, presided over by oil paintings of two whiskery men who could have been twins. Previous iterations of the Hamilton-Sweeney line, apparently; beneath the accessories that dated them—a pith helmet on one, a pince-nez on the other—they had the same egg-shaped skull and prominent forehead as Regan's father. Who, incidentally, seemed emboldened now, as if the absurdly long table in front of him and the gloom in which he sat offered a measure of security. Here he was, practically shouting to make himself heard by Keith.

"Beg pardon?"

"I said, how did you and my daughter meet?"

A furlong away, at the foot of the table, William groaned. Keith wasn't sure how to respond, but neither Felicia nor the future stepuncle, seated opposite him, gave any sign of having heard, and he couldn't turn to Regan without appearing to conspire. "Regan was in that play before Christmas, *Twelfth Night*, I'm sure you saw it."

There was a throat-clearing, oddly nasal. Possibly a shake of the head. "You're in the theater, then?"

"No, no, just a theater-goer. I had to introduce myself to her afterward." Every word of this was true, though Keith omitted the fact that he'd been dragged to the play's very last performance by another Vassar girl, whom he'd deserted at the wrap party. "She's quite a performer, your daughter."

The woman who'd earlier taken his flowers now deposited in front of him a bowl of tawny liquid. He wasn't sure whether you were supposed to wash your hands in it or what. Regan must have noticed, because she touched his leg under the table. A series of muted nods and glances indicated that he should do what she did. He guessed which spoon he was to take from among the three on offer and politely slurped from it the salty broth he would later learn to call *consommé*.

There followed a course of salad, and a course of fish, and between the questions issuing from the head of the table and the bright ribbon of chatter kept up by the fiancée, awkward silences were mostly avoided. During the meat course, Felicia explained to him in a confidential tone that her cook had trained at the Cordon Bleu, and was on loan to the Hamilton-Sweeneys. All part of a slow process of preparing for the move across the park, away from this house and its ghosts. She turned to look at the oil painting hanging above her future husband, or maybe at the ancient elephant gun mounted on brass hooks on the wall below. Yes, it certainly had been a long engagement, she agreed, but they hadn't wanted to uproot young William before he graduated. Down there at the table's far end, the object of her solicitude looked profoundly unhappy. He hadn't spoken in half an hour.

As for the other brother, Amory Gould, he might have been a doll stuffed with sawdust, at least until the pie-plates were empty and the coffee appeared. Then he picked up his silver and raised it quizzically toward the light. The gesture was so odd—so conspicuous—that even Felicia stopped talking. "Now, Keith," he said, when he had the table's full attention. The spoon remained aloft; his eyes stayed on it, as if checking retroactively for spots. "It is Keith, isn't it? Did you ever consider finance, I wonder?"

Keith had just been telling Regan's father how he was having to double up on science courses, preparing for medical school. Yes, he would have liked to have gone somewhere like Yale, but frankly hadn't really applied himself in the way he could have, prior to the injury. "Finance?"

"Banking, my boy. Investing. The family business, as it were." The voice was soft, insinuating, as if you were eavesdropping on it talking to itself. Involuntarily, Keith leaned forward to hear. "The business of trust, is what it really comes down to. Now me, I'm afraid I lack what you'd call the charisma to be a public face. I remain in the background, I put people together. But a good-looking kid like you, always ready with a smile, I can't help thinking you could sell unicycles to a paraplegic. Which is of course where fortunes are to be made. Figuratively speaking. No background necessary, no special training, just an ability to think on your feet." Down came the silverware. "Our world is expanding, Keith. If you'd like to have a conversation about your place in it, I could make that happen." A mild, blue, unblinking gaze held Keith's across the table. Next to him, Regan's silence was deep, but he couldn't see her; it was as if she'd been pushed into shadow by the glacial pallor of the man's face, the patent reasonableness of his voice.

Then a chair shrieked across the floorboards. "May I be excused?" William asked, already halfway up. Just before exiting the room, he shot Keith a significant look, though signifying what? And Keith could have sworn William lingered in the corridor for a minute afterward, waiting to hear his response. He cleared his throat. "That's incredibly generous of you, Mr. Gould," he said, "but I'm already on a path now. I might as well keep on it."

There was a pause. "Of course," Amory said. "I wouldn't dream of diverting you."

Later, after he'd shaken hands and promised not to be a stranger, Regan followed Keith outside. They'd planned for her to stay overnight on Sutton Place while he took the late train back to Connecticut, and he assumed she'd come out to say goodbye. Instead, she said, "I had to get out of there."

"Why? Was I okay?"

"Oh, sweetheart." She paused on the wet curb, as if startled by the question. He was standing in the gutter. The rain had stopped, but inch-deep water bearing the sodden white petals of flowering trees parted around his shoes. "You were great. You were perfect."

They were almost the same height this way, and he had an urge to reach for her, to secure her to the ground, so that she couldn't slip away again until he'd understood her every last mystery. "Your brother liked me?"

"He'll love you, when he gets to know how much there is to you. Like I did."

It was the first time she'd spoken this word, "love," and, characteristically, it was in a context that left him no way to respond. Also: How much of *what*?

"Let's go somewhere," she said, suddenly. "I'm signed out of the Chi Omega house until tomorrow."

"Are you sure?"

For once, she didn't pull away. Her thighs were soft against his, her mouth was open to him, and he could feel that for this one night, she was going to let him do to her anything he wanted. A dim alarm in the back of his head was already warning that it shouldn't be like this, like some kind of reward for good behavior, but another voice was telling him that it might be months before she would feel this way again, and they were reeling back, stumbling against the parked Karmann Ghia, and she had taken his hands and put them on her sides, and of its own volition one was moving up to those wonderful, small breasts, warm under the firm armor of her brassiere, when he caught himself. They were still less than a block from her family. "Hold that thought," he said. "Okay?"

They ended up at a hotel near Grand Central, under the name Mr. and Mrs. Z. Glass; he would have to subsist on canned tunafish for the rest of the month, but it was worth it. They didn't even turn on the light or turn down the bed, but made love standing up, against a picture window to which rain still clung. It was like standing on the edge of a giant excavation pit. When he closed his eyes, she seemed to be somewhere out in the middle of it, amid tiny, floating lights, calling for him, but there was more of it the deeper he went. It was only just before he came, hugely, baffled, that he understood that this was not her first time, any more than it was his, and that he had still not quite managed to reach her. And even now, in his memory, as he lay cooling in the darkness of his dormitory, Regan was a world unto herself, pleased with him for reasons he could not understand . . .

17

WHEREAS HER BROTHER WILLIAM, at seventeen, was separated by only the thinnest membrane from the world that contained him. Which is to say: a city boy, definitively. He knew exactly which spot on which subway platform corresponded with which staircase on which other platform. He knew an empty subway car was to be avoided—someone had pissed in it, or thrown up, or died. He knew how to pretend you'd never heard of the famous person to whom you were being introduced, and how to pretend to buy the famous person's pretense of never having heard of you. He'd learned the previous summer how to pick up grown men in public lavatories, and all the places in the Park the vice squad never visited. He couldn't make a football spiral to save his life, but give him a broomhandle and a spaldeen and he'd hit the river from here.

At intervals over the last few years, he'd been shipped off to tired dorps like Putney, Vt., and Wallingford, Conn., and Andover and Exeter, N.H., stocked lakes into which the nation's tributaries of wealth and privilege emptied. Other kids liked to make fun of his accent. To boys from Grosse Pointe and Lake Forest, *Gothamite* was only one step from *Jew*. But never once had he envied them, or cultivated, as his sister did, that deracinated East Coast drawl. He believed his connection to Manhattan would sustain him, like an anchor plunged into turbulent water.

And sustain him it had, right up until that summer—the summer he finally graduated high school. But sitting up into the wee hours on the eve of his father's wedding in June, he could feel the chain straining, the connection about to snap. Or was it already morning? The sky beyond the ogeed bars of the kitchen window on Sutton Place had brightened enough to disclose the heavy-headed roses entwined there, his mother's. They seemed to nod at him, admonishing; they knew what they would have done in his place.

He went to the dining room. From the brass hooks on the wall, he retrieved his Great-Grandfather Hamilton's safari rifle. He checked the chamber; the bullet he'd discovered when he was a little kid was still there. Dress socks silenced his feet on the stairs.

The second-floor hallway was hardly identifiable as the one where he and Regan used to stage parades. Its rug had already been moved to Felicia's palace across the park, along with most of the furniture. Tomorrow—or, strike that, today—cleaners would arrive to prepare this house for its new owners. The guestrooms, though, had been left intact for the various male relations and business associates who'd traveled here for the wedding. He'd heard them come in from the rehearsal dinner around midnight and stay up dissecting the scene he'd caused there, the disgrace he'd brought upon the family. It was unclear whether they'd known he was awake directly below them, making his miserable way through a pint of Irish whisky stolen from the banquet room bar. At any rate, they hadn't come down to the kitchen. And the whisky had a funny effect; beyond a certain point, each slug from the bottle unfogged his thinking, until the whole house seemed to tremble with clarity. The dormer window at the end of the upstairs hall. The sealed entrance of what had once been his parents' room. And beside that, the guestroom where a bony collegian in orphaned bits of tuxedo sprawled snoring on the floor, his French cuffs blown open like flowers. Was this the guy who'd done it? This had to be him. The ones passed out in the beds were too old.

William stood in the half-light for what must have been minutes with the rifle's long barrel wavering above the guy's right ear. Just do it, you pussy. Pull the trigger. If you were any kind of man, you would do it. But where was Regan's boyfriend, or fiancé now, Keith, whose job this should rightfully have been? Because the best William could do, in the end, was leave the rifle on the guestroom floor, hoping the fucker passed out there would see it upon waking, and know how close he'd come to dying. Or maybe finish the job himself.

Shaking, William ransacked his own room for clothes to fill a gymbag. He grabbed his guitar, the book of Michelangelo plates brought back from Regan's semester away, his hand-me-down shaving kit, and keys from the nightstand. After a last jolt of liquid courage, he was out the door and down to the line of parked cars at the curb. Sweat and formalwear made a paste between his back and the driver's seat of Regan's Karmann Ghia. Beyond the window, dew coaxed scents from inert earth: the loam of treeboxes, the faintly salty asphalt, the whole summer perfume of rotting fruit peels and *faisandés* coffee grounds wafting from the trash piled at the curbs. The stop-sign at the corner glowed. If he'd known exactly how long it would be before he was back on these streets, he might have wanted to itemize things even more minutely, but to act in some valedictory way would be to make real to himself what he was doing, and if he did that, he might never go through with it, so he didn't.

He'd been behind the wheel only once since Doonie taught him to drive, out past where the subway ended in Queens. It had gotten him kicked out of his third school (or was it the fourth?), but the engine turned over on the first try and purred like an animal when he gave it gas. The lights of Third Avenue were on a timed circuit; at twenty-seven miles per hour, you could coast all the way up to Harlem without stopping. There was hardly any bridge traffic this early on a Sunday, and soon he was flying toward points north, weaving only minimally.

It was when he stopped to pump gas near New Haven and spied through the tiny rear window the gymbag half-unzipped on the backseat that anguish again took hold. Where, exactly, did he propose to go? Vermont? Versailles? Valhalla? From a phone booth hard by the road, he gave the operator a name pulled from deep in memory. It was a big state, she said; she couldn't find the number unless she knew the town. "Can't you just look?" he said. "It's an emergency." Something in the voice—some crackle of pain—must have been persuasive, because a minute later came the familiar Continental inflections.

"William? How could I forget? If you are in the area, then you must stop by."

"In the area" was putting it charitably; it was another eight hours before, following punctilious directions, he pulled off a switchback mountain highway and into some woods. At the end of a mile-long drive, on a steep hillside, was either a large cabin or a small lodge.

The sound of the car had drawn Bruno Augenblick, William's former drawing teacher, to the door; he was barely visible there, in the shade of the deep porch and behind a layer of screen. "Leave your things," he called, over the dying engine. "First let us get you a drink." The city boy, still shaking inside, was not to see the city again for half a decade. By that time, he'd be twenty-two years old.

WILLIAM HAD FIRST ENCOUNTERED Herr Augenblick while attending the school before the school before this last one, whose generous ratio of carrot to stick, it was thought at the time, might benefit a young man of his . . . idiosyncrasies. Friday afternoons, the boys who'd behaved were bused thirty-five miles east to metro Boston, where for a few hours they were free to walk around Harvard Square and breathe the air into which, God willing, they might one day matriculate. William had made only a couple of friends at the new school, both of whom lacked his hard-won skill at dodging demerits, and so he often found himself wandering the Square alone, while his classmates hit the movies. He liked particularly to slip behind the walls of the college and pass himself off as a student there. He could smoke his cigarettes openly. He could cadge free lunch in the residence halls, so long as he carried a book to immerse himself in (and if he hadn't brought his own, one could always be nicked from the library). One such Friday, he saw a cluster of students with Very Serious Expressions sitting on one of the quadrangles, reproducing in their outsized drawing pads a bronze statue of some dour old Puritan. He was curious, suddenly, to see just how far his imposture might go. A sketchpad cost fifty cents in the campus bookstore, and pencils set him back another nickel. He found the students where he'd left them, arranged on a brick curb facing the statue. No one looked up when he sat down among them, or looked over at the pad where he'd begun to sketch. He'd actually lost track of time when a pair of hands clapped once. Standing over him was a man in seersucker, maybe forty, with owlish tortoiseshells and a skull shaved bare. "This brings to an end our session." The accent was German, or Swiss. The shirtsleeves were buttoned to the wrist despite the Indian-summer heat. "Please leave your work on the bench. I shall avail you of my judgment next week." The students began to shuffle away, but the man held William back. "And you are . . . ?"

"William Hamilton-Sweeney. I transferred in."

He indicated the pad under William's arm, which William handed over. The face stayed unreadable as it scanned his drawing, which had started out as a cartoon and ended up halfway serious. Finally, without warning, the instructor ripped the page off, balled it, and deposited it in the wire-mesh trashcan to his left. "Start again."

That fall, William would become the most diligent student in the Friday-afternoon drawing class, though he pretended not to look forward to it. The instructor never offered him so much as a word of praise, but always set aside time to review his work at the end of the session, and after the last class of the semester he pulled William aside. He had planned a little gathering that Saturday night, "a kind of salon. A few of the more advanced students will be there, and local artists, and some of the tenured faculty. You might find yourself edified." To reveal his inability to attend would be to admit that all along he'd only been a boarding-school refugee, and so that night he snuck back off campus and walked the two miles to the bus station on Route 117.

The house on Beacon Hill was like a museum, with paintings hung willy-nilly on every wall. The food was every bit the equal of Doonie's. Herr Augenblick—now just Bruno—lived awfully well for a visiting instructor, it seemed. William let himself have a glass or two too many of champagne and, mustering all available perspicuity, inserted himself into various conversations. It didn't bother him to hear people murmuring as he moved away that this was *the one Bruno had mentioned, the Hamilton-Sweeney;* he was pleased to find the other guests—all older, almost all male—hanging on his jokes like hollyhocks on a line. Occasionally, he caught Bruno watching from the far side of the room, but it was only at the end of the night, as guests were putting on coats, that the drawing instructor approached him. "Those two are walking back toward the college. Perhaps you would prefer an escort."

"No, thanks," William said, pretending to look through the pile on the bed for his own jacket. "I like to be alone."

"And you are not in fact headed that way, no?"

"Beg pardon?"

Bruno gestured toward the green-and-gold rep tie trailing from the pocket of the blazer William had uncovered. "The colors of one of our local lycées, I believe."

"You knew this whole time, didn't you?"

"Don't pretend to be surprised. You never appeared on my class list."

"Okay, but why didn't you say something?"

"William, an artist is someone who combines a desperate need to be understood with the fiercest love of privacy. That his secrets may be obvious to others doesn't mean he is ready to part with them." What the hell was that supposed to mean? William wondered. But of course, he already knew. He'd known what Bruno was since the very first day of that class, when the sunlight had gleamed off of the shaved dome of his head, but he had not realized that Bruno had seen quite so far into him. "But now the term of my visiting lectureship has expired. You will have to decide on your own what path to pursue."

"And what happens to all this?"

"This? This is Bernard's," he said, nodding toward the fresh-faced chair of the Art History department across the room, whom William had met earlier, and to whom, come to think of it, Bruno had been attached all evening. "I have a place in Vermont where I repair between appointments. It is country that reminds me of my home."

And maybe it was true that William needed to be understood, because how else to explain how crushed he was to learn that Bruno wouldn't be back in the spring? But it turned out to be a moot point. After insisting on finding his own way back to school, he got caught sneaking in at dawn—the squawking birds of suburban Mass. betrayed him to the headmaster as the louche, late-sleeping pigeons of New York never would have—and, this being a third offense, he was expelled before completing the term.

SITTING NOW ON THE FRONT PORCH of the mountain house, watching his highball glass sweat and mosquitoes moil around a smudge-pot, he wasn't at all sure he'd made the right decision. Bruno looked different than he remembered; heavier set, less coolly überhuman. Perhaps sensing his guest's distress, Bruno didn't push him, except to ask about his tux.

"What, this?" William had forgotten he was wearing it. "I ran out of laundry. Only clean shirt I had. Where is everybody? Where's Bernard?"

"Bernard is in Boston."

"Oh." The shadows of the mountains were like the ridged backs of dinosaurs. Just twenty-four hours earlier he'd been at that restaurant in Central Park, surrounded by oligarchs with champagne flutes. The glass he'd raised to toast his father had been narrower than the one now trembling in his hand, and he could honestly no longer remember what he'd said to cause so much trouble.

"You're welcome to stay as long as you like, William."

"You're not going to make me tell you what's going on?"

"I do not need to know 'what's going on.' Guests come and go all summer. There are three bedrooms currently vacant. You may take any one you like."

But William stayed on the porch long after Bruno went to bed, and not only to avoid the possibility of being asked to join him. By now, his father would be married to Felicia Gould, and it was something to which, after years of adjusting, and adjusting, he just could not seem to adjust. That Daddy had declined to call the wedding off at the last minute should have come as no surprise. Indeed, if William III was being honest, he may even have been looking for an excuse to break with William II, the way a rocket's liquid stage might long to escape the solid. What he'd been unprepared for was Regan, the only person besides their mom and Doonie he'd ever really trusted, taking sides with the enemy. If he was to survive it, she would have to be burned away, too. And sleep now was an impossibility. The wind shifted. The mosquitoes writhed, as if on fire. The ice was exploding in his Drambuie.

HE'D ASSUMED BRUNO was just being polite about guests coming and going from the mountain house, but it turned out he'd meant it. It started the very next weekend, with a carload of pale men from one of the urban centers—Boston or Philly, he hadn't really been listening—crunching up the gravel drive. They emerged in straw hats and sunglasses, shirts half-unbuttoned, drinks seemingly already in hand. Stood with arms over open car doors and stared past the figure of Bruno waiting on the porch steps and beheld the valley beyond, midge-swirled and smoky at midafternoon. They didn't actually say, *Well, would you look at that*; they didn't need to.

And it was strange: once, William would have preened for them, acted the ingénue, but he could barely bestir himself from his deck-chair to wave hello. Stranger still, none of them seemed to mind. He was almost certain Bruno would tell them something later, in private—*Give him his space*, maybe—but what accounted for the fact that now, at the moment of their arrival, the men tromping past him in the shade of the porch looked at him with the kindly expressions of people who had been there before? No one, William thought, could have possibly ever been *here* before. Amid all this bounty, yet unable to think about home without his espresso cup starting to quake on its saucer and the stilled cars of the driveway and the long ragged wildflowers starting to swim a little beyond the porch's cool enclosure, like things glimpsed through a fever. At some point, he stopped rocking. Shouts echoed uphill from a swimming hole, fractured by boulders and gulleys. Through the black trunks of pines he caught a flash of flesh as one of the guests mounted the diving rock; there was a pause between its disappearance and the answering splash.

After sundown, at a communal dinner, William sat quietly, doing his best not to ruin anyone's good time. The other faces around the table, flush with wine and exercise, were like the faces of prisoners who've had their convictions overturned. Anyway, it was pure narcissism to think his inner devastation could have ruined this for them. He was just some beautiful boy, a sylph, a runaway, furnished for the pleasure of their gaze. Only Bruno—powerful, patient, impenetrable Bruno—cared to notice that William had hardly eaten. And even this he took in in a single flicker of attention, saying nothing.

Soon William was making excuses to eat on the porch. He set the plate of veal or spätzle or spaghetti on the stumpy rattan table and didn't bother lighting the lantern. Laughter leaked through the screen door. Around it and around the ember of his cigarette, insects swarmed, along with the smells of smoke and room-temperature red sauce, like a rancid picnic. He tried to imagine the darkness of the porch merging with the darkness beyond, and himself with it, an animal crashing around in the underbrush. He tried to imagine Bruno coming to the door later, when the dishes had all been washed, looking for Narcissus and finding only the infinite dark. Even this—the old fantasy that there was still someone in the world who would chase after him, ask him what was wrong—now gave him no pleasure.

At times when the guests had returned to the other, urban halves of their lives, William was theoretically freer, yet he felt, if anything, worse. He could not read, could not sleep, could not tune his guitar. Only a few activities, pitched exactly halfway between stupidity and concentration, could still absorb him, and it was out of these that he had to cobble together a day. A baseball game on the radio; a crossword puzzle in the newspaper; a glossy magazine story about Elizabeth Taylor or Marilyn Monroe. He would send lists of magazine titles along when Bruno drove into town to do the shopping. William offered to pay (once he was legally adult, he had full control of the trust fund his mother had left him—plus the cash from selling off Regan's Karmann Ghia through the local classifieds), but Bruno always refused, in a way that should have been welcome but that just felt patronizing. He came back laden with bags of free food, but William still had no appetite of any kind. Even the beauty of the landscape was an abstraction, like the beauty of a man in an advertisement for a cologne you could not smell. Between him and it, dead time piled up: so many seconds, so many hours, so many years. So many tons of food and cubic hectares of liquid to dispose of before he died, which he would probably do right here, in the Northeast Kingdom, on a day much like this one, at the tail end of ten thousand days just like this one.

One mid-July evening, after unloading groceries from the car, Bruno sat down in his own rocking chair. More guests were due tomorrow, and William thought he was going to say something about this—thought, with a kind of weird thrill, that Bruno had finally lost patience—but Bruno just said, "I brought you something." He nodded to the paper bag on the end table between them. Inside was a sketchpad. Bruno rocked and sipped his cocktail, looking out to the far hills in which William had been feigning absorption.

"Bernard hasn't been up here," William said, finally. "Will we be seeing him?"

"Bernard and I had a parting of ways."

He had figured this out long ago, but the point was to wound. "Hence the generosity."

"No one is keeping you here, William. You are free to go at any time."

"You have a position you're looking to fill. Admit it. You want to fuck me." The tears in his voice surprised him, tiny hot beads of helplessness, but he couldn't stop himself: he didn't *want* to let go of whatever was killing him. Didn't *want* to change.

Bruno sighed. "As ever, William, your way of seeing the world is sui generis." He got up to go inside. "And no, I wouldn't take advantage of you even if I had no one else to amuse myself with. You are a child."

He wanted to get up, to stop Bruno from leaving. He wanted to feel the hard Teutonic fist connect with his cheekbone. Instead, when the last of Bruno's going-to-bed sounds had subsided, he stole into the bathroom and pulled the pullcord and looked in the mirror. It was true: he was a child, greasy and pale and thin and ungrateful, unloveable and unloved. Even the mother he carried inside him was less a memory than a dream. He turned the water on, loud, and wrestled the ancient razor-blade out of his shaving kit and considered for a long time the image it made against his fishbelly wrist. But once again, life proved too much for William Hamilton-Sweeney. What could one do but strop the blade sharper and attack the child's bad moustache lately sprouted on one's upper lip?

IT WOULD BE FIBBING to say the blackness lifted off William all at once after that; diseases don't work that way. But he did at least start sleeping through the night more often and shaving every morning. In the afternoon, he'd hike down toward the lake on paths of mulchy leaves, or what appeared to be paths, human-sized spaces among trees whose names he taught himself as he drew them. His sketchbook slowly filled with hemlock and mountain ash, and with the little animals that would come stepping into the clearings if he sat very still, or reveal themselves as already there, squirrels, sunbathing turtles, once a deer. He would eat the sandwich he'd brought and not even notice that it had begun to taste again, and then would resume his hike. The creek that descended from the swimming hole babbled nearby. The orderly old wilderness would split for a huge slab of rock down whose face tumbled a falls, and here, in the light, on the sunbleached rock, with the breaking water in his ears and the ozone of peaking vegetation in his nose, he was granted what he'd hoped for those first days after his arrival: he was no one, with no past and no future, nothing beyond the now and now and now of the white water surging into the clear.

And at night, at the long dining table, he started to open up a bit. If anything, the men's laughter was harder than it had been at Bruno's salon in Boston, and the part of him that lived for it was apparently still alive. Now, though, there was a second part, an artifact of his recent illness, as if his melancholy had, in a universe adjacent to this one, claimed his life. As if he were his own ghost, standing slightly behind himself, observing. He observed that he would at this point have gladly become Bruno's concubine, out of pure gratitude. And he observed that behind the indulgent smile, there was a part of Bruno, too, holding back, as someone once burned will keep his distance from flame. Bruno was careful now never to leave his bedroom door open, literally or figuratively. Sometimes late at night William heard through it the sound of something swishing through the air, a grunting in pleasure or pain.

BY MID-AUGUST, heat was draped over the mountains like a wet carpet. Back in New York, he could allow himself to think without too much bitterness, envelopes from Yale would be piling up on the mail table in the West Side penthouse where his father now lived: letters about course registration, about inoculations, about Selective Service, about extra-long sheets, letters with his four full names stamped into them by typewriter, William Stuart Althorp Hamilton-Sweeney III. It had seemed a problem, at first: how to go off in the fall to this machine for the perpetuation of class privilege without also returning to the family for whom its earth sciences building was named. Then, like a magician's knot, the problem resolved itself; he simply wouldn't go. And once that decision was made, his future seemed secure. It was part of the enchantment of this valley to make anything seem possible.

Here, for example, stood William, poised above the swimming hole on a rock the size of a Volkswagen. His bare feet gripped the warm uneven granite as though made for it. Below revolved the ivory bodies of men. On the banks where their clothes lay in neat piles, two of those bodies had been lumpy and dangly and ill-proportioned, but in the water they became gods. Through the undulant glass of the surface, parts swelled and subsided, now a thigh, now an arm, now a lunar white ass as the young one, the handsome one, turned to shout up good-naturedly, "What are you, some kind of sissy?"

He glanced over at where Bruno sat in his long sleeves and wide-brimmed hat, reading the *Frankfurter Allgemeine Zeitung*, which took eight days to reach him here by mail. Last night, when the house was quiet, William had stolen down the hall and slipped into bed with the man who was now goading him, and after he'd sworn him to discretion, they'd athletically fucked. Even when he'd gone with strangers into their cars, or into the lavatories of Grand Central, William had never allowed things to go beyond the oral, the manual, the intracrural, and he now understood why they called this other thing *consummation*. He wondered, though, if Bruno had heard. He wondered if he'd wanted Bruno to hear.

"Come on! Jump!"

William shook off the shadow of his betrayal, reached down and peeled off his chinos, stood there with the wind on his skin. He was beautiful here, protected, admired. There was no prurience to it. Just men enjoying one another without shame or secrecy. And it was Bruno who'd made Eden possible. Bruno who sat reading and did not look up at the lithe body, now eighteen, as it took two quick steps and cannonballed into frigid water.

Later, he stretched out on the sand next to Bruno, unsure anymore if his body was so worthy of attention. "You should go in."

"Ach."

Except for the single syllable, Bruno might have been sleeping behind his dark glasses. And of course Bruno never swam. His skin was defenseless before the sun, he'd said. Now his right sleeve had slipped up his arm, revealing a blue tattoo, a number. William felt certain Bruno would have covered it if he'd known it was showing. Embarrassed, he retrieved his own pants from where he'd thrown them. "I'm just saying, you might as well enjoy it if you're here," he said, pulling them on.

"William, there is something we should talk about."

"Is there? Talking is such a drag."

"You have had, I think, a good summer. You look healthy. It is a great country that makes this possible. But what will you do in the fall, when I leave for New York?"

"I didn't know you were leaving."

"It is nearly September, William. Every season has its end."

The architecture of the future was suddenly reorganizing itself, corridors becoming dead ends. Was this his punishment for last night? "I could stay here. Take care of your house."

"I found your sketchbook in the living room this morning. I took the liberty of looking through it. You have improved."

"That's private," William said.

But Bruno appeared not to hear. There was a college a hundred miles south, he said, well-known among artists. He had several acquaintances who taught there, men and women he knew from stints at other institutions. He thought William might easily be accepted. "It would be a way for you to stay in these mountains, if that's what you want."

William looked out at the pond, the men, the otterlike sport. "Bruno, I still don't understand. Why are you making this all so easy for me?"

Bruno now noticed the sleeve and began to roll it down over his arm. It wasn't clear this was connected to anything, though he did say, "Believe me, this is not for you."

THAT THE COLLEGE WOULD INDEED ACCEPT WILLIAM on such short notice was probably meaningless, given that it never rejected anyone. It was one of those progressive schools that were springing up across the land in the wake of the Eisenhower administration like mushrooms after a long rain. In practical terms, this meant William could do whatever he wanted, which suited him far better than the "rigorous character building" whose beneficiary he'd lately been. He took Drawing, and Philosophy, and Philosophy of Drawing; Social Realist Cinema, Latin, Psychoanalysis, Ecology of Mind . . . One course had him spend a whole semester painting a single still life; in another, he sat on the floor and glued together bits of cut-up magnetic tape. This is not to mention the on-campus performances: a concerto for transistor radio, another where the music was silent. Or afternoons spent lolling under the big pin oak at the heart of the Arcadian grounds, bullshitting with his new friends about the Bhagavad-Gita. Most of it was bullshit, on some level, but it was bullshit he felt passionate about, and in two areas—music and visual art—the passion was strong enough to burn through the veil that separated the two Williams, the real and the revenant.

By his second year, he was holding exhibitions in the little cottage he'd rented on a hill outside of town—what would later be called "happenings." William strummed along to tape loops on his Spanish guitar while faculty members circulated in a fug of marijuana and red wine, inspecting his friends' paintings. (William's own paintings never made it onto the wall; unlike music, they were a thing, not an event, and somehow they never felt *done*. How could you know when you were done when you worked as he was learning to, splashing paint onto canvases in big, bloody gouts? How could you know when you'd bled all the feelings out?)

Over his five years as an undergraduate, he would have love affairs with teachers and students, and even once, unsuccessfully, with a woman. Why not? Barriers of all kinds were coming down. In 1964, he ate LSD with several other students and lay in a Busby Berkeley formation in a peach orchard on a summer night watching the stars throb like ventricles on the inside of a vast, blue heart. "Wow," two people said at the same time, and everyone ended up kissing everyone else. That was the year of driving stoned and never crashing. Of wandering into classrooms in the dark and covering the chalkboards with automatic writing and leaving without turning on the lights. Of taking speed and hanging mirrors in the forest around the college, and painting themselves and the trees different colors.

Color more broadly was still an area of interest, as it had been when he'd watched footage of the Oklahoma City sit-ins on the TV back on Sutton Place, with Doonie in the doorway behind him. He had no TV now—he was a conscientious objector—but he followed the Birmingham Campaign and the March on Washington on the radio and wished there were any blacks here in Vermont to whom he might demonstrate his fealty. The best he could do was set up an Alice B. Toklas bake sale on campus and send the proceeds to SNCC—a down payment on the day when someone like him might actually have to work for a living, rather than rusticating here at art school, and someone like Doonie might retire to the Riviera, rather than to Hollis, Queens.

Still, some barriers remained meaningful. In a moment of champagne-induced weakness, he had called Felicia's on the phone at Christmastime of 1962, planning to apologize to Regan, belatedly, for having stolen her car. Instead, he got Stinking Lizaveta, Felicia's new *femme de chambre*. "Who is this?" she said, while he fought to silence his breathing. "Is anybody there?" And there was the barrier of the mountains, which kept the seethe of the cities at bay. When President Kennedy had been shot in Dallas, it had felt like fiction, like a report from an imaginary place. After graduating, he moved even farther out into the countryside—and farther into his painting. His grasp of current events was therefore even more tenuous, and it was not until a couple weeks afterward, stopping into the post office in town to pick up his mail, that he would find his "Order to Report for Armed Forces Physical Examination," covered in stamps marked **FORWARD**.

God only knows how the mailman had found him. He was supposed to have reported to his local draft board office two weeks ago—and that office was still, according to this document, the one on Church Street in Lower Manhattan. There was probably some simple way, he thought later, to change his address and thus avoid the three-hundred-mile haul back to New York in the ancient truck he was driving by then. But the sudden prospect of seeing it again, the city, his city, set his heart struggling like an animal in a too-small cage. The next morning, with his canvases and guitar and the boxes of art books he'd accumulated blocking the passenger's side mirror, he was rattling back down the switchback highways, toward the Hudson River Valley and the vertiginous homeland beyond.

THE SERGEANT WHO INTERVIEWED HIM didn't believe him about the homosexuality. "Of course," he said. "Right. Just like every other wiseacre who walks through here."

"No, but I mean I'm *practicing*." What shame there had ever been his five-year exile had burned right out of him. And the thought of being bombed or shot at tended to focus the mind. Beyond the little glass room, fanblades whirred, long strips of flypaper wriggling eel-like, ends affixed to the fans' steel cages. There were rows of metal desks with typewriters, and every time a form was pulled from a roller, it got tucked under a paperweight to keep it from blowing away. The interviewer, an apple-cheeked Southerner who still had a narrow strip of white at the back of his neck where his hair had been shaved, looked reasonably cool, but despite the tremor of the glass from all these pounding typewriters, not the faintest zephyr made it to where William sat, uncomfortably close to the desk.

"With a last name like yours, pal, you'd think there'd be easier ways to get a deferment."

William was starting to get genuinely nervous. He'd long ago concluded that the loving God of his mother was a cartoon character, and he'd never much believed in even the nail-paring old man who stood back and let the Hamilton-Sweeney bullion pile up in the vaults, but at moments of high anxiety, he was not above imagining a pedantic and capricious demiurge out to punish him for his sins. "I smoke pot, too, if that counts against me."

"If we let it, Mr. Hamilton-Sweeney, we'd lose half our conscripts."

"Sergeant, what do I have to do to prove that I'm a fag?" What, indeed, was he doing? He was reaching forward, touching the man's hand. "If necessary, we could go somewhere more private . . ." The din of typewriter keys seemed to die down. In a lower voice, he added, "Not that I'm attracted to you personally, you understand, but in the name of science—"

Then a bright pain buzzed in his ear, where the sergeant had struck him. "There are rules here, son," he said, a minute later.

"Do they involve abusing your examinees?"

"You try to make a scene out of this, and I will have you in jail."

"I'm not leaving without my paper," William had the presence of mind to say, from his doubled-over position. The rubber stamp came down like a hoof. *Unfit to Serve.* The guy didn't even look at him.

On his way out, he passed another officer, who had presumably come to see what the commotion was about. William brandished the paper, gave his ear a final rub, and paraded out into the waiting room where rows of ungroomed young men in bluejeans sat or stood, looking uniformly uneasy. If he expected them to applaud, he was mistaken; they stared as if he were an ostrich escaped from the pullet factory, and themselves condemned to become dinner. No matter; he was free. He hustled down the stairwell and burst through the double doors and into the brightness of the fatherland at noon.

It was 1966—the year of Black Power and Jerry's Kids and "Eight Miles High." Behind the bright blue flag of the sky, a man was roaming outside a space capsule, tethered only by a rubber umbilicus. Meantime, down below, the kempt façade of the world he'd left behind was crumbling. Streamers of pot rode the lunchtime air; swirls of graffiti had bloomed on the postboxes and on the cornices of municipal buildings; near where William had parked, two white kids, a boy and a girl, sat on a flattened box on the sidewalk asking stockbrokers for change, as if this were no more morally significant than asking the time of day. And it all seemed to William to betoken not decline but progress—to presage the breaking through of some more ecstatic and penetrating way of life. For how could his own father, the very incarnation of bourgeois order, have appeared on the streets where the son now stood? No, William thought, digging what little change he had out of his pocket to give to the coyote-faced girl: New York now belonged to the future. And it was going to protect him this time, he was sure of it. Never again would they let each other down.

18

THE 1973 NATIONAL MAGAZINE AWARDS were held in a flyblown banquet room way up near the Columbia School of Journalism—an area not known for its elegance. Then again, neither were journalists. And so, if you'd scanned the crowd before the lights dropped, your eye might have come to rest on a table not far from the stage, and a tall man whose nobility set him obscurely apart. It wasn't in his clothes; the way he wore his rented tuxedo, it might as well have been a sportcoat and jeans. Nor was it in his bearing, exactly (a few crumbs from dinner still clung to his beard). Rather, it was something inside, something his physical surroundings couldn't quite touch. This was the magazine reporter, Richard Groskoph. And as the plates were cleared and the PA system crackled on, he wasn't even here. He was five minutes into the future, where his life's work had just been vindicated.

He was a perennial nominee, it's true, in the category of "Reporting Excellence," but this year, he'd finally made finalist. The article in question had been pegged to the cancellation of the lunar landing program. Somehow, though (as was often the case with Richard's work), it had metastasized into something else altogether. It had taken him the better part of two years to report and write, and when he looked around at his colleagues at nearby tables, the cream of ink-stained New York, he knew the competition was his to lose. He was close enough to the podium to see filaments of lint on the emcee's black lapels. To picture the guy, a second-tier local Jerry Lewis, rehearsing his jokes in a kitchen in Rego Park, in boxer shorts and garter socks while his wife ironed his pants. Kids were wrestling on the floor of the next room and the teakettle was shrieking and there was too much going on for anyone to notice the shabby state of the jacket, and suddenly Richard's colleagues at the table were applauding. Had he won? Had he really won?

He had not. An editor from *The Atlantic Monthly* was making his way forward to accept the award—slower than necessary, rubbing it in. Well, the prize had been meaningless all along, Richard reminded himself. Still, there were certain kinds of meaninglessness you wanted to experience from the inside, feeling flashbulbs caress your skin as you hoisted the little coppery statuette over your head.

It even had a name, he learned afterward; the "Ellie," in tribute to the more glamorous Emmys. The chief fact-checker at the magazine was a sometime member of Richard's Wednesday night poker circle, and he must have said something to the other guys, because that week they started in before Richard could get his coat off. "Don't look so glum," said Benny Blum, from City Hall. "Ellie comes to those who wait."

"Though maybe this is a case of an Ellie in the hand . . . ," someone said.

"It's not the writer the Ellie goes to, anyway. It's the editor," said the checker.

"That true, Rick? It was never your Ellie to lose?"

"Hey—don't call him Rick," another voice interjected. This was the bridge-and-tunnel baritone Richard had been bracing for: "Dr." Zig Zigler.

He and Zig had been best friends as cubs in the city room of the *World-Telegram*, where the bulk of the table had met. Like many a drunk, Zig was a lot of fun, right up to the point when he wasn't. Only Richard knew the details of the crack-up. Instead of resigning to protest "the whole canard of journalistic objectivity," as he liked to claim, Zig had been fired for fabricating stories, and some combination of that secret and a subsequent fistfight in which he'd broken Richard's nose had caused the rift between them. Zigler had emerged from a long drying-out period less fanciful and more caustic. More recently, he'd earned a measure of renown hosting an early-a.m. talk show on local radio. Each weekday, he took the calls of a dozen or more devoted listeners, along with headlines from the morning paper, as pretexts for a running state-of-the-city lament. Still, he envied Richard. And now, with everyone turned toward him, he dropped the other shoe. "A little respect, please. That's National Magazine Award Finalist Richard Groskoph you're talking to."

Improbably, the name stuck. Your deal, National Magazine Award Finalist Richard Groskoph. National Magazine Award Finalist Richard Groskoph raises . . . calls . . . folds. Richard did his best to smile and nod, as if to say, yes, go ahead, have your fun. Only Larry Pulaski seemed to notice anything was wrong. Back when Richard first recruited him for the game, some fifteen years ago, the newspapermen had treated the diminutive cop almost as a mascot. He'd long since made detective, though, and the Assisian gentility of his manner, the air of martyrdom his polio conferred, belied a ferocious ability to read tells. "You okay?" he asked at the end of the night as, twenty bucks poorer (Richard) and richer (Pulaski), they put on their jackets to go home. "Right as rain," Richard said, and declined the ride Pulaski offered. He would walk instead, albeit only as far as the nearest bar.

ANYWAY, HE WASN'T IN THIS FOR THE GLORY, was he? When he'd been twenty-three, just back from Korea and stuck on the city room's rewrite desk, there had been no Ellies, no journalism school, and no such thing as a twelve-thousand-word feature. Someone called in sick and someone else shoved a pencil in your hand and aimed you in the direction of a burning building somewhere and told you not to come back without a quote from the fire marshal, kid, and that was it: you were a reporter. Well, that and a steady drip of spirituous ethers. Even now, at seven a.m., in this shift bar near Penn Station, newspapermen hunched over their drinks like some lower order of monks. You knew them by the volume of their talk; they were half-deaf from a night of jangling phones and Linotype rattle and barking sub-sub-editors. It was part of the dignity of the thing, the long suffering, the shitheel pride.

And in truth, this promise of collective identity was what had drawn Richard to the trade in the first place, for the quality that set him apart was not a quality at all, but its absence. He'd known since

puberty that he had what a shrink might call "a weak sense of self."
(Unless, that is, his strong sense of not having a self itself constituted a self.) The other kids at school seemed to carry some inner
map of where they were going, who they were becoming, that stabilized them through all the outward transformations, but Richard,
the world's first 6'3" thirteen-year-old, felt as if he'd been cast into
the wilderness without so much as a stick of gum. Or as if there were
more than one of him: a whole multitude, good and bad. He never
knew when he woke in the morning which Richard he was going to
be. And rather than soften with time, the dissonance grew harder to
tolerate. On graduation night, he plowed his father's car into a tree,
half on purpose. It was decided in the clearer light of morning that
maybe the best thing for him would be the army, and within the
week his father was driving him in a new car down to the recruiter's
office.

The expectation—even on Richard's part—was that military discipline might mold him into something definite, but in fact the void
within proved unmoldable. His buzz cut and ill-fitting uniform only
made it clearer that he was no G.I., any more than he was anything
else. Overseas, he spent any free time he got reading, or hunkered
over his portable turntable, listening to records a cousin sent from
back home. The other fellows tended to interpret this as arrogance,
but in fact what Richard was mostly doing, with his Lester Young and
his serviceman's paperbacks, was groping for a different way out. One
night, on the way back to the barracks from KP, he noticed a group of
foreign correspondents huddled at their end of the mess tent, playing
cards under a bug-swirled light. "Fuck me," one of them said, grinning. Richard had seen them before, of course, but he'd never really
seen them, their shambolic rumple and manifest travail (he was working his way through Faulkner at the time). And he'd thought, out of
nowhere, *That's* an army I could be part of.

It was the kind of intuitive leap that would serve a reporter well.
As would, it turned out, a lack of fixed personality. Richard's first
beat back home was the Village, and when there was no news to
report—no strike on the docks, no murders, no robberies to go pes-
tering Larry Pulaski about—he spent hours in the jazz clubs, soaking
up the between-sets patter of the musicians who came down from
Harlem to play. He could hear his accentless voice echo their argot as
he sat with them, urging them on. The stories they told would form

the early installments of the column that began to run under his byline in the Metro section. Notes from All Over, he called it, with the self-deprecating self-aggrandizement that was the column's sense of humor. "All Over" in this case meant all five boroughs. He profiled freak show performers on Coney Island; a man who played cello on a Long Island City subway platform; a woman in Mount Morris Park who fed both pigeons and bums. It was news only in the sense that it appeared in a newspaper, but there was nothing New York liked reading about more than itself. For a few months in the early '6os, the name of the column, in foot-high cursive like the name on a bakery box, decorated the sides of the newspaper vans, *Now with 'Notes from All Over,' Tuesdays and Fridays*. It should have been a triumph: everyone else out there knew who Richard was, even if he didn't. But he wanted more.

Earlier that year, Truman Capote had come out with his "nonfiction novel." Richard had heard rumors of its greatness, of course, when the thing had been serialized in *The New Yorker* at 100,000 words—an indulgence previously granted only to the bombing of Hiroshima, and at a quarter a word, enough to dine out on for at least a year (though maybe a little less, if you were Capote). Now, from the window of the bookshop on the corner, pyramids and campaniles of *In Cold Blood* taunted him, along with a propped-up photograph, like a French postcard, of the author recumbent on a dark divan. It was out of date; the last time Richard had seen Capote at a party, he'd been older and fatter, though still vain as hell and oddly impish. Yet he couldn't help pausing to look at it, drawing so close that his own face hovered in front of Capote's in the polished glass. Finally, after checking to see that no one who knew him was around, he went in and bought the damn book. It was ten in the morning. He finished reading it at ten at night. And, it pained him to admit, it *was* great. Truman had demons of his own—anyone who'd emptied a glass with him could tell you that—but no one could take away what he'd pulled off here: to disappear this completely into other people's lives. From here until eternity, he would be able to look in the mirror and see the author of *In Cold Blood*. And so, when the editor of one of the glossy magazines approached Richard with the offer of higher word counts, longer deadlines, more various subjects, Richard threw himself on it as if it were a life-preserver.

The newspapermen in their egalitarian scrum had bitched about the self-indulgence of the emerging "New Journalism." (Q: "What do you call someone who neither contributes nor edits?" A: "A contributing editor!") But now, on a magazine salary, Richard could spend an entire morning taking a single sentence apart and putting it back together again—*Friday nights the West Side gathers . . . It is a Friday night and the West Side is gathering itself*—with no outside voices baying across the room for copy. What he wanted above all to get right was the web of relationships a dozen column inches had never been enough to contain. Family, work, romance, church, municipality, history, happenstance . . . He wanted to follow the soul far enough out along these lines of relationship to discover that there was no fixed point where one person ended and another began. He wanted his articles to be, not infinite exactly, but big enough to suggest infinitude.

Some of the universes he explored, as the '60s gave way to the '70s: Negro league baseball, folk rock, TV evangelism, stand-up comedy, stock-car racing. It was this latter, in a roundabout way, that had led to that awards banquet. He'd been lurking on the edges of a big post-race party in Daytona, Florida, when a pit mechanic had invited him to a wee-hours bonfire on the beach. Some hippies had gathered there to watch the launch of Apollo 15. The odd part was, they were stone cold sober. Talking to folks, he discovered a kind of leaderless cult, devoted to the eschatology of rockets. The launch was their sacrament. They believed, they told him with disarming frankness, that the earth was due for a thousand-year flood ("Aquarius, man . . . get it?") and that in time the rockets would carry them to the safety of a new home in outer space. He knew at once he was in possession of a story.

To report it, he went native. Grew his hair out, grew a beard, shacked up with a lovely twenty-four-year-old airline stewardess who wore what she insisted was a chunk of moon-rock on a leather thong around her neck. She was otherwise wonderful: articulate, passionate, well- if eccentrically read, and he often thought later he should have stayed with her. Who cared if she believed life on earth was coming to an end? Who was to say it wasn't? On December 7th of 1972 (which he didn't tell her was to be his last night before leaving), he found himself back on the same beach. Surrounded by what he'd come to think of as his people, acid casualties and alligator wrestlers and Jesus freaks, he watched the last of the Saturn V rockets lift off like a great Roman candle. And certainly there was a sense of *something* ending—being dragged up behind that rocket, never to come down again. They all felt it, there on the beach. Getting down what it was in words, it occurred to him, was what he'd been trying to do now for nearly a decade.

Or so he would tell the editor at Lippincott who contacted him after the awards banquet. There was a clause in his magazine contract that allowed him to republish his pieces in book form, and ever since *In Cold Blood* he'd oscillated between certainty that what he wrote wasn't fit for bathroom reading and imagining how it would look in hardcover. "I'm almost seeing it," the editor said. "That whole 'Death of the American Dream' trip, Hunter's done very well with that. But looking at the manuscript, I think what we need here is one more piece, a capstone, something to kind of distill and connect the big theme."

He was right. Whatever change Richard had sensed in the *zeitgeist* remained tantalizingly inchoate. Something about loss, something about innocence, something about desire, and America, the individual and the altogether. . . . It was a half-complete metaphor, a tenor in search of a vehicle.

"You could sell it to the magazine, too, of course," the book editor said. "Get paid twice, and promote the book in the bargain. You think you've got it in you?"

He knew better than to take an advance before a book was finished—and had his defeat at the hands of *The Atlantic Monthly* not reawakened his hunger to be somebody specific, he might have been strong enough not to. But here was something, finally, to launch him into the firmament inhabited by Talese, Mailer, Sheehy . . . and, of course, Capote. He would be Richard Groskoph, author of *The Loneliness of the One-Hit Wonder*, or whatever they decided to call it. "I'm sure I'll come up with something," he told the editor, and two weeks later, they cut him a check.

IS IT ALREADY OBVIOUS the money was cursed? He sat down at his desk at half past eight the next morning and found he had no idea what to write about. He tried itemizing the contents of his desk. It sometimes helped him to do this, as though together they might reflect a way forward:

a) one tartan-patterned insulated thermos bottle;

b) one Halloween mask, never worn;

c) one ancient photograph of a Lower East Side knife grinder;

d) one dried-out starfish;

e) one paperback edition of <u>Webster's New Collegiate Dictionary</u>;

f) one fedora-style hat;

g) one bit of perforated rock, strung on a necklace;

h) LP sleeves: <u>Live at the Apollo</u>, <u>Forever Changes</u>;

i) one Underwood typewriter;

j) one battery-operated police scanner;

k) assorted unopened utility bills and sheets of A4 paper;

l) highball glass with orange peel, pencil shavings, old toothbrush;

m) stack of <u>The New York Times</u>, roughly nine inches in height;

n) stack of the <u>New York Post</u>, roughly 14 inches in height;

o) one bottle rocket, unignited;

p) one 40-watt light bulb missing its filament;

q) <u>The Prefaces of Henry James</u>;

r) stack of the <u>New York Daily News</u>, roughly 12 inches in height.

But by ten he was out of things to list. Be patient, he told himself. Something will turn up. He'd acquired at a police auction a few years back a Wurlitzer jukebox from the seized possessions of a mobbed-up social club. A hubcap full of quarters and slugs rested atop it, and he sat for the next several hours with his head back, listening to his 45s, trying not to think of the word "blocked."

RICHARD HAD ALWAYS, RITUALLY, REWARDED HIMSELF for an honest morning's work with a drink or two at lunch, but that summer it got difficult to see his coffee down to the dregs before reaching for the bottle. At three—another ritual—he would allow himself to go buy the daily papers, but now, just to get away from the silence of his typewriter and his phone, he went as early as noon, and to news-stands farther and farther afield. On a Thursday afternoon, Union Square was Rabelaisian: people were strung out in broad daylight. On a bench under a tree, a long-haired boy and a flat-chested girl or vice versa stuck their tongues into each other's mouths, their eyes closed as if in sleep. Farther down the square a student with a mega-phone demanded justice for the Cambodians. They were everywhere he looked, suddenly, these kids who no longer believed in prog-ress. And why should they? Progress was Watergate and Mutually Assured Destruction. Progress had looked on as tracts of jungle and thatched huts disappeared beneath a carpet of flame. Progress had raped villagers at My Lai and bayoneted babies. How to approach all this, though? How to get your arms around the craziness left behind, when the orderly Rand McNally map of the world you've been rely-ing on has rolled up to the ceiling?

There had been a time when he might have looked to music for consolation—indeed, he had vague ideas of stumbling across some band whose story might perfectly emprism the passing of the age—but even music now betrayed him. From the little jazz and folk clubs where he'd ridden out his twenties and thirties and from church basements and union halls issued new sounds that, rather than har-monizing what was discordant, made more discord. One afternoon, he was wobbling down one of those sidestreets whose denizens he'd once written about so well, when he heard a sound like white noise from over on Broadway. In the plantered median, a woman in an unseasonable overcoat slumped on a bench, next to a cart swollen in every direction with possessions. A radio unit on top seemed to be operating under its own power, and despite himself he stopped to listen. Threaded through the crunching electric guitar chords and roiling drums was a Farfisa organ, like the calliope of the minor-league ballpark of his Oklahoma youth. Then a voice that sounded English began barking words he couldn't quite make out. The side-walk yawed under Richard like the low-gravity surface of the moon.

He thought about a phone call he'd received that very morning. Instead of one of his army of sources (*Have I got a story for you*) it had been that stewardess he'd shacked up with, calling long-distance from Florida. She was eight months pregnant, she said. She didn't expect anything from him, not after the way he'd up and left her, but now that it was too late to change her mind, she felt it was her duty to let him know she was going to have the baby. Richard stared down the street to where cars were crawling along on the West Side Highway, and to the sun on the Hudson beyond. To anyone passing by just then, he would have looked no saner than the madwoman in the median, awaiting the day of judgment. And if the great God Jehovah, tall as the Pan Am Building, should come driving his chariot down the avenue just now, what would His judgment of Richard Groskoph be? Coward. Failure. Drunk. If he kept up like this, he'd be lying in Bellevue before the summer was out.

When he got home, he called his travel agent. He shoveled into a trashbag all the food in his refrigerator and wiped down the inside with lemon juice and water—the first time he'd done so since leasing the apartment. He unplugged the jukebox. He set his houseplants out on the curb, for neighbors to take, and purged the bathroom of anything with an expiration date. He packed his suitcase with all that would fit and then sat by the window and watched the sky go pink and had a glass or three of bourbon, for old times' sake. The next morning it was already falling away under the silver wing of a plane rising out of Idlewild, or JFK it now was, the thousand square miles of ravaged earth, highways, power plants, apartment blocks, and the tiny, scuttling selves he'd been this close to becoming one of. Picture a burrowing insect running from the light. Or picture a Ulysses trying to outsteer fate. Picture thumb and forefinger poised millimeters apart.

19

A S A LITTLE KID, he'd loved to run his fingers over the spines of the LPs, the heavy cardboard sleeves. He'd loved, too, how little their motley colors (cream, orange, blue) revealed about the music inside. His dad would slap an undistinguished black dinner plate on the rubber mat of the spinner, and it might turn out to be organs, violins, or Gene Krupa banging his drums like pots and pans. Then Dad would sink back into his recliner with his newspaper as though he didn't notice Charlie playing on the floor at the far end of the room. Sometimes, though, the corner of the paper would come down and behind it would appear one quadrant of the face Charlie loved to look at, thin and mild and clean-shaven, and he'd be able to tell from the one visible eye, magnified by reading glasses, that his dad was grinning. Charlie would grin shyly back and pretend to conduct with a Lincoln Log.

At that age, he could often be found on the floor of whatever room his parents were in. It was as if the house was divided into two kingdoms: one that started at knee height, the other belonging to Charlie. Under the kitchen table, the hanging edges of the tablecloth formed a jungle canopy. Wooden legs were the stout trunks of trees. Die-cut army men with little fins of extra metal at the neck where the machine had stamped them out scrambled up these trunks to perform recon missions on a Friday night in winter. The radio on the counter wasn't supposed to be on—Charlie knew this because, whenever his grandfather visited, there was no music from sundown Friday to sundown Saturday. Now, though, it played a big band song from before he was born, a slow, nostalgic, glimmering chandelier of a thing, around which a clarinet swooped and dove like a bird had got into the room. When he edged forward out of the jungle, steam made a gray half-curtain on the bottom of the kitchen window. His mom, bending to the dishwater, didn't notice. There was a small bunching of pantyhose near her ankle where you could actually see the color of the hose as distinct from the skin. The dishes made their own music beneath her moving hands, a mellow clanking, like the sounds Charlie heard when he held his breath and became a submarine in the tub. Then Dad was pulling Mom from the dishes and bringing her swaying out into the open space. Their feet, hers in slippers, his in his work shoes, found a rhythm, and Charlie's disappearance was complete. It answered to some deep, sweet need he had to be a part of them—a sense of being, himself, imperfectly stamped out—which was maybe connected to still other music, back beyond the caul of forgetting that covered whatever faces had sung the newborn Charlie to sleep at the Home for Unwed Mothers out on the East End.

Of course, Charlie couldn't stay this close to his mom and dad forever. At six, he started trundling off to the red brick box of Charles Lindbergh Elementary. The other kids sometimes teased Charlie for being a redheaded Jew, but his knack for marginality helped him here, too. And anyway, the broader community from which the school drew was more than half ethnic: Slavs, Italians, and even a few Greeks. The men held union jobs or clung to the lower rungs of the professions; the women worked part-time or stayed home. They owned one car per family, American-made, drank moderately if at all, and dedicated weekends to lawn care, to hobbies pursued in basements, or to watching golf in the afternoon with the living room lights off, ostensibly to reduce the glare off the tube but really so that no one noticed if they fell asleep. They were the very middle of the middle class. And this was why they'd moved out from the crumbling boroughs—not for the freedom to do whatever they wanted behind closed doors (though there must have been some of that, too), but to lose themselves in the great mass of America. Normalcy was Long Island's chief industrial product. Over time, its specs had been drummed into Charlie. As long as your hair was long, but not too long, and your collar was wide, but not too wide, and your slacks were neither too expensive nor too cheap, and you watched the requisite eight hours of prime time a week and kept up with the adventures of Captain America and Iron Man and didn't bring in anything too weird for lunch, you were pretty much okay.

Charlie's best friend in those days, Mickey Sullivan, was a redhead, too. In theory, this should have imposed a certain distance between them; one carrot-top per homeroom was necessary to establish balance, but two together was too many. Mickey was big for his age, though, and had older brothers, and was a hitter, so the other kids let their friendship stand. And because Ramona Weisbarger seemed to have mistaken for loneliness Charlie's failure to obtrude, she would give him permission to ride his bike over to Mickey's after school.

Mickey had a collection of 45 r.p.m. records purchased with his and other people's milk money, and always had three or four of the newest ones with him at school to show Charlie. At home, he had a Fancy Trax portable record player with a built-in speaker, and they could kill hours doing goofy dances in front of the mirror or playing tennis-racket guitars. (What, did he think they were made out of money? is what Charlie's mom said when he asked if he, too, could have a Fancy Trax record player.) For fast numbers, Mickey always insisted on playing the solos, relegating Charlie to rhythm. For slow numbers, they would turn their backs on each other and wrap their arms around themselves and make mwah-mwah smooching noises until they couldn't pucker anymore from cracking themselves up. And so the high-charting hits of the Dave Clark Five and Herman's Hermits and Tommy James and the Shondells were also among the songs Charlie would associate with his Long Island childhood. By junior year of high school, they were stacked in a jukebox in his chest, on heavy rotation.

Somewhere in there, too, was the sound of a rehearsing cantor seeping through the nicotine-stained ceiling of *MEETING ROOM B* in the basement of the Flower Hill synagogue, where the same fifteen kids were dragged together for Hebrew school every Sunday. Rabbi Lidner was a smoker, and seemed always to have a cigarette burning in one hand and another going in an ashtray tipped into the chalk-holder of the blackboard behind him. The ash on this untouched cigarette would grow to the length of a pencil eraser. Of a golf pencil. Charlie kept waiting for the mythical moment when it would reach the filter, creating an entire ghost cigarette, but like the moment when the playground swing swung all the way over the bar, it never came. Rabbi Lidner would invariably decide to supplement his monologue with Scripture, which was, after all, what qualified him as a rabbi, and the fumbling of his sausage-shaped fingers on the chalk-holder or the scratch of the chalk on the slate would jostle the ashtray and crumble that magnificent ash. Charlie, due to his asthma, watched from the far pole of the circle of folding chairs, by a window he cracked even in winter. At that distance, the English phrases on the board were no more intelligible than the Hebrew ones he'd forgotten to practice. He might as well have looked for guidance to the tannish blots above.

The last minutes of each class were set aside for open-ended scenarios in which loyalty did battle with honesty, or honesty with wisdom, or wisdom with courage, and the rabbi expected Charlie and his peers, who could hardly keep their fingers out of their noses, to say what a Jew was to do. "Suppose you're rummaging in your father's study—," he might begin.

"I'm not allowed in there," Sheldon Goldbarth would blurt. Charlie had it on good authority that Sheldon Goldbarth's mother let him drink coffee in the morning, but Rabbi Lidner was used to these outbursts.

"So you've already broken a commandment, good noticing, Sheldon. But while you're rummaging, let's say you discover your father has broken one, too. He has—"

"Coveted his neighbor's wife!" said Sheldon Goldbarth.

"Coveted his neighbor's ass," Tall Paul Stein muttered, to giggles.

Commanding obedience was not Lidner's forte, nor that of Reform Judaism more generally. "Your father has . . . stolen something from his job. What are you going to do?"

The implication, as Charlie read it, was that Jews were held to extraordinary standards: courage *and* wisdom *and* honesty *and* loyalty, all at the same time. It was this assumption of extraordinariness, paradoxically, that allowed Shel and Paul to cut up in class. Ultimately, the bloodline marked them for better things. It was like the origin story in a superhero comic—the drop of radioactive goo, the faint golden glow descending through the mother. There was only one problem: by this account, Charlie had no superpowers. Sure, he'd seen strawberry-blond Hasidim on the train with their forelocks and patchy beards, and Rabbi Lidner had pointed to stories of adoption in the Torah; Moses was adopted, he said. Yes, Charlie thought, but by Gentiles. And all the really great feats were performed by Hebrews from whom Charlie couldn't claim biological descent, besandaled heroes and warrior kings. It was said that, in a pinch, you should seek out the help of a Jewish stranger before that of your best Gentile friend. And who was to say that Charlie's real parents, whoever they were, were the friendly kind of goy? Who was to say that his *real* grandfather hadn't, like the witch in Hansel and Gretel, tended a German oven?

ONE SUNDAY IN MIDDLE SCHOOL when Charlie was riding his bike back from the synagogue, he happened to pass the church at the bottom of the hill his house was on. The bell had just rung, sailing little boats of sound out over the green world, with families pouring out onto the lawn and an almost military double line there of kids Charlie's age, boys in slacks on the right, girls in kneeskirts on the left. Perhaps it was how still they were that drew his gaze, for when had Charlie ever known a mixed-sex group to stand so still? A person in penguiny robes crouched before them. At her signal, they turned and headed back into the now-exhausted church. Mickey Sullivan's red head, taller than the others, turned right past the spot where Charlie was standing, foot propped on a pedal, but if he saw, he made no sign.

Charlie was nervous asking about it the next day—nervous Mickey might give him an Indian burn or a titty-twister, as he tended to do when some awkwardness arose between them. To his surprise, the question seemed to make Mickey five years older instead. Sophisticated. Blasé. Looking past Charlie to where the lunchtables were already filling up, he reached into his pocket. Inside the fist he brought out nestled a gold chain. A small cross rested across either the love or health line of Mickey's palm. When Charlie reached for it, the palm snapped shut. "I don't get to wear it until after I make my first communion."

"What's a communion?"

"What you saw us practicing for, dummy. You go and kneel on this little like pillow and they give you this wafer that's the body of Jesus and then you drink his blood."

"You guys drink blood?" Grandpa had warned him about this stuff, but then, Grandpa was full of weird superstitions.

"Not real blood, you homo."

"Oh," Charlie said, pretending to understand.

"And there's a party, and you get presents"—the goys got presents for everything—"and then you're basically a grown-up."

"So like a bar mitzvah."

"I guess." Mickey showed Charlie the right way to put one hand over the other, waiting for the wafer, but punched Charlie in the shoulder when he did it to the lunch lady, asking for creamed corn. This was sacrilicious, he said. It was like Mickey had lost all sense of humor—like he'd become a grown-up already.

Knowing what his mother would say, Charlie prepared a list of reasons why he should be allowed to go to Mickey's first communion. The church was right there down the street, and how could he expect people to come to his bar mitzvah a year from now if he didn't go to their things? *Absolutely not*, she said. But he went anyway; it would be easy enough to fib about Rabbi Lidner keeping them late at Hebrew school. It was like one of his little moral antinomies. Honor thy mother and father, the commandment said, but how was it possible, really, to dishonor what was simply an extension of yourself? Weren't his folks still facets of that unity he'd felt under the kitchen table? Sure, it could grow more or less distinct in the shuffle of daily life, like a lake glimpsed through trees from a moving car, but the lake was always there, wasn't it? The Benny Goodman Orchestra was always playing somewhere.

Though if he had stopped to think about it—if he had stopped pedaling for a minute—he might have noticed the disorienting blur the postage stamp yards and telephone poles and other solidities of his childhood had lately become. His parents had been more distracted than usual, more excitable, more anxious. His mom had grown lax about making sure he didn't wear the same shirt or take the same lunch two days in a row. And Grandpa was about to arrive from Montreal that morning for a visit, hastily announced and of unspecified length. But Charlie was still a child then. He saw what it pleased him to see.

The new communicants sat on the church's frontmost bench. Even from way back, he could see Mickey's big red head. You weren't supposed to clap or anything. The music from the organ was thinner and more plastic-y than he would have expected. It sounded like the organ at an Islanders game. The weirdest thing, though, was the way the people in front of him kept talking to Jesus, as if he were not dead but floating right over their heads. As indeed he was, a glazed, roughly life-sized plaster figure, glossy as a waxed apple, bolted to the baby-blue wall. *Hear us, Lord Jesus.* It was as if the church was a house Jesus was haunting. He tried to imagine Moses or Abraham haunting the temple, but couldn't. The patriarchs who haunted Jews were those, like Grandpa, who were still alive.

Afterward, at the Sullivans', there was a big white store-bought cake decorated with a cross. He wondered if this, too, stood for something—if he was plunging his fork into the spongy brain of Christ, and if so, if he should eat it, or if the Jewish or the Christian God would consign Charlie Weisbarger, who at this particular moment was faithful to neither, to the flames of hell. Yet he couldn't help himself. The cake was drier than it looked, but the spun-sugar flowers, hardened to a crust, gave him a pleasantly headachey feeling.

"So what did you learn today?" Grandpa asked when he got home. He was a tall man, thick in the middle, with a head as big as a cigar-store Indian's, and impossibly lush nose-hair. Two deep creases framed his chin, making it look hinged. His suitcase sat beside him on the living room sofa. Dad, as if to give his father room, had perched on the decorative hearth. Mom reclined in the recliner, where Dad should have been. Obviously, Charlie had interrupted something.

"We're up to, um, Deuteronomy."

"He's not talking about with Rabbi Lidner, Charlie. Maimie Sullivan called to say you'd left your sweater at Mickey's. And you've got icing around your mouth."

"Mom, I'm sorry. I didn't want Mickey to think I didn't want to go to his party."

"You don't need to explain it," Dad said. "Your grandpa just wants to know if you learned anything."

The set of Grandpa's jaw seemed even more wooden than usual. Charlie did his best not to look. "Well, they're a little weird about their Messiah." They were quiet, so he went on. "It's confusing. If he was really the Messiah, then why would Hashem let him die? On the other hand, if we're always waiting around for Messiah, aren't we going to miss him when he comes?"

"This is what I'm talking about," Grandpa said, mysteriously. Then again, everything he said was mysterious.

Dad said, "From a party, you got all this?"

"Well, not exactly." He could have tried fibbing again, but couldn't stand the way secrets seemed to make a distance among them. "I went to the service, too."

"Charles Nathaniel Weisbarger."

"What? I don't see what the big deal is, if I can go to the party."

"It's this deception, Son."

He couldn't help thinking some of this was for Grandpa's benefit. To his surprise, though, the old man took his side. "Why wouldn't the boy be confused? You want honesty, and meanwhile you're keeping this from him."

"Keeping what from me?"

"Dad—," his dad said.

"Kid, you're going to be a brother."

"What?"

"David—"

"Dad, you're going to have to go now. Go take your nap. This is our affair."

It was the first time Charlie had ever known small, mild-mannered David Weisbarger to stand up to Grandpa, and the old man took it better than he would have expected, except that at the threshold of the room, he turned and looked straight at Charlie. "Remember, there are two ways to pull a bandage off."

"How is this a bandage?" He turned to his mom. "I *want* a brother. A brother is great. A sister is fine, also, if that's what you pick. I just don't know why you wouldn't tell me. Is this something you decided just now?"

When they'd heard the door shut upstairs—it was Charlie's room Grandpa stayed in when he came to visit, demoting Charlie to an air mattress down here—Dad said, "What your grandpa was trying to say, Charlie, is it's not another adoption. Your mother is pregnant. We wanted to tell you, but it's never a sure thing early on, especially at her age and with our history, and we didn't want to upset you. Things have been touch and go; it's why your grandpa's going to be here until the babies come. Mom's on bed rest . . ."

"But it looks like you're going to have siblings, honey. Two of them. Twins."

For a minute, Charlie hesitated. Twins. He felt like the needle on *The Price is Right*, when the big wheel goes around and around, different possibilities ticking past, the possibility that you've won big, won nothing, something in between.

"You know this doesn't mean we'll love you any less," Mom said.

Charlie put his hand on her shoulder. He felt very calm now. The big wheel stopped. He had only to open his eyes to see where he'd landed. "Mom?"

"What, honey?"

"How do you think I should feel?"

Did it mean something that it took her a while to answer? "You should feel however you feel. But what I'd hope for you to feel is that this doesn't change anything. The fact that we adopted, that should tell you how *much* we wanted you."

"Okay, then, that's how I feel." He tested it; it felt sturdy enough to hold for now, and anyway, he hated it when she cried.

That night on the air mattress, though, he couldn't get comfortable. Whenever he pushed down a lump, another surfaced elsewhere. He ended up spread-eagled, the blanket anaconda'd around his thighs, in light that reminded him of movies where they shot day through a filter and called it night. A toothy mass by the hearth resolved into fireplace tools. He could pick out the poker and the brush, and if he focused he could read, or imagined he could read, the word *Harmony* on the front of the upright piano. Houses made ticking noises at night, like cooling engines; he wondered what the physics of the thing could possibly be. Air escaping from wood? Continental drift? Mostly, though, he tried to suss out what was coming. On the surface, everything was the same, Mom and Dad and Grandpa sleeping upstairs. On the other hand, there was the great seriousness with which they'd told him, as if he was supposed to feel it had changed everything. He wondered how the Goy Messiah would have felt, when they'd told him he was getting a brother. He'd been adopted, too, in a sense. Of course, being perfect, he would have handled it perfectly. At some point, he heard the creak of the front stairs. It was his father, he was almost sure, watching him. He pretended to be asleep. And then he really was, and a hippie Jesus in a paper hat was smiling over the counter of a hamburger stand, asking could he take Charlie's order.

IT MUST HAVE BEEN IMPORTANT that Mom was thirty-nine, because no one—not Dad, not doctors, not Mrs. Sullivan—seemed able to talk about the pregnancy without mentioning it. *A blessing*, was the other thing they all said. People at temple would start out talking about the Summer Olympics, or the new electric juicer they'd seen advertised on TV, and quickly it would lead to, "Well, you know, she's thirty-nine . . . it's a blessing." A double blessing, Charlie thought, with two heartbeats. But he could feel the world rearranging itself, with the equator located somewhere along her expanding waist, on the sofa where she spent most of months seven and eight on bed rest, and Charlie way away at the North Pole.

In smaller ways, too, the terrain of his life was shifting. Dust began to gather on surfaces where she never would have let it before—the tops of towel rods and teakettles, the white knobs of the kitchen-counter radio. Nor did Dad ever turn it on anymore, even when preparing one of his specialties (tuna casserole, franks 'n' beans, fish fingers) or the heat-n-serv pierogi Grandpa had brought back from a Polish market in the City. Finally, Charlie asked if he could take the radio up to his room. His dad, seeming exhausted all of a sudden, didn't look up from the pot he was stirring, but said sure he could, which made Charlie wonder what else he could have gotten away with. *Can I have the car keys? Can we get a dog?* The next day was when you were supposed to bring your dad to school to talk about his career, but Mr. Weisbarger couldn't come. "My mom's due in a month," Charlie told the teacher, borrowing his dad's phrasing. "She's thirty-nine. It's a blessing." So Grandpa came instead, and explained how to make shoes, until people were crying with boredom.

He would have a memory later of Grandpa's arms scooping him out of a molded plastic seat in the hospital waiting room, like sherbet from a container; of expressway lights flicking past the car door against which he slumped; of waking up in the top bunk of Mickey Sullivan's bunk bed. His bond with Mickey was already dissolving, and the adult orchestration imparted a weird flavor to what remained. They shot hoops in the driveway the next morning (or in Charlie's case simply tried to avoid missing the backboard), but didn't talk much, and when they did, Mickey was like a hostage reading lines on TV.

"My mom says sometimes it just takes longer when they're older."

"I know," Charlie said.

"Must be some kind of vagina thing."

"Okay, Mickey, I got it."

"My sisters had scales when they came out. They peeled off everywhere. And gross black bellybutton stumps."

The insistence from all directions that everything was all right gave him a terrible premonition that it wasn't, but on the second day, Dad and Grandpa came for him, and four days later Mom was home with two wrinkled little black-haired people poking out of cowls of blue blanket. Boys, apparently. Moon men. He held his breath and kissed their heads, which were hot and tiny and faintly moist, like nostrils turned inside out. He wanted to please his mom, but didn't want to breathe in baby-scales, or space-dust. It was the reverse Mom was worried about. "We have to be very delicate. I know you're going to be a great protector." Then it was time for them to sleep again. Them meaning everybody but Charlie.

His inconspicuousness now was like the proverbial wish you should be careful about; it went everywhere he did, and instead of sealing him in with his parents, it sealed him out. When Mom and Dad talked to each other or to him, it was about the babies, or through the babies. Every gaseous smile, every clutch of their miniature fingers, turned out to be full of meaning. "Look, Charlie. He loves you." Even when Mom could return to the dinner table, she kept getting up to check the crib upstairs, where Abe and Izz reliably fussed.

Then one day his dad drove him to the electronics store and led him to the aisle of gleaming stereo equipment. They'd remembered! He almost ran to the Fancy Trax record players.

"Are you sure that's the one, Charlie? Because I'll get you whichever you want. Under let's say sixty dollars."

On carpeted plinths sat ranks of wood-paneled eight-track decks, chunky-buttoned built-in phonographs, Fisher brand tuners with their etched and glowing frequency stripes, all that luminous bandwidth. At least four radio stations could be heard. Fragments of light scattered off passing cars and went wide around him. But something held him back: the sense, perhaps, that he was being bought off. He would become a bystander in his own home now, and the stereo would be his only consolation.

On the other hand, he wasn't so far beyond the cold compass of economics himself that he failed to see these were the best terms he was likely to get.

At home, they'd turned his room into a nursery and moved him down to the basement—had rolled a harvest-gold deep-pile carpet over the poured-concrete floor. *An entire level all your own*, was how it had been put to him. Dad now set up the new stereo—a Scott 330R receiver with five inputs and a headphone jack and switches that said FILTER, MODE, TAPE, and LOUD—near his bed, as he'd requested, and then went back upstairs to those other sons on whom his mind had clearly been. He'd see Charlie at dinner, he said, which Charlie knew would be Stouffer's chicken cutlets, or breakfast for dinner, again.

As soon as he was gone, Charlie lay prone on the bed, his arms stretched out like those of the savior in whom he wasn't supposed to believe. The synthetic coverlet depicted stars and planets at distorted scales. It still smelled like the plastic it had come wrapped in. Above the ceiling, one of the twins started crying again, which made the other cry. He reached out and, having let the tuner warm up as the salesman had shown them, flipped on the speakers. There was a thunderous voice—the volume must have gotten jostled in transit—but when he turned it down, the frequency knob was still on the station it had been tuned to in the store. Over a majestic piano figure, the voice sang that Mars was no place to raise a kid. "In fact, it's cold as hell." The line shook something loose in Charlie. With his nose pressed to the space-age blanket and his arms now tucked under him like wings, he was crying, though not with such abandon as to carry over the music. This way he could tell himself that the reason no one came to comfort him was that no one heard.

ELTON JOHN BEGAT QUEEN, and Queen begat Frampton. How Charlie would cringe, years later, to think back on the Frampton concert at the Long Island Arena to which he dragged his father—the memory of Dad pretending not to smell the pot-smoke wafting up to the frightening nosebleeds. Of trying almost desperately to make Dad see the magic that had happened when Charlie was alone: the small Englishman down there on the stage *literally making his guitar talk*. And Frampton begat Kiss (the singer had grown up on Northern Boulevard!), who begat Alice Cooper, who begat Bowie . . . who, for a long time, begat only more Bowie.

By then, the storm of puberty had descended, turning his basement room into a kind of loamy lair, laying waste to his body, from which pimples and hairs and all manner of protuberance swelled, and filling his ribcage with feelings oddly shaped and too large to fit inside. Abe and Izzy could go for a few minutes without being held, restoring some of his mother's autonomy, but neither she nor Dad came downstairs much, maybe on account of the smell. Not that it mattered, in the cosmic scheme of things. The planet was dying, said the ugly scary friendly androgyne staring up at Charlie from the *Ziggy Stardust* sleeve. *Five years, that's all we've got.* And the album had been out awhile. According to Charlie's calculations, the year that *all the fat-skinny people and all the nobody people* would cease to exist was 1977.

This wasn't to say it was all apocalyptic gloom, his Ziggy Stardust period. When they weren't crying or monopolizing his parents, he loved having brothers. He loved watching them spit up on different relatives at his bar mitzvah in June (and loved the chance to make Mickey Sullivan as uncomfortable as Mickey's first communion had made him). And fear of Grandpa aside, he'd always loved French-speaking Montreal, where the Weisbargers went again the following August, squeezing all five of them into the wagon. That was also the year Grandpa started showing him a strange and special solicitude—the winter they snuck off to Radio City.

It was his close hot solitary hours in the basement he would dwell on later, though. Turning the music up loud and stripping naked and watching himself in the mirror hung on his wall among the posters and album covers he'd tacked to the millimeter-thin wood veneer. Despite Mickey's claim that he himself never did it, that you got seven years in purgatory for each infraction, Charlie couldn't keep his hands off himself. He pressed his midsection to the mattress and saw big dreamy tits like ice cream bells. He would try to come without touching himself, thinking that might lighten the penalty, but at the last minute his will would give out. Every time, he felt more and more excited and then, suddenly, so ashamed. Which should have been his confirmation that Mickey was right. And the week after the first of David Weisbarger's two heart attacks, Charlie would realize that the penalty had been visited not upon himself, but upon his father. It was as if each little handful of pearl jelly he brought out of himself had cost seven years of his dad's life. Or—let's be honest—seven weeks.

Again, Grandpa had come to stay, though this time it was Dad and not Mom in the hospital, and Charlie stayed home. He preferred Grandpa's silence to being sent to the Sullivans', where Mickey was mostly interested these days in lifting weights in the garage. And he preferred either to the hospital and its lunchroomy smell, green beans, bleach, which he now knew to be the smell of death. With the plastic tube running to his nose, like the tubes of Mickey's older brother's bong, Dad looked faded, all his color sucked away into the machines. And at night, through the basement ceiling, Charlie heard crying he knew was not the twins'.

THE MONTH AFTER THE FUNERAL, Charlie would feel as if something huge and mechanical was bearing down on him—as if the sky itself was just one dull plate of a vise too vast for him to have noticed it before. As if all the music had gone out of the universe. It was hard to get out of bed in the morning, and hard to keep his head off his desk in second period Chem. Shel Goldbarth and Tall Paul Stein knew his dad had died, of course, and went easy on him, as did anyone whose folks read the paper. To the anonymous jocks and preps, though, he was just the same freak kid. *Sorry*, they kept calling him. *Sorry Wastebucket.* He wasn't about to tell them why he deserved better; he didn't care, really. What hurt is the way Mickey Sullivan didn't say anything when they used the name in front of him. The way Mickey had withdrawn his protection.

One night, he went to the kitchen phone and mashed the familiar digits for the Sullivans. Of course, the odds against getting Mickey in his large and intact household were 7 to 1; it was Mickey's mom who picked up. For a second, Charlie was paralyzed. "Hello?" said a woman who used to cut the crusts off his sandwiches and remove the sweaty yellow square of supermarket cheese he wasn't allowed to have on his bologna. "Hello?" He hadn't thought this far ahead. There were the old standbys, refrigerator surveys, Prince Albert in a can, but in this intimate intracranial buzz, they seemed less hilarious than they did at the lunchtable. Plus Grandpa was watching TV in the next room. What was the term? *Heavy breathing.* He exhaled into the receiver's mouthpiece, left a fine mist of condensation on the plastic. "Hello? Who is this?" He hung up.

The next night, he got Mr. Sullivan, who said this was *not funny at all*, that whoever this was, he would *find out, and when*—

Except it *was* funny, actually, the way the most random compulsion could become something to live for. The last few periods at school began to lengthen uncomfortably, like a telescope turned the wrong way. The entire day was a narrowing funnel leading to this one moment, just before the hang-up, when the Sullivan on the other end would know it was the Unknown Caller, and know the Unknown Caller knew they knew.

Then one night came the knock on the door. Maybe it was the timing that tipped Charlie off, because no one knocked on the Weisbargers' door these days except Mormon missionaries or women from Congregation Beth Shalom bearing casserole dishes—it was too sad a house for social calls—and they would not have come at night like this, in the rain. No, this was the other shoe, coming to stomp out his life like a bug's. He stole upstairs to his old bedroom, now shadowed with cribs and playpens and toy shelves from which stuffed animals watched and disapproved. He dared not turn on the light: it might be seen from the sidewalk below, and he didn't want to wake the twins. On cat's feet he made it to the window, lifted the shade. He was too late to see whoever it was on the stoop; he caught only an arc of black nylon, cut off from the rest of its umbrella by the chord of the roofline. It trembled a vigorous accompaniment to words Charlie couldn't make out. He could hear their melody, rising into frustration. A man's voice, which was interrupted by another man's—his grandpa's. "Why don't you leave the poor kid alone?"

Grandpa would never mention the visit to Charlie; nor, evidently, to his mother. But the next day at school, Mickey, newly huge, found him near the loading dock behind the cafeteria and silently, dutifully—almost apologetically—pummeled him. And that was the formal end of the friendship.

But was it really the end of the Unknown Caller? Back in the good days, Charlie used to have this intuition that timelines were a fiction. That time seemed like an arrow only because people's brains were too puny to handle the everything that would otherwise be present. He'd tried to explain it to Mickey once, when they were bullshitting ideas for their own comic book—for parallel universes and so forth, but also for how to fit the simultaneity of things into the relentlessly forward-moving frames. His theory led pretty swiftly to ridicule, but was a private comfort. Now, though, he saw why Mickey might have wanted to defend himself against it. Because if every moment of a life is present in every other, so is every old self you've ever tried to outrun. And then how to know—the present self having always felt flimsy, somehow, compared to the one so acutely alive under the kitchen table—which you, specifically, is the real one?

UNLESS CHARLIE WANTED TO TAKE THE SCHOOLBUS—and he rode the same route as Mickey—he had to walk the half-mile home. In March on the Island, the ground was still too hard for planting, so the people who were home stayed indoors. Underdressed, because in muzzy post-sleep he'd mistaken the brightness outside the basement for warmth, which anyway wouldn't have survived the afternoon's clouding over, he jammed his fists in the pockets of his coat and did his best to lose himself in the empty sidestreets. It was impossible, of course; they were a perfect grid. He passed the ballfield where he'd played pee-wee league, co-sponsored by the Jaycees or Kiwanis or something. When the wind kicked up, the loose cord from the yard-arm made a racket against the flagless metal flagpole, an alarm that made his heart tense up like something was about to happen. Which was ridiculous, because what ever happened on Long Island, except people being born and people dying? Still, he decided for once in his life to be a mensch. He hopped the fence and trotted out to right field, blowing on his hands for warmth, and secured the cord to the cleat at the bottom of the pole. Coming back across the dead grass, he stopped. Someone was watching from one of the dugouts.

It was a girl, he realized, when he'd moved close enough to see into the gloom under the tin roof. A tall, slender girl with brown hair to her shoulders. She had on enormous headphones, with an antenna. Her army jacket and the tallboys of beer next to her on the bench could have been a drifter's, but her posture was pure Amazon. And the voice—the voice, hoarse with cigarettes, absolutely killed him. "Good Samaritan, huh?" She didn't take off her headphones.

"I just figured that sound must drive the neighbors crazy. I mean, it was driving me crazy. Hey, do you get music on those things?"

"No, I just wear them so strange guys won't come up and bother me." She studied him through the diamonds of the fence. "You want a beer?"

He did, if only because she was the one offering, but he told her, truthfully, that he shouldn't. His mom was part bloodhound.

"You sure? You look like a man who could use one."

He'd forgotten all about his swollen face. "I fell," he said. "My name's Charlie."

Now he could see quite clearly a Cheshire grin spreading in the shadows behind the fence. "Well, don't let me keep you, Charlie. I'd only get you in trouble."

"Right," he said. "Right," and made his feet move across the brittle grass, toward the fence he now saw he'd have to climb right in front of her. It trembled under his weight; his jacket snagged for a second on a twist of metal at the top, but miraculously he did not fall.

When he got home, Grandpa was watching TV with the sound off. He didn't mention Charlie's lateness, and Mom, apparently, was sleeping, as she often was these days. Still dazed, Charlie sat down in the living room, his swollen eye facing away from the old man. On screen, the camera panned drunkenly across bleachers full of cheering people, zoomed in on an overweight woman who was jumping up and down. At the same time as it advanced the storyline— this woman would become the game show's next contestant—the sequence conveyed a dense set of messages about luck, fate, prosperity, community. In his old life, Charlie wouldn't even have registered them. Now they seemed obtrusive, artificial, like the bouncing mass of the woman's hair, the gauzy orange of her university sweatshirt. Maybe because he was Canadian, Grandpa, in his armchair, didn't change expression. But when the show cut to commercial, he pushed himself up with a grunt and shuffled to the kitchen. When he came back, he placed in Charlie's hands a frozen bag. A mound of Eagle Eye shelled peas gleamed on the packaging, more seductive-looking than any real-life pea had ever been. Had something happened to Grandpa's brain? "For your eye," he said. "Take the swelling down."

While Charlie arranged the bag of peas over his tender brow, Grandpa turned the TV off. In the next room, the icebox whirred, replacing the cold air he'd let escape. "Some kid at school does this to you, eh?"

"I don't want to talk about it."

"Did you deserve it?"

"Grandpa, I don't want to—" Something in the old man's face stopped him. It was like he was deep inside Charlie, and had been for some time. "Yeah. I pretty much deserved it."

"And no one stood up for you?"

Charlie shook his head.

"Then you learned something, didn't you? Now next time some-one asks you what happened, if you're all right, you say, 'You should see the other guy.'"

"You should see the other guy."

"But confident. With a smile. Like your face might break open."

"You should see the other guy."

20

ARRIVING AT THE PORT AUTHORITY BUS TERMINAL in July of 1975 with his cardboard suitcase in one hand and his letter from the Wenceslas-Mockingbird School for Girls in the other, Mercer felt divided as to how long he might stay in New York. Even before the letter he'd been divided: one part of him swanning with Jay Gatsby around an imaginary Gotham; the other part stolid and earth-bound, nose to the deep fryer, in the stifling, sizzling South. He'd told himself—at night in his childhood bedroom, with its too-small bed and its clutch of overdue books on the nightstand—that the ten-sion between the two was insupportable, that he must flee or, like the purer products of America, go crazy. He'd pictured himself how many times snapping shut his typewriter case, binding up his mea-ger pile of manuscript pages, standing out by the highway with his thumb jerked north. It was just as plausible, though, that it was the divisions keeping him sane—his waking life excusing the impossi-bility of his dream-life, and vice versa. Had his former Shakespeare professor not invited him to come up like this for a job interview, he might still be back there in the bedroom he'd outgrown, turning his paper hat in his hands, the most literate short-order cook in north-eastern Georgia.

He'd showed the letter to his mother first, in a kind of dry run, and watched her mouth purse as if he'd served her a slice of cake she knew to be poisoned. "You don't know anyone in New York," she'd said

finally, but he was out ahead of her. He knew Professor Runcible, for
one, and C.L. had an army buddy who had a spare room in his rent-
controlled apartment. And hadn't she wanted to be a teacher once
herself, before she fell for Pop? "I'm twenty-three years old, Mama.
There's no guarantee I land a position, but I ought to at least go up
there and talk to the man."

In Shakespeare, tragedy was the flame struck from the clash of
moral principles; here her maternal desire to see him meaningfully
employed warred with her Old Testament mistrust of cities. Her lips
pursed tighter. "I suppose it's only polite. But you'll have to ask your
father." Which would turn out, as he feared, to be another order of
drama altogether.

Afterward, in the mothball heat of his bedroom under the eaves,
he tried to convince himself it was Pop he was running from, or C.L.,
or the cultural drought of the little town whose distant water tower
he could see from his window. Or that he dreamed of New York
because it was where the saviors of his youth had hung out. Melville
and James Baldwin and especially Walt Whitman. But Pop obviously
suspected him of having other motives, which Mercer couldn't quite
put out of his mind, or see.

Next morning, he was boarding a Greyhound bus, on a thirty-
dollar See America Pass. Through day and into evening he rode with
his legs folded into the cramped space of the window seat, a back-
broken paperback of *The Age of Innocence* propped against them, his
brown suit laid out carefully on the rack above. Clearly, his chief
weakness as a novelist heretofore had been his inability to keep pace
with the complexity of real life. To imagine, for example, that the triumph his fugitive hero would feel at the pine forests whooshing past
and the taillights of his countrymen strung out jewellike ahead might
be tempered by an equally exquisite guilt. Or, on a purely physical
level, by discomfort. With the sun still out, it was too hot, but when
night fell, Mercer got cold. No matter how wide the window went,
the bus smelled like the rotting carpets of the coloreds-only motel
rooms of his distant childhood. He read and slept but mostly stared
through the glass and tried not to make eye contact with the passengers alighting serially on the seat beside him: a bantamweight old
farmer on a hemorrhoid pillow, an ex-con picked up at the gates of a
jail, a Jehovah's Witness in support hose who from midnight to two
a.m. read audibly from a marked-up Bible. That he could hear her
wasn't an accident, he was pretty sure; she wanted his immortal soul.

But she disembarked in D.C., and the seat remained blessedly empty until the bus pulled into the blasted parking lot of a minimall somewhere in New Jersey.

The sky was by then pink with morning. The only viable tenant appeared to be an Orange Julius. For having so far husbanded his cash pretty well, Mercer rewarded himself with one of the eponymous beverages. He returned to find the bus's luggage hold open and a G.I. in mufti doing pushups nearby. Two women too old for teddy bears played with teddy bears. The driver, a small, raisinesque Pakistani whose nicotine dependency had them stopping every forty minutes, stared out across the asphalt. In the absence of parked cars, the brushed-metal cobra-style streetlights seemed contextless and creepily regular, as though deposited there by UFO. A sunburned white kid with a ballcap and a zippered case of tennis rackets shifted from one sneaker to the other, waiting to board. He had a strong chin, clean cheeks, delicate little triangles of down on the back of his neck where the cap ended. Mercer knew in a flash the kid would be his seatmate.

Riding toward the coast, they exchanged not a single word. Then they crested the ridge of Weehawken, and there it was, New York City, thrust from the dull miles of water like a clutch of steely lilies. As they rumbled down past billboards toward the great churn of the tunnel entrance, the seatmate's arm sort of flopped against his own on the armrest, so that they were barely, just barely, touching, the brown and the beige, a plane of contact one atom wide, and the huge opposed feelings inside Mercer swelled until he thought he might burst right here, a firework on the heights of New Jersey, never to reach his destination. But fifteen minutes later, watching the driver unload his typewriter in the oily gloom of the bus-station subbasement, Mercer would be squeezing the moment back into some inner oubliette. The kid had made off with his rackets, never to be seen again, though Mercer would ever after equate the Manhattan skyline with the smell of English Leather cologne.

He ascended through Brutalist atriums and Byzantine stairways, his arms feeling yanked from their sockets, his eyes that special brand of bus-ride dry. Mostly, though, New York was the people. He'd never seen so many as confronted him that morning. Before him on the sidewalk, at head height, were too many other heads to count, moving up and down with the bodies they were attached to, like ripe fruit bobbing in a barrel. Fat faces, thin faces, pink faces, brown faces, bearded and naked, hatted and bald, male and female and everything in between. Dazed unto stillness, his heart doing calisthenics in his chest, he was an obstruction, an abstraction; the masses could have trampled him had they so desired. Instead, they broke around him at the last possible second, jostling him bodily, perhaps, but leaving the essential Mercer Goodman untouched. Not to put too fine a point on it, but who the hell in this bustling city even cared who the essential Mercer Goodman was? It was this, as much as anything, that made him feel he'd stepped into a dream.

C.L.'S BUDDY CARLOS lived above a one-screen porno theater on Avenue B. The spare room he had to offer was more like a closet, only minus the privacy. There were chewed-out places in the doorframe where the hinges should have been and a discolored bedsheet to separate it from the kitchen. After some haggling, Carlos agreed to sleep there himself, and for the privilege of taking over the larger bedroom, with its locking door and ceiling fan and a mattress about which the less said the better, Mercer coughed up $220 for the month, which was $70 more than Carlos paid for the entire apartment. This arrangement worked out well enough for Carlos, who'd had trouble holding down a job since his discharge; unemployment checks and the vigorish he charged his roommates were his only visible sources of income. But it was an unforeseen blow to Mercer's own budget. As soon as he'd settled in, to the extent that settling was possible, he called Wenceslas-Mockingbird to schedule a meeting.

Dr. Leon Runcible, recently installed there as Dean of Faculty, had been something of a legend on the campus of the University of Georgia when Mercer was there. He was about as eminent as it was possible to be without tenure. Head boy at Groton, chosen by W. H. Auden for the Yale Younger Poets series while still in his twenties, subsequently the author of a well-regarded volume on the poetry of the metaphysicals. . . . His manner was still faintly Grotonian—especially the voice, declaiming iambs—but when Mercer's Shakespeare class got to Lear on the heath, he'd raised his arms toward the ceiling and grasped at the air with an intensity that made the veins on his hands stand out. Then, just as quickly, he was back to that patrician poise, tossing off an allusion to Whitman Mercer would later pursue in the paper that won him the freshman English prize (making him the first Negro ever so honored). For a semester or more after that, Mercer had led his mother to believe he was still leaning toward an accounting major. In fact, most mornings found him in the second row of the modern language building's great lecture hall, watching the young professor produce sentence after sentence of exegesis, like loaves from a bottomless basket.

The massive desk of a dean's office now did nothing to reduce the Runcible dazzle, but Mercer felt his undergraduate laurels as a withered garland upon his brow. As a secretary brought tea and cookies, he heard himself venture a Freudian reading of Countess Olenska, arguably the heroine of the book Runcible had enclosed with the letter. He had just begun to generate real insight when Runcible sighed. "Hearing you talk, Mercer, makes me wonder why I left the classroom for the thanklessness of administration." He gestured with the back of his hand as if to dismiss the leather-bound books, the fieldstone hearth, the huge windows onto Fourth Avenue. "But my late mother was an alumna and donor, and I suppose in some sense I hoped to honor her devotion to her alma mater. Now about the position. The board here, the prior administration, they can be rather old-fashioned in their thinking on certain matters. They do not always hear the varied carols I hear. The carols that for that matter the city council, on whom we depend for certain zoning exemptions, increasingly hears."

Wait a minute; it was Mercer's *mind* they were after, right? Runcible swept on.

"As I'm a newcomer to the school, it only makes sense for me to install some exemplars of my point of view. For instance: I look at you, Mercer, and I see an articulate young scholar, to have whom any graduate program in the country would be lucky. But as circumstance has it, here you are, available, and here we are with an opening in fourth-form English—that's an Anglicism for tenth grade—and I have only one concern, really."

"It's okay. I'm used to being the only black guy in the classroom."

Runcible coughed, as if a shard of cookie had gone down his windpipe. It went on long enough to be alarming, ten or fifteen seconds, and when he'd recovered, the face behind his hand remained claret-colored. "Oh, no, Mercer. For me, it's not a question . . . Rather—can I speak in confidence? It's that you are a male." The word landed with an odd spin. "Adolescent girls can have the appearance of women, but they still see teachers as figures of great power. I speak from experience. The fellow who would be your predecessor departed under certain clouds. A line had been crossed, if you follow. I need to be sure you follow."

Mercer promised Dr. Runcible there was no reason to worry. If given a chance here, he would do nothing to reflect poorly on his patron, or on the school, or on the memories of Wenceslas and Mockingbird (whoever they were). "On that you have my word."

HE WASN'T TO BE ADDED OFFICIALLY TO THE PAYROLL—wasn't expected to turn in a syllabus and prep a classroom—until the week before Labor Day. And so, for the rest of the summer, he had all the time he should have needed to make serious headway on his first opus. There were only two problems. The first was that he could barely afford to feed himself. The second was the apartment. All day, moaning and warmth from the movie theater below wafted distractingly through the floorboards. And Carlos seemed never to leave, not even to do laundry. His habit of sitting in the living room, studying his own shadow in the mud-gray screen of the unplugged TV, was unnerving, as was the cigarette perpetually asmolder between his swollen knuckles. After Mercer came back from a coffee run one day to find his Waterman pen missing—it had been a graduation gift from his mother—distraction shaded over toward paranoia. And when he worked up the nerve to tell Carlos to stay out of his things, Carlos just shrugged and said the rent would be going up in September.

Mercer began locking his room in the morning and heading for the big library on Forty-Second Street, where you could call up any of three million books from the basement. He sat facing away from the clock, under a powerful vent blasting marble-cool air. A shabby woman in fingerless gloves sat nearby, filling stacks of paper with huge words, five or six of them to the page, letters so big Mercer couldn't quite read them. If he could fill a page with his own normally sized words, the day was a success. It had taken Flaubert a week, after all, to manage that much. Provided you believed Flaubert. Afternoons, he made notes for the next day's work and, in the name of research, sank himself into *The Red and the Black* and *L'Éducation sentimentale* and nibbled at the edges of Combray.

And then, to save subway fare (and to forestall his return to Carlos, and the armpit heat of Avenue B), he walked. Manhattan turned out to be situated on a series of barely perceptible hills. They lifted you up every half-mile or so, offering a vista of foreshortened intersections, a fleshtoned sea. The busiest crossings—Seventh Avenue and Fourteenth Street, Sixth Avenue and Eighth—acted as catchments for panhandlers and street vendors and West Indian women like the one from the bus holding out little tracts like takeout menus, warning Mercer that the end was nigh, that only cheeses could save him. The farther south he walked, the more godless the city became. He occasionally even saw men holding hands, as if daring anyone to say something. It was fascinating—just anthropologically—that they could coexist with the traffic cops and the street-corner preachers, in universes that overlapped but somehow did not touch. And every so often, someone must have become confused about which of these universes Mercer belonged to, because he would feel that he, too, was being picked out of the crowd. He'd turn and see a Hispanic in white jeans appraising him frankly across an avenue, or an older man in tweed watching from a sidewalk café, cigarette floating in lazy semaphore. It would be Mercer who had to lower his gaze. But this lowering apparently signaled something, too; once or twice he even felt himself followed, and couldn't be sure he hadn't invited it, however accidentally.

One ominous evening in August, under the first thunderheads in weeks, he was mooning around the labyrinth where West Fourth Street crosses West Eleventh Street, absorbed in not being absorbed in these things, when he felt a hand on his shoulder. He turned to find a mussed-looking white guy grinning up at him. "Hey, I think you dropped something." With his dark hair and lynx-like features, the fine white clavicle showing between the lapels of his leather jacket, he was . . . you wouldn't say classically handsome, but striking. In one hand was a guitar case; in the other, a yellow pencil, held eraser-end first. It took Mercer a minute to shift his frame of reference. "Oh," he said, taking the pencil. "Thanks." And snuck another look at the storm-colored eyes before turning to go.

He wondered now if he hadn't been unfair to Carlos; if he hadn't just dropped his Waterman somewhere. On a deeper level, he wondered if perhaps he wasn't, like those curiously incomplete protagonists he'd been reading about, the Luciens and Juliens and Marcels, somehow wrong about himself. Then he wondered if he hadn't had the frame of reference right after all, because there, a block behind him, was that small man, in pursuit.

Mercer ducked into a shop, short of breath. He was embarrassed to find that it mainly sold sex toys. He grabbed from a shelf of books the most plausibly literary title—*For Whom the Balls Toiled*—and waited by the front window for his pursuer to pass. The man seemed in a hurry now; the guitar case trailed along behind him. That he didn't so much as glance in the window came as a curious disappointment. Before he could think about what he was doing, Mercer had laid aside the erotica and hurried back out of the shop and was following the man east, toward the lettered streets, as if there were something he could not wait any longer to find out.

At the entrance of Tompkins Square Park, though, his quarry disappeared. The pathways under the trees were jammed with teenagers, white boys and girls in dingy shirts and do-it-yourself hair. He was wending his way forward (*Pardon, Excuse me*) when a metallic shriek nearly deafened him. All around, hands spiked up into the greeny air, as if to call down the storm. And then the noise began.

In a clearing near the base of a streetlamp, a drummer bashed away, dwarfed by speakers. A large Hispanic man in a sexy-nurse costume bent over a small electric organ. A shirtless singer—shouter, really—barely touched the guitar around his neck. Tattoos bulged and jumped on his chest as he screamed his weird manifesto into a megaphone *Connecticut*, it sounded like he was saying. *Connecticut. Connecticut.* The layers of sound that nearly drowned it out, though, were coming from the other guitarist, Mercer's pursuer, who aimed his face upward at the boiling clouds, the tendons of his throat a startled, ghostly white. As he flailed at his instrument, the kids around Mercer shoved and bounced. "What is this?" he asked a fellow with green hair who pogoed nearby. But any response was inaudible.

There would be five more songs that day (the last five songs, as it turned out, that Ex Post Facto proper ever played). Then the sky flashed white and ripped and the rain began, a real five o'clockalypse, and when the guitar stopped, whatever cohesion or pressure had held the audience together dissipated. Kids hustled back under the sheltering trees. Mercer joined them, straining to see through the steam rising off the pavement what was happening there in the clearing. The bedraggled drag queen had already started to break down the organ, to coil the orange extension cords. The singer continued to shout into his megaphone, but you could hardly hear him over the pounding rain. Then came police lights, whirling. Mercer watched the singer get right up in the face of an officer, like a baseball manager bumping chests with the umpire. He noticed the other guitarist leaning against a nearby treetrunk with his case in his hand. The kids closest to him were too awed to approach, though they clearly wanted to. What would it be like, Mercer wondered, to wield that kind of power? Though maybe, were such a gift entrusted to you, you wouldn't have any idea. He moved closer. "I just wanted to tell you, that was . . . It was really something."

"Hey, Pencil Guy. Didn't realize you were a fan."

Could a nod count as a lie? "How would you have?"

"Anyway, I hope you got your fill, 'cause you kids won't have Billy Three-Sticks to kick around anymore. I only came out of retirement for Nastanovich." Nastanovich, evidently, had been the bassist, right up until his overdose. This farewell show was for money to pay off the funeral home.

"I'm really sorry to hear that."

The guy looked away. "What are you going to do?"

"Billy Three-Sticks, though—that's you?"

"My secret identity. A *nom de plume*."

"*De guerre*, you mean. *De plume* is for writers."

The guitarist's eyebrows twitched. Then he set down his guitar case and, from some recess of his leather jacket, retrieved a flask. "Really it's William. You thirsty?"

At the risk of being thought prudish, Mercer said he didn't drink. Or, come to think of it, maybe prudishness would serve to put the brakes on whatever was transpiring here. But William just said, "Don't tell me you don't eat food, too, because the best pizza in the city is just around the corner."

IN HIS OTHER LIFE, William was a visual artist, a painter, and when he learned Mercer was new in town, he offered to take him on a guided tour of the Metropolitan Museum that very weekend—that is, if Mercer was free. "Summers in junior high, I practically lived here," he would explain, leading Mercer to the ticket window. The two-dollar suggested donation was going to just about clean Mercer out for the day, but William only handed over a dime, and indicated by a look that Mercer was to do likewise, which he did, a little guiltily.

"You grew up in New York?"

"More or less," William said, "until they packed me off to prep school."

"I start teaching in a couple of weeks at the Wenceslas-Mockingbird School for Girls. My first real job, unless you count manning a grill."

But as they wandered through the galleries, it was William who did the teaching, riffing on the artworks on the walls and the contexts that had, he said, produced them. If Mercer hadn't known better, he would have thought it was *William* trying to impress *him*. "Look," he said, stopping in front of a Renaissance painting.

"Jacob and the angel, right?" Mercer said. "My mother's church has an entire window."

"But here." William pointed to an incongruity. The angel's muscled leg was lifelike, subtly three-dimensional, where the tunic it disappeared into was crudely geometric, more like an icon of clothing than the thing itself. "This is the entire history of Western painting, right here. The struggle to represent things accurately. And then, when we develop a language for rigorously rendering 3D shapes in two-dimensional space, what do we find? We're as far from the truth as ever. The robe here may be less real-looking than the hand, but at least it's more honest about its status as representation. And of course, both are in service of a fairy tale. It's the old Nicholas of Cusa thing."

Something roused itself in Mercer. "Remind me . . ."

"Well, Nicholas was this monk who pointed out that the more sides you add to a regular polygon inscribed in a circle, the more it looks like the circle. By definition, though, it's becoming less and less like a circle, because a circle only has one side." William unwrapped a piece of hard candy and popped it into his mouth. "Or maybe no sides, I can't remember."

"So it's like a paradox?"

"Depends on whether you buy Nicholas's solution."

"Which is?"

William was inches away now, though they both continued to look at the painting, and Mercer could smell sweat and leather and what was either butterscotch or rum. "Nicholas says you can close the distance between the two only by an act of belief. A leap of faith." And he reached out and pressed a finger to the paint. "Hey, I touched a masterpiece."

This would always be where William excelled, the discussion of ideas and movements and things, the matrix of the very abstract and the very concrete that made up the culture. Mercer's own sense of culture, formed first in the Greater Ogeechee Public Library and then under Dr. Runcible, was essentially nostalgic: greatness had ceased to occur in the arts right around the time when his father was off fistfighting with Hitler. It was William who would introduce him to Schoenberg and La Monte Young, Situationism and West African tribal art and Fluxus. Right now, as they ate hot dogs on a bench behind the museum, he was riffing on Susan Sontag's "Notes on 'Camp'" and the artistic merits of the graffiti that seemed to be swallowing New York's lampposts and trashcans. On the great green rug of the Park, brown circles had begun to spread like cigarette burns. The haze of August blurred the apartment buildings opposite. A trumpet somewhere was blowing a tune by Harold Arlen—not Hoagy Carmichael, as William said, but Mercer didn't correct him. It was too easy to remain in the passenger's seat and be carried along wherever William wanted to go. To lie back, so to speak, and let him delve into the ideas that had animated his own band, back before the whole thing went to hell. More recently (one thing being as good as another, in Sontag's reading), William's tastes had been running toward disco and reggae, he said. Punk rock was frankly too white. The generic terms were meaningless to Mercer, but he knew this last bit was for his benefit. He watched William rip off pieces of hot-dog bun to toss to a pigeon. He watched a nearby college kid, twenty-one or twenty-two, proposition an older woman. He watched the sun come out from behind a cloud, and the branches of the elms thrown up like dancers' arms, and the green garments they held to the wind. Incidental, all of it, of course, but this was what this city bestowed that novels couldn't: not what you needed in order to live, but what made the living worth doing in the first place.

THEN FALL ARRIVED, blowing the stink off the sidewalks. The riffle of drying sycamores softened the traffic noise. By late September, there were premature garlands scattered on the ground, so that if you squinted, you could almost imagine the sidewalks as browning pastures, and yourself as a wandering bard. Or perhaps this was Walt Whitman bleeding beyond the ruled margins of the school day; Mercer had been shepherding his students through "Song of the Open Road." He found he liked the work—liked these girls with their first names that might have been last names, their braces and bony knees, the chewing gum that couldn't quite cover the smell of illicit tobacco. He didn't mind that they blushed when he called on them; it wasn't that he was male, or black, he told himself, but that he had separated one of them from the herd. He tried to do this gently, fairly, to use the power Dr. Runcible had warned him about for good rather than evil. He liked the way they attempted to conceal beneath an air of sophistication the anxieties it nonetheless caused. And he liked the way that, from the safety of groups, they gabbled over him maternally, with their awkwardly personal questions. Was he settling in okay? Was he getting home-cooked meals? In their fumbling propriety, they reminded him of himself. Most of all, he liked the chance he had to offer "his girls" (as he came to think of them) larger, freer selves—selves that had read Cervantes and Aphra Behn, and could quote from memory the sonnets of John Donne. He was like a chef presenting fabulous new dishes, lobsters of intellect, figs of sensibility, the very tastes that had freed him from Altana.

After the three o'clock bell had tolled and his last laggard pupil had slogged off to field-hockey practice, he would pack up the Italian-leather satchel he'd splurged on with his first paycheck and strike out toward the brownstone blocks north of Washington Square. This was another thing he liked: proximity to the glamour of attainment. The days were ending earlier, and in softened light he could see through the buffering trees into homes unlike any he'd known. Sing, Muse, of high, molded ceilings and built-in bookcases chockablock with hardcovers! Sing of armchairs with scarlet upholstery and high-boys lacquered like mirrors and the elegant shadows of potted palms! Sing of a chandelier made entirely of antlers! Of what looked to be a genuine Matisse on the wall above the hearth!

Of course, he had still not yet divulged to William his plans to become a great writer. Why would he? They were just friends, after all, who, on the cosmopolitan model, owed each other neither explanation nor apology. After an evening of Chinese food plus drinks, someone's loft party plus drinks, or just drinks (Mercer's always virginal) they would find themselves at the top of a set of subway steps and Mercer would mention the pile of papers waiting for him back in Alphabet City, and then he would extend his hand for a collegial shake, trying not to imagine where William, who had no such stack of papers (though half the time neither did Mercer), would spend the rest of the night.

Even when he did in fact have papers to grade, Mercer often forgot them, staying up late daydreaming instead. For daydreams were safe, as secret identities and well-defended boundaries and watertight compartments were safe. He confined his friendship with William to west of Broadway and below Houston Street, confident no one from work would discover it. He must have been doing something right, because for three glorious months—a fall that ripened and reddened like some champion apple—life came easily, more or less. Weekends, when his mother called, he had to work to keep from gloating.

Then one evening at the end of the semester, just before he was to fly home for Christmas break, he found himself coming out of a subtitled movie in some section of the city he hardly knew. Or *film*, to borrow a word from William, who bounced on the balls of his feet to the beat of some inner metronome, grinning up at the egg-shaped moon. "God. Don't you feel like you've just been taught to *see* again? When she smashes the jar of strawberries against the door—I feel like I need to hold my head perfectly level, so that nothing I just saw sloshes out."

Even as he said it, he was spinning to take in Mercer's reaction. They'd known each other only fifteen and a half weeks, but already Mercer had embraced the role of straight man. He suspected that William enjoyed his diffidence, his potential corruptibility, his unease with his own instincts. Halfway through the film, his hand had come to rest for a full minute on the thigh of Mercer's corduroys, inches from his crotch, and now Mercer was feeling flushed and giddy and a little dangerous himself. "I would have written it differently," he said. "Where was the plot? I think I dozed off once or twice."

"Plot is incidental. Those strawberries!"

"Yep. Must have slept through them."

"You little philistine!" William gave his arm a hard punch. "I am appalled."

"Matter of fact, does the theater offer refunds? I might have to go back and ask for one."

But William caught him as he pretended to turn and pulled him into a doorway, one hand on each arm. There was liquor in his mouth—it must have been in his soda cup—and then it was in Mercer's. How often, in later years, would he return to this taste, and to the heat of William's hands, and to the friction of their whiskers in the dark! It was why, he now saw, the city had summoned him. Or it was why William had. And he had apparently as early as December of '75 already stopped bothering to distinguish one from the other.

21

THE CONCEPT, ORIGINALLY, had been a four-piece. Venus handled keys and wardrobe; Big Mike banged on the drums; Billy Three-Sticks was guitars, vox, art direction, and most of the songwriting, and Nastanovich, who had never touched a bass prior to 1973, provided the loft they practiced in. When Nastanovich lost his day job, though, and had to move back in with his mom in Queens, they no longer had anywhere to play. William sure as hell wasn't going to invite these guys up to Hell's Kitchen, to make fun of his unsold paintings and start trouble with the sixth-floor Angels. Then, at the record release party that summer, a kid came up and ID'd himself as a fan. He'd heard they were looking for a space to jam, he said. Well, the house where he was living had an unused utility shed out back. It was right off the Second Avenue F. Were they interested?

It seemed like the perfect solution, and at first, the kid was all solicitude (though his handle—Nicky Chaos—might have served as a warning). He'd borrowed a soundboard for them to run their instruments through, and even a four-track, for if they felt like laying anything down on tape, and had brought in a friend of his named Solomon, a window-washer with some high-school vocational training, to run it. Nicky watched every session, seemingly without blinking, gargoyling forward from his perch atop an amp. After a month or so, though, he began offering constructive criticism, and then just criticism, full stop. The voice William sang in, he said, was too Anglophile to be truly revolutionary. Too Mockney. Here's how he'd do it. And he hopped down off his amp and took the microphone, and though the screaming that followed evoked stuck pigs, you had to hand it to the guy—he knew all the words by heart.

Soon he had insinuated himself into the band as a second guitarist. And here was the problem with running a band on a non-hierarchical model: even if they'd been in a position to say no to Nicky Chaos, which by this point they weren't, who would speak for the group?

Now, when Nicky got overbearing or temperamental or William simply got tired of hearing his voice, he walked over to the record store on Bleecker to remind himself why he and Venus had started playing music together in the first place.

The staff there was always happy to see him. This may not have been unrelated to a sideline William had in those days, '73, '74, which was scoring cocaine in small amounts for various friends and acquaintances, record store clerks not excluded. *Hobby*, was probably a better word than *sideline*. He did it not for the money—his trust fund was still more than enough to live on at that point—but as a species of philanthropy, a way of doing his small part to combat the overall hassle that seemed to be creeping into the process of securing good drugs, because, he figured, what went around came around. And besides: he was in a position to do it. One of his conquests from uptown had become a dealer and, even after they stopped fucking, extended to William a discount that allowed him to cop in family-sized quantities, which he would then take around like Santa Claus visiting the Nice list. He liked the way it opened doors for him, the way it made people happy to see him, not because he was William Hamilton-Sweeney III, the wastrel heir, or Billy Three-Sticks, frontman of the storied Ex Post Facto, but because, he felt, he was himself.

As for the coke *it*self, it made him funny and good-looking, but he was already those things, so he could take it or leave it. He generally abstained Sundays through Wednesdays, and never got high before painting. He might knock off early as the weekend approached to do a bump before happy hour, or break out his stash on a date that had started to drag, or if he was headed to the Village bars, or to Grand Central to cruise the men's rooms, for old times' sake, but that was more or less the extent of it. Coke was like the Democratic Party: he went along with it on principle, but it did not speak to him personally.

After the first time he did heroin, though, in the slant-ceilinged manager's office of that record store, he would spend the rest of his week calculating how he could slip away as soon as possible to swim down into himself, into the delicious blankness of that canvas, again.

This was in the fall of 1974, a sweltering day in September. He was carrying some 45s for the store to sell on consignment. "Kunneqtiqut" b/w "City on Fire!" They'd recorded the tracks in preparation for the second LP, back when Nicky was still confined to his amplifier top. Now it seemed that record would be going in a different direction, or at least that it would take time for William to reclaim the helm of the band, so he'd paid to get them pressed up as a seven-inch. Before handing them to the clerk, he dropped into the hole at the center of the stack of records a bag of coke. The guy waited until the little heat-sealed sleeve was already in his pocket to tell William he didn't have any cash.

It was cool, William said. Consider it a gratuity.

"I mean I know I got a drawer of cash here, but I can't touch it, man. I've been fired like five times already. But if you can come upstairs for a second, we can maybe work something out?"

The ceiling fan spun woozily, and the door to the street was open, a frame of green light and the ambient noise of the traffic.

"Watch the till, honey?" the clerk said.

The only other person in the place was the chubby girl in overalls and a halter top scouring the rack of fanzines by the door. Did William know her from somewhere? Then his friend was leading him upstairs, to a tiny office whose ceiling sloped to one side, beneath another set of stairs. There were old concert posters peeling from the wall, a safe with a stereo sitting on top of it, a loveseat, and some big, uncovered speakers. You could hear the upstairs neighbor kids running around, like shoes tumbling in a dryer. The friend switched out the reggae record on the stereo ("I hate this shit. This is the owner's shit.") for a white-label bootleg. Then he produced from a drawer a tiny sachet of what looked like sand. "Brown sugar, my friend. A favor returned."

William was by this point projectile sweating. There was no fan up here, and the only window, cracked onto an airshaft, was too yellow from smoke to see through. He'd observed the junkies under the El tracks up at 125th, and nodding out on the front steps of his building, and at that moment, he had not a self-destructive bone in his body. He should have said, *No thanks*, and turned and not looked back. Should have gone back to Hell's Kitchen and put in another couple hours on his painting. On the other hand, was this not life, too, trying to tell him something? And was his job, as an artist, not to hear what it was saying? He said, All right, cool, and the friend—or was it acquaintance, really?—said, "Hey, wait wait wait wait wait. You don't want a taste?"

William got out his blade and looked around for a surface to cut some lines on, but again the guy, whom frankly William was starting to wonder if he even *liked*, stopped him.

"No no no no, man," he said, as if William were a child playing with a can of roach spray. "This is caviar. You've got to boot it."

As the guy tied him off, William looked away. His fear of needles, when he was a kid, had been legendary. Every time Regan retold the story of his tetanus booster, the number of nurses who'd had to help Mom hold him down grew. Apparently, though, fear was merely the mask fascination wore to hide itself from itself. Or at least he was fascinated now, a little aroused, as if perhaps this was the thing he'd been looking for these last few months, as the band's future grew dimmer. *The distinguished thing.* Now where had he come by that phrase? The smell of cooking drugs was like burnt hair or corn, or like dental work, acrid but sweet. There was a hand on his upper arm and a vituperative little pinch. "Keep still, brother. You're squirming."

"I don't feel anything," he said. And then he was descending arm-first into a body-temperature bath, wondering disinterestedly as it reached his waist if he was going to come in his pants. His face was traveling away from his what, his soul, which was swimming down into the warmth, which was where God was. And this was only the first ten seconds. He felt his jaw hit his chest, where it was clearly meant to be.

Righteous. Am I right? The voice came from far, far away.

He heard another voice an octave lower than his own, a beautiful lush voice, purr, "Righteous." He was only dimly aware of the first voice, owner of neither purr nor jaw, tying itself off now, and then later telling William he could stay up here as long as he wanted, when really what William wanted to know was was it possible to get higher.

The speaker cabinets went up and up. The record was about Cortés the conquistador, the killer, and it was angelic, big coppery clouds of guitars sailing like galleons toward the rise where William stood watching, stark naked, in a breeze sweet and chaste off the pavements and dumpsters outside. There was something infinitely sad, and thus infinitely beautiful, about these ships and the green sea and the Yucatecan sunset and the little particles of ash in the follicles of the carpet. He wanted to paint the gray specks, the distinguished green. The *distinguished thing* was death, of course, Death was coming already from the far shore to which it had removed his mother, but if this was what it felt like, then as Nicky said, *Who gave a fuck?* The ships were too far off to hurt him anymore and he watched for a while, naked in his skeleton mask, as someone came and someone left and the cannons sparkled on the hillsides like beads of drool on an armrest. He could barely get the needle moved back to the beginning of the side, and then after a while he didn't need to. The music was inside. He had crawled inside the speaker.

22

THOSE FIRST FEW WEEKS OF GRIEF COUNSELING, Charlie took the LIRR in. He was always late, though; invariably his train would get hung up in the East River tunnel. He couldn't tell how much time had passed unless he asked other people—his dad's watch still lay in a coffin-shaped box in his underwear drawer—and they were already looking at him funny because he was doing his nervous humming thing. The stares only made him more nervous, which led to more humming, and when he came out of the subway he'd bolt the last five blocks to the doctor's and arrive sweaty and short of breath, sucking on his inhaler. Dr. Altschul must have said something to Mom, because after he got his driver's license, in May, she insisted on his taking the station wagon, as she'd insisted on the counseling in the first place.

The office was on Charles Street, in the half-basement of a brownstone you wouldn't necessarily have known was anything other than a residence. Even the discreet plaque below the buzzer—*All appointments please ring*—made no mention of specialties. This was probably for the peace of mind of clients (patients?), so no one in the waiting room would know what you were there for, who needed board-certified grief counseling and who needed whatever it was Dr. Altschul's wife (also, confusingly, named Dr. Altschul) did. Honestly, that Dr. Altschul should be married at all was a mind-bender. He was the kind of bosomy overweight man who could make even a beard look sexless. Charlie kept trying to memorize the doctor's zippered cardigan, so that he could determine at the next session if it was the same one. But as soon as he'd settled in, Dr. Altschul would sort of tip back in his large leather chair and place his hands contentedly on his belly and ask, "So how are we doing this week?" Charlie's own hands stayed tucked under his thighs. *We* were doing *fine.*

Which could mean only one thing: Charlie was still *in denial.* For eight or ten weeks now, he'd been resisting the pressure of Dr. Altschul's questions, the Buddha-like invitation of those flattened but not knotted fingers. Charlie focused instead on the oddments of the therapist's desk and walls—diplomas, little carved-wood statuettes, intricate patterns woven into the tasseled rug. He'd had the suspicion, from the very first, that Dr. Altschul (*Bruce,* he kept telling Charlie to call him) meant to vacuum out his skull, replace whatever was there with something else. It was connected with the doctor's studious skirting of the word "father" and its equivalents, which of course kept the person they referred to at the very front of Charlie's mind. But suppose they were right: the school guidance counselor, his mom. Suppose the dead father lodged in his skull was making him sick, and suppose Dr. Altschul could pry Dad out, like a bad tooth. What, then, would be left of Charlie? So he talked instead about school and pee-wee league, about the Sullivans and Ziggy Stardust. When given a "homework" assignment—think about a moment he'd been scared—he talked about the terrifying dentist his mom used to make him go see on the thirty-eighth floor of the Hamilton-Sweeney Building; how old Dr. DeMoto once scraped his plaque onto a saltine and made him eat it; and how the window, inches away from his chair, gave onto a sheer drop of six hundred feet. Mom had this idea that for the finest care, you had to go to Manhattan. In fact, maybe ponying up for a fancy headshrinker now was contrition for Dad; maybe she thought if he'd been rushed after the second heart attack to a hospital in the City, he'd still be alive. "Heights—that's what scares me," Charlie said. "And fires. And snakes." One of these wasn't even true. He'd put it in to test Dr. Altschul, or throw him off the trail.

Then one Friday, a month before school ended, he found himself holding forth with unexpected vehemence about Rabbi Lidner. This had been another of his "homework" assignments, to "recover" his feelings about his adoption. "Abe and Izz will do fine with the

Torah study, it's in their blood, but honestly, sometimes I feel sorry for them. They don't know what they're in for."

There was a twitch, a resettling of fingers on the cardigan, like a cellist's on his instrument, a movement at the corner of the therapeutic mouth too quick for the beard to camouflage. "What is it you feel they're in for, Charlie?"

"All this stuff about being shepherded, watched over . . . You and I both know it's bullshit, Doc. If I was any kind of brother, I'd take them aside and tell them."

"Tell them what? Shall we role-play?"

Charlie let his gaze rest on Dr. Altschul's pantheistic tchotchkes. "You know. You are alone, you were alone, you will be alone."

"This is a worldview you have."

"I've only been saying this for like two months now. What I feel is, basically, you're an alien dropped on a hostile planet, whose inhabitants are constantly trying to tempt you into depending on them. Have you seen *The Man Who Fell to Earth*?" Charlie's face was hot, his asthma tightening his throat. "I realize that maybe sounds like a metaphor, but you listen to David Bowie, he's thinking about what people will face in the future. I guess I'm trying to, too. Because there's two ways of taking off a band-aid."

Was it the cardigan he was allergic to? Its lurid flamestitch pattern seemed to fill the room. And right then, in that moment of weakness, was when the doctor pounced. "Charlie, what do you remember about your father?"

All of Charlie's beautiful rope-a-dope had deserted him. "You make it sound like he died thirty years ago."

"This is what we call an evasion, Charlie."

"What if I just said fuck you? Would that be an evasion?"

"It makes you angry when I ask about your father?"

"Is our fifty minutes up?"

"We've got another half-hour."

Charlie resolved to sit there silently with his arms crossed for the remainder of the session, but after a couple of minutes, Dr. Altschul offered to pro-rate. He seemed to feel a little bad, but probably this, too, was a ploy. They obviously trained them not to have feelings. As Charlie rose to open the door, the doctor told him that his "homework" this week was to *think about it*. A red-haired lady out on the waiting-room couch looked up, curious; *Think about what?* He had an urge to grab the magazine from her hands and rip it in two. Instead, he said something a girl at school had said to him once: "Take a picture, it'll last longer." And fled through the narrow basement door, grazing his head on the overhang.

It was midday now, the air hotter and stiller than it had been when he went in. The lime-green pelt of pollen on the cars boxing in Mom's wagon let you know they hadn't been driven in a while. Nor had the street been swept; rotten mulberries from the trees littered the asphalt like dog shit. Charlie kept walking. As the blocks piled up between him and the grief counselor's office, his indignation ripened into something almost like pleasure. Messiness, death, righteous anger: this was Charlie's world. It *pleased* him that the berries were spoiling and the brownstones were falling apart and the plastic window of a convertible he passed was slashed, wires spilling from its dashboard where the radio had been. It was Dr. Altschul who was the freak, hunkered in his anal little cave, trying to sell Charlie on a world that made sense. It was Dr. Bruce Altschul who was in denial.

On Bleecker Street, a speaker out front of a record store blasted Jamaican music. He saw two leather-jacketed boys, one black, one white, loitering inside between deep bins of LPs. Charlie's normal move would have been to hurry past, but the bright, clear flame of defiance was still lit; woe betide anyone who tried to fuck with him now. Not that the boys even saw him come in. They were not so much loitering, actually, as pretending to loiter, while a person he hadn't noticed snapped pictures from across the store. "Good," she said. "That's great. Except can you try not to look at the camera, dumbass?"

All it took was the voice. It was *her:* the girl from the ballfield. The hair was different, or maybe it was that the headphones were gone, but her features were still larger than life: the pierced nose, the wide, expressive mouth. He flipped through some nearby records. Quick glances took in more of the boys across the shop. Or men, possibly, in a kind of uniform. Slogans in various hues covered their black jackets, superseded by an identical logo freshly painted on the back of each. The white guy's hair was short and uneven, as if cut by lawnmower. The black one wore a stocking cap. The camera would make them look lost in contemplation of the record stacks; click, click, it went, a devouring sound, or so Charlie imagined. In reality it was impossible to hear over the deep-dish bass thumping off every surface. Then the white one, the giant one, announced he was bored. "Are we done yet?"

"Are you kidding? You do this like every day, Sol."

"Yeah, but not in front of a camera. You didn't tell us that would make it be so boring. Plus Nicky would kill me if he found out. No more cameras, he says."

"Nicky, Nicky, Nicky. Why should I listen to someone who refuses to even meet—"

"—only 'cause you never put down the fucking camera! Anyway, I got to get to work."

"Fine, whatever," the girl said. "I'm out of film anyway. Go screw." But once the guys drifted out the door, she started aiming her lens around at the perfunctory record store crap, the posters on the wall, the smoldering joss sticks, the caged ferret, et cetera, et cetera. It landed, eventually, on Charlie. The eye not blocked by the camera opened and then narrowed, as if to bring a memory into focus. "Hey, wait a minute. I know you. How do I know you?"

When he tried to speak, the heavy patchouli odor became a tickle at the back of his throat, leading to a coughing fit, and then wheezing, and ultimately to the inhaler. "The VFW field," he managed finally, little tears in the corners of his eyes. "You had headphones on." And did the universal sign language for headphones.

"Oh, shit, that's right. What are you doing here, though?"

He looked over at where the matching jackets had been. "What's anybody doing here?" he said. "Getting the hell off Long Island."

Back there in the dugout, the girl had been a schoolkid, like Charlie; now she was the emissary of some more adult world. "Listen, I've been up since yesterday morning, and I've got to get some caffeine. You want to come with?" He wondered if she wasn't hustling him out of the store to spare herself the embarrassment of being seen with him, should her friends return, but outside she stuck out her hand. "I'm Sam, by the way. I didn't mean to give you the third degree back there."

"Jesus, no. It's just weird running into you again like this. Shouldn't you be in school?"

"Shouldn't you?"

"I had a doctor's appointment. Otherwise, my mom wouldn't let me drive in."

"Right, the bloodhound. I remember." She lit a cigarette. He willed himself not to cough. "My dad can be pretty bad, too, but he thinks I had a volleyball tournament last night. All he'd have to do to verify I've never touched a volleyball in my life would be to pick up the phone, but then he'd have to have me around and, like, talk to me instead of hiding out in his workshop. And anyway, who would want to miss all this?" It was true. Greenwich Village on a Friday at lunch-time was the opposite of everything Charlie hated about the suburbs. People everywhere, street musicians, smells of fifteen different foods floating out of the propped-open doors. In a smoky luncheonette, she led him to a booth by the window and ordered two coffees. The waitress stared at her until Sam said, "What?"

"You couldn't order egg salad or something? This is becoming an everyday thing, Sam."

"I'll make it worth your while—promise."

The coffee came in paper cups, as if inviting them to vamoose, but she picked hers up and blew on it and took a drink, black. "So what's wrong with you?"

"Huh?" he said.

"Your doctor's appointment."

"It's, um . . . not that kind of doctor."

"Well, obviously, in this neck of the woods, and if you're driving in by yourself. It's a shrink, right? I meant, are your folks splitting up, or what's the story?"

"My dad—" Charlie coughed again. When he'd finished, his voice came out quieter than he meant it to. "My dad died in February. Right before I saw you, I guess."

"Fuck! You should have said something. Are you okay?" she said, and put a hand on his hand. His heart almost stopped.

"I don't want to talk about it."

"I respect that. Most guys, they'd just use something like that to get in your pants."

Outside, pigeons scrabbled over scraps at the curb. He pretended to like coffee, and after a while did. "You must come here a lot, to know the waitresses."

"After my mom split on us, my dad decided to spring for a fancy school." He admired the casual way she repaid his confidence with a confidence. "It's right around the corner. And I start at NYU in the fall. I should only be a senior, but I skipped a grade."

"And your friends, the guys at the record store . . . ?"

She smiled. "Sol, the tall one, I know through his girlfriend, who I know from shows. I've been putting together this little like magazine thing, trying to document the scene. But it took me three months before his friends would let me take photographs. One of them still won't. They can be funny about who they let in."

"I meant do they go to school with you."

"School's not punk."

"Punk?"

"I can see I'm going to have to educate you."

He used a spoon to dredge up the coffee-browned sugar crystals from the bottom of his cup and licked them, like a bee harvesting nectar. "I'm highly educable."

For some reason, it made her laugh. "Anyone ever told you you're a charmer, Charlie?"

He shrugged; no one ever had.

"Seriously, Sol and those other guys, the Post-Humanists, their idea of changing the world is just to say no to everything. I don't think you can really change anything unless you're willing to say yes. No, I've already decided. Us Flower Hill kids have to stick together. You're going to be my project."

Charlie felt that perhaps there was something not right about this, implying as it did a need for improvement. On the other hand, it was a nice day, he was no longer in the therapist's office, and he had the attention of a beautiful girl. Out on the street again, they dumped their empty coffee cups into an overfull trashcan. Charlie wasn't deft enough to avoid bringing a whole mortifying mound of soda bottles and newspapers and Styrofoam takeout containers crashing down around his Hush Puppies, but Sam just laughed again, and it wasn't the kind of laughter that subtracted anything; it was a warm breeze lifting him up.

Then Sam was planting her fingers around Charlie's shoulder-blades and propelling him back through the door of the record store. The register was on a raised platform near the back. The bearlike clerk, too, seemed to know Sam, for he nodded at her from on high. Charlie drifted over to the *B*'s and began to flip through *Ba, Be, Bi, Bo*. The Bowie selection was impressive, at least compared to the cruddy little strip-mall storefront he was used to. There was a colored-vinyl single of "Suffragette City" and an expensive live recording with a sticker that said *Import*. He wanted to look at it more closely, but as soon as he saw Sam coming he put the record back in its place and reached for another tab at random.

"George Benson? Yikes!"

"What? No. I was just goofing around."

"Well, here's your first mission, should you choose to accept it." She handed him a 45.

There was a turntable near the register where you could listen to records pre-purchase. Sam placed the headphones on Charlie's head—a weirdly intimate gesture—and cued up the B side and watched his face while he listened. At first, he thought there was something wrong with the headphones; the music was a distant tempest of revved-up drums and guitars. But when the instruments locked up and the chanting started, he understood it was a style: amateur, noisy, aggressive. It was anger heated to the boiling point where it became a sort of joy—the very feeling Charlie had felt this morning, storming out of the doctor's office. When he looked up, Sam's mouth was moving. He took off the headphones. "What?"

"Amazing, right?"

"It is amazing. But I don't have any money."

"I'll buy it for you."

"I can't let you do that."

"Sure you can. Anyway, I owe you."

"For what?"

"You said you have a car, right? You're driving me home."

And so he did, doing his best to kick his eight-tracks under the seats of the station wagon so she wouldn't be able to read the labels. She lived on the other side of Flower Hill, where the development stopped, in a white-sided ranch house with a hill sloping down behind it. As they sat at the curb out front, she made no move to go. From the backyard came a noise like the drone of a plane. "What's that?"

"Nothing," she said. "Only my dad. If he's not sleeping, he's working."

He felt like he should say something else, ceremonialize the moment. Not that this had been a date or anything like that, but it had been more or less the happiest he'd been since back before the twins.

"Well, thanks for the education."

"Yeah, no sweat."

"Maybe we could hang out again some time."

"Do you think you could get this car? We could hit the city in style."

"Sure. My mom never goes much of anywhere these days. She's studying for her real-estate license. And she's got to take care of my brothers."

"You didn't say you had brothers."

"Twins, yeah. They're just babies."

"You're a real mystery man, Charlie. I didn't know we had any of those left in suburbia." She used a finger to write her phone number in the dust on the dash. "Call me this week and we'll figure something out. And don't forget to listen to the A side. There will be a quiz."

As she tripped across the lawn to her front door, he tried to file away the contours of her jeans and the exact shade of her hair. Brown was too . . . prosaic somehow. More like a butter-rum Life Saver. Then—what was he, some kind of numbnuts?—he scrabbled under the seat for a pen and copied her phone number onto the crinkly paper of the record-store bag. That night, as he began wearing out the grooves on "City on Fire!" by Ex Post Facto, he would touch the inked digits every five minutes or so, as if to reassure himself that the wind hadn't blown them away.

FOR THE PROPHET CHARLIE WEISBARGER, that would be the year punk started: 1976. Later, as he learned more, it would seem like other years had a claim on the title, 1974, 1975, late Stooges, early Ramones, but that spring-into-summer was when the culture first made itself known to him. On Fridays and Saturdays and sometimes Sundays, he would pick Sam up at her house or, if she'd stayed out the night before, meet her in the Village. They would goof around, shoplifting from drugstores, magic-markering song lyrics on the boards surrounding demolition sites, and collecting discreet photos of the ratty kids you saw more and more on the streets of Manhattan, down where the grid went crooked, the ragged and dispofucking-sessed. Often in her bag she had a bottle from the liquor cabinet back home—it had been her mom's; her dad's drink of choice was beer—and when she found out Charlie couldn't smoke grass on account of his asthma, she proved adept at coming up with airplane glue and Quaaludes and painkillers, the greens and the blues. These latter made time stretch; he had memories of looking up from stoops they'd plopped down on, smiling at the various freaks who paraded by. The City comforted him in a way the Island never really could, because it was impossible, just statistically, for him to be the freakiest person here. Once, he squatted with her near the entrance of a Carvel store watching strange hats, ripped pants, cosmic boots go marching by, with chocolate ice cream running down his fingers like mud. (His left hand felt like it belonged to someone else—occasionally handy in private, but awkward most of the rest of the time.) A passing homosexual in tiny shorts clucked and shook his head at the pair of them, the poor lost children, and Charlie couldn't help making a wisecrack, as if Mickey Sullivan was still around. But he backpedaled when Sam, citing the principle of freak solidarity, called him on it. "I meant it as like a tribute," he said. "The way certain kinds of blasphemy refer to God."

"You're not as dumb as you look, are you?" she teased him, and he could feel a bubble of warm liquor expanding and rising in his head.

"You're the one who skipped a year, College Girl."

"No, I'm a lot of things, but I'm not smart like you, Charlie. You're like the smartest dimwit I know."

Then came the endless hours at that luncheonette of hers, trying to sober up on coffee before the drive home. She told him more about how her mom had taken off with a yoga instructor, and he talked a little bit about his adoption, and his dad.

Mostly, though, they talked about music. Punk was a jealous god, who could not abide the existence of other musics besides itself, so Charlie didn't dare tell Sam about his enduring affection for *Honky Château*, but having steeped himself in photostatted 'zines, he could now talk knowledgeably about Radio Birdman and Teenage Jesus and the Hunger Artists and argue the relative merits of Ex Post Facto and Patti Smith. In private, he thought *Horses* might be the greatest album ever made; a song called "Birdland" he must have listened to a thousand times. Out loud, though, he agreed with her that the demise of the bassist, and subsequently of the band, made Ex Post Facto's *Brass Tactics* the more valuable document. She'd dubbed it for him on eight-track, and they sat in the car near the West Side Highway coming down off glue and soaking in the majesty of the music. He cranked the volume as high as it would go, because he wouldn't be able to give it the decibels it deserved at home; his mom was a master of defeating the purpose. That whole time he was hanging out with Sam, she thought he was at therapy or at the beach with Shel Goldbarth, or seeing *Jaws* three times in a row at the Hempstead Triplex. Consequently, the latest he could manage to stay out was his ten o'clock curfew. Just when Sam was getting ready to head to the Sea of Clouds or CBGB, he'd be exiled again to Long Island. He would stop at a gas station to rub soap on his shirt to cover the smell of Sam's cigarettes and to gargle away the pasty aftertaste of pills with the travel-sized bottle of mouthwash he carried. Mom never mentioned how clean he smelled; she was usually in bed when he got home anyway. He suspected she was just relieved he'd found the *friends* he seemed to be spending so much time with, per Dr. Altschul's "prescription."

Only one thing about it bothered him, really: What was in it for Sam? She had this whole other p.m. life in which Charlie couldn't participate, except to drag out of her on the phone the next day every ecstatic detail of whatever show she'd been to. She could have spent the days, too, hanging out with her cooler friends, Sol Grungy and the others. And yet, when Charlie was around, those long afternoons, it was just him and her. He wasn't a total moron; he knew she liked having the Weisbarger family wagon at her disposal. But was that really why she was spending so much time with him? Or did she, like . . . *like* him, or something?

"CHARLIE, THIS ISN'T about our last session, is it? Because we're going to have to talk about that sooner or later. I'm a grief counselor, remember."

"That has nothing to do with this, Bruce. It's a decision I came to on my own."

"And how does your mother feel about it?"

"She's not the one who has to come sit here. I'm old enough to think for myself."

"The goal of therapy isn't really for you to be . . . how did you put it—"

"Cured."

"Cured. Besides which, we've never really gotten down to what you're grieving about."

"But if I can't be cured, what would be the point of doing all this? Or can't you imagine there's any way for a person to grow or change without a shrink being involved?" He and Sam had practiced. "And why doesn't therapy ever seem to make anyone better? It's like some kind of perpetual motion machine."

"I'm hearing hostility in your voice, Charlie, that makes me think there's a personal element here. If that's the case, you should know that there are many other counselors with different approaches. I'd be happy to refer you across the hall to my wife, for example, or to a different practice altogether."

"Nope, Doc. I'm telling you. Cured."

The counselor studied him. The ends of his fingers pushed up from the nubbly cardigan like a range of small mountains. Charlie had never before noticed he was double-jointed. "Well in that case, I guess we're done here. Though I'll have to bill you for the whole hour."

"Send it to my mom," he said, and walked out of the office and toward the end of the block, where Sam was waiting, whistling the opening bars of "Gloria." The Patti version.

23

I'S HARD TO EXPLAIN to anyone up North, but Southern winters are their own kind of harsh. The milder climate means no one knows how to insulate a house, and as the day gets colder, light runs off the harrowed fields, receding toward the pines. Between here and there is this sense of utter emptiness, like if you hollered even animals wouldn't hear you. And all the dread of it Mercer had felt growing up returned, with interest, over the Christmas break of 1975. Despite the fact that his father hadn't said a word to him since his departure for New York, his mother contrived multiple excuses for them to gather 'round the armchair where Pop was now confined and behave as if things were normal. *Normal*, in this case, meant Mama performing her monologues about which of her church friends was in poor health and how well C.L. was doing in residential treatment in Augusta, as Mercer shifted uneasily on the ottoman. He felt like an asshole with his trim new moustache, his department-store clothes. Mama seemed not to notice how much of his native drawl was gone, but though Pop's eyes never left whatever object occasioned the gathering (plate of food, Christmas tree, TV) he winced visibly whenever his son spoke. When Mercer felt that he'd had enough—that he would explode literally this time, leaving bits of brain hanging from the wallpaper—he volunteered to let Sally out, followed the arthritic old collie out to the dead grass the porchlight didn't reach. He was shocked each time by all the stars you could see out here, the same ones the Greeks and Trojans had looked upon, a reminder that you were adrift in an insane vastness where nobody knew your name.

It was only on returning to New York that he could finally breathe again. He found all the lights off in the apartment, but that was nothing new. He didn't think Carlos had gone anywhere for the holidays—wasn't sure Carlos even had a family to go to. Waving away the cigarette smoke near the door, he shouted a greeting. Any sympathy he felt for Carlos, though, vanished when he reached his own room. A draft was lifting the covers of the exam bluebooks stacked by the head of his mattress. Or not a draft—the ceiling fan was on. He scanned his papers and clothes, trying to remember how he'd left them. He walked back out to the living room, searching for Carlos's eyes in the light from outside. "Hey. The ceiling fan in my room is on."

There came a sucking sound like a dry kiss. A face bloomed briefly, orange in the gloom.

"Carlos, did you go in my room?"

"It gets smoky in here."

"Did you go in my room, Carlos?"

Mercer thought he saw a glint, a shrug. "You're just like your brother, you know that?"

He was almost shaking now. "Carlos, I pay you money. It's my room. You can't go in my room."

"You should have seen old C.L. in the jungle, boy. Real twitchy."

Carlos's decision not to leave his chair now revealed its tactical brilliance. If Mercer went over to give him what was coming he would almost certainly end up in traction; yet because Carlos was sitting, it would appear that he, Mercer, had been the aggressor. He had visions of sirens flashing up the tenement façade, of being wheeled out handcuffed to a stretcher and remanded to Altana. Finally, he retreated to his room. He turned off the ceiling fan, turned the thing on the doorknob that would lock the room behind him. He would figure out how to jimmy his way in tomorrow; for the time being, his things would be safe, assuming Carlos didn't have the energy to break down the door. Just in case, he slid the forty pages of manuscript, untouched since that summer, into his Italian-leather satchel.

"MERCER?" Through the bright strip between the jamb and the door of his loft, William seemed perplexed—not unhappy to see him, but unprepared. Had there been a mistake?

"I had a fight with my roommate," Mercer forced himself to say. "I was wondering if I could maybe crash on your couch tonight, while things cool down."

William glanced back into the interior before taking off the chain. "It's a futon, not a very good one, I'm afraid, but you're welcome to it. How was Dixie?"

"Terrible." But his mouth had broken of its own accord into a grin and was moving toward William's. It was as if that ottoman back in Georgia had been positioned over a cellar door, holding it shut, and what was inside was the fact that he'd all along been dreaming of this. "I missed you."

"Don't say that before you've seen the apartment."

The only other time Mercer had come up, the loft had seemed reasonably tidy (though admittedly, William had hustled him out to dinner in minutes), but now it looked like a tornado had hit. There were clothes covering every surface, plus soda cans, cartons caked with rice, milky jars of paintbrushes, candy wrappers, a shopping cart full of coffeetable books, canvases aslant against walls. From the mouth of a vortex of jockey shorts, the cat, Eartha K., stared coolly. Mercer couldn't not laugh. "Gracious! You're a secret slob."

"When I really start working, I get a little . . ."

"Do you realize how completely touching this is, that you would hide this from me?"

William looked sheepish.

"Let me take care of the counters, at least, William. My way of saying thanks."

He had already started in on the dishes when William cracked a beer from the fridge and plopped down on the futon behind him and began to tease out of him the dreadfulness of Christmas. His own holidays, he said, had come and gone unnoticed. Ex Post Facto used to play an annual New Year's show; without band practice, he hadn't known what to do with himself but work work work.

The warmth of the water on Mercer's hands and of the eyes on his back were a single sensation. "Work work work," he repeated. "Poor you."

William, standing, reached around him and took the dishtowel. "You're adorable, you know. But you've done enough."

"Have I?"

And then they were grappling on the minty floorboards. Belts, shirts came off. Lights went dark. Hands found skin. Everything that could happen happened, right up to the irrevocable, but at the moment when fear pulled him away, Mercer was still, technically, a virgin. "Do you know what I like best?" he asked, panting (as if he knew).

"Mm."

"Just sleeping with someone. Just being next to someone while I sleep."

William seemed willing to go along with this, if not thrilled. And it freed Mercer somehow to change his mind, and then they were grappling for real, two bodies painfully merging.

Afterward, leaving the lights off, they made their sweaty way over to the sleeping area. William shoved some boxes off the bed. He turned to the wall—don't take it personally, he said, but he couldn't sleep without facing a wall. Mercer, for his part, lay awake listening to the motorcoaches downshifting on the street below and the come-ons of hookers working the orifice of the Lincoln Tunnel. He felt roughed up, distantly, but then there was this sense of suspension, of not yet having drifted back into the size and shape and color of his own personal body. Of depths he'd forgotten he was immersed in going clear, like he could swim right down and touch the bottom of his life. He tried to ground himself in his surroundings. There must have been a breach in the window at the foot of the bed, for ice had formed in the corners between the two panes. Outside, the winter-bare fingers of a solitary tree played across the violet sky. How many words would the old Mercer have thrown at this tree, the bones of this tree, the dappled black bones of this wind-whipped tree, and at this sky? And how much farther away would they have carried him from the feeling still gathering inside? Here he was, six months into his new life, and already this creature beside him, white in the streetlight, in whom wild dreams might even now be unfolding, was his.

OF COURSE, history had a way of persisting, as it did now in the person of Carlos. Mercer's solution was to avoid Alphabet City altogether. He might slip in at five a.m. to change for work, or some mornings not at all. He'd installed a travel iron at William's place to flatten the wrinkles out of the previous day's clothes. He would consecrate them with drops of aftershave and then head straight across town to teach. The nights of his own education in Hell's Kitchen were often long, but he felt, purely as a pedagogical matter, that the benefits to his mental health more than offset any exhaustion.

Sexually, William was a naturalist, and preferred to make love at home, in the buff, unaccessorized, on the firm surface of the living room floor or in the little walled-off sleeping nook. The one quirk was that he sometimes asked to be slapped. Well, that and the mirror he'd hung by his side of the bed. But Mercer didn't want to let on that he was too inexperienced to know whether this was anything to feel uncomfortable about. Afterward, cooling, sighing, chafed, he would study the reflection of his sleeping lover there, and would compare it to the unfinished self-portrait tacked to the wall. The hair in the drawing was shorter than that now on the head he loved, but the eyebrows were heavy in just the right way, charcoal for charcoal. To anything William said, they added intensity. The nose: crooked, busted once, William had told him, with that vagueness that let Mercer know better than to ask. But that was where the drawing ended. Below was just white space.

ONE NIGHT in mid-February, or rather, one early morning, Mercer found himself in a phone booth outside a discotheque on Third Avenue. He'd just dropped his key through Carlos's mailslot and moved the last of his things into William's apartment, and they'd stayed out late celebrating. Now it was time to explain his change of address to his mother. He was counting on the absurd hour and the arterial pulse of the music still throbbing inside him to propel him into saying what needed saying. But his courage ebbed at the sound of Mama's voice, muzzy from sleep, as though she were talking through a corner of her scratchy nightgown. "No, you didn't wake me, honey. I was just about to roll out the biscuits."

"What time is it there?"

"Same time as where you are, Mercer, you know that. Is something wrong?"

Nothing is wrong, he thought. *I've met someone. Say it.* The empty phone-book holder dangled like a broken hand. Beyond the light-smeared glass, its acne of fingerprints, a feral-looking man picked through a pile of trash.

"Son?"

"It's nothing," he said. "Nothing's wrong. Just, I'm up, and I was thinking of y'all."

The silence that followed made him wonder how much she already knew. "You haven't been drinking alcohol, have you?"

He closed his eyes. "Mama, you know I don't drink."

"Well, it's nice of you to think of us, honey, but can I call you this weekend? I hate to run up your long-distance . . ."

That he'd placed the call collect was beside the point. Less than a minute later, they'd said their goodbyes and hung up.

Whereupon another of William's virtues came to light: he recognized the limits of words. When Mercer didn't get up from bed the next morning, he didn't ask what was the matter, but simply laid a hand between his shoulderblades.

In fact, everything important about their domestic arrangements had been decided on, like the cohabitation itself, without the indignity of talking about it. It had been decided, for example, that William would move his artistic operations to a studio space he could rent for next to nothing way up in the Bronx. It had been decided, too, that they would not talk about William's family. There were no photographs anywhere, nor any signs of a life prior to this loft apartment, and it seemed natural, almost, that William should have no past. Hadn't he always been for Mercer a kind of mythological being, sprung fully formed out of a fire or a lake or a forehead somewhere? Yet, in almost direct proportion to his reticence on the subject of his own origins, William loved to hear about Mercer's. After dinner, when he'd poured himself a few too many glasses from the economy-sized Chianti he kept on hand, he would get Mercer to shake out the Goodman family laundry again. He loved especially to hear about the utopian ambitions Pop had brought back from the war—his kibbutznik streak, William called it—and about the almost biblical struggles between Pop and C.L. "You know, I never saw it at the time, but I guess I had a little temper, too," Mercer confessed one night, drying the dishes. "Or not so little, actually." And he told William about how he'd knocked his crippled father down the night before he'd left for New York that first time. Back when he'd still believed life moved in Freytag lines, he'd thought this might make a fine early climax for his novel.

"And this is why he won't talk to you?" William was in his usual postprandial posture: stretched out on the futon with his hands on his beltbuckle and his head propped up to watch Mercer clean the kitchenette. "Well, I guess it either has to go outward or inward."

When Mercer looked back, puzzled, it was as if a mask had slipped. William had been thinking out loud, remembering something, and for a few seconds his face didn't know what to do with itself. Mercer suddenly felt the full measure of his disadvantage in age, in financial independence, in skin tone and sexual worldliness—in how much he worshipped William, and wanted him, and needed him. He was sure William, who didn't believe in needing people, wouldn't have wanted him to feel anything but equal, but there was such a thing as power, not granted to everyone equally, and that's just how it was. So, rather than ask, "What goes inward, honey?" he kept his mouth shut like a good boy. And how did this not qualify as trust?

IT WASN'T UNTIL THAT SUMMER, and the Bicentennial celebration, that Mercer had the first inkling there could be anything wrong with these arrangements. After watching the tall ships from up on the roof, they'd made their way down to one of the basement boîtes just starting to spring up south of Houston Street. The fleet was in town, the trains full of sailors. Mercer thought it odd to be going out to dinner rather than watching the fireworks, but the friend who had chosen the venue had plenty of reasons to be suspicious of nationalism, William said. As who didn't. "You've got to stop being so *au fait*." He seemed keyed up, in his white dinner jacket and ripped jeans. But maybe it was just that he'd already had quite a lot to drink; Bullet, the Hells Angel who lived upstairs, had invited his crew over to party, and had been passing out bottles of malt liquor on the roof.

It was nine o'clock when they reached the restaurant. Outside waited a shaven-skulled older man in seersucker and tortoiseshells, and an Oriental woman, much younger, who appeared to share Mercer's ambivalence about being there at all. With fireworks booming invisibly to the west, the introductions were only semi-intelligible: Bruno, Mercer; Mercer, Bruno; William . . . Jenny? Jenny. The woman shifted in her heels, as if longing for sneakers. She said something about the kitchen closing early due to the holiday, but Bruno knew the *maître d'hôtel*—which he pronounced flawlessly, even at high volume.

Anyway, it was a European restaurant, at least as someone who'd never been to Europe imagined it: free jazz on the stereo, butcher paper on a wobbly table, delicate little lamb's-cheek croquettes, candles heating the un-air-conditioned and otherwise unlit storefront to a disorienting degree, turning wine ruddy in the glasses. Since the place had no liquor license, William and Bruno had brought several bottles each, and by the main course were well into the third. Mercer, not wanting to seem a hayseed, had allowed himself a single, tiny pour, and now felt adrift on a sea of warmth, his face slick with it. Laughter would gong out from somewhere in the dimness and he would laugh reflexively, no longer caring what the joke was. He had a sense of similar scenes playing out elsewhere in the city, similar little expatriate conspiracies of good food and good drink while ashes rained down over the Hudson and the Soviets rattled their sabers and scientists in the Midwest moved the hands of the doomsday clock one tick closer to midnight. All you needed was a person who could pay for it.

In this case, he assumed, that patron was Bruno Augenblick. Mercer gathered that Bruno was some kind of art dealer, which might have explained William's nerves, and the purpose of dinner, except that the vibe between them felt non-commercial. At any rate, Bruno was pretty clearly not heterosexual; the companion, the small, possibly Japanese girl who worked at his gallery, and whose name Mercer had already forgotten, seemed to be along mostly to illustrate to William that Bruno had a protégée of his own. Since Bruno was monopolizing William, she and Mercer wound up talking diagonally across the table. He was going into his second year of teaching, he said, carefully, when she asked what had brought him to our fair city. He was thinking of shaking up his syllabus in the fall. As a former high-school girl herself, maybe she could help. Had she read Balzac's *Lost Illusions*?

She'd read *about* it in college at Berkeley, she said, still looking like she wished she were anywhere else. Was Balzac the one Marx liked so much, or was that the other one?

Mercer didn't know, but *Lost Illusions* was one of his personal favorites. Basically, a young poet from the provinces comes to Paris to make his fortune and, in the fullness of time, discovers that he's been wrong about everything. All the people he takes for geniuses are idiots, and vice versa. "This is like a venerable French genre. I've actually been working on an update," he heard himself confess. "In the original, the historical background is the Second Empire, but in mine, it's Vietnam."

The smile across the table seemed to tighten. Because Jenny *Nguyen* was Vietnamese, not Japanese! Oh, cursed, cursed wine.

"I mean, it's early going," he added. "A lot could change."

"Autobiographical?" asked Jenny.

He could feel the blood rising in his head. He hadn't meant for this stuff about the novel to slip out in front of William. "Oh, not at all," he said.

"I just thought, because of that whole 'write what you know'—"

"No, I'm just feeling my way in. Forget I mentioned it."

"It sounds not terrible, actually. You know, I'm sure Bruno knows people in publishing. God knows he knows people everywhere else."

"Oh, no. I didn't mean to suggest . . ."

He looked to his lover, embarrassed, but William was still deep in argument with Bruno. And had somehow obtained a cigarette. Though Mercer had never known him to be a smoker, he had to admit that William looked regal with it, exhaling through his nostrils, and then—just when the ash seemed dangerously long—leaning forward to flick it into the neck of an empty wine-bottle. The ash sailed neatly through the green gloom inside, touching down at the bottom like a horse high-diving in a circus. "Personally, I have high hopes," William was saying, apropos of . . . well, what, exactly? "Failure is so much more interesting. All the evidence suggests that God considers mankind a failure. Things get interesting just at the point where they break down."

Bruno smiled, as if he'd been trying to explain ethics to a headstrong toddler. "You and I only have the luxury of feeling this, of course, William, because our entire lives are nourished by capitalism. We are like the little mushrooms on the log."

Oh, right. This fiscal crisis thing. *FORD TO CITY: DROP DEAD.*

"Which is my point exactly," William said. "Growth from decay."

"An ungainly metaphor, fine. But let us be factual. Let us take your friend, the one who usurped your musical enterprise."

"Nicky Chaos was never my friend. He was just some kid who hung around at shows and happened, Mr. Big Shot Gallery Man, to offer us a practice space when we needed one. I didn't know he was going to take over the damn band."

"You should have seen an insurrection coming. This is one of those people who carries Nietzsche in his pocket with a bookmark halfway through. Did he tell you he came to see me about taking him on as a client?"

"This is Captain Chaos you're talking about?" asked Jenny Nguyen. "The nihilist you can't say no to? I hate dealing with that guy. He called like every day last fall. Seemed a little desperate, honestly."

"Probably because the band had broken up," William said.

Bruno continued. "He believes he is a great artist who also makes music; really he is a bad musician trying also to make art. And what is this art? Spraypaint. For him, *kulturkritik* is moustaches drawn on ladies in your Sears catalogue. He thinks a safety pin is jewelry. He confuses brutality with beauty. This is very American."

"I sometimes think he's trying to become a version of me," William said.

"A more bankable version of you, you mean."

"Don't tell me you agreed to represent him! Jesus, Bruno, I thought better of you."

"As you yourself have discovered, Nicky Chaos takes persistence to the point of obsession. In a way, he is himself a work of art. A fact of which he's no doubt unconscious, or else he would ruin it. But more to the point: One day, I arrange to sell the only canvas he showed me to an acquaintance of mine, a banker. 'An investment,' I tell him. He will never know the difference, a thousand dollars is a rounding error for him. But for Nicholas? He can now afford groceries for a year. Do you think this is possible without the help of the bourgeoisie, all the beautiful, helpless children renting brownstones and dining on osso buco?"

"That place on East Third's a squat. I don't think he's ever paid rent."

"We are like infants, William. I include myself, of course. We may not believe Mama and Papa exist when we cannot see them, but that doesn't mean we don't depend on them."

"But really, this is your definition of 'interesting'?" William had another cigarette lit. For a second, Mercer had the impression he hadn't extinguished the first. "Because if so, look at how your beloved free enterprise system has deformed the word. I mean it. When it comes to replacing your dreams with its own it turns out to be as efficient as any Central Committee."

"But why do the alternatives have to be either corporatocracy or the gulags?" said Jenny, exasperated. You got the feeling she could have ended the argument in about three seconds, had the men bothered to invite her into it. Which maybe was why they didn't.

"Except in this case the dreams are wet ones rather than nightmares. America isn't that far from totalitarianism, Bruno. You just happen to like the perfume she's wearing."

"Only an American would say this."

"Look around you. It's the end of the week, how do we express our dissatisfaction with the system? We go to a restaurant and bitch over screw-top wine. We make ourselves into a bourgeoisie-in-waiting, in case anything should happen to the real McCoy. It revolts me to say this, but I'm with Nicky Chaos on this one. Choice isn't the same thing as freedom—not when someone else is framing the choices for you."

Mercer had the uncomfortable sense of being some kind of case in point. The napkin in his lap was stained like a surgical gown. What would the parents of his students have thought of all this?

"And William, you prefer to the general welfare . . . some Platonic ideal of freedom."

"How could anarchy be any worse for the general welfare than this? I say let the city go bankrupt, the buildings fall, let grass take over Fifth Avenue. Let birds nest in storefronts, whales swim up the Hudson. We can spend mornings hunting for food, and afternoons fornicating, and at night we'll dance on the rooftops and chant shantih shantih at the sky."

"But why leave the band, if you're so politically sympatico with Nicholas?"

"I can agree with him on certain things and still believe fundamentally he's a sociopath."

"In a world with no law, it's the sociopaths who rule. The Stalins, the Maos, you know this, William."

"What do you think, Mercer?" Jenny now interjected; he couldn't tell if she was trying to do him a favor by dealing him into the conversation or calling him out for not extending the same courtesy to her. The skronking jazz from the kitchen had ended abruptly. Three pairs of eyes settled on him.

"I think it may be true," he said carefully, "what Bruno is saying, to the extent that I understand it. But that doesn't mean it's not depressing. The reason we can say anything we want in America is that we know it makes no difference."

Whatever pride Mercer had felt in this little *aperçu* dissolved when he saw William and Bruno clink their glasses and drink to it; he'd been mistaken, somehow, about how serious they were. Then William was asking the waiter where the *little boys' room* was. The waiter apologized; it was out of order, awaiting a plumber.

"Well, I suppose I'll have to do this the old-fashioned way. I'll leave you three to talk."

Still grinning, William stumbled up the stairs into a part of town people talked about as if it were the Wild West. Mercer, abandoned, rearranged his napkin. He could feel the owlish gaze returning to him. "So," Bruno said. "How does it feel?"

"Are you going to be obstreperous all night, Bruno?" Jenny asked. "Because if so, I'll bow out now." Another favor, Mercer realized; for motives he could not imagine, Jenny Nguyen had been trying all night to throw him a rope.

"You are right, my dear, as usual. I withdraw the question."

Still, Mercer wanted to know. "Wait. How does what feel?"

"To be the latest addition to William's collection."

He looked around, but the only help he found was his own bewildered face blinking at him from the mirrored wall. This was why people smoked cigarettes, he saw now, or chose ridiculous glasses. Sans accessories, you were naked.

"See? He had no idea," Bruno said without turning to his companion, who by this point was making a conspicuous show of interest in the contents of her own purse, perhaps looking for cab fare. "Shall I enlighten you?" He crossed his arms. A cigarette burned between two fingers. (It was remarkable how much you could tell about a man from the way he held a cigarette, Mercer thought fleetingly. Bruno, like Carlos, had a considerable threshold for pain.) "As far as I can tell, Mr. Goodman, you are a gentleman. But you should know that our dinner companion has a history of bolting at the first sign of emotional complication. I would hate for you to not be prepared for this."

"You must think you know William pretty well, then."

"He loves to play these what-if games about the coming of the revolution, but there is still in him that thing that is used to having every whim answered, every challenge smoothed away. It's what comes of being raised a prince."

"A prince of what?"

"A prince of New York, of course." His eyes narrowed. "You must know our William is, or was, heir to one of the largest fortunes in the city."

It was as if, Mercer would think later, he had discovered a birthmark William had been hiding—a big one, right at the center of his chest. Why had it been kept from him? (And by whom, really? Mercer couldn't claim not to have noticed the elasticity of his lover's funds, funds as deep as underground springs, and possibly as inexhaustible, or not to have gotten the distinct feeling at times that William had settled in the blighted old factory building in the West Forties not out of poverty, but out of spite.) Furthermore, why was Bruno telling him now? He was about to tell Bruno, untruthfully, that he didn't believe him, when William reappeared, rubbing his nose with his pocket-square. "What did I miss?"

Bruno's fingers steepled in front of him as he watched. *You are an adult*, Mercer reminded himself. But then why did adulthood, the part of your life when you were theoretically freest to pursue what you wanted, always seem to require these compromises? "Nothing," he said. "You didn't miss anything."

"So who's got room for dessert? Anyone?"

Even though Bruno made a show of trying to fight for it, William did end up picking up the check, pulling a roll of twenties from the breast pocket of his dinner jacket. "No, I've got this." Mercer pretended not to see Bruno's knowing look.

Outside, after the foursome had dissolved, William said he would pay for a taxi home. "We can't afford it," Mercer told him. "I don't mind taking the train. Or even walking, it's a nice night"—which it wasn't, it was a sweltering, tropical, miserable night, with the gunpowder stink of the fireworks just ended, and already, out of the humid desertion of post-celebratory streets, a cab had materialized, a big yellow answer to a question Mercer didn't know how to formulate. He let his burning forehead rest against the inside of the window and watched the empty streets scroll by, sparkler sticks, downtrodden little flags, the metal gates of loading docks graffiti'd with the hundred secret names of God.

"How did that go?" William asked.

"You make it sound like an audition. But I feel like the fact of my being black or whatever settled any questions Bruno might have had."

"It's true that Austrians aren't known for their sense of transracial brotherhood."

"You can joke all you want, but I don't like you showing me off like that." The Papaya King on Sixth Avenue was still open. A hunched shadow out front appeared to be vomiting into a gutter, but when Mercer blinked it was only a postal box. "He tried to warn me about you, you know."

"What, that I tried to sleep with him?"

"You tried to sleep with Bruno?"

"I was a kid, Mercer, it was the '60s. Anyway, as I recall, he wasn't having it."

"I mean he tried to warn me about who you are. Where you come from."

"Ah." William's hand, on the back of the seat, brushed Mercer's shoulder gingerly. "But I sort of assumed you'd figured that out already."

"Well, I didn't. I was trying to respect your privacy."

"Don't you see, Mercer, that this is something I love about you?" It was too loud; the driver's eyes swung to the rearview mirror, but William glared fiercely back, and the guy turned up the radio and kept driving. "You're the first person I've ever met who, if I left a diary lying around open, would close it without reading."

"Only because I'd feel guilty. It doesn't mean I want us to have secrets, William."

"Then why didn't you tell me you were writing a novel?"

"You weren't supposed to hear that. It's embarrassing, that's why."

As William touched his cheek, Mercer felt himself, against his will, leaning into the soft, white palm. "So let's give each other some room, some mystery. Make our own utopia. Let Bruno be jealous; he doesn't have what we do." The driver's eyes flitted back to the mirror, and William dropped his hand. But when they passed into a black patch, a sidestreet where all the lights had been knocked out, their fingers found each other on the seat again.

IF ONLY MERCER COULD HAVE LEFT THINGS THERE. But the next day, while his lover slept off what he didn't yet realize was probably cocaine, he headed across town to the library. He trudged up the marble steps between Patience and Fortitude, two leonine friends he hadn't seen since those uncomplicated days when he was just another reading-room arriviste.

The periodicals division was a grotto off the first floor, redolent of burnt coffee and aged paper. That afternoon, and for several that followed, he hunkered down at one of the macrocephalic machines, pages of microfilm spooling past too fast, really, to read. It was like his life, somehow—a thing you watched go by much too quickly, and the only real decision in your hands was to stop or keep going. It was hard to know how far back to look—'69? '65? Finally, from 1961, he found a society page article on the impending marriage of Felicia Marie Gould of Buffalo, New York, to William Stuart Althorp Hamilton-Sweeney II, Chairman and CEO of the Hamilton-Sweeney Company. In a photograph, the couple stood shoulder-to-elbow, attended by family. The groom was dignified, the bride-to-be resplendent. When Mercer attempted to adjust the size of the image, the machine whinged nervously. Not pictured: the bride's brother. To one side, though, stood a woman identified as the daughter of the groom, flanked by her own fiancé . . . and then the son, a late-adolescent William. Mercer had never seen a picture of him from this era before, and a great tenderness or forgiveness welled up in him. William was even skinnier than he was now, his body slumped like a question mark in its too-big suit. And something was wrong: he looked as if it were consuming him whole, from the inside. No wonder he didn't want to talk about it.

Outside, the big old plane trees heaved in amber light, as though signaling to the rush-hour buses on the avenue. A door spun behind him—it was closing time, shouts of guards were echoing under the vaulted ceilings, telling all the pale, sedulous scholars it was time to go—but it was as if the air dissolved them on contact, or as if the broad spaces of the raised plaza diluted them, because the only people left out here seemed to be mendicants and the mentally ill. A woman with fingerless gloves approached, and Mercer had foisted a handful of pocket-change on her before he recognized her as his erstwhile colleague, the one with the giant handwriting. Watching her walk away, he felt guilty for not letting her finish whatever she was asking him; why was he in such a hurry? Was it mere forgetfulness, or something graver? He would wonder again a week later, when, wandering toward the foot of Madison, he turned and saw the inscription chiseled like a bad joke into the limestone pediment of the tallest structure there, the one with the golden finial. *The Hamilton-Sweeney Building*, it said.

24

WHEN HE'D LEFT AMERICA IN 1974—its dirty wars, race riots, drug culture, Watergate—the whole country had seemed to Richard Groskoph to be in flames. What he was looking for was a place without news, and on a small island in the north of Scotland, he'd more or less found it. Why Scotland? It was the country of his mother's grandparents, for one thing. For another, he wouldn't have to learn a new language. There were Park Avenue high-rises with more residents than the village where he found a farmhouse for rent. The money would have to be paid back eventually—he'd abandoned his hypothetical book, that search for a last story—but eventually was so far off, and in the meantime, his advance remained surprisingly fungible. For companionship, he bought a terrier from a neighbor. He called it Claggart because he'd always thought Melville had been too hard on Claggart in *Billy Budd,* and because the name seemed to fit the squat furry body, the officious muzzle butting at his shin, demanding food or a walk.

By day, Richard gardened and read and carpentered to the accompaniment of bad pop radio. By night, he ambled down the shoulderless road to the village for the one drink he still allowed himself. And were it not for television, things could probably have gone on this way. He didn't keep a TV set in his hermitage, as a matter of policy—easier just to saw a hole in the roof, or in the roof of his skull, and call back down the demons—but on a high shelf in the pub sat a small color model, years out of date, used mostly for football matches. One night he came in to find it on. From her stool near the door, the widow Nan McKiernan tipped her sherry his way, in obscure congratulation. He followed her gaze to the TV. The smoggy pink sky pictured there was unmistakably not Scotland's. And now here came the greening copper of Lady Liberty turning slowly past the helicopter window, and great white flocks of boats and the airy towers of Manhattan heaving into view behind. How could he have forgotten? It was the Fourth of July, the American Bicentennial. Which meant he'd been at large now for two solid years.

As he splurged on a second drink, and then a third—calling it *Scotch*, like a tourist—the sky onscreen faded to the color of the one outside. Sparks burst across it, lapidary handfuls of blue and red and gold, like memories of his earliest summers in Manhattan. Only not really, the BBC was saying: in the wake of the fiscal crisis, the City had switched contractors, and for the first time ever, these fireworks were being directed by computer. Did it matter, Richard wondered, that it was robots instead of men in the boats, lighting the fuses? But then, wouldn't some nuance, some human thing, be lost? And would the computer remember to mail a special program of music to the radio stations, keyed to the detonations? Surely they still did that. Surely "Rhapsody in Blue" was even now ringing from every car on that other island, to which he'd once belonged. And suddenly his whole journalistic apparatus was up again and humming, for here, he saw, was the vehicle he'd been waiting for, the missing story. History, scenery, fate, impermanence, disaster, politics, the city, all packed into a single shell, awaiting combustion. Music made visible: fireworks.

The display went on and on. Rehearsing the million ways one might narrate it, Richard barely noticed the dog's plaintive whimper at his feet, or the ring of the till discharging its drawer, or the chairs being turned upside down on the tables. He didn't even want to blink. Then, just at the start of the grand finale, the light onscreen dwindled to a point and died. The barman had pulled the plug. Down by the window, the widow Nan McKiernan had vanished like an apparition, leaving only empty stemware. Richard dropped too many pound notes on the bar and made to follow. Claggart hesitated, looking fretful.

"What?"

But somehow Claggart must have known, even before Richard did: a week later, he'd be back in New York with the dog under an arm, unlocking the apartment, steeling himself for the dust and the mouse droppings that had doubtless accumulated there in his absence, and all the other imperfections that never showed up in memory.

THE LONG ISLAND ADDRESS HE GOT FROM A SOURCE didn't look like the third-largest pyrotechnics outfit on the East Coast, or really the third-largest anything. It was just a gravel drive at the end of a cul-de-sac, leading back past a modest, ranch-style house. God, these houses! He stuck a twenty in his cabbie's hand and told him to keep the meter running. Batik curtains gave the windows a closed, impassive look. Richard pushed the front doorbell, pressed his ear to the storm door's glass. Nothing. Or not nothing; there was another, deeper sound—a kind of low thunder gathering not within the house, but behind it. Hoping his old fedora and necktie made clear he wasn't an intruder, he walked around to the neglected backyard. In a tree near the patio, a treehouse was collapsing. And then tucked into a copse at the bottom of a slope was a corrugated metal hangar the size of a small bungalow. Its sides rumbled. A panel truck was parked alongside: *Cicciaro & Sons Am seme ts*. For ten or fifteen feet in every direction, the grass grew high, an inordinate, overfertilized green.

His knock on the hangar's door brought no answer, but a smell of sulfur seemed to issue from behind it. He knocked again, louder this time, and the rumble deepened, as though downshifting. A voice yelled something he couldn't make out. He called back, "Hello?"

A beefy man in flannel appeared in the doorway before him, lowering his ear protectors to his neck. He had hair the color of iron. A workingman's blunt features, like the face of an Orkney plowman, only darker, more stubbled, streaked on one cheek with grease.

"Carmine Cicciaro?"

The man didn't respond.

Richard introduced himself, showed a credential from the magazine that hadn't published a piece of his writing in almost four years.

"I don't read magazines," the man said. He was missing part of the ring-finger on his left hand, Richard noticed. Behind him were the sources of the shuddering: big, industrial fans attached to ventilation ducts. And was that, just visible on a table, a twelve-gauge shotgun?

Richard explained that he was just looking for a comment or two about the Bicentennial fireworks. (This was an old ruse—give them a chance to set the record straight.) "A friend of mine in the Mayor's office said the City decided to go with another contractor this year, and I wanted to make sure I understood the reasoning." It felt good to be reporting again, to feel eye and mouth and memory sync together like parts of a machine. But Carmine Cicciaro had already returned the ear guards to his ears. "I'll give you fifteen seconds to get off my property."

Had Richard's touch deserted him? "Mr. Cicciaro, Benny Blum gave me your name personally, said you were the man to see if I wanted to know anything about anything about fireworks. For what it's worth, he also said he thought it was a mistake for the city to bid the job out to a conglomerate. 'Injustice,' was the word he used."

Cicciaro gave him a look as if, during this whole speech, there had been a piece of spinach in his teeth. "How do you know Benny Blum?"

"We were in Korea together," Richard said. Which was true, technically, though they'd not met until years later, at the poker table.

"You really rode all the way out here from the city?" Then Cicciaro sighed. "Give me a minute." He retreated into the hangar, where the drone of the fans died. When he emerged, he put a padlock on the door. "Can't be too careful nowadays. Anyway, I need a beer."

They ended up in grimy deckchairs, drinking cans of lukewarm Schlitz from a cooler whose ice had long since turned to water. "I keep 'em out here, my daughter won't be tempted," Cicciaro said. "You got kids?" Richard shook his head, no, because "kids" made him think of presences, personalities. Though at this point, his own progeny with the stewardess, boy or girl, would be what? Almost three.

"Can't say that I do."

"Well, it keeps you up nights."

"That's what they say."

"I'd compare it to a constant, low-grade hangover. Luckily, I have extensive training. That's a joke." Cicciaro looked off toward the hangar. "Sammy's got basically a good head on her shoulders, but with a reckless streak she didn't get from me. In the old days, she used to climb up in my lap and talk. They hit thirteen, though, they're women, with all that goes along with that. Hardly ever here these days. And when she is, I can't even describe the noise from the stereo. I have to put up with exhaust fans, but I get paid for it, you know? Or used to. She'll be in college in the fall." He took a long drink of his beer. At this temperature, Richard thought, you could really taste the aluminum.

"You and me, we're a different generation," he hazarded.

"You can say that again. I can remember when there were still horse apples on Mulberry Street. But this isn't what you came here to ask me about."

"Wait a minute. You grew up on Mulberry Street? I used to live on Mott, when I first got to the city."

"We were at 270 Mott, my granddad's old place. We had the apartment above."

"Right across from the church there, the old St. Patrick's," Richard said. He had prepared for this.

"That's the one."

At some point during this beer or the next, Cicciaro would explain how his grandfather had come through Ellis Island in 1907 or '08. "The family legend is that Granddad got chased out of Sicily because some villagers thought he'd made a deal with the devil. Fireworks were in his blood, you know? He knew how to make the powder do what he wanted to do. That's old-time magic, from back to Marco Polo. Came up with the formula we use to this day, six, seven times as potent as in your average grenade. They probably would have let him stay if he didn't use it anymore, but the thing about this job is, you don't choose it, it chooses you." Behind the stoic front, he was obviously as hungry to tell his story as every other person on earth, but Richard didn't want to spook him by getting out too early the folded A4 he habitually kept in his pocket for notes. In America, Cicciaro continued, the grandfather started shooting off rockets even before he found a place to sleep at night. For years, on feast days, the neighbors down on the Lower East Side would gather on stoops and in windows while he rolled up his sleeves and made the fire dance. "Then this guy, this Tammany fixer, spots my granddad one day, looking like he's setting off bombs in the street. People didn't trust Italians then. Sacco and Vanzetti and all that, not to mention the Black Hand in everybody's pocket. So he has him hauled before the ward boss, and my granddad's standing there—or this is how they told it to me—and inside he's falling apart, because those old folks, always in the back of their mind was the threat of being shipped back to Palermo, where people still kept time with sundials. But from the outside, he looks like he's made of stone, which is a Sicilian thing, too. Authority? *Vaffancul'*. Anyway, they weren't going to throw him out of America," Cicciaro said. No, it turned out they wanted him to shoot off bombs for Independence Day, courtesy of the Democratic machine. "Like I said, it chooses you."

Richard saw his opening. "You know, Benny had mentioned some of this to me, but listening to you talk here, I'm wondering if your grandfather's story, and your family's, might become a bigger part of this article than I had imagined. It's a great story, and it might help City Hall see what they're missing when they go with these computers."

"Five years from now, everybody's going to go with computers. But I guess that would be all right, if you wanted to say some things about my granddad."

And here came the part that was always so delicate. "It would mean sitting down for a talk or two, at your convenience. I'd take notes. Things would go on record."

"Oh." There was a pause. The bug zapper zapped a bug. "I don't know, Mr. Groskoph. I'd really have to think about it."

IT WAS HIS DAUGHTER, Carmine would say later, who convinced him to agree to Richard's proposal. He never admitted that he himself did anything other than tolerate the interviews; he would spend the first ten minutes after Richard's arrival puttering among the kitchen cabinets, amassing two baloney sandwiches on crustless Wonder Bread and a warty dill pickle and a can of Schlitz, all to preserve the conceit that this was merely lunchtime, he'd been planning to take a break anyway. But by the time he stopped talking, it would be late, the sandwiches a distant memory. And even then, when whatever gust of self-disclosure had passed, they'd keep sitting out on the slack plastic deckchairs, drinking beer from the mossy cooler, or soda if Richard was feeling virtuous.

Afterward, he would pilot his old Schwinn back through the conurbations of Nassau County and Queens to the number 7 subway terminal in Flushing. Bringing the bike took about an hour extra each way, but it saved cab fare, and what was better than this? The route was bucolic, mostly, through neighborhoods of ersatz-Tudor rowhouses and detached homes, little parks with shade trees that might have dated back to the Dutch. The sun shimmered through the thinning elms and poplars, the air was cider-crisp, the chain hummed, the back wheel ticked. He felt then, and really that entire fall before the shooting, as if he'd managed to convey back across the Atlantic the equilibrium he'd worked so hard on the far side of it to achieve. And sometimes he would stand in his pedals, six-three, forty-six years old, and steer a long, loose arc toward a knot of scrabbling birds at the curbside, just to see them detonate into the air, to freeze one mid-flap with the camera of his mind. For he had made his peace, finally, he thought, with the fact that this was who Richard Groskoph was: a camera attached to a tape recorder. A disappearer into all that was not him. A receiver, a connector, a machine made exactly for this.

25

O N SECOND THOUGHT, maybe Keith had understood more about Regan than he'd admitted to himself back in '61, their last semester before adulthood. At the very least he'd known better than to tell her about his second run-in with the Demon Brother. It had followed hard upon his final exam in organic chemistry, which had revealed, inarguably and somewhat majestically, the depth of his inaptitude for the medical profession. The afternoon the grades were posted, he'd found himself at a payphone in the back of the campus rathskeller. Was it possible he was drunk, though it wasn't yet dark out? Sure, but he felt no more responsible for the former than for the latter. Things happened, he imagined himself explaining to Regan. And now this was happening: his hand was reaching for the receiver. His mouth was asking for Amory Gould.

His datebook would record a meeting the following week at a café on Seventy-Ninth Street near Madison. At the time, Keith couldn't figure out why they didn't just meet at the Hamilton-Sweeney Building, but maybe this was how high finance worked. The greater the altitude attained, the fewer the hours spent behind a desk. And then there was the matter of properties—accoutrements. In his office, Amory would have had only the separate phone-lines Regan had mentioned and maybe a pen and some paperclips with which to fiddle and beguile, but here there were coffee cups, sugarcubes, napkin rings, steak knives, long spoons designed to reach the bottom of milkshake glasses . . . all of which he handled restlessly while leading Keith through a half-hour of Welcome to the Family chitchat. You would have thought Amory had requested the meeting himself, for the purpose of mending, with these arcane instruments, whatever had been breached between himself and Regan. When he slid the laminated menu across the table and told Keith to order anything he wanted, they still had not come within shouting distance of the question of Keith's future.

Yet as Keith ate, Amory's gestures grew somehow quantitative, like the gestures of a man trying to purchase fabric in a language he doesn't speak. The *Quanto costa* gesture, the *No, I couldn't possibly*, the Lachesis gesture of measuring something out to have it cut off. And when the leatherette envelope enclosing the check had been returned to the waiter, he drew his hands into his lap. "Now then. To business."

The effect of the abrupt cessation of movement was to make his head suddenly vivid, as though it had come zooming across the table. Previously, Keith felt, he had glimpsed the man through a fog of unknowing. Now he was seeing the tiny blemishes at the tip of the nose, every capillary in the white of the weak blue eyes. "You have come to me, I gather, in the aftermath of some setback in your education. And because you want solid ground under you before proceeding with my niece-to-be. You want to be sure you can support her in the style to which she is accustomed. You are thinking, in short, of a shift in field."

Keith nodded, like a bird following a bit of waved seed.

"Now as I've said these are exciting times, expansionary times, for the Hamilton-Sweeneys. I'd love nothing more than to make a place for you at the firm."

"Is there a reason you can't?"

"Think, Keith." It was practically a whisper. "You want Regan to see you're landing on your own two feet. She's very particular, as I'm sure you know, about being in anyone's debt. No, what I've taken the liberty of doing instead is arranging for you to meet with my old friend Jules Renard at the firm of Renard Frères. I had only to tell him about you, and he is eager to talk. Provided all goes well, you save up for a couple of years . . ."

It was the same line of argument Keith would use with Regan

after graduation, after the Renards had offered to bring him on in the bonds division in the fall. He even adopted elements of Amory's crabwise approach, inviting her first to the finest French restaurant in Poughkeepsie. But as he broke the news, he could see he'd bumped up against something in her that caused pain. "I thought you'd be happy," he said. "I was never smart enough to be a doctor, we both know that, and this way we could really stand on our own feet. I mean, if that was something we ended up wanting to do."

"Why are you trying to make this my decision, Keith?"

But he was off and running, as he'd so often been since that night in the hotel, with their future tucked like a football under his arm. "We could rent a place in the fall wherever you wanted, and in a few years, I'd have enough saved up to buy. You could keep acting. And you'd be close to your brother, which I know is a concern. Are you crying? Why are you crying?" And why in a restaurant this expensive was the table so damn big? He ended up having to scootch his chair around the side to hold her hand, though to other diners it must have looked impulsive; Regan's distress had again become nearly undetectable, except for that little stone or lozenge stuck in her throat. "I love you," she said.

"I love you, too."

"And I trust you, honey."

"You make it sound like a warning."

"It's not, but—"

"So trust *us*, then," he said, and stroked her ring-finger with his thumb. By the time of her father's wedding, which is to say her brother's disappearance, he'd have placed a diamond of her own there, bought on installments that, on a bond trader's salary, he figured he ought to be able to pay off by the end of the year.

RATHER THAN SUBJECT NEW HIRES to any real training process, the Renard frères threw them in among the veterans and saw who had the will to survive. Keith assumed he would be one of that select group. He had a wife, after all, who'd thought she'd be marrying a doctor, and to whom he felt he owed a reasonably quick, reasonably large success. But the Demon Brother's influence had its limits. That first week after passing his Series 7, Keith sat eight hours a day in the semi-privacy of his cubicle, watching the black leather oblong of his trading book atrophy like cooling lava on his desk. Beyond the pebble-glass partitions, the ringing of phones formed a vivid, angelic continuum, but his own phone stayed mute in its cradle, until, Friday morning, the head of the guy at the next desk rose like a balding half-moon above the glass. Tadelis, was his name. Every name here was a last name, or ended in a vowel—Mikey, Matty, Bobby—or both. "Wake up, Lamplighter. You're making us look like geniuses out here."

"I can't seem to get anything going."

The noise Tadelis made was not what was traditionally thought of as laughter; it was more in the way of a spasm ground out between tectonic plates of anxiety. "What, do you think you just wait for the phone to ring and then you pick it up and money flies out? Look around you. Is that what you see? No, seriously, stand up and look."

Renard Frères had adopted an Action Office floorplan, with only these low walls to separate the junior traders. The goal was the free exchange of ideas—a kind of happy medium between the organization man and godless socialism. But all around, in the shallow prisms of the cubicles, were guys like Tadelis, jackets off, hunched over phones in extreme, almost defecatory postures. Hands jiggled pens. Raked thinning hair dark with sweat.

"No, what you see is a bunch of guys nobody ever handed nothing. You see Jimmy O over there? Made the firm a million bucks last year. I'm not sure he even went to high school." Tadelis's voice was somehow both bumptious and conspiratorial, his mouth a pink cloud behind the glass. "Now you come nancying in here like dead weight, and we're all trying to figure out, what's the underlying value of this asset?"

"Pure nepotism," Keith confessed. "A favor to a friend."

"Bullshit. To a big swinging pair like the Renards, there's no such thing as a favor." He narrowed his eyes. "No, I see it now. You may not have an idea in that pretty head of yours, Lamplighter, but people want to do things for you. Look at me, I'm barely clinging to the lower rungs, I should be sandbagging the hell out of you, and here I am offering a hand. You're a salesman. You can sell."

"Not if nobody calls, I can't."

Again, the laugh. "You think those are incoming calls you're hearing? Those are call*backs*, my friend. Now the way this usually works is, you go through that book you've got there, Jimmy Schnurbart's old book, Fat Jimmy, we called him, God rest his fat ass, and any entity you see on the other end of a trade, you dial." Fair enough, Keith thought, but Tadelis wasn't finished. "Except frankly, it's all dead wood at this point."

"Beg pardon?"

"Me and Jimmy O already picked off anything of value for ourselves. Think of it as a gentle nudge. A guy like you should be upstairs as a stockbroker, chasing rich old WASPs who are waiting for you to call up and say, Let me make you a hundred grand."

"And how would I make them a hundred grand?"

"Jesus, Lamplighter. You take a percentage coming and going. What do you care if they make a hundred grand?"

Keith wasn't sure how literally he was to take Tadelis's analysis, but testing it couldn't be any less productive than sitting around playing with himself all day, as he now realized he appeared to have been doing. He opened the book. He dialed. And dialed. But what he discovered over the next month was that his interest wasn't in entities, it was in people. The last call he'd make from that phone was to Jules Renard, to ask about a transfer over to equities.

TADELIS TURNED OUT RARELY TO BE RIGHT, but he was right about this: Keith could sell pretty much anything to pretty much anyone. The secret . . . Well, there were two. One came from growing up Catholic, this habit of compassion he had back then. There was a moment before any trade when you'd positioned your client right on the fulcrum between yes and no, and the slightest breath could tip him in either direction. At that moment, Keith would close his eyes and sort of send his spirit outward, as in prayer, until he was sitting right next to the client on the other end of the phone, willing the deal to be good for him.

The second secret was that it was easy for Keith to believe in what he was selling. This wasn't to say he always understood it; in fact, he still found the mathematical ins and outs of bond yields and liquidity spreads surprisingly hard to hold in mind, like slippery fish in a basket. But in the Action Office, that Darwinian milieu of gristle and blood and genital metaphor, there'd been a certain contempt for theory anyway. It was said that each of the world's great ideas—the wheel, *Hamlet*, Newtonian gravity—could fit on the back of a cocktail napkin, and Keith was a cocktail-napkin kind of guy. He would get three or four jumps out on a cost-benefit tree, a single choice having branched into eight, or sixteen, and then, partway into examining those, would throw up his hands and go with his gut. "I think you're really going to come to feel as good about this as I do," he might say, hopefully. You only had to be right 51 percent of the time to beat the market, and in those years, Kennedy, Johnson, it was hard to lose money. The same libidinal energy coursing through the television and the streets outside seemed to be making the money multiply.

He brought the two secrets to bear on his home life, too. Number one: love other people. The night after the first time he booked a ten-thousand-dollar trade, he burst in the front door in a golden fog of beer from all the rounds he'd bought his coworkers and lifted Regan off her feet and kissed her until her thighs parted to admit his. "Easy," she said. "The baby." Probably she just meant that she'd be more comfortable on her back—the doctor had assured them, periphrastically, that they could continue to enjoy the fruits of marriage. But there were gentler ways to obtain them. Once he'd carried her to the bed, he lifted her nightgown and moved down between her legs and lapped at the spiced copper there until, across the quivering swell of her belly and breasts he saw the flush leap into her throat, her hands twisting the sheets by her head.

He was wild for her in those days, in the two-bedroom newly-wed apartment in the Village, and in taxicabs and Broadway theaters and the little cabin on Lake Winnipesaukee where, that third year of their married life, the kid had been conceived. Keith thought he could fill, with his body and his money and his soul, the lonely places Regan's mother and brother and whoever else had left. And she'd let him think it, he would come to see (as if, had he realized what had been taken wasn't replaceable, he'd have ceased to love her).

When the child was born, they called him William. Keith had always liked the name anyway, and if he understood correctly, William III was unlikely to produce an heir of his own to carry it on . . . even assuming he someday returned from the wilderness into which he'd vanished the night before Old Bill's wedding. Once a Social Security card had been issued, they went down to her bank and Regan transferred into the boy's name her entire trust fund, minus her inheritance from her mother. For his future, she said. For college. Keith, who was the trustee on the new account, asked if she was sure she wanted to do this. But she was capable of great decisiveness. And now that she'd finished signing the documents, Regan was free of the Hamilton-Sweeneys.

Or as free as you could be, living in the same town, sitting on their Board, seeing them at holidays. Christmas with the Spocks, Keith took to calling it after the advent of *Star Trek*, Old Bill remaining galactically remote and Felicia proving somewhat colder than she'd initially seemed. (Amory, to Keith's great relief, would always be off doing a deal in some foreign territory, so his name rarely came up.)

Aside from these family visits, with their forcible cheer, Regan had by then given up acting. It had been clear since Will's birth that she'd never really meant to continue, that motherhood was where her talents would go. But Keith encouraged her to keep up with her play-reading group. In fact, he'd supported her in all her Greenwich Village hobbies: meditation, book club, health food, neighborhood preservation. When she had to go offer testimony at a hearing over one of the City's endless redevelopment plans, he took off work to watch Will. He would always remember, he thought, how he'd gripped the seat of the boy's new bike and jogged around the park the smart money still said would be razed to make room for a highway, and how, at the end of the umpteenth circuit, Regan had arrived amid a cluster of women in skirts, the youngest and prettiest among them. How she'd blushed and raised her fists in victory. He felt just then as if his soul had swelled to fill his skin—as after scrimmages in high school, when he'd walked home tossing the ball to himself in the fast-descending night, replaying sixty-yard touchdown runs.

That was probably, come to think of it, the geometric apogee of his life, because the salesman's Second Commandment (again) was Believe What Thou Art Selling, and this proved to be a little trickier than the First, when what thou werst selling wast thyself. In 1970, for example, with Regan pregnant again and Will nearing school age, Keith started to feel he wasn't making enough money. Each new tax bracket was a kind of elevation from which you could survey all the things you couldn't yet afford. If Regan liked the book club that met at her friend Ruth's house, how much more might she have liked a home she could actually entertain in? If she liked the community garden she and the other mothers had made in the vacant lot down the street, how much more might she have liked her own private yard? Or at least a balcony where she could pot her herbs?

By the time he confessed to Regan that he'd been talking to a real-estate agent, he had made up his mind. Uptown, in a Classic Six, Will and the baby would have their own rooms, and wouldn't have to be around the hopheads and barking lunatics who had lately taken over the Village. It would mean working harder, of course, to take home more money, they both knew that, but in truth Keith had grown bored in the upper-middle echelons at Renard. He had a solid list of clients; what if another firm let him bring them over and start a named advisory business of his own? He sincerely believed, as he laid all this out for her, that this was what he wanted. The charity dinners, the harbor cruises, the corporate picnics where you plucked new business . . . he enjoyed them, didn't he? He enjoyed having to turn on the charm, having had a little too much to drink. And he would be someone now, the head of his own group—Lamplighter Capital Associates. With his Brooks Brothers shirts, his fancy Swiss watch, and a driver waiting downstairs, he would finally feel he deserved her.

IT WASN'T LONG AFTERWARD that Keith began exploring the wonders of leverage. The cocktail-napkin version looked like this: if he combined two dollars borrowed cheaply from the bank with one dollar from a client's account, then each dollar made on the three-dollar investment more or less doubled his client's money. The particular sector he was experimenting in was military. Personally, Keith was a dove, and had written some large checks to Hubert Humphrey during the '68 election. He'd nonetheless ridden out the bear market that followed by taking big positions in Dow Chemical, in Raytheon, in Honeywell, both for clients and for himself. And though there was some risk in maintaining them—the war couldn't go on forever, could it?—Nixon's expansion into Cambodia and Laos seemed to open up demand for all kinds of new product lines. If Keith was right, he was going to have leveraged himself into a nice modern house in New Canaan by the time the next correction came. Meanwhile, in the name of diversification, Keith was now long on the City itself. That is, he'd begun moving his clients into long-term New York municipal bonds.

They'd first drawn his eye toward the end of 1972, when he was certain they were undervalued. True, the later part of the war years had been punishing for the local economy. In the early '60s, the Lower

West Side in the a.m. had still been so dense with shipping pallets you could barely walk; now the loading docks were all sealed up and shrouded with graffiti. You could hear pigeons brooding there behind the corrugated steel. Tax revenues were suffering, and there was talk, if you listened to Dick Cavett or the "Dr." Zig show, of a permanent shift to a symbolic economy, or a service economy—an economy based on anything other than measurable human production—but this struck Keith as the worst kind of eggheadery. And what about real estate? It used to be that from eight to eight the whole city was musique concrète: drills jackhammers belt-sanders electric saws and the pizzicato plink of hammer on nail. He remembered scaffolding marring the long-in-the-tooth face of every other building in Midtown, wrecking balls like slow fists clobbering the tenements. Will, at two or three, had loved to watch the cranes, and flying above the operator's cabin or aerie the big bright American flag. Now the smug numbers of the ticker machine said real estate was depressed. It made Keith want to take the ticker machine up to the top of the Hamilton-Sweeney Building and show it the limited landmass of Manhattan. What happens when the 2 percent of American males eighteen to thirty-four currently wading through the rice paddies of Southeast Asia return to rent apartments, look for jobs, consume durable goods? The tax base comes roaring back, obviously. This isn't Soviet Russia. This is America we're talking about. For God's sake, this is New York City.

The oil shock a few months later made him feel prescient. The Dow Jones took a bath, but the ratings agencies had returned city debt to AAA status, and Keith had already put $4 million into thirty-year munis and even picked up a $100,000 bond for himself. And when, in early '74, those same munis dipped down to 20 percent below face value, he went back to the well with another $4 million. This time, he bought the bonds on margin, matching each dollar of equity with a dollar of debt. If he didn't seek his clients' explicit permission, it was only because it was so clear leverage was what they would want. His personal accounts were even less liquid, but he managed to scrape together enough cash to buy another five bonds on margin for himself.

By the fall, he had $6 million of other people's money, $300,000 of his own, and $2.2 million of the bank's in a tax-free and virtually risk-less instrument. A strange thing had happened, though. Not only did the global market remain slumped, but nothing in New York seemed to be performing: not private housing or public housing, not urban renewal, not office space. Occupancy rates at the newly built Trade Center hovered around 30 percent. Even Radio City now was on the auction block. It shouldn't have been a surprise; the last time Keith had been there, the five thousand seats had been so empty you could hear not only a cough but the rustle of a cough drop being unwrapped. It was a Thursday matinee of *Herbie Rides Again,* but he'd needed a couple of hours away from reality. Because, amid talk of the federal government having to backstop the city budget, his $8.5 million muni spree was now worth not the $10 million it should have been, conservatively, but $6.4 million. A margin call from the bank would force him to realize losses close to 50 percent; here in the corporeal world, leverage, depressingly, turned out to be just a synonym for amplification. And in any case, if his clients woke up to what he was doing behind their backs—on their behalf!—he could lose his business.

Thank God, then, that his military-industrial speculations continued to thrive, tossing off their soporific dividend checks. At the 1974/75 Hamilton-Sweeney New Year's gala, men in tuxedoes, their faces barely recognizable, queued three and four deep to shake his hand. They had no idea about the great, sucking hole in his balance sheet.

Neither did Regan. "It's like you're a celebrity or something," she said afterward, perched on the edge of the bed, leaning forward to roll down her hose. She had always gone to these parties grudgingly; he had the feeling she'd rather have stayed home and watched *The Brady Bunch* with the kids, but there was a new thing in her voice as she sat up to watch him struggle with the knot of his tie. "I'm proud of you, you know."

They'd both had several glasses of champagne, but he wanted to believe that if they made love that night, for the first time in—had it really been a month?—it wouldn't just be the alcohol. They lay on their sides with the lights off, barely moving, trying not to wake the kids, and as part of him slipped into Regan, inching down the path to freedom, another part of him thought, So this is what it really feels like to be a man. Not the fullback carrying home the golden cup, but the compromised, muddled, and not entirely forthcoming creature now trying to pretend to his wife that he's as lost in the moment as she herself is.

OR IS PRETENDING TO BE. For Regan seemed to have struggles of her own. Cate had been a difficult pregnancy, leaving her housebound for long stretches. And Regan would have been an uneasy transplant to the East Sixties regardless; she'd been happier in the rockier soil downtown. Now that her various personal pursuits—and the larger pursuit of the right pursuit—had lapsed, much of her time not occupied with Board matters was lavished on one kid or the other. It wasn't that Keith was jealous, exactly, but the way all their conversations became about the kids worried him. Then again, he could hardly ask her about it, because it was just as likely his fault. He'd long since lost track of who'd started hiding first.

He began avoiding home, staying late at the office after everyone had left or going to the Y to swim laps until his eyes were bleary with chlorine, or jogging down along the FDR as shadows stretched over the city, devouring the blown-out tires and heavy shopping bags and encrustations of guano that lined the pedestrian path until it was just auto fumes blasting into and out of his lungs and ghostly horns and the disembodied taillights moving at a sluggish jogger's pace along the drive.

When he finally reached the big new apartment, his dinner would be in foil on the dining room table. Will might still be on the rug on his stomach in that adorably defenseless way of his, with his homework all around him. But Cate would be in her room asleep, or busy with the hamsters Regan had bought her. And Regan would be curled up in their bedroom reading plays in what he'd come to think of as her chastity sweatpants—formless cotton things. Even they couldn't disguise that she'd lost weight, more than was probably healthy. Sometimes he had the dim intuition that he was supposed to ask her about this, but what if she told him it was nothing, and left him there extended over the abyss by himself? Or conversely: What if she told him something he didn't want to hear? And asked him, in return, why he was avoiding the apartment? How could he make her see that it wasn't that he didn't love this; that in fact he loved it too much to contaminate it with the infection that was, apparently, him? Instead, he would pour his drink and put on his Scottish bagpipes LP and stand by the window, looking out over the city. He was in his own transparent hamster ball, he thought, rolling around, unable to make contact.

THE DAY THE WORD "DEFAULT" first began to percolate through the papers—the day people started to wonder if there was even any bottom to hit—he saw nothing for it but to call in sick. He took Will to the Park after school, to practice with the lacrosse stick. When Keith was a kid, "sports" had meant football, baseball, and basketball, but weren't they paying tuition precisely so the kid could have choices? Well, that and because the public schools frightened even Keith. Besides, he had to admit he liked the resinous warmth of the wood on his palms, the ultraquick rip of the pocket through the air when he sent the little ball streaking deep over the Great Lawn—his old friend leverage, again. Will, though, as regards hand-eye coordination, was a Hamilton-Sweeney through and through. Clambering back across the green, his awkwardly long shinbones kicking up high in front of him, his shirt billowing like a sail, he resembled for a second his namesake, Regan's vanished brother, who, Keith dimly remembered, had also played lacrosse for a semester or two. It was so striking that he almost didn't notice the glum blankness on Will's face when he returned.

He stood behind the boy, adjusted his grip on the stick, trying to reverse-engineer the mechanics of the trapping move he himself had mastered. (Why hadn't he just stuck to what he was good at?) "No, like this." The relative positions of their bodies recalled some other day, years ago, when he'd taught Will how to fly a kite, or throw a Frisbee or something, he couldn't quite remember anymore, his senses were too full of his current son, ten years old, his hair level with Keith's chest. When had it stopped being whitish-blond? And when had his pliant body, which once would have done almost anything to be close to his dad, grown so stiff, as though there was something unmanly about their hands meeting on a lacrosse stick? "Okay, okay, I've got it," Will said, and backpedaled away. Other grown-ups and other kids floated behind him, little colored no-see-ums against the grass. "Fire it in here, Dad. No weak stuff." Keith, who for unexamined reasons had to win any competition he found himself in, wound up and threw the ball as hard as he could. It shot past Will's shoulder and into the field beyond, and Will cursed as he turned to chase it, as if his father, who'd never heard him use the f-word, weren't standing right there. Keith thought again of the rumors that had been flying around Wall Street all morning. One held that New York munis were trading at half off. Another, which he was afraid to check out, was that *no one was buying these pigs at all*. But later, Keith would decide that this was the moment he had really given up—the moment when he'd become invisible even to his son.

HE DID PLAN TO OPEN UP TO REGAN about his mistakes—at this point, he'd begun borrowing from Will's trust fund just to cover family expenses—but on the night they sat down together over lo mein after the kids were in bed, they talked mostly of her need for a change. She'd found herself wondering lately, she said, whether her brother hadn't been right to get out of New York altogether, all those years ago. She'd believed in the promises of the '60s, after all, even if she'd participated only indirectly. Hadn't they told themselves they would not be like the generation of their parents, trapped in choices they'd made at twenty?

There were still worlds within Regan not confined to wifehood, to motherhood, he saw. But even as these glimpses thrilled him, they pained him, too, by reminding him of all he'd forgotten . . . and for what? He could barely remember. On his finger was a ring he'd worn now for fourteen years, nicked and scratched and lovely white gold, and when had he last really noticed it? It was as if, Keith thought, he had acquired his own Demon Brother: the depresh, the megrims, the black dog that followed you wherever you went. It was as if every American now had his own dark twin, the possibility of life lived some other way, staring back at him from store windows and medicine chests. Had his parents had this? His grandparents? He realized it was Regan staring at him.

"What?"

"If something's on your mind, honey, you can tell me."

But how could he tell her? How did you find your way back to the mirror, and the proper life that lay on the far side of the glass?

DEUS EX MACHINA, was how. He had signed up for a three-day conference of financiers on The Future of the City, hoping to glean some way out of the disaster he'd gotten himself into. It was false advertising; for the word "Future," they should have substituted "Crisis," because that was all anyone would talk about. Oil crises and demand crises, crises in confidence. Some believed that, in the age of floating currency, confidence was the only thing keeping the system from collapse. And these were the optimists! The people who, like Keith, held on to old-fashioned ideas about value as something empirically ascertainable—they tended to think everything was *really* fucked.

On Friday morning, having learned next to nothing, Keith stepped out of a session to get some air. The lobby was empty, and the sound of his wingtips on the polished marble struck him as somber, though perhaps this was the accumulated gloom of yet another presentation. *The American city is over,* the presenter had been arguing, as slides of post-riot Detroit or Pittsburgh flickered on a screen behind him. *There won't be ground broken on another major development in New York for twenty years.* This very New York into which Keith was pushing—it still seemed to him impossible that it should fail. Speaking of impossible: Who should be sitting on a traffic bollard there, in a bespoke suit, but Amory Gould?

Not wanting to be rude, Keith went over to say hello. In lieu of a greeting, Amory held out a pack of cigarettes. He could have afforded Dunhills or Nat Shermans, Keith thought, but the ones on offer looked cheap, with a Spanish name: Exigente. For etiquette's sake, he accepted. The first drag made his head swim; he hadn't touched tobacco since the sulky week or two that had followed his football injury in college. "Thanks," he said. "I didn't expect to see you here among the gloom-and-doomers."

"Oh, I never miss a chance to see people trapped in a category error."

Keith looked up. With his white hair, Amory had once seemed so much his senior as to hail from a different century, but now they could have been contemporaries. Indeed, of the two of them, Amory was probably the more vital. "You think they're wrong in there?"

"What I think is that liquidity and vision, my boy, can still do great things. Everything else is smoke and mirrors."

"You must know something I don't."

"Supposing I did. Would sharing it be to my advantage? Wouldn't you do better to assume I was obfuscating?" Amory narrowed his eyes against the drift of his own cigarette. Keith had never realized he smoked; he did so like a man in a hurry, or one who had grown up in an extremely cold climate. As in fact, Keith remembered, he had. "I always liked you, you know, Keith."

"I guess I do. I guess I wouldn't be here if it wasn't for you."

"Oh, I don't mean to imply that. No, what you've got you grabbed for yourself, and for that I salute you. But it doesn't alter the fact that I've always felt you and I could do great things together, given world enough and time."

Keith, a little flummoxed, suggested that Amory seemed to be getting along just fine without him. Weren't new markets still falling open across the globe for the Hamilton-Sweeneys? Hadn't last quarter's year-over-year earnings, miraculously, almost doubled?

"You haven't taken my meaning exactly. I mean I've taken a liking to you, Keith, you're practically my nephew. And those I like I take an interest in. And those I take an interest in I have ways of looking out for. And now once again you need some looking out for, don't you? Yes, there's something you need your Uncle Amory's help with."

The tone struck Keith as off, but he was now beyond the place where he might have showed it. At that moment, he thought he understood why Regan didn't like Amory. "Now how would you find out a thing like that?"

"You assume I'd need to go looking. But your face has always been an open book."

Armies of pigeons, rustling, plummeted down a building face across the street. Then, just when it seemed they were about to hit the pavement, they surged back upward to roost again in high windows. They repeated their performance several times, rendering it inexplicable. Why these windows? Why leave them? It was as if the birds were caught in the repetition of some primal trauma, stuck between what they had and what they wanted. There was no point trying to hide things from Amory. Keith found himself explaining about the bonds on his books, now far below junk, the losses that were about to become insolvency. The nicotine must have gone to his head. Still, it was a relief just to tell someone. Even this someone. "I've turned out to be quite a disappointment."

"Not at all." Amory lit another cigarette. Reflected. "Let me tell you something, Keith. When I was a younger man, people dressed up to go on airplanes. The seats on the subway were made of wicker, and a gentleman always yielded his seat to a lady. Everything had place and proportion, and a man like you . . . well, you would have simply thrived. Now things are different, naturally. It is harder to find people you can trust. But what once was true remains so. There is still money lying all over the streets." His voice sounded as if it were coming from much farther away than it really was, crossing tundras and seas, rather than merely the square of sidewalk between them, on which Keith, when he looked down, half-expected to see loose currency. "Not everyone is bold enough to collect it. People are waiting for someone else to go bring down the buffalo, are you following me? Now I've watched you from afar all these years, you've been a comer. You have earned. There is a vulgar term for this, I remember. You have shown yourself, Keith, to be capable. It is a fact of this world that a capable earner can fall on hard times. But then who will feed the tribe? Where will that leave them? We can't let that happen— not for our own sake, but for *theirs*." He paused. Leaned forward. "Eighty-nine cents on the dollar. Would that be enough? Because that's what your father-in-law would be prepared to offer."

Keith, stunned, found it hard—or harder—to calculate. With that kind of money, he would be able to pay back the bank and get his clients back to neutral, though he'd still be somewhat in the red personally, after patching the holes in the kids' trust funds.

"You'd take a commission, of course," Amory continued. "Let's call it thirty-five."

"Thirty-five thousand?"

"Everything aboveboard. Which doesn't mean we couldn't keep this to ourselves."

"I don't know what to say."

"Say nothing. Go forth and sin no more."

"Jesus," he said. "Thank you. You have no idea what a favor you're doing me." And took Amory's hand in his own, before Amory could take back these too-generous terms.

"We are no longer in the world of favors, Keith. Think of it as a trade."

"Then what do I owe you?"

Amory tamped out his cigarette decorously on the bottom of his shoe and then smiled a placid smile. "Oh, I'll be sure to let you know, when the time comes."

THE HOLE PLUGGED, his balance sheet rebalanced, and summer stretching out before him like a shoreline, Keith should have felt like a new man. He wanted to reach home on time, or even a little early, to take them all out for pizza to celebrate. But when he did reach home, he found a note saying they were already out for pizza. And even if they hadn't been, what if they should ask, *Why this munificence all of a sudden?* It was then that Keith understood that his mistake wouldn't be escaped so easily—that he was living in a post-mistake world. The parasite may have gone, but it had left him hollowed out, a man apart.

Though maybe that was just the knowledge that the Demon Brother was not through with him. For long after the sale had been executed, transferring the bonds from his accounts to Regan's father's—after Felix Rohatyn had stepped in and arranged for the rescue of the city budget, netting the Hamilton-Sweeney Company a neat $900,000 on a strategy that had been Keith's; after Regan had taken a job of her own (albeit at her family's company)—Amory would reach him at the office. His voice, normally so distant-sounding, receded even further, as if the connection was bad. He had an errand, he said, that he wondered if Keith might run?

IN GENERAL, IT WENT LIKE THIS: On a Thursday or Friday, late in the day but not yet at close of business, Keith would pick up his brief-case. Inside would be a manila envelope, which would have arrived by courier in a larger envelope in the morning. Making some excuse for leaving early, he'd pass Veronica and the secretarial pool and board the elevator to the street below. His destination was a derelict townhouse east of the Bowery, the kind of place that sent a little bit of itself with you whenever you left it, in the form of dust on your shoes, on your cuffs, fine gray film on the pads of your fingers where you had rung the dusty buzzer. Keith never rang the buzzer, though; Amory had said nothing about hand delivery. Easier, instead, to use the mailslot.

What was in these envelopes? Subpoenas? Payments to a secret mistress? To an illegitimate child? He knew better than to ask. Amory maintained a far-flung network of contacts, not only in the intelligence circles he'd moved in as a young man, but also with the tremendous data machine that was taking over finance; he saw information as his business. Not Keith Lamplighter. He just stooped and pushed the envelopes through. The arrangement was a little uncomfortable, sure. Grandees of old New York had once lived in these brownstones, but now it was territory openly hostile to his social class. And what if someone he knew should see him down here? But of course, not even the natives saw him. People were too busy getting high, or too scared to come out on the streets. The closest he would come to human contact was the bark of a dog or the muffled noise of a stereo.

Then, after the fourth or fifth time, he was walking back over to the safer blocks to find a cab when a sick feeling overtook him. He balanced his briefcase on the rounded top of a postal box and flicked open the clasps, and there inside lay the long, unmarked envelope he'd been supposed to deliver. This might not have troubled him so much except that its fraternal twin, a sealed stock warrant awaiting the signature of an important client, was missing. He tried to recall the moment when he'd slid the envelope through the mailslot, but couldn't. His mind had been already back uptown, already home. He returned to the townhouse. The noise coming through the walls of the basement and the battered steel door with its giant hieroglyphic graffito now had the deep, amphibious thud of live music, but it couldn't quite be called music. It was more as if someone was shooting up a music store. He knocked until his hands hurt and waited for some lull in the noise, but there was none. August of 1976, with the air thick, the sun beating down.

At some point since he'd last noticed it, the buzzer had been ripped out like an eye from its socket; a single, twisted ganglion of wire corkscrewed from the doorframe. He squatted and lifted the squeaky flap of the mailslot, to see if he could see his envelope lying on the floor inside. Sweat trickled from hairline to eye. He could feel watchful presences behind drawn curtains across the way. Did people ever call the cops down here? And if they did, did the cops dare to come? Maybe if he fashioned the buzzer-wire into some sort of hook. . . . He was about to shout through the slot, to ask if someone could let him in, when a shadow fell over him. He looked up. There, suspended against the humid sky, were two very long legs in denim. The young woman they belonged to was cradling a stack of records against her hip. Her black tee-shirt was cropped short to reveal a pale strip of belly. Her brown hair went gold where the sun hit it. She squinted down at him fiercely, but her voice, when it came, was curious, rich, throaty—almost amused, he might have said, long after he'd forgotten the exact words she spoke.

Which were, for the record: "Hey—is there something you're looking for?"

THE FIREWORKERS, PART 1

~~The Runaway~~
~~In My Father's House, There Are Many Mansions~~
~~What a Kingdom It Was~~
~~monkeys invade the heavenly palace and chase out the dragon~~
~~Year of the Snake~~
~~No One Goes There Anymore~~
The Fireworkers

THE HOUSE WAS A WHITE, ALUMINUM-SIDED RANCH SET BACK
off a cul-de-sac amid the ramifying suburbs of Nassau
County, Long Island. Save for its relative isolation
there, it might have been any of ten thousand others.
The plumbing was temperamental. The walls bled sound.
But when Carmine Cicciaro, Jr., drove his young wife
out from Queens to look at it in the spring of 1963, he
saw that it would serve: out back was just enough flat
land to fit a patio, a cottage-sized outbuilding, and a
stand of pine and elm to screen the traffic on the Long
Island Expressway, toward which the rest of the lawn
ungently sloped. I was living in Manhattan then myself,
and, in the years after the Cicciaros moved to Flower
Hill, I must have passed the place a dozen times on
summer treks out to Montauk without giving it a second
look. Certainly, I never imagined that one of America's
greatest indigenous artists made his home there. Then
again, until the Bicentennial summer of 1976 and the
events that followed from it, I probably wouldn't have
thought to call what Cicciaro does for a living "art."

What Cicciaro does for a living--or did, until very
recently--is shoot off fireworks. To his colleagues, the
show he put on over New York Harbor on July 4, 1971,

remains the greatest achievement in his field in a
generation. So neglected is this field in the outside
world, however, that no one can even agree on a name
for it. Its seminal texts are all hundreds of years
old. Casimir Simienowicz's <u>Artis Magnae Artilleriae</u>,
from 1650, uses whatever is Latin for "firemaster,"
while other period works refer, somewhat cryptically,
to "Wild Men" or "Green Men." More recent sources speak
of "pyrotechnicians," but I have found that the men
themselves (and they are all men) prefer "fireworker."

They are of Italian descent, largely--the Rozzis of
Cleveland, the Zambellis of Pennsylvania, the Ruggieris
of France--and they are clannish and recessive and
tight-lipped and gruff. Indeed, when I first found my
way to that house on the hill, Carmine Cicciaro, Jr.,
was reluctant to talk about himself at all. Asked about
his accomplishments, he fell back on platitudes. "You
don't choose it so much as it chooses you," he must
have said three times in as many minutes, as we stood
in the doorway of his workshop. When I pressed him to
elaborate, he said only that firework was in the blood.
Growing up, he'd watched his older brothers, Frankie
and Julius, load shells onto the family barge. He'd
watched his father pilot it out into New York Harbor.
Later, he'd watched from the deck as the sky lit up and
thousands of heads along the waterfront tilted back,
mouths widened into "o"s. My suggestion that this was
rather an extraordinary way to spend one's youth yielded
only a shrug and another truism: "No one goes into this
job for the glory."

As if to underscore the point, Cicciaro carried
himself less like an American master than like a pirate
exiled to the mainland. He had eight o' clock shadow
and a belly like a catcher's pad and a checked wool
shirt several sizes too big, as if his own big frame
might disappear inside. His left hand was missing half

its ring-finger (most fireworkers are missing some appendage or other), but he never made reference to this, or to the silver band he wore below the remaining knuckle, except to turn it around and around while I made my pitch for an interview. On a table in the workshop was a shotgun. He might have turned me away entirely, but when my military service in Korea came up, it seemed I had passed some test. We were soon seated on his back patio, drinking cans of Schlitz from a cooler.

Beer, I found, relaxed him. Provided the subject was remote enough, he could be positively digressive. When I told him my research into fireworks had gotten little further than a 16th-century Sienese named Vannoccio Biringuccio, he said, "You've just got to know where to look." He must have spent hundreds of hours when he was a teenager digging around at the library. "Chinese history, technical manuals in chemistry and metallurgy, military history around the Hundred Years' War . . . Did you run across Francois de Malthus? Back then, the guy firing your shows in peacetime would also be the one mixing your gunpowder in battle. I could probably come up with call numbers, but my memory's not what it used to be."

This was another feint, I thought. Cicciaro was only 48 years old; his memory was manifestly good. Moreover, he wanted to talk. That summer and fall, we would spend many hours on his patio, where I coaxed out of him the story of his profession, a Spenglerish tale of triumph and decline. We got comfortable enough with each other that he seemed not to care if I went inside to freshen the sodapop I switched to, rather than try to match him Schlitz for Schlitz. But when I confessed that I hadn't expected him to allow me back after that initial meeting, he said I'd gotten lucky. His daughter could talk him into just about anything.

Her name was Samantha, she was 17, and she was the first truly personal subject he'd been willing to broach. This was back in August. In a month, when the dorms opened, she would enter NYU's School of the Arts. Cicciaro didn't seem to connect the word "arts" to his own work. "Music, movies, poems . . . she's crazy about all of it," he said, though he hoped, given what he was paying, that college would steer her toward something "more practical." He lifted the beercan perched on his knee and gestured to me. "Maybe even journalism. She's been making this whole magazine by herself, with pictures and everything. Not that she'd let me read it."

Later, he would have reason to speak of Samantha and her secrets with anger and with sorrow. But that first time, his mouth contracted as if he'd snuck in a lemon drop. Then we sat in pleasant ignorance and talked some more and watched the wind-tossed trees at the end of the yard, whose leaves were going gold at the edges. It was three o'clock, and then three thirty, and the traffic was thickening on the L.I.E. and the sun was going down.

WHEN WE TALK ABOUT FIREWORKS, WE'RE ACTUALLY TALKING about three distinct things. Roughly half of the 653 members of the Confederated Pyrotechnics Guild work in military ordnance, and wouldn't know a Roman candle from a hole in the ground. The rest are in "amusements," which further subdivides into stationary "set pieces" and "aerials." Any self-respecting fireworker knows how to fashion a set piece. At the holiday shows I saw growing up in Tulsa, a burning frame spelling out "God Bless America" was a ubiquitous coda. A scant few decades earlier, the grand finale itself would have been a life-sized palace or Catherine wheel spewing sparks onto earth or water. Improvements in technology, however, have left the aerial branch

ascendant. The staple of a professional show today
is the mortar-fired shell, which you'll rarely hear
referred to in the trade as anything other than a bomb.

The basic science behind both set pieces and bombs
Cicciaro traced back to the nameless Chinese villages
where gunpowder first appeared some 2,000 years ago.
"Of course it wasn't gunpowder then," he told me,
"because there weren't any guns." Still, to judge by
their efforts at monopoly, the emperors of the Tang
dynasty must have recognized the powder's martial
implications. By the seventh century, fireworks were a
fixture of court occasions, and fireworker an official
position, like magician or Lord High Executioner. Then,
around 1300, Marco Polo succeeded in smuggling a few
unfired shells back to Venice. "Or anyway, that's the
story." But the alchemists working for the doges would
prove no better than the Tang emperors at containing
the supply; over several centuries, fireworks spread
down the boot of Italy.

By the 1850s, when they reached the ancestral home
of the Cicciaros, the village of Pozzallo in Sicily,
the Italians had made modifications. One was to replace
the closed spheres the Chinese favored with open-ended
cylinders that tumbled in the air, spraying sparks even
before they burst. Another was "polverone," a black
powder alloyed with various dampening agents to slow
the burn. And in the early 19th century, fireworkers
discovered dozens of other alloys that broadened
their palette beyond the traditional off-white. There
were strontiums for red, sodiums for yellow, bariums
for green. As a general rule, Cicciaro said, colors
become less and less stable as one moves up the visible
spectrum. Blue is generally thought to be the most
volatile, and the hardest to produce, but Pozzallan
lore holds that while still in short pants, Cicciaro's
grandfather, Gian' Battista, found a way to go beyond
it, to a purple that verged on ultraviolet.

However true this was, Gian' Battista Cicciaro
would land around the turn of the century in the
New World, where fireworks became one of the first
mass entertainments. The American city of that time
was primarily an economic unit, not a cultural one,
and ethnic and class factionalism threatened to rip
it apart. Yet the impromptu infernos Gian' Battista
mounted on holidays gave the restive Italians and Irish
and Germans and Jews something in common--at least
while they lasted. This was not lost on Tammany Hall.
The firm of Cicciaro & Son Amusements was swiftly
chartered and granted renewable ten-year contracts
for Independence Day, New Year's Eve, and the Feast of
San Gennaro. In 1934, with a gang war diverting the
Chinatown tongs, Gian' Battista's son and successor,
Carmine Sr. added Chinese New Year to the list,
consolidating the family's control over what fireworkers
call the "Big Four."
    Carmine Jr., who by this point had already witnessed
dozens of shows, claims to remember none of them.
What he remembers, he says, is lying awake afterward
in the family apartment on Mott Street, waiting for
his father's feet to creak the front stairs. The smell
was pungent, vaguely diabolical. "It stood out almost
like a yellow or red in the dark," he said. "And then
next day there'd be a ring of black powder left in the
bathtub for my mother to clean. You could write your
name in it with a knuckle." It was by scraping this
residue into a Knickerbocker mint tin, drying it out
on the rooftop, mixing in some illicit compounds, and
inserting a match end for a fuse that Carmine Cicciaro,
Jr., age seven, manufactured his first bomb.

I'D BEEN GOING OUT TO THE HOUSE FOR ABOUT TWO MONTHS
when Cicciaro offered to "show me the shop." I thought

he meant the outbuilding below, his private workshop, whose noisy exhaust fans were why (I supposed) no houses had been built nearby. Instead, he drove me out to the compound his father had erected in Willets Point, Queens, near the end of the Depression.

Today, Willets Point is a zone of razor-wire and dog bark and wastewater in open ditches backed up against the IRT trainyards. Until a modern sewer system is built, no residential buildings are permitted, so its chief tenants are metalworking shops and salvage lots and unmarked warehouses toward which tankers and semi trucks rumble. It can be hard to believe you're even in New York until you glimpse, past the nippled domes of the water treatment plant, the finials of Midtown. Just next door is the Cicciaro & Sons compound, 17 numbered Quonset huts on an acre or so of grassless land. A copper plate has been grounded to a pole beside each door; before entering, you touch the plate to discharge any static electricity you may have accumulated. (Watch a fireworker carefully, and you'll see it becomes a habit: at the doorway of any kitchen or bathroom or gas station kiosk, a hand paws unconsciously at the jamb.) When a light is turned on in one of the huts, a red bulb outside lets everyone know it is occupied. And behind the last row of sheds is the back acre known as "The Lab": a scrabbly emptiness sheltered on all sides by man-made dunes whose inner slopes, scorched an igneous black, are dotted at all hours with dozens, sometimes hundreds, of the local gulls. It's the nitrate buildup in the dirt that draws them, Carmine told me. "Like you crave the iron in a steak. Some mineral imbalance in the blood."

He began coming out here to work after school in the early '40s, when both his brothers shipped out for the war. His main duties were to tidy and secure the premises when the technicians had left for the day. Left

alone among the combustibles, though, Cicciaro began to
tinker. It quickly became clear that he had inherited
his grandfather's gift for color. He was able to see
distinctions between shades that escaped others; to
smell, via a mild form of synesthesia, the precise hues
that would result from various admixtures of chemicals,
and to sense just how far he could push them and still
survive. One of his earliest triumphs was what the
writer and fireworks enthusiast George Plimpton has
called "one of the great, rare blues." It burned both
deep and bright, though Cicciaro's secret formula was so
potent that the shells couldn't be packed more than a
day or two ahead of their firing.

Then, in November of 1944, a U.S. bomber carrying
Cicciaro's brother Frankie went down over the Pacific.
Julius Cicciaro was killed in Belgium not long after.
There was a posthumous medal for valor. Their mother
became one of those black-clad Catholic women who only
leave the apartment for daily Mass. The father simply
worked harder, as did the remaining son. Winter has
long been when the fireworker is busiest, building
bombs for the summer shows, and the shop in Willets
Point stayed open Monday through Saturday. By the time
he officially left school at 16, Carmine Cicciaro, Jr.,
was logging ten to twelve hours a day in the sheds.
Then on Sunday, after church, he headed back to the
big public library on 42nd Street and sank down into
brittle-paged books.

Even as he immersed himself in history, though,
Cicciaro had an eye toward the future. All around him,
the world was standardizing. People no longer had to
wait for an opera performance; they could buy a record
album and listen to it over and over, the same way each
time. Yet firework remained immune to even the most
basic notion of composition. In the absence of his dead
sons, with whom he'd had a sort of telepathy, Carmine
Sr. had to rely on flash-blind technicians running

around lighting fuses by hand, trying to read the
waving of his arms in the dark.

One day, Carmine Jr., reached Willets Point to find
these technicians gathered around the radio in his
father's office in Shed 8. The networks were reporting
the detonation of Fat Man over Nagasaki. It was the
largest man-made explosion ever devised, and the
war would be over, with ample retribution for his
brothers' deaths. The men seemed mainly preoccupied
with the bomb's engineering. One explained that the
key electrical problem had been getting the explosive
material to ignite evenly around the core. . . .
Seeing the bereaved kid nearby, he broke off. But
Cicciaro himself was already puzzling out schematics.
The A-bomb was almost the inverse of an aerial shell:
a transformation of order into heat, where fireworks
turned heat into order. Yet the need to control the
ignition rate was much the same.

Within a month, Cicciaro was out among the dunes with
a crude circuit board he'd built to sequence and fire
multiple fuses. This device, later called a "Cicciaro
board," would permit the elaborate synchronization
we have come to associate with fireworks shows. It
therefore played a big role in readying those shows
for television broadcast. As for a patent application,
however, Cicciaro told me that it never occurred to him,
any more than it had occurred to the fireworker who'd
discovered that magnesium perchlorate burned a bright
pink. Which is to say that, not for the last time,
Carmine Cicciaro, Jr., had brought himself one step
closer to obsolescence--to being consumed by the fire
he was making.

A BOMB ESSENTIALLY CONSISTS OF A CASING, A FUSE, AND
two charges. The first of these, the casing, is a
corset of butcher paper several layers thick and up to

12 inches in diameter. Once the fireworker has removed
the casing from its wooden form, he fastens a long
match, or passafuoco, inside. This will ignite the
lifting charge, even as the fire proceeds more slowly
through the polverone and the fuse proper. At the
center of the bomb goes the smaller metal tube called
the cannula, which contains the most powerful powder:
the bursting charge.

On the Sunday when we visited Willets Point, the
compound was mostly empty, but inside Shed 15, a
technician named Len Rizzo, recently divorced (another
occupational hazard) was using empty San Marzano
tomato cans to prepare some shells for a "First Night"
celebration down the Jersey shore. I watched him pack
the space between each can's outer wall and the paper
casing with finger-length noisemakers and chemical
nuggets the size of bouillon cubes, known as "stars."
These latter were the bomb's colors. Their volatility
was why they got loaded in before either of the charges,
Carmine told me--"Always build from the outside in"--
though I can't say this precaution made me any less
tense when he invited me to try it myself.

With the color and the sound ready, the shell
traveled to another shed, where the cannula received
its bursting charge. This was sectioned off to give the
shell several "breaks" in the air, like a multi-stage
rocket. Into the bottom, in yet another shed, Cicciaro
inserted the lifting charge and a paper "bochetta" of
firing equipment and sealed off the ends. The final
step was to wrap the finished shell in Italian twine,
in a kind of cat's-cradle pattern. This added to the
shell's integrity, I was told, but I wonder now if it
wasn't done simply for beauty's sake, as a set-dresser
might fill a desk drawer inside which the audience will
never see. Pulling bakery twine from the dispenser that
hung from the ceiling of Shed 7, Carmine's scarred and

mangled hands became almost delicate, and though I
never got the hang of the wrapping myself, I could have
stood there all day watching him.

The finished shells were stored in Sheds 1 through 3,
cut off from the rest of the compound by a stagnant
drainage ditch. I observed to Cicciaro that, in its
discrete plotting, the compound was an outsized version
of a bomb: each element in its own compartment. "Mixing
them too early is what gets you killed," he said. When
one fireworks family in Omaha saw its shop go up in
the spring of 1973, merchants ten miles away reported
broken windows. "The son who died was a careful guy.
But you never know. Well, the dogs knew. Neighbors said
they were barking half an hour before the explosion."

It was getting dark out, and I asked if we could
shoot something off. Not here, he said. "The city only
lets us fire Thursdays through Saturdays. But I guess
I know a place we could go. You got anything special in
mind?" I said I'd like to use one of the bombs we'd just
made. For all his warnings about safety, he came back
out of Shed 3 carrying one barehanded and handed it off
like a football. "Just don't drop it," he said, so I sat
with it on my lap in the pickup truck, jumping at every
noise as we jolted past Dobermans and over potholes and
onto the expressway.

We stopped at a secluded state park half an hour
out onto Long Island. Cicciaro had some mortar pipes
in his truckbed--that's what I'd heard banging around
back there--and he sank one straight into the graveled
parking lot, angled toward an adjacent meadow. He
dropped the bomb in. The leader fuse he draped over
the mortar's lip and lit as casually as if it were a
cigarette. He walked the few dozen feet to where I was
standing. The slowness of that fuse was almost painful.
Then the flame went over the lip and disappeared
inside.

Nothing happened at first, and I must have moved to
investigate, because he grabbed my arm. Sure enough,
there came a whooshy thud I could feel right through
the sand and a scream like the rending of air and a
blurt of light up in the moody night. He'd packed the
bomb with multiple colors, one for each of its seven
breaks. First came a burst of high-altitude blue, then
a cautionary orange, somewhat lower. Then green drowned
these out, with an even richer green at the center--like
a shell inside a shell. Then amber, gold, and finally a
deep incarnadine red as it fell toward earth. This last
was bright enough to etch Cicciaro's slack jaw, and it
hit me that he looked like nothing so much as a kid in
the grip of an obsession. He might have been standing
here the year after his brothers' deaths, alone in the
apparently private language of his work.

CICCIARO WAS USUALLY IN HIS WORKSHOP WHEN I ARRIVED,
but on my next trip to Nassau County, the Friday after
Thanksgiving, I found the door triply padlocked, the
pickup truck gone. I'd been counting on him for a ride
back to the train and had already sent my taxi on its
way. Walking would take an hour, in the rain. It was
this as much as anything that led me, passing back
around the front of the house, to ring the doorbell.
For a time, no one answered. As I was about to go,
though, the inner door receded, and there was Samantha,
the daughter, watching through the storm glass. In
the childhood photos taped to the fridge she was still
roly-poly, but in person, the first thing you saw was
how rangy she'd become. The second was that she didn't
know what to do with it. She had the slouchy diffidence
you sometimes see in wading birds before they're
startled into flight. Her hair, chin-length and bottle-
black, made her face look severe, but then her mouth
relaxed, softening everything around it. I wondered if

she'd been expecting someone else. "You're the magazine guy, right? Dad's not here."

I gave her my most winning smile and said our wires must have gotten crossed. "I was wondering if I could use your phone to call another cab. And maybe bend your ear for a minute, since you're home."

Her eyes narrowed. Then they were huge, dark, pensive again, and the door was opening. She didn't watch while I flipped through numbers in the kitchen, or even linger in the room. I should have gone to wait at the curb after hanging up the phone. Instead, I followed the house's one hallway to the bedrooms. I found her sitting on an old canopy bed, looking down at her fingers on the frets of a green electric guitar. There was a record on the stereo; she was trying to teach herself to play along when my knock on the doorframe interrupted her. "I never got a chance to thank you," I said.

"For what?" On the wall behind the bed were dozens of photographs of rock musicians.

For lobbying Carmine to keep talking to me, I said.

Her shrug was her father's. "I figure someone gives you a shot at fame, you take it."

"Fame's a pretty exalted term for what I have to offer," I said.

"Not if you're in the business he's in." She idly strummed a chord.

She wasn't tempted to go work for him, then? I asked.

"Is this what you wanted to bend my ear about? Because if so, it's already pretty well bent."

"This is what fathers do," I said. "They worry."

"Just because he's talking to you now doesn't make my life your business." Again, her thumb summoned a chord, the wrong one, and well behind the beat. "Anyway, I hope you don't take it all as gospel, because he's a little unreliable these days." The song was an old Van Morrison number. When she bent to play it, I noticed a child's plastic bandage on her neck, a pattern of white animals covering what I assumed to be an injury. The strings made a dead, detached sound. I had a brief sense of her as in mourning about something. "Or paranoid," she said. "He thinks people are trying to get him to fold his tents."

"You mean people from the old neighborhood? The mob?"

"Please. I mean the competition. We've had the contracts for the city for like fifty years, and now these assholes, or their subsidiaries, come along and snatch them." I had heard about these lost contracts before I'd ever met Cicciaro, but so far he'd mentioned them only in passing, like the failure of his marriage, and I knew better than to press him on matters touching his pride. But surely this was just business, nothing personal.

"I'll admit I was curious as to why he keeps a gun back there."

"It's the Sicilian in him. Like we're in some medieval village where property has to be protected by the sword. Though if anyone did cross him, I'm sure he could handle it. He's a tough old guy, my dad."

"Runs in the family, huh?" It was supposed to be a compliment, but came out too solicitous. Then a horn honked outside.

"There's your ride."

"E D A," I said. I can still see her puzzled look. "The chords. E-e-e-D-A. Glo-o-o-ri-a." And there, for a second, was her smile.

I WOULDN'T THINK OF THOSE CONTRACTS AGAIN UNTIL A FEW weeks later, when, to compensate for standing me up, Cicciaro finally made the offer I'd been waiting for: he wanted to know if I'd come help fire a show. "Don't expect anything fancy," he warned me. It was just that

rinky-dink First Night he'd contracted for on the Jersey
shore. "Fifteen minutes, a couple hundred shells, Happy
New Year's, that's it." Still, this looked to be the
future of the independent fireworker, and if I wanted
to see it, I might as well come along.

The show was to be fired from a refurbished garbage
scow set adrift on a brackish inlet on the inland side
of the town. Neither Cicciaro nor the other technicians
who'd driven down to meet us seemed to notice the
smell of souring trash, or the snow that had begun to
slant through the parking lot's lone streetlight. With
the barest vocabulary of grunts and nods, we loaded
up the scow. Some kids in parkas stood watching at a
distance, ready to skitter off into the dark. For all
they knew, notwithstanding my necktie and fedora, I was
a fireworker, too.

Around eleven, we pushed out onto the water, Cicciaro
himself at the wheel. We anchored in sight of the
parking lot's light and the black cattails on the shore,
but far enough away, I noted, that should anything go
wrong, the casualties would be limited to those of us
on board. Then there was nothing to do but wait. The
technicians kept to the end of the boat farthest from
the mortar arrays, but the distance between them and
their boss seemed less spatial than spiritual. He'd
recently confessed to me that he'd had to undertake a
round of cost-cutting back in the spring. Technology
had made it difficult for an unaffiliated shop to
compete on price. Big conglomerates could have the
Taiwanese build shells for pennies a day, and hire a
consultant to come in and program their Cicciaro board.
Indeed, as New York dug out from the fiscal crisis that
had pushed it into technical bankruptcy, Cicciaro was
told that in order to win back city contracts, he would
need to halve all his bids. He went to the shop one
day and gathered his men together, most of them with

families to support or alimony to pay, and announced
that, for the first time in history, there would have
to be layoffs. Then, once those jobs were gone, he was
told that his outfit was too small to compete for the
Bicentennial.

I hadn't asked him about New Year's, but now, as if
overhearing my thoughts, he spoke up from the pilot's
compartment. "You know there's a better show up in New
York tonight. Same folks they got to do the Fourth. I
never could figure out why you aren't talking to them."

I told him I'd much rather be here, with someone who
knew the traditions, than with some schmuck feeding
cards into a computer.

"I don't mean to throw cold water, but pretty soon you
won't be able to tell the difference." The first flare
lifted off like a rocket, reddening the clouds. Even
for this lowly job, he'd come up with something special:
a shell that scattered across the snowy sky a dozen
fizzing orbs of gold. They hung there as if on strings.

"I doubt that very much, Carmine," I said.

"You work and work to make something of value, and
then the money moves in." He seemed to be weighing
something. "I wasn't going to tell you this, but that
day we missed each other, at Thanksgiving, my little
workshop out back had just been broken into. Three
grams of my polverone was missing. Now why go to all
that trouble? I can't prove anything, but I think
someone wanted to let me know they can reach me."

Three grams was nothing, I knew by now. A rounding
error, or at worst, a prank by some kids like the ones
I'd seen back on the shore. "I've got friends who are
cops," I began.

"You don't go to the cops, where I'm from. And that's
not--"

But Len Rizzo, the technician, must have gotten
impatient up in the bow, or hit the wrong button,
because just then a dozen more lights streaked up

from the boat, a great volley of pops. They were more
of Carmine's latest shells, and, hard as it may be
to credit, the two things that happened next would
conspire to knock the story of the theft into some far
corner of my consciousness for months. The first thing,
slower to unfold, began with the stroke of a churchbell
on shore. It was midnight, New Year's, 1977. Which meant
that, fewer than 100 miles away, Carmine's daughter
already lay in Central Park, two bullets from an
unknown assailant or assailants in her head, the snow
going pink from her blood. Yet this was still remote
from our awareness, and the sudden thing, the thing
that struck me dumb at the time, was that, instead of
just hanging there, or lilting slowly earthward, as a
lifetime of gravity had trained me to expect, the gold
orbs before me began to rise.

BUT THEN THERE
two
cha
tec
aga
lay
con
thei
enta
    To
come
fanz
Thou
Sout
out
And
frag
larg

BOOK III

LIBERTY HEIGHTS

[JANUARY–JULY 1977]

Marcus Garvey was inside of Spanish Town District Prison,
and when they were about to take him out,
he prophesied and said:
"As I have passed through this gate,
no other prisoner shall enter and get through,"
and so it is until now;
the gate has been locked—so what?
Wat a liiv an bambaie
when the Two Sevens clash.

—CULTURE
"Two Sevens Clash"

26

ALMOST A DECADE HAD PASSED SINCE RICHARD GROSKOPH'S last
trip to the Bronx—it had been the late '60s, he'd been wrapping
up a piece on the klezmer kings of the Grand Concourse—and now,
as the 4 train went elevated beyond the river and the lights cut out,
he had an image of himself as an astronaut hurtling toward some
inhospitable planet that was really a future version of his own. Stark
brick monoliths, blue in the moonlight, thrust up from a landscape
nearly treeless. Cranes stood here and there, fossils with wrecking-
ball heads. Above loomed columns of smoke too thick to blame on
incinerators. Then the lights were back on, and none of his fellow
passengers seemed to realize they'd ever been off, or that anything
out there was burning. They stared instead at newspapers or at the
letters and numbers scratched into the windows. *Stash, Taki 8, Moon-
man 157*, incantations to keep the passing world at bay. Not unlike,
come to think of it, those ads overhead, peddling podiatry, plastic
surgery, orthodontia. The doctors were all white, the patients brown.
Richard was the only gringo in his section of the train. And no one
else was rising to get off at the next station.

Down below was a stretch of asphalt where paper cups and plastic
products collected around girders, their colors obliterated by winter.
There were Rent-to-Own circulars. There were syringes. Graffiti
suppurating on the metal shields of storefronts. When he stopped

to peer through a grating, he could make out tipped-up chair-legs. Mott Haven had once been a promised land for working folks tired of slums. Now the sole signs of life were a trashcan fire in a lot down the street and the takeout joint on the corner, the counterman ghostly behind bulletproof glass. Of course, one possible definition of the word *city* might be *a site of concentrated change*, and these transformations had been under way long before Richard had left. But he'd somehow imagined that his leaving might affect the rate of decay. Wasn't this what Heisenberg said? Apparently not. Nor—he thought again of Samantha Cicciaro in her hospital bed—did it pay to turn your back on these streets. He flipped up the collar of his sportcoat, shoved hands into pockets, and pushed deeper into the ghetto.

In a concrete plaza between two housing-project towers, emergency vehicles idled, screamers off. Firemen with small bare heads sat smoking on bumpers. Red lights raked the crowd gathered behind catenaries of police tape. Richard again felt acutely Caucasian, but no one appeared to notice him. For maybe ten minutes, they all watched cops move in and out of the nearest building. Then, through the vestibule's smeary glass, Richard spotted a plainclothesman lurching toward him on crutches. He would have recognized him anywhere, despite the hair gone largely gray. The Little Polack. Larry Pulaski.

Back when they first met, there had been no crutches. Richard had been twenty-two or twenty-three, beating the bushes for copy. One strategy was to hang around a certain tavern on Jane Street, which, if you could tolerate potatoes like wet newsprint and the occasional chit of bone in your beef, had the advantage of proximity to the Sixth Precinct. Off-duty patrolmen swarmed the bar. A round of drinks might dilute their natural antipathy to the point where they'd cough up something useful, a name, a number to call. These were physically large men, most of them. Pulaski stood out for being so small, and for always sitting down to drink. There was this hunch only Richard seemed to see; when he rose from his table, his shoulderblades pressed like tentpoles against his starched blue uniform. Later, having discovered their mutual love for Patsy Cline, Richard was moved to ask him if he ever played cards.

Now he watched Pulaski, in a child-sized wool topcoat, address the cab of an ambulance. Its aspirated idle grew louder. The crowd parted to let it pass, even as the rollers went dark; it was in no hurry. A woman started muttering. Boys in ski jackets and stocking caps—he wasn't supposed to think *boy* but that's what they were, young men with the wispiest of facial hair—jived with an edge of hostility. How long since Richard had covered a crime scene? He wanted to flee back to Chelsea, a dozen stops away, to forget again the intimate terms on which people live with death. But if Carmine didn't have that luxury, neither should he. When the last fire truck had rumbled away, he ducked under the tape. *I tried to pull that shit . . . crack my head open*, the muttering woman muttered. Pulaski looked up from where he'd braced himself against an unmarked car to peel off latex gloves. Extending a hand was probably not the move here, but Pulaski rebalanced himself to take it. His expression was benevolent. Even grandfatherly. "Richard Groskoph, for Pete's sake. Where you been all my life?"

"It's been a while," Richard agreed. Time had worsened Pulaski's spinal condition, cramped his torso into the shape of a comma. His legs made contact at the knee, but splayed below like a tripod's to support the uncentered weight up top. Obviously Richard, getting older himself, wasn't allowed to mention this. He tilted his head toward the apartment tower. "Can I ask?"

"My guys call this the Mitchell-Lama Fire Drill," said Pulaski. "Jam the elevator, pull an alarm on a high floor, set up with a gun in the stairwell near the lobby and jack people up as they come down. Except sometimes the gun goes off. Two bodies here."

"That's awful."

"It surprises me, though, to see a reporter this far uptown. You can firebomb whole blocks these days and not attract a single tape recorder." His gaze was a tailor's, eyeballing measurements.

"To be honest, Larry, I'm not really up here in my professional capacity. You got a minute to talk?"

Pulaski turned toward the building lobby, where subordinates did their best to look busy. "Doesn't look like we'll be making an arrest tonight. Let me tell the primary, and then we can go somewhere quieter."

He was surprisingly swift on his crutches; he looked almost batlike, gliding through the slatted shadows of what lights survived above the El tracks. Back at the takeout place, an orange formica counter facing the street offered enough room to eat standing up. Richard, suddenly ravenous, ordered a cheesesteak. Pulaski settled for coffee. The counter came up to the middle of his chest, but he said nothing about being uncomfortable, so Richard tried not to disguise his own height, or to feel uncomfortable on Pulaski's behalf. And it would have been easy to dwell in the safety of small-talk. No one had *asked* Richard to come up here; no one had made the dying girl his personal affair. But how else was he supposed to bridge the distance between the body hooked up to a breathing tube and the one that had sat before him two months ago, strumming an apple-green guitar? "Truth is," he said, crumpling his napkin into the cardboard basket the demolished cheesesteak had arrived in, "I wanted to talk about a case of yours. Cicciaro, is the victim's name."

Pulaski glanced behind him as if someone might be listening, though the only other person in here besides the counterman was the elderly Chinese who manned the grill. "Remind me . . . ?"

"New Year's Eve. Central Park. Seventeen-year-old white girl. Comatose. It's been in the papers."

"I'm sure it has been, in that ZIP code. But where'd you get her name? We're not releasing it."

"I happen to be what you might call a friend of the family."

"Who, the father? This is a friend of yours?"

"Or associate. Subject. I've been working on a profile."

"You're kidding."

"Fireworks and all that. It's been five months, you get to know people."

"Odd, though, that this would be the first I heard of it," Pulaski said. "I'd remember if he'd mentioned you."

"Probably didn't seem important at the time." This circling put Richard in mind of the courtship dance of crabs: each looking to grab without getting grabbed.

"And I don't suppose in those five months, Richard, you've learned anything I need to know?"

"Like what?"

An eyebrow rose almost imperceptibly. "Friends of mine, friends of ours, guys who know guys . . ."

Richard had the same disoriented feeling he'd had on New Year's Day, answering the phone. *Which hospital? Are you there right now?* Carmine's voice had had the tough flat affect of a kid talking himself into something. For three minutes in the OR, he'd said, Samantha's heart had stopped. Then Richard understood. "Come on, this is because they're Italian? The guy's the furthest thing from mobbed up, Larry. He'd go live on Mars, if he could."

"I have to ask, you know that. This is all off the record, by the way."

"Which is exactly the thing. I came up here to ask if there's a way to keep him and his daughter out of the news. I counted eleven follow-up articles the week after New Year's, and that was just off the pro forma you guys put out. I'd hate to have a gaggle of reporters descend on the Cicciaros' lawn. Or whatever the collective is, a herd, a murder."

"For them, you'd hate this?" Then, when Richard refused to be drawn in: "Believe me, I need the press in this like I need a hole in my head. Pardon the expression. But what's left to cover? It's an anonymous victim and a random shooter. We've got no leads, no case, and right now, you're the only one who knows who she was. Even the people I talked to at the college assumed she just dropped out. Give it another week, and everyone moves on to the next story."

"Have you looked at the file, Larry? She turns eighteen tomorrow. As of"—he checked the clock on the wall behind the inch-thick glass—"as of a couple hours from now, Samantha Cicciaro is no longer a minor. Everything about her becomes public record. Starting with the name."

For a minute, Pulaski was completely still. His reflection was a shade on the window. "Her date of birth. Cripes. Someone should have caught that."

"I caught it. And I'm telling you now. Do you really want her life story all over the six o'clock news, and then another month of coverage?"

Pulaski took a swig of coffee, tamped away the drops that clung to his moustache. "But what's your angle? You planning to crack this on your own?"

"I'm just trying to wrap up my profile. Probably won't even publish, now that all this has happened." He wanted to believe this was as much thought as he'd given it. But was there, briefly, a skeptical look from his old friend?

"All right, Richard. Let me see what I can figure out. Meantime, though, not a word of this. And no more surprise visits." Pulaski put his cup down, a hollow sound, and handed across a card with his new title, Deputy Inspector. "Anything occurs to you, that's my direct line." Clipping crutches to forearms, he seemed suddenly vulnerable, like a mollusk climbing back into its shell. "You know, for a minute there, I thought you'd left us for good."

"What can I say? It's obvious I don't know what's good for me."

"Well, selfishly, I'm pleased. Wednesday nights haven't been the same without you and 'Dr.' Zig. I miss having an easy mark around."

"Wait—what happened to Zig?"

"Tune in to the radio sometime, you'll see. It's like 1962 all over again. That's the year you two fell out, isn't it?" It was odd: Richard had believed that his break with Zig Zigler, like its cause, was a secret. And then what else might Pulaski know? "But drive safe, Richard."

"I took the train."

"In that case, God help you, I guess." As the men shook hands, each took care not to squeeze too hard, or to let the other know this care was being taken. Still, something lingered between them that Richard would only later come to realize wasn't quite an understanding.

27

THE PARK ON NEW YEAR'S DAY had been a blasted whiteness, or a series of them, hemmed in by black trees like sheets snagged on barbed wire. Snow had melted and refrozen on the paths, leaving a thin shell that collapsed under Pulaski's shoes and crutches, soaking his socks and lending each step a jerky quality. Of course, where Larry Pulaski was concerned, "jerky" was a relative term. Maybe when he'd bought the coffee this morning to soften up the Goodman kid, he should have stuck to decaf. Now it was getting on toward noon; CSU was winding down its canvass, there were no more witnesses, and it wasn't even Pulaski's case, technically. He could have been back in his bed on Staten Island an hour ago, dry of foot. So why had he returned to the park instead, to limp the perimeter of the crime scene one more time?

What answer you got would probably depend on who you asked. His detectives, McFadden and the others, would have said Pulaski was fastidious, a *control freak*, nothing ever done right unless he did it himself. And there was maybe a grain of truth to that. In 1976, there had been almost two thousand homicides in the City of New York, and Pulaski's crew caught a fifth of them—one for each day of the year. The aggregate clearance rate was about 30 percent. After the third time he'd personally worked back on a case to discover a neglected eyewitness, he'd announced that he wanted a copy of every case-jacket on his desk. Now two or three times a week, he would show up at a scene like this, insert himself into an investigation, just to keep people on their p's and q's. Crunch.

He turned off the path. Between it and the wall was where Mercer Goodman claimed to have found the body, and though there was a strong circumstantial case for his being a heroin addict, Pulaski's instinct was to believe him. Techs with plastic baggies tucked through beltloops now squatted there. But to the east were woods, and beyond that the Sheep Meadow. Pulaski toiled up a hill, breathing heavily. He'd always told himself he didn't need the crutches, they were only just in case, but to be honest, he wasn't sure anymore. At one point, he slipped on some rocks, but no one was watching.

Pulaski found a certain tactical advantage in being underestimated. His bosses thought that because he was a cripple he wasn't up to legwork, so they'd promoted him to Deputy Inspector, supposedly a desk job. His supervisees—kids, essentially, with long hair and muttonchops and clothes like they'd never heard of dry cleaning—thought that because he knew how to dress and kept his fingernails clean, he lived like some kind of monk, when in fact he and Sherri still had terrific sex after fifteen years of marriage. He thought it was terrific, anyway. If you'd asked Sherri, though, why he was putting in more overtime lately than he cared to count, she might have suggested it wasn't so much zeal for the job as unease about what waited at home. There was likely some truth to that, too. A decade his junior, Sherri was thirty-eight this year, and it was increasingly clear that even terrific sex wasn't going to produce kids, maybe on account of the polio, maybe on account of something with her, he was afraid to find out, as she had been once.

He told himself it was for the best. His own dad had been a drunk, and not a nice one. Larry had long ago forgiven him. Watching your kid boil with fever, eyes rolling up to the whites, must hurt even worse than the fever itself. You knew *you* were going to die, after all. It was fear of this, of his imaginary kids, of screwing them up or worse, that sat like a patch of black ice high in his chest, invisible but heavy, whenever Sherri showed him some article about new advances in treating infertility. He'd broken the news to too many parents after finding daughters under highway overpasses, panties bunched at ankles. Finding sons tangled in the limbs of a tree in a courtyard between Avenues C and D, bloated from days of rain.

Secretly, shamefully, every childless year that passed brought a kind of relief.

Except lately Sherri had switched to talking about getting out of New York altogether. And sometimes to crying in the bathroom at night. She ran the shower to cover it, but forgot to get her hair wet. And he couldn't face the fact that, after years of making her happy, as he'd vowed to do, he didn't know how to fix this. So he worked. A lot. Maybe he was supposed to; maybe this was why they couldn't conceive. Although oddly, now, he looked back at his adult life, day after day of stepping off the ferry, sometimes not even home yet at nine at night, and at the quiet orderly adult-like house, and whereas Sherri had maybe started to make peace with it—having at least learned to cry—Larry himself did appear to have regrets. Kids were getting knocked up right and left, he saw it all the time. But maybe that was God's will, too. Another advantage over more physically vigorous men was that he'd learned not to try to understand God's will. He assumed that the heavenly father who'd crippled him must be like his earthly one: distant, arbitrary. The job of the child was just to love Him. Because He said so, was why.

The sun was out now, clearing bald patches on the meadow. Last night's snow was like a dream. Kids shaped woeful snowballs out of what remained. The detectives behind Larry were invisible; none had thought to roam this far. He felt sharp, somehow. Called out of his thoughts. Something glinted in a bush near where he'd emerged.

He tottered over. Birds, flushed from undergrowth, beat out across the white. He extracted a mound of damp fabric. Bluejeans. A pocket rivet was what had winked. A lump inside one leg turned out to be a wad of jockey shorts he pulled on gloves to handle. Urine stains along the venting. In one pocket, a half-punched round-trip Long Island Rail Road ticket. In the other, a mimeographed sheet, ripped in half. **ex nihilo (ex-ex post facto) / get the fuck out**. And above this jumble a weird little glyph or symbol; hadn't he seen it somewhere?

Probably this was nothing. The queers came here for assignations, there were vice raids all the time, one of them had lost his pants. Still, it was about the only evidence produced so far, and he hated to put it into the clumsy hands of McFadden, whose case theoretically this was. Out of habit, he carried a supply of forensic baggies. He returned the paper to the jeans, bagged the jeans in plastic, and squeezed the whole package into a large inside pocket of his brushed-wool greatcoat. He wouldn't mention it to anyone just yet. He wasn't sure he trusted the system, or any system, not to mishandle it. And no one would bother to mention that Pulaski looked lumpy, since that's how he looked most days, these days.

28

AT THE END OF THE FIRST WEEK OF JANUARY, a memo had circulated, convening a plenary meeting of the upper tier of management: representatives of the Board, corporate counsel, financial officers, vice presidents, and, from the Office of Public Relations and Community Affairs, Regan Lamplighter, née Hamilton-Sweeney. The only person missing was her father, who was at home, recuperating from the "shock to his system."

Or so, at least, went the story that circulated in the fractious period before the meeting came to order. In point of fact, Daddy's system had long been in decline, and the arraignment had come as no shock. By the time Regan had reached him by phone in Chicago, Felicia had already warned him about the federal marshals camped out at LaGuardia; this, and not the snow, had been why they'd waited until Monday to fly him home. In New York, the marshals had agreed not to cuff him, had allowed his chauffeured black towncar to ferry him directly to the courthouse downtown, where Regan waited at a side entrance with his legal team. Though the bond the judge set seemed to her exorbitant, Daddy had trundled out under his own power two hours later, free until the case went to trial. No, the thing keeping him at home wasn't shock, or even the longer-term corrosion of his faculties. It was that someone had tipped off the media. There had been two dozen reporters waiting for them out on the courthouse steps, a swarm of white locusts. Deep in the background, vans hoisted fifty-foot antennae into the gelatin-gray sky. Regan should have been ready for this; it was her job. But the lead image on the evening news that night would be a two-second clip of her father, looking bleached and confused, while an unidentified and slightly blurry woman clung to his elbow. "We have no comment at this time," she repeated over and over. The angle varied subtly depending on which channel you were watching.

And it was ridiculous, the way they all covered this! He hadn't been found guilty of anything, and notwithstanding federal insinuations of profiteering, the worst crime he stood accused of, according to some of the most expensive defense lawyers in the free world, was two counts of insider trading amounting to less than a million dollars—a tiny fraction of what the firm grossed annually. But no one wanted the scene from the courthouse repeated outside the lobby of the Hamilton-Sweeney Building every time Daddy came or went. And so, even as the conference room's long table filled up, the chair at the head remained empty.

There were some moments of unease after the door closed. Without Old Bill, who would run the meeting? Then, from a seat halfway up Regan's side of the table, a white head rose. The eyes didn't seem to see her. The voice should have been inadequate to fill the big room, yet she heard the Demon Brother as if he were broadcasting from her inner ear: "As I'm sure you all know, Bill thought it best he remain at home this week, working on his defense."

No one spoke, but there was a shift in the texture of the silence, a discomfiture that passed for assent. All heads having turned to him, Amory Gould sat back down. He didn't bother to cover his mouth when he coughed.

"In his absence, the facts we face are these. Our fearless leader has been charged with running afoul of the securities statutes. Ahem. Which we know have been put in place to harass successful Americans." His face was bland, but his hands seemed to want to exact some revenge on the pen in front of him, and tugged at both ends. "We have every confidence—every confidence—Bill will be cleared of wrongdoing. Our task in the meantime is to coordinate a response, such that this firm, a legacy of his hard work and, ahem, vision, can rise to the challenges of the moment. To chart, in short, a strategy." *Legacy* made it sound as if Daddy were not recuperating, but dead.

And who was this *we*? In the time it took Regan to formulate these objections, Amory must have opened the floor to ideas, because now ambassadors from the various departments began to speak up.

Legal advocated a policy of company-wide silence as it pursued dialogue with the U.S. Attorney. Accounting was conducting an audit. Global Operations required stability above all else, lest vital revenue streams be threatened. For all his showy circumspection, his refusal to move to the head of the table, the nervous coughs he produced at almost algorithmic intervals, Regan knew her step-uncle well enough to see he was enjoying this. Indeed, most of the men contributing to the conversation were allies of the Goulds, and seemed to be competing to say whatever would please him most.

Then she noticed the blond man taking notes in the corner behind her. Still pretending to listen to Amory pretend to listen to everyone else, she snuck a glance back over her shoulder. He had to be the youngest person in the room. His hair was like wheat germ mixed with honey. Shampoo-commercial hair. It was longer than Keith's, but somehow wholesome, neat, even as it tumbled down past the collar of his arrow-collared shirt. In fact, she'd seen it once before, in the commissary on the thirtieth floor, back around the time she learned of her husband's infidelity. She'd bumped into him with her tray. At that point, she'd been too distracted to get his name; in her head, he was just the Guy with the Hair. Now, as the syllables of functionaries closer to the empty seat of power flattened and warped into nonsense, she found herself wondering what the Guy with the Hair was doing here. "—Regan?" someone was saying.

She turned back to the yellow pad in front of her, heat rising in her cheeks. "I'm sorry?"

"Artie suggested we hear from Public Relations." Her step-uncle's voice was full of something she couldn't decipher. Farther down, next to the empty chairman's chair, old Arthur Trumbull, eighty-eight and half-deaf, looked at her with eyes like a horse's, wet and black and kind. He'd been a Director since her grandfather's time, and a faithful retainer to the family. "Did you have something to add?"

She cleared her throat in anxious echolalia, trying to remember the points she'd wanted to make. "Well, first I think it should be noted that Daddy is . . . that my father hasn't been convicted of anything." She looked back at her notes from this morning. "I mean, I understand the position of Legal, and wanting to leave room to bargain, but if there's no proven wrongdoing, why act otherwise? Not having him here right now sends a message to the media people out there. Anything we do will. It seems important—and this is the view of the department—that the message we send is, we're prepared to fight."

As she spoke, Amory had risen to gaze at her over the domes of intervening heads. His thin lips smiled. "What an asset to have someone so eloquent here to represent the interests of the family. But things must also be looked at from a business perspective, and I'm afraid sticking our heads in the sand and pretending nothing has happened . . . well, it's a tactic, Regan, not a strategy."

His attention was uncomfortable, hot, like the light on the surgeon's forehead just before you go under. "Fine. So here's a strategy. Pretrial kabuki will take until at least, what, July? And meanwhile, the press is only going to get worse. If we're going to have any shot at a decent jury, we need a fair hearing from the public. Which means reconsidering the overall corporate image. We have to be seen again as the benevolent giant, the job creator. So what I'd like to do"—crafting this second point, she'd thought of the stadium plan Amory had shown her, but now she wasn't thinking at all so much as trying to drive a rhetorical thumb into his eye—"what I'd like to undertake these next few months is a comprehensive review of any business we're doing that affects the local market. Of course, I'd need data on every acquisition, every big position we take for our portfolio, every development project. Once we've completed our study, we can think about integrating them into a campaign. Like, Hamilton-Sweeney: Making New York Work."

"My dear—" Amory turned to his colleagues. "What you're proposing isn't practicable. The sheer volume of . . . An office of, what is it, two people? Ahem. Impracticable."

From the corner, the Guy with the Hair spoke up. "Well, actually, as far as influencing public opinion, she's right. Just taking out full-page ads and tossing ducats to orphans, New Yorkers are too jaded not to see through that stuff. You ever listen to that show, *Gestalt Therapy?*"

Amory had teleported to a spot behind the chairman's chair. His hands rested on its back.

Artie Trumbull looked up at him. "I agree, Amory. What Regan's saying makes sense. Leverage the good we're already doing, we might have more of a fighting chance at the voir dire. Or convince the U.S. Attorney we do, should we choose to pursue a plea."

As the senior person in the room, he still had influence; his motion to broaden Regan's mandate passed so quickly that it surprised even her, and the best Amory could do was pretend it was his idea. Unless it was only her first point he really cared about. "Evangelizing for our work, indeed, will be essential. But as far as Bill's day-to-day schedule, I have to say, I'm not sure this sabbatical isn't for his own good." He looked around the table. "Until Bill is cleared of all charges, as he no doubt will be, best to keep him out of harm's way, no? Absent any objections, it will be proposed at this afternoon's Board meeting that an interim chair be named." There was quiet now, even from Artie Trumbull. Even from Hair Guy.

And thus there would be no point in lingering to work the room, Regan was to decide as the meeting broke up. The day's inevitable outcome would be an assumption of power by Uncle Amory—or a formalizing of the power he'd already, over many years, assumed. She tried to calculate whether she could make it uptown to look in on Daddy and still be back for the start of the official Board meeting at five. Maybe, just barely, if she hurried.

The Rothko canvas near the elevator bank flashed past her, a red wound to match the blue bruise back at the penthouse. The elevator was empty, but then, at the last second, someone stopped the doors from closing: Hair Guy. They stood in mannered silence and watched the numbers count down. The building was a dinosaur, a neoclassical monstrosity from the days before elevators broke the sound barrier. Only when the door opened onto the lobby did she permit herself a look at the man's face. "I just wanted to say thank you."

For what? he said.

"For what? For being there, I guess."

He had a name, he said. It was Andrew. Andrew West. "Well, thanks a bunch, Andrew West." Then she tapped out into the cold, not daring to look back. *Thanks a bunch?* She sounded like a third grader. And still there was this stupid gauze on her hand, from when she'd nearly sliced her thumb off. Jesus, Regan, when did everything go so badly off the rails?

29

THE FIRST CHRISTIAN BIBLE Charlie had ever seen was in a motel room when he was six or seven. Usually, to save money, Dad liked to make the trip up to Grandpa's place in Montreal in a single day-long sprint. The wide new traffic-lightless interstate made it easy. That particular December, though, the stretch that ran through the Adirondacks was subject to fog and ice and closures, and when the darkness caught them north of Albany, they were forced to stop for the night. Dad showed Mom the little dresser-drawer Bible with a look of mild irony, like a man handling someone else's underthings. He must have thought Charlie, trying to tune in *Petticoat Junction* on the rabbit ears, didn't see.

But a decade later, the shooting of his best friend and the subsequent appearance of the Lord Jesus Christ to him personally would send Charlie scrounging for a Bible of his own. He found a copy—several, actually—at the back of the storefront Salvation Army in downtown Flower Hill, where the books smelled like mildew but were only a quarter apiece. He picked a pocket-sized edition stamped inside with the words **GIDEONS INTERNATIONAL**. Its green-and-gold fake-leather cover wouldn't have been out of place on a T. Rex record, but that probably wasn't what made him choose it. Probably it was the memory of that motel room upstate, which he hadn't thought about once in the intervening years.

Over the next week, cocooned in blankets in his cold basement, he had begun to read. Or re-read; the first few books he'd covered in Hebrew school. Now they worked their way deeper into memory. But it was the Gospel of Mark, mysterious and unJewish, he kept returning to. It said: Forgive yourself, Charlie. It said: Onward. It said: Today is the first day of the rest of your life.

The problem was, each new day was just like the previous one. He awoke to the fact of his friend lying in a hospital twenty miles away, comatose (or so *Newsday* had indicated in a blind item on the shooting). What would Jesus do? Jesus would be on the first train to the City, to be at her side. Charlie, for his part, couldn't make it past the LIRR. Afternoons after school, he'd stand shivering on the platform, gazing down the empty tracks to the east, as westbound riders always did. As he had with Sam on New Year's Eve. But what if he got to the hospital to find her eyes open, staring at him like, *Why weren't you there, Charlie?* Or what if they stayed closed? What if, while he stood there, her heart stopped? So he ended up back in his room, trying to fathom the workings of the goyish God. (E.g.: If there was no sin so bad as to be unforgivable, why had He withdrawn again into deistic silence after that night in the church? Or, supposing the voice was simply something Charlie had made up to comfort himself, why couldn't he make it come back?)

Then one afternoon, after weeks of trying, he made it all the way to the City. Rising above the little park that ran between some churches and Second Avenue, Beth Israel Hospital looked like the tower of Barad-dûr, a blinking red eye at its summit. There was so much of it up there, and so little of him down here, where everything was gray: gray paving stones, gray treetrunks, black wrought-iron fencing sooted down to gray. The only spots of color were the knit hats and mittens of the homeless scattered nearby. And copper-topped Charlie, tremendously exposed.

But this wasn't what stopped him. What stopped him was, he still didn't know what he'd find inside. What if the bandages made her look like a mummy? What if one eye was missing, its soft pink socket gaping like the eye of a painting that follows you around a room? As long as he stayed out here, everything remained potential, including the possibility that Sam might leap up any minute now to light up a smoke. And then it wouldn't be that big a deal that he hadn't come to visit. He felt the weight of the Bible in his pocket. He waited once more for God to speak to him, but all he heard was the wind clacking the bare trees and a bus whooshing past and, closer in, the apocalyptic grumble of an old guy on a bench.

Then, as he tracked the bus down the avenue, it hit him that he couldn't be more than a dozen blocks from the crash-pad where he and Sam had ended up the night of the Bicentennial. He wondered if her other friends, her City friends, still lived there. He wondered whether they'd been to see her. Whether, indeed, they were still her friends; she'd seemed so keyed up, going to see them play on New Year's. It was as if something had happened to her that autumn, while Charlie had been grounded out on Long Island. If he could find out what it was, he might, belatedly, reach her. Of course this was mostly an excuse for not having the balls to march this instant through the doors of that hospital. Still, he let himself be tugged south, into the East Village.

Though the blocks were ruler-straight, the way they all looked so similar made the house hard to locate, especially if you'd forgotten the number of the street. Another thing he couldn't quite remember, once he finally found it, was whether its front door had been this banged up last summer. He seemed to recall instead a big graffiti piece like a Burger King crown spreading across the steel. They'd both been high on mushrooms; he'd probably been seeing things. But he did know that it was kept unlocked. (*What do you think this is, a country club?*) When no one answered his knock, he stepped inside. The ramshackle parlor to his left had been full of black light and kegs of beer and music and punker types he'd done his best to avoid, drag-walking his semiconscious friend to the safety of the basement. In January, it was empty. There wasn't even plaster on the walls.

He climbed one flight of stairs. Then another. Still no sign of habitation.

Which made him no less nervous than that party had.

Finally, on the top floor, he heard voices. The windows were too dirty to admit much light, but a bit of gray sun fell in from a trap-door in the ceiling. This must also have been why it was so cold in here—why Charlie could see his breath. As he approached the ladder that led to the roof, his heart went John Bonham on him. He hadn't been lying when he'd told Dr. Altschul he was acrophobic. But to chicken out now would be to admit that he'd chickened out back at Beth Israel; that these investigations weren't serious at all.

He emerged behind a chimney. Or half a chimney, rather. The rest had collapsed on the swaybacked roof. Around the broken bricks came voices, one male and one female. The girl he'd danced with at the Ex Nihilo show was passing a joint to the black guitarist who'd plied Charlie with beer. He was saying, "I don't understand why we can't get rid of them . . ."

"That's why they're called homing pigeons, D.T."

The guitarist scratched his lymon-colored hair. "Fair enough, but why have they all decided to call that shed home? There weren't more than ten of them a week ago."

They were staring down at an outbuilding in the back garden, whose roof, Charlie saw, was covered not with snow, but with roosting birds. There must have been a hundred. The chickenwire coop the guitarist leaned against stood empty. "We could just shoot them . . . ," he said, thoughtfully.

"And bring the cops? Plus Sol would kick your ass. It's his coop to begin with. Or anyway, he stole it fair and square. Hey, Sol—," she called.

All of a sudden, Charlie was being hauled aloft by the collar of his jacket. The winter sky wheeled around until he was face to safety-pinned face with Sam's so-called friend, Solomon Grungy. Fee-fi-fo-fum. "Look what I found."

"It's that kid from the show," said the girl. "What's he doing here?"

"Get off me!" Charlie sputtered. And when he'd been set down again: "I'm buddies with Sam Cicciaro, remember?"

"Yeah, but like what the fuck are you *doing* here, kid?" said the black guitarist.

Charlie was terrified, so close to the edge. Someone seemed to have stolen the saliva from his mouth. "We were here last summer. He invited us." Nodding toward the hulking Grungy. "I don't know if you know, but Sam got hurt real bad over New Year's."

"Of course we know. What are you trying to say here—that we wouldn't know?"

Charlie didn't know what he was trying to say.

"Nicky should hear about this," the guitarist decided. "Anyway, let's get him downstairs, before Sol's pigeons come shit all over us."

"I already told you, motherfucker. Those are not my fucking pigeons."

They forced Charlie onto the ladder and then back down the stairs.

On the second floor, in a room whose walls were papered entirely with record sleeves—dozens of copies of Herb Alpert's *Whipped Cream & Other Delights*—they found someone sitting lotus-style on the bare floor. Nicky Chaos. How had Charlie missed him on the way up? The other three seemed proud of themselves, or expectant, as if waiting for Nicky Chaos to recognize the value of the human sacrifice they'd brought him. But he was wearing steel-rimmed spectacles now that made him look surprisingly civilized. He put down the book he'd been holding. Scratched his chin-beard. Rubbed a tattoo on his arm. "No, no, it's coming back to me. Backstage Charlie, right?"

A funny thing about charisma: the same people who can make you feel an inch tall can also make you feel huge, fortified, sometimes almost simultaneously. Charlie was all of a sudden eager to explain. "I just followed my feet here. I was at the hospital."

"They let you in? We figured that place would be crawling with pigs."

Charlie hadn't meant to imply he'd actually made it to Sam's room. "She's in a coma."

There was another bristly silence, and then Solomon snorted behind him. "So what, you want a shoulder to cry on?" The green-haired guy, D.T., started laughing, coughing, cough-laughing. But Nicky Chaos's speaking voice, a resonant baritone from which only a lunatic would have extrapolated his musical stylings, quieted them down.

"Sol's right, people want things, what did you come down here for, Charlie?"

"I don't know, you're machers, right? People who . . . who *do* stuff. That's what Sam said."

"And what does that mean to you? You want to paint some posters? Call the call-in shows, march around singing protest songs, that's going to make you feel better?"

Charlie took a step forward. Solomon started after him, but Nicky, still sitting, waved him off with a tattooed hand. Charlie's own hands clenched. He towered over Nicky Chaos. And vice versa, it seemed, weirdly. "I want judgment. I want to find whoever did this and bring vengeance down on their heads."

How naked his voice sounded, here in this cold house, in the gloom. But Nicky's came just as soft, like the two of them were alone. "Is that what you're about, kid? Avenging angel? Harbinger of doom?" When Charlie didn't answer, Nicky nodded, and hands from behind began patting at his sides, at his pockets, little nuzzling animals. By the time Charlie realized he was being searched, the hands were holding his shoulders. *He's clean.* Nicky rose and made the sign of the cross. "*Te absolvo.*" Then: "Jesus Christ, man, I had no idea you were one of us." His laugh reeked of reefer. "But let's get you fixed up. Sewer Girl, I need to powwow with your old man here for a minute, but why don't you go and see if we've got some medicine downstairs for the Prophet Charlie."

The girl led Charlie down to the kitchen, where all the doors had been taken off the cupboards. Inside were mostly mouse droppings—he could smell, he thought, the chemical tang of the poison—but she managed to come up with a teacup. After rinsing it and putting on some water to boil, she plopped down across from him at a crippled cardtable. By daylight, her vibe was maternalish. And at the same time still sexy. She probably outweighed Charlie, but it was all kind of pushed to the right places. A belly you could lie against. The big, warm thighs he'd felt against his own, dancing at the Vault. She didn't seem to mind him staring at the shadowy place her tits made when she leaned forward, either. Having shed her coat, she was wearing only the thigh-length Rangers jersey and scuffed white go-go boots; with her sleepy eyes, she looked kind of like that one sexy Muppet who played in the band. "Are you cold?" When he nodded, she reached for his hands and rubbed them between her own. Then she took out another joint, lit it, shook out the match. "You want?"

"I've got pretty bad asthma."

"How old are you, Charlie?"

"Eighteen," he said, rounding up. And, slightly defiant, "Why? How old are you?"

"Twenty-two. But I've been here before, if you know what I'm saying."

"I don't believe in reincarnation." He imagined test-driving the word: *I'm a Christian now.*

"It's because you've got a young soul. But that's cool. *Chaque a son goût.* My mom used to say that." She paused for a coughing fit that sounded like her lungs climbing out of her mouth. Her big face went lovely with color. "It means each to her own, something like that. She was kind of a hippie, there at the end. Now she's probably a bird or a deer or something terrific." She took another puff, considered him through the harsh, sweet smoke. "You know your friend Sam was missing a mom, too. We bonded over that, way back when." And when he didn't say anything: "I'm kind of the den mother here."

"Can I ask something, though? You guys go by initials, right? S.G., D.T.—"

"D. Tremens. D. for Delirium."

"I get that. But why do they call you Sewer Girl?"

"Nicky says I'm stuck on a lower level of consciousness. Because I'm from Shreveport, or whatever. It's like, if you didn't grow up in the city, it's hard for dialectical materialism to be your bag. I still get sentimental about moms and deer and my horoscope and stuff."

"That was like Sam's least favorite word, though. Sentimental. Did you ever read her 'zine?"

"You don't miss a trick, do you?" she said, and rose to pour the tea. From inside a go-go boot, she retrieved a little baggie of pills. Methodically, she crushed one under a spoon and scraped the crumbs into his tea. "You've had a rough day, this way we'll be on like the same wavelength." He couldn't do more than sip the tea, almost choking from the heat, but he could feel the pill working pretty much immediately, unless that was his imagination.

"Hey, are you hungry?" she said. "I always get hungry this time of day. The getting-high time of day." She laughed. "Which is every time of day. I could run out and get us a treat."

He didn't have any money. But that was cool, she said. It was like part of her job, to welcome novices. She'd be back in a flash. She put a long, fake-fur coat on over her jersey—no pants—and went out, leaving Charlie alone. He got up to examine the kitchen, staggering a little. The Quaalude, or whatever it was, was stronger than what Sam used to get, or else he was more receptive to it. Waterstains swelled and subsided like big, brown jellyfish on the plaster above. Soon, he was lost in the maze of cracks winding down from the molding. In one place was a fist-sized hole. He pushed at a bit of plaster experimentally; it skittered down into darkness, but the sound of it hitting bottom was lost behind what seemed to be a gray metallic buzz back in his fillings. He realized this was the fume hood, which for some reason was over the sink and not the oven. He turned it off.

The others were tromping now down unseen stairs, heading out into the backyard. Through the cigarette-stained window, he watched them disappear into the outbuilding, under a lintel of birds. Plant life rose thigh-high between here and there. It spilled over into the next yard, and the next, these yards flowing together, walled in by tenements, all surrounding that little aviary, or fortress. He was still standing over the sink with his tea, swimming down into the dark cursive of winter weeds, when Sewer Girl returned.

"Oh, geez," she said, reaching for the fume hood. "Charlie, the fans have to stay on. There aren't many rules here, but that's like number one." She offered him a crumpled-looking pastry. Had he ever tried *pasteles*? "I live on Long Island," he said, and when the synapses fused in her brain she started laughing again; it really was the squarest place on earth, wasn't it? Charlie didn't mind. He liked sitting there stoned and pretending not to watch her tits jounce around like grapefruits in a sack. He knew it was the drugs making him feel better, but after the day he'd had, was that so wrong? And wasn't this how Sam had felt, hanging out here? Maybe he'd said this last part out loud, because it seemed like they were talking about her again. It was amazing, said Sewer Girl, how devoted people were to Sam. Men, especially. "Nicky wasn't always happy about that, but that's because he sees so much more than the rest of us. He always puts these things in terms of like how is it going to affect the Phalanstery. You know   is it going to compromise the project."

From within the gauze of the drug, something solid struggled to surface. He could make it out: shape, size, and color. "What project? You mean Ex Nihilo?"

"You're probably going to want to take that up with Nicky."

But when Nicky came in from the cold a few minutes later, he put his hand on Sewer Girl's shoulder and said Charlie had had a big day, maybe it was time he headed home. The rest of them had work to do.

"Can I come back?" Charlie asked.

Nicky's smile then was a thing of beauty—an artful rip in the denim of time. "Oh, sure. Oh, most definitely. We *expect* you back, Prophet. Once you're in, you're in."

30

THE RANCH HOUSE OFF THE CUL-DE-SAC had shrunk since the fall, like some kind of withered organ. But at least there weren't news-wagons everywhere, sinking into the slushy lawn, klieging up the siding, waiting to endow with sinister significance images of its last remaining occupant checking his mail. Richard walked around to the backyard, but for the first time that he could remember, the alumi-num hangar was silent, its great fans immobile. Maybe Carmine had gone to the hospital, and they'd passed right by each other at some point in the last hour, one commuting out, one in. Then Richard thought he saw movement behind the sliding door to the kitchen. He mushed back up to the icy patio. On the other side of the glass, the fridge was open, a little parenthesis of light; Carmine, wearing only a towel, had bent to place something on the bottom shelf. The sight of his friend peering in seemed not to startle him when he straightened. The door slid open. "Sorry," Richard said. "I came out to see how you were doing."

"I was about to shower," Carmine said, as if the words took a sec-ond to reach him.

You should have stopped there, Richard would think, looking back; far be it from him to stand between a man and his shower. But when had he ever known when to stop? "You mind if I come in for a minute?"

Carmine, unembarrassed by the graying sag of his own chest and gut, or possibly unaware of it, stepped aside to let him pass.

The kitchen table was still set for two. On one of the placemats sat some rosewood beads; on the other, a cylinder of Duncan Hines cake frosting. "It's Sammy's birthday," he explained.

"I remember."

"I was hoping to get the icing on quick while the shower warmed up, but the cake's too hot. The stuff just melts. They don't tell you on the package."

"How's she been, Carmine?"

"Depends when you saw her last." It was entirely possible that this was an honest statement, not meant to make Richard feel guilty about his two-plus weeks of radio silence.

"It was the last time I saw you. In the waiting room New Year's Day."

"Critical but stable, is what they're saying now. Whatever that means. Like, 'It's bad, but it's not getting worse.'" Richard could hardly stand to look at Carmine's biblical near-nakedness, or even at the hands closing around the frosting tube. They wanted work to do, cartridges to pack, necks to wring. Outside, the sun had withdrawn from the sky in defeat, but not a single light was on in here. "You need a beer?"

"I'm pacing myself," Richard said. "I'd take a glass of water, though."

Carmine went to the tap. There was a groan, a shuddering, a curse. "The goddamn pressure in this house. I forgot the shower was still on."

"Don't worry about me, go take your shower."

"No, no, let me go shut it off."

"Please, Carmine. I can wait here until you're done."

Carmine muttered something to himself and padded off down the hallway that led to the bedrooms. Richard had been back there once before. Now the avocado shag looked gray. Dimness made the water in the pipes seem louder.

Samantha's room, he had reason to know, was the second door on the right. The blue curtains, batiked with sunflowers, had been left halfway open. Other remnants of girlhood lingered here and there—the dressing table with stickers on the mirror, the canopy affixed to the bed. Back in the fall, dozens of Kodachrome photographs had been clothespinned to lengths of twine on the wall opposite the window, but those were gone now; he could just barely make out the darker rectangles on the paint where the sun hadn't bleached

it. Carmine must have let the cops take anything that could conceivably be evidence. Not that this was any of Richard's business.
It was only that cynical omnivore, the newspaperman, who would
have allowed himself to be excited by, for example, the plastic bucket
of laundry parked in front of the closet, as though the room had
been vacated only minutes ago. Still, just hypothetically, what might
Richard have been looking for, were he looking for something? The
dressing table's center drawer was locked. He thought about checking under the mattress; it was where, as a kid, he'd kept the dirty
playing cards Cousin Roger had brought back from the Italian front.
Then he spotted the film canister on her nightstand. Inside was the
key. The drawer slid open with a woody squeak. He found at the
bottom a trio of homemade pamphlets or magazines, unlined paper
stapled twice in the fold. Each cover was a jumble of text, some of it
written, some of it typed, some of it cut out of magazines and stuck
on like a ransom note, all of it photocopied. *Issue 1. Issue 2. Issue 3.*
The last had a piece of Scotch tape still clinging to the outer edge.
25¢ at the top. *You want this.* But now the water sluicing through the
walls had stopped, and Richard, with his sharpened senses, thought
he heard doors opening and closing. He jammed the pamphlets into
the back of his waistband, covered them with his sportcoat's tails,
and hastened out into the hall, trying to remember how many inches
ajar her door had been. He'd just taken his hand from the knob when
Carmine spoke up. "You need something back here?" Richard had
never seen him like this, in a starched white shirt. Comb-lines in his
slicked-back hair.

"Just the can, Carmine."

"There's one off the living room. You know that, you've used it
before."

"Right."

He slipped past Carmine without meeting his gaze and went to
try to piss in the front bathroom. As he stood above the robin's-egg
toilet, with its carpeted lid, various selves did battle. Some part of
him sensed some other part trying to meddle with what was clearly
now the story. And he'd sworn he wouldn't get himself mixed up
with his subjects this way again. Not after Florida. Hadn't he told
Pulaski that the goal was just to finish the profile? And yet there was
this dissembling body, this conglomerate Richard, returning to the
kitchen, reiterating that he was sure Samantha would be okay (which

he wasn't), and that Carmine should get some sleep (which he probably couldn't), and just generally knitting that doily of horseshit you were expected to insert between the bereaved and the fact that no one, in the end, made it out of this life alive. "I meant to tell you," he said. "I managed to track down my friend, the Deputy Inspector."

Carmine had taken the cake back out of the refrigerator to smear on icing with a butter knife. Now he paused, considering his handiwork. "Why'd you do that?"

"They're supposed to release her name to the press now that she's legally of age, but I got him to hold off. I know how you feel about your privacy."

"And what if somebody out there has information—did you think about that?"

The knife, perpendicular, let drop a dollop of white goo. Whichever Richard was in charge now felt a little sick. He'd been so sure it was his better angels leading him up to the Bronx. "You've got to trust me, the broadcast media can be merciless. And with a random shooting, it shouldn't make a difference whether her name's out there or not."

"I'll tell you something, though, Richard, in confidence. I sometimes wonder how random things really are."

IIe studied Richard's face, as if daring him not to take this seriously. For a moment, something rustled among the crowded file cabinets of Richard's mind. But it was wishful thinking, he knew. Hadn't Samantha used the word "paranoid" to describe her father? Richard's own paranoia was currently that the pamphlets, now sweaty, might at any moment fall to the linoleum. He said gently that he sometimes wondered himself; a logical cause would mean things weren't out of control. But in his experience, looking too hard for one could lead to feeling guilty, to making *yourself* the cause, when you were the furthest thing from it. "Honestly, Carmine, I don't know how you're doing what you're doing. I was just hoping to buy you some space to do it in without jerks like me getting in your way."

For a second there above the cake, Carmine seemed to weaken. Then he was himself again, a stoic piece of Italian marble.

"Anyway, I should be getting back," Richard said. When he stood, it was with extreme care, trying not to dislodge his contraband.

"You don't have to do that."

"No, I mean it. You want me to let myself out?"

"Wait, Rich. I was going to take this cake in to her. Why don't I drive you?"

Crawling along the grim and salted expressways of Nassau County a half-hour later, they would listen to sports radio, but the details were lost on Richard. He could think only of the pamphlets clinging to his lower back and whether he could somehow sneak them under the seats of Carmine's truck before it reached the city, to leave them there as if Samantha had dropped them. He didn't, though, in the end. Because wasn't this, if he was being honest, the sort of thing he'd come out here hoping to find in the first place, an hour of travel each way? At any rate, as soon as he was safely back behind the deadbolt of his apartment he took out the pamphlets and began to read. And so began his first, tentative descent into the daughter's secret life.

31

THE FOLLOWING THURSDAY WAS INAUGURATION DAY, a half-day at
school, and after the last bell, Charlie returned to East Third
Street. He told himself he'd stop by the hospital, too, to wish Sam
a happy birthday, but knew already there wouldn't be time before it
got dark. Instead, he would spend the last hours of daylight in that
tumbledown kitchen, drinking more of Sewer Girl's special tea . . .
At best, she might illuminate for him, finally, the mysteries of Sam.
At worst, he'd have someone to whom to make his own confession:
that he had been—that he was *still*—in love with his best friend. And
maybe if Solomon wasn't on the scene, Sewer Girl would offer poor
Charlie the consolation of a mothering embrace. He would crawl
into the chasm of her cleavage, never to be seen again. But neither she
nor Sol was around, nor anyone except for Nicky Chaos, who came
to the door (which, strangely, had been locked) in the muscle-tee that
read *Please Kill Me*. "Good timing," he said, like he'd been expecting
Charlie, and took a bite from a half-eaten nectarine. "I could really
use a hand."

Apparently, the outbuilding in the backyard had sprung a leak.
Some kind of crack in the foundation had let snowmelt seep in, and
it was going to be essential, Nicky said, that the floor stay dry. Real
temperamental equipment out there. So what they were going to do
was put down a tarp and then repurpose the carpet that was in the

basement. This was what a Phalanstery meant, by the way: meeting your own needs. Each according to his means. "You ever ripped up carpet?"

Charlie was afraid that if he said no they wouldn't let him come back, plus Nicky had a way of putting things that made you really not want to disappoint him. So he followed Nicky down to the very basement where six months ago, for the first and only time, he and Sam Cicciaro had kissed. Most of the furniture—a cracked mirror, the gutshot couch where he'd sat with her head in his lap—was now gone. And so, when he turned around, was Nicky Chaos.

It took Charlie over an hour, working with needle-nosed pliers and a boxcutter, to get the carpet up, and the moldy foam padding, and the vicious-looking staples that held it down. It was sweaty work, despite the chill of the house; first his jacket and then his sweatshirt came off. By that point, his arms ached. His throat was tight, his eyes rheumy from dust and fiber particles. The big roll of carpet and padding was too heavy to carry out in a single trip, so he sliced it into sections, like cutting up a hot dog for his brothers' beanie weenies. When the last section had been hauled to the top of the stairs, the basement was featureless. Then again, you couldn't live inside a memory. And there was the small bathroom built out of the wall, where he'd helped Sam clean herself up. He went in looking for something to wipe off his sweat, but when he pulled the pullcord, there was still no towel, no bathmat. Instead, the shower was filled with plastic crates of what looked like milk bottles, like a milkman's unrefrigerated and slightly watery milk. The exhaust fan couldn't quite suck out the same chemical tang the kitchen had had last week. He killed the light and backed out, but not before being spotted by Nicky Chaos, who again stood at the bottom of the basement stairs.

There were maybe ten seconds when neither of them said anything. Charlie felt like he'd been called before the principal, though he didn't know for what. Then Nicky squatted to pluck something from the folds of Charlie's sweatshirt. He brandished the little green Bible. "What am I thinking, Prophet, assigning you to manual labor? We've got to work on your head, man."

The house out back, to which he led Charlie, was still serving as a rookery for pigeons—even more of them, if possible—and Charlie had to pretend not to be bothered by the smell. Inside, its windows had been covered over with tinfoil, blocking out the day completely. The only light came from a single, bare bulb. Massed at one end of the concrete floor, opposite where the rolls of carpet and padding had been deposited, was a mountain of gear—guitar cases, amplifiers, mixing boards, tangles of wire. Hard to say if these were the same instruments from the New Year's show, or if any of this stuff had been used to record *Brass Tactics*. It was like one of those barricades the French were always throwing up in European History. A thicket you couldn't see too far into.

Stacked atop one of the amplifier heads were wobbly towers of books, which Nicky could reach only with the help of a stepladder. He plucked them off one by one and handed them to Charlie: Nietzsche, Marx, Bakunin. Charlie kept taking them until the books got too heavy and he had to find a dry place to set them down. Maybe this was supposed to be a test, like on *Kung Fu*, where David Carradine had to stand all day with a bucket of water on his head. But when he looked back up, Nicky was dragging two rolls of carpet out into the center of the room. He sat on one, drawing his legs up under him, and Charlie understood that he, Charlie, was to take the other. Finally, Nicky held out the Gideon Bible. Right up until the moment his hand closed around the binding, Charlie wasn't sure Nicky wasn't going to yank it away.

"Look. I know what you're thinking," he said, doing his best to mimic Nicky, to fold his own ungainly legs into a lotus. There was something disquieting about sitting like this, with no barrier between them. His thumb stroked the pebbleized binding for comfort. "But Jesus was into some pretty punk stuff."

"You mean that 'love thy neighbor' shit?"

"I mean giving hell to the moneychangers. Raising the dead."

"Charlie, that's liberal accommodationism, is all that is." Whenever Nicky's fingers moved, the tattoos on his thick arms swam. There were so many they were like sleeves, basically. Maybe that's why he could wear a muscle-shirt and not get cold. "Look, you seem pretty serious to me, a serious kid. And Sewer Girl tells me you want to know about our little project here. What's tricky is, you know, knowing about something and understanding it aren't the same thing. I did five semesters at City College, but it took coming downtown, starting the house here, to sort of get my head around the difference. And we're not even beginning at the same place. Me, my old man was half-Guatemalan, my mom only speaks Greek. You and Sam are from what, like Great Neck or something?"

"Flower Hill."

"Flower Hill." While he was speaking, Nicky had removed his belt. Now he tapped what looked like baby powder from a vial onto the back of the big silver buckle. He lowered one nostril to the buckle, then the other, pinched his nose, shook his head; sighed deeply. "What I'm saying, Charlie, is you're still at level one. Your defenses are up."

"They're not."

"See what I mean? And the thing you've got to figure out before you can really *understand* what all this is, is, exactly what are you defending? Here, *mi casa es su casa.*"

Charlie waited for something to stop him from bending to the beltbuckle in Nicky's palm, but then realized there wasn't anything. It was surprisingly easy. Surprisingly quick. From somewhere behind his hard palate came a cool metallic tingle, like licking the top of a double-A battery. Nicky was still talking.

"Tell me—look around you. I don't mean right now, I mean in general. What do you see? The land is exhausted, corporations control our brains, the politicians are criminals. I could cite you chapter and verse, but that's what the books are for, and anyway, you know it's true, or you wouldn't be much of a punk."

Charlie nodded gingerly, like a guy on a rope bridge he wasn't sure would hold his weight.

"And what do we do, Charlie? We react. We defend. We surrender our birthright, which is the power to define our own field of action." Taking another big rip of the cocaine. "I mean, on the one hand, there are, what, forty katrillion nuclear weapons out there to secure the status quo. On the other, nice, bright college kids read *One-Dimensional Man* and think, Hey, I'll go lobby my . . . whoever . . . and then we'll get rid of the warheads. Without seeing that what they're doing is shoring up the very system that brought us the warheads in the first place. I mean, you can vote for the donkey or the elephant, or you can stay at home, sucking on the cathode tit, but any way you analyze it, you've consented to an immoral system. The can of shaving cream you buy at the Duane Reade, that money goes to manufacture napalm. The system's whole goal and *raison* is to be total, you know what I'm saying? A closed loop. Speaking of which . . ."

Over among the snaking extension cords and foamless speakers was a television set, which Nicky now got up to turn on. It must have been after five, the early news was on, images of that afternoon's inaugural in Washington. Had so much time passed? Nicky snorted, without really interrupting the rhythm of his words. His shoulders bobbed like a boxer's.

"I'm getting to the part where I explain about the Phalanx, Charlie. But first, ask yourself: This immoral system, how do you get outside it? Option one, you drop out, sever the connections. They got that far in '68, okay? People went as far with that as they could, to say, I'm free, you're free, kumbaya and barbaric yawp and yadda yadda, and look what happened. The problem with the whole Rousseau trip is that man is primordially a social animal, in the sense of clan or tribe. Marx says this somewhere. You detach completely, you not only find yourself way out on a limb, against your nature, but you've lost any power for group resistance. And eventually, you come crawling back, clutching credit-card applications, begging to be let in."

The man from Georgia had one hand on the Bible, silently pledging to uphold or defend or what have you. The screen, weirdly, kept going white, as if something was interfering with the signal.

"Option two: organized resistance. But the problem with any organization is that it recapitulates the system. Hierarchies and parameters. The Bentham, the Mill, but also the Barthes and Marcuse. Ontogeny and phylogeny, you see what I'm saying? Look at Heidegger and the Nazis. Prepare to be incorporated. Or this is how I started to feel, anyway, Charlie, pursuing my little philosophic studies up in Hamilton Heights. There's ghetto all around City College, did you know that? As far as the eye can see. And I'm supposed to tell myself I'm making things better, just 'cause I'm not following my old man into the Marines? All I'm doing is smoothing over the tensions. Making the system more efficient. The energy all stays within the system, is why it's a beautiful system. The system of liberal humanism."

He was talking faster now, or Charlie was listening faster, all of the words miraculously falling into the sweet spots of his brain, as if he were the world's greatest all-purpose utility fielder, with eighty-two arms and as many mitts and always positioned exactly under the popups Coach was sending out to center field.

"Except. Except Fourier, Charlie, not the utopian but the other one, the scientist, he tells you there can be no such thing as a total system. There's always energy escaping. Tension. Friction. Heat. The Western gestalt is like, hey, bring that energy back under control somehow. Aestheticize it. Market it. Jujitsu it into an identity, a product, a political party, a romance, a religion, like your little Bible there. Something, anything other than what it is, which is the possibility of change. But what I start thinking, looking out those classroom windows, is, what happens if instead of trying to palliate the friction you make it worse instead? This is the '70s now, the death trip, the destruction trip, the internal contradictions rumbling and grumbling, the return of the repressed. It's the system, having swallowed everything, having indigestion. Through the miracle of dialectics, a third path appears, which is, you nudge it along. You make things better, people relax. You make things worse, they revolt. I mean, things have got to get worse before they get better. So it is written."

"I don't understand, though. What does any of this have to do with the band?"

"No more band, Charlie. No more art. No more trying to change the culture with culture."

"You can't do both?"

"We tried, and look what happened. Look where Sam ended up." His face darkened. "Call it a New Year's resolution. We're starting over again. Defining a new field of action. We refuse to be duped anymore. We refuse any further complicity with a corrupt system. Because you know who was complicit? The Germans. The French."

"You're saying Ex Nihilo is like Vichy France?"

"Charlie, we are beyond all that art shit. That Walter Pater shit. We are Post-Humanists. The Post-Humanist Phalanx. We redeem the claim of disorder on the system. And we're just getting started. You dig?"

Did Charlie *want to* dig seemed the more relevant question. He thought for a minute. *I work in the darkness for him who will come in the light.*

He realized he'd said it out loud only when Nicky asked, "What's that?"

"Just a thing I read somewhere." He was still flying, but sober enough to turn down another bump of cocaine. It was already dark out; the emergency AV Club meeting he'd concocted for his mom's benefit would have to be over now, or close to over, depending on the scale of the AV emergency.

"Thus endeth the lesson then, I guess," Nicky said. "I want you

to take those books, though. Educate yourself. Reach your own conclusions." Charlie was a little worried that, as with the voice of You-
Know-Who, this would be the only hard sell he got. Still, he carried
with him all the books that fit in his bookbag. He even left his History texts behind, to make room—though not, in the end, his Bible.
Nicky made a compelling case, but Charlie couldn't be sure yet what
would be required, if there was to be any hope of saving Sam.

32

THE FACE BEFORE HIM was hardly a face. More like a tissue of bruises, Keith thought. A sack of bone china, cast before bulls. Then he hated himself. This was supposed to come later: the flight into metaphor, the escape from the phenomenal world. He forced his mind to be still and simply see what was there. To see the lines of stitches creeping down from her gauze-covered forehead. To see the eyes bruised shut from where they'd broken her nose getting a tube in. To see the tube itself, striped by the shadow of the blinds, like the sheet it lay on, the bellows pumping robotically under glass, the birthday cake gone stale on the bedside tray. There was another tube, this one opaque, less flexible, running into her throat. Her name, when he said it, was too loud in the empty room, and he worried that someone would come running. He knew on some level he was the bad guy here. But on another level—the level on which he'd always been the golden boy, whose every action was good *a priori*—he still couldn't quite imagine this. As he hadn't quite been able to imagine, short of seeing her in the flesh, that it was really his Samantha who'd been shot.

Maybe this was why, in the weeks after New Year's, he'd failed to make any connection between his twenty-two-year-old paramour and the nameless minor in the tabloids. Or maybe it was that he didn't read the tabloids, and had other things on his mind; all you saw in *The Wall Street Journal* were headlines about Regan's dad. In fact, when the doorman had buzzed one evening to tell Keith he had visitors, his first thought was of the Feds. There would be two of them, as in the movies, in cheap haircuts and matching black suits. One would do all the talking; the other, at the pivotal moment, would unsnap a briefcase of documents related to the unloading of eight and a half million dollars' worth of municipal debt. Margin requests, pricing history, records from the trusts. He'd plucked his coat off the hook and buzzed back down to the doorman. "Can you tell them I'll meet them out front?" At least this way he might avoid the indignity of being manacled in his own building, paraded before the neighbors.

But when he'd reached the street, he'd had only the one visitor: a storklike man with longish hair and a salt-and-pepper beard. He had a good two or three inches on Keith, and his corduroy sportcoat was more a humanities professor's than a G-man's. When he said the name of the magazine he wrote for, everything clicked into place. For a single lapse in professional judgment, Keith Lamplighter was going to be dragged before not only a court of law, but also the court of public opinion. And what would he tell his kids?

"Please, Mr. Groskoph, I can't talk to you here," Keith had said. He moved briskly toward the corner, the local public-school schoolyard. They'd be less exposed there. The man followed without a word. Which was good, it meant Keith could still be persuasive, though inside he was a quivering ephebe. When he reached the basketball court, he drew himself up to full gridiron size and rounded on his visitor. "Let's get something straight. I don't appreciate you coming to my home, invading my privacy."

The reporter looked genuinely unprepared for this. "If you could spare only a couple minutes of your time, Mr. Lamplighter—"

"Am I to assume you got Amory's side of the story first, then?"

"Beg pardon?"

They reassessed each other uneasily. How did Keith keep getting so far out ahead of himself? "I'm sorry. What are we talking about?"

"You haven't let me get to that: the shooting in Central Park last month. I was hoping you might remember something about the victim."

"Huh?" Pugnacity gave way to confusion. Relieved confusion. He tried to recover. "You must have me mixed up with someone else. I don't know the first thing about it."

"But I was under the impression you'd corresponded with her? The girl. She left this." The man held out a small sheaf of pages. On the back cover was Keith's name. The front resembled the one he'd seen once in Samantha's dormroom. **LAND OF 1,000 DANCES**. And he almost had to sit down right there, on the icy blacktop. *The victim, New Year's. . . .*

He turned toward the school building. Instead of meeting Samantha that night, as they'd agreed, he'd been watching underwear fly on Third Avenue. And now some junkie in the park had been careless with the trigger, and Samantha was—was she . . . "Is she . . . ?"

"She's alive, Mr. Lamplighter, but she's not been conscious since. I apologize, it didn't occur to me her subscribers wouldn't have heard. I'm just having trouble tracking down any of the people mentioned between the covers here. But you weren't in contact, then?"

Keith wondered if he was visibly shaking. "Not personally. I mean, obviously, I was a, um, subscriber. Trying to keep up with the new music. But this is insane. I need a cigarette."

After he'd tried a couple times with his matches, the guy had offered him a Zippo. The schoolyard disappeared behind the lighter's flutter. The smoke scraped like fiberglass.

"I guess the name Sol doesn't mean anything to you, then? Iggy? Or the initials D.T.? PHP?"

Keith shook his head. "Where did you get that thing, anyway?"

"The other mystery is, this is a long shot, but I'm wondering if you've heard about a house in the East Village where she might have had some friends. I can't seem to run down any kind of address."

Keith saw again the sealed mailers that had filled his in-basket that summer and fall. But what did they have to do with anything? "Sorry," he said.

The man moved around to study his face. Whatever kind of reporter he was, it obviously wasn't an investigative one. In fact, his mood seemed strangely buoyant, as if Keith's answers were an afterthought to the questions themselves. "She never mentioned it?"

"Like I said, I never really knew her, personally." Was that it? Was he free? He'd pulled his coat tight against the winter wind, which sobbed around the playground equipment. "The cops know about her little magazine?"

"They've got copies, I'm sure. Though I can't see how it's going to help crack a mugging gone wrong. If it's a concern . . ." The reporter removed a card from his pocket. "That's a direct line you can use, should anything come back to you that might be useful."

But it wasn't even Groskoph's card, Keith had seen, once he was back inside the apartment. He'd bolted the door behind him and gone to the pile of newspapers next to the kitchen trash. There it was, in the *Times:* the Central Park victim had ended up at Beth Israel. He was afraid to breathe as he looked up the hospital in the phone book. He'd forgotten his niece's room number, he told the woman who answered, and gave her Samantha's last name; he wanted to send flowers. He waited to be told there was no such person. Instead, the woman said that gifts weren't allowed in surgical recovery, but that his niece was scheduled to be moved back to intensive care on Monday. Visiting hours were seven to seven. Hello? Was he there?

And now that he *was* there, or here, the thing he couldn't stop thinking was that it was true: he'd barely known her. There were only eighteen candles on the cake. He'd counted twice, to make sure. And she looked even younger than that—ten years younger, at least, than when he'd first met her, on the stoop of that goddamned brownstone. Far younger than she'd pretended to be, standing over him, looking straight into his eyes and smiling with one side of her mouth at the roles they found themselves playing. And he'd let this deceive him. In a by-the-hour room with rain lashing the windows, with the ripe berry of her nipple in his mouth and her long legs clinched around his back in a sweet misery of barely moving, he'd wanted to be deceived. Those legs were lost beneath the medical-green blanket. Her skull, shaved for surgery, reminded him of the soft skulls of infants, and he wanted badly, for a second, to bend down and smell her there where the bone had fused, to feel the roughness of hair coming back, to close his eyes and press his nose to this lineless pale scalp that hadn't seen the sun in not twenty-two but eighteen years—as if she were his daughter, rather than his mistress. Or not even that. He'd taken all the inadequacies of his marriage and his life and shaped them into a fantasy. Consciousness stripped away, she was a stranger. He was carrying flowers from the gift shop downstairs, in case the nurses got suspicious. Now he placed them on the tray by the cake. Neutral white irises. "Happy birthday, Samantha." He kissed his fingers and touched them lightly to an unbruised patch of arm. And then, Keith knew, it was time to leave, before someone—her father, the law, or just a less credulous journalist—got wind of the fact that her old lover, a fraud and a married man, was still out here roaming free.

33

REGAN WOULD RATHER DIE than admit it, but the Demon Brother was right; she'd had very little sense of what it would mean to check every pie in which the Hamilton-Sweeney octopus now had a tentacle. She hadn't considered the sheer number of these pies, or the volume of paper that went along with each: earnings reports, public utterances, letters of interest, memoranda of understanding. This was in addition to divorce papers, analyst bills, summer camp applications for the kids, and her duties as the juniormost member of the Board. Every morning when she unlocked her office, a ziggurat of paper two feet high awaited her, as if it had rebuilt itself overnight. Her job had become, in essence, to vanquish the ziggurat, and with her only employee out on maternity leave, she was more or less an army of one. Though sometimes, looking up from some document she didn't understand, she would see a head of golden hair floating above the tops of the cubicles outside, or its owner, tall and broad-shouldered, flushed out briefly into a transverse corridor. She would pretend their eyes had met. She would make silent contracts with herself: if I sit and work for the next half-hour, then I will let myself go to the water fountain. Andrew West, the Hair Guy, was never there, of course, and she would have to punish herself by tacking the minutes she'd wasted onto the end of her workday. It was an old pattern, rules to rebel against, rebellion leading to further rules, but she kept this insight below the level of conscious recognition, for if she were to allow herself to see it fully—to admit to Dr. Altschul, for instance, that she'd become infatuated with a man who wasn't her husband, or ex-, or whatever Keith was to her now—it would be just one more reason to punish herself.

Then one morning, she pulled out her chair to find under the desk a plain brown tube she'd requested from Archives several days back, along with supporting documentation. She moved the ziggurat to the floor and unrolled what was in the tube. On top was an elevation of a treeless waterfront, your typical urban minefield, but overlaid with a transparent dream-city: green meadows studded with retail kiosks, mansarded condos with hanging gardens, two beaming office towers, and that stadium she'd seen a model for at New Year's. Artists' renderings of pink-skinned people hoisted stemware in open-air cafés, a few darker faces for contrast. LIBERTY HEIGHTS URBAN RENEWAL, PHASE TWO, said the legend at the top, *renewal* being the current term of art for slum clearance. Since losing the bid for Lincoln Center at the turn of the 1960s, the Hamilton-Sweeney Company's investment arm had diverted most of its energy to international concerns, Exigente cigarettes, El Bandito coffee (whose mustachioed spokesperson, Pepe Rodríguez, she was in a position to know, was actually an Armenian from South Jersey). Meanwhile, the real-estate slump had all but halted construction in the five boroughs; you couldn't get a project a tenth of this size built anymore, even with City Hall behind you. And hadn't the city's new overlords in Albany, even before the indictment, scrambled to distance themselves from the old machinery of power that had led to the fiscal crisis—and thus from the Hamilton-Sweeneys? Yet this, Liberty Heights, was the hundred-million-dollar initiative toward which Amory had driven the company. And it turned out he'd been right! A simple Blight Zone decree had changed everything, turned breakdowns to fast-tracks. It was as if he'd known even back in '75, the year on the blueprint, that such a decree was inevitable, and now here she was, raising and lowering the transparency: reality, fantasy; fantasy, reality. A knock at the door interrupted her. An immaculate head of hair angled into her airspace, like a retriever nuzzling the slipstream. "Ms. Lamplighter? You asked to see these?"

The Guy with the Hair approached to place an accordion file on her desk. He was younger even than she'd thought: he moved with that carelessness that gets knocked out of you by about twenty-seven. "Thanks," she said. "This is awful, but I don't remember what you do, exactly, Andrew. Are you in Real Estate, or Legal?"

"Global Operations, actually."

"But these are accounts, right?"

"The accounting department of Global Ops." He gleamed at her like a diamond with a single facet.

"We have two accounting departments?"

"And now Global Ops has swallowed Real Estate. It's complicated."

Fighting down doubt, she fed the blueprint back into its tube. "Do you think you could stay for a minute and translate these?" His voice was lovely, and as he walked her through various charts and tables that first day, she sat with lapped hands and let her brain go slack, until his words, *receivables, carrying charges, standard depreciation*, became avant-garde poetry.

By the third such session, though, some genetic disposition for figures kicked in, and she could hear the skepticism Andrew was doing his best to conceal. Even for him, the Global Ops books were a maze, credits and debits darting across columns and around corners, and then at every third turn you ran into a matryoshka doll of shell companies. Most seemed to be registered in the same Central American republic the cigarettes and coffee came from, but Andrew having returned to his desk, it wasn't clear whether the net capital-flows were toward or away. What was clear, from his departure if nothing else, was that this haziness couldn't be accidental. And *cui bono*? Well, here and here again was her father's school-ruled signature. Not to say that complexity was in itself criminal, but did she really want to have to turn this stuff over to the government in discovery? Especially when the media, led each day by the four a.m. transmission of that motormouth on WLRC, was more hostile than she'd imagined? At this rate, they were going to have to get the trial relocated to Albuquerque.

Still, she couldn't bring herself to press her father on any of this when she swung uptown on her lunch-hour to check on him. Behind the desk in the library where he still spent his days (though he couldn't make heads or tails of the new data terminal), he was too much the Daddy of old: towering, proper, vaguely imperial in his dark blue suit. And his rectitude was heroic, Regan felt, given the arc of his cognitive decline, and even before. She'd learned long ago that what read as reserve was really just a way to protect the things that mattered.

THEN ONE DAY his new neurologist scheduled a house-call. It was only a preliminary visit, questionnaires and bloodwork, but Regan had taken the afternoon off to run interference—Felicia found other people's medical appointments draining—and when she arrived, a table like a masseuse's had been unfolded in the fitness room. The patient sat in a gown the blue of a Mylanta bottle. His feet swung back and forth, a kid's splashing in water. His shins, hairless from a half-century of socks, filled her with unreasonable dread. But any minute now the neurologist would reappear. "Daddy?" He seemed to return from whatever childhood dock he'd been visiting. That he could still do this was a good sign, she thought. "We need to talk. About your case."

"Yes. Okay." He'd never been verbose, exactly, but lately he'd pared his word-hoard even further, to these clipped affirmatives that obscured how much of what you said was getting through. Which may have been their purpose. The doctors at Mayo hadn't been able to arrive at a definite diagnosis, any more than the other specialists, but the more she thought about these dodges of Daddy's, the more she wondered if he'd been deteriorating for much longer than she'd thought: ten years, or even fifteen.

"Remember how we talked last month about fighting this thing in court? Amory wanted to look at a plea, and I said, No, Daddy, you should stand up and fight. Do you remember?"

And then sometimes there would be this: the flash of lucidity, even when it was least welcome. "Of course I remember. Why wouldn't I remember?"

"This is important, and I need you to listen. When you meet with the lawyers on Monday, I think you should tell them you want to push for a deal."

"I want to push for a deal."

"That's right."

"But sweetheart, Regan, why would I push for a deal, unless I'd done something wrong?"

Oh, what wouldn't she have given to have her mother back? Or the next best thing, which since she was eleven years old had been her brother? It should have been William sitting in all those Board meetings. William fending off Amory. And it was William, she felt now, who could have explained to his namesake this sense of foreboding. No matter what he'd believed when he'd taken off all those years ago, he'd always been the one Daddy loved best. But then she remembered Andrew West. "It's complicated," she said.

34

HOW YOU SKIP SCHOOL IS, you lie. You shower like it's any other morning, or run a wet comb through your hair for lifelike simulation. At a quarter to seven, you turn off "Dr." Zig—this city is not a machine, it's a body, and it's ly—and with your army-surplus bookbag full of Marx and Engels and the moldering remains of yesterday's uneaten lunch, you trudge upstairs. You pour your brothers their Lucky Charms, making sure neither bowl has more marshmallows than the other. (The oaty bits don't matter; they'll end up all over the table anyway, or crushed to calcium-fortified powder on the floor. Incidentally, when did you ever get Lucky Charms as a kid?) To test your invisibility, try grumbling about the sleety wait awaiting you at the bus stop. Your mom could offer to drive you, torpedoing your plans: far harder to escape from the hall monitors at school than from this defenseless little house. But this assumes Mom will be listening to you, which she won't. Instead, she'll be circling in and out of the kitchen, trying to figure out where she left a) her keys, or b) *the other earring that looks like this* (holding up earring), or c) both. Her eyes are puffy. She's been up late again. On the phone, again. You may want to ask her who that was on the other end of the line, but remember that at a time like this, her attention is unwelcome, and nowadays, it is always a time like this; her attention is always unwelcome. As is its lack. In any case, you already know who she's been talking to. You are the Prophet Charlie, after all: seer, teen visionary, adept of noumena. Everything that is to unfold has done so already in your head.

When the Lucky Charms are just lurid milk, your mother still waiting for the babysitter, head out the door. After a couple of minutes at the bus stop, start walking, ostensibly to keep warm, ostensibly just to the next bus stop. No need to look to see if your former home has vanished yet into the humdrum gray behind you; you'll be able to feel it, the sudden eclipse of the tractor beam the house puts out. Of its forcefield of sadness.

HOW TO MAKE A REVOLUTIONARY CONSCIOUSNESS IS: educate yourself. On the train, for example, read the same two pages of *Das Kapital* over and over, willing them to make sense. Or give up and flip back through dog-eared pages in the Bible you're still not quite ready to abandon. Behind the closed doors of the Phalanstery, the four core phalanges and various hangers-on are already murmuring in ardent exegesis, or prepping for secret missions that will someday (once you're ready) include you. How will you know you're ready? You'll just know, Nicky says. Meantime, he lets you sit in with the little clique of grad students that gathers weekly to talk Nietzsche with him. He'll even let you stick around for a private lesson after he sends the other novices back toward dorms and classrooms. Still, you'll get left behind when he and S.G. take off in the battered white van Sol stole from a gig he used to have as a window-washer. Sol steals anything not nailed down—meaning, you suppose, that he has already achieved revolutionary consciousness. You, you're still fighting your way free of *Thou shalt*.

HOW TO TURN ORDINARY OBJECTS against the system that produced them: "Take a wet paper towel and pour some flour in the center. Then wrap it up tight with a rubber band. It'll throw like a softball, but anything it hits will be covered in what, as far as your victim is concerned, is a strange white powder." Or: "Pick up the phone. Call a politician to have a rumor confirmed or denied. Call another politician to have him confirm or deny the first politician's confirmation or denial." Or: "Take a needle and poke a hole in the top of each of a dozen eggs. Let them sit in a warm place for about a week. Then go up on a roof and do what comes naturally." Not exactly likely to unshackle the species, right? But there are many things that are beyond your understanding. Sol Grungy, who's come in at some point during this little practicum, will be sneering, as if sensing your reservations, but Nicky will reach up to smack him on the back of the head. Now watch out a window as the two of them disappear into the little house out back. Or rattle off in the van toward points unknown. Wonder: If you're not ready now, in your yearning to go there with them—how will you ever be?

HOW? You'll work your ass off, is how. They'll leave you with orders to staple more tinfoil over the Phalanstery's front walls and windows. Sol has stolen this foil, too, thirty or forty rolls—*From each according to his means*—for reasons no one bothers to explain. Maybe it's supposed to drive the pigeons away? In any event, you roll out great sheets, staple them with a staple gun. Tucking it into crannies where the floor has pulled away from the wall . . . there's something kind of sexual in the motion. Something rhythmic, something angry, like the Stooges record on the turntable behind you. You should be sitting in Trig right now in Nassau County, but no one out there cares, not even the hall monitors. Your suburban life is closing down like an aperture, while the city swells to fill the sky. It occurs to you that it's been an hour since you thought of Sam.

At some point, as you work on the walls, Sewer Girl will bring you pills and a beer; her tread on the floorboard makes "Gimme Danger" skip. Now imagine the warmth of her big white body raising the air temperature near your neck a few degrees, just before she touches a cold can to the skin. The fact that the two of you are here alone signifies they're starting to trust you. You can complete this part of the revolutionary program without direct supervision, assuming that Sewer Girl hasn't been left behind in a supervisory role—that she's as clueless about the big picture as you are. In fact, it's tempting to think she's been sent just to tease you, to swell your 'nads beyond the limits of endurance, but such thinking is self-regarding, neo-Humanist. Look: Isn't she already retreating to work on her own little patch of unfoiled wall? The lath there looks naked, like bone.

But back home, in the mirror, the muscles of your arms will have gotten a little bigger. How surprised Mom would be, if she found out you've been doing chores. Voluntarily!

HOW TO MARK YOURSELF AS DIFFERENT: Grab a Sharpie from the coffee can on your desk and copy, to the best of your memory, the tattoo everyone seems to have—the one Nicky has, the one Sol has, the one Sam has. The mark of the Post-Humanist Phalanx that proliferates on the cornices of apartment buildings, on housing-project handball courts, on the notebooks of the grad students, on the sides of parked cars, on subway station entrances, scratched into the plexiglass of a phone booth, as if mechanically reproduced all over the East Village, stamped out in some factory of the image. Once, on your way to Penn Station to catch the LIRR home, you'll see it inked on a stranger's forearm, someone you don't even think knows what it means. Maybe you'll look now and see you've gotten it upside down. There are still things to learn, obviously; you aren't ready yet. But the capital you do have, Nicky would say, is time.

WHAT WILL MOVE YOU DECISIVELY CLOSER is spraycans. Bombing, they call it. They tell you to dress all in black: black sweatshirt, black jeans, black watchcap. You would think your mom would notice this, but she's just pleased your Ziggy Stardust phase is over.

You work in teams of two, one to spray, one to look out for cops, and at first you're the lookout, lingering on the corner in a posture of forced nonchalance. No sweat. Your entire life, or anyway the last few years of it, has been a posture of forced nonchalance. No one but Sam has ever guessed at the tensed interior, the turmoil in your guts. Down the block, in profile, green-haired D. Tremens moves his arms in front of a tenement building, as if doing tai chi. He's not a big fan of yours, you can tell. But maybe it's not personal; D. Tremens is not a big fan of anything. What he is is committed. And he trusts you to be ready, at the first sign of cops, to skitter off into the darkness, letting loose your war-whoop. Here is the bloop of a siren. Do it, Prophet. Run.

The slap of combat boots will echo in the mazelike grid for seconds after you've stopped. Your laughter will surprise you. When was the last time you laughed? (Don't answer that.) Here you are, deep in

Alphaville, where even the cops won't follow at this time of night. But you're a part of the lawlessness now; it can't hurt you. Your partner, having caught up, hands you a tallboy. You raise it in the air. "Here's to Mickey Sullivan," you say, because you've used him as an alibi again tonight. D.T.'s eye-roll can be made out even here, under the busted streetlight. "Famous revolutionary," you say, and the laughter pumps out of your chest like blood, great almost painful spurts of it splashing up the building faces toward the marquee moon.

Then it's your turn. You are the one crouching before the metal security gate of what during daytime is a dimestore. You are the one shaking the can. The liquid thunk of the ball inside the cylinder seems deafening; you are tensed, listening for any hint of trouble. But everything has been teed up for you. There are still other levels, you're becoming aware, whole echelons of activity beyond those you've encountered: the milk-crates, the foil, the whispers in honeycombed rooms; the heavy-looking duffelbag you saw Sol and Nicky lugging through the dusk toward the little house out back; the changes under way out there, where only the two of them go, plus wherever they've all been disappearing to in the van . . . but you know that you are here tonight for a reason, locking into your fate. The rush of paint sounds like the blast of a hot-air balloon. *THE SYSTEM IS A CRIME*, you write. *THEY DON'T DESERVE A DIME.* Then the logo, blooming out of nothingness, the symbol you've perfected in the margins of tests and in Wite-Out on your boots' steely toes: the five slashing strokes. The little crown of flame. Like this:

35

THE WONDERS OF THE MAGAZINE began with its title: a nod to the R&B magus Wilson Pickett, himself nodding back to Chris Kenner. Though perhaps "fanzine" was the better word, as its formal debts were less to any national glossy than to the small-batch booklets that had started cropping up in head shops and record exchanges at the dawn of the 1970s. Cheap xerography blurred the images, and Samantha's prose was likewise loose, a trying on and discarding of styles. Yet with these crude tools, she'd managed to fix to the page a story far richer and stranger than anyone back in Flower Hill could have imagined for her. It was as if she'd been afraid her life might otherwise fly away, and knowing the fear was justified—wanting to reach in somehow and warn her—was surely part of the compulsion Richard Groskoph felt in the waning days of January, sinking deeper into *Land of a Thousand Dances*.

The greatest part, though, was just the intimacy of the thing. Reading it was like subletting a small apartment in someone else's head, right down to the cryptic signifiers she assigned to her friends: S.G., Sol, N.C.—Iggy? To an outsider, they meant nothing. There was, however, a subscription label on the back of one of the issues, and on the third night, after his fifth or sixth read-through, Richard had let the name there carry him to the phone book, and then to the Upper East Side. He should have guessed Keith Lamplighter would be just another white-shoe midlifer clinging to splinters of the rock 'n' roll cross. *By his name, by his neighborhood will you know him.* But the degree of tangency almost didn't matter; for a few minutes, Richard was connected to someone who was connected to Samantha. It was only later, back at the desk, that he began to worry the guy might really for some reason get in touch with the cops, tipping them off that Richard had secured his own copies of the fanzine. Or no— wasn't the worry really that he'd now divulged to a stranger the very name he'd been trying to protect?

Probably not, he decided, pouring himself a drink. The victim's continued anonymity had done little to quell the tabloid fascination with what had happened in Central Park that night. Maybe the fascination and the anonymity were even related, in a way that belied everything Richard knew about what made arrangments of ink on paper come alive for readers. Given the number of unsolved shootings in the city, it was at any rate striking that this one had now migrated from the police blotter to the op-eds, which from a scant few details—female, white, seventeen—had conjured up a sense of her as a symbol.

As Richard himself was conjuring, he realized, when he should have been finishing his article, his book. In the past, bouts of procrastination had tended to anticipate a more total block. He wasn't sure he could bounce back from another one. And he still felt ethically iffy about the fanzines—especially now that, amid the mess of his desk, the third issue, the one he'd taken uptown, could not be found. So the next morning, when the booze wore off, he sealed the other two in a weighted plastic bag, sunk it in a bucket of water, and stuck the whole package in his freezer.

Where it should have remained forever, really, amid boxes of frozen veggies and pizza slices gray with frost. But as the specifics faded from memory, the fanzines' general mise-en-scène came into sharper relief. It was with him at night as he fell asleep and in the morning when his eyes opened: the scuzzy rock clubs, the unlocatable brownstone she'd discovered in the middle of 1976. There seemed to be a whole secret city out there, reached through hidden panels and swinging doors. The only points of congruity between it and the New York he thought he'd returned to were an air of abandonment and the omnipresent graffiti.

It wasn't long before Valentine's Day that one of his p.m. rambles took him downtown—and that he realized the two New Yorks had flipped. Punk had picked all the locks, sluiced out into the grid. Tatterdemalion kids crowded St. Mark's Place, their clothes held together by dental floss and wishful thinking. And from all around, rooftops and stoops and passing cars, came that other adhesive: the music. Had music not delivered Richard, too, on more than one occasion, from a life he'd believed himself trapped in? The tempos had changed, but that almost didn't matter. The point, now as then, was to tune in to something bigger than yourself, and to feel around you others who felt as you did.

He ended up at a record store on Bleecker Street. It was where he'd bought nearly every long-player put out by Blue Note Records in the 1950s, and countless Stax/Volt sides in the '60s. Where he'd acquired the collected works of Hank Williams and all those bubblegum 45s that twanged his auditory sweet tooth. *Highway 61 Revisited*, the day it came out. *Let It Bleed*, the day it came out. But now face-out on the wall were sleeves he didn't recognize. At the counter, a furry young man rang him up. Let's see. *Rock n Roll Animal*. *Agharta*. "Anarchy in the U.K."?

"I'll take this other forty-five, too."

But any perplexity the clerk felt at Richard's choices dissolved when he saw the **Wrecking Ball** credential. He was from Missouri, he offered, unbidden. He'd come here to study photography. He held up one of the records, flipped it over to reveal a black-and-white shot of three guys in leather jackets and a woman a head taller. Backed up against an alley wall somewhere, they looked ready to take on all enemies and not fight fair. "Used to hang out with this one here a little bit, actually," the clerk said, tapping the smallest of the four, who shot the camera the bird. "Billy Three-Sticks."

It was the other kind of name that had come up in Samantha's fanzine: Rotten, Vicious, Hell & Thunders, like some firm of malign lawyers. But the devotional context had made Richard forget that the musicians these handles attached to had lives independent of her needs. Maybe you were supposed to forget; maybe this was the point of a pseudonym. Apart from the fact that Billy Three-Sticks had fronted her favorite band, Richard hadn't thought to find out the first thing about him. Until now.

"Well, far as I know," the clerk said, "he's still living up in Hell's Kitchen. Hell, my boss probably owes him some dough for these records. I could scare up an invoice, if you want."

THE PLACE IN QUESTION WAS A SOOTY FACTORY in the old industrial district west of the Port Authority; from street level, you could see the tops of rusty letters spelling out *Knickerbocker Mints* welded to a scaffold on the roof. As with the surrounding buildings, there was nothing to suggest that it had gone residential, or was in use at all, save for a pair of gleaming Harleys on the sidewalk out front, the only vehicles in sight still in possession of their chrome. Indeed, the cars lining the street seemed not so much parked as aborted. All this Richard took in through the sheer plastic sheeting hung from a bodega awning on the corner of Tenth Avenue to protect the flowers underneath. Or rather, the empty flower pails. He'd walked straight up from the Village in the cold, stopping only here, at this last outpost of civilization before dystopia began. Theoretically, he was waiting for the coffee he'd bought to warm him up, but it was equally possible he just wasn't ready to discover that there were no buzzers in the vestibule, that it was bad information, and so surrender once more the sense of higher purpose now flowing through him. And if there were no such purpose, then why, within minutes of his watching, did a small, pale man who was unmistakably the one on the record sleeve emerge from the building's entrance and head this way?

Richard half-expected him to tack across the street, to enter the bodega and walk right up and put out a hand, but there were no course corrections. Billy Three-Sticks must have been headed toward the subway. There was something furtive in his gait. Richard tossed the rest of his coffee back and was just about to go accost the subject when another figure, similarly furtive, appeared on the near side of the street: a black man in ill-fitting coveralls. This second man moved rapidly, keeping the lines of cars between himself and Billy Three-Sticks, yet glancing over at him frequently. What the hell was going on here? Richard shivered. He was a layman in the wings of a vast cathedral, waiting for his cue to step into the light. When he did he could see Billy Three-Sticks and the black man reach Ninth Avenue. Were the police running down the same lead? Unlikely. Anyhow, the way you knew an undercover was by looking at his shoes—and the pursuer's, when Richard drew closer, were authentically battered, the canvas upper peeling away from a heel covered in ballpoint pen. Stenciled onto the coveralls was a stick figure washing a window. The man's watchcap was riding up in back. Some tonsorial mishap had befallen the hair there; was it green? Before Richard could decide, though, hair, shoes, and coveralls were tailing Billy Three-Sticks around a corner onto Eighth Ave. And by the time Richard had caught up, both men had melted into the crowds around the bus terminal. So why did he feel like rejoicing?

36

MERCER USED TO PASS THE TIME, during his post-grad months of flipping burgers out on Route 17, by polishing his opinions on life and literature for that future date when they would grace the pages of *The Paris Review*. For an interviewer, he always pictured the same person: a tall, graying white man, neatly but casually dressed, with expressive eyebrows that offset a certain coolness of voice. He looked, come to think of it, like a bearded, less chesty Dr. Runcible. As Mercer imagined it, he sat in a folding director's chair, notepad in lap, leg crossed at the knee. Whenever Mercer expressed an idea of particular promise, the knee would begin to jiggle up and down. Mostly, though, the pen raced over the paper, as if under its own power, hurling lariats of shorthand at the unfettered brilliance of America's Preeminent Man of Letters—a title Mercer humbly disavowed.

Q: *Your work seems to represent a qualitative break with some of the minimalist tendencies coming into vogue among younger writers at that time. Some might even call it old-fashioned.*

A: "Well, we lived, people of my generation, in an age of uncertainty. A whole set of institutions we'd grown up trusting, from the churches to the markets to the American system of government, all seemed to be in crisis. And so there was a fundamental skepticism about the ability of any institution, even one like the novel, to tell us anything true."

Q: *But it sounds like you're almost in sympathy with the opposition, Mr. Goodman.*

A: "I see that as my job, basically. To be in sympathy. But I've long felt, perhaps perversely, that when you hold theory up to experience and they don't match, the problem must be with the theory. There's the critique of the underpinnings of these institutions—justice and democracy and love—and then there's the fact that no one seems able to live without them. And so I wanted to explore again the old idea that the novel might, you know, teach us about something. About everything."

Later, though, when Mercer's manuscript fell into neglect, his imaginary interviewer disappeared. And by the time he resurfaced, this January, he'd changed. For one thing, he was no longer content to remain in his chair, in the otherwise featureless studio of Mercer's head. So strong now was the sense of someone hovering nearby, amassing footage of the loft and the world beyond, that Mercer had once or twice found himself peering out the front window for cameras on the street.

For another, the questions had grown uncomfortably personal. A month had passed since the Deputy Inspector had produced, as if by magic, a bag of heroin from the Coat of Several Colors. Mercer's putative reason for not confronting William about this—that he was too traumatized by everything else that had happened that night— had meantime come to seem like an excuse. This wasn't to say that when he closed his eyes at night he didn't still see on the backs of his eyelids a bloody form spread-eagled in the snow. But a week had passed since he'd last jolted awake before sunrise with a gunshot in his ears and a sheen of fresh sweat on his skin. *So why*, his interviewer wanted to know, *did he not now say something?*

Well, for one thing, how would he explain to William what he'd been doing on the Upper West Side in the first place? For another, did it logically follow that if 1) the coat was William's, and 2) the drugs were in the coat, then 3) the drugs must have been William's? Because what if, in a crowd somewhere, someone had slipped the dope into William's pocket? It happened all the time in movies. Or what if William had been carrying it as a favor for . . . for Bruno Augenblick, or . . . for his old bandmate, Nicky Chaos, whose new act he'd gone to see that night? In fact, hadn't he claimed this was why he'd quit the band in the first place? That he couldn't afford to be around a bunch of junkies?

Or maybe those hadn't been drugs at all. Police on TV were not uniformly opposed to faking evidence when it suited them. Maybe the little cop with the crutches was looking for leverage; maybe he was going to call at some point in the near future and force Mercer to confess to everything he knew about the Hamilton-Sweeneys.

And here was yet another reason for Mercer to keep his mouth shut about the drugs: it would have been unfair to add to William's burdens. Not that they ever talked about his father's case, but he could hardly have missed the updates on the news, and he'd been behaving oddly (even for William) since the arraignment. *Ah, but did this not corroborate . . . ?* Fine. Yes. Mercer's phantom interviewer, who was proving to be fucking tenacious, had gotten it out of him: lately, William had been acting more and more like a junkie.

For example? Well, for example, he'd been spending inordinate amounts of time up at his studio in the Bronx, returning hours after midnight. Sometimes when Mercer peeked up at him undressing in the moonlight, or in the light pollution that passed for it, he could swear William was wearing sunglasses. And in the morning, William would be dead to the world. He'd never been an early riser, whereas on work days Mercer had to be presentable and reasonably conscious by seven a.m. But lately he would come home near sunset to find William still in his bathrobe, watching soaps or sports and slurping pastel-colored offslew from a bowl of the pre-sugared cereal he now moved through at a rate of five boxes per week.

So fine; start over. The real reason Mercer didn't ask if William was shooting up again was that he was scared to confirm it was true.

What made it worse—what made it, yes, since you asked, even harder to ignore—was that Mercer had seen all this before, when his brother got back from Vietnam. He remembered how Pop had asked if he wanted to ride down to the bus depot the Saturday after C.L.'s discharge, and how he'd jumped at the chance to get out of the house. Mama had already cleaned every room three times by that point; if he stuck around, she was liable to start vacuuming his shirtfront with the hose attachment.

It had been high summer then. Pop had let him drive, which is how you knew his mind was elsewhere. "Hard to believe in less than a month I'll be at U. Ga.," Mercer said, for the sake of having something to say. Pop, in the passenger's seat, stayed silent, except for the faint or imagined noise of his hands rubbing the thighs of his trousers. The knuckles were like hardened magma: black, swollen, craggy from having worked the land for two decades, making it safe for the pigs and the chickens, for the towering green corn that rose around them in every direction, staining the sky beige with its exhalations. Mercer's own hands, at ten and two on the wheel, were an infant's, comparatively speaking.

Since his brother had left for basic training, Mercer had developed an idea (based partly on a Maxwell House commercial) that C.L. would return reformed. He'd be waiting for them in pressed olive drab, his bag over his shoulder, his face shaved down to handsome planes. He would crush Mercer's hand and snap off a salute for the old man and then commandeer the wheel, and Mercer would fall asleep in the bed of the pickup, watching those dirty Georgia clouds barely move while peaceable man-talk drifted back from the cab.

The depot had been empty when they arrived, however, and the person who climbed off the bus fifteen minutes later had in common with Mercer's imaginings only the canvas bag. He wore a dingy tee-shirt. His hair was a clot of wool; a beard half-clouded his face. Pop, himself a veteran of both the Second World War and a lifetime of shaving bumps, was visibly steamed (or scared, it now occurred to Mercer), though, to his credit, all he said out loud was, "Get on in the back, then." Climbing over the tailgate, C.L. looked distant, passive, almost dreamy. As he would three years later, the morning Mercer found him buck naked in the north field with a machete in his hand, blood on his face like warpaint, standing over a throat-slit shoat.

William wasn't yet at the point of blood atonement—and who knows, maybe it wasn't drugs so much as preexisting instability that had landed C.L. in a padded room in Augusta—but he'd had that same shell-shocked look lately. He, too, had grown a beard, claiming that his Yuletide contusions, still unexplained, made it hard to shave. When Mercer observed that he was losing weight, he said it was because he was going vegetarian. Then one day Mercer fished a White Castle wrapper out of the trash. "I said *going* vegetarian," William said. "I didn't say I'd got there. And what are you doing rooting through the trash?"

What Mercer was doing was looking for some final bit of proof, some *casus belli*. He still wanted to imagine he could outrun the Goodman family legacy, the mistrust and fear layered densely as phloem beneath a tree's tough bark. But wasn't this all William's fault, for keeping things from him? (Assuming William *was* keeping things from him? (Which he definitely was?)) Mercer was going to have to just come out and say it. He opened his mouth. "Let's go away together."

"What?"

Mercer hadn't known this was something he'd been considering, but evidently he had it all worked out. "You've been working awful hard. We both have. Presidents' Day is a three-day weekend." William hesitated for a moment. He would have to say no; how would he be able to last three days without a fix? And then Mercer could lob his accusation. But instead came a shrug that made Mercer wonder if he still somehow had everything backward.

"Sure, if that's what you want."

"I just feel like we've barely talked lately."

"I said yes, Mercer."

"I know." They were looking right into each other's eyes. It was Mercer who had to turn away. "There's that travel agent over on Ninth Avenue. I feel sorry for her, no one ever seems to go in. And Florida's only a three-hour flight."

"Why don't we head north instead? Bruno's got a place in Vermont I'm sure we could use for free."

"In February?"

"I'm a little cash-strapped at present, Merce. Plus it would be romantic. Snowy midwinter, nobody around but us chickens . . . isn't that the point?"

"Of course."

"So let me phone Bruno as soon as this game is over." As William turned back to the Knicks, Mercer continued to stare at the side of his face, unable to shake the feeling of defeat snatched from the jaws of victory while someone looked on from nearby. Then he told himself: No, this is good, this is perfect. They'd go far away from the drugs or William's family or whatever was tearing them apart. Somewhere William wouldn't be able to hide like this in plain view. Either he'd tip his hand, and Mercer would pounce, or Mercer would know for certain he'd been a damn fool, letting his imagination run away with him again.

37

J ENNY NGUYEN WAS FIVE FOOT TWO IN SNEAKERS, small-chested, hippy (she thought), but with a fine, intelligent face. At rest, it could seem aloof, or wary, but when she laughed, which was often, her whole body relaxed. Her nails were bitten, her teeth even and vigorously white. She was a child of the suburbs. Also: an unreconstructed socialist.

Moving east, at twenty-four, she'd been a couple years out of practice, and was hoping New York would allow her to become again a force for justice in the world. This was the heart of the empire, after all, a powderkeg of alienated labor. Instead, she had ended up somehow as a wage-slave herself, dependent for her daily bread upon the *rentier* Bruno Augenblick, and the alienation that increasingly preoccupied her—quite against her will—was her own. She agreed with Bruno, for instance, that Valentine's Day was a mercantile conspiracy meant to gin up commerce in the middle of February, otherwise the armpit of the year. But that didn't mean it felt particularly righteous to be spending it alone.

Leaving the gallery that evening, she found another reason to curse her luck. She listened every morning for the weather report on WLRC; today, the weatherman had predicted *wintry mix*, rain turning eventually to sleet. But among the several ways she continued to fail to become a New Yorker was her perpetual inability to remember an umbrella—her assumption, when the sun was shining, that it would never stop. And now the sky was prematurely dark. Here came a cab kiting past with its sign lit, but a cab was an extravagance she wouldn't be able to afford even if it were already raining, so she hurried toward the subway. She felt a drop, and then the sky opened like the hold of some great black bomber. By the time she reached her new building, she was soaking, hair in eyes, her canvas bag and the one-sheets within it a freezing, sodden mess.

Something about her absurd appearance or the sanctuary quality of the vestibule's white light made it seem perfectly natural that the tall, bearded man then checking his mail should ask if she was all right. It was as if the rain had turned the costume she'd been wearing—competence, urbanity, purpose—translucent. As if he could see through to what was beneath, though his blue eyes would have had that penetrating quality anyway. His mailbox abutted hers, which meant his apartment must, too. Since moving in last fall, she'd sometimes heard music through the walls. She was fine, she said.

His voice was a broadcaster's, unaccented. "You're not fine, you're soaked."

There was a moment of awkwardness here, a little hurdle of activation energy they might never have cleared.

"Maybe I'll catch a cold," she said, "and then I won't have to go to work tomorrow. It's pretty much a win-win."

The muted thunder of his laugh made her joke seem less lame. His name was Richard, he said. In his experience, a little Scotch would knock the damp right out of you. "The old ounce of prevention."

"I just moved from the Lower East Side a few months ago. My cupboard's bare."

"I've got a bottle that's currently just going to waste."

At this, all kinds of flags went up, stories splattered across the *Post* in inch-high type, her father's face when he'd pulled up to her first building, on Rivington Street, in the moving van. There was a whole set of codes governing the interaction of apartment-house neighbors: you stuck to small-talk and looked suspiciously on favors. But something about Richard—the gray in his hair or the casual slump of his shoulders, the assorted newspapers under his arm—made him seem safe. When she told him she was going to dry off and change, and then maybe she'd oblige, she didn't think she meant it. Yet there she was fifteen minutes later in a tactically frumpy sweatshirt, being shown into his apartment. She appreciated that he didn't lock the door behind her.

It was a two-bedroom unit, an L whose arms embraced her studio next door, yet the mess in the living room testified to his bachelorhood: loose typewriter ribbons and carbon papers, mountains of old magazines, terminal moraines of LPs jutting from the walls. A terrier emerged from this documentary chaos to snuffle the cuffs of her jeans. "Don't mind Claggart," Richard said. "He's harmless." Then she spotted in the corner, glowing wonderfully, a Wurlitzer jukebox. "Holy shit!" It was like being on a commuter train through the Bronx and seeing among the piles of crushed cars a pasture with a lone white horse. Richard seemed almost embarrassed. He'd snagged it for fifty bucks at a police auction, he said. He invited her to take a quarter from the hubcap that sat up top. Resisting the urge to linger, she punched in the first numbers she saw, a Sam Cooke, a Patsy Cline, and "Drift Away" by Dobie Gray, while he cleared a spot on the couch. Two glasses appeared. She waved her hand to stop him after an inch and a half of liquor had sloshed into hers. "*Sláinte*," he said. They sipped and watched the rings of overspill evaporate from the faux-maple coffeetable. He made an unconscious sigh after swallowing. His radiators, like hers, were hyperactive. The little dog, achieving his lap, went still.

Jenny would have described the ensuing silence as not uncomfortable. And she would have described the man as elegantly disheveled, with his sleeves rolled to his elbows, his collar open, his shaggy beard. He'd brought the Scotch back from Scotland, he said finally, his eyes soft in the velvet light. Over there, it was just called *whisky*. Was it all right?

It was indeed, a soft blaze, a bloom that opened in her chest and moved outward from there, sending warmth to her extremities, filling her head with sweet fire. She asked what he'd been doing in Scotland.

He flushed. "A sabbatical, I guess you'd call it."

"You're an academic?"

"God forbid."

"A priest?"

"Just a guy who had to get out of New York. When I need to pay the rent, I write." And before she could say anything: "But what about you, Jenny? What do you do?"

In her experience with the men of this city, talking about work was the conversational equivalent of a general anesthetic. They would nod along and pretend to listen, but afterward would retain nothing. The gap between the enormous (to her) fact that she'd sold out and taken the job with Bruno and the scant impression it made on them left her lonely. Which was why she tried not to mention work, hewing to such comparatively scintillating topics as weather, sports, and that old standby, real estate. Besides, half the men the gallery brought her into contact with were gay, anyway. The mere fact that she'd given Richard this opening showed how rusty her social skills were. But he seemed genuinely interested, and she was surprised to find herself holding forth at length about the sorry state of contemporary art and the culture industry from which, on the Marxian view, it had become indistinguishable. "Actual artists are like mythological creatures," she heard herself opine. "You hear about them, but a sighting's pretty rare."

Violins kindled on the jukebox. What about Warhol? he asked.

She'd seen him once coming out of a donut shop on Union Square, she said. And she had to admit that her heart went pitty-pat. "Sure, I'll have a little more, thanks." (Her host, she noticed, limited himself to the one glass.) "But can pop really be the endpoint of everything? Adorno and Horkheimer must be rolling in their graves." The music ended. "Jesus, did I really just say that? This is why I should steer clear of hard liquor."

He smiled. "This? This is mother's milk. Though that's if Mother's a Celtic warrior-princess." He rose to plug another few quarters into the jukebox. Trucker music, songs from the stray frequencies, from flyover country. "Which yours isn't, I'm guessing." She was used to the clumsiness of white people—their covert impatience to know which pan-Asian drawer to stick you in—so his relative straightforwardness was a nice departure. Besides, the whisky had softened her defenses.

"I grew up in L.A. My folks came from Vietnam before it was Vietnam," she said. "On a plane, not a boat, but . . ." L.A. had always fascinated him, he said. It was one of the few places he thought he could live. And this somehow got her opening up about her old neighborhood, student radio at Berkeley, the activist years—stuff she didn't ever talk about anymore. Sitting in an armchair under yellow lamplight in front of a black window in an apartment whose only other light was the milky rainbow of the Wurlitzer, Richard was like a giant, welcoming ear. Or a reflecting device, beaming her best self back at her. "Hey, this is kind of fun," she said. "You want me to run next door and get some pot?"

Then something crackled on his desk. Richard glanced over at the mess of paper there.

"A mouse?" she asked.

"There seems to be a poltergeist around here lately. You believe in them?"

"Um. Not per se."

"Sorry, it's just my police scanner."

"Oh, God. Look at me. You've probably got work to do."

"That wasn't a cue to go."

But she was already on her feet, reasserting her independence. "I should. I've got things to take care of, too, and I've got to open the gallery in the morning for some rich asshole to come in and not buy things. But thanks for the drink, Richard. Any time you need a cup of flour or an egg . . ."

There was a twinge of pain in his face, as if a headache long deferred were now returning, and she had the sudden intuition that maybe he had been the one in need of human contact. And this settled the debt, took away whatever was starting to seem weird. Later, from her own apartment, she would think she heard through the wall a reprise of Dobie Gray. Where was that guy now? was one of her last thoughts as she plummeted toward unconsciousness. Because, talk about art, "Drift Away" was a fucking masterpiece. She was half in love with Dobie Gray.

A WEEK WOULD PASS before she spotted Richard again, this time at the homuncular grocery across the street, fishing in a pocket for change to pay for three different newspapers. "Parallax," he said, mysteriously, placing a finger alongside his nose like a character from a novel. He waited for her to make her purchases and saw her back across the street. They watched the lighted numbers above the elevator door diminish, in a silence stiffened by its once having been breached. Then he mentioned, as the doors rolled back, that they'd barely made a dent in his whisky. That was an oversight that should absolutely be corrected, she said.

Soon they were in the habit of having a nightcap together, not every night, but close enough that she looked forward to it all day, and was disappointed if it didn't happen. *A tasting*, he called it. *Duck on over for a tasting.* She was fascinated, in particular, by *his* fascination with everything except himself—a quality you rarely encountered in a man. He seemed to know the life stories of every other tenant in the building, past and present, and would tell them to her if she asked. "I hope that's not because you're inviting them all over for a tasting," she said.

"Matter of fact, I've got an appointment at ten with Mrs. Feratovic, the super's wife, if you wouldn't mind hurrying things along."

Or she would drape her legs over the arm of the couch and curl her unpainted toes and talk wryly about California, and about all the things she used to imagine her life would be like, back before she realized she wasn't going to be able to save her own family, much less the world. His way of listening, of asking questions, made her feel funny and charming and, underneath that, needed. Unless that was just the whisky.

Or was she, she began to wonder, the teensiest bit attracted to Richard? He had to be pushing fifty, with wings of peppered brown hair that swooped down over his ears like a Hapsburg monarch's, his nose had been broken in two places, and she'd decided in college that Freud was no friend to women, and so didn't believe in the Electra complex. But compared to the men she'd met so far in New York— parties too loud to hear anyone speak, dial-a-dates in the cryptic style of Harold Pinter plays—the whisky ritual felt like what her father would have called an elegant solution. And if he were to make a move on her, she couldn't say with one hundred percent certainty she would have resisted. Though what could anyone really say these days with one hundred percent certainty?

38

T O THE QUESTION of what he was doing in an idling van on the west
side of Manhattan, the Prophet Charlie had no answer. Nicky
certainly hadn't offered one; had just yanked him off tin-foil duty on
a day when he should have been in school and handed him a pair of
the coveralls the Post-Humanists seemed to buy in bulk. *McCoy*, said
the name over the pocket. Cool, thought Charlie: another field trip.
With any luck, he'd be paired with Sewer Girl this time—maybe
even get to watch her slip into her own coveralls and out of that ratty
hockey jersey, now seriously the worse for wear. Instead, it was again
D. Tremens who waited in the van out front. He finished wiring the
radio back into one of the dashboard's holes, yawned, and muttered
something about thieves. Then, without so much as a greeting, he
floored it around the corner.

D.T. was also the one who handled the binoculars once they
reached their destination. He trained them on a door a half-block
away, as if something big was about to happen . . . but on this street,
it soon emerged, "big" was a relative term: a bag person pushing a
shopping cart past Charlie's window; a schizophrenic shouting about
a "box of nightmares"; a lady of the night limping by on a broken
heel. True, there was the one time D.T. ducked and hissed, "Don't let
him see you," and when Charlie looked across the street he spotted
the huge tattooed mulatto who worked the door of the Vault, now

climbing onto a motorcycle. A suspect! "He's getting away!" Charlie hissed back, caught up in the spirit of the thing. But D.T. shook his head. "He's not the target, Einstein." And the only further developments were a couple of lights going on here and there in the buildings above. There was a target, fine, but knowing what that meant was apparently for D.T. alone.

Indeed, Charlie came to believe he'd been brought along simply to keep his partner from losing his mind with boredom. Which wasn't easy, with a partner who was already too bored to talk. When Charlie tried to play deejay with the radio, D.T. said to leave it where it was. And when Charlie offered to run over to the bodega a block back for snacks, the reply was a groan. "Christ, bro, I'm not your sensei, you're not my apprentice. You want to go, go." This meant, of course, that Charlie couldn't go. So they listened to the radio and watched the sky get dark, and at a certain point, some secret meridian was crossed, or (what amounted to the same thing) D.T. had seen enough, and they took the van back downtown.

Subsequent shifts monitoring this spot, though, would change Charlie's assessment. The problem wasn't so much that D.T. couldn't be bothered to talk as that when he did now, it was like a negation of the whole purpose of talking. His favorite words were *no*, *shit*, and *really?* followed closely by *nothing*, *fuck*, *whatever*, and *man*. They came together in a surprising variety of utterances, but the underlying message was always the same: D. Tremens really did not give a fuck, dig? It almost made you wonder about his role in the Phalanstery. Nicky Chaos had a negative streak, too, but he was a prodigious maker of connections. D.T. denied them. When Charlie asked how he'd ended up with the PHP, for example, he insisted, "I'm not *with* anyone, okay? I'm my own thing." Maybe it had to do with people always thinking they had you figured because you were black. Charlie knew a little bit about people thinking they had you figured. Though not about being black. Then he realized he was doing it, too, and felt guilty, and so basically gave up on conversation himself.

But there was a more labile side of D.T. that still came out when he was drunk, and by the second week of their stakeout, this was a fair portion of the time. His sauce of choice was beer, the cheaper the better, and as the hours piled up, so did the empties. Charlie liked beer as much as the next guy, but the heap of crumpled cans outside the driver's-side door seemed to puncture the plausibility of their disguises. Well, sure, there were alcoholic window-washers, just as there were alcoholic lead guitarists, but maybe, Charlie suggested, he should go scout around for a trashcan? "Not the Mary Poppins bit again," D.T. said. "You have to have figured out this deep-cover bullshit's just to keep Nicky happy, anyway. Or did he not tell you about his old man?"

"I know his dad was a Marine, if that's what you mean. And half-Guatemalan."

For the first time in a long while: a laugh. "And I'm fucking Chinese. You've heard Nicky try to speak Spanish, right? They spent a year or two in the tropics when he was a kid, but I'm pretty sure that's only 'cause Papa was in military intelligence. Which is obviously where Nicky got all this. The disguises, the code words, the stupid fucking foil, like there really are listening devices . . ."

"But I thought Nicky hated his dad."

D.T. rolled down the window and sent a can clattering to the curb. "Fucking *exactly*, Prophet." Then, between gulps of his next beer, he told Charlie a story. Back in '74, he said, before the Post-Humanists were Post-Humanists, Nicky started having them keep tabs on the members of his favorite band, Ex Post Facto. It was the first principle of tradecraft: he was going to figure out what his future bandmates needed, Nicky said, and then offer it to them. Sol had been working as a window-washer for dough. "So we already had these uniforms," D.T. said, plucking at his collar. "And the van." To which Nicky added a crash-course in how to avoid getting noticed, unless of course you wanted to get noticed. Dress like a square. Fake whiskers, if necessary. But D. Tremens didn't like being told what to do, see? "Hell, I first started dyeing my hair partly hoping it would be too conspicuous for Nicky to send me out spying. Like, I assume if this shit was so important, he'd go out and do it himself."

"Couldn't you just point that out to Nicky?"

D.T. shrugged. "In a perfect world, maybe. In this one, you need a roof over your head."

His surveillance portfolio had included Venus de Nylon. There was a sister, too, whom he'd been sent to check out once or twice. "But mainly he had me watching Billy, who he was obsessed with even then. Nicky never gives up on anything. It's what makes him effective."

"Wait—are you telling me it's Billy Three-Sticks we're watching for here?"

"Shit, kid, they really keep you in the dark, don't they?" When no answer came, he sighed. "You see that cinderblock up on the fire escape? That's Billy's window right there."

Charlie's first urge was to go throw rocks at it, to shout up what was going on below. It didn't seem fair, somehow, to repay *Brass Tactics* with an invasion of privacy. "But what possible purpose—"

"That's what I'm *saying*, Prophet. You do enough drugs, you start to get these persecution fantasies." He played a funky little kalimba rhythm on the pulltab of his beer. Charlie couldn't figure out whether it was unconscious or to make a point; by now, D.T. might as well have been talking to himself. "But maybe it's catching. I mean, the way Billy came around on New Year's Eve rapping about a blaze of glory . . . That could have just been loose talk about the flashpots we were planning to use, but Sol swears he was acting suspicious even back as far as Christmas, and whatever you want to say about Sol, he's pretty hard to rattle. And then that record, the one about the world coming to an end this year—"

This, Charlie knew, described a surprising array of records. "You mean the Clash, '1977'?"

"I mean the one Billy brought backstage that night. 'Two Sevens Clash,' right? A message, he called it. Or a peace offering. And I agree he's been looking haunted. No, Billy definitely knows at least as much as I do." Fair enough, Charlie thought, but about what? Reggae? Numerology? Even if he'd felt like revealing the depths of his bewilderment, though, Charlie wouldn't get a chance to ask, because just then D.T. told him to shut up and make like wallpaper. "Here he comes." Charlie expected to see the unkempt figure in the motorcycle jacket. Instead, it was another black guy, well-dressed. "That's Billy's boyfriend."

Hang on a sec, Charlie thought. Billy Three-Sticks—the man who'd penned the deathless lyric *Wasted, tripping, / basted in the drippings / of your love*—was gay? But then, hadn't Charlie been taught not to look down on his fellow underdogs? D.T.'s indifference seemed, in this light, nearly Sam-like: what people did with their genitals was their business. "Now watch. I've seen this before. A half-hour or so after the boyfriend leaves, Billy comes out all sneaky. He'll go down to the Meatpacking District, then up to the Bronx. Or just to the Bronx. He goes straight uptown, I don't even bother to follow anymore."

In fact, what happened was that fifteen minutes later the boyfriend pulled up to the vestibule in a late-model white hatchback. Then Billy Three-Sticks, unshaven and looking even thinner than at New Year's, hurried out with a suitcase and got into the shotgun side. D.T. sat up. "What the fuck?" But as the car pulled away, he was too drunk to give chase himself. He made Charlie switch seats and ordered him to wait until the car was a block away before they tailed it onto a highway by the river.

For miles, their quarry would stay at exactly the speed limit, a hundred yards ahead. Only way up near the George Washington Bridge, after they lost the white hatchback in Jersey-bound traffic, was Charlie allowed to turn back. And thank God: he was due home anyway. Still, as they picked their way through traffic on Broadway, he asked if they should have done something to stop Billy Three-Sticks.

"Orders are, not unless it looks like he's going to meet with his uncle, or the fuzz. Force was never supposed to be our first option. Like, if we saw him entering the Hamilton-Sweeney Building, we'd know for sure he'd sold us out, and that would be a whole 'nother kettle of shit. But hey—Nicky doesn't need to know we let him off our radar just now, okay? Nothing to report. Another dumb day."

And like that, Charlie was the one with power. Did it make him automatically immoral? He thought back over the various kinds of instruction he'd been absorbing. "Fine," he said. "But only if you level with me about what the hell this all really is. Nicky's working on something major, isn't he?"

They were stuck behind a bus somewhere north of Times Square. Horns rose around them in peevish disputation. D.T. seemed to hold his breath for a minute before reaching for another beer. "Look—you know Billy's uncle's one of the biggest wheels in New York, right? An old crony of the Dulleses, may they rot in hell."

"No, I didn't know that. I'm in the dark, remember?"

"Consider yourself enlightened. This guy, the uncle, he's plugged into every network you can think of, public and private. Like a gauge that registers every flicker. And over the years, he's done us some favors, so you might say he's plugged into the PHP, too. Of course, we kept that from his nephew. But when Billy shows up on New Year's dropping hints—when he *just happens* to be hanging around Grand Central at Christmas as Sol's coming back from some top-secret mission in Queens—what's the logical inference, if you're Nicky? Like, what if the uncle's using Billy as an agent to see if we've turned against him? There's no manipulation he isn't capable of. Nicky claims Billy used to call him the Demon Brother."

Charlie felt a twinge, like he'd heard the phrase before—the title of a lost Ex Post Facto song, or an Ex Nihilo one yet to be recorded. He reminded himself to focus. "Nope. I still don't get it. 'If we've turned against him?' Why would the PHP have anything to do with a big wheel like that in the first place?" (Or frankly, given what he'd seen of this operation so far, vice versa?)

A burp brought D.T. back to the present—a present in which he was compromised. "Suffice it to say, before you wager with the devil, you'd better see his trump card. Nicky didn't, until November. The city made that Blight Zone in the Bronx, opening a hundred acres to development. And then the thing with Sam . . . there's just no way Nicky's going to roll over and accept he's beaten. The latest thinking is that we need a Demon Brother of our own."

Not so fast, Charlie wanted to say. Go back to that. To Sam. It had been a month since he'd heard anyone, even himself, speak her name. But they'd reached the Phalanstery, and D.T. had his door open to get out. Charlie reached for his arm. "What do you *mean* a Demon Brother of our own?"

"You may be Nicky's chosen one, Prophet, but if I'm not ready to be read in on the details, you sure as hell aren't. Listen, you asked me last week what I believe. Someone comes at you, comes at something that matters to you, you blow up in their face—that's what I believe. Which reminds me," he said. He pulled from the glovebox a small suede sheath with a switchblade handle protruding. "Nicky thought you might want some protection." But that just went to show that they were right about things, that Charlie really wasn't ready, because he'd never imagined Nicky was this serious. He couldn't use a knife on someone, no matter how bad his need. He tucked the switchblade, still folded, into his uniform's pocket. D.T., for his part, was sobering up. Which meant souring. "I mean it about keeping your trap shut, okay? I figure Nicky wouldn't send us out together if he didn't want you to know we had Billy under watch. But if he heard I'd let on about the Demon Brother," D.T. said, nodding at the pocket, "he'd probably use one of those on me."

39

B RUNO'S HIDEAWAY, as Mercer couldn't help thinking of it, sat at the end of a deep lot forested with hemlock, so that it was invisible from the road. But though William had been talking it up all week, the accommodations were one-star at best: a few bedrooms, a bear-skin rug before the fireplace, a shelf of discontinued board games. Everything smelled like mothballs; it had been shut up since the previous summer, Mercer surmised, or maybe the one before that. And they could have been on the beach right now! He kept his disappointment to himself, but couldn't help going around to open windows. William took this as just another opportunity to expound upon the freshness of the twenty-degree air.

For dinner, they unearthed from a cupboard a box of pasta, a decade old if it was a day, which Mercer whipped together with olive oil and some canned Parmesan of equally dubious provenance. Then they sat up side-by-side on the wicker couch playing Risk. They had this game at home, but hadn't touched it, he didn't think, since the night he'd told William he loved him. The Summer Olympics had been on then. William had moved his feet to Mercer's lap, and something about the gesture had led him to blurt out the sentence he'd been turning over in his mind for weeks. William's response was to look just this way: preoccupied with his next move. Now Mercer wondered if he'd been jonesing for a fix, or whatever the slang was.

William pushed his armies into Kamchatka. "I know what you're thinking, Merce."

"What do you mean?"

"You think I'm cracking up. Going crazy." That last word—a significant one, in the context of their relationship—seemed to twist in the wind for a minute.

"I think you're reckless, maybe. Asia's always hard to defend."

"Come on, Mercer. Be honest with me a little."

"What do you want me to say? Good artists are always crazy, one way or another."

"That's an old wives' tale."

"Try me," Mercer said, moving to firm up his own forces in Eastern Europe.

"Rauschenberg."

"You know I'm no good with painters."

"Fine," William said. "Who is it that you like so much. Faulkner."

"Faulkner was a dipsomaniac. And a womanizer."

"Dostoevsky?"

"Compulsive gambler. Rabid anti-Semite. Did love his wife, though." Mercer laid an awkward arm across the back of the couch. "Honestly, honey, sometimes I think *I'm* crazy." Which was true; he periodically suspected himself of neurosis, though he was also aware that this suspicion, itself the source of the neurosis, was evidence of basically sound mental health. But William was looking straight at him now, smiling.

"Okay, you pass." He swept the game board onto the floor, a gesture of pure cinema, and then shoved board and table out of the way to clear a patch of bearskin big enough for both of them. "You'll have to be careful," he said, "my bad arm's still tender." But elbows out, fingers on buttons, he was leading again, as in the early days, and all Mercer had to do was let himself be carried along.

Afterward, they lay together sweating, staring up at the dark-stained rafters. Blood vessels expanded, cooled. Little game pieces dug into Mercer's back. It was so quiet here—the quiet of the country, which he realized he'd missed. Wind in the eaves. Birds calling and responding. Those had been some of the best times, early on, after they'd finished fooling around but before he'd returned to himself. He felt that his mind had clarified, like thick white butter exposed to heat—some sense of emergency lifting away.

Then he must have fallen into a dream, because he was in a movie house, trying to find a place to sit. The theater, sloping toward the screen, was somehow both bright and dark. There were no empty pairs of seats, only single ones dotted here and there. People stared at the back of his head, wanting him to hurry up and choose, but what if the theater held only a finite number of groups and couples, and they were already here? He ranged deeper into the tortuous upholstery. He found a couple of empty seats together, but they were perpendicular to the screen. Actually, every seat was, except the screen was no longer where he'd thought; it existed in every direction. He was seated now, at just the right distance, not too close, not too far, but anxious, because how would William find him? He turned to discover William standing in the aisle next to him, holding a popcorn and Cokes and smiling patiently down. And as he reached for William's leg, the way a small child will reach for its mother's, there welled up through a small hole in the bottom of Mercer's soul a relief surpassing any he'd ever known in waking life.

HE ROSE THE NEXT MORNING to the sound of whistling. He couldn't remember the last time William had been up first, but here he was, bustling about the cabin. He'd put away the game pieces, washed up last night's dishes. A blizzard was howling outside the windows, but he seemed so pleased to be back in this place—so nostalgic, perhaps—as to almost invite suspicion. When he went to go get groceries, though, he asked Mercer to come. "There's no one I'd rather get stuck in a snowdrift and freeze to death with," William said. The trip was uneventful, the roads well-plowed. Mercer watched through the rental car's whitening windshield as his lover sprinted toward a tin-roofed country store. There was another car a few spaces over, its muffler exhaling fog, but the strip of trackless skin exposed when William hiked his motorcycle jacket over his head to keep dry felt again like Mercer's alone.

For lunch, they roasted hot dogs in the fireplace. Then, when the storm had passed, they bundled up and went out into the silent woods. "There's something I want to show you," William said. It was a swimming hole, meager and now frozen solid. He scrambled up onto a giant black boulder slippery with ice and stood there with arms spread wide, as though embracing all of space. Or all of time—

the beard and sunglasses made him hard to read. When Mercer called after him to be careful, William beckoned him to follow.

He was right: the view was worth embracing. The sky was low and broody, but from here, near the treeline, you could see the forest rolling down into the valley, the lake tucked away like a pocket mirror. "Remind me again why we don't live out here?"

"Did you really think I'd steer you wrong?" Then William pointed to the wide-open country beyond the next ridge. "New York's that way. My compass is unerring."

THE WEATHER WOULD HOLD for the rest of the weekend. They got up each day with the sun, wore themselves out on a long walk through the snow, and then retreated to the cabin for a nap. Then dinner and Scrabble and sex. William looked happier than he had in a year, healthy and sober and whole, as if it had only been the city light making him seem like an addict. Alas, part of the definition of an idyll is that it can't last forever.

They left for New York Monday morning, to beat the evening rush. Because their shoes were still wet from the woods, William took his off when he curled up in the passenger's seat to sleep. They were coming out of the Lincoln Tunnel when his foot came to rest against the parking brake. His big toe poked through a hole in his socks. There were dark bumps near the base, like carbuncles. "What *are* those?"

"What are what?" William asked, stirring. "Eyes on the road!"

A delivery truck roared past, its airhorn a long, descending moan. Mercer's palms were slick. "Those things between your toes. Are those bruises?"

William adjusted his sock so that the toe disappeared again. He was inviting Mercer to play along, to pretend he hadn't seen anything, and Mercer might have done it, except that his interrogator, quiet these last few days, had returned, but with a different voice. It was the voice of Pop, demanding that he act, for once, like a man. "You've been using again, haven't you?"

"Why are you saying this? We were together all weekend, Merce. We had a great time, didn't we?"

"Before, though. This winter."

William's laugh had nothing to do with humor. "You know, we're not each other's property. My body is not your body." He reached out to turn the radio up, but Mercer was finding his way past the lump in his throat.

"Can you not see this is a big fucking problem?"

"You're being theatrical."

"I'm theatrical?"

"I'm not going to argue with you, Mercer." His voice rose. "I just—Look. I just went a whole weekend. Doesn't that tell you something?"

"Listen to yourself!" Mercer's hand hurt. He had banged, apparently, on the steering wheel. Of course, this was what William wanted. To be yelled at. Made the victim. Mercer turned the radio back down, so that they might, he pointed out, actually be able to talk for once.

Which was exactly why, William said, reaching for the knob, he'd turned it *UP* in the first place. "And don't pretend like you haven't known the whole time. You've always been a terrible liar."

"We're not done here," Mercer said, but got no response. He was shaking inside, afraid of what he'd done, but also furious. William, though, was ever resourceful. Just when you thought you'd cut off all the angles, he would find a maneuver that led toward liberty, and now, at a stoplight a few blocks from the car-rental place, he simply hopped out of the passenger's seat. His door slammed behind him, echoing up the fronts of the buildings. He moved onto the crowded sidewalk and disappeared around a corner. And then it was as if the weekend had never happened—almost as if they'd never left. Once again, Mercer Goodman could barely see sky.

40

SHERRI HAD BEEN GETTING the real-estate circulars for a while now. You wrote in once, to one, and all of a sudden they all had your name and address. Farmsteads in Connecticut, time-shares on the Jersey shore, rustic Adirondack retreats. Of course, to Larry—though he never would have thought of telling her—this three-bedroom house on the north shore of Staten Island already *was* a retreat. He'd bought it at Eisenhower-era prices the year of their wedding, and as his F.O.P.-backed raises outpaced inflation, they'd been able to add amenities like the wet bar in the basement and the handrail in the bath, the cutaway in the dining room wall through which he could pass plates to the kitchen without having to get up from his chair. Lately, though, Sherri had grown serious about a change. He'd taken her for Valentine's Day to an old-timey resort upstate, and she'd wanted to drive around the next morning to look at property. Slowing down so she could peek back up some random driveway that dissipated like a jet trail among the conifers, he'd understood that the imaginary life she was sketching for them—*you could have a workshop, we could rent out the basement*—was really a way of talking about early retirement. With the fiscal crunch, the force was looking to trim payroll anyway, and she was tired of sitting up waiting for the phone to ring. The idea, when she turned back to him, was clear: he was supposed to volunteer to get the paperwork started. And then a week later a photo of that very house, the one they'd been idling in front of, had appeared on the corkboard above the wall-mounted phone in their kitchen. He'd tried to picture himself crutching his way down that grainy and nearly vertical driveway to check the mail. Having that be the highlight of his day. Scrabbling back up again, making wooden toys at a workbench.

He found her out back by the covered pool, wrapped in a horse-blanket, reading a library book while a mug of tea steamed on the arm of her Adirondack chair. It couldn't have been more than fifty degrees out, but that was warmer than it had been in months, and Sherri had always had this need to be outdoors. He lowered himself onto the chair's other arm, doing his darnedest not to wince. She obliged him by moving her reading glasses up onto her hair, still sandy-colored but now with streaks of gray. He wouldn't have thought it possible that a woman could get more beautiful as she got older. He pulled the clipping from his pocket and pressed it to the weathered wood. "I found this pinned to the corkboard."

"Of course you did, sweetie. I put it there for you to find." She didn't move to take it.

"Is there something you want me to do with it?"

"I thought you might want to call it. See? I circled the number. Pretty transparent, as ploys go." She'd closed her book. She had that faint little line she got around the corners of her mouth, like she was teasing him, but her voice was dead earnest. "Don't you remember this one, from Valentine's Day? It's the one with the gables, north of New Paltz."

"That hotel was full of hippies."

"You said you liked it."

"New Paltz is like a magnet for them. Energy fields or something."

"Honestly, Larry, I'm starting to feel a little strung along here. Do you know how much you were home this week?"

He reached for her hands. Strong, warm from the tea. "Why would I string you along?"

"Twelve hours, not factoring sleep."

It was his turn to sigh. He let go of her hands, turning to face the taut blue skin that covered the pool. They'd been among the first people in the neighborhood to put one in, back when they thought they'd have kids. In-ground, because Larry had trouble with ladders. Once in the water, though, he could move like anyone else. Summer mornings, he used to do laps. Afternoons, neighbor kids wore a wet path through the kitchen, where Sherri baked Toll House cookies and mixed pitchers of lemonade. But those kids had grown up, had stopped sending graduation announcements and Christmas cards. A couple of them had run off to the West Coast; one was in jail. A chainlink fence with green privacy netting had risen on one side of the yard. On warm days, you could hear a new group of kids behind it, laughing and experimenting with swear-words and splashing in pools of their own.

"There must be a case," she said.

"There are a lot of cases, honey. That's the problem."

"No, there's a specific one. What else could it be? Certainly not how much your bosses appreciate your efforts, ha ha. But when you won't talk to me about it—"

"That was your idea, to stop bringing work home. I knew it was going to bother you."

"What am I supposed to do?" she said. "You know I've never wanted to put you in a position, but what about my position? If I don't speak up, you'll put this paternal thing you have ahead of me. It's a kid, right? Or a lost cause. Or both. Oh, God, don't tell me it's both."

It was true. Even before New Paltz, the Cicciaro case had begun shunting the others aside. He hadn't admitted this to himself because he was never going to close it. It was uncloseable. Yet it was the one that had followed him home. That had entered his dreams. "You should come work for me. Replace McFadden."

"I know you, Larry. I know your little messiah complex you think is such a secret. Wait. Hear me out. I understand that you feel like you can't walk away from this. But we're not getting any younger. And your spending seventy hours a week on the job isn't putting us any closer to getting out of here. There's always going to be another case."

"Are we fighting? Is this some kind of ultimatum?" He was still on the arm of the chair.

She placed a hand on his back, her fingers parting around the mis-aligned vertebrae. "We're talking, like adults. Look at me, sweetie. I wouldn't have married you if I thought you were going to be the kind of man who needed ultimatums."

"I promise you, Sherri—"

"Or promises either," she'd said, as he leaned down to kiss her.

Yet it was strange; that Monday, when he slipped away from the office early and took his afternoon paper over to Beth Israel, he would be nagged by the feeling of having given her his word. Why else had he come back here, at the end of visiting hours? He flipped off the beige Magnavox in the corner, which the girl's father had left tuned to daytime TV. The window was supposed to stay closed, to keep dust from penetrating this nominally sterile environment, but Pulaski cranked it to its maximum width of three inches. There was ice-melt on the sill outside. The girl would never see the birds tippling at the puddles, but he liked to think that somewhere deep inside the shell of her body, she would feel the fresh cold air, hear the sounds of city buses sloughing past and the drug commerce from the park across the way and know she wasn't missing anything. And maybe she liked the smell of loose tobacco as much as he did. He'd barely gotten his pipe lit, though, when an intense nurse swept in to tell him he couldn't smoke on this floor—did he not see the machine she needed to breathe?—and cranked the window shut again. He resisted the urge to flash his badge; she knew who he was. Anyway, she was right.

As afternoon turned to night, newspaper sections accumulated like geologic deposits on the floor beside him. The breathing machine breathed. The heart monitor monitored. Other nurses came in and out; the bed went up and down; the fluid bag running into her arm was empty, full, empty. The goal was leave-taking: less immersion, not more. But the patient under the sheet was somehow a comfort. He tried to imagine what Sherri was up to at this hour, on the far side of the deep-rock harbor. Sure, she had friends, tennis, her part-time job at the library, but when was the last time she'd lunched with a friend? Or lifted a racket? He stayed here, perhaps, because in the sad fact of the dying girl on the motorized bed beside him he felt closer to Sherri's loneliness than he had yesterday on the arm of her chair. Her in her little box of light on that island, him in his box on this one. For a moment, he thought he sensed, beneath the visible world, some blind infrastructure connecting the two of them, or the three of them, and connecting them to still others. People he hadn't even met.

And you wanted to make a suspect from this circle of connection, the acquaintances or acquaintances of acquaintances from whom a perp nine times out of ten emerged. You still hadn't ruled out the black kid who found her, for example, despite what you may have let him believe. (One of the private-school coworkers Pulaski had discreetly approached described the guy as a little eccentric. Though another said she thought he was working on a novel, which explained a lot.) Or you wanted to make the father, a Sicilian with a damaged hand and a tendency to say as little as he could get away with. The vanished mother. The mother's lover. Whoever it was who'd been leaving those flowers. A DD-5, that was the form you used, a complaint follow-up. You filled them out in triplicate. The problem was that the DD-5, with its blanks for facts, left out everything else. Like intuition. Like feeling. Like the question of just how far these connections extended. Richard Groskoph. Mercer Goodman. "Dr." Zig Zigler, who when he wasn't filling the airwaves with the depredations of the business class was now ranting about virgin sacrifice and the monsters in the Park. All these threads, like the ley-lines he'd read about in his Time-Life history books, converging on the Cicciaro girl, who lay there unaware, a glass-coffined beauty whose kingdom was in ruins. But of course, this was true of everybody; who didn't exist at the convergence of a thousand thousand stories? At the center of forces, circuits, relays Pulaski could sit like this all evening and not be able to make connect. Which meant the shooting was meaningless. A chance encounter. Just one of those things. And he had promised (hadn't he?) to do his best to get free of it.

Or so he was thinking when he noticed for the first time the shadow on the back of her neck, trapped against the pillow. To touch her would have broken some unstated rule, but then he realized he could just move the pillow itself, and her head flopped sideways—he shuddered—revealing a black tattoo an inch in diameter just below where the gauze had been cut away. It looked to him like an icon, goggles and spiky hair. Familiar, somehow. Why? Because it was the same image he'd seen on the paper he'd found in the pocket of those bluejeans in the Park.

41

WHEN REGAN RETURNED TO THE APARTMENT, the only light in the living room was the TV, and Mrs. Santos was in a wooden chair she'd dragged in from the kitchen, using her knitting needles to transmit her silent judgment: it was after dark, a mother should be home with her babies, not staying late after work. Then again, she was the only sitter in Brooklyn Heights Regan could actually afford. Keith may have thought she was living the life of Riley over here, but short of reclaiming stewardship of the kids' trust funds, it was hard to make rent and tuition and insurance premiums, even with the child support checks. Asking Mrs. Santos to stay through dinner tonight had meant packing her own lunch for work for a week. And times must have been tight for Mrs. Santos, too; Regan had left ten dollars to order pizzas, but there was evidence—ketchupy plates, the smell of grease in the air—that the old woman had pocketed the money and found things in the fridge to whip together burgers. "The kids are in their rooms?" Regan asked, from the doorway. *Sí*, yes, said Mrs. Santos. "Would you mind sticking around until nine, then?" She was about to explain—she could just squeeze in a quick run—but if Mrs. Santos saw the leather couch as self-indulgent, what would she think about recreational jogging?

On her way to change, Regan noticed Will's door was closed. She opened it to find her son face-down on the floor, perpendicular to another boy, his new friend Ken. She wanted to like him because he lived on the block and Will needed friends, and because Ken was Japanese, and a Yankees fan, but the kid was so damn secretive, or, more charitably, oblivious to adult authority. In his presence, Will became secretive, too. The second she'd come in, they'd whisked their cards and dice into the shadows under their chests. They'd taken up some kind of game about magic—wizards, hobbits, stuff like that. *Eldritch Realms*, it was called. Mothers were, it went without saying, non grata. "What are you guys up to?"

"Nothing," Will said.

"Hello, Ken."

She couldn't tell if Ken mumbled a response or not. It was odd: his mother, at the park, was always so friendly now. Regan decided to see and raise his ruse of not seeing her.

"Well, whatever you're doing, honey, I wish you'd include your sister."

"Mom," Will said, without looking up. "You. Are. Embarrassing. Me."

"This isn't the easiest time for her."

"Do you not see I have a friend here?" he said.

"It's after eight. Maybe it's time Ken went home."

That was all it took for the boy to scramble to his feet, flash a hand at Will, and, eyes hidden by the brim of his ballcap, zoom past her into the hallway. "Bye, Mrs. Santos!" The front door clicked shut. She waited for Will to say something, but he just lay there in his own cap—the Mets, Keith's team—staring at her ankles. When she left him, he was adding Ken's cards and dice to the pile under his chest, like a dragon smothering his hoard.

By now, Regan knew herself to be the worst mother in the world—it was the very crest of the wave of guilt she'd been riding for the last three hours—but she was afraid that if she didn't run tonight, she would resort to some other, less innocent set of penalties. These must have been more obvious than she'd thought, too, even before the crisis became overt, or what had Keith meant by giving her a pair of running shoes for her thirty-fifth birthday, telling her it would be good for her health? She'd been slow to admit it, but he was right. Most people lost weight when they started training for a marathon. Since Regan had taken it up, not long after New Year's, she had gained four pounds, according to the bathroom scale. There were times when she'd even felt capable of living without a bathroom scale.

With the running shoes on, she felt like that again, freer. She streaked down the Promenade toward the glowing arms of the bridge. Breath. Breath. Breath. Breath. Like Lamaze. She wondered, was it just the divorce that was eating at her kids? That sense of abandonment she'd been warned was unavoidable? Or was that the damage of junior year, twenty years ago, still making her see herself as bigger in the minds of others than she really was? At least part of what was bothering Will was his grandfather. Upon returning from Keith's last weekend, he'd asked her to explain the difference between a grand jury and a regular one. He knew her work was to make Grandpa's company look as good as possible, so when she told him everything was going to be fine, did he assume she was just doing her job?

She began to climb the bridge now, blood humming in her head. Thoughts of work became thoughts of Andrew West, who was the real reason she'd been late getting home. He'd been tactful in his choice of restaurant. The casual décor, maracas and other mariachi trinkets, the anonymity of the neighborhood, had set her at ease. Who could possibly want to fool around after Mexican food? But when, post-appetizers, she'd broached the question of how they might shore up Daddy's position in his talks with the U.S. Attorney, he'd told her she deserved a break from thinking about work all the time. He took a long drink from his margarita, then squinted and rubbed his forehead. "Ice-cream headache."

She'd been titrating wine into her own system by the milliliter. She needed her wits about her.

"So, do you like music?" he asked, once he'd stopped squinting.

"Doesn't everyone?" It came off as defensive, glib, and she could already feel herself shrinking. How ridiculous she must look in this windowless restaurant with this beautiful . . . well, kid. "I used to think I'd be in Broadway musicals when I grew up. I remember dragging my dad to see *My Fair Lady*." She told him how Daddy had ended up crying, he laughed so hard. Daddy wasn't much of a laugher, even then.

"And do you dance?" he asked.

"Why? Do you?"

"I won some trophies in high school," he said. Then: "I'm only kidding." But he did know this little disco where they could go.

After dessert, of course—"They have the most amazing flan here." Now her knees throbbed. She'd reached the summit of the bridge's pedestrian walkway, a couple hundred feet above water, but if she couldn't make it the whole mile without giving up, how was she ever going to manage twenty-six and change? Luckily, there was gravity to carry her downhill toward Manhattan. The city doubled in the water below her. Like those two images of the South Bronx. Before and After. Despite her expanded powers, there was still an awful lot she didn't know about the company that bore her name. She didn't even know, really, the first thing about the stranger she was thinking of letting into her bed: where Andrew West had worked before, to whom he reported now . . . For all she knew, he could have been hired by Amory to keep an eye on her, compromise her—who could say how far the Demon Brother's reach extended?—though Andrew had been nothing but kind, and Dr. Altschul would have pointed here to a pattern of self-sabotage.

"Andrew," she'd said matter-of-factly, as the dinner plates were cleared. "I'm worried I've misled you. My husband and I only just separated, and what I really need now, more than anything, is a friend."

He didn't fight back. The gleaming teeth that had probably never seen a cavity, the sculpted hands that absently twirled the air, searching for the squash racket he'd left back in Webster Groves . . . they could have slipped into a janitor's closet for seven minutes of heaven or parted and never seen each other again, or anything in between, and Andrew West would have been just fine. And the fact that he carried it so lightly shook her. Stupid! How could she have thought this meant anything to him? After some coffee and more small-talk, he'd kissed her chastely on the cheek and closed the door to the cab.

At the foot of the bridge, she slowed to a trot. The leafless trees of the park behind City Hall beckoned like black hands. She longed to stop for a minute and take a breather, but she didn't dare; a park at night, even one this small, was no place for a woman alone. And that was what time had finally made out of Regan. A woman alone. She saw again the yellow police tape stretched across the end of her father's block, turning white in the New Year's snow. The white sheet being fed into the ambulance. To be minding your own business, immersed in the mess of your life, and then for it all to go black. This was what religion had been for, supposedly, a place to put your fears about whether there was anything beyond that black. She wished someone else were here right now. To be honest—and it killed her—she wished Keith were here right now.

But she let the shadows chase her back onto the bridge. At speed, the lights of the cars on the lower level blurred and disappeared. The water below was a great erasure mark. There was only her breathing and the rhythm of her feet on the pavement. She could have been jogging home to the old place, an intact marriage, undamaged kids, except. Except there was no Manhattan anymore. She was Brooklyn-bound.

In the living room, Mrs. Santos sat in her hard chair watching Telly Savalas watch a building burn on *Kojak*. The lights here were still off, and the interaction of the yellow overspill from the foyer and the blue flicker of the TV gave this, the theoretical center of the home, a bleak and migrainous aspect. Regan advanced into the room, digging in her purse for money, glancing over at Kojak's enormous lolly because sometimes she didn't feel comfortable looking Mrs. Santos in the eye. "You didn't let them watch this, did you? Because Will's so curious about everything, and I'm not sure he's old enough . . ." She realized she'd insulted Mrs. Santos, but she couldn't apologize without altering a power dynamic that was already—face it—fucked. Besides, her homework from therapy this week was to stop apologizing so much.

Mrs. Santos continued to knit. "A man calls for you while you are out."

Regan's pulse was still up, tympani in her chest. "Did he leave a message?"

"No, just a name." Regan was completely in her power now.

"Well, do you remember what it was?"

Mrs. Santos smiled to herself, in private triumph. "We do not have this name in my country. Merced, is something like this. But the family name, I remember. Is *Buen hombre*. Good man."

42

THE NIGHT OF, or the evening of the day of the Night Of, Mercer stripped off the necktie and Oxford-cloth shirt of his teaching costume and sprawled prone on the bed, hoping sleep would make the hours between five and eight pass quickly. His eyes stayed open, though. The days were getting longer again; this time a week ago, he wouldn't have been able to make out much of the portrait tacked to the wall, save maybe for a mitre-shaped tangle of hair. Now those eyes that were not quite William's seemed to accuse him. He turned the other way, to face the window and the beaded curtain that hid the rest of the loft. Out there, futon and armchair had been drawn together, in an angle open toward the door. And there was a place of honor for William, too, a fraying nylon beach chair Mercer had found up on the roof—which, for all he knew, belonged to William, anyway.

They used to sit up there on warm nights, William drinking beer with the sixth-floor Angels while Mercer perched nearby on an upturned bucket, studying the fires that broke out uptown every summer. Once, the enormous Angel named Bullet had waved his beercan toward the burning horizon. "You know this guy Maslow? He has this triangle I heard about on 'Dr.' Zig. When you're down there on the bottom of it, you can't appreciate what's higher. This is why niggers, man, you can't give them nothing. No offense." Mercer did his best not to take any. The invitation to participate in Bullet's delusions—that Mercer was not, in fact, black; that he and William were merely dear friends—was, properly viewed, a gesture of solidarity. And on second thought, Bullet himself looked awfully swarthy in most lights; Mercer couldn't be sure he wasn't speaking brother-to-brother. But William, who had appointed himself Surrogate Defender of the Brown People of the Earth, now proceeded to shoot holes in Bullet's theory. It was obviously the landlords who paid to have the fires set. Insurance purposes, cutting losses. And landlords were, by and large, honkies. The practice was well-established; Jewish lightning, was the unfortunate term of art. Mercer braced for carnage, in case Bullet saw himself as white (or Jewish), but Bullet had always had a soft spot for William. Had Mercer had the guts to ask, he probably would have agreed to take part in the intervention—to host it, even.

Instead, the first person Mercer had called was Bruno Augenblick, who'd said, "You really don't understand William, do you?"

To which Mercer had wanted to reply, *So explain him to me, then.* "I'm just supposed to wait around until he ODs, that's what you're telling me?"

"Is that what you think I want, Mr. Goodman?"

Mercer had assumed since their one disastrous meeting that Bruno, unlike Bullet, actually hated Negroes, or at least this Negro, but now he wasn't so sure. He fingered the brochure from the Substance Abuse Treatment Center on Twenty-Eighth Street. The phone's rendition of silence was as imperfect as its version of the human voice. There were faint pops and crackles, like bubbles in a glass of 7-Up. "I frankly don't care what you want, Bruno," he said. "What I want is to help William get off this stuff. I guess I was foolish enough to think you'd pitch in, seeing as how you're old friends, or whatever it is you are."

Bruno's voice remained stiff, chilly. (How was there such a thing as German-language poetry?) "I'll have to trust you to understand that this is precisely why I can't have anything to do with your . . ."

"Intervention."

"Precisely," he said again. And that was that. He hadn't even wished Mercer luck.

Now the curtain on the window was gray with dusk. It had been blue when Mercer had bought it, a thin fabric to replace the butcher paper William had taped across the glass. The headlights and taillights of the buses slouching toward the Port Authority traced the history of Western civilization on the cotton. It was, substantially, a history of soot. Though a few feet separated the curtain from Mercer's head, he could make out individual particles of blackness, the democratic meaninglessness of them scattered at random across the gauzy gray cloth. Airbrakes sounded like breaking bottles. Stuck buses bleated like sheep. He'd been a passenger down there, once, his head filled with a mixture of fantasy, superstition, and the vestiges of childhood religion, a running monologue aimed at God. (*Da ist keine Stelle, die dich nicht sieht.*) And had he really been so different, fretting about the apartment this afternoon, setting out mismatched mugs, as though this weren't an intervention but a tea party? He still acted as if the proper arrangement of surfaces might call down benediction, or grace. Of course, there was no telling when William would be home, though he'd been promised (falsely) a special dinner, to be served at eight. Mercer could only hope he wouldn't show up at seven thirty. Or ten.

There came a sound like a shot. It must have been a garbage truck hitting a pothole—one of thirty-two distinct sounds he'd categorized that interfered with sleep in this city. But garbage trucks came with the dawn. So maybe he'd slept through the intervention, and now it was morning: same traffic, same crepuscular light. The fact that "dusk" could mean two nearly opposite things seemed indicative of something, if only that the membrane between the real and the cognitive had grown perilously thin. Then the sound returned in multiples—wham wham wham wham WHAM—and he realized the night hadn't happened yet. The Angels had left the inner end of the vestibule unlocked again. Someone was banging on his door.

Before he could get it all the way open, Venus de Nylon, the Farfisa wizard of Ex Post Facto, swept into the apartment as if it were her own, and Mercer merely a butler or footman. The last time he'd seen her (Him? Her? Her.), she was in nurse's whites and a Tina Turner shag that swayed side to side as she made dainty stabs at her organ. Now she'd shaved and waxed her head. With her gold hoop earrings, she looked like a Dominican Mr. Clean. She seized a picture frame from a bookshelf, a Polaroid of himself and William on the patchy grass of Central Park. "Well, this is cute."

Mercer held out his hand. "We haven't been formally introduced. I'm Mercer."

Something stirred in her alligator-skin purse. She reached in and scooped from it a ball of white fur.

"And I see you brought your dog."

Set down on the floor, the beast scrabbled under the sofa. There was a yowl, and Eartha K. streaked out and shot through the beaded curtain of the sleeping nook. The dog gave a few yaps at the swinging beads, as if gloating. "I wasn't going to leave her tied to a lamppost, if that's what you're suggesting." Venus's eyes flicked back to Mercer. "Honestly, I never understood why a Hamilton-Sweeney would choose to live in this neighborhood anyway."

"Like I said on the phone, I do appreciate your helping out with all this."

"I knew the day would come. Billy's always had to take everything to the end of the line."

"Please, sit. Can I offer you coffee?"

"Aren't *you* the Donna Reed of this motherfucker? But I don't drink it. Weak heart."

Venus took the futon, lifting her big knobby feet from their flats and curling them up on the cushion like a mermaid's tail. Mercer couldn't help but speculate about the body under the velour tracksuit. Had she had the surgery, the great final chop? Strategic bagginess made it hard to tell. He handed her the brochure. The idea here, he said, was to make William see how many people cared about him, the real him. The him he was with other people.

"And how many people is that, exactly?"

"I've got three confirmed, at this point."

"Three plus you?"

"Three including me."

"Shit."

"I did get his sister to come."

"I got to warn you, Mercer, you could get Jesus Christ himself to come and still not stop a serious habit. I learned that from watching Nastanovich. Our first bassist, you know. I really thought when he passed, it would scare Billy straight. Or at least back to coke. But a junkie's going to do what a junkie's going to do." She touched his thigh. Mercer, suddenly disconsolate, didn't remember to pull away. "Don't take that amiss. I don't want to see your boyfriend in jail or with a toe-tag, but you've got to accept that some people think the real them is whoever they are when they're *not* around other people."

Another knock at the door brought Mercer back to himself. Or to the version of himself he'd fashioned in order to make it through this. "That'll be Regan."

Since he'd last seen her, she had acquired a patina of health, as if she'd been on vacation, or to one of those new tanning coffins. Of course, the weeks around the solstice were when white people in general were at their whitest. Regan hesitated a moment before crossing the plane of the door, but no alarm began to sound.

"This is William's friend, Venus," Mercer explained. Venus extended a hand palm-down, as if to be kissed. Regan shook it and then, rather than sit on any of the available surfaces, walked around surveying the reclaimed furniture, the scrappy congoleum, the yellow ovoids of lamplight on the cracked plaster walls. The jacket of her business suit was a boxy armor. "Can I take that?" he asked. But she was cold and wanted to keep it. He apologized about the heat. "The landlord likes to turn it off and see how long he can go before anyone notices. I was just about to make some fresh coffee."

"That would be lovely, thanks."

"This is what we have." He held up a yellow can of Café El Bandito, careful not to open the cabinet door wide enough that she'd see the wood-grained roach motels within. (Really, though, why did he care? Why, since they met, had he been so desperate to impress her?)

Regan approached the dog. "Can I pet him?"

"Her. Shoshonna."

While the percolator burbled intestinally, Mercer took some creamer packets from the fridge and got down the sugar box and did a surreptitious roach check. He sought to verify in the glass-fronted cabinet that his guests were getting along, but instead, Regan had moved to the window, and was gazing down at the cinderblock on the fire escape, the dead flowers. The street below, full of stalled automobiles, would be a trench of bloody light. From down there, she would look like a portrait. "I don't see why this shouldn't work," she was saying. Her voice had gone small and hard, as if a walnut were lodged in her windpipe. "He's been looking for a home all his life, and now he's got one. He can't want to just throw that away."

"Is that the choice?" Venus said. "Either/or?" Mercer set down the tray of coffee fixings. He hadn't the heart to tell Regan that the beach chair she'd sunk into was meant for William.

Then, downstairs and a world away, the vestibule door opened, and there was a surge in the volume of car horns. The dog growled. Even before the keyring took up its rhythmic jingle in the stairwell, Mercer knew it was William. His face must have telegraphed it, because Regan and Venus had tensed, too, like teenagers in a monster flick.

They listened to his feet on the stairs. Or maybe Mercer had it backward: maybe William was the hapless victim at whom the audience was shouting, *Don't go through that door!* He couldn't remember if he'd locked it. Some fumbling ensued, and then it opened and William's eyes were swinging around the room. There was Venus on the couch, and he could see William struggling to seem glad to see her. It must have taken a second to correct for the suit-jacket and the hairstyle, to recognize the other woman as the sister he hadn't seen in a decade and a half, but the instant he did, his face shut down.

And why couldn't he be high right now? Mercer wondered. Why choose this of all moments to be sober? Also, why was Regan crying? It gave William the advantage, standing there in his beard with his keys in one hand. "Why don't you have a seat, and I'll get you some coffee," Mercer said. He wanted to flee in shame, to the kitchenette, to the next room, to the fire escapes and rooftops and the places where the city ended.

"Why don't *you* tell *me*, Mercer, what she's doing here? What are you doing here?"

Venus sighed. "Your sister's here, O Best Beloved, because you're strung out again."

"Oh, no. Uh-uh. We're not going to pretend this is somehow on my behalf."

"William—" The nut in Regan's throat had swollen; her color was deepening to bright red. Venus's dog chose this moment to trot over and investigate William's high-tops, which were spattered with paint like pigeon shit.

"I can't fucking believe this. I'm going to go out in the hall now and count to ten, and when I come back everything is going to be sane, okay? How does that sound?" He made no motion to go. Venus, however, had retrieved her purse from the floor, preparing to jump ship. This was not what Mercer had pictured at all. Even three-on-one, William was winning. (But *what* was he winning?) That's when Regan, God love her, rose. She was exactly the same height as her brother.

"William, I love you. You know that."

"So does Mercer here, supposedly, so how come you're all ganging up on me?"

"I do love you," Mercer said quietly.

"We'll discuss it later, Mercer." He turned back to Regan. "Let's be real. First that invitation, and now this. You thought I couldn't last a month without you, and that was like 1961. So why the fuck are you back in my life all of a sudden?"

"That's how long it took me to find you!"

"You can't have been looking very hard, Regan."

"I had a marriage. I had kids, two of them. And now Daddy's in trouble—"

"And what—you expect the other heir to like race back in and reclaim his birthright? I never wanted what Daddy has, Regan. Whatever he thought. Mom left me more than enough." It was a deft change of subject, but Mercer was too riveted to try to steer things back to the drugs.

"He grew up in the '30s, William. People didn't wallow in their feelings. That didn't mean you weren't like the little prince in his eyes. Why do you think the Goulds wanted him to pack you off to school?"

"—which he promptly did."

As Regan hugged herself, she seemed to get smaller, as if trying to hide in her coat. "Have you never in your life made a mistake? Have you never deserved a second chance? Maybe it's time to try forgiving people."

"Anyway, you were the one who bore the brunt of their attention, as I recall."

"Please don't—"

"And whose side did Daddy take then? Whose side did you take? Fifteen years, Regan, and have you said a word about what happened?"

There was a silence. William seemed powerless not to press his hand.

"You lost the right to judge my choices the day you let the Goulds off the hook. If you need an ally now, go ask your husband."

"But did Mercer not tell you? At New Year's?" *Damn it*, Mercer thought.

"Tell me what? What does New Year's have to do with anything?"

"Mercer, you didn't tell him about the divorce?"

"This is all a bit *Peyton Place* for me," Venus said. "*Vámonos*, Shoshonna."

"No, wait," Mercer said, trying to recover the script. "Look, we all love you, everybody loves you. We want you to get help."

"Who says I need it?" William asked. "Is it you, Venus, who dresses in women's clothes and bottle-feeds your dog? Or you, Regan, who'd rather die a slow death than admit what they let happen to you? Or is it you?" He turned to Mercer, and his voice softened. "Who can't accept a single goddamn molecule the way it is? You don't love things, Mercer, you love the ideas of things. You're asleep and don't even know it. Now if you'll excuse me—"

The little dog tried to follow him out into the hall, and he had to use his foot to keep it inside, compromising somewhat the majesty of his exit. But by the time the door closed, Regan had turned back to the window. Her hands, nearly lost in her sleeves, were balled tight; it was impossible to tell whether she was crying again. Mercer leaned against the counter, feeling punched in the gut. At last, Venus reached down for her dog. She had preserved a certain dignity in the midst of all this, and intended to leave with it intact. The dog, oblivious, plunged into the purse and situated itself there. Venus hoisted the strap to her shoulder and looked back at them just before leaving. "Well, *that* went well, don't you think?"

43

WILL WAS A NOTORIOUSLY LIGHT SLEEPER, and his bedroom was right next to the kitchen, so the noisy percolator was to be avoided. Instead, up before dawn that Saturday, Keith heated the coffee in a pot on the burner, the way they used to in college. It came to a boil faster than expected; he found himself rushing around in stocking feet, looking for something to strain it through, a colander or sieve or any other porous vessel his wife might not have thought to deprive him of. As the airshaft beyond the kitchen window brightened, he grew almost frantic, like one of those coyotes that occasionally wandered onto the Upper East Side. There was already a note on the fridge in case the kids woke up—*went running*—but he'd been hoping to get back quick enough that they'd still be in bed, and he wouldn't have to lie. Something with holes . . . The best he could do was a slotted spoon. He wrapped a paper towel around it and made a mess filtering the molten mixture into his cup. The coffee tasted like water colored brown with a crayon. Grounds stuck to his lips. His heart, he felt, was a porous vessel. He was in the front hall zipping his windbreaker when Will appeared behind him, rumpled with sleep, the note in his hand. "Running where?"

"Just around the Reservoir," Keith said. "Supposed to be like spring today."

"In those, you run?"

He looked down at his loafers. "Shit, I forgot. This is what happens when you get old, champ. Your brain starts to go." Then, recalling his father-in-law, he felt like a jerk.

Under Will's watchful eye, he switched into sneakers. He would have to remember to get some mud on the treads on the way back. His son was becoming the kind of kid who would check. He seemed not only to bristle with secrets lately, but to suspect everyone else of keeping them, too—though maybe this was what Regan had meant when, citing her shrink, she'd accused Keith of *projection*. Anyway, the sneakers came in handy; after waiting fifteen minutes for the poky Sunday morning local, he actually did end up jogging down to Bryant Park, where, provided the forecast held, he'd arranged to meet Tadelis at seven.

"Look, Lamplighter," Tadelis said, even before Keith took a seat. "You have to go talk to them. As your friend, I advise this. If I was your lawyer, I'd drive you there myself." He'd brought bagels, and already had a poppyseed lodged between his upper incisors. Keith was in no position to tell him, though. For several weeks between Thanksgiving and Christmas, when the terms of the separation were being worked out, Tadelis had put him up on his couch. And now, for free, he'd agreed to look over the target letter that had come from the U.S. Attorney's office two days ago, precipitating Keith's panic. Tadelis was the only guy he knew personally who'd ever been through an insider-trading investigation. Since losing his securities license, he'd been scraping by teaching business communications at City College. Notwithstanding which, he still pronounced "attorney" so that it rhymed with "horny."

Keith handed him the letter, which shook slightly. "I'm sure you've heard it's Regan's dad who's under indictment. I just feel like I can't say anything to these guys."

"What could it hurt if you did? You're innocent, remember?"

Tadelis wasn't really capable of keeping his voice down, but the old ladies taking in the morning from some benches nearby had their own lives to worry about. Somehow Keith kept forgetting this about other people, as they no doubt did about him. On the surface, he was healthy, prosperous, talented, good-looking. Inside, though, he was suffocating. He couldn't let Regan's divorce lawyer get wind of his potential exposure in *U.S. v. Hamilton-Sweeney*. Nor could he let the U.S. Attorney get wind of his involvement with a shooting victim.

And about the Demon Brother, whose silence he took as a warning, he didn't dare say a word even to Tadelis. If the spheres of his life that—just barely—contained one mess or the other came into contact, it would all explode. "They don't seem to think I'm so innocent."

Tadelis, who'd been intent on the letter, looked up. "Think like a prosecutor for a second. You're a little fish. Your father-in-law's the big kahuna. We already know there's a confidential informant somewhere in the firm, no? So they must have granted whoever it is immunity, thinking they were going to get an airtight case. But my read is, either the immunity freed the person *not* to talk, or the evidence is shaky. Now they've got to build leverage to push for the toughest possible settlement for Regan's old man, so they put the screws to anyone they can think of to corroborate what they've got. This much publicity, they'll want him to plead to at least a few felony counts, plus some jail time, a hefty fine."

"You're saying if I don't talk, there's a chance Old Bill gets a better deal?"

"I'm saying you've got to look out for number one, Keith. Unless there's something you're not telling me, I don't see where's the breach of fiduciary—but at any rate, go in, meet with them, and if necessary, you'll be protected."

"But that would be a kind of betrayal, you know?"

"A bigger betrayal than getting indicted yourself? These are your peak earning years, my friend. You've got kids to think about. And soon enough, alimony. Here, have one of mine."

From his own battered soft-pack, Keith had been able to fish only two ends of a broken Exigente. Which amounted to yet another thing Regan didn't know about him: last fall, he'd taken up smoking, a reminder of the license, the chaos that persisted beneath the superficial order of his life. Sometimes, late afternoons, he used to take the elevator down to the street. The day's last cigarette was all it took to separate those who had a reason to be idling there, at 3:55, at 4:10, from the loiterers, the drifters, the scarecrow homeless. There was a kind of fellow-feeling, never expressed with eye contact, exactly, but a glancing, sidelong sense of something larger than the self. Of course, it struck him now, he was already part of such a something, called a marriage. Samantha may have been the white rabbit leading him down to Underland, but all the while, it was Regan he'd been chasing. For it was only with her that he'd ever felt that powerful powerlessness he knew was love. And it was Regan he needed here in the open air, really. Her beautiful good sense. Her hand holding his, reminding him of exactly where his apparent gift for subterfuge had gotten him. If this were about anyone else but her dad (and maybe even then), she too would have pushed him to talk. "Just remember," Tadelis said, around a finger mining food from his gum line. "My advice is worth every penny you paid for it." But he was right, Keith decided at last . . . as was this Regan who remained inside him. What could it hurt to set up a meeting?

44

THAT HIS OLD FRIEND AND RIVAL should land such a large chunk of early-morning radio had always seemed miraculous. "Dr." Zig's mouth alone should have disqualified him; it was one of the filthiest Richard had encountered (and the competition, among newspapermen, was stiff). Now, more than ever, you could feel him running right up to the edge of the Seven Dirties, longing to jump:

—so far we've got Ed from Far Rockaway on public fornication, the lady from Brooklyn with the hobo on her stoop, and then, working our way up, muggings, rapes, the merchant princes fallen into disgrace. The Yackline's still open at KL5-YACK—that's 555-9225 for all you illiterates out there in the gritty city. But before I take another call, New York, can I speak freely? I feel like you're only getting half the picture . . .

Richard had first tuned in three weeks ago just to see if Pulaski was right. But now he found himself waking earlier and earlier, leaving his police scanner's AM radio function set to WLRC. "Dr." Zig was drinking again, it seemed. And he got too close to the material, saw everything as personal, including what he made up wholecloth; that had been his problem at the newspaper, too. But in ways Richard found hard to account for, it made *Gestalt Therapy* even better, as radio. He was not alone in feeling this. According to the Arbitron ratings he'd last checked in '73, Zig's audience had lately more than doubled. Every morning, tens of thousands of masochistic tri-staters were tuning in to hear him rant about the shooting of the unnamed minor in Central Park. Or this other thing, some insider-trading case. Or their symbolic link to entropy, to decay. For paranoia was Zig's late style: How else but through networks and conspiracies could he fashion a target big enough for his outrage? Richard usually found paranoia uninteresting, insofar as it swept away the incidental, which was the real grist of history. But maybe this was precisely why he couldn't stop listening to "Dr." Zig now: it reminded him that he was comparatively sane.

What he'd been chasing these same weeks, he kept telling himself, was not any particular set of connections, but simply background, the last incidentals of the story that had flashed before him forever ago in a bar in the north of Scotland. Sure, he'd made the rounds of the classrooms and dorms Samantha had abandoned, but the purity of intent was there; police had already exhausted any leads. And sure, the terse employees sweeping last night's cigarette butts out of the rock clubs on the Bowery seemed to look on him with suspicion, but all he was asking for was someone who'd admit to remembering her. In the evenings now there was his neighbor, Jenny Nguyen. He sat with her making little birdbath stabs at the one glass of Scotch he allowed himself and pretending that this was his life: another item or two of due diligence crossed off the list, someone warm and funny and human to come home to.

But then why every couple days did he find himself back in Hell's Kitchen, at that bodega where he always got coffee—the one whose owner claimed there was no such person as Billy Three-Sticks? The man didn't like him loitering, so Richard had started walking Claggart all the way up there as a cover. He'd drink the coffee down a bit and unleash the dog from the lamppost outside, and together, they'd start toward the old mint factory. He kept telling himself that today would be the day he at last reached the buzzer. If nothing else, he could tip off Samantha's idol about the oddballs in coveralls who were staking him out. But then Claggart would stiffen, and Richard would spot a shadow in a doorway down the street, or in a white van, watching. He'd had to resort to surveillance a few times himself in the '50s, and knew the little tricks: these were no more window-washers than that lamppost was a time machine. Yet whatever of the cub reporter remained in Richard kept coming back for more.

What he'd established, after nearly a month, was that Billy Three-Sticks rarely came out before late afternoon; he seemed almost to shun the light. And if he did walk over to the Times Square Automat, say, for food, his pursuers would trail along unseen a half-block behind. If he then ducked into the OTB to place a bet, they would linger outside. More often, he left his apartment only to scurry to the subway, where they would or wouldn't follow him, depending on which entrance he used. Even in the latter case, Richard didn't feel he could follow Billy down into the tunnels; someone was always watching.

Except he hadn't yet tried the crack of dawn, had he? So now, as *Gestalt Therapy* rolled into its third hour, he ran Claggart out for an expedited walk and wrapped an egg sandwich in wax paper, in case he got hungry—the bodega wouldn't have opened yet—and headed uptown alone.

This early, the street was devoid of vans, or any life at all. As he approached the old factory, Richard felt again the humming inside, as if he were about to get lucky. And perhaps he was, though not in the way he thought, for a dozen yards shy of the door, he heard an echo from a loading dock farther down the street. Ignore it, he told himself, but he'd never been a match for his own curiosity. And what he found on the dock, a few feet off the ground, was a tableau: a young woman rooting among some shipping pallets. With her go-go boots, she might have been one of the neighborhood's many prostitutes, but the grimy athletic jersey beneath her unbuttoned fur wasn't the sort of plumage that lured tricks. "Hey," he said. "Did you lose a contact lens or something?"

"Keep walking."

"No, really. It's cold out. If you're looking for something, let me give you a hand." He had already hopped up onto the dock; he intuited a connection with the window-washers, even before she told him it wasn't a contact she'd misplaced, but some binoculars. "I come here to bird-watch," she explained, a bit tightly. "This is the best time of day." For a few minutes, they searched together in silence. The most he found was a featureless white outline, not quite a stick figure, spraypainted onto a side wall. She kept edging toward the dock's lip, but he made sure to stay between her and the street, lest she try to bolt. Then he saw, near some steps, a sleeping bag. A leather strap poked from the top of the roll. When he pulled at it, out came the binoculars. Heavy. Military surplus. "If these were a snake they would have bit you."

She shrugged. "Must have rolled them up inside."

"They're not really for watching birds, though, are they?" he said. "You know you shouldn't sleep on the street."

"Why? You reckon some perv is going to try to chat me up?" As he handed her back the binoculars, though, the wrapped egg sandwich fell from his pocket to the ground, and her expression shifted from sarcasm to interest. "Hey, are you going to eat that?"

"I'm afraid it's not hot anymore," he said, but it seemed the offer of real food was too good to pass up; she looked like she'd been getting by entirely on Twinkies.

They sat on a step as she wolfed the sandwich down. She was careful to finish, he noticed, before telling him that he wasn't fooling her, she already knew exactly who he was. "You think I haven't seen you down by the bodega? You're that guy writing about Sam's dad, aren't you?"

Something clicked for him. "And you must be S.G." Her reaction was one he'd seen in maybe half a dozen courtrooms: a down and leftward dart of the eyes while the facial ice reset. He took from his pocket the folded paper he'd made notes on, but had no time to consult it. He was flying blind now. "You know, I've got a complete published run of *Land of a Thousand Dances* at home, so I've learned some things about you and your buddies. But the fact that you're up here spying on Billy Three-Sticks doesn't have to be part of the story. You and D.T. and Sol, and who's the other one? Iggy, right? I'm sure there's a reasonable explanation for what you're doing. Is there something you're trying to protect Billy from? If you could bring me back down to that house to meet the others I'd only take up a few minutes of everyone's time."

"I just came here to pack up my stuff, jack. How about you? What's *your* explanation?"

He struggled to recall. "I'm trying to get a better picture of what Samantha was like."

"Well, you're sure going about it all wrong, hanging around the West Forties." The graffiti'd figure seemed to ripple on the wall behind her, as on a television with bad reception. It wasn't waving, as he'd thought. Its hands were in the air. "Off the record," she said. "That's a thing, right? It means you can't use anything I say."

In a less caffeinated state, he might not have agreed so quickly. But she had something to tell him. He wondered if this was it. "That's very much a thing. We're off the record right now."

She turned the wax paper around in her lap, studied it like a mirror. "What you have to understand about Sam is that she was screwy about men. She could never see that they were all in love with her." She glanced up. "Hell, you seem like you are, too. And people in love are not to be trusted. I mean, when she got a boyfriend for a little while, we gave her no end of shit, like we thought it was beneath her. 'Loverboy,' we called him. Sam's Loverboy. But that whole time before Thanksgiving, before she came crawling back to live with us . . ."

"She was living in the house."

"Just for that last month, Thanksgiving to Christmas. But there were a couple months before that when she was barely even coming by to say hi, and I know it hurt Nicky's feelings. Which he really does have, no matter what anyone says."

"Nicky? I thought his name was Iggy."

She looked confused. Stricken. "Crap, what time is it? They're going to start to wonder where I am. And if he thinks I've been talking to a reporter . . ."

He *who*? Then *what*? But he knew better than to push her now. "How will I find you again, though, if I let you go?"

"What makes you think you could stop me?"

And then she was bringing the binoculars down with great precision on his testicles, and he was on his side on the oily cement, watching her walk away. He struggled to speak around the pain: "Wait." Her tall white boots paused at the edge of the loading dock, just where day started. He had a feeling it would be the last he ever saw of her. "You didn't tell me why you were packing up your stuff."

"You're not much of a detective, are you, old man?" She seemed to reach a final decision. Pulled her fur tight around her. "Billy Three-Sticks went to ground four days ago. Hasn't been back since."

45

INCREASINGLY, AFTER WILLIAM'S DISAPPEARANCE, Mercer would find himself returning to that winter, trying to nail down some turning point, some moment about which he could say, *It all started when.* . . . The search wasn't orderly, or even continuous; he could go for hours caught up in questions of test preparation, of dry-cleaning, of Middle-Eastern affairs. But then on the subway or on line at the place down the street where he went when they were out of toilet paper—or rather, when *Mercer* was—he'd be accosted by a memory. Here was William shaking a handful of change as though preparing to shoot dice. Here was William rummaging for a token in the pockets of the bluejeans heaped on the sleeping-nook floor—picking them up and tossing them aside, without it ever occurring to him to deposit them in the hamper. And here was William, spied on once from above, stealing away from the building in the bloody pre-rush-hour light. If he were truly headed uptown to paint, he would enter the subway on the far side of Eighth Avenue, but here he was turning downtown instead. Here was William, in other words, leaving by slow degrees.

The night of the intervention—the night he'd walked out the door and not come back—had merely literalized it. Nevertheless, the effect on Mercer was baleful. He held it together for his girls at work, but afterward, as in his earliest days in the city, he walked home via the most circuitous route possible, looping up toward Central Park rather than face the emptiness of the loft. It was getting on into spring, and under the glass globes of streetlamps the trees were pushing out green. Sound carried farther in this oxygen-rich air; he might hear laughter from the entrances of restaurants on the east side, where valets helped expensive people out of the interiors of cars. He peered through the lit windows of the apartments where they lived—apartments he'd once pictured himself inhabiting. William had come from this world, had been a natural aristocrat, which was maybe what Mercer had fallen in love with in the first place. (Though who's to say? Who's to say why a kid at the state fair picks a particular five-dollar animal pinned high on the corkboard behind the sideshow barker, that particular one, and will then spend ten dollars trying to shoot a balloon with a BB gun?) Anyway, for Mercer, there would be no transfiguration.

If he put off reaching home until eight or nine o'clock, he believed, he might find William waiting there on the futon, rocking forward in that way of his, hands between knees, penitent. *I've thought about it*, he'd say (for he always had to let things sink in before he could really hear them). *You were right.* Instead, when Mercer switched on the lamp by the door, there was only Eartha K. In the first few days after Mercer took over the management of her food supply, she'd dabbled with lesser degrees of aloofness—even once rubbing against his leg when he came in. But she'd soon learned that his sense of duty alone was sufficient to keep her fed, and now they were like inmates in a prison yard, circling each other uneasily, in orbits as wide as the cramped apartment would allow.

Then one evening after work, he went to dump her tin of Friskies onto a saucer, a chore William knew he found disgusting, and couldn't find the can-opener. Or the pliers he thought to use in its place. Come to think of it, where was the TV? Or that pile of jeans? Yes, at some point since this morning, William had been back here. Mercer imagined him pale and hunched, moving through the loft with a bag and throwing things in at random. Maybe he was pawning them, or bartering them for heroin. But upon closer inspection, the pattern revealed an unexpected forethought. Mercer had bought a four-hole toothbrush holder, e.g., to sit by the kitchen sink. It now bared a poignant third hole. And for William to think about oral hygiene meant he must really be serious about not coming back.

MERCER HAD ALWAYS BEEN what his mother called a *good eater*, in contradistinction to C.L., but that night he could barely choke down a meal. There was no pleasure in it. And this seemed to be the new order of things. Where once he would have raided cookbooks for challenges with which to woo William, he now settled for the four food groups of bachelorhood: Frozen, Cold Cuts, Breakfast Cereal, and Takeout. His energy level ebbed, to offset which he drank more coffee. There was perpetually a half-pot souring in the faculty lounge at school, and visiting it gave him a way to mark time. Every few hours, between periods or even during them, he dragged himself up the three flights of stairs and stood at the window with his paper cup of joe. No one cared what he did anymore—not unless you counted the little cop who'd apparently been asking around. Outside, office workers carried bagged lunches from the deli. This was how he would end up, too: aging and anonymous and alone, on a numbered street the sunlight never quite reached.

Once or twice, at night, he planted himself in front of the type-writer, trying to get back to the book he'd come to New York to write. It was supposed to be about America, and freedom, and the kinship of time to pain, but in order to write about these things, he'd needed experience. Well, be careful what you wish for. For now all he seemed capable of producing was a string of sentences starting, *Here was William*. Here was William's courage, for example. And here was William's sadness, smallness of stature, size of hands. Here was his laugh in a dark movie theater, his unpunk love of the films of Woody Allen, not for any of the obvious ways they flattered his sensibility, but for something he called their *tragic sense*, which he compared to Chekhov's (whom Mercer knew he had not read). Here was the way he never asked Mercer about his work; the way he never talked about his own and yet seemed to carry it with him just beneath the skin; the way his skin looked in the sodium light from outside with the lights off, with clothes off, in silver rain; the way he embodied qualities Mercer wanted to have, but without ruining them by wanting to have them; the way he moved like a fish in the water of this city; the way his genius overflowed its vessel, running off into the drain; the unfinished self-portrait; the hint of some trauma in his past, like the war a shell-shocked town never talks about; his terrible taste in friends;

his complete lack of discipline; the inborn incapacity for certain basic things that made you want to mother him, fuck him, give your right and left arms for him, this man-child, this skinny American; and finally his wildness, his refusal to be imaginable by anyone.

It might have helped Mercer to talk about how ill all this made him feel, but inability to talk about it was one of the illness's symptoms, as well as an underlying cause. He was like a person with a full-body rash just beneath his clothes. The fear that the rash would repulse people was stronger than the hope that fresh air might help it heal.

Of course, there was one person from whom he couldn't conceal that something was wrong. On Sundays, when his mother called, he filled the dead air between them with perfunctory reports about teaching and meteorological conditions and whatnot, but couldn't lift his voice into the melodious register of well-being. She never asked about his *roommate* anymore, he noticed. But she continued to speak in the anodyne phrases for which he'd compiled an imaginary translation table:

MAMA		PLAIN ENGLISH
We'd love you to come visit sometime.	=	I wish I could take care of you.
I hope you're eating your vegetables	=	I'm worried about you.
Is it still cold up there? I don't know how anyone puts up with the climate; you couldn't pay me enough; etc., etc, ad nauseam	=	I told you so,

And she was right. It seemed impossible that he'd chosen to live here, at a latitude where spring was a semantic variation on winter, in a grid whose rigid geometry only a Greek or a builder of prisons could love, in a city that made its own gravy when it rained. Taxis continued to stream toward the tunnel, like the damned toward a Boschian hellmouth. Screaming people staggered past below. Impossible, that he now footed the rent entire, two hundred bucks monthly for the privilege of pressing his cheek to the window and still not being able to see spectacular Midtown views. Impossible, that the cinderblock planter on the fire escape could ever have produced flowers.

Which didn't prepare him for Mama's threat, in early April, to come visit *him* instead. It was the vision of her in Easter clothes and a large floral hat bowling through the hustlers at the bus station that finally coaxed out of him the admission that he might be able to make it down for spring break after all. *We'd pay for you to fly*, she said, *if that made things easier.* Some meaning he couldn't quite translate danced just out of reach. "No, Mama," he said finally. "I'm not a kid anymore. I can pay for things myself."

46

THEN OUT OF THE BLUE CAME THOSE WEEKS in March when Jenny didn't hear the Wurlitzer through the walls or see Richard in the hall or elevator. She contrived reasons to linger by the mailboxes on her way into the building, or to run across to the superette where he bought his three daily papers: she needed milk, or a knob of ginger, or a Chore Boy sponge. (What didn't they carry, tucked away on high shelves the manager reached by means of a mechanical claw?) But she never saw him. Maybe he'd gone back to Scotland. Maybe he wintered in Miami Beach. They hardly knew each other, after all. Maybe they were no longer friends.

It was the middle of April when she saw him again. She was teaching herself yoga out of a coffeetable book, determined to whip mind and body back into shape. She'd torqued herself into Elephant Pose: hands flat on carpet, torso arched, one leg cramped into place behind her, the other rampant, trembling, seventy degrees overhead. A few feet from her face, a celebrity in a headband beamed orgasmically. Then a sound from the wall distracted her, and she collapsed onto the floor. Just another of the city's noises, she told herself, come to unhorse her. Her first few months in New York, she used to sit and get high and listen to them, for fear of listening to the voice inside. That voice now repeated the centering chant from the book: *Tat tvam asi*. It meant: *You are that*. But how could she be sure yoga wasn't just another form of commodified quiescence? This was a sometimes attractive and sometimes frustrating wrinkle of the dialectic, she'd found: everything turned out to be the superstructure of some other thing. And here you were, thinking you were free . . . The sound came again, in triplicate, through the wall between her place and Richard's. It was definitely a knock; it was meant for her. And it was all the excuse she needed to abandon her attempts at bourgeois self-actualization. She threw on sweats over her underwear and hied her butt out into the hall.

She'd never seen Richard actually drunk before, she realized when he opened the door. She said something like, "You're back," and he just stared at her with a tight smile stuck to his face like a shaving plaster. There was a single light behind him, the green-shaded banker's lamp on a desk now covered with newspapers. Only when she reminded him that he'd knocked did the old courtliness return. Of course, yes, come in. He cleared space for her on the sofa. Then he dropped his long body into the deskchair, perilously close to tipping over the bottle on the desk. "Taste?" he said.

It took her a second to remember what he was talking about. "I'm sorry, were you busy? I don't want to get in the way of . . . whatever you've been up to."

"Oh, it's too late for that," he said. "I've pretty well fucked that up completely."

She couldn't stand to just sit silent like this, facing him through dim air. She got up to look out the window. Great reefs of light thrust up from downtown. Even more intolerable was the idea that they didn't really know each other. If she didn't know this man, she didn't in this city of eight million know anyone. She turned to find him cradling his glass in his hand like a kid whose pet bird has just died. "Fucked what up, Richard?"

"Take a look." He pulled a newspaper from the stack and sent it flapping toward her through the gloom. If not for her quick reflexes, it would have hit her in the face. Instead, it crashed harmlessly into the blinds. Then he was apologizing, but it was a man's apology, meaning she wasn't sure he even realized what he'd done wrong—he still seemed so abstracted, so far away. But now the orderly freight-cars of her thoughts were derailing, tumbling down embankments, because on the front of the newspaper was a yearbook photo of a pretty young woman blown up so the dots of the halftone were visible, a dark pointillism that made the face somehow instantly nostalgic. She'd seen it on every newsstand she'd passed today, she realized, but without really seeing it, the way you didn't really see parking signs, or bus-shelter ads. It was the girl who'd been shot in Central Park several months ago. The one in the coma. But now she had features, a biography, a name. **Cicciaro**, said the caption. Right. There had been an outburst about it this morning on the radio, when she'd been waiting to hear the weather.

"This is someone you know? Is she going to be all right?"

"No one realizes yet it's another dead end," is all he said, and the way he stared down at his hands filled her with pity. When you were young, you had the resources to rebuild after each crater fate blasted in your life. Beyond a certain age, though, you could only wall off the damage and leave it there. She'd seen this with her dad. She wanted to tell Richard, You're wrong, there is no such thing as a dead end, all setbacks are temporary. Or she wanted to show him, or herself. College had laid bare the ideological strutwork of such desires, but without them, there was only the dilemma: troll the singles bars for one-night stands, or go for she'd honestly lost count of how many months without sex. She watched her hands press themselves to his face. And then she was drawing it forward. His whiskers scraped against her chin, and she could taste chewing gum and Lagavulin. He was a surprisingly good kisser until, abruptly, he drew back. "You don't want this."

"You don't know what I want," she said softly, still holding his head.

"Neither do you, dear Jenny," he said.

If she hadn't suspected he was right, it might not have pissed her off the way it did; she might not have stood up so abruptly, or forgotten her balance—her *tat tvam asi*. But she did, and it did, and she did, pausing only to say, "I'll see you around, I guess, Richard."

Which, as it turned out, was exactly wrong.

47

PULASKI EYED AGAIN the rolled-up tabloid wedged between the passenger's seat and the door. He'd put it there precisely to get it out of his sight, but the picture of the girl called his gaze back and back, like the blood the lady couldn't get off her hands in that *Macbeth* Sherri'd taken him to see once. Today was the first day the Cicciaro case, now known to all as such, was front-page news. It wouldn't be the last. He'd realized all along, of course, in some little-visited backroom of his consciousness, that her identity would out, the way you can tell one of your teeth is rotten long before you give in and go to the dentist. But as with a rotten tooth, he'd hoped ignoring the consequences might make them go away.

Among those consequences was the fact that he was currently cruising up Central Park West in a marked car, bound for a housing project in Harlem. His driver, a patrolman, was black. Afro-American, rather. Though this was officially Pulaski's case now, and so Pulaski's team, the Deputy Commissioner had made sure a liberal helping of Afro-Americans was scattered in among the two dozen officers detailed to this morning's raid, to deflect the inevitable cries of racial bias. Pursuant to Pulaski's arrival at the Frederick Douglass towers, the officers would sweep through hallways in their head-breaking boots, banging on doors, looking for excuses to collar any and all young men in the fifteen to twenty-five age range, to drag them outside for questioning as to their whereabouts on the night of December 31. Why outside? Because that's where the cameras would be. And why these kids? Because it was the nearest housing project to the crime scene. Because people uptown didn't vote. Because some rider of municipal buses, reading the fuller account the NYPD had more or less been forced to give, had suddenly recalled seeing a black man run into the park near the time of the shooting. In fact, this story seemed to back up the one Pulaski already had from that black man, who thus really had probably saved the girl's life. *In a tuxedo, right?* he'd asked the detective who took the bus rider's statement. *No,* the guy said. *Dressed . . . you know, like they do.* Uptown, dark bodies sat in small apartments, coils of potential energy, powder awaiting the flame. He could already hear hollering: *What the fuck, I didn't do nothing!* Someone was bound to overdo it, and some rookie, white as Wonder Bread, would overreact, the nightstick would come out while women in housedresses watched from the curb, and at that point you just hoped Bill Kunstler and F. Lee Bailey weren't picking up their phones.

Then again, what choice did he have but to go along with this? Since the girl's name had leaked, it was as if the city's vast reservoir of grievance had finally broken its dam. Details were what turned a symbol into a myth: Italian surname (granddaughter of "striving immigrants"); freshman at NYU ("full of promise," never mind her grades); Long Island origins ("new to the city"; "chasing her dreams"). And then there were the pictures from the yearbook and the junior prom. She was "attractive." "Innocent." Because victims always were. Not that Pulaski was any better, when it came to privileging her over all the other hurting people out there. Despite the lack of forensic evidence, he'd ordered McFadden back in January to leave open the possibility that she'd been sexually assaulted; it was a way to extend to her the anonymity accorded in rape cases, even after she was no longer protected as a minor. And though he was certain there had been no such assault, the idea persisted in the leer of yesterday's headlines. **INNOCENCE LOST. NEW YEAR'S EVIL.**

Though not until he reached the City this a.m. had he seen the degree to which all this was going to complicate his job. Three separate news teams had set up on the bricks out front of 1 Police Plaza. Must have scurried over from the federal courthouse where they more often camped out these days. One reporter had spread deli napkins on his shoulders to catch falling makeup as he touched up his face for the cameras. Another was already intoning into a microphone, in a beam of light that made the spring day dull by comparison. No one seemed to notice Pulaski limping toward the stairless side entrance. His face wasn't known, his cases never got much press, which was part of his not being taken seriously by the brass at 1PP—of him having reached the zenith of his career at Deputy Inspector.

His office here was back off a forgotten fifth-floor hallway whose overhead light had burned out. He'd unclipped his crutches, leaned them precisely against the desk, lowered himself to the cushioned chair. His hands were curved from the rubber grips; he pressed them against the desk blotter. Deformation, was the word for the flattening of three dimensions down to two. Funny, the things that popped into your head when you just learned to sit still. Maybe if he locked the door, unplugged the phone, closed his eyes . . . but the phone at that moment began to ring. It was his bosses, summoning him downstairs.

A meeting, they called it, but he knew it was an interrogation. The Chief Inspector's office, with its burled wood and deep-pile carpet, seemed out of place in this building, like an antebellum parlor crash-landed in the Brutalist '70s. Pulaski had been in it maybe twice before, to witness the dressing-down of one of his detectives. This time, he himself was the lucky contestant, and they didn't even wait for the secretary to close the door.

"Looks like you've got a real shit-storm on your hands, Pulaski." This was the Deputy Commish, enthroned in a high-backed chair of imitation oxblood leather. "I've got the Mayor's office calling to ask why we've been suppressing your victim's name," he continued. "You know what that looks like?"

"Like shit, is what it looks like," said the Chief Inspector, who stood to the side of his own desk, in a zone of false neutrality. He lobbed a copy of the *Daily News* onto the blotter. Pulaski knew better than to reach for it; the bosses were a long-running vaudeville act, they couldn't help themselves, and this was part of their show.

"We know it's not true, of course, that this particular case isn't on your very frontmost burner, Pulaski, but frankly, we're having a hard time explaining the thinking here."

"So why don't you explain it to us, Pulaski."

It seemed to Pulaski self-evident. "You're saying you wanted the

Fourth Estate queued up outside months ago? One Son of Sam isn't enough?"

The Deputy Commish looked at the Chief Inspector, or vice versa.

"Why don't *I* explain something to *you*, you little prick. You know how many bodies we caught in this city last year? That's assuming your victim doesn't kick? We've got federal funds riding on our clearance rate. Next year's an election year."

"You're taking it away from me?" Pulaski asked.

"The mouth on this guy. No, you dumb shit, you're going to go out and hang this on someone if it kills you. You're going to drag somebody before the cameras and say, by God, the city's safe again, and then it's the D.A.'s problem. Or you know whose ass it is?"

He had a pretty good guess.

"Your ass, Pulaski."

"Well, I can't work it all by myself. I'm going to need some men, some overtime."

"Of course you are," said the Chief Inspector. "For starters, a little canary tipped off Channel 5 and Channel 9 you'd be conducting a roundup this morning at the Douglass Houses." He looked at his watch. "Camera trucks will be on the scene at eleven, which gives you about an hour to get organized. I want to see cuffs, Pulaski. I want Afros ducking into cars. The personnel requests are right here. All you need to do is initial."

He'd barely had time to grab his coat, and whatever else he might need. Now shadows of the Park's trees, newly in leaf, raked the windshield of his squad car. After weeks of rain, the sun was out, a bulb in a toy oven. Coffee had leaked from the lid of his cup and soaked a neat half-moon into the thighs of his trousers. "Pull over," he said, out of nowhere.

His driver looked startled. Subordinates often seemed to have little idea of how to respond to Pulaski, but he couldn't very well drive himself; he'd taken the ferry in this morning, leaving back in his garage the Plymouth the city had customized for him.

"Just pull over for a minute, please."

He opened his door, dumped a third of the overfull coffee onto the paving stones that edged the sidewalk. It collected in runnels, ran toward the curb. You wouldn't have guessed a slope was there. As he reached for his crutches, the radio crackled on the dash. *Kilo, alpha, five, nine. Come back.* The driver looked over, tense eyes, dark brow.

"Tell them to sit tight. I have to see a horse dealer."

Another upside of being a cripple was that people eventually stopped expecting you to spell things out; they figured an unplanned stop like this, you must be making for your health.

"You want me to come with?" the driver said. "That mud's slippery. I almost broke my tailbone this morning getting out to the car."

"Just sit tight," Pulaski said. "I'll be right back."

It took him five minutes to pick his way back along the path Samantha Cicciaro had followed that night. She hadn't been dragged, obviously, or it would have showed on the snow, which meant what? She'd known the shooter. There were already a couple of Santería candles near where the body had been. Soon, it would become a shrine, heaps of flowers and stuffed animals. But when she God forbid died, or the case went cold, this would become just another path again, these bushes just bushes. Who remembered what block Kitty Genovese had lived on? Who remembered Daddy Browning, or his child-lover Peaches?

He emerged onto the Sheep Meadow almost exactly where he'd stood three months ago, the morning after the shooting. In his overcoat pocket was a plastic bag containing the wadded jeans he'd found then. He'd kept the discovery secret because he'd wanted to follow it up alone. Which had led to the tattoo. Which had led nowhere. Yet if he produced it now, it would look suspicious as all get-out, someone would figure out eventually he'd sat on evidence. But he saw again a mother in a housedress, in the shadow of a housing project, watching a nightstick draw blood. He saw Sherri, the mother she would have been, charging like a lioness into the fray. All he wanted, really, was to deserve her.

He emerged from the Park doing his best to hold the evidence aloft and still maintain control of his crutches. He knocked on the window, waited for the driver to lean over and roll it down. "Call off the rodeo."

"What?"

"Tell them it's off, I'm calling it off. Have them send the whole team down here instead. We've caught a break. But we need to re-sweep the park."

Again, with the eyebrows: skepticism, concern . . . relief? "You sure?" the driver asked.

"Of course I'm sure, darn it. Pick up the radio—or no, give it here. I'll do it myself."

48

THE WOMAN BEYOND THE WINDOW was coughing and coughing. One could hear it even over the *corrido* and the few other patrons at the bar—and that was before a spasm of particular violence so racked her that her head struck the glass, not three feet from where a solitary man sat, brooding over his gin. To judge by the square of cardboard he'd seen on his way in, the story that had brought her to this milk crate in the East Village in the coldwater spring of 1977 was rather involved. It hung about her neck on a length of twine, whole magic-markered paragraphs of extenuation and woe, but the cough broke her off at *Hey, Mister.* . . . He'd had a tickle in his own throat a few weeks ago, which spoke to the promiscuity of the local microbes, but hadn't let it ripen into this noisome hack. Or was it a play for sympathy? Among the persistent errors this city's news media made was to deny the poor any capacity for ratiocination. They were like animals, only worse, as actual animals knew better (not to mince words) than to shit where they ate. It was a measure of Amory Gould's seriousness, his heroic objectivity, that he knew this not to be the case. For two years, as orphaned teenagers, he and Felicia had lived in a house without electricity, burning furniture for warmth, eating out of such cans as Amory could buy on a delivery boy's pay. They weren't animals. Just, circumstantially, closer to the threshold of survival. But there in the lizard brain, you learned you would gladly crawl over others of your species if it meant moving up.

Fellow-feeling never got anyone out of Buffalo. Or remade the Bronx in its image. Now, as the woman coughed again, he set aside the predictable headlines of the *Daily News* and headed for the payphone by the lavatories.

The phone number came to him quickly. When he'd paid to have it established—or when a subagent of the tobacco company had—he hadn't quite known its purpose. He'd learned by that point simply to give himself options and use whatever came of them. When the Presidente was in power, one worked with the Presidente. When the Subcomandante, the Subcomandante. But he could not deny a little sizzle, as of a closing circuit, when he discovered the reason a thing was as it was. Why this number? So he could dial it now. And on the fourth ring, someone answered. Female, a bit slow. "Huh? Speak up."

There was a low mechanical noise in the background. Calibrating rapidly, Amory decided it was better she not get the sense he'd noticed. Was young Nicholas there? Seconds passed. "Nicky's, uh . . . he's not disposed at the moment."

"Not disposed, or not at home, my dear? I'm more than happy to stay on the line."

There was the sound of a mouthpiece being covered, of life at the other end being extinguished. Returning after two minutes, minus the noise. She seemed agitated about something. "I'm not your dear, though, bub. You got a message?"

He had the impression Nicholas might in fact be as close as her shoulder, listening, and he made his voice resonant again, that it might be overhead. "Tell him his benefactor is in the neighborhood." He checked his watch. "I have installed myself at Don Jaime's Cantina. By five thirty p.m., I will be gone." He hung up, walked to his booth, and, ignoring the coughing woman, returned to his pocket the nickel he'd got back.

He could be confident they knew the place; it was hardly a block from the house he'd just called. And this had been calibrated, too (as had this morning's paper). The idea was that mediation take place in light of the utter ease with which, at any hour of any day, Amory Gould could reach Nicholas, relative to the difficulty of someone like Nicholas reaching him. It might indeed have made a nice show of fearlessness to march right up East Third Street, whistling if that wasn't too much, and to knock on the door. This way, he could note any evidence of change. That noise, for example. But he'd been intrigued to find himself apprehensive about entering the house again. It was this same apprehension that had read Nicholas's silence since mid-November as a sign the boy was more dangerous than he seemed. (Though as with any game, two could play at silence.) In the end, Amory had simply made sure to pass the house en route to the bar. The door had been repainted; the gray at the center was a shade darker than the gray around it. To further the air of abandonment, they'd done something to draw birds to the roofline and windows, sprinkled seed possibly, so that guano whitewashed the stoop below. And good for them. What he did not understand was the tinfoil in the windows. Why not butcher paper, something less flash? Perhaps he would suggest it, a show of magnanimity.

In any case, a bar was a worthy Plan B. Its darkened interior limited the number of observers. Yet it was public enough to convey a sense of up-and-upness, of having nothing to hide. And if one's interlocutor had things to hide and still agreed to the venue, then it also conveyed a sense of power. Besides, he felt at home among Spanish-speakers. These people knew where they stood. *El hombre invisible*, they called him on his junkets south, though with his current tan, he was nearly one of them. He raised a hand to signal the waitress. Far from rendering the prompt service to which he'd grown accustomed, she chattered on with the bartender. But fine. It only went to show Amory had been forgotten.

That is, until Nicholas entered and approached the booth with a girl in tow—likely the one who'd answered the phone. Amory had long known women to be unreliable (even his fool sister); how could he possibly be construed to have invited one here? Nor had either of them bothered to change into civilian garb, or otherwise play down their difference from the cheaply but neatly dressed Latins. If anything, it was played up. The boy's short-sleeved sweatshirt, too light for the chill, showed off his million tattoos. His beard was Amish-ish. The girl wore some kind of insalubrious sports uniform and carried a bag with a broken zipper. All of which was interesting, as data. They wanted it known (thought Amory) that they didn't care who was watching. That they too had nothing to lose. Well, we would see.

"I'm thrilled you could fit me in on such short notice." He held out a hand.

Nicholas just grunted and slid into the booth. Jerked his head. "S.G."

"The pleasure is mine," Amory said. "Shall I order something for the table?"

Nicholas started to decline, but here the girl spoke up. "They've got food?" He associated her dull-eyed look with factory workers, but, now that the waitress was paying attention, handed off his untouched gin and asked for three mezcals and a bag of potato chips. He'd noticed some clipped to a stand by the door. The waitress went again. He waited for Nicholas to say something, but Nicholas had discovered the first rule of negotiation. Well then, small-talk it was. "You've been to Don Jaime's before? I thought because it's so conveniently located, vis-à-vis the house . . . and once you get used to it, the atmosphere is almost convivial. One could imagine making a habit—"

"But we're not here to swap notes on watering holes, are we?" The boy was really too easy to needle into speech. "I mean, unless you're planning to buy the place."

"Any plans, on either side, I would hope could be discussed privately."

"We can talk in front of S.G. What there is to know, she knows."

"I'm sure." Now the waitress slid Amory's newspaper to the edge of the table to make room for drinks. The girl was struggling with the mylar bag of chips when the boy reached over to open it for her. He wanted her attention freed for whatever passed between him and Amory Gould. In all probability, then, she knew next to nothing, but was along as an insurance policy, a witness that on thus-and-such a date, at thus-and-such a time, this meeting had transpired. There was an implied threat, but this was part of why the PHP had appealed to him all along: Who would ever believe anything any of them said?

Nicholas downed his mezcal. Made no sign of noticing the burn. "To be honest, I'm impressed you'd show your face down here."

"I've always suspected this neighborhood's reputation for criminality was at least one part hysteria. Look around you. Salt of the earth."

"It would show more nerve if you'd stay after dark."

"I'll make a note to avoid it. That means our time is limited, though."

"Why don't you just say why you came? I assumed we'd served our purpose," the boy said.

"Ah. But this was exactly the thing I hoped to hear."

"Hear what?"

"Did I ever conceal that I had a purpose in coming to you?"

Nicholas reached for a chip. "No, no. I wouldn't say concealing was what you did."

It should have set Amory at ease. But as the woman kept coughing and a car slid by, scattering the rainy light, he thought back to the time when he himself had been closest to feeling his plans had come to nothing—the spring of 1975. He'd spent the previous dozen years swelling his firm's coffers with Central American lucre. Through two successive coups and a *guerra civil*, he'd kept the Bandito beans harvested and the Exigentes rolled and a black market in American-made munitions profitable. Yet the fiscal crisis in New York, for all the little opportunities it opened, threatened to foreclose bigger ones. Again, though, what Amory's dealings with Bill's children years ago had taught him was not to try to create from nothing. Instead, he shaped such conditions as could be shaped; as for the rest, he waited.

Then one day, in the course of checking up on his nephew's activities, he'd learned of this house on East Third Street, and of the intriguing alias of its occupant. To wrest further information from the city bureaucracy was easy enough, but slow. By the time the files reached him, Ex Post Facto was no more. The carbon-copied rap sheet of "a.k.a. Nicky Chaos" should therefore have held little interest. Vandalism, disobedience, possession. But just as he was about to shred the document, an item stayed his hand: an arrest for attempted arson in Bushwick that June. There'd been a string of more successful fires in the same area, Amory recalled, but in this case no pecuniary motive could be discerned; the building spared from flame had already been condemned. Two accomplices had fled on foot, but the accused had evidently made no attempt. High on narcotics, no doubt. For though Nicholas would later be freed via long-distance bond, in the police file was a most fascinating set of notes from the night of the arrest. Suspect made no attempt to deny ownership of the kerosene and the matchbook. Suspect instead claimed solidarity with the oppressed. Suspect argued that fire dramatized the material conditions, the collusiveness, the need for change . . . the awful banality of the ideas, in flatfoot prose, hurt Amory's eyes to read, and yet, and yet. Something about these ambitions, the scale perhaps, had reminded him of nothing so much as a young Amory Gould.

It was how he'd introduced himself a week later on East Third

Street: as a man of ambition. When it came to ends, they were on opposite sides, naturally. Still, it had been remarkable to discover in Nicholas's own words a potential congruence of means.

The boy had edged backward through the front hall, baffled but already, Amory saw, inflamed. "I don't understand. I never signed the confession. How did you get a copy of that?"

One could have said anything here, so long as one kept beaming and spoke quickly and in hushed tones and did not appear to be steering one's audience toward the parlor. Amplify the plumminess. Establish a debt. "Success in this life depends on connections. I'm fortunate to represent, in my business dealings, a family rich in them. For example, I believe you have a history with my nephew. William Hamilton-Sweeney. Billy."

"But we're at total loggerheads, Billy and me."

"I trust, then, I can count on your confidence about this visit. And I should add that on my side, I'm acting as a free agent. Not a soul knows I'm here."

The windows in those days had been blocked only by dust and pollen. An even, golden light filled the room they sat down in, saturated the boy's strong chin, his rawboned features, and underneath, his air of quick intelligence. An ape of God, was the phrase that occurred. As a child smarter than the rest he must like Amory have been subject to schoolyard taunts, but with the total stillness of the house, and the heat—the casements were open an inch or two—it felt as if they were beyond all that. Beyond time. Something shifted in the boy's expression. Hands on knees, he leaned forward. "Holy shit. Billy's uncle. You're the fucking Demon Brother, aren't you?"

Amory had found the nickname distasteful when it first reached him. But then he'd seen the beauty of it. It was a giant puppet, a white screen he could hold over his head. The fear, the desire, others would supply.

What he proposed to Nicholas was a kind of wager. Charges dropped, records sealed, the boy could resume his arson campaign, though this time in the already smoldering Bronx. And provided he kept within boundaries Amory defined, he could be sure the police would not stop him. Budget cuts had left holes in their deployments. Indeed, Amory had access to the triage plan, and would pass along certain sites and times where the game could be pursued with immunity, he said. "Or I understand you studied social science? Think of it as a test of competing theories." When the last claimants to the torched acreage had been driven out for urban renewal, per Amory—or when the spectacle of the system's neglect finally galvanized the underclass, per Nicholas—it would be clear whose vision of human nature had won. Whatever the case, Nicholas would get to stay on in the house. Amory had taken the liberty of having a corporate investor from south of the border secure the deed.

"And if I don't go along with this, you're going to kick me out? Make sure I go to jail?"

"I don't work by coercion, young man. When people enter into a bargain, they must do so of their own free will."

"But how do I know you'll hold your end up, once my fires do their thing and you see the people start rising up?"

"The same way I know you won't mention my visit here today to our mutual irritant, William Hamilton-Sweeney the Third. We proceed on faith."

In the event, of course, it was the reverse he needed to see now: that Nicholas, five months after the Blight decree, had accepted defeat. For what Amory had neglected to mention was that he need not assume control over the South Bronx property by property: that, once the arson had passed a certain threshold, his plans could be accomplished by fiat. Toward the girl, who'd made short work of her chips, he now nudged a glass. "Please. Drink."

"No," Nicky repeated. "I guess you told me how it was going to be, and I guess that's how it is. You didn't need to come all this way for a victory lap."

"I'm afraid your friend has me all wrong." He had turned to see what the girl would do. What she did was finish her mezcal and then shoot a look of despair at the empty glass in her hands. She would rather, in other words, be anywhere else. Amory wondered what Nicholas had over her. "I'm here to ensure there are no hard feelings."

"Do you think that's what it was about for me?" Nicky said. "Feelings?"

"We can agree then that we've reached the end of our walk together."

"That's a little poetic for me, but yeah. What do you have, if not your word?"

"You don't know how immensely pleased I am to hear it. And just as a gesture," and that there should be no lingering tie between them,

"I've had my *compadre* the investor burn the deed on East Third Street. The house is yours to do with as you wish. Your property."

"I guess there's no getting outside that, is there?" Just then a horn honked. A beaten-down van had pulled alongside a hydrant. Its driver was lost in shadow, but it wasn't impossible, given the light and the angles, that whoever it was could see Amory Gould. "That's you, S.G.," said the boy, and after shaking the last drops of mezcal onto her tongue, the girl rose and slung her satchel onto her shoulder. From under the flap peeked weathered volumes. She caught him looking, and he was surprised to find, before her mask went up, that her despair was hatred, and meant for him alone.

Then he and his protégé were eye to eye, in a silence that echoed the long one from '75. It was only in the fall, on the phone, that Nicholas had made excuses for taking all this time to decide, and Amory could repeat the gesture of indulgence he'd first used years ago, on Block Island, with that other boy he'd thought to use then— what should have been a beautiful killing of birds, relative to the number of stones. The problem, really, had been a misapprehension about control. You couldn't trust people to be tomorrow what they had been yesterday. Yet he knew now that with fear, as with fantasy, you didn't need to. They would control themselves. And if he'd just observed that these so-called Post-Humanists had found a new object for their rage, then he also needed to know they were afraid. Afraid of all Amory knew. Afraid of all he could do. He left off rubbing his arm and raised his hand to signal for the check, and when the waitress came he thanked her in the same florid Spanish he used on the Subcomandante. Then he turned to Nicholas. "*¿Y me olvido de algo primordial, quizás?*"

It was time the boy saw that he'd been caught out: his father was neither a Latin American ethnic nor an intelligence officer, but only a pleasant-looking former medic, a widowed surgeon living in Newton, Mass. And the son was, among other things, a world-class dissembler who'd watched one too many James Bond films.

"That is to say, there's one other thing we should cover." Amory moved the drinks from the middle of the table and returned to its place the *Daily News*. He'd never before seen Nicholas speechless. He admired the effect of his hand resting there, a white spider tapping a leg. "This unpleasantness in Central Park . . . I feel I should assure you I had nothing to do with it. For if I had, if either of us had, it would be entirely outside the scope of our agreement, and the protection that extends."

"What unpleasantness? I have no idea what you're talking about."

Nicholas stared him in the eye, to avoid looking at the paper. Which was another mistake; that he felt the need to lie here was so revealing. The Blight Zone he'd helped bring about not only hadn't defeated him; he was planning to retaliate . . . and something would have to be done about that. But no sense rushing anything. Amory played the long game. "No? Even now, no idea?"

"Not a one," Nicholas managed. "But I think I'd better split before someone gets the wrong idea about the two of us."

Only after the boy was gone did Amory reach for the remaining mezcal. And oh how it did burn. The woman outside coughed again. He felt in his pocket for the nickel from earlier. He could always have moved to another booth, but you acquired a taste for self-assertion, a kind of pride. For Amory, there had been no diplomas from a Princeton or a Yale; he hadn't had the connections of his witless brother-in-law. But since acquiring the Block Island house, he'd kept on the walls the family pictures of the people who'd owned it before, the way tribal chiefs hang on to scalps. And look at him now—facing, and accepting, the colder burning that was life on earth. He would force the rest of them to accept it, too. He looked to the woman outside the window, rapped the nickel on the glass, right by her head. And when she turned and he showed her his true face, her cough died in her throat. He didn't even have to motion her along.

49

O N THE SUBJECT OF HATE, Charlie's Bible remained ambiguous. Which probably, given the ambiguity of every other power that might have guided his misguided life, he should have seen coming. Like how on the first day of high school his mother had told him to be himself, even as she reached out to straighten the clip-on tie she was making him wear. He could hear her upstairs now, her feet pressing faint concavities into his ceiling as she roamed from oven to fridge, humming along with the old countertop radio she hadn't touched in years. She must have wanted something to fill the silence, since tonight the person she would normally have been on the phone with was speeding toward them through the dark. She'd sent the twins to the sitter's; it was to be just the three of them at dinner. Any minute now, she'd call down for Charlie to come up, which meant he was running out of time to figure out how to feel. He continued to page halfheartedly through the little green Bible. Taken as a whole, the thing offered not much of the frictionless and abstract lovingkindness he'd found back in January in the eleventh chapter of Mark, the love of bumper stickers and old pop songs. Instead, God the father was largely a god of sticking it to your enemies—"Happy shall he be, that taketh and dasheth thy little ones against the stones"— and even meek Jesus threatened the disloyal with everlasting fire.

A car door slammed outside. The doorbell was the same cheery two-tone that a few years ago would have summoned Dad to the front hall. The whole house was disloyal, Charlie thought. And here came Mom calling down for him. Well, screw that. Let them greet each other, shake hands, hug hello, whatever, he refused to be rushed. From along the baseboard, he retrieved the red tee-shirt he'd worn back in pee-wee league. There'd been only the one size, extra large, because no one wanted the fat kids to feel self-conscious. Some of the iron-on letters had begun to peel off, but you could still make out Charlie's number, unlucky 13, and the name of the team, which had also been the name of the sponsor, Boulevard Bagels. (*Go . . . Bagels!*) Last summer, he'd cut the sleeves off and sliced big vents from mid-torso to armhole, exposing tufts of armpit hair. He appreciated the way the shirt turned his ugly body into a weapon against the world. The way it said, *See what you did to me?* It fit so tight now you could count his ribs. In the mirror, he mussed pomade into his regrown hair, got it to stand up in small orange hedgerows. He stuck out a sick-looking, grayish-pink tongue and placed on it an eggy white spansule. *Disco biscuits,* Nicky called these, which was why Charlie had to fight embarrassment every time he asked for more. Disco sucked and would always suck, Every Good Punk Preferred Speed— but the Phalanstery was a kind of potlatch for narcotics, and given a choice, Charlie would take the slow drown of downers every time.

The pill's coating had started to melt on his tongue, and soon its bitter innards would reach his taste buds, so he swallowed it dry, relishing the little pain as it passed the Adam's apple. He snapped shut the old mint-tin where the rest of his stash was stashed. (The 'ludes wouldn't fit in his Pez dispenser.) He lifted his big, black combat boots and clomped slowly up the stairs, enjoying the tremendous noise each step made, imagining his mother and the faceless man cowering. He paused behind the door, hand on knob. Even now it wasn't too late to fall back downstairs, to hurt himself bad enough for an emergency room visit. It might have been a respectable way out. Instead, he committed a disloyalty of his own: he opened the door.

The man in the foyer was neither as grotesque as Charlie had hoped nor as handsome as he'd feared. Just alarmingly chipper as he held out a hand. Charlie, a foot taller, could see down onto the lush carpeting of his head. And the toupée was only one of a number of ways in which the man was the opposite of Charlie's father. They also included his rabbity front teeth and his Star of David medallion and his turtleneck; Dad never wore turtlenecks. "Morris Gold," he said. "Call me Morrie."

The drugs and the costume were doing their jobs: they gave Charlie distance and power. He ignored his appalled-looking mom and seized the hand and didn't let go. "I was starting to think you were imaginary." It oozed from his mouth like refrigerated syrup.

Mom chuckled nervously. "Charlie doesn't normally dress like this."

"This is fashion, Ramona, my daughter's friends all wear this stuff." The pressure of the man's hand was perfectly calibrated, neither over-firm nor effeminately limp; he didn't seem to realize that Charlie was crushing it into powder. In his other hand, the neck of a jug of pink wine looked diminutive, sweat dampening the label. "I wasn't sure red or white, so I split the difference."

"Should I get that into the fridge?"

"I'll do it." Charlie watched his own hands, at the end of hundred-foot robotic extensions, grab the bottle. Mission Control, his brain, had to issue distinct commands to get him safely through the swinging door. *Rotate 110 degrees. Extend left foot. Extend right foot. Lower arm.* And then the long bulbs in the kitchen were lighting the countertop like porn: rods of sweaty cheese prodding cocktail olives, spinach lolling in wooden bowls, pale crisp lettuce leaves cupping ice-cream scoops of tuna salad. There were six of these, in case anyone wanted seconds, and for dessert, her famous apricot balls, toothachingly sweet. And amid it all, irrigated by a paddy of its own juices, the brown bulk of the brisket. The smell was too much for Charlie. He braced himself over the sink for a minute, waiting to throw up, but had the presence of mind to reach out and turn off the radio, so that if the voices now moving into the dining room were to rise above a murmur, he might be able to hear what kind of impression he'd made. When it turned out he wasn't going to puke up the pill, he decided he needed a drink. He removed the wine's little foil collar and stared at the corkscrew until it became apparent how to use it. David and Ramona had never been drinkers. He hadn't even known they owned proper wineglasses, honestly, but there they were, in a cabinet above the range hood. He poured three, one substantially fuller. He drained that one down to match the others. He turned the radio back up, turned it to a station playing one of the hirsute wanker bands beloved of his peers. It had the virtue of being loud, at least. *Activate thumbs. Two hands around three stems. Back through kitchen door; rotate.*

One look at his mother's flushed face told him they'd forgotten him completely. Had there even been, as he turned, the flash of a hand retreating from tablecloth to lap? He set the glasses down hard, imagining the stems breaking loose from their vessels, the vessels toppling, but they didn't. Nothing was ever to Charlie's satisfaction, any more than he ever was to anyone else's. As he loomed over the lovebirds, a gawky obstacle, Mom was obviously weighing whether to say anything about the wine in his hand; he'd never drunk alcohol in front of her before, not counting the Manischewitz at Passover. In the end, though, she was the picture of sophistication. Morris raised his glass. "To old friends and new." Only when his mother went to start bringing out the food did it occur to Charlie that maybe she was as scared as he was. And now he was alone with the suitor.

Silent treatment didn't work. Morris Gold was one of those people who was comfortable with silence, believing he could make it stop at any time. "So, Charlie," he said, after a while. "Your mom tells me you're a musician."

"Nope," Charlie said, and took a gulp of wine. The glass clinked against his teeth.

"Now where did I get that idea?"

Charlie resented the mildness of his adjustment, the way he sought to dispel the friction by treating Charlie as an adult. Trying to offend this man was like trying to offend a coat-rack! "But I listen to a lot of music," he blurted, finally. "My mom hates it."

"I remember when I was a kid, the grown-ups all thought our music was the devil, too. Bo Diddley on the *Ed Sullivan Show*. I figure it's one of the great privileges of youth, to cut loose from your folks. That about how it seems to you?"

He had that well-meaning, man-to-mannish thing that good junior athletic coaches have, and Charlie's traitor heart longed to respond. He tried to feel the monitory shade of his father nearby, but he felt so little of what he wanted to feel these days. Luckily, his mom chose that moment to come back with the tuna salads, resuscitating his anger, like a hand around a guttering flame.

Right up through the main course, Charlie did his best to be unresponsive, and to savor the weird holes this punched in the grown-ups' talk. It was mostly vapid anyway: *What a long winter it's been! Heating oil's spiking. Did you hear the County might cut the school year to 180 days?* He felt almost sorry for Mr. Gold. How could he stay interested in a woman whose idea of conversation was to recite the contents of that morning's paper? Then Mom surprised him by changing the subject to the City. It had gotten so bad, she said, she was afraid to send Charlie in even for a doctor's appointment. There had been that thing on the news. From right here in Flower Hill. Had he seen it? Charlie tried to focus on what she was saying, but his head felt packed with gauze. Like no one could reach him in here, where it hurt.

"Oh, I don't know," Mr. Gold said. "I think if you keep your wits about you, and stick to the good neighborhoods . . . I was just last week at Russ and Daughters. You know Russ and Daughters, Charlie? Whitefish like you wouldn't believe." He inspected his coffee with a twinkle, as if he expected to find a whitefish swimming there. Then he pushed his dessert plate, streaked with the entrails of apricot balls, out onto the tablecloth. "Delicious."

Mom dabbed her mouth with her napkin—the good kind, linen. Softly, she said, "Those were always David's favorite."

"No they weren't," Charlie blurted. "They weren't his favorite."

It was like he'd snapped his fingers in front of a hypnotized person; it was the first thing out of his mouth all night she seemed to have heard. "I beg your pardon?"

Dad's name had been another knife to the solar plexus. Or no, it wasn't the name. It was the ease with which she tendered it, with which Mr. Gold took it, *as if they had talked about David Weisbarger before.* All this time had passed with Charlie and his mom avoiding the subject, which he'd told himself was because it was still so painful to her. "His favorite was German chocolate cake, with the coconut."

"It's a figure of speech, honey. He always liked the apricot balls, you know that."

"Stop that."

"Stop what?"

"Stop turning him into a figure of speech!" Charlie was rising now, and rising and rising, thin as a wisp of smoke.

"Honey, are you okay? Your hands are shaking."

"Don't turn this on me! You're the one using Dad."

At which point Mr. Gold spoke up. "Charlie, why don't you take the dishes in and let your mother and I have a word before I go."

It was clear Charlie had won. The word would be *soon*, as in, *Maybe it's too soon, Ramona*. But instead of triumph, he felt a kind of helplessness. "God hates an adulterer, just so you know." An elbow attached to Charlie knocked over a glass, spraying dregs of rosé. Impossible to say if this was intentional, but some of it got on the white turtleneck of Mr. Gold, who was standing now, too, looking down at the spreading stain.

"Jesus Christ, Charlie," his mother said. But he was already stomping downstairs, sucked into some black hole where he could barely see what he was doing. He scooped up a wad of clothing from the floor and stuffed it along with his seven-inch of "Kunneqtiqut"/"City on Fire!" into his bookbag. Almost as an afterthought, he grabbed his Gideon Bible.

In the front hall, Mom was apologizing. "Where do you think you're going?" she asked as Charlie stormed past, but her voice was just a noise in his head. He plunged into the damp spring night, not bothering to pull the door shut. He thought about making a dash for the car, but she'd taken his keys from him. And his bicycle had a flat, God damn it. Then he spied, leaning against an unpruned bush, one of the too-big BMX bikes Grandpa had bought the twins. He had to pedal furiously to muster any speed, and his knees kept clipping the handlebars. The training wheels groaned and squeaked. But it was mostly downhill to the train station. He kept waiting for someone to call him back, to jog after him, but no one did. So what, he thought. Good riddance.

AN HOUR AND A HALF LATER, he was on the crumbling stoop of the Phalanstery. The rain running down into the corners of his mouth had a sawdusty taste that reminded him of his special red pillow, sucking on the corner of which had been his trick for getting to sleep when he was five, or eight. That's what he must have looked like now, a five- or eight-year-old with a scanty bag of supplies and a face slick with what could have been tears. But Nicky Chaos had always seen deeper. He was blocking the doorway, only a step up from Charlie but also as tall as a god. From behind his tatted shoulders came a corona of light made strange from the yards of supermarket foil designed to jam up cameras, microphones, whatever. Or were the drugs in Charlie's system causing him to see things? That reggae record Nicky liked so much was playing somewhere. There was a faint wistful whiff of pot. "You said I'd know when I was ready," Charlie said. "I'm ready."

"Good," Nicky said. "Because something's happened to force our hand."

Inside, a party was under way, people Charlie didn't recognize shuffling like vagabonds from parlor to kitchen and clogging the stairs and hallways. Musician-types and druggie-types and the slumming philosophers of the universities. A beautiful black girl in an Afro and a shirt the size of a moist towelette slid past without appearing to see either of them, but Charlie had no time to feel upset about not having been invited; they were already out back, Nicky backhanding the door of the little garage. He muttered something through the peeling wood, and various bolts and locks clicked open. A wall of cinderblock had been put up, screening off the far end. On the near side, on the colorless carpet, Sewer Girl and Delirium Tremens sat in black hooded sweatshirts, passing a j. Between them was a newspaper with a picture, worryingly, of . . . Sam? Nicky placed a hand on his shoulder. "The Prophet here's got something to say."

What did he have to say? The Prophet had forgotten.

"He's ready. He's going out tonight with us on our run."

"He's going to stick out like an asshole in that shirt," said Solomon Grungy, looming from behind the cinderblock. There must have been another stereo, another copy of the record, because the song was playing out here, too. Culture, "Two Sevens Clash." Which, viewed from a certain angle, was exactly what the PHP logo looked like. And Sol had done something to his eyebrows. Shaved them off, maybe? Nicky was telling him to shut the fuck up, but Sol was right: red cotton shrilled between the zippers of Charlie's windbreaker like a warning. Sewer Girl dug into a duffelbag. "Here's something black."

SINCE THE LAST TIME CHARLIE HAD SEEN IT, the van had acquired a busted rear window. Someone had taped a piece of cardboard where the glass should have been. It had been someone else, presumably, who'd spraypainted *PUSSYWAGON* in red over the name of the window-washing company on the side—unless this was some elaborate head-fake (wheels within wheels) so that no one would suspect the Post-Humanists of whatever it was they were really plotting. Tablets of speed were distributed, swallowed dry. Then Sol and D.T. climbed in back, while Nicky told Charlie and Sewer Girl to double up in the shotgun seat. They must have loaded up the cargo area earlier; that chemical odor was coming from back there, and every time they took a corner, bottles clanked invisibly. Nicky kept the window down and his arm propped on the door, so Charlie did the same. Sewer Girl was a squirming warm mammal on his lap. If she could feel him getting hard, she didn't seem to care. Indeed, she shifted around so much he got the idea she might be doing it for his benefit.

Then they were flying over the East River, amphetamines kicking in, the lights of the City dwindling to toy size, smaller than nightlights, smaller than Lite-Brite, and the breeze was whipping S.G.'s hair into his newly arid face. They swung out onto a scythe-blade expressway. "Music," Nicky demanded. "Music is essential." S.G. leaned forward to wire the radio into the dash, though the metal frame of the van and the girders of overpasses and the shitty FM signals of metropolitan New York messed with the reception. When the snags of static did yield to an identifiable sound, it was Donna Summer. "I hate this shit," Sol groused from the back. Charlie was ready to hate it, too, but Nicky reached out to stay Sewer Girl's hand. "No, this song is genius."

"And shouldn't we be there by now?" D.T. added. "Magellan I'm not, but . . ."

"You know Nicky likes the scenic route," Sewer Girl said.

Energy was streaming and colliding all around, but Nicky seemed to have withdrawn into his own cool microclimate in the driver's seat, and Charlie could hear him crooning falsetto, *Aaaah . . . love to love you, bay-buh,* his eyes never leaving the road. They'd scooted off a hairpin exit now and were coasting past desolate hulks of buildings. These were not the good neighborhoods. Nicky slowed to a near-stop. "You see that?" Beyond was an old tenement with a charred façade. The top story looked stove in, and most of the windows were missing. Something twitched on a sill: a bird tucking its head away in shame.

"What happened there?"

"What do you think happened, Charlie?" There seemed to be no one else in the van but him and Nicky.

Oh, Charlie realized. *We* happened there.

"When I said we were readying for revolution, I was serious. But don't worry," he said, sensing Charlie's unease. "No one was living there. No one got hurt."

As they drove on, Nicky pointed out other buildings in similar estate. It was like a filmstrip: one flame-licked sight flicking away, another taking its place. "We weren't the first crew up here, Charlie, and we may not be the best, but we're the only ones with a program."

So this was Nicky's big rebellion? And had Sam known about this? Did she know?

"Obviously she did, Prophet," Nicky said. "Just think about where she was found."

Through the haze, Charlie glimpsed a time when thinking about her was all he had cared about. He tried to make contact with that person. "In Central Park?"

"Central Park West. Like a thousand feet from that party."

"But maybe she was just going there to meet Loverboy," Sewer Girl said.

"Yeah, maybe she was going to rat out your change in plans."

Nicky, scratching furiously at his chin-beard, ignored these theories from the back. "No way, not our Sam. Those bullets were a shot across our bow—they changed everything. Preparing for the new target is taking longer than I thought. But we might as well hit back, now that he knows we know. By the time he's calculated angles of response, we'll be ready to hit again, even harder."

For Charlie, much of this was confusion. What new target? And what was the point of torching these derelict buildings again? Before he could ask any more questions, though, Nicky had cut the lights and was snapping at S.G. to turn the radio down. They'd pulled alongside a section of plywood fencing that seemed to run on for miles, blocking whatever was behind it from view. *LIBERTY HEIGHTS PHASE ONE. A HAMILTON-SWEENEY PROJECT,* a sign said, with a picture of glassy towers. *IF YOU LIVED HERE, YOU'D BE HOME BY NOW.* And maybe Charlie did see the point after all. There was a shadow with a weapon running swiftly along the fence, and he almost called for Nicky to watch out. Then he saw it was Solomon Grungy, who'd bailed from the back of the van, and the weapon a bolt-cutter he was even now applying to the gate. A chain snapped like a wishbone; its loose ends fell. Sol gave the gate a shove and then hurried back to the van, which rolled toward the opening.

The excavation inside was massive, a hole probably a quarter-mile long, filling all the acreage between road and river. Trailers and port-a-johns skirted the rim, along with a line of pickup trucks. In the hole itself, in yellow moonlight, sat a dozen or more bulldozers and backhoes. Here and there, rebar jutted from concrete.

Charlie followed his fellow Post-Humanists. His legs had pins and needles where S.G. had squashed them; on the plus side, his stiffy had subsided. She and D.T. knelt behind the van, stuffing rags into the necks of bottles. Sol unloaded more milk-crates from the back. Nicky was somewhere far away and feeling no pain. He stooped, retrieved a bottle, pulled a lighter from his pocket, and then hesitated. "You want to do the honors, Charlie?"

"Me?"

"You've got about five seconds after you light the rag." Charlie took the lighter and bit his lip. "The dozers are a little far. Try aiming for that trailer over there. Vengeance is mine, saith the Prophet."

Nearby, Sewer Girl stopped her work to watch. Not wanting to seem like a pussy, he took the bottle from Nicky. It was either light it soon or pass out from the fumes. But he'd always been told he threw like a girl. Sam, the star by which he was navigating, offered no direction. Nor did any god. He hadn't even touched the flame to the rag, he still thought he was making up his mind, when there was a whoosh and a wave of heat like the grill when his dad would squirt on lighter fluid. He eyed the distance to the trailer. Imagined Sam standing in this very spot. This had to be for her, somehow. And then the bottle bisected the night, end over end, the perfect pitch he'd never before been able to muster. It shattered on the roof of the trailer, just wide of the wall, and sent waterfalls of fire streaking down the side.

"Beautiful," Nicky said, and handed him another bottle.

Still others were whistling through the dark around him, ten, twenty, fifty bottles; he soon lost track of which were his own. To the crash of shattered glass, blue flowers of flame bloomed all around the yard, consuming the trailers, the dozers, the electrical box of the crane, two dirt piles, and a truck bed. A port-a-john buckled sideways and began to melt. Small shadows he realized were rats scurried up the flickering walls of the foundation pit. The various sounds of the fires became one hungry hiss, and the flames merged, too, until he could see quite clearly the faces of the people he was with, no longer stoned.

As Charlie looked on, empty-handed, Nicky stripped off his own tee-shirt, doused it with liquid from one of the bottles. They were all watching now; Nicky was their captain, primordial, savage. He was shoving something into the gas tank of one of the trucks. Lighting the shirt. There was a shift in the air, a thickening in the quality of attention. When he glanced up, he looked almost surprised, Charlie thought. Almost frightened by his own daring. Then they were all running hell-for-leather for the van.

They barreled out of the yard with one of the back doors agape, swinging on its hinges, he could see it appearing and disappearing in the sideview, and here was the first whoop of a siren, like a game, like his brothers playing the game they called Emergency in their room upstairs. If Mom could see him now, he thought, or if Sam could— the power he had to strike back at the world that had struck him. And then there was the deep cannonball thud of the gas tank going behind them, a concussion he'd still feel in his chest in the morning. A blue blaze he'd see again when he closed his eyes, shot through with weird sparks of green.

50

S O HOW'S LIFE IN THE BIG CITY?" Mama said, rumbling away from the airport in the truck that had been Pop's. Her face was worn but handsome, with that dignity folks of their generation had, and when she reached across the gearbox to pat Mercer's knee, his squirm was reflexive. Her opener, back in the terminal, had been, "You smell like a brewery." He'd discovered on his last flight home a lack of faith in the physics that kept planes aloft, and so an hour into this one had caved and ordered a beer. But it had quickly receded into the larger universe of his failings. Down in Georgia, late April could pass for June, but the arm he offered for support in the tropical parking lot got swatted off. There were still rules, apparently: the arrow of need pointed only one way.

"Oh, you know. *Plus ça change.*" He cracked a window. Sown fields exploded in his nostrils. He had a sudden vision of his parents aging in time-lapse, crumpling into matched rockers angled toward a window unit. "Listen, I was up late last night grading papers. Do you mind if I catch a little shut-eye?"

"Why on earth would I mind? That's what you're here for, isn't it? To get some rest?" You'd have thought he'd accused her of infanticide.

"I appreciate it, Mama."

"You know, when you were a baby, Pop used to have to put you in the truck and drive around the back-roads at bedtime to settle you. Your little mind was always working."

Invisible hands were trying to squeeze him back down to the size of his prepubescent body, that container he'd worked so hard to escape. "Mama? I'm just going to try to sleep."

He feigned slumber for the couple hours it took to reach Altana, and the ten minutes from there to the farm. When he opened his eyes, he was facing a plain, tin-roofed house, pale in the dusk. It might have been someone else's except for the complicated things it did to his heart. Pop, who was watching TV in his Barcalounger, naturally didn't speak when Mercer came in. But maybe he was just waiting for his son to go first—to offer an account of himself—because when Mercer asked how he was, he started squeezing the nubby arms of the chair. "Oh, can't complain." They were the first words he'd spoken to Mercer in almost two years. "Your mother says you got yourself in some kinda trouble up there."

Mercer thought of the crippled detective. He did his best to stand up straight. Porchlight from beyond the screen door flooded the spaces around him. "Nossir. I'm just visiting."

"You don't have to talk so loud. I hear fine."

"The TV's on," he said, helplessly.

"You got rid of that moustache, I see."

Mama and Pop were different this way; with her, the pressure was broad and constant, a kind of floor you learned to walk across, whereas with him, it was a thumbtack hiding in the carpet. Mercer was finding it hard not to look at Pop's missing foot. But Mama chose this moment to come in from the porch and whatever she'd been affecting to do there. "Your brother's sorry he couldn't be here to greet you. He's gone to Valdosta to see about some stereo equipment. He's starting a mail-order business, you know."

Since C.L.'s discharge from the treatment facility, she'd talked about him becoming a pilot, a soybean trader, a personal-injury attorney, and some other things Mercer couldn't quite recall from their phone conversations. How could there be so many different careers for which one person was uniquely unqualified? "You let him drive?" He looked to Pop for some acknowledgment that this was a legitimate question, but on the subject of C.L., Pop was still evidently mute. "Forget it," Mercer said. "I'm going to sleep off this jetlag."

It seemed to be in everyone's interest now to respect his conceit. But the flight had only been three hours and had never left the Eastern time zone, and later, after his folks had gone to bed, he would still be lying awake studying the slantwise paneling of his bedroom ceiling. It was temperate enough out to keep the windows open; the breeze smelled like damp asphalt and rare earth metals, coppery but not quite. Every great once in a while a truck would pass by on the highway, an all-night express he could hear from a mile or two off. But in the gaps in between, there was only his brain, like a radio with the knobs busted off, broadcasting the questions from which coming down here had been supposed to free him. Would he ever see William again? And if so, what would they say to each other? Would anyone else ever find him attractive? Would he be able to trust them? Would he ever make love again, or even want to? And why love things you were destined to lose? Why let yourself feel things if the feelings were doomed to die? (And away on another channel: Was it possible that the basic unit of human thought was not the proposition, but the question? What was the logical content of a question?)

On and on it went, even as something in his chest softened and the claustrophobic world around him—his *Encyclopedia Americana* and his shelf of picture-books and the framed picture of him and C.L. flexing their little-boy muscles at Atlantic Beach and the palm-sized rocking horse Hercule the farm manager had whittled shortly before his cancer diagnosis—began to melt into multi-hued moonlight. He tried to keep from making any sound that might leak through the floor to the room where his parents now slept because Pop hadn't been able to climb stairs since the accident. If you could call it an accident. The morning after, the morning of the bonfire and the north pasture and the sacrificial pig, C.L. had been high on PCP. As he probably had been when he'd run the harrow over Pop's leg, said the doctor at the state mental hospital. This was not to mention the self-reported abuse of cocaine, hasheesh, and the sedatives the V.A. had prescribed. Basically, the doctor told Mama in a soothing voice Mercer could just hear from the hallway, C.L. had spent the last two years trying to burn out his cerebral cortex. The things these kids saw over there. . . . Then a truck was approaching on the highway, or maybe a car. Or one of each, the low engine and the high commingling. As they came into range of Mercer's window, he could make out the thump of disco. Even unto Ogeechee County this foursquare beat had penetrated.

Just when they should have started to fade, the vehicles turned in toward the house, carrying enough speed to slip around on the driveway. He heard oyster shells kick up and hit an undercarriage, saw rhomboids of light distend on the ceiling. A door slammed, but the headlights hung there overhead for what felt like forever as the radio pulsed on. *Love to love you, baby.* In the old days, Pop would have got up and run whoever it was off with a pitchfork. There were voices. Finally, the lesser of the two engines pulled away. Mercer could hear C.L. stumbling up the stairs. The next thing he knew, the light on the ceiling was morning, and someone had stuck his brain in a paper sack and smashed it with a hammer.

ONE OF HIS MOTHER'S ANTIQUATED BELIEFS involved the curative power of manual labor, and though she framed it as a favor he could do for her, he knew she was thinking of it the other way around when she asked him, at breakfast, to mow the north pasture. They were down to one cow now, and the grass was knee-high, she said, an eyesore. An eyesore for whom? Well, for *folks*—the same ones, presumably, who would have been scandalized if it turned out one of her boys was light in the loafers and the other one sick in the head. These *folks* were imaginary, it was true (the nearest neighbors were white people who hadn't much spoken to the Goodmans since Pop had wrangled his loan for the land all those years ago), but they were, for Mama, a necessary fiction. They answered the problem of how to keep oneself upright, given the horizontal eternity that awaited us all just over the figurative rise.

As he drove the mower over the uneven acre—he could actually feel the dullness of the steel blades when they whacked into a patch of wildflowers—Mercer fantasized about insurrection. But the house was too small to contain even the two men already fighting over it. Anyway (*whack*; he accelerated toward a ragged patch he'd mown twice already, weeds that were simply playing dead), Pop was at least talking to him again, which meant that he was still in compliance, the good son.

Afterward, he left the mower in the meadow, in case Mama spotted a patch he'd missed, and went in search of water. The footpath wound over the hill, past humid green ditches, fields rented out for usufruct now that Hercule was gone and the dream of self-subsistence Pop had brought back from his own war had collapsed. Green bonnets of cotton peeked from the ridged dirt; soon they'd be the size of medicine balls Cresting the little slope by the rope swing, he heard a sound like nails being pounded into wood. It was a basketball, caroming off the side of the utility barn where Pop had mounted a netless rim. From this distance, the person chasing down the rebound didn't resemble anyone who'd ever played here. He was heavier, for one thing. His hair was blown out in a huge 'fro his blue bandana couldn't contain. And he was barefoot; cowboy boots sat side-by-side under a shade tree. Nor was C.L.'s jumpshot the pure ecstatic arc Mercer remembered, objective correlative for all his brother's unattainable perfections. It was a flat line-drive lacking innocence or English. Though it did, to be fair, go through.

Without saying anything, Mercer slipped in and started guarding him. Soon they were grunting, banging. C.L.'s cheeks dimpled like a kid's when he smiled. He was a step slower, thanks to the beer-gut, and Mercer beat him for a couple of easy layups, but he pulled even with a jumper from outside, and when Mercer checked the ball to him on the next possession, he fired it back almost too fast for Mercer to catch. Those dimples. "What, Negro? I thought you were a city boy now."

Mercer never did have much of an outside shot, and with this grin right up in his face and whatever chemicals C.L. was sweating out of his system clouding the air, he had no confidence he could sink a fifteen-footer. He dribbled and dribbled, trying to remember his brother's weaknesses, and to guess which of them remained. He head-faked right and drove left, wheeling at the end to protect the ball. He was about to toss up a baby hook when C.L. fouled him—hard—retrieved the ball, and stepped back to drain a j. "That's game," he said, still with that idiot grin. The skin of Mercer's forearm tingling, a phantom sting where C.L. had slapped it. There were two options—call the foul or don't—and either way, he would lose, but there was a thrill here in this moment when actual combat might have replaced the shadowboxing he'd been doing for months now with every last person he loved. They squared off, breathing hard. Then C.L. reached out exploratorily, touched the arm, and, when he saw Mercer wasn't going to react, extended himself further, a one-armed hug that was inches from a headlock. "Aw, you still got it, Brother."

"Got what?" Mercer asked.

"If you don't know, I can't explain it to you. Come on."

This was less an invitation than a command, as the arm on Mercer's shoulder doubled as a yoke. They ended up on the shady side of the barn, where dew still clung to the ground. There used to be great curved divots left by the horses that had stabled here, but that was back when Pop was one of the first black men in Georgia with this many acres, and he and C.L. had towered over Mercer like some more enviable species. C.L. threw the barn door's sprung lock near Mercer's feet. The door fell into histrionics. The square of barn it disclosed was as dark as a tunnel but blessedly cool. "Watch for snakes." C.L. must have come here often; a couple of carpeted shipping pallets had been dragged near the door, and on the ground were beercans pale with age. To refuse C.L.'s invitation to sit would have looked precious, so they plunked down on adjacent pallets and gazed out the open door. All of their father's Arcadian designs, his soil-management systems, all the changes he'd wrought on this land disappeared in the prospect: grasses and skies and a small bitter crab-apple tree. . . . C.L. lifted his pallet and fetched from underneath a Mason jar he began to unscrew. A lighter snicked. C.L.'s face flared orange in the dimness, and then a familiar smell cut through the rich animal aura of the vanished horses. He extended his fingers.

"Acapulco Gold. Not that seeds and stems shit you get up north."

"I don't guess you've got any water squirreled away out here," Mercer said.

"Come on, Merce. B-ball and a little weed, helps get the toxins out."

"Toxins?"

"Why you think you want water? They put all kinds of chemicals in that shit to keep you hooked." C.L. took another toke, continued talking without expelling breath. "This here comes straight from the earth. A guy I know knows the guy who grows it."

C.L. had brought back from his war a head full of these *idées fixes*, like a trunk whose contents had been jostled in transit. Worse, he assumed you shared them. Refusal to go along would only make him angry, and you didn't want to make C.L. angry. As ever in the family Goodman, someone would have to swallow feelings here, and it was easier that it be Mercer. Besides, the eventual horror of that night had not erased his memories of smoking marijuana on a balcony with William's sister. If anything, it made them dearer to him. He took the joint, comfortable now that he could once more find an approach to his brother. A cough swelled inside.

"That's good, coughing will get you higher. Take another toke if you want."

When he focused on it, Mercer could feel his mind ballooning outward, sort of, and tight little bundles of tension in his joints relaxing. He inhaled again. How long had it been, since that night at the Hamilton-Sweeneys'? The in-between was contracting, bringing closer things he hadn't wanted to think about, but there was no urgency anymore; he had all the time in the world. He handed back the joint. "You happy, C.L.?"

"As a pig in shit. Speaking of which, how's Carlos?"

"Carlos? Carlos is kind of a nightmare."

"Yeah, that he is, isn't he?" C.L. laughed. "But then, you lived with me all those years, so that can't be why you moved out on him, can it?"

"What are you talking about?"

C.L. was doing something to the joint, fixing it so it would draw better. "Mama told me you found a new roommate. Let's not bullshit each other, Little Bro."

Mercer looked around. There was no way anyone could hear. But the walls could, and the earth, and the ghosts of horses, and the state of Georgia.

"Honestly, I don't care what makes your prick stand up, Mercer. There were a couple brothers in my company known to share a sleeping bag over there in the war. We're out God knows where in the dark, listening to mortar rounds coming down, wondering which one's got our names on it, and I start to think, at least these guys have each other. Turns out there are atheists in foxholes, but still, craving pussy wasn't helping me none." He put a finger to his lips, held up two fingers vertically, then jabbed them toward the back of the barn and the house beyond. "And the ones who do care would be telling you what to do regardless."

"Oh my God. Do they know?"

"If they did, they'd never know they knew. But that's why Mama hates you being up there, getting out from under her. She knows you've always given your heart away too easy."

Mercer grabbed for the joint again, stood up. He was thinking for some reason of that picture in his room, the trip to the beach when he was a little kid, all that beautiful flesh gleaming in the sun. C.L., already adept at hurling himself into things he couldn't control, had stood waist-deep in the chest-deep water, explaining to Mercer how to bodysurf. How to bend the knees and crouch and wait for the moment when the wave started to take you. But Mercer could never time it right; he was always a second behind the break, and would end up stranded on the sandbar, watching his brother's long ride in to the shore. "We lived together for about a year before he left me. William, is his name."

"He white?"

"Jesus, C.L."

"He is, isn't he? Damn. There's your problem right there, trust me."

"It's not that. It's . . . Listen, what do you know about heroin?"

"The drug? Bad shit. Hard to kick. People try to take it away, you resent them."

"But you're clean now."

C.L. licked his fingertips and pinched the end of the joint, producing a tiny sizzle of extinction. "Never cleaner."

"Hey. You don't have any more of that grass handy, do you?"

"How many days you staying?"

"'Til Sunday."

"We might have to make a little run."

His brother lifted again the pallet he'd been sitting on, only without fully rising, an Archimedean feat. Mercer's eyes were now like a cat's, able to see into the hole that had been hollowed out beneath. "What's that?"

"What's what?" C.L. was tucking a revolver into the back of his jeans. When he reached under the pallet again, he came up with a roll of currency.

"Is that a gun?"

"You got to learn to take care of yourself, Merce. It's a red-assed world."

THE POT CAME FROM PRINCEVILLE, an all-black community on the far side of the county line. And, more proximately, from a quadriplegic dealer named "Boot." C.L. was welcomed like a dear friend. Meanwhile, as a stranger, Mercer was forbidden to enter the guy's dumpy house, and had to sit out front with the chained-up dog who shared his owner's distinctly malevolent cast of eye. Their own dog, Sally, had died last summer. Had C.L. been released in time to bury her?

Mercer wondered, even as he girded himself for the sound of gun-play. Stereo equipment indeed.

But then again, smoked out the window of his room under the eaves that afternoon, the stuff restored Mercer's appetite for dinner. This was worth the price of admission, which was having to sit through the meal without looking too intently at Mama or Pop, lest they see his incompletely Visined irises, or at C.L., whose own empinkened gaze might make him crack up. Nor did his parents look too intently at him, for to notice a thing is to become responsible for it. What Mama did notice was that he was looking sturdier already. "Must be this home cooking." And in his mellow frame of mind, Mercer almost agreed. You couldn't get food like this in New York: pork shoulder and butter beans and cornbread. Instead you got what? Let these salt and pepper shakers stand for the Garden and the Coliseum. Let that tall candlestick be the Hamilton-Sweeney Building. Somewhere beyond that, near the floral arrangement, a young woman lay dying in a hospital bed. It was all Mercer's students could talk about last week; she'd turned out to be an alumna of a rival prep school, and the hallways buzzed with intimations of a "Kneesocks Killer." A serial killer would, by definition, require at least two victims, yet the rumors had made him even more afraid for William, roaming those streets alone. But that was all behind him now, right? The pot made it easier to think so. It was rhubarb season, and little berries were starting to come up in quantity, and he took seconds, thirds, of Mama's pie.

With sleep, too, the drug helped. Aping C.L., Mercer had pinched out his afternoon j., saved the end bit, the roach, for later. He'd thought he might try writing some, here in his room where it all had started, but instead he just lolled on the bed. One or the other of his parents was now a snorer; he could hear it a floor below. How many years of wire-to-wire labor, of worries, of pains in the neck and ass their boys gave them had they gone through just to get to the point in life where it was acceptable to fall asleep halfway through *The Jeffersons*? It wouldn't have been fair to them to dwell in the lonesomeness welling again inside him, and now he had an alternative. Which was to relight the joint. In the springtime dark with the windows open and the smell of leaves drifting in, he again grew casual, expansive, unraveling like an old sweater. He devised a little game wherein he gripped the business end of the joint with his lips and breathed in and out, feeling the temperature near his face rise with each breath. The trick was to pluck the joint away just before it burned him. And soon after it either did or didn't, he would feel the world begin to slope away underneath him, the surface of a gathering wave.

ONLY ONE THING CONTINUED TO GNAW AT HIM, he thought: that Saturday Night Special C.L. kept stashed in the barn. Out pulling weeds from Mama's vegetable patch the next morning, he ran through the reasons not to worry. First: They'd both been handling firearms since childhood, when Pop had issued standing orders to kill on sight any crow that came within a country mile of the corn. Second: After two tours in Vietnam, maybe C.L. just felt safer with a weapon nearby. Third: These days, C.L. seemed at least as *compos mentis* as his brother. On the other hand, Mercer now knew himself to be a kind of catechist of rationalizations. Had his experience with William taught him nothing? Had Chekhov? And if that thing went off and killed anyone, it was liable to be C.L. And so, that last night before he was to fly back to the city, he resisted the pull of sleep. He waited for the domestic creak and shuffle to subside. Then he slipped down the back stairs and out the screen door, which he was careful not to let slam. The crickets were louder here, and a full moon threw the house's shadow over half the yard; beyond, trees took over, and he stole from one to the other, a shadow himself. Only upon reaching the shell drive did he look back. The house was dark, except for one window flickering on the second floor. He hadn't been aware C.L. had a TV in his room. Clearly, he hadn't been aware of a lot of things.

Pushing deeper into the farm, the blue land swollen under all those stars, he felt like a figure in a dream. The heavy barn door screamed like an alarm, but then came the old, sure thunder of the wood rolling back. As he groped around in the hollowed-out place beneath the shipping pallet, he tried not to think of the snakes C.L. had warned about, of wriggling millipedes, of eyeless soft insects. At first he felt only the Mason jars of grass. They no longer seemed quite so valueless, but to steal from C.L. would have compromised the purity of his dream-mission. He thrust his hand deeper, holding his breath. It came upon a solidity of metal. Carefully, he oriented the barrel away from himself and dragged the gun out.

Black irregularities in the moonlit pasture outside betrayed his mower's oversights like ink on an exam book. If his girls could see him now . . . He felt a sudden kinship with them, their feigned composure, their inability to imagine the repercussions of choices they were presently making. With his hands, he dug up a patch of damp earth, maybe eight inches deep. The land of his upbringing was under his nails and in his nose, as Pop always meant it to be. It seemed a shame to let it dirty up a good gun, so he used the shirt off his back as a wrapper. He was a priest now, pagan, half-naked in the night, performing obscure rites of interment. Or he was the lead player in his own novel, or in one of those new arcade games William loved, compelled to repeat some totemic motion until he got it right. Only once did he feel, as he had on New Year's Eve, that someone was standing among the trees, watching. Well, let him watch, damn it. Something was being enacted here, as if it had been this deeper mission calling Mercer home all along. And now that he'd completed it, maybe he would be allowed to advance through to the next level, to a world where no one got shot.

51

REGARDLESS OF WHATEVER HE'D SAID TO HIS SISTER in the heat of his outrage, William was finding it hard to husband his dough. If he took twenty, or thirty, or forty bucks out of the bank, he'd burn through it in a single day. On the other hand, some recent lost weekends in the war zones of the outer boroughs had him too spooked to carry more. Several times on lonely streets late at night, he'd had the sensation of being followed. This had started when he'd still been living with Mercer, actually; you'd sense yourself being watched and then turn around and there'd be no one there. And then once, in a flyblown Bed-Stuy shooting gallery, too zonked to move, he'd felt a friend of a friend of a friend lift his graven head, heard him whisper to someone else, *Shit, man, do you know who this cat is?* as if there might be enough cash in the wallet of Billy Three-Sticks to take them all on the Permanent Nod. Which just went to show you had to be careful of other people.

The rule applied to domestic life, too. The first few weeks after moving out, he'd been crashing in Bruno's guestroom in Chelsea. He'd assumed his old benefactor would be pleased to see him free again, but some inkling of the circumstances seemed to lurk behind Bruno's Austrian restraint. Failure to ask what had happened read not as tact, but as evaluation, as disappointment, and perhaps even as a subtle pressure to get clean.

So William had said sayonara and moved the few things he had to his studio in the Bronx. Sure, he was the only white guy for blocks, but he felt sometimes that being raised by Doonie made him an honorary brother. Anyway, color wasn't the source of his agita up here. It was the half-finished canvases gaping from the wall. *Evidence*, his magnum opus was called. The title had come before almost anything else. He'd planned to finish before telling Mercer much beyond that. Perhaps at first he envied Mercer's sanity about his own work, his refusal to boast about his productivity, which must have been considerable, for all the hours he put in. Later, though, after he realized he himself was procrastinating, William had kept quiet out of shame. And now not having spoken about *Evidence* made it seem even less real. He still forced himself at least once a week, out of a kind of spite, to mix up his pigments. But the daily discipline of brush and canvas had long since deserted him.

Indeed, by April, his main discipline was forestalling until early evening, or at least late afternoon, an experience infinitely more beautiful: the leisurely walk over the Grand Concourse or the long plunge down to the Deuce to cop. As a surfer reads waves, he'd learned how to predict the intervals when the government tightened the supply, and how to ride out dry spells. (If they weren't only temporary, cops would have been out of jobs.) And he'd learned to appreciate rush hour, the scoring time, when he flowed out to be with the world for a few minutes before diving back into himself—it had the form of anxiety, only drained of the content—and to relish the pellucid air of five o'clock, the colors of the medium he was moving through.

One day, when the supply was good, he was back in Times Square. Daylight Wastings had just ended, but even this early, the neon flashed come-ons above his head, *Peepland* in red, *Peep-o-Rama* in blue and red, to match the come-ons catcalling from all around. "Reds." "Blues, blues." "Ten dollars, the hand; twenty, the mouth; fifty, full service!" It was a glimpse of the alternate future: not a nuclear holocaust, or a communist utopia, but a life organized completely on market principles. He wanted to stop and admire all these people living like it was the day after tomorrow. Instead he angled head-down into the crowd, trying not to be recognized. In the pocket of his old Ex Post Facto jacket, in the little hole he'd cut into the lining, was a paper envelope of heroin, like the sleeves they put stamps in at the post office.

Hard to say, then, what drew his eye up toward the marquee of a porno palace as he approached the corner of Broadway. He must have felt a disturbance just beyond the boundless world his eyes perceived. Maybe like dogs we know when we are being hunted. Anyway, in a single glance, he comprehended a body bigger than the bodies around it and somehow distinct from them. It was a white guy, a real hulk, damn familiar-looking, with whiskers and flyaway hair and a slightly fantastic or spectral gaze that raked the crowds from the shadow of a hat brim. William had seen this getup once before—from the window of the loft, he thought—and suddenly his anxiety was just anxiety again; he *had* been followed. This was the follower. Some kind of narc, it seemed, with that silly hat, the unconvincing length of that hair. He was waiting to bust William. But he hadn't spotted him yet.

William's instinct, oddly, was to do exactly nothing he hadn't already been doing. Or not so oddly. Wasn't this what you were supposed to do in the presence of a wild animal? Move calmly away. Running will only enrage it. William didn't look again but resumed his businesslike pace across Broadway. His hands sweated in his pockets; he could dump the drugs, but loved them too much. Fortunately, the block between here and Sixth Avenue teemed with New Yorkers as degenerate as himself, and when he felt dissolved among them, protected by them, he looked back and saw no such person waiting on the traffic island.

Later, locked safely inside his studio, he would wonder if he was imagining things. In any case, he was going to reward himself for keeping cool with a dose large enough to make him puke. Somewhere nearby a building demolition had been in process all day, but it registered at present only as intervals of rumble in the floorboards and a felt compassion for the rats of this city, surrounded on all sides by predators, made homeless by the rubble. Of course, it was not the rats he kept seeing as he hunkered over the blackened spoon. Or as the knot inside him untied and dropped him on the dusty floor to lie in his jockey shorts and drift in and out of the portal the shifting sun drew across the wall. It was the shadowy face of that presumptive stranger. No stranger, really, than the one he'd see if he got up right now to examine the mirror. For William, too, was haunted. Hunted, maybe, for something more than his drugs. Or Billy. He'd been jumped a few months ago, and had not wished to repeat it. But he had lost the will to move, or possibly the ability. And so what, he thought now. Fuck it. Let them come.

52

YOU COULD TRACK Mr. Feratovic, the super, by the sound of his walkie-talkie in the hall. Mostly it picked up stray transmissions from vacuum cleaners and passing taxis; the only person who ever used it to contact him was his wife—or so Richard had told Jenny, during one of their late-night bull sessions. He could tune in the signal on his police scanner, hear Mrs. F. calling her better half down to dinner. Didn't he find eavesdropping a little unfair? she'd asked. That day at the start of May, though, she had a question about some contractors' scaffolding that had appeared outside her window—about whether renovations prefigured a rise in rent—so when she heard the telltale static approaching the door, she disabled the police lock and stuck her head out. She found the super attempting to corral Richard's Scottish terrier, Claggart, into a corner with his big brown boots.

The poor dog, obviously traumatized, allowed her to swoop in and rescue him. As she moved toward Richard's door, though, the super shouted, "Not home, miss."

"Excuse me?"

Mr. Feratovic was what you might call well-preserved. He could have been as old as seventy, but wore short shorts and a starched undershirt year-round, and his arms and calves were knotty with muscles. He squinted and leaned toward her, as if into a stiff wind.

The wet cigar-end in his mouth made it hard to decipher what he was telling her, except for the last bit: "You let the dog go, see what happens."

So she set Claggart down. Mr. Feratovic held open the stairwell door, and Claggart bolted for it. The boots stumped down the stairs in hot pursuit. Jenny had little choice but to follow. By the time she reached the first floor, Claggart was sitting rigid in the vestibule, facing the street. Nose-prints smudged the glass. "You see? I find him here, exactly like this. Your friend, Miss Nguyen, he is not home."

"We're just neighbors," Jenny said, wondering why she was so quick to correct him.

"You want I should lock him up until your friend gets back?"

"No, I'll watch him." She picked the dog up and, afraid to look at the super's face, slunk back upstairs. Claggart whimpered a little and tried to get a view over her shoulder, his canine heart thumping from exertion. But how had he escaped in the first place? Steel doors barricaded the stairwells. The recessed elevator buttons were ill-suited to paws. And to protect his record collection, Richard kept his front door locked. Everyone did now. Even socialists.

That night, she kept waiting to hear the snap of Richard's deadbolt, the three claps with which he summoned Claggart whenever he returned home, the golden enchantments of the Wurlitzer leaking through the wall. But when she used the spare key he'd given her and fetched Claggart's dogfood, the flat next door was cold and dim and somehow creepy. It didn't look like the home of a man whose return was imminent. Still, there had to be a reasonable explanation— Richard loved the dog, and wouldn't have just abandoned him. It was a conviction that would stay with her, however illogically, even after Richard's body turned up a week later, waterlogged, bleached, knocking against the pier of a boat slip in Brooklyn.

SHE'D HEARD IT FIRST from Mr. Feratovic, who'd heard it, he said, from the police. She would remember later how the super had looked so seriously down at Claggart, who crouched behind her, growling. How he'd shifted his unlit cigar from one side of his mouth to the other without using his hands. How he'd steamed away, leaving her clutching the doorknob for support. The eeriness of the hallway then, as if she were the only astronaut left on a space station orbiting the earth.

But she would not cry, she'd told herself, as great, silent tears rolled down her face; she would not give Mr. Feratovic the satisfaction, when there had to have been some mistake. She would spend hours flipping stations on the radio, searching for it. She got no word either way. By midnight, she was ready to hurl the appliance out the window, watch it shatter in a cheap supernova on the black street below. Then she remembered: the goddamn scaffolding would catch it.

IT WAS GRIMLY FITTING that the *Daily News*, that first weekend in May, should bear testimony of Richard's death (an "apparent suicide"). After that, word spread through the building like a contagion. Was it true? the neighbors said. Have you heard? But to a person, they fell silent at Jenny's approach. She wanted to tackle them, to sit on their chests until they confessed their suspicions about her and Richard, to make them repeat after her: "We were just neighbors!" Even at work, she felt conspired against. Paperclips scuttled to the bottom of her totebag. Paintings lost themselves in storage. The frosted skylight above her ticked with a shower that didn't let up for weeks. What light it let in was murky and aqueous, and she kept imagining sinking into water herself, the light on the surface receding, her breath stuck in her throat. How could anyone just give up like that? she wondered. And again: How could he have walked out on the dog? Unless his death had been an accident? Was it worse to be an idiot or a coward? No, coward was worse. It would mean she was going to have to hate him forever—and hate herself, for not having stopped him, the night they'd quarreled. Never before had foul play seemed like something to wish for. Still, if his wallet had been missing . . . Or if he'd, like, been in a love triangle, mixed up with the wife of a KGB assassin . . . But she'd left paranoia behind her. The unaligned miseries of life on earth were proving to be more than enough.

Then one day near the end of the month, a coffee cup appeared on the desk before her—not one of the blue paper numbers the deli used, but a diminutive porcelain mug filled with espresso from her boss's special machine. Steam curled off the *crema*. She didn't dare look up; five seconds ago, she'd been muttering under her breath, imagining she was alone. "If you like, I can take it away," Bruno said, finally.

"No, thank you," she said. "It's really thoughtful."

He seemed to hear this as an invitation to take the chair next to her desk, his preferred place to sit and bitch about the caprices of his artists—though as far as she'd ever been able to tell, his days were spent mostly in upmarket cafés. "Something is bothering you, *Liebchen*."

"I'm fine."

"You should be sleeping more." He would have liked nothing better than to manage every detail of her life, like a kid with a doll. It was the transparency of this instinct that Jenny appreciated, or the transparency of the transparency; Bruno knew himself to be living vicariously. In fact, he'd started to look lately like there was something keeping *him* up late with worry. "I have a doctor friend who could write a prescription."

"I get more sleep than I know what to do with, Bruno. I'm the Wilt Chamberlain of sleep. I don't need pills."

"Ah. Well. I apologize, then . . ." This was new: he was offering, as if at great personal cost, to respect her autonomy. It was a kindness that almost made Jenny burst back into tears. She wanted to reward him, but how could she begin to explain the complications? Her hands wrestled on her desk. When she looked up, Bruno was giving her that X-ray look of his from beneath his shaved dome. "You know, when you first started here, Jenny, men turned to watch you walk down the street as if you were one of the ikons in the old paintings, a gilded circle around your head. Being men, they would be only too happy to collect you. But not Jenny Nguyen, I said. She's too smart to be taken in. Of course nothing is more attractive than someone who needs saving."

"Wow," she said. "How much do I owe you, Dr. Freud?"

The weary look had returned to Bruno's face, tempered perhaps by heat, or sadness. He took the cup and downed the espresso in a single draught. And then, oddly (because Bruno never touched anyone), he patted Jenny's hand. "You will figure it out, is all I mean to say."

CLAGGART'S EYES, moist and brown and rimmed with amethyst, were able to grow to a size that made the rest of him seem pitiably small and defenseless, and to project the purest distillate of melancholy— a melancholy from which only Jenny could save him, he would have claimed, had he had the power of speech. Every night, arriving home, she found him cowering under the U-bend of the toilet. His face furrowed, intelligent beneath its fur. The eyes sorrowed at her; at the door; at her again. She wanted to collapse on the couch, but whatever wraith had let him out that first time was no longer on hand, and invariably she surrendered. "Okay, hang on." Perhaps selflessness would earn her a reprieve from grief.

Seven o'clock was some kind of citywide dogwalking hour, when hordes of ostensibly autonomous individuals, still in permutations of professional attire, rushed out of their co-ops tugged by leashes taut as waterskiers' ropes, at the other end of which, straining like hairy engines, were spaniels, shih tzus, bichons frises. Jenny would just as soon have waited until later, avoided the butt-sniffing do-si-do that followed each time Claggart encountered another animal, the entanglement of leashes and compulsory good cheer, the conspicuousness with which she then had to hover over him with a baggie as he choosily chose a place to evacuate, so that no one would mistake her for one of *them*, the vast negligent army of dog-owners who left every sidewalk a mound of desiccated doo. Better, like the Puerto Rican guy from around the corner with his awful Chihuahua, to wait until midnight, to let the dog go where it went and leave it—an assertion of freedom she secretly saluted. But she needed to get to bed as soon as possible, because despite what she told Bruno, he was right: she'd contracted insomnia.

It wasn't falling asleep that was the problem; one floor up from the avenue, where a dump truck's unsecured tailgate could sound like an exploding shell, she'd gotten used to keeping a pillow over her head. But something inside kept rousing her hours before dawn. The bedsheet clung like a greasy bag. Her pulse thrummed in her head, a cloud of importunate bees. She would have said she'd been having a nightmare, but she couldn't remember having dreamt about anything. The sleeping pills Bruno's Dr. Feelgood eventually prescribed only made her more anxious. The major risk was you stopped breathing.

It might help her calm down, she thought, if she knew how long she'd have to wait for the sky to get light outside, so she bought a new clock-radio: a cheap, squat, vaguely toadish thing with a face that glowed when the batteries were in. Which just went to show how little Jenny knew about insomnia. What the glowing clock did, actually, was help her track how many hours it was taking her to fall back asleep, while the radio part got her hooked on an early-a.m. program called *Gestalt Therapy*. She recognized the form, or formlessness, from her hitch in college radio, and was fascinated despite herself by this fellow practitioner still beating his head against human foibles. But recognition wasn't the same thing as rest.

Then came the morning walk, slaloming among the strollers. They appeared in clusters, as if by prior accord: fat white babies lounging like satraps in conveyances of aluminum, canvas, and elastic. The silence of these children gave her the creeps. And she resented the women who pushed them, their modish footwear, their secret reservoirs of income, their breasts swollen into the likenesses of fruit. The petit-bourgeoises. The Bettys, she used to call them, for short. This resentment, though, had begun to seem less political than she'd hoped. It was the resentment of the eight-year-old who wanted to be picked for kickball at recess, if not first, then at least not last. Anyway, the Bettys seemed not to see her, or the city dying around them. Spring was at its peak, and they moved toward the park's cruddy grass like sun maids, two or three abreast, singing hymns of fecundity.

It was at this point that Jenny began to contemplate the likelihood that she was not gifted with any special world-historical mission or insight, that she'd never been any different from—by which it seemed she'd meant "better than"—anyone else. At nineteen, she'd built a whole belief system around the premise that there were two kinds of people, those who fought for a better world and those who only wanted what everybody else did. Now there seemed to be just one kind of person, inching from the former column to the latter. Indeed, she'd begun to see a peculiar symmetry between the Marxist narrative of progress to which she still wanted to subscribe and that of triumphal capitalism. That is, they seemed equally fantastic. Maybe she'd been a rube to believe in anything but the blind ontic quest to ensure one's genes survived. And if there were an Invisible Hand, its finger would have been wagging at her; she never should have gotten her own leash tangled with a middle-aged alcoholic's. But at least there was Claggart. "Come on, puppy," she'd say, and would lead him gently away from the fancy treebox he'd been sizing up for a deposit. They were wronged parties, both of them, and whatever this thing was, they were in it together now.

53

CORRIDORS GONE DARK after the last bell; the puddled light of trophycases; the squeak of sneakers on a gym floor; corkboard announcements stirred by cross-breezes; vapors of ammonia; summer like a flash of thigh beyond a janitor-propped door . . . so this, Keith thought, was what six grand a year got you. It took him a while to find the Lower School, and really he only knew he'd arrived there when he spotted Regan in a small plastic chair at the hallway's far end. One leg, crossed over the other, bobbed impatiently in the air. But what did she want him to do? He'd had a two-thirty phone conference with the U.S. Attorney's office to set ground rules for an actual sit-down. Not that he could tell her that. She held her head stiff when he bent to kiss her cheek.

"Sorry," he said. "Traffic. You look terrific."

It was true; a little jolt of jealousy shot through him whenever he saw her leading a press conference on TV. She'd taken up running, Cate had said. She was still in work clothes now, signifying, perhaps, her willingness to drop pressing business and race uptown for the sake of the kids. Though in fact she could have been an hour late and no one at the school, with its Hamilton-Sweeney Memorial Library, would have said anything. And if Regan was always the Virtuous One, the Punctual One, what did that leave for Keith, except irresponsibility?

There being only the one chair, he leaned against the wall to wait. She obviously didn't want to talk, but he had to assume he'd been summoned here, two weeks before final exams, because of Will. He'd been so withdrawn lately. Though it was hard to establish a basis for comparison. Once, during the dark years—or what he'd thought were the dark years—Keith had gone out to run some errands, completely forgetting Will was even in the apartment. Returning, he heard a noise from the bedroom, and stuck his head in to find his son sitting on the floor, utterly absorbed in some megalopolis he was engineering out of tinkertoys. In this, as in so much else, the boy took after his mother. Keith was thinking about the affinities between self-effacement and self-assertion when the door to Regan's left opened. "Miss Spence will see you now."

"Why'd you wait out there?" he murmured, following Regan into a beautifully appointed waiting area. Eames chairs surrounded a table of austere and vaguely Nordic wooden toys. Their names would be impacted, diacritical: Jûngjø. Fërndl. On the wall a white canvas held a single blot of red, menstrual in exactly the same way the toys were Swedish. Even the secretary was cute, but given the various givens, checking her out would have been a mistake.

She'd wanted to present a united front, said his wife.

"You sure you weren't just trying to rub in that I was late?"

Before she could answer, they were being pushed—metaphorically, of course—into an inner office.

The headmistress was not the one he'd been expecting . . . not, at any rate, the portly old lady with whom he'd clinked glasses at a Hamilton-Sweeney gala long ago. She'd been whatever was the female equivalent of avuncular, and he'd felt so good about entrusting his son to her that he'd written out a donation to the annual fund the very next day. But that event, along with the rest of the early '70s, seemed sunk now beneath layers of tawny hilarity, like a waterlogged cherry at the bottom of a champagne flute, and the woman resettling herself behind the desk was, by contrast, a string bean. Her office was lit by a half-dozen floor lamps, as if direct light would have turned her to dust. And according to the stenciling on the door, she was not the *Headmistress*, but the *Head of School*. Each school—Lower and Upper—must have had its own *Sturmbannführer*, under the supreme command of that jolly fat dowager whose company he wished for now.

Transitions being for the intellectually frivolous, Miss Spence turned to Keith. "I'm sure Regan has told you," she said, "I asked you both here today to discuss your son."

"Amazing kid, isn't he?" Keith said. "And you've done a great job with him. We're thinking one more year and he'll be ready for Groton."

"One of us is thinking," Regan interjected. This had become another bone of contention; he'd decided boarding school might be just the thing to pull Will out of himself, the camaraderie of early manhood, the sense of being liked and likeable that never really goes away. In the New England of Keith's imagination, it was always autumn, always football season, auburn light from over the Berkshires raking long shadows of uprights across the manicured fields . . .

"These obviously are decisions to be made, important ones for William's future," said Miss Spence.

"Will," Keith said. "William's his uncle."

"But what we're here to focus on today is the present." She slid a document across the desk. "As you've no doubt heard, they've been reading Shakespeare in his English class. I wanted to share with you a recent assignment."

Her neutrality of tone could not disguise the fact that she was about to criticize his son; Keith's impulse was to defend, to argue. "What is this, *Hamlet*? Seems like a heavy lift for sixth grade."

"Rigor is what we offer here, Mr. Lamplighter. You'd find they follow a similar curriculum at Groton."

The paper had been typed, with few obvious errors, on the old Remington that had gone missing from Keith's study after Regan had moved out (along with, it seemed, everything else that had made home home). He recognized the crooked *z*, the number *1* used for lowercase *l*s to get around the broken key, the faint ghost of a *t* that haunted every *g*. **THE HERO OF PASSIVITY**, ran the title. And above that in red pen: **See Me**. Regan made only a token attempt to peer over his shoulder. As he asked for a few minutes to read, Keith's heart was in his throat; he had a distinct feeling of being ambushed.

In addition to being well-typed, the essay was surprisingly well-written. The sentences were blunt and lucid, yet the argument was intricate. According to his son, *Hamlet* had been misunderstood for centuries. Its protagonist was the victim of "outrageous fortune" only to the extent that the audience took his word for it. What if, on the contrary, Hamlet was a kind of unreliable soliloquist, hid-

ing from us—and perhaps from himself—the full range of his homicidal impulses? That is, what if Hamlet had gotten exactly what he
wanted? The plot, far from being a farrago of hems and haws, might
be seen as a series of wish-fulfillments. And in this resided the play's
uncanniness: each act hinges on a death the hero has secretly longed
for. `For Example`, Will wrote,

> ```
> The murder of the father, which my research says
> is Hamlet's big conflict, in fact solves a bigger
> one. Looking at the textual evidence supplied
> by his subjects and his widow, Old Hamlet was a
> terrible sovereign and husband. (Let's not dwell on
> his failings as a father, but please note the huge
> guilt trip he lays on his son.)
> ```

Keith skipped ahead.

> ```
> Say Hamlet knows it's Polonius behind the curtain?
> The "accident" removes both a person who would
> punish him for deflowering Ophelia and the
> pressure to make her "honest" (i.e., a wife).
> Throughout the play, there's a part of Hamlet that
> shrinks from women's natural whorishness. We can
> see this when
> ```

Will had been experimenting with comments like this about
women on recent visits to the old apartment. Almost as if he wanted
to see what his dad would say. Keith knew this to be divorce static,
deviations from the boy's gentle and Regan-like mean, but when he'd
heard Will one day, on the phone with some friend of his, refer to his
mother as a *bitch*, he'd grabbed his beautiful smooth little aristocratic
chin and insisted that if he was looking for someone to be mad at, he
should be mad at *him*. At Keith.

> ```
> Ophelia's like the inverse of Gertrude. Hamlet
> becomes more obsessed with her the more she
> holds back what he wants. Once she gives up her
> "virtue," he gets bored. So Ophelia's suicide frees
> him to not have to feel guilty anymore about his
> own horniness. It would be a stretch to say Hamlet
> ```

```
ki11s her, but in her death a11 his repressed
wishes come together--punishment, purity,
ob1ivion--in a symbo1ic "conf1ict" that removes
any rea1-1ife obstac1e he might have to dea1 with.
Which may be why it's on1y a hop of a few scenes
to the so1ution of the other "prob1ems." Or rather,
to the p1aywright waving his wand to make them go
away. In conc1usion, if we 1ook at the origina1
Greek meaning of the term "hero"--"chosen of the
gods"--Ham1et emerges as one, despite because of
his apparent passivity. Or wou1dn't you say that
if he wants exact1y what he gets, he must get
exact1y what he wants?
```

Keith continued to stare at the page, puzzled. When he raised his head, finally, both women were looking at him as if he were the one who'd written it. He forced a smile. "Well, I think it's safe to say it's not plagiarized." The string bean asked if he didn't find it unsettling. He scanned her face for subtext, but found none, which freed him to be irritated. "It's an argument. Isn't that the point of the exercise?"

She leaned back in her chair. "There is an attitude toward women here that his teacher and I find frankly disturbing."

Funny that she should say this; the impression he'd got was of an absolute contempt for men. Selfish, careless, predatory men. "I can assure you, Will has nothing but respect for women. He's a sweet, sweet boy."

"Intelligent, too," Miss Spence said. "He was probably hoping you'd see this."

Grudgingly, because it felt like giving up, Keith admitted that, yes, he could see that.

"The question is, what is he trying to communicate?"

"I think what Miss Spence is saying is we need to do more to address his feelings about what's going on at home," Regan said. By *we*, she meant *you*, to which Keith wanted to say, *Well, you're the one who asked for a separation.* But it already felt as if they were sitting here in nothing but their underwear, baring their slackening waistlines and winter-pale skin to the impassive Head of School.

"I'll talk to him, Regan. I'll take care of it." Regan searched his face. "I swear."

Sometimes, Miss Spence was saying, it was hard for grown-ups to remember how delicate children could be. Keith hated the way she said "grown-ups." Also the way she kept referring to Will as a child. She talked, in fact, as if he himself were a child. Over-enunciating, gesturing with her prehensile hands. "Next year is a placement year, and without more continuity between home and school in terms of helping him emotionally through what may be a difficult time, we're frankly concerned he may not be ready for the rigors of Upper School."

"Are you kidding? Have you seen his Stanford-Binet? Besides, the freaking library—"

Regan jumped in. "Okay. That's enough. You heard my husband. He'll talk to him."

Miss Spence appeared to have tasted something sour. He imagined her face freezing this way, but this was probably just the kind of misogyny she'd been getting at. He had the uncomfortable sense she'd turned her teacher-vision on him, and could see everything.

It was with gratitude, then, that he followed Regan back outside minutes later, into damp fresh early June. To anyone watching the front of the school, they would have seemed like routine parents on a routine visit, except that Regan kept slightly ahead, tapping down the steps in her black pumps. He touched her arm. "Hey. I appreciate your standing up for me in there."

Only then did he see the blood rising in her cheeks. "Did you think I . . . You embarrassed me, that's why. Honestly, sometimes it's like you're the teenager, Keith."

"She's overreacting. He's a great kid."

"He's *been* a great kid. There's a certain kind of kid like this, people love him, but he hits thirteen and—"

"He's not going to turn into your brother." She turned a shade redder. He tried to steer them back onto more familiar ground. "Honestly, I really do wonder if boarding school wouldn't do him a world of good. And then it would give him a decent shot at Harvard—"

"You think Harvard is what I care about right now?"

"Of course not," he said. "I'm only saying . . . Obviously, what we care about is if he's happy."

"Well? Does he seem happy to you?"

In fact, the opposite. Last week, out the window, Keith had watched Will skateboarding down on the street. And only at that distance, cutting sloppy ellipses between parked cars, the wind in his too-long hair, had he seemed to cut loose. At the boarding school, he could be free to feel the thing he felt down on the street—free from the spectacle of his grandfather's case, free from the depressing custody visits, free from the toxic presence of Keith himself. He was willing to deprive himself of his son, if it meant allowing Will to stay young a little longer. Or did he simply want to escape from the sense that Will, too, could somehow see inside him? "No, I guess he doesn't," he said.

"Then don't try to sell me on this, please."

"I don't understand the hard line here."

"William went to boarding school. You know that." She seemed on the verge of saying more, but was Regan, and so held on to herself.

"Maybe we could consider sleepaway camp this summer. As a trial run . . ." He couldn't seem to stop talking about this. It was the one form of connection available right now.

But her arm was up, a taxicab sloping toward the curb where she stood. "I have somewhere to be."

"We could split a cab," he said.

"I'm not going where you're going."

"You don't know where I'm going."

"Wherever it is, I'm not going there."

He watched her slide into the backseat. In its sober skirt, her ass was possibly a bit broader than the Lower School secretary's, but had more character. It had always been one of her best features, and anyway, he was glad to see her looking healthy again. Separation suited her. Unfortunately, what suited her didn't always suit him. This maybe had been the problem to begin with. Still, he'd seen the look on her face back there; no matter what she said, she really had jumped in to defend him. Didn't that point to the possibility that she still loved him, too? And as the yellow cab lost itself in a school of its fellows, as he stared after a sunstruck rear window that may or may not have been Regan's, he had an urge to take a knee, kiss the ground, cross himself for luck. Because what she wanted, she'd obviously been signaling, was for him to act on those feelings. To change his life. To finally figure out how he was going to win her back.

54

WHAT SHE WANTED, ACTUALLY, was an airtight door to come down behind her, cleaving them cleanly, so that she could be angry at Keith without being angry at herself. Yet the boundaries were still so porous that a mere backward glimpse at him dwindling on a streetcorner could leave her reeling. Outwardly, of course, she kept her composure; these last months had taught her how to stand up to cameras, to deliver careful non-answers into fascicles of microphones. But inwardly she was a trained animal, inclined to leap into Keith's arms the second he showed her kindness. The only solution would be to create between them some obstacle so large neither of them would be able to get around it.

The obvious candidate was Andrew West. He'd been helping her with the recent "setbacks" at Liberty Heights. (The Bronx had been in flames since the late '60s, but as soon as the inferno touched one of *their* projects, it required a public statement.) And with how to sell to the press the plea deal that was now going to keep Daddy out of jail. Well after the twenty-ninth floor's other denizens had packed it in, they remained in her office. The night janitor's Hoover could be heard worrying a patch of carpet nearby. Light pooled on piles of prospecti and spiked phone messages. And on Andrew's neck, bent over the desk at the same angle as the anglepoise lamp. His smell reminded her of Keith's aftershave, a ceramic bottle of which had followed her to the new place. In the first days after the move, looking through boxes in search of something else, she used to brush against the raised sailboat logo, used to lift the stopper and breathe in the simple blue scent. But Keith's simplicity was the kind that made complications for everyone else. Like how he used the aftershave to cover the smell of the cigarettes she knew he smoked. Which she herself had smoked, the year before he rescued her. Andrew, by contrast, wore only Speed Stick, and sometimes now in the warmth of their little conspiracy, she imagined she smelled his sweat. He hadn't asked her out again, after that once, so she was going to have to take the lead here. Yet she couldn't quite do it.

Later, she would lie in bed with her eyes open until the dark became a palimpsest of grays: chair, nightstand, the small gray stack of plays she'd checked out from the library back in March, determined to become again the literate person she'd once been. What had happened? Marriage had happened. The indictment had happened. The thing with Will. Work and cabs and dinner and dishes and every other blessed thing that left her here in a pile on the bedclothes, almost teary from exhaustion but still not ready to sleep. She'd been having this dream lately about a kind of gate, an alabaster thing as tall and deep as the triumphal arch down on Washington Square, but with a central passage too narrow to see through. The gate was unlocked now; she was supposed to enter. But she didn't know how things looked at the far end—only that you couldn't come back to what you'd had to let go of in order to fit through. And what if no one waited there to receive her?

On a Friday afternoon in the heart of June, she was supposed to meet with Daddy's lawyers to vet the terms of a revised proffer. She decided to take Andrew with her to the offices of Probst & Chervil, down in the Financial District. She'd been in the conference room once before, and it should have been spacious enough, though no one had told her Amory Gould would be in attendance, already occupying the extra chair. It struck her again how physically small he was, for as large as he'd managed to make himself in her mind.

"Regan, how goes it on 29?" Only someone who'd known him for a long time would catch the note of challenge. She acted unfazed. Things were fine. Surely he remembered Andrew? "I gather Mr. West has been lending a hand," said the Demon Brother. "But I wonder if he'd allow us a tête-à-tête. There's been a development that might affect your work."

"Andrew's been deep in the books, Amory. Whatever it is, he can hear it, too."

One of the lawyers offered to get a chair. "I don't mind standing," Andrew said.

If this registered as a blow, Amory didn't show it. And it occurred to her that he, too, had been acting—that this was all to be disseminated as office gossip. "Well, I wanted it to come from family first." He paused. "Your father has once again changed his mind."

"Excuse me?"

"About the plea," another lawyer blurted. "Your uncle means we're moving to trial."

"I know what he means," she said, her knuckles whitening on the arms of her chair. "But this is not what has been discussed."

"As we both know," Amory resumed, "Bill has a way of forgetting. He now seems quite insistent that he admit no wrongdoing. Understandably. The risk of exposing assets . . . And he still hopes to return to run the company. Which as you know is a sticking point for the government."

"But if he wins, people will just say he got away with it. And what if he doesn't win?"

"You don't think he'll lose, do you? Nothing's been proven, you yourself have said. And if he's to run the company, surely he's competent to make his own decisions? The trial would likely start in mid-July. Our counsel here just filed the relevant motions."

The lawyers were obviously meant to be his amen chorus, for each one she tried to look at looked away. "I can't believe this."

Amory gestured to a telephone on the conference table between them, and only now did she see that it had been turned to face her, even before she'd come in. "Call him, if you like." And here again was the gate rising before her. On one side was the old Regan. The new Regan, though she had no idea how she could fight back, wasn't about to plead with Amory or his Gouldettes for mercy.

As they all made their courtesies and departed for the weekend, she and Andrew were urged to linger as long as they wanted, to talk over next steps. But she felt, in the room with its door left open, as if everyone out there could see every last thing about her. Andrew took the chair next to her, and they sat for a long time in silence.

When his hand reached for hers, she brought it to her cheek. There was an emptiness that ran the length of her, a sweet oblivion now on fire after so many months. She wanted to move the hand to her mouth, to kiss it, but when he tried to scoot his chair closer, she drew back. "Geez, I'm sorry," he said. His flushed cheeks nearly melted her again.

"Please don't say that. It's my fault. Or not my fault. . . . It's just the timing, Andrew. Can you just be patient with me a little longer?"

55

THE CLOCK-RADIO WAS HOW SHE KNEW, the day the noises came, that they started pretty much exactly at 6:30 a.m.: sharp barks out in the hallway and beyond the construction scaffolding out front, the heavy thud of bodies against an interior wall. They'd likely been instigated by the super, but Jenny found herself unable to reach for the phone to call him. Instead, she played dead on her hide-a-bed, letting the bar beneath the mattress subtly reconfigure her lumbar region. She was too old for resistance, she'd decided. Easier to say nothing than to say something.

Gradually, though, the voices outside grew more insistent. They were foreign, of course, Eastern Europe being Mr. Feratovic's preferred labor pool. Hopes of getting back to sleep began to seem ahistorical. She carried her other radio into the bathroom so that she could catch the tail end of "Dr." Zig in the shower. But her focus was shot. Even when the slamming in the hallway stopped, she was primed for it to continue, and after rinsing the conditioner from her hair, she killed the water and the radio and pressed an ear to the shower wall. All she heard was a kind of low rumble, punctuated by distant clunks and clanks. She stepped back; the sound was gone. When she listened again, there it was, the neutral gear of a great submarine, the sound of the apartment house itself. It should have alarmed her—to think that this sound had been here all along, without her knowing!—but somehow she found it comforting, as if indifferent gods were puttering nearby. Then behind the dripping shower and the building's murmur came the squeak of wheels, echoing in the emptiness of the apartment next door. What had they done with all of Richard's stuff?

She threw on an old tee-shirt over her panties and looked for her missing huaraches and then, failing to find them, galumphed barefoot out into the hall. Two white guys who couldn't have been any older than she was lounged there in weightlifting belts, their cigarette hands draped over the handles of dollies. Richard's coffeetable stood on end between them. She demanded to know what they were doing. One said something to the other in what sounded like Russian and smirked in the direction of her breasts. She recrossed her arms to make sure she wasn't poking through the fabric and rummaged for useful phrases from her Red Brigade days, but all she could remember was *Na zdorovie* and *Komsomol*, and anyway, who's to say these guys weren't Polish? Finally, she just pushed past them into the dead man's apartment. It pained her to see it so bare in the too-bright light. To smell the turpentine a gangly kid was applying to the baseboards, and the dust on the carpet, embossing where things had stood in paler blue.

She went to put on a bathrobe. Down in the vestibule, Mr. Feratovic was roosterish, his walkie inert. The V-neck of his tee-shirt made a topiary of his chest hair. As he leaned toward the glass to look out at the curbside traffic jam of Richard's furniture and boxes, a tiny cross glinted in the sun. "I hope you're not planning to throw all that away," she said.

He turned as if only just noticing her and then, with an ostentatious lack of comment, turned back to the glare. When it came to the question of who was using whom, the super-tenant relationship was the strangest this side of politician-constituent. Or reporter-subject. His cigar twitched. "Two months, Miss Nguyen." His habit of addressing her formally was obsequious to whatever degree it wasn't patronizing. She also hated the way he made her last name sound like *unguent*. "Nobody steps forward to claim this crap. Anyway, your friend does not need, where he is now."

Maybe he meant *in an urn in Oklahoma*, she thought, as a hired man crabwalked past them and crashed the coffeetable like a great blimp onto the curb. But it sounded like he meant *in hell*. "This stuff doesn't belong to you. You can't just throw it away."

"Is not throwing away. Is what-do-you-call. . . . The good furniture is in someone else's flat by nighttime."

"That jukebox should be in a museum."

He shrugged. "Call a museum." A rumpled-looking girl in a bikini top, some kind of voluptuous transient, had stopped to pick through a box of records. Jenny couldn't just stand there, it was like watching a buzzard pick at carrion—indeed, actual birds seemed to be eyeing the loot from the fire escape—so she blew down the steps in her bathrobe and lifted the first box she saw. It was heavier than it looked, but, no longer caring who gawked at her bare legs, she carried it to the elevator. She couldn't afford to renew her lease come September, anyway.

By midday, the clutter of Richard's larger apartment had been reconstituted in her own. There were towers of books on the hide-a-bed and LPs in the bottom of the closet. Boxes swamped the kitchenette counters. She would have made room for the Wurlitzer, but it turned out Mr. Feratovic had already sold it—to cover the last three months' rent, he said. From the doorway, sweating through her gallery clothes and three hours late for work, she watched Claggart scamper to and fro among the piles, as if searching for something. It looked like a crazy person's apartment, she thought, the home of a lost Collyer brother. Then again, the junk formed a body of evidence: Richard had existed. And who, in this city at the tail end of this century, wasn't crazy a little?

THAT EVENING, she began to go through the boxes. They were legal-style cartons, sealed at the ends with bits of string wrapped around plastic buttons. In the first, she found sealed envelopes with crinkly glassine windows, an ashtray in the shape of Richard Nixon, a plastic backscratcher, and a hunk of gray rock with a hole you could fit your pinky through. Did this last even count as a possession? Mr. Feratovic's goons had just taken heaps of whatever was at hand and stuffed it in, like leaves into a bag. The next four boxes she merely took the lids off and dug around in with her arm.

At some point, she realized she'd forgotten to eat dinner. The dissembling sun had dropped halfway down the sky without seeming to traverse any of the space in between. Dust hung in the shafts of light the window scaffolding admitted, and it was strange to think that at least some of this dust was Richard, dislocations of skin, of bitten fingernail. She was sitting on the floor with the final box before her. She unwound the string, only half-remembering what she was even looking for. Inside, a mess of twisted hair and flesh confronted her. Only after she looked away, gorge rising, did she realize there would have been a smell, had it ever been alive. It was a Halloween mask, a Wolfman, turned inside out. A girl in grade school had been able to do this with her eyelids, turning them a glossy, whitened pink. Jenny had to kind of steel herself to get the mask out, but underneath was a stack of magazines. She lifted them from the box and rolled off a rubber band dry with age, which snapped before she could work it free. A manila folder that had been bound in with the magazines fell to the floor. She tucked it gingerly back into place, between the issues of August 1965 and April 1966. She had been fourteen then. She had been fifteen.

These were Richard's archives, and she was to spend much of the weekend perusing them. The obits were right. Colorful characters— bartenders, minor-league ballplayers, owners of Russian baths— emerged from his sentences without apparent effort, as if he'd become each of them in turn. By the night of Monday, July 11, all that was left was the folder—a typescript she already knew was not a last will and testament, but what he'd been working on when he died: The Fireworkers. She'd saved it for last because reading it would be weird. And was. The surface was drier, cooler than some of his efforts from the '60s. But beneath that she could feel a greater passion struggling to break through. After fifteen or sixteen pages, she decided she needed to ration herself. She marked her place with some pictures he'd clipped in and balanced the folder on the arm of the hide-a-bed and doused the light and lay for a while in the darkness, more baffled than ever about what might have compelled this man to destroy himself. An actual artist, living right under her nose.

Still, it was as if through his art she'd finally started to heal. She would sleep through the night that night for the first time in months. And when she left the next morning for work, she would remember to lock the door. She was absolutely sure of this, she would tell the cops later. When she left, the lights had been off, the door locked, and the windows that looked out on the scaffolding closed.

56

NICKY WAS RIGHT: you couldn't really understand Post-Humanism until you'd seen those bottles of fire whooshing end-over-end through the air. Even now, Charlie wasn't sure what to feel about it. Or rather: he could imagine what he *should* feel, but didn't quite know what he *did*. Order and rules and property were things he'd been brought up to respect. This being America, some rebellion was to be anticipated—even welcomed—but there had been no question of him not finishing high school, for instance, any more than there would have been of ripping up the Constitution and starting from scratch; he would someday be an accountant or a podiatrist, with kids and a mortgage. Instead here he was, living out of a single bag of sweat-stiffened laundry in the attic of a revolutionary cell in the East Village. And things around the Phalanstery had changed in the weeks since their raid on the Bronx. The graduate students and punk-rock groupies who used to drift over to smoke the Post-Humanists' dope and engage Nicky on the finer points of *Ecce Homo* had disappeared. There was now a police lock on the front door, and two padlocks on the little garage out back; one on the inside, for when Solomon Grungy was holed up in there—which was most of the time—and one on the outside, for when he was out.

What was constant was the birds. By the start of summer, the roof out there held so many that it threatened to cave in, and Sol was

constantly at war with them. He'd tried poison; he'd tried install-
ing a row of spikes along the dented gutters, he'd tried electrifying
them; once—this was before the rear windows of the Phalanstery,
too, got covered with foil—Charlie had been arrested by the sight of
Sol pacing around back there with a heavy pistol, muttering to himself. Later, when Nicky had taken Sol aside and reminded him that
they couldn't afford to attract attention, he'd heard Sol say something
about how even the birds were out to fuck him up.

At the time, Charlie put this down to increased drug consumption. In the morning, Sol would toss back whole handfuls of amphetamines, and in the evenings, when he came in from whatever he was
doing out there, he collapsed in a chair shaped like a satellite dish
and smoked massive amounts of weed. It helped, he said, with his
hand. He'd injured his left thumb and forefinger not long after Liberty Heights—had burned the tip of one, apparently, and damn near
lost the other—but refused to see a doctor. Now he would peel off
the white leather driving glove he'd taken to wearing, and Sewer Girl
would bend over him in her bikini top, her tits almost touching his
chest, and massage cactus oil around his wounds and then, while he
waited for it to soak in, pack him bong-loads and hold the mouthpiece
to his lips. "What?" he'd say, when he saw Charlie watching. But the
sneer had become a sort of comfort. If Sol's paranoia meant locked
doors and covered windows and banished outsiders, and if Charlie
remained here, in the front parlor, with him and his old lady, did it
not then stand to reason that Charlie was part of the family?

YET, AS WITH HIS OLD FAMILY, his new one kept him on the margins.
There a basement, here an attic, but still: no one who adopted him
ever seemed quite able to forget the fact of his adoption. And so, two
months into his stay, there remained these deeper recesses, things
Charlie felt he wasn't being allowed to know. There was, for example,
the fact that Sewer Girl was also fucking Nicky. More than once,
while Sol busied himself in the little house out back, Charlie had
jerked himself off listening to his own comrades go at it, not particularly subtly, on the far side of the floorboards. ("I love you," he heard
her say over and over, as if in a trance, while Nicky, usually voluble,
just grunted.)

Then there was what he'd found in Sol's clothes drawer one day.

He'd been foraging there for pills, because he was tired of being rationed, or having to filch them one or two at a time from the pockets of Sewer Girl or D. Tremens. And Sol had indeed been sitting on the motherlode, blue codeine and sky-white 'ludes, each in its own jar. The pills glowed like jewels in the light of unshaded bulbs, the artificial day that now reigned throughout the house. But when Charlie reached back in to see if there was any Percodan, he bumped up against something hard and metallic. The gun, was his first thought, but in fact what he discovered, tucked carefully, almost tenderly, inside an athletic sock, was a black Nikkormat camera. What was Solomon Grungy, of all people, doing with Sam's camera? Charlie wrapped it back up, but not before winding and removing the film.

THAT WAS THE NIGHT HE BEGAN ACTIVELY TO EAVESDROP. Well past midnight, after brushing teeth and stripping down to skivvies (not having any pajamas), he would kneel on the dusty floor he'd been sleeping on, and rather than saying his prayers, he'd find himself pressing an ear to the wood. Maybe he was hoping to catch again the distant sound of sex (and it was funny, come to think of it, that he never heard Sol and Sewer Girl fucking). Mostly, though, it wasn't a planned-out thing, this listening. Or so he told himself. One minute, he was clasping his hands in front of his chest; the next he was bending down, in animal attunement, the draft from the trapdoor to the roof raising gooseflesh on his thighs.

Down, down went his attention. Past the pale hairs that edged his eustachian tubes, past the trapped volume of air between ear and wood, the scuffed surface of the floor and its tough intractable heart, the narrow-gauge pipes, frayed wire, rat-runs along the joists. With his eyes closed, the Prophet Charlie could see all this, as well as strabismic whorls and irregularities on the undersides of his eyelids, from the pills. (His pre-bed routine usually included a couple painkillers, to bring him down off whatever he'd been on that day.) Down through flaking tin ceilings, through plaster and lath; unimpeded, he should have reached all the way down to the cathected utility lines and subway tunnels. Instead, he stopped ten feet down, in the room where Nicky slept, surrounded by *Whipped Cream & Other Delights*. If it was late enough, he might hear murmuring there, halting, as Nicky and Sol forgot the ends of their sentences, sparked a joint whose peppery essence seeped up to where Charlie was trying with all his might to ward off an asthma attack.

Nicky's voice was low and insinuating. D. Tremens, when he finally showed up, cracked wise. But Sol, for whom a whisper was an alien concept, spoke in a hiss, a concentrated version of his usual basso, which meant it squeezed more easily through the intervening layers of wood, paint, and air. "Do you have any idea how tricky it is to circuit all the parts together with any precision?" Charlie heard. And, "Well, you damn well *better* think about it, D.T." And, "It's the scale that's the whole problem." Charlie thought he heard Nicky say something here about geometry, *like that, plus three zeroes*, which was simple enough, but a thousand what? Inches? Seconds? He suddenly understood why Mrs. Kotzwinkle had been so adamant about units back in eighth-grade math. But no—he couldn't follow shit, and now he'd gone and drooled on himself. He really needed to lay off the codeine.

Then, some time past the Fourth of July, he came down to the parlor to find the front door wide open, and Sewer Girl and D. Tremens humping furniture out to the back of the PHP van. When Charlie wanted to know what they were doing, D.T., straining under the weight of his own mattress, gave him a look. "Are you going to ask questions, or are you going to help?" So Charlie grabbed a couple of folding chairs. *Each according to his means*, he thought.

The Phalanstery aesthetic had always been Spartan, but now the parlor was totally bare, save for the stereo and the single lamp D.T. had told him to leave behind. They moved on to the kitchen. Nicky, sitting Buddha-like on the one small countertop, smiled approvingly as Sewer Girl carried out the cardtable where Charlie had once been served tea. Where, just last week, ten identical travel clocks had appeared and then, just as quickly, disappeared. "Nicky, what's going on?" he asked. "Where are they taking that stuff?"

"Whatever doesn't fit we'll dump at Fresh Kills. You know it? A trash-mound out on Staten Island, so big it's got its own ecosystem." He drained his beer, threw the can in the sink. "The vanished remainder, made manifest. For the rest, who can say? Amarillo. Winnipeg. Whoever needs a wake-up call, or call-up, or wake." He'd laid hold of more coke, you could tell when he started in like this with the puns. "You look distressed."

"I just don't get what's changed?"

"Everything's always changing, Charlie. We become who we are. The mask melts into the face."

"But if you get rid of all the chairs, the novices won't have any place to sit."

"There won't be any more novices, not here. You Post-Humanists have labored long enough in darkness. It's time for you to think bigger than New York, go launch other Phalansteries in other places."

"Leave New York? But what about you?"

"Like you said, Charlie: I'll remain in the light." It was true, it sounded like something he would say, but then, he'd said a lot of things. Nicky reached under himself and produced the dog-eared Bible Charlie couldn't remember the last time he'd consulted. Flipped to a page. " 'We will not serve thy gods, nor worship the golden image which thou hast set up.' You were right, there is good shit in here. Nobody escapes in the end. And now it's almost time to pull the golden image down."

"I thought that's what we were doing at Liberty Heights."

"Do you see chaos in the streets? Phase One was just a dry run. Next to Operation Demon Brother, it'll look like a cherry bomb."

Charlie waited for Nicky to look away, as if he'd inadvertently let slip a clue, but instead he seemed to be staring straight into Charlie. And it was Charlie who turned to go, unable to bear the maniacal steadiness of that gaze. "Hey." Nicky stopped him and held out the book. "You don't want to leave this lying around where just anyone can find it."

AND SO THERE WAS THIS, finally, jamming him up: doubt. There'd been a brief once-upon-a-time when, no matter how he'd drawn the line between insider and outcast, pure and impure, oppressed and oppressor, his little Bible had reassured him he was on the side of the righteous. Its insistent second person had seemed to address him specifically, just as that voice in the church had—just as Nicky's did now. It was a seductive proposition: You, Charlie, are the subject. The hero. Yet when the pills wore off, another voice, his own, still let loose a stream of what Dr. Altschul would have called insecurities. For all the theoretical sexiness of election, of inner-city revolution, Charlie was beginning to suspect that Long Island had ruined him for it, somehow. That there was something irredeemably common about him.

For here he was the next day—having just received an object lesson in the vanity of material attachments—sneaking off to the laundrette around the corner to wash all his worldly possessions with a box of vending-machine soap because Western culture had trained him to hate his own, natural smell. He supposed he'd have to get used to taking care of himself, if the Phalanstery was truly, as Nicky suggested, winding down. The denim jacket he'd sliced the sleeves off and painted with the PHP icon was green from grime. His tube socks were crispy and brown on the bottoms, like cookies left too long in the oven. As he loaded the pair of jeans he wasn't currently wearing into the machine, he went through the pockets, as his mom had taught him. In addition to some linty pocket-change, he found the roll of color film he'd shoved in there a week ago and then forgotten. And when he passed a camera shop a few doors down, he went in on impulse and, before he could change his mind, dropped off the film to be developed.

He was feeling awfully low now, slinking back to East Third Street, though he couldn't be sure why. Secretive, maybe. But how many times had Nicky told him that excess attention to these interior states was another symptom of the humanist disease? What mattered, he wanted to believe as he turned the corner, was the world beyond the self, the world of action—and that's when he spotted the cripple.

It was clear in an instant that he was out of place. There was the shirt, for starters, a short-sleeved madras model like the idea of leisurewear held by someone who'd never known leisure, and the creased blue trousers redolent of golf courses. There was the old-fashioned straw hat, and the brushy gray moustache below, in a region of blinding sun. It was true that impressive whiskers flourished all over the Loisaida, but they were either curly, as with the Hasidim, or in the case of the Spanish-speaking men in their folding chairs, a sumptuous beetle-black. This guy looked, in other words, like a tourist, in a neighborhood tourists ran from, screaming. Or with his crutches, maybe a refugee from one of the nearby medico-psychiatric clinics. But as Charlie looked on, he seemed to be hiding behind the trunk of the struggling sapling opposite the Phalanstery, and—yes—making notes in a flip-top pad.

57

AFTER THE NIXON SCANDALS, the various law-enforcement agencies had been sealed off from one another to prevent abuses of power, but there were still nodes of contact where favors could shuttle back and forth. Larry Pulaski and an old friend of his from the Police Academy constituted one such node. The friend—let's call him "B."—now worked for the U.S. Attorney's office, and so they made sure only to talk in informal settings. That first Tuesday in July, for example, Pulaski had gone up to meet him at Yankee Stadium. It was B.'s choice; last time it had been Pulaski who, having come into some information about a Bonanno family capo, called up and said, "Let's go see the Jets." B. had put on a few pounds since then, but as they began the slow limp up the endlessness of ramp, Pulaski told him he looked like a million bucks.

From the nosebleeds, the inner face of the stadium was wall-to-wall carpet, little nubs of pink and brown stretching in either direction amid filaments of red (for the visiting Indians), but chiefly of Yankee blue. Innings, hot dogs, and remarks were passed. Games always moved slower in person than on the radio, particularly when an eight-run bottom of the third put the outcome beyond doubt. Or when you were waiting for a companion to get down to brass tacks. But it wasn't until the seventh-inning stretch—another reminder of Pulaski's physical limitations—that B. asked, out of the side of his mouth, how the case was going. Pulaski, reflexively, played dumb: Which case? The one that was all over the papers, wiseguy. In that case, "going" wasn't quite the right word, Pulaski said.

"Come on," said B. "You've got it easy. All you have to do is make an arrest. The prosecutors are the ones who have to convict on your weak mess." The calliope tootled drunkenly behind ten thousand other conversations. B. bent to scribble an address on the back of a ticket-stub. He handed it to Pulaski. "You heard of these guys, the PHP? One of the fringe groups, like the SLA, the PLO."

"I'm guessing P stands for People? Or is it Power?"

"So far as I can tell, just some dropout with delusions of grandeur and a couple friends. Though who can say what folks are capable of. Anyway . . . the office has been busy with something bigger, but in the course of due diligence, someone ran across the acronym, did a little poking around. Nothing came of it that we could use. But word is, your vic spent time with them." When Pulaski gave him a look, B. wiped mustard from his mouth and held up his hands in the gesture for *I swear, Your Honor, I never touched her.* "You think the lead's a piece of shit, you're probably right. Throw it away, burn it, my lips are sealed."

"Exactly what kind of poking around are we talking about? And who's this 'someone'?"

"My salary line is GS-9, Pulaski. I just get whatever trickles down." It took Pulaski about a second to know when something wasn't being said, and B. knew he knew. A few drops of mustard trembled on the underbristles of his moustache. "Fine. What about FBI? Those initials mean anything to you?"

"But what's their jurisdiction on this?" Pulaski asked.

"Like I said, they're working on something unrelated, which isn't what I came here to talk about. I just thought maybe you'd seen this." B. took back the ticket-stub. His pencil began to sketch two eyes and a spiky head of hair. Or a number. A tattoo. ⚡ "PHP, get it?" The sound around them seemed to go hollow, as though receding into cans. Pulaski felt exposed. See-through. Even here in the shade behind home plate, they were visible to thirty thousand people. There were cameras everywhere. The people behind them suddenly seemed *too* plausible, with their spanking new caps and giant foam fingers. Then B. ripped off the little stub of stub he'd been doodling on and crumpled it and dropped it among the peanut fragments. "Don't say I never did you any favors, asshole."

BUT WAS IT EVEN A FAVOR, really? At this point, with the retirement plan in dry-dock and the Deputy Commish breathing down his neck, Pulaski was about ready to listen to Sherri, to go to the doctor who fudged his annual bill of health and say: Let's get me on disability, already. It was he, not Sherri, who had arranged to drive up to the Catskills to look at acreage the very next day.

On the ferry home from the game, he stood at the back rail watching the lights of Manhattan recede into dusk. The city, from this angle, was so small. Uptown buildings hid behind the towers of the Battery and dwindled until he could blot them all out with his thumb. His native Jersey was terraced housing projects and trees gone umber from summer heat and smog. He'd spent the last couple months trying not to think about Richard Groskoph, but he couldn't help himself now. The scuffed shoes. The water churning below. He'd worked his share of suicides. He could never grasp, though, how anyone lucky enough to be born in this country, in this century, could want anything other than as much life as he could possibly lay claim to. And Richard had been survived by a child! A three-year-old living somewhere in Florida, the *Times* had said, which just went to show you never really did know anybody. Of course, Richard had only spoken to him twice in the last half-decade, and had been so hacked off that last time, after the Cicciaro girl's name leaked out. But surely this was a symptom, rather than a cause. Surely he, Larry Pulaski, had been the farthest thing from Richard's mind . . . A few violent-looking clouds edged in from the west to menace the trade towers. The breeze was thickening. But rain did not come, and the end of the thought sat cooling within him, plated on some nerve ending just beneath his tongue.

Sherri was asleep when he got home, but he stayed up, looting beers from the rec-room fridge, wearing an uneven path in the carpet with his crutchless pacing. Assume it's accurate, he thought. Assume the Cicciaro girl had these connections to some lefty agitators, fine. But the guy who'd found her body had been a guest of one of the city's richest families, the very model of the Establishment. Pulaski had never been one for the overwrought plot; any entanglement he could imagine between these two lines of evidence was willful to the point of insanity. Still, his work had taught him better than to believe in coincidence, either. That a hundred yards from the Hamilton Sweeney New Year's gala (as "Dr." Zig Zigler never tired of pointing out) she'd crossed paths with a random mugger—he'd stopped buying it a while ago. And it was manifestly not a serial killer, per the *Post*. Streaks of reflected light on the sliding door blotted out whatever was outside, but he could hear the wind-chimes rattling. The creak of stairs behind him. "Honey? How was the game?"

"Oh, fine. You know how I feel about the Yankees."

"Overdogs," Sherri said. "But what are you going to do?" Then she stood there in her nightgown. He couldn't figure out why until she said, "We've got a big day tomorrow. Are you coming to bed?"

AT A.M. MASS, he would struggle to be interested in the homily, as he would struggle on the way home after to be interested in the property descriptions Sherri was reading aloud from the classifieds. He could hear his own distracted monosyllables, yet felt no more able to improve upon them than if he were watching himself on closed-circuit TV. Sherri waited until they were passing through downtown Port Richmond, in sight of the New York skyline, to say, "I'm guessing you want me to drop you at the ferry?" Her smile might have been wry, triumphant, had he not known her well enough to see she was furious.

"I just need to go in for an hour or two, hon. I should have mentioned it, I know, but I'll be back by lunchtime, we can hit the road. Promise." At the ferry terminal, he leaned in to kiss her, but she turned so that his lips glanced off her hair.

THE ADDRESS ON THE CRUMPLED TICKET-STUB took him east of Bowery, to a neighborhood of old tenements and townhouses. It had been a rough enough area even back when Pulaski had only been a beat cop, but at least there'd been life on these streets. Now, for blocks, the only greenery was spindly ailanthus sprouting through the stoops. From broken upper windows, pigeons came and went on inscrutable errands. Other windows were boarded over. The summer sky was a blue beyond blue. The rowhouse itself looked uninhabited (though it had become hard to tell which, if any, of these houses were occupied; did a padlock mean someone lived there, or someone didn't?).

He made a halting circuit of the block, but any glimpse of the back of the building in question was blocked by others. He returned and knocked on the big windowless door, which to his surprise was steel, rather than wood. A few patches of green paint clung like graveyard moss. His hand, flattened against it, didn't look much better: splotches the color of coffee rings. He thought he smelled marijuana, but then, the whole Lower East Side smelled like marijuana.

Breaking in was an option. He tried to picture his misshapen shanks shimmying through a basement window. On one hand, he had no warrant, and if the Feds really had this place on their radar, he could get in big trouble for tipping off the occupants. On the other hand, what surer guarantee of an exit from the department than official misconduct? But perhaps Sherri was right. Perhaps he had no intention of making an exit.

He took up a vigil from the far side of the street, in the shadow of a lone tree. Bending to copy license-plate numbers into his notebook, he had an intuition he was being watched, but when he looked down toward the corner of the avenue, there was no one. And then, for a long time, no movement; the heat, merciless as a specimen jar, was making it seem there might never be movement again. Not to mention immersing him in sweat. The vague sense of crisis that had begun on the ferry last night, or at the ballpark, had never really subsided. He told himself he needed to cool down.

He followed the old streets west and north, to where there was likely a bodega. And there was still some life down here, it was true. Sleek golden kids who could have been anything from Puerto Rican to Egyptian prowled the sidewalks of Third Avenue, fighting and flirting, at ease in their bodies. A boy spritzed a girl's shirt with a can of seltzer. Hand-lettered signs crowded the window of the Gristedes: *HALF CHICKEN 89 CENT LIMIT FOUR PER OFFER CREAM-SICLE 12 PK 2-4-1!* He thumbed a dime into the cup of the junkie out front, reflecting that for a dollar he could have bought the guy half a chicken, and also that the guy probably didn't want half a chicken. No doubt his sense of being under observation was not the FBI, but his conscience, which now no longer wore the face of God, but that of Sherri.

At Astor Place, the grid opened up to admit prospects to the north and southwest. Here, too, were kids, but older and less innocent, mohawked and safety-pinned, with the stringy look of stray dogs.

Some had actual stray dogs. It was as if, Pulaski sometimes thought, the '60s had tipped the entire country on end and shaken it like a box of cereal until all the flakes ended up in the East Village. He wanted to ask them, Why do you keep coming here? Can't you see this city is dying?—but maybe underneath he was jealous of their freedom. And of course Samantha Cicciaro had been one of them, he'd seen from the photographs now filed neatly away at 1 Police Plaza. Around him men in African prints sold incense and sunglasses from long bingo tables. Drugs and money changed hands openly. He might as well have been invisible. He found a deli and bought a cold beer, keeping it in a paper bag. He was somewhat surprised at himself, but why not? This was what liberty was. There was no real law down here anymore.

He could no longer sit on a curb or a Siamese connection—his spine wouldn't permit it—but out front of St. Mark's in-the-Bowery were benches and some old big shade trees that had withstood the centuries. It had a tiny graveyard, too, one of a handful on the island, and he'd always found graveyards comforting, somehow. A city where we'd all dwell. He sat for a while imbibing tepid foam. With each sip, the world turned a degree, or a second. He'd really believed, apparently, that on this day, in his hour of need, God Almighty was going to swoop down and reveal what had happened back there to the Cicciaro kid, but maybe this was all he was going to get: a memory of his senior year in high school, when his father had driven him in from Passaic to see the V-J Day parade. Afterward, in a cool yeasty bar with sawdust on the floor, Dad had treated him to his first-ever foamer and said, "Don't tell your mother." Then they'd walked back to retrieve the car. Passing directly behind the spot where he now sat, not thirty feet away, his eighteen-year-old self had felt about as good as he'd ever felt in his life. Summer in New York City, with the clouds above going copper-colored and a Negro with a trumpet playing for pennies by the subway station, the shimmy of buses echoing up the fronts of high buildings, as if God were on a person-to-person call, saying, *This is where you belong.* He'd always assumed that it was this feeling that had led him here. But what if time worked the other way around? What if what his adolescent self had felt then was the ghost of his present one, sitting here on a sagging bench, beckoning him into his future? He wove his hands together and touched his forehead to them. He could almost feel his father's eyes on him, swimming with liquor. But when he turned to where the eyes were, it wasn't ghosts he saw. It was a carrot-topped teenager with a terrible haircut, staring in through the wrought-iron bars.

It was the purposeful way the kid looked away and drifted down the street that let Pulaski know he'd been watching. He reached for his crutches, but the boy was already half a block away. As Pulaski limped after him, the kid glanced back and began to run. Pulaski, too out-of-shape for pursuit, pursued anyway. The red head floated nearer, and despite the fact that the kid was at a near-sprint now, a design was visible. Pulaski crossed against the signal, looking no doubt like just another of the crazy people who haunted this place. If his hands had not been occupied with rubber grips, he could have reached out, could have grabbed . . .

Then the sky was swinging behind him and he was pried off his feet, undone by a crutch-tip in a sewer grate. Asphalt exploded against the side of his face. Tires screeched. Horns. A circle of faces appeared above him, peering down in concern. "Gracious, mister." "Are you all right?" Someone offered to get him water.

"I'm . . . all right," he said. But getting up seemed beyond him, and he could tell that stitches were in his future, and that he'd have to call Sherri to drive him home in his work car. He could feel himself already in the passenger's seat of the Fury, with a bruise that was going to hurt like hell, being borne away from this mysterious kid, and this moment when the world and the case—which by now were practically the same thing—had seemed so close to breaking open.

58

As SPEED APPROACHES INFINITY, time and space begin to skew, and what once seemed knowable divulges a deeper strangeness. Which helps explain why the awnings and building fronts Charlie is racing past now look so unfamiliar, and why the blocks are so much longer than he's used to. Where could he be? East Fifth? East Sixth? The street signs have all been painted over or stolen. Even the instinct behind his flight—that the neighborhood will enfold him, that he'll disappear here among the natives—reveals itself as a misconception. Old women in housedresses gawk at the crazed white boy streaking past their stoops, but at least they don't call the cops.

Then again, maybe they don't need to call the cops. The little cripple back there in the crosswalk obviously was one; Charlie had seen it, looking down into the guy's coplike face, just before he'd bolted again. And should he feel remorse for this, for not reaching out a hand? Other people had stopped to help. But that was liberal accommodationism, right? And who was to say the guy's crutches weren't a prop? Curiosity had been part of why he'd followed. Plus maybe if he could show that he'd actually picked up a few tricks on his surveillance runs, the PHP would see that their trust in Charlie was well-placed. That he was fully Post-Human after all.

Not that stealth was easy. The cripple's course had been fit-and-startful—a long pause at Cooper Square, while Charlie crouched

behind a parked car pretending to tie his shoe—and then into a deli
for a brown paper bag. Then they were backtracking, it seemed, to
that church on Second Ave., the one where Sam claimed to have seen
Patti Smith read "Piss Factory." There was no way for Charlie to
follow him into the fenced churchyard without giving himself away.
The man's posture on the bench among the graves was slumped,
defeated, almost like David Weisbarger's after a rough day at work.
Charlie tried to dismiss this as a trick designed to lull him into lowering his guard, but it must have worked, for in the second after the guy
turned and their eyes met through the bars, the only thing Charlie
could think of was to flee.

Now, the sirens he's braced for having failed to eventuate, he slows
to a walk. A blister has formed on his sockless left heel. This block is
a mystery, but at the end of it, pigeons circle, flashing, blind or indifferent to his lostness. Their order is the order of leaves whipped by
a helical breeze. Of kids determined to ride the Tilt-A-Whirl until
their money runs out. Or of something else Charlie's whacked-out
brain can't remember. He tells himself they have no message for him,
he's just happened to look up at their moment of peak agitation, but
they keep going round and round in urgent epilepsis, until he recognizes the trees beneath them as Tompkins Square Park. Somehow
he's run clear around it and is approaching from the river side. He
checks back to make sure no one's following and then uses the park
to orient himself toward . . . well, what? You couldn't quite call it a
home.

The little garage out back is unlocked, and he intrudes as far as
he dares if he doesn't want to get yelled at. A fan whirs on the other
side of the cinderblock divider, and when he clears his throat, loudly,
two figures appear from behind it with goggles on. They stare at him
through the safety glass, astronauts at an alien life-form. Then Sol
uses his good hand to push his mask up above what would have been
his eyebrows. His eyes are high, wild. The burnt hand's driving glove,
soaked in disinfectant nightly, gleams like a futuristic fashion statement. Otherwise he looks quite ill. "You scared the shit out of us."

"It was unlocked," says Charlie, lamely.

"We thought you were COINTELPRO or some shit."

"I don't even know what that means," Charlie says. "But listen, I
saw someone out front, watching. I tailed him." At this, Nicky's own
goggles go up. Charlie puts his hands on his knees to help him catch

his breath. That smell. Like a dentist's drill. "It was maybe an hour ago, I had just gone out to . . . uh, get a muffin, and I saw this little crippled guy with a moustache watching the house from across the street, like casing it, honest, I swear. So I followed him."

"And?" Nicky's face is covered in sweat and missing its chipped smile. This is the moment when Charlie realizes he's not going to tell them how it really turned out.

"He was pretty slick. He lost me."

"It could have been the reporter guy," Solomon says to Nicky, who momentarily blanches.

"Obviously it couldn't have been the reporter, Sol. Don't you read the paper?"

Another thing Charlie's not going to do: he's not going to beg them anymore to explain themselves. "I thought if I saw something I was supposed to . . ."

"You did right," Nicky says, "to bring us these concerns, and I'm going to think on this real hard, I promise. But it's kind of the critical juncture here, Prophet. Would you mind?"

Sol has already pulled his goggles back down to return to his work, and after shooting Charlie a meaningful look, Nicky joins him behind the concrete shield or barrier. The fan, wedged into a window, stutters the light like a nickelodeon. Despite which, Charlie seems doomed to stumble around in the dark, clutching pieces of a puzzle he still can't see.

THAT NIGHT, when he returns from drying his clothes—they sat in the coin-op washer around the corner for hours before he remembered, but were apparently still gross enough no one wanted to steal them—it's like old times again. The doors have been thrown open, figuratively speaking, and on the floor of the denuded parlor, the grad students eat rubbery pizza straight from the box. They recognize Charlie now as one of the chosen ones, and nod at him as he picks his way through with his knapsack of laundry. At first, he thinks the Post-Humanists are partying for the benefit of whoever might be watching. A diversion-cum-alibi: nothing to see here, Officer; just kids having a good time. But then from the kitchen floats the scent of Sewer Girl's pot brownies, which isn't what you'd serve if you thought there were cops nearby. He's sampled these brownies once before, but this time she's made them special for him, remembering his asthma.

"What's the occasion, though?" he says, around a mouthful of acrid chocolate. "Is it somebody's birthday?"

She spins him by the shoulders until he's facing the doorway he's just come through. Above it, someone's spraypainted on the wall *Two Sevens Clash!* attended by winged iterations of the PHP logo. Of course, he thinks. July 7. 7/7/77. "It's like our last hurrah," she says, as he reaches for another brownie, hoping it will cover over the pit opening in his stomach, "now that the timing problems have been worked out. Well, actually, Nicky says getting another meeting set up may still take a week. Tonight would have been perfect synchronicity, but, you know . . . *laissez les bons temps rouler.*"

Out in the parlor, swollen green jugs of wine are going hand-to-hand around a circle, and Charlie, already stoned and seeking further refuge, drinks twice his share. No one seems to notice when he dribbles some down his chin. Even Charlie himself hardly notices. This shirt, now on its fourth consecutive day of wear, smells like bad bologna or steak gone blue on its surface, so the spreading stain is at best a remote concern. As is the conversation. There are ten or twelve people, mostly boys, thrice as many as have ever comprised Post-Humanism proper, and the stereo that is the room's only remaining equipment is wailing reggae. The words spoken over it decay into a tone-poem:

> *I know Hegel says somewhere . . .*
> > *. . . wants to see ID, I'm like, motherfucker, I'm trying to get ID . . .*
> *. . . stumblebum was too drunk to even play . . .*
> > *. . . missing a piece off the . . .*
> > *. . . stencil it on the . . .*
> *. . . why do I need ID? Nobody checks those things, anyway.*

Nicky sits unusually quiet in a corner, licking pizza grease from the side of a pinky, the only person with enough distance to make sense out of what everybody's saying. *I can see with my own eyes,* goes the singer of this album he loves so much, *It's a scheme that divides.* Charlie is convinced for a second that Nicky has orchestrated *everything* this way, kept them all in their separate compartments. And for just the smallest subslice of that second he wonders if he's content to be on the receiving end of Nicky's benevolent administration. (And if this would really constitute freedom. (And like, what's the difference between that and liberation? (And is true freedom even possible? (And all kinds of stuff like that, the pot has screwed up time again and his thoughts are slo-mo billiard balls.)))) But then Nicky catches him looking down and takes a long swig from a passing jug and says to D. Tremens, "Turn the music down. We're forgetting something."

"What is it?" Charlie can't keep himself from asking.

"Well, if this is really going to be our Last Supper, don't you think somebody should bless it? Or what good was all your Bible study for? Invoke for us, Prophet."

The request catches him off guard, like a pop quiz. Like being shoved out onto a spotlit highwire above a crowd that didn't realize you had any training. He's not even sure what Nicky means by "invoke." Does he want a confession? A renunciation? Or more characteristically, a plundering of someone else's language for his own ends? Would it be cheating to just read something aloud? This is a moot point; he's hidden the Bible in his laundry pile in the attic, along with the camera he decided to take from Sol after all. Charlie rises, sees he's the second-tallest person in the room. To cover his embarrassment, he lowers his head, looks at his feet. He thinks about begging off entirely—indeed, maybe that's what he's being pushed to do—but it seems equally possible that backing down would be the only way to fail the test. A snatch of Scripture, read over and over after the shooting, flutters around inside his skull: *The Lord, your God, is in your midst, a warrior who gives victory.* It's got the militant note Nicky likes; even D. Tremens would approve. And then what was the next bit? *He has come to overturn. Ye Ethiopians also*—Nope, not really germane, reggae or no reggae. What else, what else. Uh . . . the flocks will lie down and the cormorant will sing in the window, for, uh . . . No, wait. Here is something. *Woe.*

"Woe to her that is filthy and polluted," he hears himself say to the now-quiet room. "To the oppressing city." And when no one responds, more lines come mysteriously back. "The city that dwelt carelessly and said, *I am:* how she is become a desolation! But fear not." Fear not! Yes! They always say that, that's essential. But how to get around the embarrassing stuff about Hashem? Well, what about this? "On the day of festival, there will be exultation and loud singing," he says.

𝔇isaster will be removed from you, so you will not bear reproach from it. 𝔄ll your oppressors will be dealt with at that time. 𝔄nd the lame will be saved and the outcast gathered, and their shame will be changed into praise and renown in all the earth. 𝔄t that time you will be brought home.

At first, when he looks up, there's only more silence. Then Nicky starts to clap, slowly—"Right on, Prophet"—and then Sewer Girl, and a couple of the outsiders, and even feverish Sol Grungy, it seems, with his maimed appendage. "Pro-phet! Pro-phet!" the novices chant. A wave of noise you wouldn't even know was a goof, if you couldn't see their faces. But inside, Charlie feels unsteady again. Menaced, somehow, by his flock. Maybe it's the drugs, but this wasn't supposed to be ironic, it was supposed to be about sanctifying what they were doing. He excuses himself and goes upstairs to take a pill and lie down.

LATER, Sewer Girl will appear alone at the head of the attic stairs. Her bikini top is already off, is what makes him feel like he's dreaming. In the moonlight through the ceiling's trapdoor, her tits look like soft blue balloons. The nipples are bigger than he imagined. Even her bellybutton screams sex—an inny, a shadowy ellipse. Before he can ask what she's doing, she has crossed the room, and is reaching for his beltbuckle. He's afraid if she sees him without his clothes on, she might not want to. But she already has his jeans around his ankles, and one hand is foraging matter-of-factly in his briefs, as though reaching into a bowl for a goldfish. With her free hand, she moves his hands to those tits and shakes her hair to one side, and then her mouth is on his and they are falling back onto the mattress.

How often and in what infinite varieties has he imagined this moment? But something is off. "Wait," he says, gasping, and gropes among clothes for his inhaler. Takes a big hit.

S.G. looks at him with an expression he can't quite see, her own breath coming steady. "What is it?"

"I can't do this."

"Why? Don't you like me, Charlie?"

"Of course I like you. But . . ." He's sitting up now, peering into the dark, the blanket of his moldy bedroll covering his exposed lower half. "But it's loyalty, you know?"

She stares at him for a minute. Then she starts laughing. "Oh, Charlie, is this about me and Sol?"

"I thought you were with Nicky now."

"Who do you think sent me up here?"

"Nicky *sent* you? Well, that's just great. I thought *you* liked *me*."

"No, that didn't come out right." Her voice softens. "Listen, that stuff you said earlier, Charlie, the reproach and the shame . . . You were right. I could just feel it shifting even as you talked. Like something being lifted. I wanted to find a way to say thank you, and Nicky said this would be cool. Said he hopes you see now you're tougher than you think." She runs her fingers through his hair like a mom, and he can feel himself recoiling, irritated.

"What about Sol? Your boyfriend? Does he know about this?"

"Well, does Sam? Or is she not your one and only anymore?"

"Who do you think I'm being loyal to?"

"Charlie . . ." She reaches under the covers for his crotch, but he rolls away to face the wall, burning like a furnace in the night. Sewer Girl lies behind him, not touching him, and will stay like that for a long time. She's not all bad. Her slave name, she told him once, was Jain, with an *i*. But when the morning comes, she'll be gone from his side, as everyone always is, which seems to suggest that it's not so much insecurity that plagues him as foresight.

HE MUST NOT BE TOTALLY RESOLVED, though, because when a week passes without anything further happening, he both is and isn't disappointed. Mostly, he feels on his own again. The twelfth of July's supposed to be when Sam's film is ready for pickup, and that morning he goes over to the camera store. In exchange for his last worldly dollars and some pocket-change, they hand him a red cardboard sleeve of single prints, three-and-a-half by five, the cheapest. For some reason, though, he can't bring himself to open it. If the pictures are Sam's, they're all he has left of her, and once he looks at them, consumes them, she really will be gone.

He returns to the Phalanstery to find Nicky waiting. There's one last job needs doing, he says, a two-man action; he wants to know if Charlie's up to it. Charlie slips the photo sleeve into a pocket, hoping Nicky won't ask about it, and half out of guilt says, *Why wouldn't I be up to it?* How much damage can two people do, after all?

Soon they are barreling uptown with the windows down and the radio up full blast, the empty rear compartment thunking every time they hit one of Sixth Avenue's savage potholes, a legal-sized mailer sliding from side to side on the dash. He's riding shotgun again, for the first time in months. Not Sol, not D. Tremens, but him, Charlie Weisbarger. Or *McCoy*, if you're going by the name on his uniform. Perhaps, he thinks, this could even be the time to ask Nicky about Operation Demon Brother. But when he does, Nicky just touches the envelope and smiles. "We'll post the invitation on our way back."

They narrowly miss the meter they park at. Charlie plugs a nickel in and Nicky checks the diver's watch he sometimes wears, now that the van has no clock. Then he hands Charlie an army-surplus backpack that feels like it's full of groceries. "What's in here?"

"Awful curious today, aren't we, Charles?" Nicky takes from the backpack another pair of coveralls and pulls them on over his jeans. No one passing pays him any mind. Someone has scrubbed *PUSSY-WAGON* from the side of the van, so that it once again looks like a window-washer's, Charlie sees, and now Nicky, too, has the uniform to match, although it's Sol's old one, and consequently several sizes too large. *Greenberg* is stitched across the pocket. Wait a minute. Is *Sol* Jewish? To ask, though, would be to prove Nicky right.

He follows Nicky down to Twenty-Third Street, a broad confluent of traffic. The huge apartment house on the corner has a construction scaffold running around it between the first and second stories, a plywood catwalk with waist-high walls. Half the buildings in the city have these things, yet nothing ever seems to get finished. The shadows beneath are cool. "You first," says Nicky, nodding at the metal struts. This seems to run counter to the incognito vibe; it's rare to see workmen actually working on anything. But probably Charlie could start screaming he was being murdered, and no one would bother to pay attention.

He gets stuck four feet off the ground, clinging to the crossed X braces. It's about as high as he can free-climb before his acrophobia kicks in. Nicky is looking tensely around. "Go on," he hisses. "Pull yourself up." Charlie reaches up, up, and grasps the edge of the plywood. Most likely, his arms will give out first, the same skinny chicken arms that were his undoing when it was time to climb the rope in gym class. At some point, though, fear of being caught overpowers his fear of heights, and maybe yields an adrenaline rush, for here he is wriggling over the lip and flopping onto the catwalk, one flight up, hidden from view.

In seconds, Nicky is beside him, on his back. They are staring up at a sky raveled with cumulus but otherwise a superheated blue. It seems to be not the clouds but the buildings that are moving, swooning, waiting to fall. Then Nicky is telling him to sit up a little, not to crush the backpack. From it, he draws a thin strip of metal. Charlie watches him work its silver length between the sashes of the nearest window. The meaning of a term that has never made sense snaps into focus: cat burglar. It has that kind of quickness. One moment, Nicky is here; the next, Charlie is alone.

There must be at least a hundred windows above and on the other side of the street. He says a little prayer, that none of the people who live or work behind them will look down to where he lies. Of course, if he could just act like he belonged here, no one would think twice, but Charlie Weisbarger has never, at least since his brothers were born, known what belonging felt like. Instead, he's always afraid that this world that envelops him—the ordinary music of street life below, the oily burn of nuts roasting on a cart—will at any moment be snatched away. And that there will be no other. The truth is, when you get right down to it, the Prophet Charlie is a moist, gaping wuss. His fears are a rock so large God Himself couldn't lift it. Which means, of course, that he is unworthy of mercy. He rolls so that he is stretched out along the foot-high lip of plywood and wedges himself as tightly as possible into what should be its shadow, were the sun not beating down like a spotlight from a prison wall. When he looks back to where he was lying, he notices the red envelope of photographs from his pocket. It has ripped open on a staple or something, and a stack of pictures has started to slide out.

They are of burnt buildings, glassless windows, scorch-marks on walls, he sees, but never, for some reason, of the PHP, or of the fires themselves. In one picture, an ambulance streaks past a sporting-goods store and a sidewalk blurred by smoke—unless it's the frame itself that's blurred. The lens has been jostled. Flicking forward, he can hear Sam's voice, bell-clear and hoarse, calling to him from somewhere as near as the back of his own head: *Wake up, Charlie.* The last shot is of a basement. Deep focus, early light. Sam naked on a rumpled mattress, startled, the sheets pulled off. This would seem to expose something about her and the person taking the picture, a tattooed action figure in the mirror, but who it really exposes is Charlie. Nicky was fucking her, too. What else has he refused to see? *Wake up*, she says again, as Nicky comes clambering back out the window. In his hand is one of those glow-in-the-dark alarm clocks. "Couldn't find what I was looking for," he says. "But you can't have too many of these."

His forehead is slick with sweat, and he's already moving toward the edge of the scaffolding when Charlie grabs his arm. Holds out the photograph. "Do you want to tell me what this is?"

For a split-second, Nicky winces. "It's time to drop the dumb act, Prophet. It doesn't suit you." Then, in a blink, he's snatched the stack of photos and shoved it into his own pocket. "All right. Let's get out of here."

A rustle draws Charlie's eye back to the apartment's open window. The thing he's been smelling, he realizes, is smoke. "Is something burning?"

"We don't have time for this, Charles. Either what we're after's in there, or it's not, and now it won't matter either way."

Charlie kneels by the sill. There's a sad-looking lily in a pot, and, touchingly, a workout book on the coffeetable. A yapping can be heard from behind the door. "Hey, Nicky? There's a dog in here."

"Sometimes you've got to break a few eggs."

Come on, wake up. But to what? To the fact that instead of some kind of heroes, they are just punks. He thinks of Sam in that bed. Of Sam training her lens on that sidewalk, as if to send him a signal. In a blacked-out house, stripped of all comforts, it's easy to turn your anger outward, to attack this city he's lying at the center of, with its filth and its pollution and its oppression, but really, New York is the only thing that's never abandoned him. He says, "You were lying, weren't you."

"What?"

"All this time, you haven't given two shits about consequences. You never cared who got hurt."

When he turns, Nicky has one leg over the side of the plywood. "Charlie, I swear to God, if you go in there, I'll leave you." But Nicky's already done that, hasn't he? Left him out here tied to that rock. A breeze gusts the curtains, feeds the fire; Charlie's face is a pillow, hot on one side. Nicky's eyes are hard black briquettes. His handyman disguise makes him look like the stranger he in point of fact is. "I'm going to count to three. One."

The dog is barking its head off now, someone is going to hear, and the flames are sweeping from the mound of papers in the kitchen sink toward the window.

"Two."

Why doesn't the smoke alarm start beeping? he wonders. Because Nicky has disabled it, obviously. The fumes make his eyes water. "You know why you're going to end up in hell, Nicky? There's no love in your heart." And before Nicky can answer—because he doesn't need to answer—Charlie is diving headfirst through the window-frame, following a dog's voice into the hungrier heart of the fire.

LAND OF 1,000 DANCES

25 ¢

beg
borrow
steal

THIS ISSUE:

REVIEWS OF CHEAP STUFF

ANARCHY, REBELLION, TEENAGE ANGST

MORE WAYS TO SCREW THE MAN

WELCOME TO BEAUTIFUL NYC

GRAFFITI (SP?)

BOMB THE SUBURBS

PLUS: POST HUMANISM: WHAT IS IT??

PUNK RAWK!

TYPOS!

LENORA'S LUNCHEONETTE

YOU WANT THIS

MORE POINTLESS RAMBLING YOU DON'T CARE ABOUT

issue 3

sept, 76

HELLO
my name is

geek

this issue dedicated to k,
For the "passageway"
+ to c, wherever he may be

A NOTE FROM YR EDITOR[1]

high school, irving place, 1976 ... graduation's still 73 days
away, but college acceptance letters have already started to
appear.[2] the headmaster sez no one's supposed to bring them
to school, but you can see kids at their lockers letting fat
envelopes fall to the floor. dartmouth, smith, williams - oops,
did i drop that? still, the truth is, if you want to name the
vibe turning the laughter brittle between periods, it's fear.
here we are in this paradise for conformity-seeking youth,
with its hierarchies and pieties, + the thought of losing it
is causing this huge reactionary spasm. i've been keeping my
nose-ring[3] in lately, e.g., instead of taking it out on the
train, 'cause frankly i just don't care anymore, but so then
i'm doing my conscientious-objector bit at gym yesterday + this
senior girl comes up to me, "hey, samantha, you've got something
hanging out of your nose" + i'm like, good luck at princeton
next year with the frat boys or field-hockey or whatever it
is you do to distract yourself from your pathetic life. See,
reader, amerikan high school is above all about safety:::::the
safety you get when you renounce freedom. irony being that
yr correspondent, who is no-shit desperate to get out, has so
far only gotten 2 envelopes, both skinny, both thanks but no
thanks. my dad's big dream was that I'd get in somewhere out of
state + escape the ancestral folkways of the cicciaros (not to
mention of my mom). but to be honest i didn't exactly bend over
backward trying to impress the admissions committees in boston,
because seriously ... boston? so these days after school instead

of bumming around with sg i find myself racing back to lawn guyland to see if in my mailbox waits the envelope that makes it official – the one from columbia or at least nyu (which apparently admits everyone). it doesn't happen + doesn't happen, but i tell myself it will. i'll be living at last for real in this city i see when my eyes shut at night. Around me now in calc goony girls are trying to get mrs. boswell to turn from the board + catch me drafting this instead of crunching antiderivatives. it may be true i'm only half paying attention, but this much has sunk in: from any point, line, or curve, it is possible to move up one order of abstraction. like, say i am a point. time is a line. the rate at which the passage of time changes is a curve. The antiderivative of that curve would be, what? the rate at which the acceleration of the future toward the present accelerates. and so i am a changed change whose change is changing, + what follows will be a document. + if you can't keep up with me, kiddies, well, too tough for you.

p. 3

1. actually, who am i kidding? it's just me here, editor, writer, designer, so send me some stuff – reviews, essays, poems, whatever. okay? okay.

2. just goes to show what kind of sadists are running the education system in this country.

3. See issue 2.

l.o.t.d.
c/o Sam Cicciaro
2358 outer bridge
flower hill, ny
11576

table of contents

YOU'RE MY SISTER AND I LOVE YOU VERY MUCH...BUT YOU HAVE AN EVIL LITTLE MIND!

L.E.S.
CONFIDENTIAL

THE POSITIVELY TRUE ACCOUNT OF ONE GIRL'S ADVENTURES
IN THE GHETTO WITH A NIKKORMAT, A HOLE IN ONE SHOE,
AND HEAVY CONCEPTS LIKE SOLIDARITY

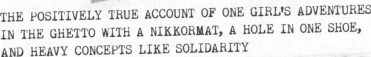

We were somewhere east of Bowery when the drugs began to
take hold ... the drugs, in my case, being a couple clove
cigarettes, the Bayer headache powder I was using to fight
off last night's hangover, and a pinner SG had found in one
of the pockets of her coat. Tame, perhaps, but I wanted my
head on straight. Despite talking a good game whenever my dad
grumbled about the Welfare State, I had never actually been
in a housing project before and was a little nervous, plus I
secretly hoped I might get something out of that afternoon's
exploits I could use for my senior Art project. Still, what SG
was smoking must have been uncharacteristically good stuff,
'cause against the dead sky further east where the numbers
start to turn to letters the cabs rolling past were suddenly
an exquisite yellow. Headlights like drops of milk in the
weak tea of the day. Cabs all aimed our way. In flight.

SG had actually been waiting for me even before school
let out - I'd seen her out the classroom window a half-hour
before the last bell, leaning up against the metal fence of
the building across the street in that mangy fake-fur of
hers, and in the second before I steeled myself and became
punk again her eagerness had almost embarrassed me. (Then
again, maybe it wasn't eagerness but boredom. Her classes at
NYU must not ask too much of her, because she never seems to
be in them.)

In any case, I went to the bathroom and unhooked the
crank from the window sash. Put back in my nose-ring. Climbed
on the radiator and lowered my legs through the window and
dropped six feet to the frozen flowerbeds out front. Some
moms waiting to pick up their middle-schoolers looked at me
like I might apologize or something, but I just put on my big
sunglasses and blew past them like butter wouldn't melt, and

we were on our way. SG's boyfriend Sol was coming from a
paying gig at a building in midtown and was going to meet us
on the L.E.S., where they had something they wanted to show
me. Make sure you bring your camera, they said.

I now think the housing project was in fact _his_. Sol's,
I mean. I knew already he'd grown up poor (there had been
a big splat of jealousy underneath all the grief he gave
me when he'd found out I was from Flower Hill, to which I
would have said, it's nothing to be jealous of) and whenever
I hinted around about needing a place to crash, he and SG
were both so vague about where they went at night after
shows that I'd come to suspect they were sleeping part-time
in that van of his. At the very least, Sol moved through
the project plaza like someone who _belonged_. To me, it was
a little intimidating. I want to think I'm open-minded, but
there were all these black and Puerto Rican guys sitting
on their different benches out front, staring or pointedly
not staring at us, at the white girls, but Sol just walked
right by and no one said anything. I guess the two SGs look
pretty heavy together. I guess that's part of the point of the
razored hair & safety pins. And I felt proud of my friends,
and then of myself, too. This wasn't private-school America,
suburb America. This was real.

The elevator inside was out of order. The stairwells
smelled like pee and went on forever. Up on the roof was a
couple making out on an old mattress, but we just pretended
not to see them and vice versa. Then we came around the side
of the monster air-conditioning unit and there it was on
the brick, in white, yellow, & blue (which you'd see in these
photos if I could reproduce in color):

POSTHUMANS LIVE!

SG knew I was into graffiti, I guess, because ever since we'd
been hanging out she'd seen me snapping pictures of it. We'd
be trolling the bins at Señor Wax and I'd see a panel truck
rattle by with a great big burner on the side, bright as an
elicit sun, and I'd be out the door to take the picture. Tags
on postboxes, throw-ups on phone-booths, bombs on buses, plus
the whole amazing front of the Vault on Bowery. Back in the
fall, when I began to really notice the spraypaint spreading

all over everything, I kept having this fear for some reason
it was going to disappear just as quickly, like a Polaroid in
reverse, and so I wanted a document, some proof that for a hot
minute life and art had come close enough to touch. Now it
occurs to me that this can be partly a way of turning yourself
into a bystander. But then again if I had a tag it would have
to be like SAM HEMPSTEAD PIKE or something, and I don't trust
my body not to fuck up anything bigger than Sharpie-ing the
stalls at school.

Maybe this was why
it surprised me that
Sol could have done the
big blow-up before us
now. It wasn't the most
technically accomplished
graffiti you'd see. If you
paid attention, as I did
in the darkroom, pulling
the photos I'd taken from
their chemical baths,
you started to see there
was actually a whole
lovely graff esthetic,
which this didn't have,
exactly. But what it
lacked in style it made
up for in size, and he
had this grin on his
face like a hunting dog
who'd dropped a rabbit
at my feet. "Posthumans,"
I said. "Is that like
'posthumous?'"

He said he'd got
the word from a buddy
of his. "It's a thing he
says about us punks.

We're post-Human." It sounded so kind of atypically
philosophical or something that I couldn't not tease him.
"The buddy SG keeps talking about, you mean. The mystery
man who broke up Ex Post Facto and now can't show his
face at shows."

But this is something I have to be careful about, this teasing reflex, because for a second Sol's sour and safety-pinned visage kind of crumpled and I saw it meant something more or different to him than I'd been led to believe, and SG looked like she could have thrown me off the roof. Or one of us, anyway. It was the moment of maximum separation, like I was still stuck back in the suburbs of the heart with walls and windows and inhibitions and fears between me and the city. And I didn't know what else to do so I backed up and crouched down and started snapping pictures. Already the piece was starting to look more impressive. It wasn't meant, really, to be judged up close; from back near the fenced edge of the roof, I could see how you'd be able to see it from down below, where there was now traffic coming toward us, too, headlights crawling along the FDR toward Brooklyn. And here was Sol, this wage-slave punk kid, who had actually thought to <u>do something</u>. It was wicked cool, I said finally, realizing that was what he'd wanted all along.

After that we bought some 40s of malt liquor out of solidarity and sat on the benches out front for a while getting drunk and talking too loud, but people weren't exactly understanding the gesture. DT had met up with us and brought 'ludes, so we ended up going to the handball court to get 'luded and watch Chinese kids play handball as it got dark. But just before it did - just before the lines between us dissolved and we melted into a puddle - I remember thinking how it was funny we still required chemicals to make this happen. In all those months since SG and I had discovered our NYU connection (her enrolled, me applying) and had started hanging out, I had never been quite sure whether I was trying to convince her and her friends I was tough enough to be one of them, or whether they were trying to prove to me they were worth the effort. Which just goes to show, I think, that the United States of Punk Rock is an ideal and not a birthright. We're all still working to perfect it. Then the 'ludes hit, with the violent sky and the soft pock of handballs and the laughter bubbling in our blood and the city rising all around us, and that's exactly what it felt like we were: perfect.

WELCOME TO THE BEAUTIFUL
VILLAGE

the coolest place!

we dedicate this issue's travel section to hangouts below 14th street, with gratitude for helping us survive senior year.

1. señor wax

is there an actual señor wax? if so i've never seen him. instead you've got the staff perpetually trying to hit on you. still, for the most up-to-the-minute in wrawk & roll, el señor is the establishment for you. + not just cuz it's the only joint in town disreputable enough to stock this rag you're now reading . . .

2. second ave salvation army

if you're willing to brave fleas, you'd be amazed at the funky shit you can find for under a dollar. (caveat emptor: all pants appear to have been tailored for someone four feet tall + 325 lbs)

3. subway tunnels

mob up with yr droogs at one end of the platform. then have one or two of you slip past while the rest stay behind so the transit cops don't notice. rats, third rail, layers of subway soot, + trains mean you have to be careful, but it's like a museum of graff down there. thousands of years from now, future humans or posthumans will move in groups led by docents with little purple hats. here we have a genuine TAKI.

4. sex shops

by far the finest people-watching is to be done outside the sex shops west of 7th avenue, cuz you'd just be amazed who you see going in to buy dildos.

5. overlooked park at bleecker & sixth

one of my favorites. mostly junkies, old people, and so many pigeons (you'll want to check the trees before you choose a bench), but cathedral-quiet, not counting the traffic, which just turns to a kind of oceany wash. it's true that it can be fun to sit in a park banging on trashcans with sticks + do chants + just generally wig people out, but i never bring the droogs to this one. a great place to take a book you've just bought from . . .

6. mcaleery + adamson (one block north of st. mark's place)

this basement bookshop is hard to find (there's no sign) and smells like the bowl of an old pipe and the staff is so basically offended that you think yourself worthy to shop there they can make you cry. all of which i find weirdly comforting. this is what happens to people when they spend their entire life inside books + never come out: real life starts to grate by comparison.

l.o.t.d. salutes: lenora's

That this "luncheonette" stays open 24/7 is but one reason to love it. Consider also:

- bottomless cups of coffee

- a ~~malieu~~ melieu of grad students, shut-ins, dockworkers, drunk oldsters who like it when you make faces with them, etc.

- the waitstaff: would you like a side of 'tude with that egg cream?

- bialys sold here

and you get to meet the weirdest people! liike i'm in there with sg and we start talking to these folks in this picture and the guy says to us, "i'm about as stable as a bottle of nitroglycerin" and i say, "why is that? does it tip over easy or something?" and he says, "naw, ya just get a drop of that shit and it goes [neat descending whistle noise] ... POW!" yeah, man, on all night.

hunger artists / voidoids @ cbgb, 26 jan.

there's been some rumblings in the so-called alternative press
about what a revellation it is to have some female faces on the scene,
but that's pretty condescending if you think about it. fact is: hunger
artists have one of the sickest sounds around + have been tearing up
the local circuit ever since their "deface the music" 7 inch. a transcendent
gig at american legion post 719 last fall showed that noli mettanger
can go toe to toe not only w/ debbie harry but w/ almost any singer
on the planet. tonight was comparatively just excellent. for me the
big discovery was opener the voidoids led by bad boy richard hell
(ex-television). rumor is there's going to be an east-coast mini-tour,
so if they're in yr town, definately check them out

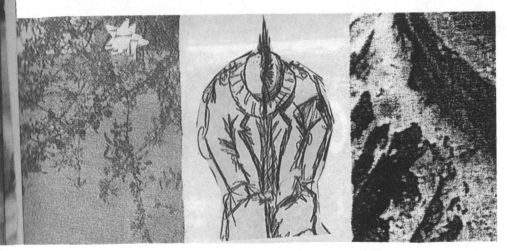

heartbreakers / some band i can't remember @ the underground, 20 feb.

okay, can i say something? it is possible to take heroin chic too far.
johnny thunders used to be so beautiful, but even with the fucked exposure
on the picture i took of him at this show, he looks like fucking keith richard.
'chinese rock' is breathtaking, but don't get high on your own supply, you know?
as for the band i can't remember ... what can i say? students at R/SD,
i think someone mentioned, so possibly going somewhere, or nowhere. more
memorable by far was dt + sol raising hell down on st. mark's before
the show + causing scenes in the narrow aisles of stupid boutiques. then
outside one sol pulls from his pocket this dog-collar necklace i'd been eyeing.
i expropriated it for you, he said. which was heavy lingo for boosted,
dt said; sol had picked up the fancy word from their friend nc, tho i often
wonder if this nc of theirs is like imaginary, as i have yet to meet him.

showed up at this one expecting music + got poetry instead,
but it's patti, so who really gives? i mean i swear when that
voice of hers got all hetted up + was bouncing all around
filling the ceilings of this little church you could hear jet engines,
you could hear guitars + whole drum corps + probably even
atheists walked out feeling a little closer to god. a real scene,
too, this one, with like a million billion people + everyone loitering
around outside afterward kvetching about how she was better
two years ago reading on the rooftop of so + so's apartment,
back before warner brothers + lenny kaye, before anyone knew about
her. this kvetching, by the way, is how you know patti is really
the real deal, + i've taken it almost verbatim from these three
dissertationist types i saw passing a j. among the graves.
    i went to take a picture of them — a perfect decisive
moment with this lightpost leaning over them at a
crazy angle — but they're all hey hey hey hey + crowding
around like, what am i, some kind of pig? paranoid
as hell. + then sol, who i didn't even know was in
attendance, comes crashing through the crowd w/ sg +
dt in tow + dt's like, "is there a problem?"
i smell violence + everybody else can,
too. my man bullet, this hell's angel
who usually works the door at the
vault, has been brought in by patti's
management or whatever as security
+ i can see him like moving through the
crowd, skinny bodies flying out of the
way like bowling pins + it's sol he's
coming for, who looks like the instigator.
hey, it's cool, i tell sol + to prove
i'm not a narc + defuse the tension
+ keep sol from getting stomped +
say fuck you all at once, i grab the
dissertationists' joint + suck down the
whole thing in a single go, a real lung-
buster. sol doesn't know how to behave
around women, as evidenced by the fact that
he doesn't even like patti. then again, if he
doesn't like patti, what's he doing here in the
first place?

FIGHT IN A PARKING LOT

a boy spinning donuts
in the snow in his boss's van
around and around till it's slicked
a thick black oily slick

and two men coming out
of a lit box nearby,
saying hey and hey
and just hey what the fuck
do you think you're doing

and the girl up on the slick top
of a dumpster, watching,
as the one stomps the shit
out of the two, doesn't like
how the kicks keep on coming
when you're down

doesn't like this brakelight, hey,
this exhaust, hey, this hanging open
of this door in this snow,
but then again, she's never been
on the winning side of anything,
and hey honestly, who's to say
who doesn't have it coming?

anarchy \ann-ar-KEY\ [[ML *anarchia*, fr. Gk. fr. *anarchos*, having no ruler, fr. *an* + *archos* ruler] 1a. a utopian society made up of individuals who have no government and who enjoy complete freedom.] *

a very real danger

THE ESSAY PAGE
-mostly political-

Everybody seems to be talking about it these days, from "Anarchy in the U.K." to "Up Against The Wall, Motherfuckers." You go to the Vault on your average Friday night, you'll see at least three kids in identically abused white tee-shirts with the circled capital-A inked on the front. Hell, I'll probably be one of them. Because this whole punk thing in some sense is about liberation. But then when I looked up the definition above and really meditated on it, I started to see this tension I at first couldn't think my way out of. On one hand: Complete freedom. Freedom to be who I want. Express myself as I want. Live where I want. Make what I want. Tune in the music I want on my radio. But also, if I want, to take your radio, deprive you of your own music. Your utopia. This looks at first like a junior-grade objection; you just insert into your anarchist constitution or whatever that the boundary line of freedom is wherever it starts to impinge on the freedom of others. But take a slightly more complicated case. Say I'm married to a person I don't love. Or whatever is the anarchist equivalent of married. Say we have a kid. It is my right - right? - to free myself from that and just go. But if I do, I'm hurting my kid. Or if I take the kid, I'm hurting my husband. But if I choose not to hurt either of them, they're in a sense hurting me. Impingement, in other words, is all around, and this freedom business is much messier than it looks at first blush.

One possible way of squaring the circle, it seems to me, has to do with that other part of the above definition, "made up of individuals." I wonder what would happen if we started to think in units larger than that. As if the collective weren't something that came after the individual, but the thing that comes before. That makes the individual possible. What if we could just define "enjoy complete freedom" in a more collective way? Is this even possible? I don't know, but the current alternative does seem to suggest that the imperialism of the self has infected even this little scene of ours. I urge my fellow tee-shirt wearers to start thinking about this stuff, seriously, because the thing we're building together will ultimately only survive - maybe we only will ourselves - if we can get beyond these screaming me-me's. This I I I.

4.2.76

straight home after school. it's eight o'clock now + the sorcerer is still in his workshop, so it's looking like tv dinners again.

1.4.76

oatmeal for the fifteenth morning in a row today + dad forgot to put in sugar. when, i turned my guitar up to 10 + tried to teach myself cretin hop he didn't even complain. still depressed over losing the contracts.

1.10.76 saturday, but not going into the city. sit around + get fucked up + pretend not to be lonely: i can do that by myself + save train-fare.

5.6.76

weirdest thing happens today. i'm hanging out at señor wax, trying to get sol + dt to sit still for pictures, when skulking by the window is this kid i know from out in flower hill. weirder: this is the second time in a month; i'm not sure i would have spotted him otherwise. i decide the universe is trying to tell me something, + anyway, i need an out, so i ditch sol + dt, + act like we're dear old chums + take him to señora s for cawfee. also weird: it felt like we were dear old chums. a long island of the mind, maybe. said we should hang out. he said, on the island? no, no, sez i; the island is a depression. lel me show you the city. my city.

5.9.76

what did i remember about c from that day on the ballfield? carrot-top, that's it. but he turns out to be maybe the funniest person i've ever known. i don't think he even realizes it, but i can hardly look at him without cracking up. his long stringy goofiness. tonight we rap on the phone for 40 minutes about nothing, not philosophical "nothing," but just ... nothing much. maybe i was meant to have a little brother.

6.7.76

For a week they'd been rehearsing us, as if it were any great complication to walk up to the riser + take the diploma as it was handed to us. underneath the robe i wore jeans + my TV tee, + at the last minute, too late for the graduation adviser to notice, i left the nose-ring in. they were going to graduate the real me or no one. from the doorway to the gym, i'd scoped out where my dad was sitting, but now i lost him. i could see him, though, in my mind's eye, with his arms crossed, nodding once, as if to say, well, you did what you had to do, but don't get too pleased with yourself. the rest of the applause was polite. + then, from the top of the bleachers, just as the headmaster was shaking my hand: an indian war-whoop. my heart leapt up.

*definition of anarchy taken from ... fuck it, i don't have to tell you, cuz i'm an anarchist

music reviews

reviewz u kin use: wreck-chordings

★ = terrible. avoid.

★★ = you are allowed to buy this + i won't make fun of you.

★★★ = pure genius. walk, don't run.

---

the clash, seen on the green (u.k. bootleg) ★★★★

rumor is, frontman joe strummer started out in a bar band + just went punk last year. but a) who was punk before last year? and b) with music this good, who cares? the long live set here is only the band's second time out in public, but the hooks flying around could really bring our message to the masses: london's burning. salute the new wave, even if the pop flourishes still feel a little put-on + there's a weird reggae rhythm going on in the last third (+ even if the july 4 show at the black swan's supposed to have been better) this is still, no bullshit, worth your hard-earned dough.

"howling fantods," by get the fuck out, b/w "soylent blue,"
by johnny panic & the bible of dreams

a collaboration by some east village neighbors, but as with most split singles, not everyone comes out looking good. "fantods" is uncomfortably close to caterwauling. there's all this theoretical jabber on the sleeve — but punk rock isn't some intellekshul thing; it was supposed to be about passion. the b-side, though, is worlds better. johnny panic has a kind of sinewy maximalist panmusical thing going on, with these moments of poetics that remind me of ex post facto in its heyday — or what i have to imagine ex post facto was like in its heyday. billy three-sticks, a nation turns its lonely eyes to you . . . ★★★

---

berlin, by lou reed

this is the most depressing song in the world:
  "they're taking her children away
  because they said
  she was not a good mother."
lou! how could you!

1. ~~Horses~~ Brass Tactics
2. ~~Brass Tactics~~ Horses
3. Radio Birdman (import)
4. Modern Lovers: Modern Lovers
5. (tie) Ramones: "Blitzkrieg Bop"
   Iggy: "No Fun"

What this human lacks in experience, he makes up for in
enthusiasm. You can show him a certain building you like, or a tree,
even, and for him it will be the coolest building or tree he's ever
seen. When you tell him a story - any story - his face lights up
like a girandole and whatever he says when you're done will be so
completely ingenuous (sp.?) that you want to take him up in your arms
and protect him from the big, bad world. He's like this great sponge
or camera (in short, the perfect LOTD reader.)

    Like I remember the day after graduation, we're hanging
out at Señor Wax, and C. wants some music he can listen to while
driving in from Nassau County. Neither of us has enough money for
an eight-track of <u>Horses</u> in addition to the stack of records,
so we go halvesies. I get a call two days later: Patti is the
greatest recording artist of all time, greater even than bowie,
which in C-land i gather is high praise indeed. He actually says
<u>recording artist</u>.

    And I'll never forget how he looked coming up out of the
Sheridan Square subway the weekend after I'd turned him on to
Ex Post Facto. It was only the second time we'd really hung out,
but he'd ripped his corduroys and done his hair up into reddish
spikes. And I said to him then what I say to him now - which is a
way, maybe, of saying it to myself. You're getting there, buddy.
Have faith.

Dinka Traditional   *Weisbarger*

The Magnificent ~~Bull~~

Weisbarger

My ~~bull is~~ white like the silver fish in the river
white like the shimmering crane bird on the river bank
white like fresh milk!
His roar is like the thunder to the Turkish cannon[1] on the steep shore.
Weisbarger
My ~~bull is~~ dark like the raincloud in the storm.
He is like summer and winter.
Half of him is dark like the storm cloud,
half of him is light like sunshine.
His back shines like the morning star.
His brow is red like the beak of the Hornbill.[2]
His forehead is like a flag, calling the people from a distance,
He resembles the rainbow.

I will water him at the river.
With my spear I shall drive my enemies.
Let them water their herds at the well;
the river belongs to me and my ~~bull.~~ *Weisbarger*
Drink. my ~~bull.~~ from the river; I am here *Weisbarger*
to guard you with my spear.

1. **Turkish cannon:** During the 1800s much of the Sudan was occupied by
Turkish and Egyptian forces.

6.20.76

today pizza + some pills (c can't smoke cuz of asthma) + we
end up at an art gallery where they're showing, b/w stm by this
photographer who used to date patti. c doesn't say anything but goes
red as a balloon + sucks on his inhaler a lot. i try to keep a straight
face. then in front of a picture of a naked guy w/ a dong the size of
a stud pony's, i just lose it, + then c loses it, i think out of relief.
we are laughing so hard the girl at the desk says we have to leave.
right at the door, we turn + shoot her the finger + run. i'm surprised
how nervous i am to show c my own pictures after that, but i've
brought my binder in my bag, not "burners, bombs + glow-ups," but the
one with all the pictures i took at shows last winter. some of those
bands are already legends now. which doesn't guarantee the pictures are
any good. we sit on some stoop in the west village looped on pills,
+ he goes quiet as he flips through the pages, blinking like it's hard
to focus, + i'm scared he's going to give me some fake compliment,
like i'd given sol's graffiti that one time, but he stops at a picture
of johnny thunders + taps it with the pad of his index finger so
lovingly that i don't even mind the print of pizza grease it leaves
on the plastic. you know what this needs? he says. a big old wang,
right here. i tell him when i get to college in the fall, he can come +
crash at my dorm, + we will be the king + queen of nyc. we will
take over this town.

6.30.76

ran into sol at the dictators show last night + he invited me to
a 4th of july party at a certain notorious pad in the east village.
his invisible friend had finally decided to meet me, sol said, + he gave
me something special too, to make it a really memorable night. he told
me not to take them until we met up. okay, i said, but i'm bringing
a friend of my own. sol turned about three shades of purple then.
jealousy: the least punk of emotions.

7.10.76

whenever i call c's house now, his mom picks up. he's grounded,
she told me the first time. i said for how long? she said who is
this, at which point i hung up. now i just hang up as soon as i
hear her voice. i'm dying to tell him about the php. i don't think
his mom is lying to me, but still, not hearing from him, it feels like
he's mad at me for something, or like i'm betraying him, throwing
him over for this punk-rock world we fantasized about the way
i end up throwing everything over. overturn overturn overturn.

It was supposed to be one of the great nights - the Bicentennial -
but when Gloria Buonarotti awoke the morning after, it was
like she was coming back from abduction by space aliens who'd
extracted all the moisture from her eyeballs and then backed
over her face with their spaceship a few times for good measure.
Here she was, in yesterday's clothes, on the cold concrete floor
of a basement whose nearest window gave onto the brick wall of
the next house over, less than a foot away. Her camera, thank God,
was still in her bag. There was a mattress, the back of a couch, a
sound of breathing nearby. She did her best to avoid all three,
making her way toward the memory of stairs. Apparently, the
aliens had left her basic ambulatory structure intact, because
she reached the top with only one stumble. Pretty much every myth
in the whole of human history recommended against looking back,
but now she couldn't help herself. In the shadows, three pairs of
legs tangled on the mattress. Jesus Christ, what had she done?

       Upstairs was a war zone: bodies slumped in corners and
along baseboards. Holes - fresh? - in the walls. The night had
concentrated the smells of keg beer and cigarettes and grass
and blended them into a single thing. It was her need for a smoke
that led her to the kitchen. There, a guy stood at the counter,
dark, not unhandsome, copiously tattooed, rinsing out
a paintbrush in what had once been a container of Cool-Whip.
He didn't seem at all surprised to see her. "Guten Morgen" he
said, his cigarette bobbing in his mouth and scattering ash in
the water. His glasses were the little ones with the steel frames,
like from the 1920s. Then he pinched the water from the end
of the brush, a little fussily, almost as if he was copying the
gesture. "Do we know each other?" she asked. This was his house,
he said. Ah. She introduced herself, shook his hand, followed his
gaze to the easel near the window, where a canvas had been set
up to catch the sun. It was still damp, but totally incoherent, a
bunch of lines crisscrossing in the center and then blankness,
save for two words, "Captain" plus something unreadable, in the
corner. She had the oddest feeling for a second that all of this,
the painting, the cigarette, his waiting here with this leering
familiarity, had been prepared just for her. She raised the camera.
There was something iconic about him, with the a.m. summer light
streaming through the rear window - he might as well have been
wearing a beret - or maybe it was just the stories her friends had
told that now seemed to gather around him ... but he said the
rule was still no pictures. "You know how to get home from here?"
And she thought: well, good question. Do I?

HEY. YOU.

harmless terror, a.k.a. "detournement," by anonymous

1) Swallow some snake bite antidote then walk into your local army recruiter's office. The antidote (most types are harmless—make sure you get that kind) will make you vomit.
Do so all over the carpet, desk, clothing, etc. Then apologize profusely.

2) You can make a very effective fuse by inserting a non-filter cigarette in a book of matches so that it will ignite some matches when it burns down that far. Then loosely crumple paper around the matches and cigarettes so they are hidden. Toss it in a trashcan or any other area with a lot of flammables. It takes about 5 minutes to ignite—by then you can be far away, though hopefully not too far away to watch.

3) Pick up some dog training liquid at any pet store—it smells like concentrated piss. If you can't figure out something to do with it then you shouldn't be reading this.

4) Stage massive searches on busy sidewalks for "lost" contact lenses telling people not to walk there or "you might step on it." Pretending you've lost something is a great cover for all kinds of subversive behavior.

5) Leave notes all over town that say, "Tuesday's the day."

ring
ring
hello you've reached the united states of amerikkka. a broken chaos mixed with interracial tensions at a congressional hearing. more at eleven robbed at gunpoint protesting a march held by some radical extremist group who doesn't like some policy says the public relations advisor to the president passed a bill rates will be increasing. if you do not pay wages have been decreased again because of fighting in some foreign country and we have to intervene in these heinous acts for this special news bulletin as we take you live to the scene of the crime. Police report the suspected of rape, murder, loitering, and jaywalking. Soon to be a made for TV movie star found in bed with such-and-such who broke up with such-and-such decay in the blocks backed up when a gass main attraction event at your local mayors race to your nearest convenience store held up again by a masked man and some sports team beat another sports team in ratings even though they came from the same factory layoffs as a result of stagflation is improving benefits to unemployment rates declining value of the dollar is up by twenty percent risk of heart disease control center issued a report that there is no illegal activity needs to be stopped in the innercity pollution ordinance to put an end of the line for criminals gaining a college education...

HOME-EC CORNER
SG'S Millennium Brownies

The secret to a good brownie isn't the brownie ... take any old Duncan Hines mix to start. What you've really got to pay attention to is yr dope. Essentially, you'll be butter-poaching at extremely low heat, for 1-2 hours. Then when yr dope is nice and tender, pull it out and dice very fine until you've got basically a paste. tip: make sure you hang on to the butter to incorporate into the batter. loads of thc in there.

There was this old church somebody knew about. You had to climb over a fence and get a boost up through a broken back window and then you were inside, trying to let your eyes adjust to the moonlight. A few steps forward and you'd be under this immense dome that as you looked up seemed to be breathing. Other people must have known about it, because from up in the organist's balcony, you could see blacked-out places down among the pews where bonfires had been kindled for cooking or for warmth. Elsewhere there were little almost art projects, assemblages of old umbrellas and shopping carts and mirrors. It always struck Gloria Buonarotti as beautiful, this urge to make something and leave it even where no one would ever see. Like the murals she'd shot in abandoned tunnels. She was here to do the same, she thought: leave big burners of graffiti running up the columns - gargoyles, vines - and then to preserve it all with her camera.

These bombing runs, as Iggy called them, had been bringing their little circle to the Bronx a lot lately. This was where people's minds were ripest for blowing, he said, but more likely it was that the cops had given up on the place, and artists were free to do whatever they wanted. The only people likely to step in would be the men who stared from out front of the bodegas when they piled out of the van. On one level, she was afraid of these men. On another, different level, she knew that was wrong. Didn't she, too, know what it was like to feel hostile and abandoned? From out on the Island, the city looked like this place of utter freedom and life and all that, but it was really shocking to see from up on the expressway when the sun went down - Iggy liked her to take the passenger's seat, so they could argue while he drove - the square miles of forsaken buildings, neighborhoods. And as her flashlight beam surfed the church's innards, she started making a catechism: What is a church anyway? The body of Christ, which is also the people. Gloria didn't believe in Christ anymore, but hadn't given up on people. She shook her spraycan, a vision of her piece coming on. What if you could have bands play up here on the altar, while the pews filled with folks from the neighborhood, drawn in by the music? What if you could have photo exhibitions up in the choirs, painting studios in the basement? A food pantry, a free clinic? What if kids could come after school to find out what they were good at? A house of worship for all. A kind of commune or Phalanstery, only turned inside out, like in that hand game little kids play: open the doors, see all the People. It was too big an idea for her to pull off in aerosol, let alone reality, but now she had friends. Then she looked down and saw them roaming the pews, splashing them with stuff from big cans she assumed to be paint right up until someone lit a match. As if they really were just the vandals the reactionaries dismissed them as.

But Iggy, naturally, had a theory. The world had become a picture of itself, he explained on the drive back downtown, and in that picture, nothing real could happen. One had to free people to see the faultlines.

I thought that's what art was for, she said. Like your painting.

MODERN CHILDREN:
CAN SOLVE MANY FAMILY PROBLEMS!

p.21

Nah, it turns out I'm no good at that.

To be an artist, Iggy'd have to be able to create, said someone from the back of the van.

That's exactly what I'm trying to tell Gloria here, smartass. You have to find some way to create a discontinuity. Strike through the mask. Jolt people awake.

"But without them getting hurt. Like that fire."

"Yeah, right, exactly."

And now the other girl, the one Iggy called Sick Grandma, spoke up, though to whom was a little unclear. I told you, she said. Don't say I didn't tell you.

confused + conflicted – the personal, the political: the political, the
personal. i feel like i spent so much time preparing myself for finally
   belonging, + now that i've been inducted into the inner circle i'm not
sure that's where i want to be. all of this is invisible to the php
of course. for them, once you're in, you're in, + they just assume i'll be
the permanent fixture i currently am. all of this comes home to me
today when i encounter this rather beautiful preppie in a jacket and
tie on the front steps of the brownstone while they're all in the little
garage out back. he's come to deliver some package, but ends up giving
me a ride uptown + we talk + for a quick minute i'm not only seeing
this entire other life i could be a part of (as he asks for my phone
#), but also seeing how my current life or semblance thereof – my
holding pattern, let's say – might look to someone standing outside it.
+ where is my c, with whom i once might have talked this over? still
            grounded out in nassau, is where.

writing this in my new dorm. classes aren't until the 7th, but
i told dad yesterday was the only day to move in, because i've got
to get out of the house ASAP. on the drive in, we sat in traffic
downtown for an hour + didn't say a word. he seemed sad, in a way
he hasn't been since the magazine guy started coming out to interview
him for an article on fireworks. + it's ridiculous, it's not as if we've
ever had like long meaningful talks, + lately we hardly see each other.
it's only the idea of me he loves. still, i felt shitty watching him drive
away, but then, at last: a place all my own.

sol + dt walk over from the squat today to see the new digs; i
have to keep them from breaking anything in the hall or otherwise
getting me in trouble. i have the last bottle of old sequoia
whisky smuggled out from flower hill + they end up killing it +
sol decides he wants to do a piece on my wall. no, i say. my
dad's on the hook for any damages + it's not like my wall. dt,
that little asshole, has noticed at some point i'm not drinking
much + starts to rag on me, like, what, does the college girl think
she's better than us? what i don't dare tell them is i've got a
date tomorrow night + i'd rather the room not look like wild
animals have been living in it. i end up giving sol a little bit
of wall above my bed to work on + now the damn room smells
like spraypaint, which is why i'm up this late writing. (or is it
nerves? the sense that something again is about to change?)

p. 23

THERE ARE NO REGRETS, NEDDY... THERE IS ONLY THE FUTURE!

LeDoux and WILSON 3-24

In conclusion, reader, I'll share with you the one interesting thing the professor said in one of the few college classes I've managed to attend to date (one of the first and, it's looking increasingly likely, one of the last). He said our concept of time isn't something we're born with, but something specific to our culture. "Clock-time is only as old as the clock." It goes back to the monks, he said, with their matins and complines and all that. And as our ability to divide our lives into little increments has improved, time itself has sped up. The professor went on to build some kind of braintacular air-castles out of this, but I was already tuned out, stuck on that one idea: the dividing of time into more and more little boxes to be filled, and how it can distract a person. The question you have to step back and ask yourself, I think   the question you don't stop to ask yourself, getting caught up in all that speed - is like: where will you be twenty years from now, or thirty? Or when you look back from your deathbed, where will you have been?

The increments that distract me from my own bigger picture, I'm realizing, are these three-month things you could practically set your watch by. Step 1: I discover something new. Step 2: I think: yes, finally, my life is about to begin, this is where I'm supposed to be. And then three months later I come out of a kind of trance and see I've been bullshitting myself again. It's like my impulses or appetites are always running a season ahead of my brain.

After I switched high schools sophomore year, the something new was sex. It took me about two weeks to sleep with Brad S. - and pretty much scotch the chance of any of the girls there ever being friends with me. I guess the size of his apartment impressed me, or at the time I needed to feel like I belonged to that world. I liked the way his parents were never home, so it was like he owned the place, like an adult. And I liked the way he seemed to know what he was doing. Who else I shouldn't have slept with: the senior class president. I learned a lot from all this, but it didn't make me happy. (Maybe it's a good policy not to sleep with people who don't make me happy.) And by the time it ended, I was already moving on.

I remember the clerk at Señor Wax trying to get over on me by comping an advance copy of Radio Ethiopia and claiming I reminded him of Patti. But it was the sound itself I'd fallen for. I would become a musician (notwithstanding my staggering lack of musical eptitude). Or at least a devout apostle. I would move to the City, be swallowed by the scene. Now that I've penetrated the mysteries of the East Village, though, and started to see its darker side, I'm wondering again what it is I'm doing. Which makes me nervous about what comes next. What if three months from now, I want out?

But the thing is, I've started to think, you can't only say no. You can't only tear shit down and assume that what springs up in its place is going to be better. You have to build at some point. To commit. Isn't this what punk was supposed to be about? Like, don't despair, people. You can still pick up a guitar and drumsticks and make something. No Future - that stuff was just the content. The form said: HERE is your future. I think even SG and DT and NC have to see this at some level. The personal and the political being somewhat indissoluble in the hothouse of that house, there's been some jealousy of the time I've been spending with certain of them lately. But at this point, having experienced what a real adult relationship looks like, if I stay interested in the PHP, it's not in the way any of them think. What I'm interested in now is minds. Specifically: in changing them.

I know, I know... you're thinking, "How can I be a part of something so awesome, well, send on your stuff, we have open arms:

articles
columns
poetry
prose
artwork
comics

+If you have the spare cash, send donations, 'cause I'm making myself pitifully broke w/this. To receive the next issue, please send $ and stamps.

p. 25

THANK YOU
Call Again

We appreciate your patronage and hope we may continue to merit it. If we please you, tell your friends. If we don't, tell us. We strive to satisfy.

HELLO
my name is

Keith Lamplighter (sr.?)
Lamplighter Capital Advisers
501 Fifth Ave., 12th floor
New York, NY 10017

l.o.t.d.
2355 outer bridge
Flower Hill, NY 11576

Adolph S. Ochs
PUBLISHER

13c USA

INSUFFICIENT POSTAGE

BOOK IV

MONADS

[1959-1977]

I too had been struck from the float forever held
*   in solution,*
I too had receiv'd identity by my body.

—WALT WHITMAN
Leaves of Grass

59

THE FERRY TO BLOCK ISLAND WAS RUNNING BEHIND SCHEDULE, and it was already dark by the time Regan reached the Goulds' rambling vacation house that last official weekend of the last summer of the 1950s—the start of her junior year. The driveway's cars looked like cultured pearls in the moonlight, or a line of cooling embers. In the lit-up windows, hired men in white jackets bustled to and fro. Laughter and surf and the pock of badminton rackets could be heard from out back; that must have been where everyone was. But where the Goulds were, her brother was sure not to be, so she carried her suitcase inside and asked a tall woman with a guest-list where she might put her things.

The woman showed her to a room under the third-floor eaves, as far from the grown-ups as possible. The dresser where Regan put the clothes she'd brought from Poughkeepsie smelled faintly of talcum, and under that, rot. She was revising downward her assessment of Felicia's personal fortune when out in the hallway a familiar voice began to count backward from sixty. Little kids, the unsupervised offspring of the guests who would be filling the house and the island's one hotel for the weekend, stampeded over weary floorboards. She found William at the far end of the hall, in a room that mirrored her own. He lay back on the swaybacked bed in his blazer and unknotted school tie. His eyes were closed. "Forty . . . thirty-nine . . . hello, Regan."

"Are you peeking?"

He patted the bedspread beside him. "Come give us a kiss."

"You're peeking, I can't believe it. Don't stop counting! You'll disappoint the kids."

"Maybe, but at least I've bought myself peace and quiet until they figure it out."

"You're terrible."

"Come on. Kiss kiss."

In his yearlong journey through the digestive system of the nation's most prestigious prep schools, William had been trying on and discarding various selves, but with this latest incarnation, there was an element of recklessness, of testing to see how much she was willing to put up with. As he pooched his lips at her, a sour scent wafted up. "Jesus, William. You absolutely reek of booze."

He grinned and opened his blazer to reveal a bottle of rum. "Bad form to let the birthday girl's hospitality go to waste, don't you think?"

They sat on the bed for a while passing the bottle as he made fun of the room's generically nautical décor and the pinheads whose laughter kept gusting up beyond the open window. And of course the posturing of the Ghouls. Each time he mispronounced the name, she heard pain. She felt it, too, obviously. On the other hand, she also felt, as she increasingly had these last years, the difference in their ages. Yes, she would rather her father have entered a monastery, but they were both adults, and if Daddy preferred to have a . . . a *girlfriend* (though the word stuck in her throat like a fishbone), the honorable thing was to smile and nod and not to stand in the way. Perhaps, too, she imagined some benefits accruing to filial diligence. Wasn't the Karmann Ghia she'd gotten for Christmas one of these? In its too-perfect congruity with what a twenty-year-old might have wanted, it had clearly been picked out by Daddy's consort, but maybe the larger impulse had been his. Maybe for the first time her superior maturity was being acknowledged. Appreciated, even. And when the little kids came back to confront William about his failure to look for them, Regan left him to charm his way out of the mess he'd made and went downstairs to join the party.

The house's sandy backyard extended forty or fifty feet. This being the year when all things South Pacific were in vogue, the perimeter had been marked off with rattan torches that puffed and guttered in a stiffening wind. Whitecaps crashed grayly beyond the dunes, nearly invisible, while within the charmed circle glowed the faces of executives and their wives and various friends of the Goulds. Daddy, dignified in his summer-weight wool, pecked her on the cheek. She'd been hoping for an embrace, but he had a drink in his hand, and this felt more sophisticated—which, with Felicia looking on, was probably a good thing. She summoned over a waiter to give Regan a cocktail of her own, in a cup shaped like a tiki god. Then the brother, Amory Gould, offered his arm. "Come, dear. There are people I'd like you to meet." Daddy's smile may have wavered a bit here—Regan would never quite be able to decide—but when she pivoted into the haze of booze and firelight and the deeper black of stormclouds piling up to the east, a kind of inner hum overtook her.

Amory's hand, soft on her lower back, propelled her through knots of guests. She kept waiting for him to get bored, but he hummed with an intensity of his own. He was barely taller than Regan, but had the impressive white hair even then, in his thirties, and that ingratiating manner; the way he introduced her as "Bill's daughter—exquisite, isn't she?" would have made her blush, had it not been as if she weren't there. Eventually, they reached the outermost orbit of guests, where a gangly boy in a yachting sweater stood smoking. He wasn't badlooking, in a sort of bland, Episcopalian way, but his only real distinguishing features were his horn-rimmed glasses and his hair, so blond it too was almost white. Regan was surprised to feel the quickening of the hand on her back, unless of course she was imagining it.

"Regan Hamilton-Sweeney, may I present . . ." and then Amory said the name Regan would subsequently expunge from her memory, leaving only the initial L. "Regan here is down from . . . Vassar, isn't it? I can't keep my Seven Sisters straight." They laughed more because it had the rhythm of a joke than because it was funny. L., said Amory, was a Harvard man.

"That makes us cousins, practically." L.'s pause here was to let Regan know that he, too, saw Amory's clumsiness, and she smiled, genuinely this time. It was all the opening Amory needed to burrow back into the crowd. L. gazed after him. "None too subtle, is he."

"Oh, he's not so bad," she said. "It's his sister you've got to look out for. This is her birthday we're celebrating."

"I mean I reckon he's assuming because we're around the same age . . ."

"You think he's setting us up?"

At which they both laughed again, anxious. That should have been out of the question, L. said. His father was the president of a rival holding company in the City, and evidently in private called William Hamilton-Sweeney II all sorts of names that didn't bear repeating. "Father can be kind of a son of a bitch, if you'll pardon the expression. I'm surprised we were even invited."

"Well, the, uh, Goulds were the ones making the arrangements," she said. "It is their place, after all."

"Yeah, we've been out a couple times already this summer. Have you seen the water yet? We should walk down."

And because the alternative was to spend another half-hour talking about their parents like good children of the ruling class, she acquiesced. L. grabbed another pair of tiki cups from a circulating waiter, and without anyone seeming to notice, they slipped down the moonlit path and out between the dunes.

They went maybe a quarter-mile, to where a rock jetty broke the curve of the shoreline. On an impulse, or maybe because adjunct-hostess duties had been wearing on her, Regan pulled off her shoes and waded into the water in her tennis skirt. It was cold, but she stayed in calf-deep, letting the shiver rise past her knees. Far-off lightning stabbed the sea. "You know," L. said, wading out to her, not bothering to roll up his pants. "You're not so bad yourself, for a Hamilton-Sweeney."

As he stared at the side of her face, she felt as she did more and more these days: excitement and nerves and transgression all mixed together so you couldn't tell which was which. She drained her drink—her third or fourth of the night, she'd lost count—and set the tiki cup adrift, a bottled message. "I think I felt a raindrop." He tried to blame this on the surf, but she knew that if she stayed here, he would want to kiss her, and she wasn't sure she liked him that way. "We should head in."

They returned to the yard to find everyone packed together, facing the wide back porch, the proscenium where stood her father and the Goulds. Daddy beamed stiffly, but his discomfort with public speaking wasn't something Felicia shared. She hoisted her pagan vessel into the air. Her voice, scrubbed of any trace of her native Buffalo, was capable of remarkable penetration. "When Bill asked, I can't say I hesitated," she was saying. Regan thought of Lemuel Gulliver lying there politely while soft-footed Lilliputians scampered back and forth with their tiny ropes. And then of the buffalo nickels her mother used to save for trips to the beach, to give to her or William, whoever saw the ocean first. "Although it's always a daunting task to bring two families together, we'll have all our friends and colleagues to help. I couldn't imagine lovelier people to celebrate with, and we certainly look forward to seeing you all at the wedding." *The wedding?* No wonder L. had been surprised; this wasn't a birthday, after all, but an engagement party. Regan looked around frantically for William, but maybe he'd already sensed it, earned the nickel no one was around anymore to give them, because he still hadn't come down from upstairs. Which was where she finally spotted him, or thought she did, a childlike head in a small, square window.

WHETHER DADDY GENUINELY LIKED FELICIA or was merely being swept along by her energies had been a topic of regular debate between Regan and her brother, back when the latter had still been living at home. It might have been some kind of silver lining here that the point had at last been settled in Regan's favor. But that night, when she broke the news, William accused her of having taken Felicia's side all along, which couldn't have been further from the truth.

The truth was that she would have been the first to scrap the diplomatic pose and join him in his fulminations against the Goulds if she hadn't seen how lonely Daddy had been. Mom had died in '51, and for most of the next decade, he'd sworn off dining and opera and the social functions they used to frequent. He gave himself over to his work, sometimes returning home as late as eight in the evening. But business and pleasure were not so easy to wall off from each other in a city as thick with both as New York. A couple years ago, he'd returned to public life, and Felicia had arrived soon after, trailing her brother and familiar. When he couldn't avoid talking about her, Daddy referred to her as his "friend," as if Regan and William were still children whose sensibilities this half-truth might spare. In fact, it had only aggravated their sense of betrayal, in that it let Daddy feel he was being more solicitous toward their feelings than he actually was. He didn't believe in feelings, really—not even his own. It was almost an ideology with him now. Regan had seen him cry only once over her mother's death, and then only through the cracked door of his study the morning of the memorial service, when he and Artie Trumbull had sat with a bottle of cognac on the desk between them (though, as William would point out, she couldn't be certain the glimmer in Daddy's eye hadn't been a trick of the light, or of memory).

But in at least one respect, William turned out to be right: alcohol made the engagement go down more smoothly. Regan had two Bloody Marys with breakfast the next morning, and lunch was similarly boozy. Brother and sister might have shared a conspiratorial look from their respective tables on the lawn, except that brother refused to come down to eat; he would spend much of that weekend holed up in his room, or out God only knew where, on the principle that the greatest punishment he could render against his oppressors was to deprive them of the glory that was William. Not that Daddy noticed; at his own table, surrounded by well-wishers, he seemed a little drunk, too. And so Regan ended up smiling over at L., who sat across from her, under the flapping white edge of a tent thrown up against the threat of rain.

Later, when the tables had been cleared and a seven-piece band brought in to approximate the golden hits of Felicia's youth, they danced together three times. Regan at that point still loved to dance, still loved the way it made her feel. She had played the Cyd Charisse role in the sophomore production of *Brigadoon,* and as her feet moved over the scrubby grass, she imagined she was back there, behind the footlights. Again, though, when L. wanted to kiss her, she shied away, she supposed because by that point she was too sloshed to feel in control, but perhaps really because she sensed in his wandering hands an impatience that gave her pause.

It was on this same sandy expanse that some of the younger men and the kids got up a game of touch football late Sunday morning, before a group luncheon at the island's one nice restaurant. Whether it was suppressed recklessness or her second mimosa or the unstable interaction between the two, Regan decided to join in. Two of the Company's junior vice presidents chose up teams, and out of deference to Daddy, she got picked early, even though she was the only girl. She and L. were on opposite sides. They ended up shadowing each other, offense and defense.

And how could she have failed to notice before how suitable L. really was, in his generic way, the summer-tanned calves beneath his rolled khakis bursting into motion, churning up the sand like a million fragments of light? Then again, maybe these thoughts were somehow emanating from her uncle-to-be, who stood on the back porch, having sworn off the sport as "too physical." Because after the ball had been handed to her for the first time all morning; after L.'s own ardor or fighting spirit had gotten the best of him and he'd burst upon her and laid her out, in flagrant violation of the protocols of two-hand touch; after she'd lain on her back on the sand with the wind knocked out of her and her hair whipping around her head and L.'s beery breath in her face and his thigh like a marble pillar between her legs; when she'd turned her head like a little kid to see how others would react before deciding whether to laugh or cry, it had been Amory, some fifty yards away, her gaze had landed on. The other man on the porch—L., Sr.—had turned toward him, oblivious to the cries of foul gone up from the sand. But Amory, hands on the railing, was unmistakably focused on *her*. She began to laugh, and the boy on top of her did, too, his golden face flushing red. It was almost like acting. You decided to feel something, and then you felt it. She could see the cracked lenses of L.'s glasses and the pores of his upper lip. Their heaving bodies pushed apart and fell together, and then he rolled onto his back. They lay with the backs of their hands touching and belly-laughed at the lowering sky.

It was also Amory who proposed that the two teams, victor and vanquished, walk down to the restaurant before it started raining. Regan felt as if it were not her but some larger force operating through her that murmured something about taking a shower. She couldn't have said to what degree something similar was at work in L. when he, too, opted out.

In the empty kitchen, over gin and tonics, they confirmed again that there were no hard feelings. "It's just that sometimes a feeling gets the better of me," the boy said. As he edged around the counter toward her, she slipped farther away and said she should really shower. There was still grit in her teeth.

Under the hot water, time moved too fast and not fast enough. She couldn't decide if she wanted the luncheon expedition to stay away or come back. She would get out once the air temperature of the bathroom matched the warmth of her skin.

L. caught her in the hallway when she had only a towel on, as if he'd been waiting there. Kissing, fumbling, they moved through the gray house. Upstairs into who knew whose silent room, reeling backward laughing. Only not so silent now. From the roof came the first experimental spatter of rain. *Plink.* She scrambled up so that the bare part of her back was pressing against cold wood. "We just met," she blurted. She laughed again a little nervously and pulled the towel he was tugging at tighter.

"Come on," he said. "It'll be fun."

The hush that followed was unsettling. In the city, the continuous buzz and shudder of planes and cars and industrial machinery reminded you that the outside world still existed, and thus that you existed for it. Now, propped up against the headboard, she could see beyond the cross-stitch of drops clinging to the windowscreen only sky . . . and so couldn't quite be sure what was real. Was it her laughter at the chill of his hand on her thigh? Or was it her knees pushing away his torso in the unlamped room? To some more sober self the scene felt sinister, like something on a movie screen that makes the audience mutter, *Don't.* "Don't," she heard herself say. But he must not have heard. He had his khakis undone, the towel rucked up around her waist. At that moment, the outside world became imaginary; if she could have gone downstairs, she would have found that everything, people and dunes and lifeguard stands and jetty, had been raptured away in an atomic flash. Was she losing her mind? She'd consented to be kissed at first, she remembered, her ear, her neck, while between her thighs his hand might have been looking for misplaced keys. Or had that been the gin talking? Was this the gin pressing against her crotch? Her body was submerged in a liquid that kept her from moving, while her head reeled through space. Should she yell for help? No one would believe this wasn't what she wanted. She was too drunk. And maybe he was too drunk, too, to know what he was doing. At any rate, there was no one around to hear. Even the servants were gone. "Don't," she begged, adding a fake laugh so he'd know she would forgive him if only he'd stop. But he had her wrists now in his surprisingly strong hands, and wouldn't look her in the face, and he didn't stop, until he did.

WHEN HE'D GONE, she slunk half-naked to her bedroom on the third floor, ducking below the windows, and locked herself in, ready to play dead at the first sign of his return. She let her crying become audible only after hearing a door slam downstairs. He'd thanked her warmly afterward, as if she'd given him a gift. But if it had really been a gift, why did it hurt so much? What she wanted now was her father, or her brother, but she was too ashamed to go find them, and scared *he* would come back first. Eventually, she crammed her things into her suitcase and limped down the back stairs, pausing at landings to listen. She hurried to the car without leaving a note. Her windshield wipers were useless against the squall that had blown up. It was to be a rough ride back on the ferry. She would spend it locked in the lavatory, kneeling before the toilet. Only on the mainland, in a restroom behind a Sinclair station, would she discover the small perfect circle of blood in her underwear.

THERE WAS A PAUSE on the phone when Daddy reached her in Poughkeepsie that Monday, a thick bolus of shame and anger and loathing that stopped her throat. "I was feeling sick to my stomach," she lied. "So I decided to drive back a little early. Sorry I didn't tell you; I didn't want to rain on your parade." He didn't think to probe the logical gaps here—just said, in his abstracted way, that he hoped she was feeling better. Having spent the whole drive back rehearsing the part she would now be expected to play, she told him she was.

It would take her another month, spent mostly in bed, to decide to tell her father what had actually happened that weekend. And then a month after that, and another missed period, to screw her courage, et cetera. She knew she wouldn't be able to get the words out over the sorority house's communal telephone, and so, on a Friday in mid-November, she drove down to Sutton Place. What she found there, though, was odd: to the usually neat stoop clung hundreds of yellow leaves, their skeletons like darker tracery. She remembered for some reason how she and William used to collect them, and how Doonie would iron them between sheets of wax paper strewn with the shavings of crayons. Stained glass, they'd called it. The reason was that she was stalling.

The first floor was silent, save for the kitchen. There, she came upon Doonie bent over a shipping carton, a wisp of hair escaping from her bun, more white in it than there used to be. Part of her wanted to bury her face in the cook's broad back, smell that old sturdy smell, let her tears soak the cotton. But Regan was older now, too.

"Miss Regan," Doonie said, looking up. "I didn't expect you back."

"What are you doing?" Regan nodded at the newspaper-wrapped parcel in Doonie's hand, hating the note of command that had entered her voice. Doonie looked equally surprised to find it there.

"Some of these pots and things I bought out of my own purse over the years. Kathryn and I always had an understanding I'd take them with me when I left."

"But you're not leaving us, are you?"

Doonie raised a finger to her lips and motioned toward the open door. "It's not my choice, Regan, but in thirty-five years, I never cooked a *haute cuisine*, and I ain't about to start. You'll have to talk to your father about it."

Regan stormed into the hall. They were getting rid of Doonie now, too? Indecent, was what it was. She'd nearly forgotten her purpose in coming here when she entered the unlit living room and saw the silhouette facing the bay window. Beyond it, in the courtyard, a Japanese maple had exploded into red, filling the squares between the mullions with fire. Amory Gould. The nervousness she'd always felt around him had now thrown off its mask. It was revulsion. Her instinct was to run, but at that moment something made him turn around, and a weightless smile replaced whatever had been on his face. "Ah, Regan! Let me pour you a drink." Without any gesture toward turning on the lights—without, indeed, seeming to notice they were off—he moved toward the credenza.

"I'm . . ." She swallowed. "Thanks, but I'm not thirsty."

"But surely you've come to celebrate the good news?" When she didn't respond, he pressed a glass into her hands. The company's largest competitor, he said, had just that morning agreed to a takeover. "This adds extensive interests in Central America to our holdings. And it stands to make you"—he clinked with his own glass the glass that hung between them—"a very wealthy young woman."

"Who is it?"

"Who is who?"

"The competitor," she said, though she already knew the answer. The wine was sickly sweet, cloying. She drank not for congeniality, but for courage.

"I introduced you at the engagement party. The son seemed to take a shine to you. I felt certain you would make a fine match." His face swam up through the gloom, a lamprey from the shadows.

"Or was there another misunderstanding? In any event, everything worked out fine, Regan, and you'll learn that sometimes self-interest means putting long-term security ahead of affairs of the heart. Anyway, let's drink to your father. Nothing, I'm sure, could spoil this moment for him. They're in the office upstairs as we speak, blowing dry the ink." And in case she didn't get the point, which was to keep her big mouth shut, he clinked her glass again, hard enough that a bit of his own wine leaped in. Almost as if he'd meant to infect her, she would think.

60

ACTUALLY, HER NAME WAS NOT JENNY. This was a condition she shared with billions of other people living at that time, but most were oblivious to it, whereas Minh Thuy Nguyen thought about it at least once a day. Her father and mother had emigrated from Vietnam back before anyone knew to feel sorry for them. Not that there was any reason to feel sorry, Dad said—the country had been at war on and off for a thousand years, like most of the rest of the globe, and anyway the Nguyens weren't living in some shell-shocked Indochinese village but in a wide white ranch house in an unincorporated canton of the San Fernando Valley where they didn't pay city taxes and where in the early evening when the light homed in low over the mountains and the DDT truck rolled through to spray for mosquitoes, the yards' synchronized sprinklers could have been the fountains of Versailles, wasting their bounty on the ridiculous desert grass. But white people turned out to be profligate with their pity, too; as early as middle school, other kids had started looking at her with that expression that said, *Vietnam . . . Yikes!* And so, on the first day of sixth grade, when Mr. Kearney called the roll, Minh Thuy had corrected him. "It's Jenny."

"Jen-yi?" he ventured.

"Jenny." She was only twelve, but already she knew he couldn't care less what she called herself. California was beautiful in exactly this way: so long as you kept your lawn green and your grades up, you could do any weird old thing you wanted. And Jenny was one hundred percent Californian.

The new name split her life in two. There was, on the one hand, home: the shady world where she continued to answer to *Minh Thuy*. Her mother, a migraine sufferer, kept semi-sheer drapes drawn through the bright hours of the day, so that the sunken living room stayed dim. Minh Thuy could barely make out the jade Buddha and the crucifix butted up like bookends on the mantel there, the photographs of overseas relatives, or the volumes of Victor Hugo on the desk where her father composed his weekly letter to the editor of the *West Covina Times*. She might hear him in the kitchen chopping vegetables, the chock of his knife on a cutting board of space-age polymer, while her mother lay on a straw mat by the coffeetable with a washcloth over her eyes, as if dead. (The softness of American beds overwhelmed her when she was having an attack, she claimed, though surely she could have found someplace less conspicuous to lie down.) The migraines provided a handy alibi for why Minh Thuy never invited friends over, for why every sleepover or Brownie troop meeting took place at Mandy's house, or Trish's, or Nell's. Only later did she realize her parents had used the migraines as an excuse, too. She would think back on Dad's wet bar, a hundred dollars' worth of liquor bottles to which he took a dustcloth each Saturday, as though at any second the house might fill with his colleagues from Lockheed. She would think of the hi-fi bought on installments from Sears, used only for the Metropolitan Opera broadcasts on Sunday afternoons. Of Mom and Dad sitting stock-still on the davenport, listening to *Samson et Dalila*. She would recall the strange smells of her friends' houses, one like fish food, one like cottage cheese; she couldn't remember which was which, but if they smelled strange, how must her own house smell to them? The world of Minh Thuy was like an odor that, terrifyingly, she could not herself detect. But within those walls she'd remained an obedient child, saying her prayers, eating soup in the summertime, practicing her violin in the garage so as not to disturb her mother.

Her growing up, however, had been done in the other world, the world of Jenny, with its miles of highways, its drive-ins, beaches, and bougainvillea, chaparral, Tastee Freez, wildfires, stucco, cineplexes, bumper cars, in-ground pools, planned subdivisions up in the foothills with grids of paved streets and manholes and streetlights, as if someone had forgotten to build the houses, or as if some B-movie bomb had vaporized them. In high school, she would drive up here with Chip McGillicuddy after double features or beer blasts. Mouths sort of sore from kissing, they'd park in one of the deserted cul-de-sacs and look out over the corresponding cul-de-sacs below. She thought of this as the essential Californian activity, gazing upon your life from a great distance, trying to infer from trees and highways and restaurants shaped like the foods they served which house was your own. (This was before she moved to New York and discovered that recasting your life in cinematic terms was a national phenomenon, possibly a global one.) From this height, and with smog framing the sodium lights in soft focus, her house looked like everyone else's. And when Chip worked his hand up under her shirt and handled a small breast clumsily, like an avocado he was testing for ripeness, she could have been anyone's girlfriend, could have been anyone, which at the time seemed like what she wanted. She reclined in her seat and stared at the leatherette ceiling of the McGillicuddy family wagon and thanked God for the Golden West.

She stayed in-state for college, on a scholarship to Berkeley. Her father clucked about it and read aloud an editorial about recent misbehavior on campus, but he was attached as only an immigrant with a doctorate can be to the idea of public education, and he knew it was the best school in the system. She and Chip continued to go steady, though he was at U.C. Santa Barbara and she was concerned about where all this was headed. He was one of those people who, set walking toward a point on the horizon, would keep on in a straight line without ever noticing that the horizon never got any closer. He would have marched straight into marriage, though what he'd meant those times he'd said he loved her couldn't possibly have been what she meant when she thought of being loved.

College stirred in her a certain contempt for virtues like kindness and persistence. She would have appeared to have been a kind and persistent person herself, but a steady diet of Antonioni films and an introductory course on existentialism had awakened her to the fact that she wanted more. She wanted to cast her self-reinvention as Jenny from the Valley in theoretical terms, as a form of resistance, or a heroic negative capability—probably because somewhere underneath, she was ashamed. It had been painful, being two people. There was a civil war inside her. Phone calls grew strained.

Then, in December, Chip invited her family to his family's Christmas party—an overture that felt like a sneak attack, in that the invitation, addressed to *The Nguyens*, came in the mail while she was still finishing exams upstate, and she didn't have a chance to stop her father from opening it, from RSVPing enthusiastically and posthaste. Her mother was seeing a chiropractor now, the headaches seemed further apart and milder in intensity and duration, and as they drove together through the weird SoCal Yuletide, the fake snow on the roofs of bungalows, fir trees in the windows of service stations flanked by palms, the massive cognitive dissonance generated by consumer culture, the Cartesian fallacy, and so forth, Jenny saw Mom flinch a little when Dad reached across the seat to take her hand.

She watched them at the party, too, a bourgeois affair where men in hibiscus-colored shirts stood around drinking buttered rum while women circulated restlessly and kids reconnoitered out back behind the pool house to watch planes streak in over the Valley and get high. The desert moon stayed up for as many as eighteen hours a day. The desert could seem, itself, like the surface of the moon.

Having ignored Chip's hints that they should go for a drive, she returned to find her mother surrounded by a little scrum of husbands. Mom's English wasn't stellar, on account of her years of isolation, encountering America through a tube, but you wouldn't have known that to look at her. She laughed almost silently at the men's jokes. There was condescension on Chip's father's face, as if he were saying to his friends, Look how easy it is to make these Celestials laugh. Also, the man was drunk. He was an alcoholic, according to his son, and this was the first time Jenny had seen him *inter pocula*, but the implications for Chip and for family life in general seemed to fall away beside the manifest injustice of being made to perform for these people like trained monkeys, of having to be Jenny, and of not quite being able to recall the country that was supposed to be hers, on whose benighted people the fascist Nixon was even now dumping his bombs. She squeezed her mother's elbow. "We have to go."

"But we have such a good time," Mom enunciated, as if it were a phrase learned from a book.

"I'm not feeling good. We need to go."

She lay on the backseat on the ride home, faking menstrual cramps and watching colored lights slide across the window. While Mom continued to practice her English—*What a lovely home*—and Dad pretended they would return the invitation, she kept seeing the way they'd bowed when they laughed, like spring-mounted toys. Kept hearing their tiny coughing fits of laughter.

Back at school, she started to go by Minh. Whereas her parents' Viet-ness had once been something to conceal, it now provoked from people—when it had been established, through decorous indirection, that she wasn't in fact Chinese, or Thai—a kind of awe. It was something she'd accomplished, rather than something she was. It didn't seem worth mentioning that her dad, a Catholic, had supported the Diem regime. Her grades suffered, but only slightly, as a result of the rallies and parties and self-criticism circles and hybrids thereof she began attending, and of nights spent doing her own small part for the sexual revolution. (Even this, she later reflected, was not an unmixed good, in that it created an unrealistic picture of the world to come. But what didn't, in those days?) As Mother Mountain, she appeared weekly on the 10-watt student radio station, punctuating excerpts from *Minima Moralia* and philippics about the aerospace industry and modern kitchen appliances with renditions of Stockhausen on her detuned violin. Relative to the rest of the student body, her drug intake was moderate-to-fair. She went home less. It was a heady time.

Then came the occupation of the deans' building, and the arrest, and Dad showing up alone to bail her out. At the start of the long drive south, he told her her mother was leaving him—for the chiropractor.

Jenny turned her face to the window, feeling at last the full force of something she must have been concealing from herself for a very long time. As if the point of the blade were aimed not into her but out. She wanted it not to hurt, the institution of marriage being such a heteronormative cop-out and all. Or was it possible to love something and hate it at the same time? For liberty to be tyrannical, and tyranny liberating?

They arrived at home to find the house empty, and finally, after so long, she could smell it, like salt and paper. It didn't smell any more or less weird than Trish's house had probably smelled to Mandy, or Mandy's to Nell, and she wanted to call them all up with a belated invitation to spend the night, so that she wouldn't have to cry alone, but she hadn't spoken to Nell or Mandy or Trish in a long time, and all she had now was her father, and later, in the chiropractor's houseboat on the far side of the 405, her mom, and the two Valiums she'd smuggled home in her laundry bag.

Philosophy seemed to require that one take a position on the questions that reasserted themselves now. Tradition vs. Progress. Reason vs. Passion. Being vs. Time or vs. Nothingness. Was she Minh Thuy, finally, or was she Jenny? But the time when there had been a meaningful difference between the two would come to seem like a tiny neighborhood where you couldn't decide which house was yours. Which felt important when you were high above, you thought, in the foothills, but not so much at the truer remove of a continent, where the lives you'd lived, and the places you'd come from, dwindled to a single point on the horizon, in the incorrigibly distant past.

61

S NOWING HELL OUT HERE. Through the windshield, Regan couldn't see the road, or even trees beyond their skeletal trunks. She kept picturing herself and the car sliding off among them, into the nothing. With the dashboard lighter. With Kotex and peanut butter and a pack of chewing gum gone brittle from the cold. Over and over her little inventory she ran, like the girl with the prayer in the Salinger story. Or the kids who sang that song on the radio. How many times had it played in the hours she'd been driving? She'd listened till their dumb sweet voices hurt too much, and then turned it off until that hurt too much, and then back on, and there was the song again. She could count on hearing it several more times, drifted in at the forest's edge, as she warmed herself with the lighter and sucked the last nutrients from the gum. Snow mounting over the ragtop. Air dimming as night fell. Blood slowing, mercury dropping. And finally miles of uninflected white. Nuclear oblivion had been a nightmare since childhood; now she knew it was what she deserved. For in these last few days, what was in her womb had seemed to stir. Probably that, too, was just her imagination, but it had forced her to examine her choices. Say she really had waited too long. She could never tell L., much less marry him, as Daddy, still in the dark, would want. And a child with no father would shackle her to the tainted fortune she planned to give up as soon as her acting would support her. True, she could change her name, go somewhere far from New York. But what if she hated the kid for forcing her into a grim life in the provinces, the way she'd hated having it inside her, this thing made not of love, but of pain?

BACK IN THE FALL, when she'd first approached one of the gentle theater boys, the son of an OB/GYN, hatred had been closer to panic. She'd asked if he could make discreet inquiries on behalf of a sorority sister who'd gotten herself in trouble. He'd come back with the names of a few places near the city, but if discretion was a concern, he thought she might be better off—the sister, he meant—crossing the border to Ontario. The laws there were even stricter than in the U.S., but his father had a colleague . . . Only later, consulting an atlas, had she realized what lay between her and Ontario. She kept wondering about her last run-in with Amory Gould. He'd expected her, as Daddy's obedient daughter, to play along with the chosen suitor, show him the Hamilton-Sweeneys weren't that bad. But *We've been out a couple times already this summer*, L. had said. So had Amory known even beforehand what L. was? At a minimum, he knew after the fact, and said nothing. Perhaps for him it was a matter of indifference. Perhaps by saying nothing herself, she was even now playing along. There was only one secret, she thought, that was still hers alone: the pregnancy. She couldn't have the Demon Brother find out what she was about to do with it. To it. And where was the one place in the world from which he'd turned his all-seeing eyes? There it was, on the map before her. The city he'd come from. Buffalo.

Tundra having failed to stop her, she reached it just after noon. The streets downtown were white and lightly trafficked, forsaken under Christmas tinsel keening with the wind. She took the bridge over to Canada, checked into a motel with her supplies. Then she called a taxi and went out onto the frozen balcony to wait. The cab that came was not yellow. It idled in the parking lot, hadn't seen her through the snow. And so there was still time to decide, she thought, on that balcony. And in the cab. And at the clinic. She was free, said the nurse who took her vital signs, to change her mind at any point. Regan meant to find out if it was possible what was in her was already a life. Instead, she said, "Why are you telling me this?" But the answer was obvious. It was the same reason the waiting room they made her pass back through was so horrifically genteel, with its potted plants and piped-in music: so she would know that what happened after they fit the mask over her mouth and nose and turned on the gas was nobody's fault but her own.

YOU WERE SUPPOSED TO HAVE SOMEONE drive you home, take care of you for the first seventy-two hours, but Regan, by design, had no one. As far as anyone in her other life knew, she'd taken off after Christmas not for Canada, but for Italy, to spend a semester studying the *commedia dell'arte*. She'd started laying the groundwork at Thanksgiving; this ancient theatrical rite, she said, survived in its purest form in rocky little Piemontese villages that would be hard to reach by phone. It had still seemed possible, so far before any quickening, that things would turn out differently, that she would carry her baby to term and then put it up for adoption. And in either case, she couldn't stay so close to home. Daddy was preoccupied as usual, but Felicia remembered, suddenly: "What about the wedding? You'll be back by June? We've always talked about a June wedding."

"But Daddy said you'd agreed to wait for William to graduate first," Regan pointed out. "And this is a once-in-a-lifetime chance for me. If you want a June wedding, you'll have to wait till '61." At which William looked up from the napkin he'd been doodling on and mouthed the words *Thank you.*

Now, lying in bed the morning after the procedure, she thought of phoning him and confessing everything. William would have been on a plane within hours and never breathed a word. Instead, she changed the two pads she'd bled through in the night and propped herself by the window. The motel was so hard-up that they'd turned off the vacancy sign to save money, and beyond it she could just see Lake Erie, the wind stiffening the waves into peaks. The room had two TVs, stacked one atop the other, but only one of them worked. She left it on all afternoon to cover her crying—not that there was anyone to listen—and ate peanut butter out of the jar.

WHEN SHE WAS WELL ENOUGH to drive, she headed back to Buffalo. The address where the Goulds had grown up was on Essex Street. She'd expected something grander than a dilapidated townhouse on a tiny lot. She got out of the car and tested the boards on the windows. The nails held; nothing in there was going to get out. Then she went to see a realtor and signed a six-month lease on a bungalow near the university, sight unseen. Insofar as she had any plan left at all, she was sure the place would be fine, and it was. The tarpaulin covering an unshingled patch of roof would remain there for the length of her occupancy, but there was a deep tub in the bathroom and a fireplace in the den, and shops and restaurants to serve the people her age nearby. She rang in the 1960s downing an entire pizza in front of a fire she'd built with her own hands. Her mom used to chivvy them into the pews at St. John the Martyr for the New Year's Day service; what you do the first day of the year decides what you'll be doing the rest of it, was her superstition. Regan wasn't sure what crappy Buffalo pizza signified, or the lone glass of wine with which she chased it, except that for the foreseeable future, she'd be doing a lot of things on her own.

SHE EVENTUALLY GREW TO FEEL OKAY about the town. It was scruffy, beat-up, depressed, but resolute. And aside from the pizza, the food was surprisingly decent, though maybe anything short of awful would have seemed that way. If she had fantasies of further investigating the Goulds, amassing proof that they weren't what they seemed, she didn't follow through. Meaning there was no plan, she had no real reason still to be here. She killed the endless hours in local diners and cafés, or in her rented bathtub, forking moo shu pork from a box on the floor while she read her way through such plays as the college bookstore carried. At Vassar, she'd been a Shakespearean, but these were mostly contemporary, the theater she'd dismissed as absurd for absurdity's sake. Now it seemed a higher form of realism. Here stood Regan, after all, on a stage cleared of other people, with no logical path forward. Just senseless stretches of time, static little vignettes separated by "blackouts"—which on the page, paradoxically, took the form of white space between starved black intervals of text.

LATE AFTERNOON, a funeral parlor on the East Side of Manhattan. Rows of empty folding chairs face a casket. The carpet is dark, the walls salmon-pink. Enter: a little girl, wearing the uniform of the private school she's been out of for a week. Her younger brother, also at home, has been told she is visiting a friend down the street, but really she has come here, an hour before the start of the viewing neither of them will be allowed to attend, to say goodbye to her mom. Such is the compromise she's reached with her father, after resorting to the tears he cannot bear to see her cry. Now, as he lingers in the doorway, she approaches the casket. The silver dress. The red hair, the eyes only slightly sunken. They've done a good job with the face; it's just, something is off about the mouth. Mom's had been so alive, always in motion, always with a smile or an ironic sigh—they should have had William come and sit for the likeness.

She had been the one big act of rebellion Daddy, from two long lines of Presbyterians, had ever managed: Kathryn Hébert, a New Orleans-born Catholic. And lately, as Regan entered her own refractory age, Mom had said that what seemed to be your problems were sometimes a function of not paying better attention to other people's. Regan thought about this often. There was a man missing half his tongue who for a few months had sat on the landing at the subway entrance up by school, shaking a cup for change. Every time Regan passed him, there came a second when the desire to give almost overwhelmed her. But to reach into her satchel for her wallet would mean letting him see that she had a wallet, which would mean she would have to give tomorrow, and the next day; and looking at him without reaching for the wallet would mean she didn't care; and using the other subway entrance would mean admitting she was ashamed of what after all everybody in this city felt, so she taught herself to hurry past without seeing. Then one night as they came back from the school production of *By Jupiter* in the company of other girls and their mothers, Mom had stopped on the landing to dig around in her purse. Twenty years in New York, and she could be so excruciatingly touristy. She met the man's eye, pressed a bill into his hand, and then they'd moved along back to their privileged world, except for Regan, who lingered to watch the man take out his own wallet, place the bill inside, and then continue shaking. Her mother's belief that you could know the first thing about anyone else's problems struck her as both presumptuous and manifestly wrong—like the belief that God would be merciful, even when you weren't asking. Hadn't Mom suffered there in the end? She'd been rear-ended at an intersection in Westchester, on her way to a luncheon. The car skidded forward into the highway. A truck struck the driver's side. It must have left no teeth, because the problem Regan has detected in the mouth before her is its dentures. Mom suffered a great deal. This is the other lie they've told William, that it was quick and painless; for two days, while she held on, Daddy had been with her at the hospital round-the-clock. It was when Doonie had become Doonie, and Mom had ceased to be Mom. What Regan knows: the universe has no author. And now neither does her mother. And so there is no one here to bid goodbye, as Daddy reaches for her hand.

THE SPRING AFTER HER ABORTION, Regan attended Mass at a Carmelite chapel near the bungalow she'd rented. On the Church's own terms, her actions were meaningless, even damnable, but the service was in Latin, which meant she didn't have to listen to the God stuff, and the nuns who mostly filled the pews felt comforting. The sisters, people in town called them, as if they were interchangeable. They never asked what had brought her. Maybe they knew they couldn't understand. But no, she decided, that too was presumptuous. Then, on Wednesday nights, with a group of surprisingly unsanctimonious parishioners, she began making the rounds in a rickety truck that delivered meals to people who needed them. Handing coffee cups and hot foil containers through the truck's open side-panel, she saw her mother in the subway. She made herself look into the faces of these men and women who slept in alleys and parking lots less than a mile from mansions built by industrialists and subsequently abandoned for the 'burbs. These houses *had* to sit empty, it occurred to her, to prevent a collapse in property values . . . in much the same way as a certain quantum of working-age Americans had to be kept jobless to ensure a buyer's market for labor. So maybe Mom had been right about this much at least: Where exactly did Regan Hamilton-Sweeney get off feeling sorry for herself?

SHE WENT HOME TO NEW YORK, and then to college, believing she'd found what she'd been waiting for up there—a return to perspective. Six months away should have been enough. But back among people who didn't know what had happened, she felt heavy again, as if more than one life remained within her. And as Felicia hinted now and then, the heaviness wasn't just imaginary. Her body was still craving whatever had sustained her up in Buffalo. She would watch herself in the campus cafeteria, in the grip of some impulse, load up on instant mashed potatoes and bland chocolate cake and milk from the boxy steel milk machine. Later she would lock herself in the windowless attic bathroom of the sorority house. With the lights out, she would recall those other sisters, the Carmelites, and fantasize that they'd helped deliver a girl—a terrible warm bundle in the crook of an arm, her sobbing perfectly calibrated to Regan's pain receptors here in the Chi-O john. Other times it was a boy. Sometimes she would hum, so quietly no one could hear, that nonsense song Daddy used to sing when William was in the pram. And now she would start to feel fat with guilt. Fat with grief. Finally, she would make herself vomit, as a fellow pledge had shown her how to do in more innocent days.

By mid-November her teeth had begun to feel funny, her hair to come off in her hairbrush, and she'd lost twelve pounds when she weighed herself, which was daily. It couldn't have been good for her—she was smart enough to know that, even when the door was locked and the crazy person inside her emerged—but there seemed to be no bottom to her shame.

THAT WAS THE DECEMBER she met Keith, at the wrap party for *Twelfth Night*. The stage was the one place that felt safe to her now, and though the Sylvia Plath equation of authenticity with suffering had come to seem like teenage flummery, pain had deepened her acting. Or the role had: Regan disappearing into Viola disappearing into Cesario. She was still wearing stage makeup when she noticed the broad-shouldered and inordinately attractive young man watching her from the far side of the student-union basement. On the hi-fi was the Flamingos' "I Only Have Eyes for You," and already the song and smoke and bodies around them were melting into a tunnel of synesthetic glass.

It was important that Keith was everything the other boy wasn't. Physically, he could have broken L. over his knee. She wouldn't find out until their first official date that he'd played football, but it didn't surprise her; the athlete's thoughtless grace, that ease in his own body, made her feel nothing was ulterior. When he said he could walk her back to her sorority, if she wanted, what was on offer was simple protection. Companionship. And where most walkers watched the ground, Keith Lamplighter looked at the moon.

He was a senior at the University of Connecticut, studying to be a doctor, but his studies seemed not to take up much of his time. During exam period alone, he rode the bus to Poughkeepsie twice to take her out to movies. On the second of these dates, he asked for her address back in New York City. The brevity and good cheer of the Christmas card that arrived there the following week would sustain her through an outwardly miserable vacation. Amory had returned from overseas to help with the wedding arrangements, and Felicia had pressed Regan into trying on bridesmaid dresses. But the Goulds could not reach her mind, or the thoughts of Keith that filled it.

By the time she brought him to meet Daddy and William—by the time he stood up to Amory with his wondrous self-assurance—her weight had stabilized, and she had begun to feel, however improbably, that she was being rescued. She wanted to give Keith something in return, to reward him for being so well-adjusted, generous, handsome, bright, uncomplicated. What she would give him, she decided, was herself.

62

W HAT NICKY DIDN'T SEEM TO GET was that music had been a lark, a joke. William and Big Mike, both painters, already spent all day taking themselves too seriously. Venus cut hair for a living. Up until the oil crunch of '74, Nastanovich had worked in a fish cannery in Union City, New Jersey. They didn't *want* to treat the band like a job. They'd chosen the name via Ouija board, for God's sake. They'd made up the track listing for the first LP before writing a single song:

SIDE A	SIDE B
Army Recruiter	Brass Tactics
VHF	Down on the Bathroom Floor
Egg Cream Blues	Dog Parade on Avenue B
Anyone Over 30 Gets It	It Feels So Good When I Stop
In The Neck	Someday, Comrade Fourier
East Village Zombies/	(The Lemonade Song)
UWS Ghouls	

Most of it had been recorded in one take, William declaiming spontaneous poetry in that mock-Cockney accent because he had no idea how to really sing. The Constructivist cover art, the uniforms Venus had sewn for their live act, the manifesto from which William would read aloud before each gig, and really the whole revolutionary mise-en-scène had just been a way to blow off steam, to fuck with people's heads. If they'd managed to reach some kid at the back of the Vault or in a crash-pad in the East Village or wherever he'd first heard *Brass Tactics*, it had been at least partly accidental. Or did the music at some point cease to belong to those who'd made it? Because here was Nicky, throat clenched, trying to show William how to replicate that hitch in his own voice from "Dog Parade" where they'd had to splice together two vocal takes—an overly literal exegete of what was for him, if not for his bandmates, a sacred text.

Once Nicky had usurped the vocal duties entirely, each rehearsal became like an audition for the Philharmonic. If it had been up to him, they wouldn't even have stopped to piss. He'd wander over to a corner of the garage in the middle of a song, unzip, and urinate in an old paint-can, still shouting into his microphone. And what could you say, really, in the face of such commitment? While Nicky practiced the same three-bar phrase over and over again, until the melody lost its meaning, William could only stare down at the guitar cords coiled densely on the floor. Sometimes, as a kind of art-school exercise, he attempted mentally to disentangle them, but the grimy little tabs of masking tape marking Channel 1 and Channel 2 were useless. It was impossible to tell anymore which cord led to his Danelectro and which to Nastanovich's Jazzmaster bass and which to Venus's Farfisa and which to the knockoff Fender Mustang Nicky wore like a talisman but never touched.

Not that William was painting much these days, anyway. He'd hit some kind of wall right around the time he'd realized no one was ever going to care what he did with a brush the way a thousand screaming teenagers seemed to care about what he and his buddies had banged out one weekend with two hundred dollars of recording time and a pile of borrowed gear. Plus his corpus to date sucked eggs. For months, Bruno Augenblick had been after him to take part in a group show at the gallery. He wanted to come by the loft to pick out two or three pieces, but to William, in the winter light through the sooty window, it all looked reactionary, redundant, underwritten by the motions of a system too vast to comprehend, the way planetary spin inflects the movement of wastewater down a drain. Another way of putting it might have been that he was blocked, but this raised questions he didn't want to think about. He experienced it instead as a second-by-second disinclination to continue.

When his shoulder started to ache under the guitar strap, William would make eye contact with Venus and then stage some interruption—a beer run, a cigarette break—knowing full well that Nastanovich would use this as an excuse (*Well, so long as Billy's gonna smoke, I might as well go grab a sandwich . . .*) and that his absence would buy them fifteen or twenty minutes of down time. Because it wasn't really a sandwich the bassist needed as he slunk out into the night; it was a fix.

Given the slightest invitation, the tiniest recognition of their brotherhood of need, William would have followed. But he'd sworn to keep his own dabbling secret, as if to deny that heroin had changed anything at all. After that first, transformative nod in the office above the record store, he had resolved to wait a week before doing it again. It was like waiting to call a phone number someone had slipped in your pocket after a grope in a club. And when, after only thirty-six hours, he did dip back into the bag, he first tried snorting it like coke, while Eartha K. looked on from the futon. At some point in the past, H would have been exactly the sort of thing he hurled himself into headlong. But it was as if he sensed the gravity of the line he was soft-shoeing around. He'd seen the kids on Christopher Street who turned tricks to feed the habit, their potholed arms, hellish smiles the telltale gray-brown of teeth gone dead at the root. Some part of him wanted to preserve for as long as possible the option to opt out, to reveal himself to have only been playing at degradation.

Unfortunately, snorting smack didn't yield the same high. It was fine for like watching TV, but he missed the visions, the religion of it. He'd graduated to smoking, with similar results, and then to skin-popping, and finally to shooting between his toes, as one of his dealers did. Ah. At last. He could be on the most astonishing nod and still look down at arms as smooth and white as elephant tusks, arms that should have been in a fucking museum, telling the world he was still in control. Lately he'd started carrying works and a little auxiliary stash around with him in his great-grandfather's shaving kit, just in case. And where once he'd resolved to get high only alone—he never had liked to share—by February he would be squatting with Nastanovich in the weird little yard behind the practice space.

It was strange, he'd always thought: this pocket of untenanted land walled in by buildings, as if it predated the rest of the city. You reached it by squeezing past a warped swatch of chainlink between two brownstones that for some reason had not been built flush. The side of each house was chalky, limestoney, and they got closer together the farther back you went, so that if you were schlepping, say, a kick drum, you began to wonder if you were going to make it. Then you were through, in the yard, looking at a squat brick building like a janitorial kiosk in a city-run park. It was unclear which of the surrounding buildings it belonged to. Back in the fall, the ground around it, under the never-quite-dark sky, had been a weedy mess glinting with pop-bottle fragments and crushed vials, but all that had vanished now under a layer of snow. Clotheslines crisscrossed crazily above. No one ever complained about the noise. Nastanovich scooped a lemon-sized ball of snow with the spoon he'd taken from his pocket and used a finger to level off the excess. Through the brick wall they hunkered against, William felt the tremor of notes he couldn't name: Venus, bored or impatient, exploring the lower registers of her organ. "Seriously, Nastanovich," he said. "That's filthy. You're going to get us sick."

"What do socialites shoot with, Billy? Holy water? Besides, I don't see no tap." Nastanovich nodded vaguely toward their sordid environs, but his attention was all on the lighter-flame tonguing the bottom of the spoon. You had to hand it to him: he was smarter than people took him for. Smarter even, apparently, than William, who could have insisted on sterility, but who had never gotten high with Nastanovich before, and didn't want to bollix the chance of there being a next time.

He rubbed his hands together for warmth and squatted down himself and concentrated on the lick, lick of the flame. He felt, in a sense, beheld; anyone who cared to look out a back window right now might have seen them, two degenerates hunched in a circle of light. More likely, of course, they would have just seen the lighter (someone had shot out the yard's lone streetlight long ago) and what could they have done anyway? People were cooking up all over the East Village. Probably even in some of these rooms. As long as you were safe in your apartment, why rock the boat? Snowmelt and dope bubbled and hissed in the concavity of the spoon and let off oily steam. Nastanovich's hands stayed solid. In William's experience, etiquette dictated that the guest boot up first, but when he reached down to undo the knotted lace of his sneaker, Nastanovich asked what the hell he was doing. "Fuck that," he said, when William tried to explain. "Give me your arm, homeboy." He took the syringe in his teeth and tied William off.

"Jesus," William heard himself say as the plunger dropped. It was the first time he'd mainlined since that day above Señor Wax, and he was unprepared for the pinch in his arm, the flush and shiver carrying him away across the bounded infinity of snow. He didn't realize that Nastanovich had already fixed himself up until the bassist rose again, sniffling, and wobbled around the corner toward a parallelogram of light that had opened. William brushed snow off the butt of his jeans and teetered after his bandmate.

Inside, the bare bulb, which before had seemed cold and insufficient, still did, except now there was something utterly specific about the light, like a memory already lived through. These were not *William's* feet moving over the stained concrete. They belonged to some previous person whose choices were already behind him. As did the grin floating free of his head, like a daisy on a stalk. As did the hands strapping on his guitar, dragging through the barre chords of "E. Vill Zombies" and a cover of the Nightmares' "Horrors of the Black Museum" and a new bit of pith called "Make Me Sick." Now, when Nicky Chaos, unsatisfied, wanted to run through the intro to "Brass Tactics" for the twentieth time—"but faster . . . and can you guys make it swing less? It should sound like jackboots"—William could just swim down into the loops and whorls of those cables heaped on the floor, like a minnow tucking itself away in kelp beds, or like an appraiser inspecting at close distance the fractal curves of what may or may not have been a Pollock.

WHEN NASTANOVICH DIED, in June, William wasn't around for it, and didn't find out until he showed up at the garage for practice one day, still a little loaded, with his leather kit stashed in his guitar case. Everyone was sitting around on amplifiers, staring at the floor. Even Sol Grungy, Nicky's personal sound guy, looked chastened. "What's up?"

Nastanovich OD'd, someone said.

"Oh. Is he all right? He's all right, right?"

"His mother found him when he didn't come down for breakfast," Venus said, looking straight at William. The whites of her eyes were pink, as from swimming-pool chlorine. "He still had the belt around his arm."

William didn't know what to do. The top half of his body weighed a ton. He sank down right on the cool concrete, all those redundant cables. "Fuck."

"I say we still play today," Nicky said, after a while. "It's what he would have wanted. If there were a life besides this one, he'd be looking down on us from that great rent-controlled apartment in the sky, egging us on. So I say we play."

"I say fuck you," Venus said. William seconded that emotion, but didn't know how to say so, so he stood and walked out.

IT HAD BEEN A LONG TIME since he'd prepared a canvas, and his toolbox was on the bottom of a shelf blocked by a shopping cart he'd found somewhere, which was filled now with old issues of *Cosmopolitan* and *Wrecking Ball* and anatomy books shoplifted from the Strand. He couldn't move it—wasn't as strong as he used to be—so he had to unload the cart and find new places for the books, which took half the morning. Eventually, though, he had the tools to nail together a four-by-four frame (a vestigial reflex, blame New York: he still had the conviction that American art should be Big). He stretched the canvas, stapled it to form a blank surface, a tight white drum. And maybe the contest between painting and dope was not as lopsided as it seemed, because over the next two days, while he waited for the layers of gesso to dry, William got by on only ten dollars' worth of drugs.

He decided to turn inward, paint whatever he found there, and when the canvas was ready, he covered it in black gouache. What came next was an off-center polygon, low and to the right, eight-sided, slashing. He wasn't happy with its color, a brown like dried blood, so he mixed up a translucent blue and went back over the edges. He built up an interior with yellow, then fire-engine red. The instant the red hit the canvas, though, he felt physically ill. Not so much nausea as a whole-body itch. Because the octagon was death, it seemed to William. A rust-colored figure the size of a bowler hat, rimmed with blue voltage. A snuffer like he'd used as an altar boy, back before his mom died and he stopped believing in God—only viewed from below as it came to put out your flame. He thought of Nastanovich intently scooping up snow, of the narcotized monotone of his basslines, of colorless fish slop squirted into assembly-line cans and the plaster-walled room in Middle Village where he'd lived with his mother. It was a life that hadn't been worth much, from the outside. Things weren't looking so hot for William's either, just at present. What he wanted more than anything was to escape, go blow some guy in a bathroom, go get so high the top of his head would blow off, but he owed it to his dead friend to stay here and force himself to wait to be told what to do. At which point he would reach once more for the brush.

IN THIS WAY, the first time around, William managed to kick cold turkey. He stayed in the loft with the phone disconnected. He threw up a lot and for a week could eat only Neapolitan ice cream, first the chocolate stripe, then the strawberry, and finally the freezer-burned vanilla. When his hands weren't steady, he listened to the radio. When they were, he painted. By the end of that month, when he started to feel like himself again, he was deep into the work. The black background had gained weight and texture, like the swimmy darkness you see right before you lose consciousness, and the foreground sported a brighter border. He felt he was painting now from memory, filling in shadows and light. There was a light source somewhere, a particular source of a particular summer light that distilled itself into a glare near the center of the octagon, like a flash seen in a mirror. And as he painted up the edges, adding blue and green traces of that flash, he could make out letters. *S T O P.* But this wasn't that flat, affectless Pop thing, the Brillo box, the soup can. If anything, it was the opposite: a stop-sign whose unique scumble of urban grit— whose peeling green pole, textured upon the canvas, whose reflection of morning light near a river in summer—made William want to cry. It was the stop-sign at the end of Sutton Place, which he'd last seen sliding past the window of a stolen car on the morning he'd left home for good. A piece of evidence, though of what, he didn't know.

HE'D SORT OF ASSUMED the bassist's death and the guitarist's disappearance would mean the end of Ex Post Facto; his phone didn't ring even after he plugged it back in, and he didn't bother to tell anyone. It pleased him, secretly, to be free of the band. For one thing, it meant that Nicky Chaos would never get his most ardent wish: to play a live show as the frontman. He found himself surprisingly bitter toward

Nicky, blaming him somehow for Nastanovich, though of course if he'd really been looking for someone to blame, he might have started with himself. Then, leaving his building one day, he found Nicky on the front step. He must have been waiting, though how he knew when William was going to leave was anybody's guess. Maybe he'd been there all night. "Hey, Billy, hold up—can we talk?" William kept moving toward the corner; Nicky followed. "You look good."

"Thanks."

"Listen," Nicky said. "It's been a couple months now, I've been thinking it's time we got the band back together."

"There is no 'we' anymore, Nicky. You have to know this. There is no band."

"Okay, I get that, I respect that, but this thing is bigger than one person. All those kids out there with nowhere to go, just waiting for someone they can follow . . ."

"It'll have to be someone other than me." They were at the subway steps now. "I'm out."

"Sol thinks he can wire Tompkins Square for sound, run it off a lamppost. I'm saying we play one last show for free, take up a collection, set up a kind of charity, like the Concert for Bangladesh. Only, the Concert for Nastanovich. Maybe record it live."

" 'Concert for Bangladesh'? I can't think of anything less punk."

"And then give the dough to his mom. She's real emotional, you know. Or maybe you don't. I guess you weren't at the funeral, were you?"

William hated him for a minute. A year ago, Nicky had barely known Nastanovich's name. "I've got to go, Nick. Why don't I think about it and get back to you?"

"I won't take no for an answer, you know."

"I know you won't," William said. "I'm just not quite ready to give you the satisfaction of yes." And without another word, he went down into the ground.

63

"THE THING ABOUT NGUYENS," said her father, from the passenger's seat, "is we always have to learn everything the hard way." They were somewhere east of the Rockies, in a rental truck with a shaky transmission. For the last half-hour, he'd been reading speed-limit signs aloud, and Jenny assumed that this was just another way of telling her to slow down. When she turned up the radio instead, he fell silent again, staring out at his adopted country, its flat confusing billboards and harvest-green heart.

In retrospect, though, a couple things would strike her. One was that he'd been talking about himself as much as about her. The other was that maybe he'd been right.

A few weeks after being allowed to graduate, she'd returned home to the Valley, flattering herself that her presence would help Dad through the divorce, but for all the good it did him, she might as well have joined the Peace Corps, or journeyed to the moon. Meanwhile, the world she'd been so eager to change—the world *out there*—was passing her by. All she could do, coming back at night from dinner at Mom and Sandy's, was sit with her father in the aquarium of the living room to watch a recap of the travails of his beloved Dick Nixon. It had taken her over a year to break the news to him that she wanted to move to New York.

They reached it now on day four of the drive, thanks largely to her lead foot. Still, they had only a few hours to unload her furniture (such as it was) before he had to go turn in the truck and catch his flight home. One of these hours they wasted navigating a warren of one-way streets before she found the address on Rivington where she'd arranged to rent a flat. The building was dun-colored, jumbled with fire escapes like orthodonture over bad teeth. The windows had bars all the way up to the fourth floor, and it had been eons, probably, since the glass had been washed. But Jenny was no stranger to squalor; she'd done four years at Berserkeley, after all. Inside, the door to 3F had been left ajar. It was less the *junior one-bedroom* she'd been promised on the phone than a glorified closet. The bathtub adjoined the refrigerator. Her dad glanced out the window at the hoodlums sizing up the moving van below. How could a landlord charge the equivalent of a mortgage payment, he asked, and not even provide a living room? She'd known it was a mistake to tell him what she was paying. She pointed out that the whole city would be her living room, which made the apartment a bargain, if you thought about it. The logic of this cliché impressed her at the time. What she'd failed to take into account was the fact that most people's living rooms didn't have weather, whereas in hers, it could rain for days. Not to mention all the other ways the blurring of indoor and outdoor would work against her, as when six-legged forest creatures came lumbering out of the broiler grate the first time she turned on the oven.

On the plus side, it was easier here to score pot. There was a store a couple blocks over, it looked like a bodega from the outside, but there was hardly any merchandise on the shelves. Set back into the wall was a padlocked door with a little window, like a castle keep. You walked up and asked for vegetables, and the taciturn Dominican in the shadows back there would look at you really hard to make sure you weren't a narc and then would slide a pre-rolled joint under the chickenwire. It wasn't the good stuff per se, but it was good enough. While the record-beating rain beat down outside, Jenny sat at the little desk or table she'd set up as a buffer between her mattress and the tub and spaced out, imagining her apartment as an ark where forsaken fauna, mice and pigeons, bedbugs and silverfish, might shelter two-by-two from the flood. She imagined Mr. and Mrs. Cucaraccia, the couple from under the oven, strolling arm-in-arm up the gangway, the husband lifting his straw boater to her as he reached the top, the wife performing an articulate little curtsey.

Other times, she amused herself by listening to the noise. It was more or less a constant, seeping through walls and ceilings until it was hard to tell exactly which neighbor was producing it. By the end of the first month, she'd developed an entirely aural picture of their lives: feet, large and small, running and walking; cop shows and salsa music; banging on the radiator pipes; a ringing phone; tap practice, sousaphone practice, someone yodeling; people fucking, occasionally; people fighting, constantly; yelling for kids to *Come to dinner, goddammit*, slamming ovens, banging doors. When she passed her neighbors in the half-lit stairwell, of course, she would pretend to have heard nothing. They would just as lief knife you as say hello. Sometimes she had to almost literally bite her tongue against the urge to congratulate the Ukrainian woman upstairs whose several orgasms had kept her awake the night before, or to offer her sympathies to someone she'd heard sobbing on the phone. The most amazing thing was how much richer their lives were than she'd imagined. These people extravagantly alive in these contexts all around her, while she, a singleton, sat alone.

WHAT WAS NEEDED—to be vulgarly materialist about it—was a job. The seed money her father had placed in her account was dwindling, and would sustain at most another few months of loosies and ramen and rent. But in fall of 1974 there were no jobs, at least not for a philosophy major with a rap sheet. She spent a couple days canvassing for Greenpeace, but found it hard to knock on doors knowing they'd be slammed in her face. Then she temped for a while through an agency. The work involved reading fine print at the bottoms of newspaper ads, hundreds of thousands of them it seemed, that were implicated in a class-action lawsuit against an evil real-estate developer. Jenny's first paycheck was signed by the evil real-estate developer. As a kind of penance, she blew half of it at a bookstore near Union Square, amassing a pile of volumes by Frankfurt School theoreticians, but it failed to make her feel better, so she just didn't go to work the next day, staying home instead and getting super-duper high. A good thing, too, because that's the day the phone rang about a position she hardly remembered applying for, at a small art gallery in SoHo.

The owner was Austrian, with tortoiseshell eyeglasses and a shaved head. If it was possible to look like a less jolly Michel Foucault, then he did. He was obviously homosexual, and preferred, he told her at the interview (watching carefully for her reaction), the company of young people. He was also, she was guessing, filthy rich. But they shared a taste for the conceptual, and he agreed to advance her the first month's pay and give her meaningful responsibilities right away. She was to be his sole employee, after all.

He showed her to her desk—actually a long dining table he'd placed near the front door, so that anyone looking to steal the art off the walls or floor would have to pass beneath Jenny's watchful eye. The notion was comical in at least two ways. One: Assuming these were your average thieves—male, burly, whacked on angel dust— how was Jenny, a buck ten in heavy boots, supposed to stop them? And two: Who besides Jenny would really want to steal this art— sculptures fashioned from cigarette butts; homoerotic jello molds; a pile of rags in one corner you might mistake for trash? Bruno had one of the world's great poker faces, but he liked her cheekiness; she could tell by the way his eyes flashed behind the glasses. "Deterrence, *Liebchen*. Deterrence." He knocked on the tabletop once.

She sat down, to get a feel for where she'd be spending her days. There was a phone, of course, and a mimeographed price guide to the work on display, and a small electric typewriter for correspondence, but, given that its surface area must have been twenty square feet, the desk looked positively austere. In this way, it was of a piece with the rest of the gallery, which in a previous life had been an auto body shop. A single panel of reinforced glass had been installed where the garage door had been. Exposed girders framed a skylight. The floors were buffed concrete. Every Austrian, she thought, was a minimalist. (Later, on a fact-finding mission to the Metropolitan Museum, she would be shocked to discover a reproduced Viennese dining room of the nineteenth century, all floral porcelain and elaborate engravery. But of course, the scale of the trauma that had taken place between Bruno's grandparents' generation and Bruno's was incalculable.)

To her surprise, he would say nothing about the mess that came to cover her desk. For one thing, she was practically *living* at the gallery. Thirty-two hours a week! For another, no one ever entered it, save for a few far-sighted investors who bought only by appointment. Even the openings were dismal affairs, with Bruno and the artists and Jenny standing around drinking boxed wine with the occasional drifter drawn in off the street by the wino's free-booze ESP. Jenny always insisted on serving them.

The largest part of her job turned out to be ghost-writing grant applications for Bruno's artists, none of whom, he freely admitted, were ever likely to support themselves on the open market. *So how do you expect to make money?* she wanted to ask. Bruno's indifference to the fiscal was part of why she was able to work for him with a clean-ish conscience, but now that their fortunes were yoked together, she would have liked to have seen a little more entrepreneurial vim. She herself had, at his urging, begun dressing what he called *more professionally.* When she checked herself in the mirror in the morning (in a *blouse*, for God's sake) she felt like a sellout, but at least now there was some purpose to getting out of bed.

COMPROMISES SNOWBALLED. By her second February, she had joined a dating service. You filled out a questionnaire, you mailed in a Polaroid, and for $12.99 you received a dossier of questionnaires and Polaroids from men whose interests had been matched to yours via punch-card. It was embarrassing—assuming something worked out, how did you explain to friends how you'd met?—but the fact that Jenny didn't have any friends was why she'd signed up for the service in the first place. The punch-cards, however, proved unreliable. The bachelors in her dossier were Leos and Geminis; turn-ons included theater, dancing, and fondue. She held out for beverage-based meetings, easy to escape. If they went moderately well, she'd invite the men back to her place. She interpreted as an auspicious sign the ability to cross Bowery without bolting for safety.

There weren't many places to sit in her apartment, if you considered two to be not many, which she did. She'd tried sitting on the bed once, with a Taurus named Frank who'd seemed like a bit of a swinger, but perhaps the ululations of pleasure leaking through from her Ukrainian neighbor put too much pressure on them, because Frank had excused himself after one glass of Cold Duck, never to be heard from again. Then she'd tried drinking too much, in order to facilitate the transition into sex, but that backfired, too. It was as if, in her post-McGillicuddy renunciation of bourgeois courtship and monogamy, she'd forgotten how the game was played. One night, she heard herself explaining to a date, out on Broome Street with the busboys carrying out the night's first trash and the players at the mah-jongg club raking their tiles together like scrimshanders sorting whalebone, about the seating arrangements at her place, and the possible awkwardness, and how they should probably just move straight to fucking. "Jesus, I sound neurotic, don't I?" Ben, was the name of that one. Nice guy, really. A Ph.D. candidate in primatology at Columbia, who might have been able to clarify certain enduring puzzles of assortative mating, had he stuck around. But he left a message with her service the following morning saying he couldn't see her anymore.

She hung up the phone and slumped at her desk, where she'd been editing a Guggenheim application. Chinks in her fortress of papers and books let through the cool morning light of the street. She stared down at the color slides she'd been studying, digging for antecedents for this artist's punctilious replicas of hotel paintings from the Midwest. It was supposed to be the shift in context, the little jolt of misprision, that made it art. She had just put her head down on her arms when the top half of a stack of *catalogues raisonnés* levitated in front of her to reveal Bruno's shaved head, which never changed so much as a whisker from day to day. "*Morgen,*" he said, before dropping the books again. He steamed across the gallery toward his own tiny office in back, where as far as she knew he sat all day sipping espresso and reading week-old news in the German-language paper he special-ordered through a newsstand on Sixth Avenue. Directly beneath the skylight, though, he stopped. "Something is wrong."

"No."

"Come now. I refuse to be lied to. Some young man has wronged you, hasn't he?" From a person who renounced on principle the possibility of a transcendental morality, she thought, it was an interesting choice of words.

"None of them's stuck around long enough to wrong me, Bruno."

He waved a hand dismissively. "Romance is a fiction anyway. A myth to sell greeting cards." Still, he seemed ready, given a name and address, to go challenge the malefactor, like some feudal-era father defending his daughter's chastity. This was all in the eyes, of course. The rest of the face stayed perfectly composed. "If you want to know what the problem is, it's that apartment of yours. They see it and judge you unfairly."

"Who says they ever see it? You've never seen it."

"Please, darling. I mail your checks. Rivington Street?" He shuddered.

"Look around us, Bruno. It's not like this neighborhood's much better."

"With a public concern, an address downtown sends a certain

message, projects a certain *vous savez quoi*. But I don't have to carry that into private life. Do you think your beloved Herr Adorno never watched television? I have it on good authority he never missed an episode of *Gilligan's Island*. The problem with you Americans is your mania for consistency." Bruno's little lectures, she'd decided, were 85 percent ironic. The conceit that she would be under his tutelage provided an almost rueful amusement. "Even now, even in New York, you haven't learned that consistency won't protect you. I live uptown, shamelessly. And you should, too. Young men will flock to a woman who appears not to need them." He seemed to have convinced himself of something. "In fact, I will give you a raise to cover it."

"Bruno, this is ridiculous. Let's start over. Good morning."

"No. I insist." He held up a hand. His checkbook was out.

"You're making me feel guilty, like I've maneuvered you into something, when I'm just having a crappy morning, is all."

He thought for a second. "An experiment then. You will come with me this Sunday to dine with an old friend of mine. He has never taken my advice. He lives, that is, in a fantasy world, believing in the same kind of bohemia you cling to. You look in his eyes and decide if this is what you want. If not, we move you uptown."

"Sunday? Isn't that the Bicentennial?"

"Do you have plans? Will you be out waving empire's proud flag? No? I thought not."

THAT DINNER WAS MISERABLE. She'd assumed Bruno was trying to make a match, and so hadn't realized, until the artist showed up towing a boyfriend, that he was gay. Instead of hitting it off, she had to watch the three men push and pull with each other for upwards of two hours. It was only as a kind of punishment that she said afterward to her employer, "Fine, I'll let you move me, but I'm not going north of Twenty-Third. And you can pay for the truck."

She told herself she wasn't abandoning the Lower East Side, wasn't forsaking its proletarian freedoms for the trappings of the middle class. After all, the new building, for all its perks, was hardly a fount of civility. The people in the elevator treated her exactly as the tenants of the old place had. And there wasn't any less noise to keep her awake at night.

The difference was that it was now all *outside*: the irascible all-

night traffic, the cabs in front of the Ethiopian takeaways, the grind
ing, saurian garbage trucks. When she awakened in the a.m. into
blind-slit shrinking nowhereness, it had all gone disorientingly quiet,
and she would imagine for a few seconds she was back there in that
mausoleum of a ranch house in the San Fernando Valley. She readied
herself for the sound of her father's wire whisk against the sides of a
stainless steel bowl, the brush of his knuckles against her bedroom
door. And as the black got light, she wondered what this all meant.
Had she left some unfinished business back in California? Or was
it simply the way a place lived in long enough imprints itself on the
still-soft tissues of the brain? Or, simpler yet, did she miss it, that
mouse-quiet house where they'd called her by another name? There'd
been a time when she'd believed herself capable of living without the
conventional comforts—career, possessions, significant other—but
her self-imposed exile was revealing her to be frustratingly human.
This didn't mean she'd given up on the dream that the larger situation might be changed, or at least analyzed. But, by the time she met
Richard, she'd begun to accept Bruno's proposition that if the revolution ever happened, it would be without, or prior to, any alteration to
the contours of her own individual existence. Here she was after two
years in New York, only just learning to scale her expectations down
to the size of her actual life. It was like trying to squeeze toothpaste
back into the tube.

64

REGAN WAS TO SPEND HER EARLY THIRTIES puzzling over the central conviction of her twenties. Where had she gotten the idea that there was no problem so big love couldn't fix it? But this was probably just another way of being hard on herself; a better question might have been, Where *hadn't* she gotten it? Wherever you turned in those years, there were love beads and love-ins, "Love Me Do" and "When a Man Loves a Woman." You couldn't be a citizen of your own time and not believe on some level that love was, as another song put it, all you needed. She'd held fast to her love through the joys and sorrows of the '60s. Through the showdown between Daddy and William, through Daddy's wedding and her own, through Keith's career change, Will's birth, Cate's . . . Perhaps this was why she was so slow to see the unhappiness creeping back in after they moved to the Upper East Side. Or to acknowledge, to herself or to her husband, that she saw it. She'd been so much unhappier in the pre-Keith past; she was still grateful to him for all he'd saved her from. In fact, she would come to wonder if it wasn't that unhappiness she'd never told him about, the child who hadn't been born, that lay between them now.

But whatever the cause, Keith gradually began to pull away. At six o'clock, she used to hear his briefcase hitting the ground, used to hear him steal toward the living room to catch the kids up in his arms before they could register he was home. Now he seemed to tiptoe for another reason: to buy himself as much time as possible before having to talk to anyone. He would go straight to the kitchen to mix himself a drink, which he drained with a pinched expression. He wasn't the kind of man to complain about the mess the kids had made, but his mouth at rest was a frown, and she could feel him dwelling on something.

He'd lost interest in sex, too. This might have been a welcome development, as her own interest was waning again. Or maybe interest wasn't quite the right word, but she often felt exhausted by the time they went to bed: bloated, unsexy, disembodied. Once or twice a week, she would get him off under the covers. He would rub her through her nightgown and she would pretend to come just before she knew he was going to, and he wouldn't question it. But the condition for her not wanting him, it seemed, had been him wanting her. As soon as he stopped seeking her hand out, she discovered she needed his touch.

One night they were out at some professional function, a fundraiser for a children's something-or-other, a drinks-and-tasting-menu kind of affair where you ate off little plates and mingled with clients and potential clients. Regan hated these things, not because the thought of abandoned children didn't hit her where she lived, but because she was no good at eating standing up. To balance heavy food on a tiny plate, to manage fork and napkin and the drink there was nowhere to set down, and then to have to talk to men who invariably knew your father, or worse, your uncle . . . You ought to be able to pay money *not* to come to these things. And suddenly, Keith was talking to, laughing with, a woman who couldn't have been older than twenty-four. She looked like a mythological creature, a silkie or dryad, long blond hair and a low-cut dress in which her breasts, without any apparent means of support, were offered like alluring canapés. This was more or less the universal ideal of female beauty, from which Regan was drifting further and further, sucked toward the Mommy Zone. Meanwhile, Keith just got better-looking. How could his love, which she'd put so much stock in, stand up to her early grays, her thickening ass, her stretch-marks and wrinkles?

She started walking everywhere: to PTA meetings, to drop Cate off at preschool, to the salon with its supersonic hairdryers. She walked one afternoon all the way down to Union Square and bought an exercise book from the four-story bookstore there, which had suddenly sprouted a fitness section. At home, she played Carly Simon on Keith's high-end stereo and practiced isometric stretches, rolling a rolling-pin over her abdomen. Then, when that didn't make her feel any better, she stuck a finger down her throat and, for the first time since Vassar, made herself throw up.

SHE COULDN'T HAVE SAID when this became a daily thing. It was as if there were two worlds, sealed off from each other by the bathroom door. When she wasn't doing it, she didn't think about it. Or she did, but only somewhere in the back of her brain, while up front she didn't even acknowledge that she was looking forward to doing it again, already rehearsing the steps. First she would turn on the faucet in the bathroom, and the radio they kept on the sill by the clothes hamper, because there was no fan to cover the sound. Then she would crack the window enough to let street noise in, but not enough that what she was about to do would be visible to the great world. She would keep the door to the kitchen open, so that the smaller, nuclear world—Will, Cate—would see she had nothing to hide. And when it was all in place, this tongue-and-groove construction of sound, running water plus talk radio plus the broken-glass noise of a backhoe four stories below—she would pull the door and secure it with a metal hook a decade's worth of warping and settling had been unable to dislodge from the doorframe.

She admired the medieval pragmatism of that hook. And she admired the scale, with its nubbed rubber mat. It presented itself as the one solid place to stand in the world. But the spin of the intricately hatched dial, the blur of numbers and the almost idiographic line segments, the yaw from side to side through the positive and negative values, made her feel less that she was on solid ground than that she was at sea, up on a tiny crow's nest, so severely many degrees out of plumb that if she fell there would be nothing to catch her but blue. She would feel in an overwhelming way how everything around her, radio, hook, scale, had been prepared for just this—an unfreedom at once exhilarating and queasy-making.

She was always careful to finish with the scale before looking into the mirror, because mirrors were not to be trusted. There was the matter, for example, of the doubling. For every thing reflected, the mirror fabricated two images: the one in the surface and the one in the silvering. You will see if you ever touch a mirror that as your finger approaches, a ghost-finger appears around it, and even with your fingertip to the glass, you will not have reached the finger trapped beneath. Nor should you count on your eyes. The world is actually upside down. Regan would be feeling sick now indeed. Sick like sex with a fever, with a stranger. Sick like slick, wet shame.

She pinned back her hair. She knelt by the porcelain bowl. She saw her shadow in the water and closed her eyes. *Pulling the trigger,* the Chi Os used to call it. It had been a sort of club, at first, you walked out of the powder room feeling you had proved something. On the radio, a doctor who wasn't a doctor free-associated about the garbage strike. Rats bit babies in East Harlem. There were lines for gasoline in Jersey and for water in Biafra. How many gallons were wasted every five minutes the faucet stayed on? She sometimes thought she heard footsteps in the kitchen making the lid on the cake stand clatter. This would be Will, roaming the apartment in long, urgent arcs, having intuited that she did in fact have something to hide. She would wait for his feet to go away and she would close her eyes and she would work her index finger past her teeth and the wet lining of her tongue and into the hole at the back, almost sexual, almost like being an infant again, plus the brief distress signal that made her want to bite down, hard, but what had she proved if not that she was tough, that she was in control, the thing men feared because they could not touch it, reach it, hurt her, her fingertip's tip was on the trigger, she swallowed the sound, prim, a cat coughing.

The sick came up out of her so fast it was a good thing she'd practiced. She'd get the finger aside just in time, and even in the hot acid swoon make sure her head was over the toilet, where another self swam and muddied as the water did. She was such a good girl there was no sound but the plop of liquid into liquid but it hurt like hell to keep it quiet. Another spasm. Little tears in the inside corners of her eyes. And then it was done, her temperature had spiked, a fine postcoital sweat was on her skin. Her forearms made a chord across the cold front of the bowl, a misericord to rest her forehead on, the smell would go away soon.

Then came the deep listening, in which she could hear each layer of sound, and beyond all of them, the wind grieving over the edges of the hole she'd now cleared in herself. Like the edges of a tarp stretched over a hole in a roof in Buffalo. The saddest part, maybe, was that the seconds that followed were the best part of her day. The ceiling would lift off the room and its walls would telescope toward the sky like a great funnel and she would feel her lost child out there, the angelic sisters, her mother departing from her. Her dear dead mother plucking at the neckline of her cosmic sweater and turning away. "No matter where you are, she sees you," Daddy had said that day, squeezing her hand and looking down into the coffin. He'd meant to comfort. It was practically the only mention. And then came the ten seconds in which Regan hated herself more than ever. Time to tear two squares of toilet paper and wipe down the bowl's rim and the bottom of the sink. To brush teeth with a nerdle of Gleem. To flush again and fill the Listerine cap half-full of Listerine and half-full of water. To gargle and drink a glass from the tap, unpin the hair, glance in the mirror again. Window down, radio off, light a match. Do not risk a third flush. And sometimes, while the tank refilled from the second, she would hear socked feet scurrying off toward a far corner of the apartment, as if in flight.

65

SUMMER IN NASSAU COUNTY was fireflies and bottle rockets and cats getting it on in the shade of parked cars and playing cards clothespinned to bike spokes—all that Norman Rockwell crap—so you can bet people freaking *loved* the Bicentennial. Through the window-screen of his basement room at midday, Charlie could already smell the sulfur trails of sparklers. It was funny, though, if you thought about it: those elegiac little flags flapping on the neighbors' lawns were just advertisements, basically, planted by a local life-insurance salesman whose name was printed on the poles. To get anywhere near the real heirs of the Revolution, the punk rockers, you had to go into the City. Not that he'd ever have put it this way to Mom. Instead, he told her he wanted to go see the tall ships. With *friends*, he said—an alibi she was only too eager to accept. They hadn't discussed how he'd be getting there; later, he could claim there'd been a miscommunication. But she'd wanted him back by eleven. "Even if the fireworks run over. Eleven—repeat it back to me, Charlie."

"Geez, Mom. Mellow out." He'd left the room before she could change her mind. That was yesterday.

Now, in the upstairs bathroom, he used scissors to attack his head. Cutting your own hair was harder than you'd think, and he almost wussed out at the sight of the first clump stuck like a reddish thistle to the slope of the sink, but then he pictured Sam's grin when she saw him. With the faucet running to cover the sound, he plugged in his dad's old electric razor and prayed it still worked. The motor whined. Hairs snowed crimson onto the formica. It came across so tough on the sleeve of *Brass Tactics*, which he'd set on the counter for reference—the strip of uncut hair sprung defiant from the scalp—but in the mirror, with the bucolic drone of some homeowner's lawn-mower and the pop of early firecrackers in the background, it looked like a starved rodent had collapsed atop his skull.

He used some balled toilet paper to sweep the hairs from the counter into the bowl of the sink, and thence down the drain. Then he knelt to check the tiles for strays. Before he'd finished, a splashing sound made him turn around, and what he saw almost gave him a heart attack. The sink was overflowing. *Shit.* He grabbed a towel from the towel-rack. By the time he reached the faucet, runoff had snaked across the sloped floor, under the door, out into the hallway. *Fucking shit.* In his haste, he'd taken one of Mom's monogrammed towels, but there was no going back now. He did his best to soak up the water and then fished in the drain, trying not to register the gunked texture of the pipes. He came up with an evil little Hitler moustache of hair. He wadded it in Kleenex and flushed it down the toilet.

Out in the hallway, towel in hand, he stood listening for Mom. Abraham, age three, appeared in the doorway of the room where the twins should have been sleeping. The blameless mouth widened as Abe took in the water on the floor and his brother's ruined scalp. He clapped a hand to his cheek and pointed just to make sure Charlie knew he knew. "You rat me out, I give you a bruise," Charlie said. "Now go finish your damn nap." It was no fair, having brothers too young to be mad at. And this was *their* lawn being mowed outside; Mom must have gotten tired of waiting around for Charlie and decided to do it herself. He dropped the towel and swabbed it around with his foot and balled it up at the bottom of the linen closet. He waited for the mower to move into the backyard. Then he bolted down the stairs and out the front door, snatching Mom's car keys off their hook en route, hoping like hell she wouldn't see him.

THE WAY SAM TALKED about her dad made Charlie kind of scared of the guy. So, notwithstanding the prommish scenario he'd envisioned—ringing the bell, being invited in to wait in the living room until Sam emerged blushing from the back of the house—he idled at the curb and honked until she came out. If she was thinking of this in date-like terms, you couldn't tell it from her clothes. She wore her same old Television tee-shirt. She did, however, say his hair looked amazing, which instantly made everything pretty much worth it. She'd brought their jointly owned eight-track of *Horses*, and on the way in they listened to it twice through, singing along as they descended the back half of the Q-Boro Bridge like a bomb lobbed at Midtown: *Coming in / in all directions, / white, / shining / silver . . .*

Charlie was worried about Mom's wagon getting stolen if he left it parked for eight hours in the Village, so they took a spot above Fourteenth and headed down on foot toward where a friend of Sam's was supposed to be getting off work. She'd been nipping from a brown-bagged bottle. He reached for it and, after checking for cops, took a swig. "This is one of those guys from your record-store photo shoot we're meeting?"

"His roommates are the ones having the party. They've never even let me see their place, so you should feel honored I scored you an invite. You know who I heard might be there? Billy Three-Sticks."

"Shut up."

"I'm serious. Sol's friend Nicky knows everybody, allegedly."

They ambled south, passing the fiery bottle of O'Shakey's Irish Whisky. The city that day was like a carnival· sailors in white uniforms clotted on corners, sidewalks so crowded tourists were walking in the actual street, irritated drivers laying on their horns. Every dozen yards or so a density of pot hit him right in the nose. Hooray, America. Everyone, even the most down-and-out people on Third Avenue, which was like the world capital of down-and-outness, seemed to be wearing red, or white, or blue.

Everyone, that is, except Solomon Grungy. They found him in front of a restaurant south of Houston, sweeping what looked like a windshield wiper across the plate-glass, leaving comet-trails of dis-colored foam. He was taller even than Charlie, but burly and weathered and so pierced as to be almost perforated, and it didn't look like underneath his bandana he had any hair at all. "Wait here a minute," said Sam, so Charlie hung back, settling himself on an iron stoop to wait for the signal to come over and be introduced. His inhaler tasted bitter. Soon Grungy was disappearing into the basement restaurant, and she'd rejoined Charlie. "Change of plans." She had to yell to make herself heard above ten thousand motorcycles that were just then passing a block away. "The dishwasher walked off the job, so they're going to give Sol a crack at it. It means it's going to be another few hours before he clocks out."

"What is he, an all-purpose washer? Like, you name it, I'll wash it? Windows, dishes, whatever?"

"He needs the money, Charlie, okay? It's either that or keep stealing. We should go somewhere and wait."

Washington Square Park, where they ended up, was a fucking zoo. Hippies playing guitar in the dry fountain. Kids everywhere. The sun over Jersey was medium rare. On a bench overlooking the playground, they ate hot dogs from a cart. Then she dug a frowsy plastic baggie out of her pocket and shook what looked like bits of dried Play-Doh into his hands. "Magic mushrooms," she said. Color Charlie intrigued—but also hesitant, having heard somewhere that it was impossible to tell poison mushrooms from the edible kind. As he watched her bolt her own handful, he wanted to warn her. But she seemed okay, so he downed half of what she'd given him and when she wasn't looking pocketed the rest. They washed away the sawdusty taste with some Coke into which she'd mixed the O'Shakey's and then leaned back on the bench.

"I remember I used to go out with my dad and his guys on the barges to help fire the Fourth of July show, once I was big enough," she said. "He would have wanted us to come, but he's not doing the city's fireworks this year. Couldn't make it cheap enough."

"That stinks," Charlie said.

"Yeah, but probably for the best. It's just a button you push, not a lighter or anything, and you have to wear these stupid goggles. Besides, can you imagine being that close to fireworks, tripping? There's supposed to be a roof at this party tonight everybody can watch from."

A mood of general benevolence massaged the nerves that should have tightened here. Or maybe it was the mushrooms. The yellow-pink sky had reached down to run a thumb across her cheek, and there was blue just below that, by the nose-ring. Her whole neck-and-shoulder area, in fact, was emitting little glycerine swirls of color as she watched tiny patriots conquer the slide. He touched her shoulder. She turned as if to say, *What?* but then their eyes met. Hers were no longer brown, as he'd thought, but goldish-green, like light in the springtime—liquid, lickable sun. "Holy shit," he said. He could actually *see her feelings.*

"I know," she said. As if she could see his, too. Assuming there was even any difference.

They sat for several lifetimes watching kids like flowers sprout over the playground equipment under the breathing trees. They *became* these kids, somehow; they didn't have to talk about it. Sam took his hand with her sweaty hand and he just *knew* exactly what she meant. Then the streetlights came on, reminding them about the fireworks, and how they should head back down to Sol Grungy. She wobbled a bit on her feet, crossing Houston, but Charlie helped her.

It was dinnertime now, and the picture windows of the garden-level restaurant were full of long-necked creatures in summer suits, but Charlie could see they only looked vicious because they were lonely. Inside, classical music was playing. Classical music was amazing! He felt like a golden beam, turning surfaces translucent, seeing down to bone. With his sword of light he parted the dining room and Sam headed through the breach. Ignoring the waiters, they pushed into a corridor. She poked her head through a curtain into the kitchen, where three people whirled furiously. "Pssst. Sol!"

"Who the fuck is this?" someone said. "Get these two the fuck out of my kitchen."

Charlie whispered, loudly, "We're Sol's friends." Sol stared for a second at the bellowing steaming silver box at which he stood. Then he peeled off his rubber gloves and redundant hairnet and came out into the hall.

"Jesus Christ. I told you it was going to be a while. I hardly started and you're going to get me fired."

"So?" she said, slurring. "You hate this shit. Let's go party."

"You see how busy we are? You can't be in here."

"Listen to yourself, man. 'We?'"

Charlie hummed along with Vivaldi, or whoever, unconcerned that Sol was looking for a way to get rid of them. "Look. You guys come back at ten, someone's supposed to be relieving me. I'll take you to the thing."

"But we wanna see fireworks. And I wanna meet this Captain Whatsis of yours." Charlie had never heard her like this before, wheedling, whining, her forehead beaded with sweat.

"I'm serious. You stay around here, I'll kick your ass. Both of you."

Out in the street, there was nothing to do but finish the whisky. It couldn't touch Charlie anymore; he was too powerful. But Sam kept belching and, when they reached the corner, put hands on thighs, leaned forward, and blew chunks into the gutter. A woman in a long skirt muttered something in Yiddish Charlie should have understood. Sam's elbow felt cold and thin to his hand. He couldn't see her feelings anymore. "Are you okay?"

She sat down hard on the curb, right there in the middle of everything. Her eyelids were heavy, her lips gray (though maybe that was just 'cause it was getting dark). "Come on, Sam. Hey." She stood woozily, collapsed against him. Something was definitely wrong. Usually she could mix beer and pot and pills in a single afternoon and still be fine by dinnertime. It was Charlie who had to watch himself, or be squired on her arm to Penn Station to catch the 7:05 home. He led her back to the restaurant. The stereo was between songs or something. The hostess was ready this time, and stepped in front of him as a diner behind her made a crack about his hair. "Look, we can wait outside," Charlie said. "Or we can sit right here, your choice. But you better go get your new dishwasher."

Sol met them out front, under a shorted-out streetlight. He looked ready to take Charlie's head off, but Charlie preempted him. "I really think there's something wrong with Sam." Hearing her name, Sam smiled but didn't open her eyes. Sol squatted to inspect her.

"Shit. What did you guys eat?"

"I don't know. A hot dog, chips."

"No, asshole. What did you *eat*?"

"Uh. We took some mushrooms earlier?"

"You ate the mushrooms?"

"Just a little, though."

"How little? Caps or stems?"

"Just stems, I guess, for me. Just the tiniest bit."

"Christ. I told her to wait." Solomon Grungy stared at Charlie. "Well, I can't fucking walk off without getting paid. You'd better take her ahead to the house, it's not far. Keep her away from the roof. Get her down to the basement, give her some water, see if she'll throw up again. She can crash in the bed when she's done. I'll come find you."

"Isn't there a party? How will people know we're invited?"

"What do you think it is, a country club? It's a fucking party, man. You just walk in."

Charlie half-walked and half-dragged Sam to the address he'd been given. Inside, there were people shouting, music coming from the upper floors, a black-lit parlor in which all you could see were kegs of beer lined up against a plasterless wall and gleaming teeth attached to Mr. Potato Head heads. The smoke was so thick he had to reach again for his inhaler, but at least no one noticed them come in. He found a stairwell and lugged Sam down to the basement. He had to stoop to keep from walking into pipes. The windows were dark. The fireworks would be starting any minute. He meant to put her to bed, but when he turned on the only lamp he could find, a dim bulb without a shade, there was still puke on her face, and he couldn't let her sleep like that.

A bathroom the size of a phone booth had been built out in one corner of the room—that's what the pipes ran to. Maybe a shower would help. He turned on the water and waited until there was steam and then arranged Sam on the toilet lid. "I'm going to leave you alone in here. I want you to get in the shower. And don't drown." Amazing, how authoritative he could sound.

But as soon as he let her go, she slumped against the wall. "Don-leavmeere." The skin of her eyelids was almost translucent. You could see the contours of the eyes beneath.

"Okay, but you have to get into the shower, Sam. It'll make you feel better. I won't look." He stood in the doorway, his back turned, but he couldn't hear anything above the whir of the ventilation fan, amplified by the flimsy walls. When he peeked, her fingers were fumbling at the button of her jeans.

"All right. On your feet." His 'shroom-induced potency now revealed itself as a pretense; really what he was was scared. He tried his best not to brush against the soft skin of her belly as he helped her with her zipper, not to consider the legs revealed when he tugged her jeans downward. He'd seen legs before, hadn't he? He squatted to get the rolls of denim past her ankles. She put her hands on his shoulders and grunted as he removed gym socks shabby like his own.

She stood above him now in the faded black shirt, and underpants of startling girlishness, thin white cotton with a faint fuzz beneath. With her eyes still shut she swayed from side to side, in obedience to the music through the ceiling. Of course she wouldn't be wearing a bra. "You can't get the rest yourself?"

For a minute, she didn't respond—she might have been asleep—but then she bit her lip and shook her head. He lifted her tee-shirt. His heart was going to blow right through the walls of his chest. There were her tits, perfect pale apples, their small stems hard from the basement chill. Her panties she'd have to take off herself—there was no way he'd get through it. He turned away, crippled by turgidity, and ordered her into the shower. He only turned back around when the curtain was drawn, her body a smear behind the moldy plastic. "You all right in there?" She sputtered in response. For both of them, the mushrooms seemed to be giving way again to simple drunkenness.

She'd been in for a few minutes when it occurred to him she'd need a towel. There were no cabinets here, nowhere for a towel to hide. He stole out into the larger room, but it was bare of anything connoting domesticity, save for the couch, the lamp, a wall mirror, a yellowed mattress in the corner. He went back into the bathroom and stripped his own shirt off. The mirror, mercifully, was steamed over, sparing him the shock of his white skin and countable ribs. The haircut he now blamed for getting him into this mess. "Okay, turn off the water," he instructed. "I'm going to hand my shirt over the bar." The fact that she took it was encouraging. "You can dry off with it." All that separated his nakedness from hers was the shower curtain and his own jeans and underpants, but any hint of sex was gone. It was, instead, as if they were small children, playing at some piece of make-believe. Or as if she were the child, and he the parent. He handed her her own clothes over the shower rod and gave her time to put them on. She handed his shirt back. He wrung it out and draped it over his shoulder and opened the curtain. He helped her rebutton her impossibly tight jeans. "Deep breath," he said. Then she pushed him out of the way and knelt by the toilet and puked up a thick brown mess, once, twice, three times, until nothing else came up. He sat beside her and held back her hair.

And now what? Her color was better, she'd regained the power of speech—*Sorry, Charlie*, she said—but she hardly seemed fit for the outside world. Nor did he want to have to explain their presence to the older punks upstairs. The mattress with its twisted sheets looked like a breeding ground for bedbugs, so he led her to the couch, wrapping her in a dingy afghan. Somehow in the process of getting her to lie down, he ended up with her head on his lap. Outside, fireworks were going off: small ones, locally, and then deep in the background the huge municipal boom. He reached to turn off the lamp. It was as dark as he supposed it ever got in this city. When she felt for his face, he noticed for the first time how small her hands were. "Hey, Charlie?"

"Hey, Sam."

"Did I ever tell you the one about the Loneliest Man in the World?"

"The what?"

Her voice was extra-hoarse from puking. In the future, she was saying, they'd have all this technology, and no one would ever realize they were lonely, because no one would ever have been anything else. Only one person would know the secret.

"The Loneliest Man in the World?" he guessed.

She yawned, arched her back like a cat, went still. He thought she'd dozed off, but then she spoke again. The Loneliest Man in the World, she said, only has room in his heart for one person, and if he can't have that person, he locks himself away. He tells himself no one could possibly love him, but really, it's that he refuses to love anyone else. With her lips barely moving, she might have been talking in her sleep. "You listening?"

He'd swept her hair back over the arm of the couch, so it wouldn't get in her face. Now he touched it. "Shh. Get some rest."

She made a feeble raspberry. "Shut up, Charlie. Listen to me. This guy won't let himself . . . not even the people like fucking *blasting* their love at him. People all around, who just want to love him."

"Why are you telling me this?"

"I worry about you," she slurred.

"You worry about me? That's funny, Sam. Do you worry like I might pass out in a stranger's basement and choke to death on my own puke?"

"I worry you're making yourself lonely, because—"

"I'm not lonely," he said, or breathed, and then, as if to prove it, he leaned down and kissed her. For seconds, his eyes stayed closed; easier this way to imagine that she knew this was him, that this was what she wanted, their lips pressing together, hers still faintly acid, and that this was why she didn't stop him. Really, he discovered when he pulled back, it was because she had passed out, head centimeters from his fly. He sat in the dark for a long time after that, trying to see her clearly.

"SHIT SHIT SHIT." He shook himself awake. His legs were numb, his face sticky. The pop of fireworks had long ago stopped. What time was it? Mom was going to freaking *kill* him.

He roused Sam and made her walk him upstairs, partly because he was afraid to go alone, but partly so he'd know she could do it. Streetlights and electric green ailanthus swam in the windshields of parked cars. Some strange insignia on the door smelled like wet paint. She was going to stay, she said. She was sure Solomon Grungy would come, or was already here. She would catch the train later.

But how would she get home from the station?

There were cabs, she pointed out. Buses.

Maybe he could pick her up.

"It's late, Charlie. You said you had to go, so go." The way she said it—embarrassed, not looking him in the eyes—was a conversation-ender. He didn't know what to do, give her a chummy shove or reach for her hand or try to kiss her again, so finally, while she watched from the stoop of the strange house, he pushed off into the riotous shadows and headed approximately north, toward where he hoped the station wagon still was.

An hour later, he was on the great artery of the L.I.E., in the protein jacket of his mother's car. Sodium lights, veiled in humidity and mosquitoes, turned the landscape alien. Big colonies of apartment buildings appeared at intervals, deserted except for lights on a few random floors. Four hundred years ago, Indian tribes had moved among the black trees that fringed the roadway. Ex Post Facto sang about this, albeit elliptically. There was that song "Egg Cream Blues," with its line about "kicking over stones in a Protestant graveyard." Or was it "kicking over *homes*"? The crude mono of the recording and the singer's strange accent made it hard to tell. Charlie chewed on a foil gum-wrapper to stay awake. He supposed it was really Sam he was mad at. After all his careful care for her, she had opted to stay with the friends who'd neglected her. He popped out EPF and felt under the seat for an old T. Rex cassette he'd hid there so she wouldn't make fun. By the time it hit side two, the late-night traffic had slowed and narrowed to a single lane. There'd been an accident; men in uniform stood in the fuchsia bloom of flares, letting cars through one at a time. And what if they chanced to look in? Did he look drunk? High? Was he? He put on his Mets cap to cover his Mohawk. He rolled down the window and leaned forward and rode the brake.

When he reached Flower Hill, his mom was waiting in Dad's superannuated armchair. He was pretty sure she'd turned off all the lights for the dramatic moment it would create when she pulled the pullcord. "Do you know what time it is, Charlie?"

"Can't we talk about this in the morning?" He was already moving toward the basement; he could hear the soft retreat of small feet on the carpet upstairs, where his brothers were out of bed listening. But now his mom was up, too, a flurry of polyester.

"We can talk right now, young man. About why your shirt is all wet, for starters."

"We should sleep in, look at this with clearer eyes." He'd almost made it through the door to the basement when she snapped on the overhead light, the better to see him.

"Charles Nathaniel Weisbarger—what did you do to your hair?"

He could feel the bare skin peeking from under his ballcap, and he froze, one hand on the doorknob, as did his shadow. Things were suddenly very serious. If she insulted his hair right now, he was never going to forgive her. She reached up and pulled off the hat. And now they were both frozen, except, perhaps, for the jackass tears gathering in his eyes.

Her voice was soft. "What is wrong with you?"

He picked a spot on the wall to stare at. "I don't know. I don't know what's wrong with me."

"Charlie, is that liquor I smell?"

"Some people I was with were drinking." It wasn't until it was out of his mouth that he realized the Innocent Bystander defense—perfectly reasonable when she'd smelled Sam's cigarettes on him back in May—made no sense for a product that was liquid, not gas. *At least I didn't eat mushrooms*, he wanted to point out. *Not as many as Sam, anyway.*

"It is liquor! You drank, and then you drove my car."

"I didn't."

She turned him toward her and slapped him. "Don't you *lie* to me. Who were you with?"

He was sitting on the carpeted floor—not because she'd actually hurt him, but out of a wish not to be hit again. He covered his head with his arms, and all the hot frustration of the day was swelling and trembling in him and it seemed anything might have happened. But he couldn't stand to have his own mother think the worst of him. "You don't know her," he said. If he thought her relief that it was a girl keeping him out late would mitigate her fury, he was mistaken; the next day, he woke up grounded. And the next, and the next, and so on into the fall.

66

LATER, WHEN TIME had gone all gluey and mutable, Keith would wonder: had it really only been three months since he'd been ordered to wait in the wrecked entryway of that house on East Third? And also: Why hadn't he obeyed? In the event, though, there'd hardly been time to think. The young woman from the stoop had continued on toward the rear of the house, where a phone was ringing, and before he knew what he was doing, he'd followed her as far as the kitchen door. A bedsheet tacked over a window turned the afternoon light to marmalade. Having set down her stacks of LPs, she stood by the wall-mounted phone with her back turned, or at least those parts of it visible where the collar and hem of her tee-shirt had been sheared off with scissors. The music through the walls drowned out whatever she was saying, but when she shifted the receiver from ear to ear, he could see the swell of her hips down below and the fine muscles rippling up where her shoulders met her neck, swift little fish beneath the glassy calm of skin. It didn't occur to him that she must have known he was watching, the way she stretched and yawned, letting him take in the whole length of her.

Then she hung the phone back on its wall-mount and flattened a hand against the crumbling plaster. As if in response, the noise fell silent. "All right," she said, turning. "You said you need something from the mail?" He was speechless. "Some knucklehead probably took it out to the garage. What should I be looking for?"

"I don't know. It's a manila envelope. The postal code is 10017."

"Stay here and don't touch anything. This'll just take a minute." She paused on her way toward the back door. "You got a name, if anyone asks?"

"Sorry," he said, like an idiot. "It's Keith."

Five minutes later, she returned with his envelope, and with a camera over one shoulder. He told her she was a lifesaver and offered her the envelope from his briefcase in exchange.

"What am I supposed to do with this?"

"I'm just the messenger—I don't even know what's in it."

"It's not often you see a messenger in a suit and tie, Keith. Especially 'round these here parts." He'd almost forgotten he was still dressed for work; he would have regretted it, were it not for the impression she was flirting with him. She raised the envelope to her pierced nose and sniffed the seam. "You're not even the tiniest bit curious what's in this?"

He shrugged. He couldn't see why Amory didn't just pay for a courier, but continued not to ask. Or perhaps sensed that the answer was something he'd be happier not knowing. There were things you didn't want to dig too deeply into. Look at what Nixon had tried to do to Daniel Ellsberg. To Daniel Schorr. "Not my business. I'm only doing a favor for someone."

The envelope landed on a counter. "Well, I'll let you get on with it. I should run."

"You just got here."

"I've got to go uptown and take some pictures while the light's still good."

"I'm headed that way myself," he said, on an impulse. "We could split a cab."

"I don't do cabs. Cabs aren't punk."

"It's on me." He picked up the envelope. "I owe you for this, after all."

He wondered what she made of his motives, sizing him up, and for that matter what he made of them himself. Perhaps it was as simple as this: he liked her grin, the crinkle at the bridge of her nose, the mouth a little large for the face. "Sam," she said, sticking out a hand, and he'd recovered enough of his quickness to realize she was telling him her name.

Finding a taxi was easy enough at this hour; everyone was fleeing Lower Manhattan as if it were on fire. Ensconced in leather that smelled like air freshener, they gobbled up Third Avenue in great gulps of nine or ten blocks. The sunlight had that rich tint it picked up summer afternoons, the red that made the blue bluer. *Take a look take a look*, the street vendors said when they stopped at a signal. She'd rolled her window down to light a cigarette. The smoke made complicated shapes in a shaft of sun between the high buildings, and then the cab lurched into motion again and the patterns were sucked out, replaced by the smell of overripe trash. "So you're a photographer?"

Photography *student*, she said airily. And before his recalculation of her age could get too uncomfortable, she added, "At NYU. The School of the Arts. Graduating in the spring, actually." Those had been friends of hers back there, whose house they'd been in. People she knew from the scene. They needed a little mothering sometimes.

He asked her about this *scene*, which he seemed to remember reading about in the style pages, and by the time she finished her explanation, they were up in the low Eighties and she was leaning forward to tell the cabbie to pull over. Across the street, where the Transverse entered the Park, someone had spraypainted a traffic bollard to look like Mighty Mouse. The shadows were starting to deepen. Will's school was somewhere nearby. "Listen," he said. "I know it seems ritzy up here compared to downtown, but it's not really safe to go traipsing around the Park on your own. You hear about muggings constantly."

"What makes you so sure I didn't come here to jump tourists for their wallets?"

"Come on."

"There's only half an hour before it gets too dark to shoot, anyway. I'll be fine."

"Let me walk you," he said.

"How will you get home?" she said.

"I live in the neighborhood." It had never before crossed his mind to be even slightly embarrassed by this fact. In any case, she let him follow her in, under the dense midsummer trees. They bypassed the Reservoir and looped north, paths he hadn't taken in years. The farther they went, the more spraypaint he saw: silver aliens doing battle on the backs of benches, wire-mesh trashcans engulfed in flame. For her, each was a kind of specimen. She would squat and raise the camera to her eye while he stood behind her, trying to remember how people were supposed to look when they stood. To anyone who saw him just then, he told himself, they clearly wouldn't have belonged together, him with his briefcase, her in ripped jeans. Not that there was much of anyone around.

They ended up at the boathouse by Harlem Meer. The city had shut it down back during the fiscal crisis, and since then the gray-brick WPA structure had disappeared under layers of what she called "tags." There must have been hundreds of them, scrawled hastily over the brick in some places but in others laid down in patient letters the size of trashcan lids. On the western wall, someone with real talent—someone who in another age might have been doing frescoes for popes—had painstakingly painted a winged nude, eight feet high. And it was this, this goddess of the park, that Samantha seemed determined to capture. Suddenly she was everywhere, all at once, trying from all angles, squatting down to shoot and also standing to gauge the dwindling light. The only sounds, besides the click of the shutter, were distant car horns and birds chattering off in the underbrush. A line from a poem he'd had to memorize in sophomore German pressed incoherently against the front of his brain. He tried to focus on the wall, on the painted image. Tapered waist sloping into hips. Breasts like bronzed mangoes. A head tilted back sideways, lips parted in ecstasy. There had been a time when Regan had looked like this, at least to him. But her body had changed, slackening from the kids, and then sort of winnowing, as if to prepare her transition from motherhood to career. If the body now moving forward once more to inspect the wall had offered itself to him, what would he have said? And at that very instant, she turned to ask him what he thought. He thought he should probably be going, was what he thought.

THE NEXT TIME an envelope appeared on his desk, he waited several days before taking it to East Third Street. Amory hadn't said anything about timeliness, and Keith was concerned—or knew, somehow—that Samantha would be there. Which she was, when he finally went and knocked on the door. "What are you doing here?" she said, answering.

He stepped inside. She backed toward the wall. He put the envelope in her hand. She leaned toward his ear, so that he could actually feel her words, the way they shaped the air: "You scare me." It was like something she'd picked up from a soap opera. And he was the one who was scared.

KEITH ONLY MADE IT TO CHURCH THESE DAYS a few times a year, and Regan had, for obscure reasons, always avoided it, but that Sunday, after ten o'clock Mass, he arranged to speak privately with Father Jonathan, the assistant rector. When, after some hemming and hawing, he confessed that he'd started to find his eye wandering (he couldn't bring himself to be more specific than that), the priest recommended he talk to a professional. "That's what I thought I was doing," Keith said.

An analyst, is what the priest said he meant. He was hairless, almost prepubescent-looking, not detectably ironic. "They can be tremendously helpful with these things. You and your wife have been married for how long?"

It was a rhetorical question; Father Jonathan didn't pause for an answer, but pressed on. There was a fellow parishioner, he said, a psychologist, who had just published a book; perhaps Keith was familiar with her column in the *Times*? Keith nodded carefully. He did know the name. Father Jonathan explained that this parishioner and her husband, likewise a psychologist, had just celebrated their golden anniversary. That was *twenty-five years*. In the book, she suggested that the secret to this longevity was that they had gone out to dinner every Tuesday night for a quarter century. "Tuesday: think of it. Not Monday, with its re-entry to the week, but not yet Wednesday, the hump one has to get over. Tuesday. They simply let nothing get in their way."

A fire seemed to kindle beneath the milk-mild pastoral face. Keith wondered what it must be like to renounce pleasures you'd never had a chance to know, to burn for some woman of the parish, to watch her tend the macaroni salad at the Rally Day potluck, her body ripe in its summer dress—to feel her hand on your arm and to know you would end up on your own that night, feeding the vestry cats. Or worse: listening to another self-absorbed layman lament the banked embers of his perfectly enviable marriage. But then another Keith, the hungry person he'd been with Samantha's breath in his ear, felt like reaching across the mahogany desk and grabbing the little white tab of the collar and saying, *Don't patronize me, goddammit*. For a moment, it seemed the room might be riven by these contradictions. That he might, like unruly Jonah, be swallowed up.

Then again, this was the twentieth century. There was no justice like that anymore. And so, on Tuesday, he took Regan across town to their old Italian place. Candlelight and red sauce. Something here had changed, but it took Keith a minute to place it: above the bar they'd installed a TV, which the bartender kept on while he polished glasses. Regardless of not being able to hear the sound, regardless of not giving two shits about American League baseball, Keith found himself unable to resist the distraction. The rims of upside-down glasses caught the grayblue light and led his gaze, no matter where he turned it, back to the screen, until he realized Regan was staring at him. "What?" he said.

"I asked you a question, honey. Have you not heard a word I've been saying?"

And that was it: die cast, *jeux faits*. The evening led not to a hotel room, as he'd secretly hoped, but to paying off the sitter and helping with homework and dealing with Cate's litany of pre-bed complaints and reading her her story and dropping into sleep almost before their bodies hit the bed. The next day, in an empty office in the LCA suites, he watched his finger dial the number Samantha had given him. Which isn't to say he was ready for her to pick up.

IT REALLY TOOK HIM BACK, the old neighborhood, though it had changed—some would say degenerated. Transvestites walked Seventh Avenue openly, mingling with nice middle-class kids doing their best to look homeless, and with students and tourists and book editors in tweed. But Keith's condescension wasn't convincing, even to himself. He missed this place. Why had they ever moved?

He spotted Samantha from halfway down the appointed block, where she sat on a stoop with a Carvel and a cigarette. She'd worn a skirt, and the sight of her long legs angled out over the flagstones swept every thought of home right out of his head. She made no move to stand, even when he was upon her—simply squinted up through the smoke. But it was a good sign that she'd dressed up. It must have meant she liked him.

At dinner, he was a perfect gentleman, a rich uncle in town for the week. (Presumably not everyone he'd known down here had moved away.) Samantha was the one who insisted on more wine, and when her knee insinuated itself between his under the table, he started away, as if it had been an accident. This was madness! Anyone might have been watching! You still haven't done anything wrong, he reminded himself. God knows he'd had the opportunity to stray before, with any number of women. He had proven himself, had he not? But now he seemed to have fallen under some powerful enchantment. Up above, the girl continued to tell him about Diane Arbus and Danny Lyon and photography's gift to painting—a nervous breakdown, she said; down below, her foot found his.

Then they were back at her dormroom, a tiny single she hadn't finished unpacking after a summer away. Most of her classmates weren't back yet, but she'd already managed to have a friend of hers, one of these graffiti artists, spraypaint a wall. He could still smell the fumes. "So much for your security deposit," he said nervously, turning to take in the scrawls of black and silver crawling up toward the ceiling. When he looked back, she was leaning against her desk with a frank look on her face. Her tee-shirt, the same collar-ripped one she'd worn the first day he'd met her, had slipped off her shoulder. He approached and placed a hand on the curve above her hipbone, gave her a second to opt out. She reached instead for his belt.

It happened right there, standing up, Samantha bent back over the desk with her panties around her feet and her shirt up around her neck. He was unprepared for how aggressive he could be, given the all clear. After Will was born, Regan had stopped wanting it like this. Even when she was pregnant with Cate, her belly in the way, it was missionary, ten minutes of it, and lately not even that. He was angry, actually angry at her, he discovered, for holding back so much. For putting him here. Then Samantha's tender little grunts, the sweat of her neck in his mouth or her hand reaching down to pull him deeper, brought him back. He was in a college dormroom, someone was pounding on the wall for them to keep it down, and this twenty-two-year-old woman was bucking underneath him, her hand gripping the edge of the desk, as he streaked out into eternity. The miracles of coeducation. Everything you could possibly want, and all it took was your soul.

They fell onto her unmade bed, striped by light through the miniblinds. "That was . . ."

"Mm," she agreed, apparently too sated to speak.

There was a shared shower room further along the hall, but he couldn't very well use it (this was an all-girls floor), so he cleaned up as best he could with the towel she offered and began to put his clothes on.

"I don't want to be . . . you know. But can I see you again?"

She told him when he could call her next. It seemed somehow too intimate to kiss her goodnight. He snuck out to the elevator bank.

In the steel of the closing doors, he looked flushed, disheveled, glowing, but inside, a coolness was already spreading. He didn't meet the eyes of the boy in sweatpants who rode down with him, who had probably been plotting to sleep with Samantha himself—how could anyone not be?—or of the security guard at his desk in the otherwise empty lobby. Emerging into the humid night, crossing under the trees of Washington Square Park, Keith found himself thinking instead of the bedtime stories he'd once read to Will. Their heroes were always straying from well-lit paths and into the woods. Or maybe it was a single wood: the dark place where the things they feared most dwelled. And so, he reassured himself, he had the advantage of knowing already how this had to end. He had stopped to admire a flower, had gotten waylaid in the shadows, but in no time at all he would be back on the path again, renewed and rededicated. For was that not the point of the woods?

67

A PHOTO SURVIVES from that fall, black-and-white, of Samantha Cicciaro on the weedy median of Houston Street, a few blocks east of West Broadway. It's daytime, afternoon, sunlight strong from the west, maybe getting on toward rush hour. On either side of her, the asphalt brims with late-model sedans, their narrow taillights and boxy grilles. A city bus has pulled to the curb to discharge a passenger, man or woman, tough to say at this distance. Somewhere in deeper focus is a building whose girders thrust straight through its walls and into the vacant space next door. Deeper still, the building that was her favorite, a tall, Victorian, red-brick structure presided over by a golden statue above the portico, a mischievous little god.

Her dad had given her the Nikkormat for her birthday a year earlier. (You had to be careful, she'd told Charlie once: if you mentioned something like that around him, or sometimes just glanced longingly through a shop window, he'd buy it for you, and then you couldn't enjoy it, because you'd be too busy wondering if you'd guilted him into spending more than he could really afford.) Now, afternoons when Keith could clear his schedule, they would ramble around the wilderness blocks north of Central Park or south of Bleecker, snapping photos. In this case, he'd turned the camera on her. But despite the city teeming all around, she appears through the viewfinder to be alone. Her tee-shirt's cut short to bare a strip of midriff; over it she wears a man's blazer, sleeves rolled and safety-pinned. She has chopped her hair to chin length and dyed it what in this picture will appear to be dove-gray but is really black, roots streaking through like paler lightning. There is a little porkpie hat. Her arms loop back behind the lightpost she's leaning against, as if chained there, and her face, lips parted, turns upward to catch the sun. Like a flame reflected in a window, the face seems to belong to a different dimension than the rest of the image. And it is this, the eyes, the mouth, one keeps returning to. What was she thinking?

Looking back, there are so many possibilities. That summer, she had found her way to the intersection of all kinds of power lines and vectors of force, some of which she was aware of, some of which not. She could have been thinking, for example, that there had to be something wrong with seducing a man twice your age—that man right there, Your Honor, crouching in the grasses with a camera for a face. Or about the envelopes she teased him about never opening, which she'd heard contained Nicky's stipend from some rich relation. Or about that house on East Third, and how much loyalty you owed friends who were so obviously fucking up big-time. She could have been thinking about the fact that it was now the Tuesday after Columbus Day and she hadn't been to a single class since the end of September. Or about her dad, who would have been appalled, a good Catholic girl like his Sammy. Hadn't keeping her away from all this been his reason for getting her on the private-school track in the first place? But Dad, egged on by Richard Groskoph with his paper and pen, increasingly existed in a world of his own devising, where his own father and brothers were still alive, and fireworks in New York still synonymous with the Cicciaro name. This was what she got, anyway, from calls home. She could have been thinking about any or all of this.

But it was Indian summer in the city, the time she spent the rest of the year waiting for, and she'd learned early on that it did no one any good to dwell on things beyond the present-at-hand. As a poet she liked had written, "You just go on your nerve." And so at the instant the shutter clicked, she was thinking mostly of a sandwich on the menu of her favorite luncheonette: salty salami and capicola piled an inch thick, good bread, sharp white cheese, mayo that dribbled out the sides and onto the wax-paper wrapping when you pressed down with your fingers.

She would make Keith follow her there that afternoon. This was part of the wonder of those days: seeing how far her power over him extended. There was something about Keith, some part of him she sensed being held back, that made her hungry for proof he cared. They sat in a molded plastic booth far enough from the window that no one outside would spot him; he had a Coke and watched her eat. In between bites she tore his straw wrapper to bits she dropped into the ashtray. She took her lighter and tried setting the bits on fire. Finally, he reached out and took her wrists with marvelous roughness. "Stop," he said. "You're going to get us kicked out." For a minute, the real Keith had resurfaced. She wanted to capture him in a jar, study him, see if he was willing to ruin himself for her.

That she didn't think he was was why she loved him.

There was also, of course, the sex: fitful, explosive, scarily vulnerable. She'd decided long ago that the second-party orgasm was a lockerroom rumor, and had resigned herself to the clumsy ministrations of the adolescent male. But sometimes with Keith, early evenings when they returned to her dormitory, or to a ramshackle hotel east of Grand Central, she could feel herself approaching the lightless place of myth. Her hands would roam on his body, or his on hers, until she almost couldn't tell which was which, and she would be frightened he would stop her, or she him, but neither did. It was like a swing on which she was swinging higher and higher, through no conscious mechanism, but simply through wanting the more open air.

Actually, maybe love was the wrong word—to be in love with a person, you had to respect him, and there were times when she didn't respect Keith, exactly. When he tried to treat her tenderly, for instance, she was a little disgusted. But these glimpses of the anger beneath his pressed exterior made her feel like she'd do anything to please him. Would she suck him off in a hotel shower? Would she get down on all fours and let him take her like a dirty magazine? She would, and she would, because that was the source of her power over him: not being quite real. And all of this—or most of it, anyway, sanitized for mixed company—she longed to confide in Charlie. There were times when she still tried to call him. But of course Charlie, like all the men in her life, had abandoned her the second he saw she wasn't going to be what he wanted.

ALL TOLD, this season of her life must have lasted a couple of months, though she felt sometimes that it had been years and other times mere days. Maybe it was the way that hotel room kept coming back and back that made time seem less like a line than like a circle, dilating and contracting. They couldn't always get the same room, obviously, but wasn't every hotel room the same? Same cigarette burns and smoke-smelling curtains, same foam-core pillow and scratchy sheets. Later at night, she'd head back to the Phalanstery to smoke dope and unwind, but a note of complex *ressentiment* had entered her relationship with the Post-Humanists. She hadn't been out in the van with them since back in August, when they had torched an abandoned church for kicks and she'd drafted a story about it she'd subsequently let Sewer Girl read. It wasn't the sacrilege of burning a church that had disturbed Sam, so much as the pure waste, because somewhere inside she couldn't quite accept that life itself was a waste. Which was exactly her problem, Nicky might have said. That, and putting too much in writing.

Then, a week or two before Thanksgiving, the five of them went to a late showing of *Taxi Driver* at the run-down cinema at St. Mark's Place. Movies were right up there with television and Casey Kasem on Nicky's list of viruses on the body politic, but in this case, he'd been willing to make an exception. The poster had appeared several weeks earlier, Robert De Niro with his army jacket and Apache haircut, and you only had to pass within a dozen yards of it to see that this was a movie meant for *them*—that, as Nicky put it, Scorsese was using the master's tools to dismantle the master's house. In the darkened theater, his arm kept brushing up against hers on the armrest, but she barely noticed. Because who *Taxi Driver* turned out to be made for was Samantha Cicciaro herself. There was the Sicilio-Catholic upbringing of the *auteur*, all those ineffable points of reference. There was beautiful Bobby D., with his chin as big as a Frigidaire, the resemblance around the eyes to her lover. And then there was Jodie Foster, who, despite her halter top and hot pants, was a child. And what did Scorsese mean Sam to feel toward the idea of them as a couple? Pity? Disgust? What you could not do was imagine that Travis Bickle's infatuation with that little girl was healthy, or normal, or durable. That it would not end in tears.

That Friday, when Keith had arranged to leave work at lunchtime, she made him take her to see the movie again, in a newer theater near the U.N. For much of the second half, she watched his face, rather than the screen. But when they emerged into the weak sunlight of a November three o'clock, he just blinked and shook his head and said, "That was dark."

"It didn't touch a nerve?"

"What are you talking about?"

She gave thanks once more for his naïveté. Another test had been passed. She grabbed his arm. "Let's go get a room."

"You've got a room," he said.

"That's all the way back downtown."

"I left my wallet at home, specifically so you wouldn't make me burn through any more cash."

A plan was forming. "Well, we'll just have to go get it, won't we?" She let her torso push against his arm and whispered in his ear a couple things she would let him do to her, if he would take her to a nice hotel.

"For Christ's sake, Samantha. There are people watching." But this was New York City; you had to do a lot worse than this to get people to watch. And the redness spreading to the tips of his ears meant she already had him.

OUTSIDE OF HIS BUILDING, he told her to stay in the cab, he'd be right back, but when she saw him pass the doorman's desk, she bolted from the backseat, possessed again by the need to know exactly how far she could take things. She mumbled a floor number to the doorman, who barely looked up from his paper. No one suspected girls of anything. She caught up with Keith by the elevators, where she slipped a hand into his pocket. "What are you doing?" he hissed.

"I want to see where you live. I think I deserve that."

He was looking over her shoulder toward the bright ribbon of street, as though calculating the odds of smuggling her back through the lobby unobserved. She looked relatively unsensational today, she knew, in jeans and a holey cardigan, but if she was a niece it would seem suspicious for her to be leaving so soon. An elevator dinged. "Fine," he said, and hustled her into the empty box.

Upstairs, he stationed her just inside the door to his apartment. "See? This is it. Now don't move until I come back to escort you out." There was a ripple of déjà vu. She could hear lights flicking on, drawers groaning, while she waited in this hallway that smelled faintly of a thousand meals, as if some giant sweet dough had been packed into the pores of the walls. There was a mat for wiping feet, an umbrella stand, a table with a dish full of pocket-change, a framed painting or print of a harlequin—it was hard to tell, blears of light from the windows at the far end of the hall turned the glass opaque in places. A single tinkertoy poked half-concealed from a corner of the rug, like someone had tucked it there for her to see. She had imagined, for some reason, that his other life was as contingent as the one he'd been leading with her. In fact, it was solid, dense, and it would be harder than she'd imagined to break its hold on him—assuming she still wanted to.

She drifted down the hall toward those windows. How large this place was! The living room had that same unbearably lived-in look, as if at any moment, Keith's wife and kids would return to take up the funny pages folded on the coffeetable, the mug of cold tea, the sad fat teabag slumped in a saucer of its own water. Which was maybe why he wanted her back by the door, ready for a quick getaway, but she couldn't help but stop by the built-in bookshelves with all their picture frames, more pictures even than she'd snapped that fall for *Land of a Thousand Dances.* Surely it hadn't been Keith who'd arranged them all there. He was too careless. It was someone like her, someone who needed the reassurance of the incontrovertible. Here was a photograph, for example, of a family at a picnic table by a lake. The little girl was blurry from trying to wriggle out of Keith's arms. But the woman, with her Kodachrome red hair, was actually beautiful, the way the silver of the lake in the background and the dark green spruce were beautiful.

Then the frame was being tugged from her hands and placed on the shelf. "What did I tell you?"

"That's not where it goes," she pointed out.

"Then put it where it goes, God damn it."

She'd never seen him quite this mad, and though it stung, it was also thrilling, as if she'd planted her flag a dozen feet farther up the slope than it had been a minute ago. "What are you going to do?" she asked. "Punish me?" As she pulled him toward the sofa, she could feel the animal in him wanting to take over.

This time, though, things were off from the get-go; as soon as he entered her she could feel him softening. When she asked if he was all right, he said he couldn't feel anything. She shifted. How about now? "I can't feel anything," he repeated, panicky, like an asthmatic saying, *I can't breathe.* It was bullshit, she thought. He did feel something; it just wasn't what he wanted to feel. And he thought *she* was a child. Finally, he slid off her and sat hunched over on the edge of the couch, fists pressed to his eyes, and in the dusky pre-rush-hour light, she seemed to feel the whole apartment quivering from the tension in his body, all that useless stiffness. Which was why, when she heard a board creak down a hall, she didn't think much of it. She contaminated everything she touched, she was thinking, and here she had done it again: taken what was supposed to be a game, an experiment, and through the impossible scale of her wanting, or through simple curiosity, pushed it past what it would bear.

68

THAT HE WOULD OVERREACT SEEMED INEVITABLE, in hindsight, but that wasn't why Regan had kept it from him. No, it was that saying it out loud meant admitting there was trouble, which Regan wasn't ready to do until their third or fourth Tuesday at the old Italian restaurant. And which Keith, to judge by the reddening of his face in the Neapolitan gloom, wasn't ready to do even then. Plus she'd been feeling shut out of his life for so long—that large, public life so unlike her own compact existence—that whenever anything happened to her that did not involve him, she was inclined to keep it hidden, as a counterweight. When he set his glass down, she thought it might shatter. "What do you mean, seeing someone?" Only now did the double entendre dawn on her: he thought she was *seeing* someone. And suddenly, there was guilt—exactly what she'd been trying to avoid.

"I mean an analyst, honey. I've been seeing an analyst." The flush was slow to leave his cheeks. The bartender had stopped wiping down the bar and was pretending not to listen. "We talked about this back in the spring, remember?"

"About your seeing an analyst?" It was true that he'd never asked her specifically about the drop in her weight, probably because she'd sent him every signal that she didn't want to be asked. She'd been down to 105 pounds when she'd caught a glimpse of her real self in the mirror—just a shimmer really, before the false image reasserted itself, but a shimmer had been enough.

"We don't talk about marital problems, Keith, if that's what you're worried about. It's really just a lot of boring family-of-origin stuff that predates you." Which wasn't wholly truthful, actually, but when there was a question of reducing or resolving tensions, her commitment to honesty was not unbending; this was one of the things Dr. Altschul had helped her to see. "You remember? A few weeks before I started work, you said something about people finding analysis really helpful. In fact, Dr. Altschul was the one who showed me you were right, I should do something professionally instead of sitting around the house all day waiting for the kids to come home from school."

"I didn't know you felt there were problems."

Of course the waiter would choose that moment to bring the entrees: ravioli for her, and, for the gentleman, *linguine vongole*. A curtain of briny steam rose between them. She spooned some Parmesan onto her pasta, then let her hand rest palm-up on the checked tablecloth while the cheese went orange. She tried to think of something else. Of how easily, for example, he could have taken that hand.

"Do you like him, at least?"

"It's the other Dr. Altschul. The wife."

"Well, do you like her?"

"Are you jealous? I can't believe this. You're jealous."

"I just feel like . . . you could have talked to *me*, Regan."

There was a window here in which they might have tackled the question of who should have talked to whom; he'd been holding back for *years* whatever it was that had made those thousands of dollars disappear from the kids' college funds that one time, before they just as magically reappeared. It was a conversation Dr. Altschul would have encouraged, even if its ultimate issue would be that it was Regan, and not Keith, who'd kept the first secret. But she still wasn't healthy enough to tell him about all that. She used the side of her fork to cut her ravioli into smallish squares, leaving her knife untouched. It was an old habit: dirty as few dishes as possible, limit the amount of trouble you cause for other people. "We're talking about it now," she said. "This is a good thing."

They finished their dinner in near-silence (or he finished while she picked at hers) like those older couples you sometimes saw who wouldn't even meet each other's eyes. She used to wonder how they got that way. One day you just became them, was the answer. But when the check arrived, Keith suggested they walk home, rather than take a cab.

It was a brisk November night, with dry leaves rustling behind the wall of Central Park. Here and there, electric lights cleared larger spheres of green and gold in the otherwise deep-blue tangle of branches. The tentativeness with which he reached for her hand reminded her of when they'd first dated, and she liked that; he was seeing her again as a person with a will not his own. He'd actually asked which route she wanted to take, rather than simply deciding, and she'd chosen Fifty-Ninth Street; these days, you had to be crazy to cut across the Park after sundown.

But apparently you had to be crazy to walk at all. Halfway along the Park's southern perimeter, with the stink of the carriage horses behind them, she became aware of another set of footsteps, following. Every thirty yards or so, a streetlamp made long shadows that shrank and shrank and then grew and grew after they'd passed beneath, and at the outer reaches of that growth, she could make out, in addition to Keith's head and her own, the top of the shadow of the person follow-ing them. She knew from Keith's rigid arm that he must see it, too. They sped up. The shadow kept pace, and now on the ground she could see its shoulders. Soon there would be a torso, arms, a blade, a voice wanting all their money. Just when it seemed, though, that the shadow would catch them, Keith wheeled around and demanded, "You got something to say?" She turned in time to see a wiry black kid frozen in the middle of the sidewalk, maybe a dozen feet away. A tuft of green hair stuck from beneath his stocking cap. His eyes were locked onto Keith's. They looked so startled that she couldn't be sure he wasn't just a fellow pedestrian out for a night stroll. At any rate, he seemed to decide Keith was trouble, and pivoted and slunk away.

"Wow," she couldn't help saying. "Where did that come from?" He shrugged, embarrassed. And suddenly her limbs turned to jelly and she was cracking up. She could barely stand; it felt good to laugh. Then he was laughing. They stood there leaning on each other, gasp-ing, relieved.

And after the sitter had been paid and the kids put to bed and the teeth brushed and the sleepwear donned, they lay in the dark reliving it. "You were incredible," she told him. Her head was on his chest. "*You got something to say?* I always wanted to do something like that."

"Regan, look," he said—which of course she couldn't, without moving her head. "I know I haven't always been the person you've needed. Or frankly, deserved."

"Keith—"

"No, let me finish. This is a long time coming. I go through my days, honey, I'm thinking, me, me, me, what about me, what does this mean for me, and somehow in my mind you're still at home, and the kids are crawling around on the rug and I'm thinking, well, at least that's one part of my life I don't have to worry about . . ."

He was doing it even now—*me, me, me*—but at least he was trying. "What *do* you have to worry about, honey?"

His chest rose under her. Paused. Fell. "That's not important right now. What's important is, I know there have been problems, and I'm sorry, and I'm going to do better from now on." And then, having discharged a burden she still didn't comprehend, he kissed the top of her head. "And you're right. Good for you for seeing someone."

She said it again—*You got something to say?*—but this time only she laughed. His hand, which had found its way under her shirt, brushed her nipple. She could feel her body answering him, tensing, opening, but her brain didn't want to put at risk what had otherwise been their first good night in a long time—to reduce his standing up for her and his baring of his soul to a mere campaign for sex. She touched his wrist. Directness was another thing she'd been practicing with Dr. Altschul. "Honey, I'm exhausted, and we've both got work in the morning. Maybe some other time?"

Sure, he said, and gave her one more caress before withdrawing his hand. His face was still invisible above her. Maybe some other time.

WEDNESDAYS BELONGED TO DR. ALTSCHUL. She'd told her new secretary that the standing appointment was with an orthopedist, because it seemed imperative that no one at the firm suspect her of being a basket case, but who ever got this keyed up about going to the orthopedist's? The morning before an appointment, she'd be unable to get anything done. Her eyes would pass again and again over the same press release or whatever, but her mind would be rehearsing what she would say to the analyst, *her* analyst. She had been right to hold out for a woman, and she loved the feeling of surrender she got, reclining on the couch. The empathetic blankness of the therapeutic voice. She even loved Dr. Altschul's office, a low-ceilinged room in the basement of a brownstone in the West Village, which she Freudianly shared with her neo-Jungian husband. Regan knew these feelings weren't real, they were called *transference*, but still, she was trying to honor them. This week, in particular, she would recount the dinner with Keith, and how she'd asserted herself, and the doctor would be proud of her. But all the voice beyond her shoulder said was, "And how did that make you feel?"

"You mean to just say what I felt, like that?"

"Is that what you think I mean?"

What the analyst was really getting at, Regan was pretty sure, was Amory Gould. For several sessions now, they'd been focusing on the period of time around Daddy's remarriage, when the house on Sutton Place had been sold and William had disappeared and she'd first met Keith. The chronology was all jumbled up now, but everything ailing her seemed to begin back there. Just last week, she'd finally broached the subject of Block Island, and strangely, she heard herself talking on and on not about . . . whatever his name had been, but about the Demon Brother. *You believe this man is somehow responsible for your rape*, the doctor had said, just that blunt. *And for covering it up. And now you work alongside him.* "Well, he's never at the office. He's really more of a phantom," she'd pointed out, because she never would have gone to work for Daddy full-time if she'd thought Amory was going to be around, would she? But it was true that shortly after she'd taken over Public Relations, Amory had been promoted from his nebulous consigliere position to Executive Vice President of Global Operations, and was suddenly everywhere, ferrying his tubes of blueprints all over the Hamilton-Sweeney Building. She knew the doctor felt Amory was a danger, though she made it seem as if it were Regan who felt it . . . unless Regan was *projecting* again, a word that made her think of a giant, two-dimensional Demon Brother hovering above and just behind her even here, in the sanctity of these four walls.

"You want to know what he does to torment me?"

"You feel your husband torments you?"

"Amory. My uncle. Since they moved everybody off the top floors to renovate, his office is on 30, not far from Daddy's. But he comes down to 29 at least twice a day to use the water fountain closest to my door." Regan studied the walls of the office, the African masks that had been hung there for the diversion of the patients. It was raining outside. Drops rolling down the window made the light ripple over the masks as though they were alive. She found herself staring at one with a single red eyebrow, a pig's snout, triangular teeth through which a long tongue lolled. "I remember right after I got married, he convinced Keith to drop medical school. Why would he have done that, if not to torment me?"

"And that was important to you? That Keith become a doctor?"

Was this analysis or an inquisition? "No. But it was right around the time when I was trying to start my own family, separate from the one I'd grown up with. I know, maybe I should have moved farther away, but Keith always wanted to be in New York."

"Did you tell him?"

"Amory?"

"Keith. That you wanted to move."

"No."

"But you were angry with him for not doing it."

Regan's hands looked ineffectual, lying there in her lap. And in fact, though she didn't say it, it was Dr. Altschul she was now angry at. (Or was that *with*?) Because she was finally doing her best to come clean with Keith, and wasn't that what mattered?

SHE WOULD MISS HER APPOINTMENT THE FOLLOWING WEEK. Missed appointments meant evasion, and could lead to a period of arrested progress, according to her reading (though all the books on psycho-analysis had been written by psychoanalysts, which seemed like a conflict of interest). But it was the day before Thanksgiving, and frankly, she felt she'd earned a break. It had been twenty-six weeks now since she'd last stuck her finger down her throat.

Thursday morning, they took the kids to the Macy's parade. Will was too old, probably—he turtled his head down into his jacket, as if to keep from being spotted by anyone from school—but Cate, perched on Keith's shoulders, could barely keep from jumping off. As Woodstock passed by, looming high over the tops of the boxed trees, a gust of wind tilted him forward. "Mommy!"

"Yes, darling. I saw it! He bowed to you!"

"Did you see it, Daddy?"

Keith, underneath, seemed barely to hear, because something had happened to distract him again. It only grew more pronounced at home. When they sat down to their turkey dinner, he seemed unable to let his gaze rest on anything for more than a second. Will had to ask him twice to carve a second helping of white meat. "What's the matter, Dad?" he said, pointedly. "You have somewhere else to be?"

"No, no, I just . . ."

It was a sentence he would never finish. Regan couldn't figure it out; had she done something wrong? Maybe it was the bird. He'd wanted to hire a cook when she'd started the new job in May, but that was just the sort of thing she'd sworn off when she'd resolved all those years ago to stop being a Hamilton-Sweeney. They already had a maid, and Regan refused to make her work on Thanksgiving. And so the pile of dishes they'd made they had to do themselves. Keith and Cate took first shift, but after a half-hour, she offered to take over, and they drifted off to the living room to watch TV. She didn't realize Will hadn't joined them until she felt his eyes on her back from across the room, as if she were a math problem he was struggling to work out. "Carl's parents are splitting up," he said, abruptly.

"I'm sorry to hear that," she said. And then, because she didn't want him to inherit the WASPy indirection that hobbled her, she cribbed a line from the analyst's playbook. "How does that make you feel?"

He paused to consider. She had an urge to turn and sweep him off his perch, cover him with kisses. But he was passing into that age where mushy stuff embarrassed him. His arms and legs seemed every morning to have grown another half-inch, and his posture was suddenly awkward. Soon patches of unaccountable hair would bloom on his blemishless body and strange yearnings would seize him like giant fists. It was a bittersweet fact that made her want to kiss him. She felt, though, that even as he became a man, the earnestness he'd been born with would not desert him, and this allowed her to keep her back turned, her hands clunking around in the warm, soapy water. "I don't know," he said, finally. "Bad for Carl, I guess."

And that was when he asked her, point-blank: "Are you happy, Mom?" The honest answer was *No.* But she could hear through the flatness of his voice an anxiety that made her feel she'd failed him. Which only went to show the limit of Dr. Altschul's vision: If expressing herself meant hurting her children, how could she? She turned, her hands still slick with dishwater, and crossed the room to the stool where Will sat and put her hands on his cheeks. She tilted his face so that it caught the light from over the sink, on the assumption that the better she could see him, the better he'd be able to see her. "I am happy, honey," she said.

He raised the cuffs of his sweatshirt to blot his cheeks. "Ew, Mom. Food water."

She flicked more water onto his face and grinned. "You make me very happy."

"Gross!"

HERE WERE THE ORIGINS of magic, or religion, or both: there were certain words that, when you spoke them, had the power to create the thing they depicted. For Regan *was* happy that weekend, wasn't she, in her own limited way? It would certainly seem so, later. She was happy to take her kids to the zoo on Friday, happy not to cook dinner that night, happy to have the annual chance to use cold mashed potatoes as a sandwich condiment, and happy Saturday morning (she would tell Dr. Altschul), as she watched her husband and son put on their jackets and head out for Will's jujitsu practice. Happy right up to the point when the mail arrived.

It was lying as usual in a little explosion on the foyer floor; the doormen sorted and distributed it within the building. Magazine, catalogue, bill, catalogue, catalogue, solicitation . . . but then she saw a business envelope with no postmark, or even address. There was something uncanny about the way her name sat alone on the long, white rectangle.

She had to have already known, then, what was in it. Had to have noticed, on some level, how often Keith called to make excuses for being late, or came home when she was pretending to sleep and headed straight for the shower. That angle he'd sat at at Thanksgiving dinner, one leg to the side, as if at any moment he'd have to spring up to block the doorway, or turn off the ringer on the phone. Or why else would she have locked herself into the bathroom to read it?

Held up to the light, the envelope revealed a single piece of torn loose leaf. She already felt like giving in, making herself sick, letting go in less than a minute all that she'd so painfully built. But now she could hear Will and Keith returning from jujitsu, unzipping jackets, their shoes hitting the welcome mat where the mail had been fifteen minutes ago, back when it had still been possible to pretend her life had not changed. She sat down on the edge of the tub, tore off the end of the envelope, blew on it, tipped out the paper. This is what it said, in lowercase type that did not sit quite neatly on the line:

`he is lying to you.`

69

L EAVING KEITH IN THE GRAVELED PARK above First Avenue four days before the holiday, Sam had felt so jittery she'd almost tripped over the stairs. Freedom! By nightfall, though, she realized she was the one who'd been left. So had she been, to him, just some dumb teen? Was all he wanted—all any man wanted—a surface to reflect back the self he wanted to see? She found herself wondering again that Wednesday, when Nicky Chaos tried to talk her into spending Thanksgiving at the Phalanstery. A true Post-Humanist would treat it like any other day, he said. Think about it: the subjugation of land, of animals, and of the red man, rolled into a single orgy of consumption. But an orgy of consumption sounded like exactly what Sam needed right now, and so, before the dorms closed for a long weekend, she crammed a backpack full of clothes and took the train out to Flower Hill.

The first thing she did there was check the mailbox, in case there was some warning from the registrar waiting for Dad. *This is to inform you that Samantha Cicciaro has not attended . . .* Right. Like anyone really cared how she occupied herself; the whole concept of *in loco parentis* had been vaporized in some kind of national encounter session circa 1973. And when she trudged around back to see if her actual parent was here, the yard looked as if it hadn't been touched in months: rusty TV aerial and forsaken treehouse, grass lifeless as the sky, L.I.E. mumbling behind the trees as it had every day since she was three. The truck was gone, the bulb above the workshop door inert. You wanted so badly for things to change, and then you didn't. She dug in her pocket for her keys and touched the touchplate on the jamb, an old reflex, like dipping into holy water before entering a church.

The space inside had been immaculate once, polished valves and ordered intricacies of tubing. Now all lay in disarray. Lengths of black hose gaped, disconnected from anything. A shotgun was being used as a paperweight. Silver nitrate dusted the floor. It was the workshop of a man losing his livelihood. Yet it was also a chance to grant the favor Nicky had asked when it became clear she wasn't going to spend her holiday with him, eating beans from a can. "He's the fireworks guy, right, your dad? Do you think you could nick us a little something while you're out there?"

Why? she'd said. So he could blow up some trashcans? Tie rockets to the tails of cats?

"Give me some credit, Sam. Or are you still sore about that church? I thought we'd moved on." Nicky had seemed edgier than usual, rolling a piece of old fruit around in his hands like Silly Putty, but he had indeed moved on. He was taking one last shot at getting Ex Post Facto back together, he told her (though aside from tales of long-ago jam sessions with Venus de Nylon and Billy Three-Sticks, there was little evidence the band had ever been his). A reunion gig had been booked for New Year's Eve. Talk about an arbitrary holiday, she said. This shitty world's a year older; what's to celebrate? "Yeah, but Billy was always funny about it. I remember he used to say, as goes that first night, so goes the rest of the year. He swore to play every New Year's, at the stroke of twelve, until he died or the world ended, whichever came first." Nicky's plan for the reunion show was to make some flashpots to light off at the end of the last set—something really spectacular. "I'm thinking a kilogram of black powder would do it," he said, but he was clearly shaky on the metric system. A kilogram would obliterate half the East Village if you weren't careful, and anyway, Dad would never keep that much lying around Flower Hill, even in his days of distraction. She decided she would take just a pinch of the slow-burning polverone instead, and hope that, with the mess, Dad wouldn't miss it.

It lived in an airtight box at the back of the shop. As in a dream, she watched herself tamp one, two, three grams into a test tube, cork it, stash it in her backpack. And now some stars, for flash. As a little girl, she'd had to memorize the contents of the thousand inch-square drawers that lined the east wall, like entries on the periodic table. The sorcerer's apprentice, Dad had called her, and she'd relished the jealous look she always got from Mom when the two of them walked up the hill at dinnertime. Later, after Mom left, Sam had renounced the family trade, but the names and cautions had stuck with her. Potassium—*Keep away from water.* Silver arsenic—*Fatal if ingested.* She spooned some nitrates into a troika of tubes and wrapped each in a tee-shirt to keep the glass from breaking. After a final survey, she turned the lights off and ambled up to the house. No one was around to see. She sort of wished, in fact, that Dad would get home already. But as the sky outside her bedroom window went dark, he didn't come, and didn't come. Hadn't she told him she'd be here for Thanksgiving? The whole point was not to have to feel alone.

IN THE MORNING, though, she drowsed as long as she could, and then found a million things to do in her room. What if Dad had been down to the workshop at dawn and discovered the theft? But when she finally went out to face him, he was still in his undershirt, watching some Fourth of July festivities from the early '70s on videotape. The volume was low. From the hi-fi came late Sinatra. And maybe he really had forgotten she was coming, because he asked if she could go pick up a turkey for dinner. "You mean because you're so busy." A dryness bordering on sarcasm was one of their shared idioms, but the joke had teeth; she was getting the impression that his work these days largely involved rehashing old glories for that never-ending magazine profile.

On her way back from the grocery, she killed an hour or more cruising somnolent sidestreets, while the turkey thawed on the passenger's seat beside her. She had half a mind to go see Charlie Weisbarger but didn't know where his house was. She returned to her own to find Dad still in his lounge chair in front of the TV, now in one of those fuzzy, faintly sulfurous wool overshirts that were what the word "home" made her think of. Had he made it farther than his not-so-secret beer cooler on the patio? Was he onto her? Impossible to say. When she told him she'd found a good bird, his grunt might have signified pensiveness, or absentmindedness, or stifled rage.

She moved around the kitchen sick with nerves, which was no way to cook, and then bounced back and forth between there and her room, but the turkey that emerged from the oven three hours later, impaled on its plastic thermometer, looked credibly brown. Dad sat across from her at the little table in the kitchen, staring at it, his fork and knife clutched Neolithically in his hands. "Let me ask you something, Sammy."

Oh fuck, she thought. So he'd been out there after all. "Fire away."

"When you got home yesterday, did you notice anything out of the ordinary?"

"Uh-uh." She had to take a gulp of water before she could ask why he asked, when the real question was: Had he called the cops? But of course he hadn't. Generations of Cicciaros would have risen shrieking from the ground, come after him with pitchforks and torches.

He muttered something to himself.

"What?"

"I said, they're not going to stop until they've taken every last thing I have."

"What's going on, Dad? What are you talking about?"

He was talking about the competition, he said. These little acts of industrial espionage. They obviously wanted to send him a message. But then it was as if the outward form of the meal, the proximity of the mashed potatoes to the Platonic ideal on the box, called him back to the present. "Listen to me running off at the mouth, when you came all this way. Forget I mentioned it." His hand, scrubbed pink with lava soap, took hers. "Why don't you tell me why you're thankful."

"Me?"

"Yeah, baby. What are we celebrating here?" It was a thing Mom used to make them do. *Gratitudes*, she called it. But what was Sam supposed to be grateful for? Keith would just be sitting down with his wife and kids. Nicky was probably at this moment in the throes with Sewer Girl, who'd been servicing him behind Sol's back since at least October. Poor Charlie was still grounded. And Dad, only two feet away, remained remote, cut off by the vials in her backpack. Stealing, dishonor, disobedience, two or three sins in a single stroke. Or did she have it backward: was it the remoteness that caused the sin? The candles she'd found under the laundry-room sink glimmered. A single, hot tear slinked down her cheek.

"You all right?" he said, as if she'd stubbed her toe.

The tear reached her mouth, salty. She sniffed. "Yeah. I'm all right."

The fatty smell of the bird filled her nostrils, making it hard not to think Nicky had a point, at least so far as animals were concerned. But to notice that she barely touched her dinner would have been to have to speak about it—so Dad tucked in, and then so did she, wondering all the while, who *am* I?

THE NEXT DAY, her dad drove into the city to talk to Benny Blum. The best revenge, he'd decided, was to get his contracts back. As soon as he was gone, she walked over to the tattoo parlor on Main. The place reeked of cheap incense, and sheets of blue cellophane affixed to the windows gave the light a morgue-like tint. The tattooist was thirty-ish, limp as a noodle, with a few discrete bristles of moustache. On the plus side, he didn't ask for proof of age, and the prices started at fifteen bucks. She'd sold her semester's meal card to another student back in October. Much of the cash had gone to pay for movie tickets and cigarettes, but enough remained for a design the size of a fifty-cent piece. On a prescription pad that was for some reason lying on the display case, she sketched what she wanted. "Right there," she said, and put her finger to the spot, just below the occiput.

The tattooist led her to a backroom even creepier than the front—a room for porno shoots or child abduction—and pushed her face into a leather ring like a padded toilet seat, and doubtless as sanitary. She could feel his breath on her neck, but didn't make a sound when he touched her hair, or when he cranked up the Floyd on the stereo, or even when the first needle went in, though he scolded her for tensing her muscles. It felt exactly how you'd expect a hot spike driven into your neck to feel. Still, pain sometimes could be clarifying.

WHEN THE MAGAZINE GUY CAME OUT THAT AFTERNOON in search of Dad, she had an impulse to show him what she'd done—to say, Fit *this* into your story. But it was only the next day on East Third with Sewer Girl that she would brush the hair back from her neck, peel off the Snoopy band-aid she'd told Dad was for a bug bite. She was hoping for an admiring whistle, or, failing that, an expletive meaning *whoa*. Instead, she felt hands on her shoulders, steering her into stronger light. "What's that supposed to be?"

Sam wanted to believe that all of this—the squinting, the withholding of judgment—was a put-on, but though Sewer Girl was full of many things, guile was not among them. Anyway, one unforeseen effect of the tattoo's placement was to make it virtually impossible for Sam to inspect it herself. The only reflecting surfaces in the house were in Nicky's basement, and she would try, through various conjunctions of the cracked glass on the wall and the mirror he used for cocaine, to catch sight of the logo he'd shown her back in July, but all she saw was a blurriness that may have been a function of the tattooist's clumsiness or her own shaking hand. Then a miniature Nicky, doubly reflected, appeared in her palm. "Who dragged *you* through the briar patch?"

"Thanks, asshole. Not everybody has a sugar daddy uptown to keep them looking fit."

For a second, his gaze went flat. Then he recovered. "Seriously, though, did you already get into my stash? Your eyes are like rose-colored."

"I'm in some pain." She uncovered the tattoo.

All he said was, "Cool. Hey, did you get my shit?"

It took her a beat to remember what he was talking about, and when she did fetch the test tubes from her bag, he seemed disappointed at how puny the polverone looked, clumped there at the bottom. She promised it would be more than enough to wow a small crowd.

"There's the rub. I don't want to wow a small crowd."

"You understand an explosion is geometric, right? Kilos would be, like, this to the thousandth power. Anyway, what you're after's not a powder burst, but a steady burn that will ignite these babies at intervals." She showed him the stars, walked him through the handling instructions. The nitrates needed to stay dry, and though she'd taken the least volatile ones, reds and oranges and a little green, you wanted to keep them wrapped in some kind of padding, so they didn't jostle too much. "And be super-wary of static electricity. If I'd gotten you my dad's special formula, you'd have to worry about off-gassing, but the worst that happens with polverone is you set yourself on fire, rather than blow yourself up."

His attention seemed to have moved on to that other powder he was cutting on the table. "Well damn, you're the expert, I guess. Want a bump?"

She and Charlie had had a gentleman's agreement to stay away from the hard stuff. It was supposed to save them from the fate of the scarecrows who populated this part of the city. Just an hour ago, she'd seen one half-squatting in the middle of Second Avenue, blocking traffic, entranced by the cherry-red popsicle melting in his hand. But were these arbitrary rules not another form of dependency? To hell with it, she thought, why not?

AND THIS IS HOW, as the Bicentennial year drew to a close, the loss of Keith Lamplighter sent her back into the ambit of her friends, albeit numbed somewhat to the consequences. It became second nature: the rolling of a bill, the shielding of a nostril, and then snow flying into the head, cooling everything. The alkaline drip. The white powder. The bill slackening on the mirror.

Nicky, not coincidentally, was a dynamo. Band rehearsals in the little house out back could stretch to three or four hours. The new players included D. Tremens on lead guitar and a person named Tutu on bass. Sometimes one of the Ph.D. candidates with whom Nicky liked to wax philosophical came over to manipulate tape loops. Sam couldn't help imagining a review of these practice sessions for her 'zine. *A toneless game of Telephone. All the Ex Post Facto fury with none of the sound.* Then again, what was "good," anyway? She would have liked to volunteer for the second-guitar slot herself—the Fender around Nicky's neck seemed purely decorative—but he'd already appointed her Ministrix of Information, which mostly involved taking pictures of him striking Iggy Pop poses with his shirt off. Between songs, Sewer Girl shot Sam dirty looks. It was clear now who was the favorite.

In general, the level of jealousy in the house was higher than it had been in the summer. As a form of personalized paranoia, this was understandable—they were all smoking hellacious amounts of grass, to come down off the blow. But it had started to infect even Nicky, despite his having rapped so persuasively about the end of property, the illusion of individuality. One day, when he and Sam were getting high in the basement, he'd looked up from the mirror between them. "You realize why you returned to the fold, right?"

"What?"

The only reason she'd been spending so much time here lately, he said, was on the off-chance she might run into *him* again.

"Run into who?"

"What? Who?" he repeated, in a high, girly voice. His face loomed downward in the mirror and then tilted back, eyes closed. She'd read somewhere that sharks could smell a drop of blood in a million drops of water, or taste it, or whatever sharks did. "I'm talking about Loverboy. You obviously haven't read those books I gave you. This older-man trip of yours is slave morality, Sam, pure and simple."

She crossed the room to the stereo and knelt to flip through the stacks of LPs. Who she longed for, at present, was not Keith but good old Charlie W. No matter how much it might have hurt, he would have made at least some basic effort to understand how she felt inside, and this was maybe what she missed most about him: his utter undefendedness. That devout, almost angry look he'd given her in this very basement, just before he'd kissed her . . . How hard was it to pretend you were enjoying yourself, if it would make someone like Charlie happy? But even 'shroomed out of her mind, she could see how her habit of moving on would have annihilated his heart, and so had pretended that night to pass out. Now, from among those Herb Alpert records Nicky collected, she liberated a copy of *Brass Tactics*. She knew it would piss him off, being indisputably superior to anything he'd ever be able to create. It was her revenge for his phrase "slave morality," which had worked itself into her flesh like a burr. He needed to know she wasn't out to impress him, that she was choosing freely. As the opening riff of "Army Recruiter" blazed out of the speakers, she turned around. "Are we going to do this, or what?"

A few minutes later, they were in underwear. She let Nicky tap out a trail of powder onto the flat skin between her navel and the elastic of her panties. Her head was a citadel she was locked away inside, while he made free with the landscape below. When he started to twitch inside her, she produced a few moans. As if he cared. But at least she had done it. Had mastered herself. "See?" she said, when they'd been silent a while.

"See what?"

"I told you I was over him."

"I don't know. You think you could convince me again?"

ALL KIDDING ASIDE, this was what seemed to clinch her loyalty, for Nicky. Not the tattoo, not the theft of the three grams, not her abstention, all these months, from sticking her nose too far into exactly what the PHP aimed to achieve. It was letting him fuck her. Frozen out of their "bombing runs" since August, she now found herself back in, zooming deeper into the boroughs. She rode shotgun, though the silence from behind suggested her presence there was not universally welcomed. Before the van had even stopped, D.T. and Sol would be paratrooping out of the sliding door to infiltrate the unfamiliar streets, spraycans (she assumed) clanking in their bags. Nicky would turn on the radio and spark a joint as, behind his mirrored shades, he went on high alert. She could tell from how he stopped trying to feel her up. He even let her bring her camera—in case there was time to document the graffiti—though he still forbid her from printing the results in her 'zine. She'd mostly shoot random throw-ups she noticed while she waited, but sometimes Nicky would ask her to take a picture of something specific. "Can you get that garage over there? The one with the burn-marks?" Or he'd direct her attention to a demolition notice on the garage door, or to the razor-wired top of a construction fence, gleaming dully in the dying light. She was still going over to NYU to use the darkroom, academic standing be damned, and watching those proofs dry—train-trestle murals, charred mailboxes, knotted Chucks festooning the blighted elms—she tried to convince herself he was right. Maybe every form of vandalism had its own aesthetic. Several times recently, she'd thought they were no more than a block or two away from that church they'd doused in gasoline; she would have liked to see it again. But if she didn't ask Nicky what had become of it, she wouldn't have to deal with an answer. So she just handed him his copy of the photos, which he sheathed inside spare record sleeves and pinned to the wall of the war room upstairs.

Then one afternoon they were idling near the nexus of two avenues and an expressway. It was almost Christmas, and a Santa Claus in a vacant lot was offering to appear in pictures for five dollars. The trim on his suit was mangy, as if it had been dug out of a dumpster, yet young mothers queued ten deep on the sidewalk, holding the hands of kids waiting to get in. Sam watched through her lens. Black and Latin kids were a fixation of hers; she could beam at them the goodwill she felt toward all people of color without having to feel any of the guilt. A bus pulled to the curb, blocking her view, and then moved away again. Out of nowhere came a boom. A cloud of smoke roiled above a shuttered sporting-goods store two lots down. Women were yelling, and there was a kind of stampede away from Santa. "Whoa. Fucking gas lines up here," Nicky said, and then fixed Sam with a curious expression, as if waiting to see what she would do. But before she could respond, D.T. and Sol were shoving back into the van. A brand-new duffelbag in red, white, and blue was handed forward. "Is that the right size?" Sol asked, breathlessly. "It's the biggest one I could find."

"Jesus," Sam said. "You guys were *in* there? Are you okay?"

"That was too close for comfort, Sol. But it looks like no one got hurt." Nicky's tone was lost in the sirens that had begun to wail. Her camera swung toward the expressway's off-ramp, where an ambulance was hitting gridlock. Click.

"Hey, you two aren't, like, in any way responsible for what just happened, right?" They had joined the mass of traffic trying to get away from the explosion. With night falling, the back of the van was in shadow.

"For a gas main explosion?" Nicky said.

"Con fucking Edison, man," Sol added.

Something between the sporting-goods store and the ambulance had slid into her viewfinder, a decisive moment. She was pressing the button when her elbow got jostled, queering the shot. "Would you knock it off already?" This was Sewer Girl, on a tilt. "Seriously, Nicky, I don't know why you'd bring her along."

"You want to know who's ultimately responsible?" Nicky asked. "Look around, Sam. It's the whole rotten country. People need to wake up to the fact that no one's looking out for them." It was true that as another ambulance screamed on the expressway, the whores by the on-ramp seemed to take it in stride, the way you accepted potholes, or the third-world wars Nicky said made for cheap bananas. Overhead, exit signs rimed with road salt slid by. Port Morris, Melrose, Mott Haven—these *were* third-world countries, practically. Still, it was the kind of talk that had made her so uncomfortable at the end of last summer. "But not to worry, Sam. We're on the same side. Our fates are all bound together now."

WERE THEY REALLY, though? Nicky was starting to treat her like a girlfriend, but she wasn't even sure she *liked* him. On top of his delusions of grandeur, he smelled like summer sausage. She would still be brooding on Christmas Day, laying out the place settings for dinner, when Dad took the phone call that changed everything. What put her on notice was his silence, the way he listened without speaking. When she ventured a glance, he was pale. Her first thought was that someone, somehow, had heard tell she'd stolen from him on her last trip out. Her second was that it was a no-go on getting the contracts back. "Yeah. Uh-huh. I understand." He hung up the phone so hard that it rang again, hanging in the air.

"Everything all right?" she said, trying to sound like him. Dry. Cool. But no longer.

"Those fuckers."

"What fuckers, Dad?"

The echo seemed to remind him she was here. So at least this wasn't about Thanksgiving. Or was it? "That was Rizzo. He goes out to Willets Point an hour ago to grab something, the lock on Shed 13 is busted, and the watchman next door's just seen a giant in a hockey uniform running toward the train. We've been hit again, Sammy. They're robbing me blind."

"Your polvcrone." Already, though, she knew it wasn't polverone. If she could just look back at those pictures she'd taken, the ruined church, the sporting-goods store, the color of that smoke, the Rangers bag . . . but she shouldn't have been doing so much cocaine. Where the fuck had her camera disappeared to? Her father squeezed her hand.

"Black powder, honey. High-test. It had to be a dozen kilos. They cleaned out the entire shed."

70

THERE WAS A PERIOD just after the inevitability of ruin hove into view and just before it smashed into the hull of your life that was the closest to pure freedom anybody ever got. The fateful decisions had all been made by some remote historical figure, a you who no longer existed. Nor would the you who'd eventually have to live them down resemble in any but the most general sense the you you were today. The oven was preheating, but your goose was not yet cooked. In the meantime, it didn't matter whether you smote your oppressors or went around writing checks to everyone you'd ever wronged or anything in between. And it had to mean something, Keith would think afterward, that what he'd decided to do with all that freedom was not return to Sam, but settle their accounts for good. So why had it made him feel worse? Those last few mornings of his married life, he'd stood at the mirrored bureau as before, baring his teeth to check for remnants of English muffin, watching his hands cruise through the involved origami of a double-Windsor knot. But the familiar a.m. chamber music—the eggy sizzle in the kitchen, the *shugsplash* of water on the vanity where Regan put on her makeup—carried an extra charge of presence from his conviction that it would soon cease to exist. At any second, she would drift into the mirror's beveled edge holding up a dyed-black hair she'd plucked from a throw cushion in the living room, or that hotel key he'd misplaced.

In fact, it wasn't until the Sunday after Thanksgiving, six days after

he'd finally broken things off with Samantha, that the shipwreck or
-burning or whatever it was really got under way. He was sitting up in
bed, reading John le Carré by lamplight. She was staring at the pages
of *The New York Review of Books*, to which she'd subscribed a month
earlier, after picking it up in her analyst's waiting room. She seemed
to like exactly those things he found most irksome about *The New
York Review of Books*: its unapologetic boringness, its privileged hostility to privilege. But they did both enjoy the Olympian self-regard
of the personal ads. She said she wanted to try one on him now. Her
voice was strangely thick. "'MWM. Smart, athletic thirty-six-year-
old. Politics, cinema, running. Seeking attractive woman for companionship, more.' Can you believe that?"

"What's not to believe?"

"'MWM' means he's married, Keith. What if his wife were to read
this stuff?"

There was a tightening in his chest, as if a rope were being cinched.
"Would she know it was her husband?"

"A wife tends to know when something's going on, Keith."

"Does she?" There was a cobweb in the corner of the ceiling; how
had he not noticed this? "So then why are you acting so scandalized?"

"It's for effect, Keith. Don't you think it's time we discussed how
you've been lying to me?"

It had a strange result, this calm of hers: it pissed him off. He rose
and went to sit on the chair, so that he could see her properly, and
found that he was shaking. "I don't know. Are we going to pretend it's
all my fault?" he said. And then her beautiful composure was collapsing, and she was covering her face with a pillow so the kids wouldn't
hear, sobbing so hard that for a long time she couldn't even speak. It
was awful.

Though not as bad as the hours to follow. He wouldn't talk about
his infidelity in other-than-abstract terms, and she wouldn't tell him
how she'd found out. Instead, what they picked apart in choked whispers was the marriage itself. Or rather, two marriages: his version
and her version. Back and forth they went over every last grievance,
like people walking on coals, until the pain seemed almost reassuring. (At least in this, the pain, the repetition, they were still together.)
And when the garbagemen started to bang around outside, heralding
the end of this endless darkness, they made love, exhausted, barely
moving, as though twice their actual age. He'd never felt so close to
her, ever; the fact of his having been inside someone else (or for that

matter, the thought of someone else inside Regan) couldn't change how deeply they knew each other. What if this was what he'd had to find out: how close they could still be? What if he told her that? But it was too late, the sex would change nothing. He would probably never be this close to anyone again.

And two days later, they were sitting the kids down in the living room. It seemed impossible that a week earlier they'd stood together on Seventh Avenue watching balloons bob brightly by, knowing that the shadows passing over them were just that, that soon they'd feel again the sun. It had been completely wasted on him! How could he have let himself suffer, on what was to be their last holiday as a family, over what he'd done to Samantha Cicciaro—a child, basically, who wasn't even his own? In the seconds before Regan began to speak, Will looked stricken. But she was never more brilliant than when the stakes were high: sturdy, compassionate, in command. Leaning forward to take their hands, she started to explain that *sometimes Moms and Dads . . .* Cate's face crumpled like paper tossed onto a fire. Keith wanted to say something, but when he opened his mouth, he found himself on the verge, too. It was just hitting him that he would now only see them on pre-set dates, weekends and even-numbered Thursdays or something equally unbearable. When he'd thought of losing everything, *everything* hadn't meant this. Not this Regan, the deep-down Regan he'd fallen in love with. Not his kids.

HE SPENT THE FIRST FEW NIGHTS of the separation in a hotel, on his expense account. After his disaster with the municipal bonds, he'd rededicated himself to business ethics, but he was going to have to be careful about money for a while now. He hadn't remembered his razor, so his face was stubbly against the pillow. What he had remembered was to tuck in among his changes of clothes one of Regan's framed photographs of the four of them from a few summers back, at Lake Winnipesaukee. He set it up on the nightstand, as if he might swim down into the past, where nothing could go wrong.

On the fourth day, the frame got returned to the suitcase and then unpacked again and set up on the coffeetable of the Tadelises' living room, after the master of the house had gone to bed. It had surprised Keith, frankly, to discover that Greg Tadelis was his closest friend. They hadn't seen each other since their days together at Renard. But when he'd called and explained that he was having some trouble in his marriage, Tadelis had said, "Please, Lamplighter. Our couch folds out. Stay as long as you need."

Mrs. T. was less sympathetic. She seemed silently pleased that the golden couple, with their fancy address and prep-schooled offspring, had got their comeuppance, and Keith suspected her of siding with Regan. He'd never thought much of Doris Tadelis back when they were all going to company picnics together, but it bothered him now that she would just assume he was the one to blame for the separation. He was, of course—but how could she *assume* it? Maybe she'd seen through him all along.

He ate dinner each night at the Oyster Bar in Grand Central, preferring to endure the shame and the cost of sitting there alone rather than face this formidable woman across her kitchen table. Still, when he came in and apologized for working late, she would snort derisively, as if to say, "You think you're too good for my pot roast, don't you?"

He had to get out of here, obviously, but looking for a place of his own, even a one-bedroom with a short-term lease, would have meant admitting the separation wasn't temporary. Then, the week before Christmas, he'd arrived at the old building for his scheduled visit with the kids to find Regan out front, supervising movers as they angled his piano, now hers, into the open maw of a van. She'd gotten her hair cut short, a bob, he thought it was called, like she'd had it when she'd been in *Twelfth Night*. The fact that it could have been short for days now without his knowing stabbed at him. When he asked what she was doing, she turned her face away. "What does it look like I'm doing?" She sounded like she'd swallowed a cough drop. "I found a place in Brooklyn Heights."

"For Pete's sake, Regan. Brooklyn? How far are you going to take this?"

"Not in front of the kids." He looked and saw them watching through the glass of the vestibule. He became aware, too, of the movers, conspicuously ignoring him. She whispered, "Our *home*, Keith. You brought her into our *home*."

"What are you talking about?" But he knew exactly what she was talking about. She'd somehow figured out one of the things he'd omitted—that he'd betrayed her even under her own roof, or had tried—and now she was moving out. As a fitting together of problem and solution, it was classic Regan.

He could hang on to the apartment or sell it, she said, or whatever the hell he wanted; she just didn't want to set foot in it again.

And how were they supposed to afford a second apartment?

"I'm not dependent on you anymore, Keith, remember? I have a job."

They stood there not five feet apart, her arms crossed, his own hanging like butchered meat at his sides. Whatever they thought of all this, the movers and the doorman weren't about to let on—they were New Yorkers. Even the kids, behind the slice of streetscape floating in the glass, had mastered the art of pretending not to see.

SUPERFICIALLY, OF COURSE, keeping the apartment made things easier for Keith. (Who he was, he was realizing, was a person for whom things superficially are easy.) Underneath, it did anything but. The living room, absent its piano and its rug and its couch, wore an air of dereliction. The kids' beds had been taken, too. He'd have to buy new ones, another blow to his already tight finances.

She'd left the big horsehair mattress in the master bedroom, perhaps not believing that he hadn't fucked his mistress on it, but too sentimental to throw it out. It had been her grandmother's, and then her mother's, and after her father's remarriage, Felicia Gould had been eager to get rid of it. They'd had to disassemble the bedstead in order to get it into the elevator of their newlywed apartment in the Village. (It was larger than a king, and probably predated standard mattress sizing.) He'd borrowed a mallet and a chamois cloth from the super, wrapped one inside the other. He could feel Regan cringing inside each time he brought the mallet up against the bedrails, but she never said a word. They'd had so much fun on that mattress, making the kind of ruckus she never let herself make later, when paper-thin walls were all that separated them from the baby. And he'd never imagined horsehair could be so comfortable, the way it conformed to you whether you slept the sleep of the guiltless, like Keith, or like Regan tossed restlessly. Now the impress of her body was never going to fade, any more than would his memory of the little alarmed noises she emitted from deep in dreams.

That first night after she moved out, he would wake from his own dream of falling off a building to find himself rolling toward the declivity she'd left. For a moment, in the dark, he thought she was still there beside him. And so he had to go through losing her all over again.

He started sleeping on the sofa after that. And when the kids came over following their real Christmas with Regan for his paltry imitation and their inaugural custody overnight, Cate ignored the canopy bed he'd bought her and headed for the horsehair. She liked it for the same reason he couldn't sleep on it: it smelled like Mommy. Otherwise, she seemed on edge. She'd packed her plastic cartoon-themed backpack full to bursting with clothes and toys, as though preparing for a polar expedition. She used to do the same thing for sleepovers with friends, he remembered, when she'd always call home halfway through the night, complaining of unspecified aches and pains. At which point he would have to throw on clothes and go retrieve her. Now he half-expected her, at midnight or at one, to insist on calling Regan.

Will, by contrast, seemed all right, at least at first. After dinner, they'd snapped together the drugstore tree and tossed on a few strands of lights (Regan having taken the boxes of decorations), and when presents had been opened and Cate had gone to bed, they stayed up flipping channels in search of Jimmy Stewart. They passed a rerun of the *Saturday Night Live* Christmas special, and he could see Will leaning forward, as if to absorb as much as he could before it was snatched from him again. Regan had never let him watch the show, though he claimed the other kids at school did, that he was culturally deprived, so Keith decided to leave the dial where it was. He'd mixed up eggnog by siphoning off half of the store-bought carton and replacing it with some rum of uncertain vintage. Now he offered a sip to his son. In the past, Will would have wrinkled his nose and declined. Then Keith could tease him. *Oh, come on. It'll put hair on your chest.* This time, Will asked for his own glass. What could a dad do but pour him a finger or two? It didn't make Will visibly tipsy; if anything, he seemed more in control, as though he'd realized his long-held ambition to bring every loose nerve-ending in his body under central command. He laughed even at the jokes that went over his head—laughed exactly as hard and as long as his dad did. Permissiveness got a bad rap, Keith thought. He was enjoying the bond it made. He poured himself another eggnog and tried to focus on this, the bond, and not on Regan. Then the telephone rang. It was almost midnight; it seemed impossible that anyone should be calling now, or that the call augured anything good, but rather than let it ring and wake Cate, he hurried to the kitchen to answer it. It had been almost a month since he'd last heard Samantha's voice, but she didn't have to identify herself. Was he free to talk? she said.

From down the hall boomed the laughter of the studio audience. There was no way anyone—even Will—could overhear him. Still, when he spoke, it was a kind of hiss. "You can't call me here, do you understand? This is my *life*." He returned the phone to its cradle a little harder than he'd meant to and stood there looking at it, the way you might look at a snake you're not sure is poisonous. He waited for it to ring again. When, after a couple of minutes, it still hadn't, he made his way back to the living room.

The fat guy from *Saturday Night Live* was chasing a longhair around with a samurai sword, and Will was on his knees, watching. "Who was that?" he asked, without turning around.

"Wrong number," Keith said. And then it went to commercial. "You can actually do that stuff, can't you, Will? The judo kick and whatnot."

"Judo and jujitsu are like two separate things, Dad. Plus I'm only a green belt."

"What does that mean, green?"

Will shrugged.

"No, really," Keith said, or the rum said, or his hatred of his own deceit and the way it walled him off from other people said. "Let's see what you can do."

Will looked him over, as if to gauge his sobriety. "Fine," he said finally, but they'd have to move the coffeetable. He made Keith stand in the middle of the rug and bow. That's how they would both know they didn't mean to hurt each other. Then he reached to take Keith's hand, as if to shake. Within seconds, Keith was on his knees, and his arm was up between his shoulderblades, where the wings would have been, and blooming there was a hot white pain. So why did they call the belt green? More pressingly: Was his arm going to break? When he craned his head back, he could see his son standing over him, upside down, face flushed with effort. And there they were again to the left, doubled in the black glass of the window, surrounded by a million winking Christmas lights, in a painterly pose he could have sworn he'd seen somewhere before. The Prostrate Man. The Fierce Boy.

Adult Wellbeing

Today's Date: 2/25/03 **Name:** William H. Lamplighter **Date of Birth:** 8/18/64

Over the last 2 weeks, how often have you been bothered by any of the following problems?	Not at all	Several days	More than half the days	Nearly every day
1. Little interest or pleasure in doing things	0	1	(2)	3
2. Feeling down, depressed, or hopeless	0	1	(2)	3
3. Feeling nervous, anxious, or on edge	0	1	2	(3)
4. Not being able to stop or control worrying	0	1	(2)	3

Has there ever been			Yes
5. ...you felt so good or ... you into trouble? (e.g., un	**BRIDGE AND TUNNEL**		☐
6. ...you were so irritabl			☒

During the past year:	No	Yes
7. Have you had 4 or more drinks (women) / 5 or more drinks (men) in a day?	☒	☐
8. Have you used an illegal drug or used a prescription drug for a non-medical reason?	☒	☐

During the last 4 weeks:	No	Yes
9. Have you had a problem with sleep more than occasionally? (This could include: trouble falling asleep, waking frequently, or sleeping too much.)	☐	☒

10. Circle the number or description that most accurately describes your daily activities, social activities and overall health in the past 4 weeks.

DAILY ACTIVITIES

How much difficulty have you had doing your usual activities or tasks, both inside and outside the house, because of your physical and emotional health?

No difficulty at all	1
A little bit of difficulty	2
Some difficulty	3
Much difficulty	(4)
Could not do	5

SOCIAL ACTIVITIES

Has your physical and emotional health limited your social activities with family, friends, neighbors, or groups?

Not at all	1
Slightly	2
Moderately	3
Quite a bit	(4)
Extremely	5

OVERALL HEALTH

How would you rate your health in general?

Excellent	1
Very good	2
Good	(3)
Fair	4
Poor	5

11. Please describe in the space below any other symptoms you may be experiencing, including relevant details of onset, frequency, recurrence, etc. Attach any additional pages.

The major symptom, basically, is this dream I keep having. I'm walking around a city where it's late afternoon. Some part of me knows nine-to-fivers should be out having last smokes of the day, but there's no one on the streets. The sidewalks are pristine, like ads for sidewalks. Above are tall buildings whose top floors catch the sun. And here's how I know it's a dream: each one's covered, roof to sidewalk, with a linen veil. The veils are all different colors, unripe lemon, rose, hazard-cone orange, alternating in no pattern I can name. From each new corner, having forgotten how I got there, I can see them luffing in and out, as if behind them aren't buildings at all but something breathing. Watching. Or wait-ing. At some point, I start to run. I know that if I turn to the side, the way in waking life you turn to check yourself in shop windows, the veils will dissolve and leave me face-to-face with whatever's hiding back there. But already great hands are pressing against the sides of my head, turning it. I try to call for help, but I no longer have a mouth. I try to fight, but I'm not in control of my body. Just at the point of maximum fear—just when I'm about to gaze upon the naked face of the Thing That Waits—I wake up, soaked in sweat, gasping. I haven't slept through the night in almost half a year.

And the thing is, I've had this dream before. The first time was when I was a high-school junior, in my first year at boarding school. I remem-ber my roommate calling me out on it in the Refectory the morning after the fifth or sixth recurrence. His name was Sean Baldwin. He was this red-headed and freakishly adult-looking scholarship kid from Rox-bury, Mass. Also—though I don't know how we're defining "relevant"—a minor celebrity with the girls from across the Quad. More than once I came back to our room to find the corner of his IRA flag peeking from under the door, per the code we'd agreed on back when it seemed like a joke. Maybe because of this, there was some shunning from the other boys. I wasn't quite an outcast myself; circa '81, being from actual New York (as opposed to, say, New Canaan, or New Jersey) gave you some social traction. But I was inward by nature, and we usually refected just the two of us. Sean would regale me with stories of his conquests. It was to tease me about the one-sidedness of these conversations, I think, that he first mentioned the noises he'd been hearing from my side of the room after lights out, which he characterized as "groaning." He wasn't going to say anything, I remember him saying, but it was going on like four nights in a row. "I think that's a symptom of gonadal inflammation. We've got to get you laid, old man."

In fact, I'd been involved with a girl from the senior class since September, a Californian, though sneaking her into the boys' dorms wasn't either of our style. It was her essential integrity as a person I'd fallen so hard for in the first place. And so she remained, like everything that mattered to me then, secret—to be pursued in the woods by moonlight, when I was supposed to be studying. But here was Sean, watching my face, holding the ends of his school scarf out from his body like the toggles of a parachute that's just blown. He probably would have actually jumped out of a plane for me, but I wasn't sure how much I could trust him, if that makes sense. Still, against my better judgment, I leaned in and started explaining about the dream. How the more it happened, the more I had to know: What was back there, behind the veil?

"You ever hear of vagina dentata?" he asked.

He could be a dick sometimes, and I told him so.

If he'd had a beard, he'd have been stroking it. "It just sounds very sexual to me."

"Everything sounds sexual to you," I said.

"Fine. You really want to know what I think?" The scarf-ends dropped, and his persona seemed to slip a little bit. "You said you're in a city, right?" In the dream, he meant. "I think you're nervous about the holidays coming up, and having to go back to your family in New York."

I said I wasn't nervous. Why would I be nervous?

"You tell me," he said. "They seemed like perfectly nice people at Parents' Weekend, but you obviously have a huge thing about your dad."

"My thing about my dad is that he's an asshole. He and Mom should have split up a long time ago. Anyway, I'm not looking for etiology. I'm looking for sleep."

Sean said he found it was what he wasn't consciously thinking about during the day that came up in dreams. "Maybe before your eyes shut you should try to focus hard on what you're really afraid of." This sounded plausible enough in the mild light of an early-winter morning, but of course I had no idea what I was really afraid of, was the problem, and that night the dream returned with new intensity, waking me just after midnight. By the time finals rolled around, I was a basket case.

I should also flag here as of possible clinical significance that I'd been a pretty steady abuser of controlled substances since the year I turned thirteen. That was 1977, the blackout year. Also a year I'd just as soon black out. My parents had just started living in separate apartments. Then, the morning after the lights actually did go out, Mom and Dad were all of a sudden back together, with no explanation of what had happened to them in the night, while the city burned.

Something else happened even later that year, for which I likewise got no explanation: One evening after school started in the fall, I came home from basketball practice to find my parents splitting a beer at the kitchen table. It had become a kind of ritual. Only between them now was a stranger: a wiry, almost vampiric little man with a leather jacket and paint-splashed pants and a cigarette, which no one else would have been allowed to smoke indoors. I knew even before my mom introduced him that this was Uncle William, her brother, my namesake. My whole life up to that point, he'd been nothing more than a rumor. But now he was giving me the chin-nod, like we'd met a thousand times before. Eventually, I moved on to my room, but I'll never forget the shock of seeing him that first time in Brooklyn Heights. He himself was a recovering drug addict, my father "let slip" a few weeks later. This was supposed to puncture my evident fascination with Uncle William, probably, but only reinforced it. Because he was also an honest-to-god artist, the thing I'd decided I wanted to be. And later still, when I found in a cutout bin a copy of the LP he'd cut with his punk band back in the mid-'70s, I more or less wore out the grooves. Those songs would come to stand, in my fantasies, for the distant planet of art and sex and possibility waiting just across the Bridge, and it occurs to me now that it was this—the possibility of this possibility—that freed me to start sneaking out at night myself.

Exactly what I found out there would be hard to explain to anyone who wasn't around in those gray years of late Carter/early Reagan, but I guess the point here is to try. Budget cuts and crime and unemployment had brutalized the city, and you could feel on the street this sense of soured anarchy, of failed Utopia. But as sad as it was, it was in many ways the ideal playground for ninth graders with preoccupied families and fake IDs. You could go hear the early rap records or the late New Wave ones or the thing disco was becoming at unlicensed clubs where black and brown and white and gay and straight still mixed openly. My buddy Ken Otani and I, having told our folks we were staying at each other's houses, would score whatever we could get our hands on—painkillers, acid, black beauties—and tromp around downtown kite-high, listening for loft parties thumping within the darkened buildings. And at three or four in the morning, wobbling back toward Brooklyn, we'd hear our voices echoing up the buildings to fill the vault of the sky. As if there were secret trails of freedom my uncle had cut through the city a decade earlier, in the Bad Old Days. Which was probably why, though they never confronted me about what I was up to, my parents decided to send me to St. Paul's.

But back in the city, that winter break in '81, my explorations resumed. And I found that by recalibrating my intake of controlled substances—lighter on the pills, heavier on the booze—I was able to start sleeping through the night again. Self-medicating, you'd call it. I slept any time I could. At lunchtime, on the pretense of going to shoot hoops, I'd head over to the Promenade and drink vodka out of a deli cup, then come home and lock myself in my room and conk out until my little sister banged on the door. My mom wanted me to play with her, but Dad said to let me alone—supposedly because he was on my side, but really because afternoon naptime was two fewer hours a day he ran the risk of my company. And by the time I returned to school, I'd forgotten my nightmares completely. It was my great gift, this forgetting, I used to think.

Anyway, the second "episode" was when I was twenty-four and here in L.A., crashing on a friend's couch and just generally going through a rough time in my life—a kind of crack-up or mid-major depression. I'd moved here to act (which after two years of walk-on parts in industrials was depressing in its own right), but also because of Julia, my high-school girlfriend, whom I'd already followed to college. We'd moved in together, co-signatories on a little bungalow with a lemon tree out front. She was in graduate school for her teaching certificate. I waited tables. My late nights plus her early mornings meant seeing each other mostly on weekends.

Except one night I came home to find her waiting up on our futon. I knew something was wrong even before she told me to have a seat. For months, she said, she'd been feeling confused. And she didn't know how it had happened, but she'd slept with someone else.

I couldn't understand; cheating was the one thing I'd told her all those years ago would be unforgivable. She knew, she said, but that was part of what had been confusing her, that I would even have told her that, as if she weren't an actual human being with the freedom to act, but some character in a scenario in my head. There was a quality I had of making the people closest to me feel lonely, somehow. Some essential cold withholding at the core of myself.

To make a long story a bit shorter, I wound up staying on this friend's couch, this friend who was a girl, because for some reason most of my good friends were girls. I wasn't involved with her, sexually, but would have been happy for Julia to think that I was. How was I doing, Julia would ask, on those rare occasions when we talked by phone, as if she cared. As if it were possible for one person to care about another and still treat him or her like this. The truth was, I was doing terribly. After several years of keeping it in check, I was drinking so much it didn't even knock me out anymore, and anyway, it wasn't falling asleep that was the problem, but staying asleep. The cushions of my friend's couch were some kind of rubberized velour, the windows were uncurtained, and at five a.m. the birds were all atwitter and the light, the L.A. light everyone goes on and on about, was right in my East Coast eyes. Give me New York any day, I thought. But when New York came, it was with fangs and claws, in a nightmare I now woke from screaming.

Wait. I've just realized that the heights of the buildings in this version of the dream were exactly those of the buildings on Broadway between Eighth Street and Fourth, where I used to spend hours at the Tower Records. But of course they couldn't really be any specific buildings, because no matter how many blocks I ran, they stayed the same. Think of a rat in a maze. And when the veils coming loose from them pulled forward or sucked back, there was now a rasping sound. If I listened hard, I might be able to discern actual words, but I didn't want to hear what they were saying. I didn't want to look to the side and discover that the ravenous thing lurking back there, which once seemed so huge, was now the same size as myself.

This relapse or whatever it was lasted longer: two months, five or six nights per week. The screaming, in particular, led to all kinds of friction with my friend's housemates. I'd hear them murmuring through the walls at night, or through the sliding door of the patio where I sat all day under an umbrella playing one of the early hand-held video games. (This being practically the only thing I felt capable of doing; I'd given notice at the restaurant a month earlier, and was living on my trust fund.) In the glass, when I turned, I looked skeletal. I've never been a physically large man, but now I was down to like 130 pounds.

Then, in July, I got a call. Uncle William had somehow gotten the number. He was in town for his solo exhibition at the L.A. County Museum of Art, he said. (By that time, he'd given up painting for photography, and had become semi-famous for it.) The opening was on Tuesday. I started making excuses, because I didn't want the state I was in getting back to my mother, but he insisted we at least get together afterward for a drink. "You're the only person I know in Los Angeles, Will, and so far the only reason not to hate it." "That's the thing," I thought about saying. "You <u>don't</u> know me." But he'd already gotten off the phone.

So I went to meet him a couple nights later, at a nightclub that was unlikely to change his opinion of the West Coast. I sat waiting for at least an hour, singularly unappetized by the lager before me in its frosted glass. What else do I remember? On each side of the room's sunken center was a fish tank, tin-hued betas in garish teal water. They reminded me of some paintings my grandfather had once owned. Dirt drumming down on a casket; unisex posses flirting by the bar. By ten o' clock, twenty dollars' worth of beer had vanished down my gullet without my really noticing. The waitress, a fellow thespian who'd at first taken pity on me, kept tromping past, a silent reminder that there were other people who would like a table. For a moment, I could actually feel myself aging, moving toward the point when only half of my life would remain, then less than half, then none. Then heads started to turn toward the hostess stand, and there he was, my uncle, still in that motorcycle jacket, all this time later. Indelibly New York, despite sleeves scrunched up to reveal his forearms.

"My favorite nephew," he said, sliding into the banquette.

Your only nephew, I replied.

He asked the waitress for a cranberry juice, no ice, and then turned back to me. "Well, you certainly look like shit." I'd done enough improv that I still could probably have vamped my way through thirty minutes of hail-fellow-well-met. Oddly, though, the impulse overrode itself. I mean, here was the person whose defenses I'd studied so closely in our dozen previous encounters and in the lyrics he'd once written. After whom I'd in some sense modeled my own. And it all came pretty much spilling out of me—even, eventually, the part about my girlfriend's coworker, which I hadn't even told to the friend I was staying with.

After a while, the fact that he wasn't saying anything started to get to me. I guess hanging on to a good woman was not something Uncle William had to think about. Have I mentioned he was gay? It was part of his mystique, the sense of outrageous freedom he carried about him. But there I went again, turning people into symbols. A form, maybe, of sublimated aggression. "Feel free to respond at any point." I meant it to sound sarcastic, but as I scratched a pinky-nail through the frost of my fifth glass, I felt myself reaching across a chasm.

"What can I say?" he said. "It worries me to see you like this, and I don't have to tell you, from personal experience, it's not something you're going to drink your way out of—"

"It's not the beer, it's sleep. I've gotten like maybe fifteen hours in the last five days. Sometimes even when I'm awake now I see hallucinations, acid trails, things that aren't there. And then at night, I keep having nightmares."

"But what do you expect me to do about it, Will?" Though I was too ashamed to look him in the face, I could feel him watching me. "Advice, disaster control, that was always your mother's thing, not mine."

"Uncle William, a person I loved fucked someone else."

"It happens. No, hey. I'm not trying to be flip, but you still love her, don't you?"

I focused on my beer, but didn't touch it. Nodded miserably. Of course I did.

And there it was again: his weird mixture of ferocity and bemusement. "Listen, do you know how a Zulu speaker greets another Zulu speaker?"

"Beg pardon?"

"I learned this recently, and it struck me as insanely beautiful: The word for hello or goodbye in Zulu literally means 'I see you.' And the answer is 'I am here.' You understand? 'Sawubona.' I see you, Will." He made no move to get up from the booth. Or to pay for his cranberry juice, I might add. But I could feel a change at the molecular level, as if he were gone already. "Say it. It doesn't work if you don't say it."

"I am here," I said. And something lifted off me, not all the way, but enough.

I realize I'm burning through your paper supplies. The condensed version of what came next is that I went to see Julia, and we talked. We talked about the past, and we talked about the future, and we talked about the ways the latter didn't necessarily have to repeat the former. We practiced our trust-falls. I sobered up for good. And a year later, we were married.

A decade and a half passed—no further nightmares. I went to law school. We had a kid, a daughter. We stayed in L.A. I turned away from history, which is what I thought people came to L.A. to do. I went back to New York only every four years or so, when it became impossible not to give my parents a Christmas or a Thanksgiving, and we would stay at a hotel, rather than in the guestroom in Brooklyn Heights, owing to some lingering static between me and my dad. And at a certain point, between work and parenthood and the ordinary unglamorousness of life in the SoCal 'burbs, I was so tired when my head hit the pillow that I didn't dream at all. And for all this, in some way so strange that even I didn't understand it, I had my uncle to thank.

It's been hard for me to accept, I guess, that he's dead. Not because I knew him well—I didn't—but because I remember him, for all his quirks, as this incredibly alive person. He was diagnosed with HIV in the late '80s, but you wouldn't have known; the drug cocktail they put him on kept him mostly out of the hospital. And when we did head east, we'd go see him in his crazy apartment in Hell's Kitchen, which he refused to renovate even after everything else was condos. My daughter loved him. Julia, especially, loved him. But in early 2002, my mother told me he'd been having some health problems, and he went quickly downhill after that.

His art dealer blamed the events of the previous fall. "I don't mean causation, exactly," he told me. "More as if whatever happened to this city had to find its mirror in him. There was a certain mood of elegy, those first few months after. He'd been pretending to be immortal for so many years, and suddenly he was seeing something that helped him let go."

But I'm getting ahead of myself. The art dealer's name was Bruno Augenblick, and I met him last September, just before my symptoms returned. He had a gallery down on Spring Street, and had mounted a retrospective of some of Uncle William's paintings from the '70s. Evidence I, said the invitation I'd received in the mail. The funeral had been in the family plot in Connecticut, and I hadn't been back to the city proper in several years, and downtown in longer than that. But I felt I owed it to my uncle to show up for the opening.

In my head, on the plane, I allowed myself to imagine that the blocks south of Houston were still the ones where I'd felt so free, but on the ground, tsunamis of capital had swept all that away. Now there was art every five feet, along with brasseries and artisanal what-have-yous, all of them at eight p.m. crowding the street with their constituencies. The gallery, once I'd found it, was an extension of that, mostly expensively jeaned young people, and in a way, it was comforting. None of them had cause to suspect that I, in my schlubby cords, was anything other than a tourist who'd lost his way.

Somewhere inside, though, I must still have been expecting the city to save me, or how else to explain the scale of my disappointment with the actual canvases on the wall? Uncle William had always had that largeness of spirit that drew people toward him. And these, by contrast, were minimalist nullities— entirely white, albeit with surface disruptions that came clearer as you approached, alabaster drips and milky salients of brush. You could trick yourself into thinking a figure was struggling to emerge from all that blankness, but one never did. The only thing remotely interesting about them were their shapes.

I was staring at an eight-sided polygon, white on white, feeling complexly bereaved, when a voice spoke just behind my shoulder. "You know what this is, don't you?"

Augenblick's shirt was blinding and wrinkle-free, his glasses fashionably clunky, his head bald, and there was something phrenological about the angle at which he held it, as if he were sizing up my skull. "A ghost in a snowstorm," I said. "I don't know. I give up."

"It's a stop sign." He extended a finger so that it almost touched the bottom of the painting, whose eight edges he traced. "He stole this off its pole. Whited it out. Of course, most people don't remember he was more than just a photographer"—was there a moue of distaste here?— "but even so, you get some insight into your uncle's mind. But forgive me. You're the nephew, aren't you? When I got your RSVP, I assumed you'd be coming with your mother."

"I think Mom has some qualms about your selling work he never showed."

"You are her ambassador, then."

I held my hands up. I wasn't sure what I was.

"In any case, there are a few matters we might clarify. Why don't you follow me?" The question was rhetorical; he was already crossing the cement floor.

His office, behind a white wall, was as spare as the rest of the gallery. A slab of table, an espresso machine, a laptop so sleek as to barely be there. I took the chair he nodded toward, but Augenblick didn't sit. He seemed to emit a faint hum. "It really is uncanny."

"I beg your pardon?"

"The spitting image, I believe is the expression. Wine?"

I didn't drink, I told him, with that embarrassed feeling I got whenever I was reminded that I had a body, that I looked like anything at all.

"Well, it's not very good, anyway. This is a thing one learns: the cheaper the wine, the sooner the freeloaders move on to other openings. But surely you won't refuse a little coffee."

He turned to fuss over the machine behind him. There was a pound, a scrape, a rumble. This was when he said the thing about the mirror. My uncle, he concluded, had been like one of those trees that's grown around the fence that contains it. When a hole is blown in the fence, what becomes of the tree? Then, as if none of it had happened, he turned and set before me, in a white cup with a white saucer and a doll-sized spoon, a black decoction with a precise ring of caramel-colored foam. It occurred to me that this was exactly what I'd wanted to jolt me out of the state I'd been in since stepping off the plane, this weird sense of parallel lives. "Of course, it's his work we must discuss," he said. "Estates can be messy things, and when art is involved, one ends up with multiple executors."

"You have to understand, this is all still hard for Mom," I said. "He was her only sibling."

"You are grieving, too."

I searched for my reflection in the little spoon. "I wouldn't say we were close, exactly. I haven't been back much since I was eighteen, and Uncle William hardly ever left."

"Well, your uncle could be somewhat . . . difficult. He was prolific when he got going, and had trouble editing his ideas. This was true of many artists at the time, but it made him a particular challenge to work with. The Evidence diptych struck me as quite ambitious, once I understood the full scope. But there was also his music, which to my ears was nothing of the sort. And then something convinced him to pick up a camera, and we had already been quarreling, and I had to insist, 'No, William, this is not art. Your gift comes with certain responsibilities . . .' So he found other representation for the photographs. I maintained exclusive rights to sell his works on canvas—though to my knowledge he attempted only one after 1977. His will made the same dual provisions for posthumous exhibition and sale. But last month, going through William's apartment, my assistant came across something I'm not sure how to handle. You'll excuse me a moment?" What was I supposed to say? I'd drunk the man's espresso, and was beginning to notice he never paused for an answer anyway.

He disappeared behind a farther wall or partition, and when he came back it was with a box, the kind reams of paper come in. On the lid, someone had written <u>Evidence III</u> in black Sharpie, and I felt the same drop in my stomach I'd felt looking at Uncle William's brushwork. "This is what your uncle was working on from October of 2001 up to the end. There was a note on the box. I believe he wanted what is inside made public in some form or another. He meant it to be his legacy." The box, when I lifted it from the marble surface between us, was heavy. I couldn't tell how old the packing tape was, or if it had been disturbed.

"So why not go ahead and mount this, too? You've got a whole gallery here."

"For one thing, William—may I call you William?—<u>Evidence III</u> remains unfinished. For another, it is not the kind of material you mount. It is documentary in nature. Or perhaps conceptual. Which means, technically, it belongs with that part of the estate arrogated neither to Ms. Boone nor to myself."

"I guess I'll take it back to my mom, then."

"Ah, but that is the wrinkle, William. This note I spoke of—it stipulated, in quite certain terms, that the box and decisions about its contents were to pass to you."

I landed in L.A. the following afternoon having gained three hours in the air, and arrived home before Julia returned from work, or my daughter from school. From the cab at curbside, our house looked both exactly as I'd left it and wholly altered. Before I could think what I was doing, I left my suitcases by the front door and lugged the box out to the pool house, where I tucked it among the bric-a-brac one accumulates over many years in a place. My daughter asked about my trip at dinner that night, but I would give her only the outlines. When it came to my family in New York, I only ever gave the outlines. Except later, after I'd fallen asleep, I found myself back there once more, on nightmare city streets, empty as if some plague or catastrophe had struck. And the next night, and the next, for months.

This time, the dream was connected with the box, somehow. It almost felt like it had been all along. I would go out to the pool house sometimes when everyone else was asleep, to put off going to bed myself, and I would turn on the light and look at it. <u>Evidence III</u>. I thought about taking the tape back off and actually diving into it, this gift or curse meant to draw me back to that time we'd all worked so hard to escape. I thought about drinking. I thought about throwing the whole damn thing into the pool. But eventually, always, I went back into the house, because frankly, it was easier to face the dream.

And then a week ago, after a night when I woke weeping with terror, when I had to tiptoe downstairs to cry in the laundry room with the dryer on to cover the sound, I fell back asleep some time after sunrise, and Julia turned off my alarm. When I got up, there was no comforting getting-ready-for-school noise, just the drip of rain hitting the sill, and the light was all wrong. I came downstairs to find her tacking up a blue nylon flag with a dove on it in the breakfast nook's bay window. I dimly recalled, through the plaque of nightmare goo still clinging to my brain, a conversation about a meeting of peace activists from her church. Also that the country was going to war again. "I called you in sick," she said.

"Why'd you do that?"

"Because you're sick, honey."

We sat down at the counter and ate lunch together. When was the last time we did this? I'd been in law school. She must have been pregnant. I swallowed a mouthful of sandwich. I apologized for any noise I might have made in the night. I told her the nightmares were back. A minute passed. "You're going to say I should try therapy," I said.

"I don't see what you have against therapy."

I don't have anything against therapy, by the way; it's great for other people. It's just that, personally, I see the enterprise as proceeding from the same premises that cause the problems it seeks to treat. For you guys, what I am, fundamentally, is a closed system, a container of ego and id and biological imperatives. That I'm not may be a fiction, but if I can't imagine a reference point larger than myself, morally speaking, then what's the use? That flag in the window—is that, too, just ego and identity and self? "Call it a block I have."

"You think talking to a professional will make you vulnerable."

"Is that the sort of powerful insight I should be prepared for in therapy?"

"Stop it. Stop it. The whole point is just to free you to talk, Will. You're so afraid someone's going to tell you there's something permanently wrong with you, you know, but all it is is someone asking questions."

"Like what?"

"Like, who exactly are you in this dream of yours? Are you still a kid?"

To be honest, thinking about it made me uncomfortable. Light from the pool stuttered across the ceiling of our kitchen. "I told you already. This is later. When I'm in junior high."

"And what's the distinction, as you understand it?"

"As I understand what?"

"Between a kid and a junior-high-schooler. Most people count the latter as a child."

"Not where I grew up, they don't." And somehow I was telling her a thing I didn't even realize I remembered: how back in '77, in the middle of the big blackout, when I was twelve and Cate was six, my father had left us alone on the streets of Manhattan.

"Jesus Christ. Your father—"

"No, this was just one of those things, you know? A miscommunication about who was supposed to pick us up from day camp. But it still stands as the longest night of my life. From that point on, I knew I'd be fending for myself."

"I can't believe you never told me this."

"Why?"

"You were abandoned, Will. You were obviously terrified. Sound familiar?"

"I guess it does sound like the dream," I admitted. "But what I was feeling just now, dredging all this up? Was the opposite of what I feel when I'm having it. Like, there was a moment back there, right around the time of the blackout, when everything seemed on the edge of becoming something else. And now I can't imagine a life besides this one."

"Maybe behind the veils is a mirror. Maybe you're scared you'll look and see your father."

I knew then that I'd said too much. That I'd hurt her. "That's not what I meant, Julia. I don't know what I meant. I love you. I love Agnes. I love having, you know, a patch of grass out back and good avocados year-round. It's just where the limits are that scares me. I'm almost forty."

"Well, I'm scared too," she said. "Because I love you, Will, but I don't know how much more of this either of us can take. Whatever else is back there, you've got to face it."

And so here I am, attaching page upon page, seemingly unable to stop. I've started to feel like I'm stuck now inside the dream. Or like I'm losing my mind. I keep thinking, while driving, while cooking, while in the office preparing briefs, about a veiled city, hiding something. And I keep returning to the night of the blackout, and the question of just what changed there, in the dark.

And then there's the last thing Bruno Augenblick showed me before I left the gallery that night. He'd insisted on calling a car to take me back to my hotel, given the heft of <u>Evidence III</u>, and out of some obscure Continental courtesy had followed me to the street. It was cooler there. We waited in the autumn dusk, listening to car horns sail up the building faces, watching headlights knife by over on the avenue, while behind us, inside, the little show went on. And finally, just to say something, I told him there were still things I didn't get. Like the title: "Evidence" of what? "And then, if those white signs on the wall in there are <u>Evidence I</u>, and this box is <u>Evidence III</u>, what happened to <u>Evidence II</u>?" At this, he smiled his clinical smile, light but no heat, and gestured at something down the block. At first I couldn't tell what was being indicated, but then I saw it: what hung from the stop-sign pole at the corner was not a stop sign, but a canvas, imperfectly octagonal and only approximately red. I moved closer. Just above and to the right of the "O" was a blue halo of sun, and most of the lower left portion was dappled with leaf-shadow. What I mean is, what at first seemed to be an ordinary stop sign was really a painting. To look at it straight on, by twilight, was to see it from below, by day. Impressionism, I guess, is the word. You could see the brushstrokes, the hand of the artist, the dead man who'd signed it: Billy III. A fissure seemed to have opened in objective space, or subjective space, or in some third space altogether, and for a second, as I stood there looking, this factitious quality spread to take in the elevator-shaft warning on the building across the street—likewise fake, or real—and the orange construction placard by a subway entrance farther off. My uncle hadn't wanted to white out the city; he'd wanted to reimagine it. To exchange the inside of his head with what was beyond. Who knew, in fact, how many more pieces of <u>Evidence II</u> I'd passed on my way down here without noticing? Who could be certain, this far from the altered skyline, that he hadn't tucked skyscrapers of cardboard in among the ones made of steel? Who knew which city I was even in? It was 2003. It was 1974. It was 1961. I wanted to ask Augenblick about the scale of all this, how far <u>Evidence II</u> extended, but when I turned around, he was gone.

BOOK V

THE DEMON BROTHER

[JULY 12-13, 1977]

The imminent awakening is poised, like the wooden horse of the Greeks, in the Troy of dreams . . .

—WALTER BENJAMIN
The Arcades Project

71

THE DAY CAMP REGAN HAD CHOSEN was all the way up on East Eighty-Second Street. This was in the winter, when slots were filling up fast, and it had seemed important that the kids have some sense of continuity with the old neighborhoods. What it had not been, especially, was logical. She wasn't thinking about forty minutes on the train to drop them off and then fifteen back down to the Hamilton-Sweeney Building for work. When she was Will's age, she'd ridden the subway alone, but nowadays you might as well have set your kids up with a drug habit and a loaded gun. If they weren't bathed, dressed, and breakfasted by ten to eight, the better part of valor was just to put them in a cab. Currently, it was 8:23 a.m., July 13, two days into a heat wave. She watched Will work to isolate a Cheerio on the end of his spoon. "Do you think you could speed it up, honey, possibly?"

He made a cherubic trumpet of his mouth, sucked the Cheerio down. What rankled was the shrug that followed. Their connection had once been clairvoyant; he would materialize beside her without her having heard his approach, as if he could sense the pressure building within and had no other means to ease it. Indeed, she suspected it was the weird way he saw through you that made Keith want to pack him off to boarding school. But she hadn't even been able to let Will go to sleepaway camp, and now he seemed to be punishing her for it. In the twenty-four hours before a custody visit, he resented even her gentlest suggestion. He would prefer not to, the shrug seemed to say.

Then Cate came kiting in from the bathroom, which in the new apartment, through some architectural oversight, abutted the kitchen. "Can I have some Cheerios?"

"You had eggs, honey, not fifteen minutes ago. Did you light a match?"

She nodded, and Regan decided to withhold comment on her mismatched socks and on the nest of hair that appeared to have been sucked through a cotton gin. "Go get your bag, sweetie." No doubt the camp counselors would look at her and think, *Negligent parent*, but that was fine, it was all a penance, besides which, there was no time. In sixty-four minutes, Andrew West would be in her office to run back over the statement they'd drafted. At 1:30, they would ride the elevator to the newly renovated press room on the fortieth floor to tell the assembled microphones that, to the charges of tax fraud and insider trading, her father would enter a plea of not guilty. The U.S. Attorney was apparently hours away from finalizing an immunity deal with a second informant anyway, and once that happened, Daddy's chance at a plea bargain would expire, along with the symbolic power of refusing it.

Everything that was going to happen would happen today.

Sixty-three minutes.

She forced herself not to say anything, knowing that if she did Will would downshift even further, to a gear somewhere between deliberate and geologic. She tried to reopen their connection. *Come on, honey.* Of course, given that he was a male, frustration was just another way of loving him. The foxed neck of his tee-shirt. The freckled bridge of his slightly upturned nose. His long hair, his probably unwashed hair, falling artlessly in his eyes.

"William Hamilton-Sweeney Lamplighter, you have exactly ten seconds to finish your breakfast."

"Can't."

"Excuse me?"

He put his hands up, as if to show he was unarmed. "I'm full."

"Then *andiamo*, already." She pretended not to see the way he left the bowl out for her to clean up later.

They were at the door, Regan one sleeve into her suit jacket, when she noticed something was missing. "Where's the overnight bag, Will?"

"Oops."

"You didn't pack?"

"You didn't remind me."

"I didn't remind you to put on pants, either, but you managed to get it done."

Again, *the shrug*, which had acquired italics in her mind. Her watch said 8:34, and she felt that if she said another word to him, he would know he'd won. She knelt and buttoned her daughter's polo shirt. Time was, it had been Cate dragging her feet and Will who was dutiful. "Honey, tell me your father keeps a change of clothes for you guys."

Cate smiled and twisted away. At some point, she'd lost a tooth. "We have TVs in our rooms now."

"It's true," Will said. "He lets us watch whatever we want."

"God damn it, Will, you can do this or I'll do it myself, and I will pick clothes that make you regret it. Don't make me count to three." It never crossed her mind that maybe it wasn't her he was resisting. That maybe, secretly, he really didn't want to go.

WHAT TO DO WITH CHILDREN IN SUMMER was a question to which she'd never given much thought, prior to this *annus horribilis*. Even working full-time for the firm, she got paid leave, and the period between Memorial Day and Labor Day was supposed to stretch into a succession of long weekends at Lake Winnipesaukee with her kids and husband splashing in the water, days passing leisurely as sailboats beyond the blue cordon of buoys.

Now the fact that the camp only ran from nine to three, with aftercare costing extra, seemed a kind of scam. She'd called ahead to let the camp people know Keith would be picking the kids up today. He was supposed to take them to a Mets game and then keep them through the weekend, and although she would miss them, as she always missed them, there was a part of her right now, and this must represent some kind of progress, that thought, Let's see how *he* deals with all of this, with Will's too-long showers and Cate's nightmares, with waking at midnight to Cate hovering out in the hall and asking in her most forlorn voice, *Can I sleep with you tonight?* as if she hadn't already assumed the answer was yes. The problem was that it probably wouldn't bother Keith. He was a man who struggled with cause-and-effect. Late for camp? No big deal. The pilfering of an entire jar of Vaseline? Boys will be boys.

No, the problem was, actually, that she missed him. She missed his laugh, missed the way he balanced her out, missed sometimes not having to be the one who let things slide, and when Cate piped up from the doorway, she had to check to make sure her own face was dry, because with the lights off, except for the tranche of streetlight from between the curtains, she kept trooping back over their life as a family, trying to find the exact spot where the ground had given way. *Climb in, sweetie*, she would say.

When she thought now about sharing her bed with Andrew West, Andrew of the poreless skin and hair-model hair, what she felt was more like this indulgent mother-love than like the hunger she wanted to feel. She had put off mentioning him to the kids for a number of reasons, one of them being that Will might view him as a rival, and another being that there was probably something to that. Andrew was only twenty-eight. She had also put off sleeping with him. Still, she'd decided that tonight, when it was all over, she was going to let him do to her anything he wanted. She hoped Will hadn't noticed the leg of lamb and the bottle of Chardonnay in the fridge when he went for the milk. Or, given that the kids were her only remaining conduit to her husband, maybe she hoped he had.

IT WAS OUT ON HENRY STREET playing Spot the Cab that Regan realized she didn't have the fare to make it all the way uptown. Will didn't have any cash, either—he'd blown his allowance on those damn wizarding cards—so her options were to be late for her meeting with Andrew or to put them on the subway alone. A pinkish fog crowned the tops of the bridges, humidity mixed with auto exhaust and the ash pouring out of the ghettos. Motes of birds hung motionless, white. Forecasters were predicting record highs today, and she could already feel her blouse starting to cling. She looked Will over. He was still a good boy, she thought, a good and bright and courageous boy, and the only people on the train at this hour would be commuters. She launched into a practicum on avoiding strangers, but he cut her off.

"We ride by ourselves all the time when we're at Dad's, Mom."

"I'm going to pretend I didn't hear that," she said, meaning she had no way of knowing if it was just bluster. When she tried to follow them down into the station to make sure they got on the right train, Will groaned. She gave him a kiss on the head before he could duck away, and then one for Cate, and watched them disappear into the ground. But why, seconds later, was she following at a discreet distance? The turnstile wouldn't let her through without paying, so she stayed there on one side of the bars, watching her progeny wait on the platform, flanked by older kids canoodling in hormonal fury and by West Indian women in nurse's shoes and by people on benches who already seemed drunk. In one hand, Will had his yellow duffel, with his school's crest on the side and a little bloom of tee-shirt caught in the zipper like a weed in the sidewalk. In the other hand, he held his sister's.

Regan wished, not for the first time, that she were someone else, someone who would trust these eminently capable children, and so wouldn't have to follow them down here, as if to jump the stile at the last minute, to scoop them up and save them from growing any older. But as they boarded and sat down facing her amid the entropic graffiti that now covered the windows completely, she couldn't look away. Cate spotted her and waved before the doors closed, but Will just stared blankly ahead like any other adult with places to be—like William, somehow, the uncle he'd never met. Between them at any rate was enough space for another child. And she knew as the train pulled away that all these disappearing kids would be the picture in her head when she spoke before the cameras about the future of the company that was her family, and later as she watched her junior colleague and would-be seducee fumble with the corkscrew, and finally in the darkness when he began to snore and Regan was left on her own again, as one always apparently is.

72

I F YOU THROW A BANANA AT A WALL, there's a small possibility it will pass through the wall. Or so, at any rate, Jenny Nguyen had thought, straphanging on an uptown bus thirteen hours earlier. It was a thing she'd heard on the radio that morning. "Dr." Zig Zigler had been ranting about riots in the street, or their absence, and though Jenny knew first-hand the futility of civil disobedience, his weird case in point for low-probability events (why throw a banana at a wall?) seemed eloquently to evoke the odds of her ever being other than alone. Her most recent dial-a-date, the one from which she was returning, had been big and russet-haired and eager as an Irish setter, which had only made her feel, by contrast, pinched and premenstrual. The entire thing, from sitting down to splitting the check, had lasted under an hour. Now burnished buildings and cars slipped free of her outline on the bus's window. She wasn't *totally* repulsive, she didn't think—she'd shaved her legs; her new antiperspirant was holding its own against the ninety-degree heat—and if she could just not have had so damn many *opinions* . . . but why futz around with counterfactuals? What the Jenny in the window was doing was lugging a totebag full of grant applications back to her un-air-conditioned apartment to order in Chinese and spend another hour working, and then, maybe, as a treat, allow herself a couple more pages of her dead neighbor's manuscript before sleeping, waking, doing it all over again. On one hand, you couldn't count on anything; on the other, on any given day, change was vanishingly unlikely.

Maybe that was even a good thing, because two and a half months after the last time something really *had* changed, she still felt a jolt of loss every time she set foot in her building, a kind of gamma signature scintillating through the metal partition between her mailbox and Richard's, and radiating from behind what she still thought of as his door. She hadn't noticed yet that the hallway upstairs was hotter than it should have been, heat wave or no heat wave. The bouquet of kerosene she chalked up to ethnic cooking in 2-J. Still, there was a slight hesitation between working the key into the sticky lock of her own door and opening it—a second in which the apartment remained a black box. One/zero. Did/didn't. Involved/uninvolved.

Then she was ahead of herself, hands flying to nostrils. A window had been propped open, loosing a cross-breeze on the charred black papers plastered over everything. Smoke drifted near the light fixtures. Drawers gaped at crazy angles. Wet clots of clothes and paper clung to the countertops like confetti to windshields after rain. The boxes she'd stacked so carefully in the corner—the boxes and boxes of Richard's things!—had been torched and then soaked, it seemed. Claggart, socketed in one corner of the sleeper sofa, looked a little rheumy-eyed, but otherwise intact. She was about to call him to her when she realized that an arsonist could still be lurking in the apartment, listening to her breathe.

She grabbed the dog and rushed down to the lobby, taking the fire stairs two at a time. It was what the fire stairs had been here for all along. But what had been the likelihood of them ever fulfilling their purpose? Then again, maybe the odds depended on whether you were for or against, the banana or the wall.

THE COPS, WHEN THEY FINALLY ARRIVED, were thinking burglary. She'd tried to point out that nothing was missing. Plus why the fire? The taller of the officers held the curtain back from the window, examined the scaffold beyond. "Usually they'll be looking for a TV."

She didn't have a TV, she said.

"How you expect she fits a TV, with all these boxes?" Mr. Feratovic was standing in the doorway with his arms crossed, scattering the napalm of his disapproval over everything. It had been his idea, over

Jenny's opposition, to involve the police, and now she saw why. "You keep this much things, is a fire hazard. Officer, you agree this place is a fire hazard?"

"Officer," she said, "would you agree that that scaffolding out there is an invitation to burgle?"

"Junkies looking for an easy score," the tall officer continued, as if he hadn't heard. "They see they aren't going to get what they're after, they decide to trash the place." When Jenny asked if he was planning to dust for fingerprints he just laughed.

Later, Mr. Feratovic brought up some fans to help pull the smoke out. He'd seen worse, he said. By morning, she wouldn't even notice the smell. But in fact she would find that night that she couldn't sleep with the windows open. The idea that someone had been here, treading her carpet, breathing her air . . . it rattled her. And there were hundreds of break-ins in the city every day, according to the shorter cop—what if these burglars should come back? Well, at least Richard's manuscript was undamaged; when she'd folded out the hide-a-bed, it had been lying in the space underneath, where it must have fallen the night before.

She decided now to turn on a light. Claggart was still a little damp from the shampoo she'd used to get the smoke out, but she placed him next to her on the invertebrate mattress and balanced a wine-glass on the sofa arm like a fetish to prevent further trouble. She flipped to the pictures she'd used to mark page 17, where she'd left off reading "The Fireworkers." The wine would knock her out after a few minutes, a few more pages, she thought. Hours later, though, she would be sitting up re-reading, pulse thrumming, certain that the break-in had been no low-probability event. Someone had wanted what was in these pages wiped out—and possibly not just that. She was going to have to take action come the morning. Or was it already morning? It was only when she turned to check her alarm clock that she realized she was missing something, after all.

73

I T HADN'T TAKEN LONG after his return from Altana for fissures to resurface in Mercer's life. The girls of Wenceslas-Mockingbird—good kids, really, their sangfroid no deeper than morning ice—kept shooting him looks of commiseration. Then one day, in the mirror of the faculty washroom, he'd seen why. Insomnia had left heavy luggage under his eyes. He'd missed spots shaving. It was the third day in a row he'd worn this particular shirt, and the sweater-vest he'd been using to hide the rumples had itself begun to rumple. After blotting his armpits with paper towels, he'd stepped back into the hall. There was this hot, yellowy stillness the air always got in the minutes before the last bell, as if it were stiffening itself to be shattered. Voices nearby conjugated *vouloir* in unison. From a janitor's closet came the odor of something burning. The door had been left unlocked, and when he opened it, two girls in field-hockey uniforms whipped around from the window. Where was their hall pass? Did Coach Curtis know they were in here? And what was that smell?

"What smell?" one of them had said, even as her accomplice, unable to hold it in any longer, coughed up a cloud of bluebrown smoke. "Mr. G., be cool, please. We're like a month from graduation."

He held out a hand. He must have looked slightly unhinged; though they'd pitched the evidence out the window, they seemed alarmed, as if he were not an English teacher but the Kneesocks Killer himself.

"Where's the rest?" The accomplice blurted that it was in her locker. He heard himself propose a deal. They had until three o'clock to turn the pot in to him for disposal. Provided they swore never to indulge again, he wouldn't say anything.

Probably he really had meant to destroy it, but he'd been unprepared for the sheer heft of what these daughters of privilege would produce: a baggie the size of his head, which it seemed a shame to waste. At first, he'd dipped into it only in the evenings, as a soporific, but soon he'd added an a.m. application as well. (Was incineration not a method of disposal?) His pedagogy grew erratic. He could feel his first-period sophomores watching his shirttail detach from his waistband as he elucidated a nicety from *Portrait of the Artist* on the board. The FORMAL cause of a thing—he wrote the word out in great big majuscules—was that it fulfilled its own definition. *(Why had William left him? Because William was no longer living with him.)* And the FINAL cause of everything, according to ARISTOTLE, was the unmoved mover. ὃ οὐ κινούμενον κινεῖ. "A.k.a. God." At just that moment, Dr. Runcible had appeared outside the classroom door. It must have gladdened his heart to see an honest-to-goodness Afro-American *wunderkind* teaching these Caucasian girls Greek. What Runcible couldn't hear, through the stenciled glass, was Mercer explaining that the first two causes were typical Aristotelian horseshit. More crucial, and not incidentally almost impossible to isolate, was the EFFICIENT cause of anything—the x that had brought about y. Or could the good doctor hear after all? Because now he was leaning in to ask if Mercer could stop by after class. Mercer sensed what was coming, but as if from a great distance. A year's worth of lessons crowded the chalkboard at eye level, cloudy eraser marks and beneath them the blurred tangle of chalk-lines like the paths of electrons. One day, he and William had been speeding toward each other; the next, careening away. But why? Why y?

In camera, Runcible had dispensed with small-talk. There'd been a complaint. "Two of our girls, at an honor-board hearing, claimed to have come to an in-kind understanding with you about their scheme to supply the entire senior class with marijuana. Testimony that would seem to comport with your recent demeanor. Do you want to try to explain this to me? Because frankly I'm at a loss."

It wasn't an accurate account, entirely, but Mercer didn't see how he *could* explain. Nor could he protest that he hadn't been warned.

"What you do on your own time is one thing, Mercer, but I don't think you grasp how serious the element of collusion is. The faculty code of conduct ties my hands. This is in your contract. I can't ask the Board to renew it for the fall unless there's some extenuating circumstance you care to share with me."

"I'm not going to try to pin everything on a couple of high-schoolers, if that's what you're saying."

Dr. Runcible sighed. "I appreciate that you've got your own code, Mercer. So did Ahab, but would you trust him with your daughter? I can try to arrange to keep you paid through exam week, provided you pull yourself together and keep your mouth shut. Now on a personal note—" But Mercer had decided not to hear the personal note, for the damage had already been done. He was not only single again, but also no longer employed. He had $247 left in his bank account. The Selectric sat unplugged in the loft, the paper inside it blank. However you wanted to measure it—materially, emotionally, aesthetically— his time in New York had amounted to nothing, and as soon as his savings hit zero, it would be Greater Ogeechee, here I come.

SINCE THE END OF CLASSES, THEN, the only thing he really had to look forward to was his daily climb to the roof of his building. Evenings were best. Hunker down in a folding chair, read the same two pages of *Leaves of Grass* over and over, get high, wait. And as dark fell, the summer fires would start to flicker infernally on the horizon, distracting him from the pathetic smallness of his life. Around the start of July, though, Bullet had begun throwing these wild parties downstairs, and on the night of the twelfth, for no other reason than that it was a Tuesday, the Angels had spilled onto the roof. Mercer had decided to postpone his ascent until the morning, when he could have the place to his lonesome.

As now he did. Not even noon and it was Götterdämmerung up here, the chairs too hot to sit in, the giant steel *O* of the Knickerbocker sign more or less molten above. He put down his book. Took a toke. Watched some pigeons nip at pop-tops baked into the tarpaper. One waddled over to him, blinking Morse code, jerking its head forward and back like a tiny Egyptian before smashing it into the roof. Of course, he could only pity its mindlessness for so long, because he had problems of his own, equally intractable, to ram his head against.

A siren's bloop somewhere in the infinite grid drew him toward the roof's edge. The vista was dizzying: ashcans like bullseyes six stories down, a lamppost with the colored spaghetti of wiring spilling from its base, an electrician clambering out of a van, heading into the building opposite . . . and, yes, the day's first patch of smoke, up past the park. Last summer, with William, it had been easier to imagine these black smudges as so many painterly flourishes on the sky. But now that even Harlem was succumbing to the fires, it was harder to forget that there were actual people involved, and that underneath the spectacle of the city's burning lay someone's shelf of LPs, or the cushions of someone's sofa, or, God forbid, someone's child. Maybe the siren was a fire truck? Mercer couldn't see one anywhere, but like some bounding St. Bernard of the metaphysical, he couldn't quite let go of the belief that there must be an objective reality out there, beyond his own head.

He took a step closer to the edge and sucked down a real lung-buster and tossed the doob and spread his arms like the Jesus of Rio de Janeiro. What one wanted was a gramophone with a trumpet the size of a churchbell, diva Leontyne Price doing the big Act 3 aria from *Madama Butterfly*. No, what one wanted, really, was the city or anyone in it to see how one suffered. Of course, this being New York, they'd likely just tell him Get over it. Was this what that bird had been trying to communicate? Was it possible that the last month had been a kind of judgment on him for ever daring to pretend that anything meant anything at all? And just what the hell, by the way, were electricians doing in this neighborhood, where the streetlights hadn't worked since the Nixon administration?

It was a scissoring of wings that sliced his musings to ribbons. At some signal he'd missed, the pigeons were on the move. There were hundreds now, it seemed, a whole confusion of them rising and flapping around Mercer's head. He tried to bat them away, but ended up yawing out over empty space, trying to cough and shout at the same time. In the feathery maelstrom he couldn't tell whether he'd turned 180 degrees or 360, and his body, panicking, must have decided that the only way to prevent a hundred-foot drop was to bellyflop onto the tarpaper, because that's where he ended up, face-down on the roof.

It took the world several breaths to become solid again. There was pain in the heel of his hand where a bottlecap had cut it. A few feet away, his glasses lay anchored to oblongs of light. When he put them back on, he could make out Eartha K. perched atop a doorway, her tail twitching in disdain. And underneath, the figure that had startled the birds: that standoffish Vietnamese girl from the Bicentennial.

"Jenny Nguyen? Do you realize you nearly just got me killed?"

"I knocked and knocked on your door. When I tried the handle, the cat escaped."

"Well, would you help me get her back downstairs, at least? I don't want her going over the edge."

Jenny seemed to define "help" as looking on skeptically while Mercer pretended to have something delicious in his bleeding hand. Eartha narrowed her own eyes at his approach—they both knew the cat was the superior creature—but allowed herself to be carried down to the sanctuary of the loft. There Mercer dampened a towel and cleaned the grit from his hands, dabbed at his sweaty face. In the mirror above the sink, he looked darker than he had that day in the faculty washroom, though maybe it was all the sun he'd been getting. Between the whiskers scraggling down his neck and the now-crooked glasses, he could have been the Black Allen Ginsberg. Jenny cleared her throat behind him. "Mercer, I have to talk to your boyfriend. Do you know when he'll be back?"

"Didn't Bruno tell you?"

"Bruno doesn't tell me anything. It's not how the relationship works."

"William and I are kaput. He moved out four months ago."

"You mean he still hasn't come back? Shit." When he turned to her, she was studying William's self-portrait. "He must be some-where, though."

"Common sense would seem to dictate. But your guess is as good as mine."

"You don't have any idea where he is?"

As she moved toward the futon, lost in some private worry, her eyes no longer saw him. And because she seemed to be taking the news of the breakup so hard, he found he didn't dislike her quite as much as he'd thought. "It's fine, go ahead and sit." He'd somehow not noticed until now the folder she was carrying. "Is this about a painting?"

She looked up. "No, but it's absolutely critical I find him."

"Aren't you going to tell me why?"

"You'd think I was crazy."

"Who says I don't already think you're crazy?" he said.

She rose to go to the window, but something stopped her halfway there. And now she was speaking rapidly, facing the glass. "Mercer, listen to me. William's got himself into trouble. I'm still missing some pieces, but someone's been watching him."

"Says who? And what do you mean, watching?" he asked, even as he thought back to Christmas Day, William's unexplained bruises.

"I mean spying. Stalking. I came here to warn him he might be in danger. I thought maybe he'd know from whom. Probably the same fuckers who broke into my apartment yesterday, trying to get this manuscript. By the end of it, you see them carrying around switchblades—"

"Let me see that."

She clutched the folder to her chest. "Now's not the time, Mercer. We've got to get out of here."

"You know what? Never mind. I do think you're crazy."

"Well, somebody should tell your friend out there." She motioned Mercer over. On the rooftop across the street was a black guy in coveralls, the electrician he'd seen earlier. He might have been looking around for a junction box, but his hair was all wrong, a vibrant lime-green. And what was that glinting in his hand? "No, stay back," Jenny was saying, but as she pulled him to the side, the man seemed to pivot toward this window.

"I think he saw me," Mercer hissed.

"Now ask yourself why you're whispering."

Well, because there was something unmistakably malevolent about that electrician. His small dark blank of a face. Though this could have been a side-effect of marijuana. Please, Final Cause, Mercer thought. Get me through this day and I'll give it up, I swear. Then he was briefly in a cemetery, with Regan staring through tinted windows at the person who'd sat here waffling while William was out there in need. "Maybe it's drug people," he said.

"Drug people?"

"Dealers who haven't been paid. Or collection agents? You know he's a junkie, right?"

"Like I said, I don't know much about William, or whatever he calls himself these days, beyond the fact that he had a double life as Billy Three-Sticks—and what's in this folder. Now is there a way out of your building other than the front entrance?"

"Why?"

"Mercer, if he moved out four months ago, and they're still watching, then you're obviously mixed up in it, too."

He could keep fighting this dream-logic, Mercer felt, but what would be the point? Jenny Nguyen would just go to some other part of the loft and produce some other artifact he didn't want to know had been here all along: a dollop of plastique, a rat's nest, a decomposing head. So he led her out toward the freight elevator.

The basement was cooler, darker, faintly minty under scattered bulbs. The few remaining cartons from the Knickerbocker days alternated with the possessions of tenants who'd fled or been kicked out, all of it forming a maze in which a distant radio babbled. Mercer found that the thought of another electrician alarmed him, but more likely it was one of the Angels out cold on a shipping pallet. The metal doors up to the street were hot to the touch, and for a second, there was resistance, but then whatever had been holding them shut came loose, and the razor-edge of daylight widened into a wedge of world. Here on the northern side of the building, the street was empty, its warehouses sealed like tombs.

"We'll head east," she said, decisively. Though, with no commercial properties to duck into, no alleyways, they were defenseless against anyone who might have meant them harm. When Mercer hesitated, just past the corner of Tenth, Jenny told him not to look back. "Keep walking. One more block and we'll start seeing cabs." Then a blur shot past on the avenue behind them. She froze. "Shit. Was that their van?"

"How could it be their van?" he asked. "The guy's still up on the roof." But ten minutes ago, I wouldn't have believed they could be on the roof, either, he was thinking, as tires screeched, and the white van he'd observed from above sped back by in reverse. Was he imagining the flash of sun on metal in the window as it turned onto this very street? "Come on," he said, and grabbed her arm.

They scrambled to the next intersection, her short legs struggling to keep up with him. Though he didn't look back, he could hear the engine getting louder. But then the signal was releasing the perpendicular traffic on Ninth Avenue, and she was grabbing the doorhandle of a taxi, and he was piling in beside her, telling the cabbie just to drive. He prayed for the van to stay stuck at the red, which it did long enough for them to sail south, and there was no sign of pursuit, no bullet smashing through the back window. If Jenny, in the seat beside him, hadn't seen the van, too, he would have thought he'd dreamed the whole thing. After a dozen or so blocks, they hit a light. The cabbie's expression in the rearview was deadpan. Another odd couple. "We going anywhere in particular, folks?"

"The nearest police station's, what, Thirty-Fourth Street?" he asked Jenny, but she tightened her grip on her folder.

"Uh-uh, no way. No more cops. Besides, those aren't what you're calling drug people. Drug people don't have vans and disguises."

"So who was it, then?" Mercer said.

Jenny checked back out the window. For a second, she looked as wrecked as he felt. "I don't want to jump to conclusions, Mercer, but I'm starting to think if I knew the answer, we'd have even bigger problems."

74

TO DISCUSS A FORMER CLIENT was not only a breach of nondisclo-
sure, Keith felt, but also a breach of loyalty, yet here he was, in a
climate-controlled room on a high floor of the Trade Center's north
tower, trying not to stare at the upside-down document poised on the
table between the hands of the government lawyer, or at the hands
themselves, pale, mushroomy things untouched by the light of honest work. The document would grant him immunity from prosecu-
tion, but for Keith, the notion of loyalty still meant something. And
were he to look down at his own hands, hands that had gripped foot-
balls, hammers, steering wheels, and to discover that they, too, had
gone pale from disuse, he might not be able to go through with this.

Luckily, there was little on this side of the table for hands to do.
There was a glass of water, now warmed to room temperature. There
was a ballpoint pen. He'd had to surrender his briefcase at the front
desk in the morning, as though he were the one under indictment,
which he supposed he'd have to get used to. No one trusted a turncoat.
But this was merely another trade, he reminded himself: information
for security. He was securing Will's future, and Cate's, as surely their
grandfather would have wanted (against whom Keith had been told
the case was a slam dunk, "even without your testimony"), and still
he felt unsteady. They'd seated him facing the big picture window, as
if to say, All this could be yours, just sign already, but what Keith saw

out there, beyond buildings arranged like crudités on a platter, were guys like himself, guys he'd gone to high school with, with welding torches in hand, with scalpels, with the black billiard knobs of the gearshifts of cranes, testing the strength of the city against their demolition balls. The Irish in him was telling him to ball up the document, take his chances, be a man. Trader, he thought. Traitor. Surely there was some other way.

The Assistant U.S. Attorney who had wooed him these last weeks had disappeared, leaving him alone with this balding, nearly eyebrowless juris doctor who spoke in a murmur, as if his every utterance weren't already confidential. Each time he scuttled up close to one of the big questions, the immunity agreement inched closer on the table; each time Keith failed to give a satisfactory response, the document slid farther away. Over repeated objections, Keith had insisted on coming to sign without his own lawyer, both because he couldn't afford counsel other than Tadelis until he was formally deposed and because he couldn't stand the idea of looking guilty. Now, asked again about his dealings with Hamilton-Sweeney *père*— "just to review what we're getting here"—he tried to stall for time. He recalled the first time he'd met the man, the high-backed dining room chairs, the oil-painted ancestors. "It was the first time I'd ever seen *consommé*. I kept looking for meat hidden at the bottom. But Old Bill never made me feel unfit to sit at his table. He's a decent old guy once you thaw him out a little. Misunderstood, maybe. I guess decency often is."

But whose idea had it been to put "Old Bill" in such a large position in muni bonds?

Wasn't this covered in someone else's testimony? Keith said.

The lawyer's fingers bridged themselves above the document, a gesture curiously puppetlike. Keith had liked the boss better. "You'll notice we keep returning to this question of the bonds."

"Maybe you can explain to me again what you think Bill did wrong. It's a pretty loosely regulated market." They couldn't incriminate Keith without his lawyer present, right?

"The principle is exchange value, Mr. Lamplighter. The sense that information is convertible into value. Information not available to everyone in the marketplace."

Interesting, how these government types avoided the word *money*. "This is something I know it's hard to get your head around, but buying bonds isn't like playing the ponies. In '72, '73, city paper looks like a rock-solid investment."

"But by the winter of '75, I don't have to tell you, the city was effectively bankrupt. The debt—on your own trading book at that point, we've established—was approaching worthless. And yet you manage to unload it to your father-in-law at eighty-nine cents on the dollar, write the difference off as a loss, and three months later when the bailout comes through, they're cashed out at face value plus accrued interest."

"With a position that big, it was still a huge haircut."

"If it weren't, Mr. Lamplighter, you'd be the one preparing for trial. That could still be arranged, by the way. But we're talking about the twelve percent the trade netted the Hamilton-Sweeneys. That's nine hundred thousand dollars. And, according to our source, your father-in-law had information the bailout was on its way."

Or, more likely, Amory Gould did, for whom information was nearly an end in itself—but the information Amory had on Keith (all those envelopes, full of God knew what) made it impossible to *say* this without risking further exposure. And that did appear to be Bill's signature, however shaky, on the carbon copy of the memo they'd showed him. Memories of holiday cards he'd seen it on led to memories of Regan, who on the phone yesterday had been hinting pretty unsubtly that she had a date . . . and then to the kids, whom he was taking to tonight's Mets game. Pain-wise, it was one long associative slide, only this time it ended in inspiration. "Hey. Are you hungry?"

The lawyer blinked, uncomprehending. It was as if there were an invisible wall, Keith thought, to go beyond which you were expected to turn your back on all animal life, all desires of the flesh. In the orderly future being prepared by the federal bureaucrats, the Amory Goulds, the Rohatyns and the Trilateral Commission, people would be as bodiless as numbers, receding into the blue. But hadn't it been precisely the animal business, the getting and spending, that had sent the numbers skyward in the first place?

"Hungry. Peckish. In need of food. It's got to be past lunchtime. If you want to stay on the clock while I duck out to eat, I won't tell a soul." He rose and turned to go. Perhaps the lawyer was too surprised by Keith's impertinence to notice he'd made off with the government's pen. Keith couldn't even have said why; it was a piece of junk, and by the time he reached street level, he'd discarded it.

Down here, the mercury had spiked another fifteen degrees. A hot-dog vendor sat on his trailer-hitch just beyond the north tower's shadow, pouring sweat. Pigeons, with a gull or two and some other species Keith didn't quite recognize, gabbled after the scraps of bun the hot-dog man threw. Keith was no Franciscan, and it seemed to him an act of narcissism to feed pigeons, who would if anything outlast us. But was it really worth interrupting this for a hot dog? He would make the long walk up to that sandwich place in the Village instead. If nothing else, it would buy more time.

He headed north through Chinatown, whose stink was summer, was the city itself, growth and its own decay. Women with wheeled carts and lean men with cigarettes hurried past. People thrust objects into his sightline, umbrellas, luggage, whole duck, a frenzied commercial semaphore he didn't need to speak the language to understand. Then, outside one of those stores that sold all the above plus jewelry and electronics, the sidewalk slowed. People had gathered to watch a TV in the window. He stepped off the curb and walked along the gutter, but the cataract had spread there, too. By Canal, he couldn't move at all.

The next cross-street had been cleared of cars, and hundreds of people were processing through the intersection, or maybe thousands. Some kind of funeral, he told himself, a New Orleans–style thing, or one of those marches in honor of a waxy saint the Italians undertook every other weekend. But this crowd was too casual to be religious. The men wore jeans and muscle-tees or work shirts with union insignia. Women were profoundly tanned, their hair piled high. The fabled white ethnics, the return of the repressed, but what did people like this have to protest against? An obscure shame crept over him even as he strained to read the scattered posters. Mad as Hell. WE'RE NOT GONNA TAKE IT. TAKE BACK THE APPLE.

At which point an extraordinary thing happened. Out of the crowd emerged that old man from New Year's Eve, Isidor, the shopping-trolley pusher. He was moving now at a normal pace. Or rather, everything around him had decelerated. Less than a dozen yards away, without breaking stride, he turned and with a strange underwater languor aimed a finger right at Keith's chest.

Even after the man had passed, Keith could feel it there, burning. (*Day allah here.* Was that what he'd said?) Everything stood out crisply in blaze and shadow, the solid geometries of soot-faced buildings and subway grates, discrete flocks of what kinds of birds were those sweeping downtown and then changing their minds, flapping bright to dark like the departure board at Grand Central. Traffic, free to move again, streamed toward the tunnel end of Canal. And how simple it would be just to follow. Swing a leg over the metal fence along the gangway. Descend into pitchy cool. Brakelight smearing the grimed tiles. By the time he reached the mainland, the sun would be slipping down the sky, beckoning him past four-in-hand interchanges and the numberless gas stations of Jersey to where the earth broadened and softened and it was okay to eat when you were hungry, fuck when you were horny, rest when your loafers started to pinch. Forty hours and one bus ticket later, he would step from the blackness of a motel room west of Oklahoma City into sweet prairie air, having slipped his own life.

But that was assuming man was a rational creature, and Keith wasn't so sure anymore which part of him, the rational or the animal, was calling the shots. Maybe the idea of parts was itself a rationalization. He'd started to feel instead like he was ruled by a congress of entirely dissimilar people—Keith at seventeen, Keith at twenty-five—all of them screaming for some last, authentic Keith to show up at the final second to save them.

Which was now, possibly.

Which was him.

Déjala ir? Why wasn't his Spanish better?

From the nearest working payphone, he dialed the U.S. Attorney's office. He left a message with the receptionist. (The under-assistant was indeed at lunch.) He was happy to face whatever music there was, he said, but they shouldn't expect him back today. The briefcase they could keep, there was nothing in it anyway. Otherwise, the deal was off. They'd be hearing from his lawyer just as soon as he got one. Then he hung up the phone and hurried up the street the march had turned onto, a man called onward by spirits.

75

SOME KIND OF DOWNTOWN TRAFFIC NIGHTMARE snarling streets all through SoHo, Jenny and Mercer eventually had to leave the cab and make their way forward on foot. Still, she was unwilling to scuttle her mission, Richard's mission. Mercer had surprised her by pointing out that if anyone knew where William was, it was probably her employer. But now, outside the Galerie Bruno Augenblick, they were at odds again, this time over who would have to enter. Bruno hated him, Mercer insisted. Jenny's suggestion that he was being paranoid didn't go over well. "I'm sorry," he said, "but when a fucking—sorry, but basically fucking perfect stranger sweeps into your building and all of a sudden you're in *The French Connection*, it does tend to make you a little paranoid." On the other hand, Jenny had called in sick this morning, and was supposed to be in bed right now with stomach flu, so she ended up waiting down the block while Mercer went in to find out what he could.

She'd been imagining this as the work of two or three minutes, but it seemed to take longer. How much was he telling Bruno? She'd gone to see if there was a way to peer in when the door swung open, sending her back behind the blind of a dumpster. It was Mercer, looking sucker-punched. Bruno followed, extending a set of keys. "Mercer, a cab would cost a fortune, the subway nearest there is a trek, and the car has to be moved for street sweeping anyhow. It's the orange one, right down at the corner. Just see that it's returned when you're done."

Jenny waited until Bruno had left to emerge from hiding. Mercer was looking around frantically. "Would you stop just *materializing* like that? I thought those people in the van had come and kidnapped you."

"I can't have Bruno thinking I'm a liar. Plus I was right, see? There's no way he hates you, Mercer, if he gave you his keys."

"That's not affection, it's pity." Mercer explained what he'd been told: that for a while after the breakup, William had been living with Bruno. "It's so obvious, in retrospect. Of course he'd go running back there. But Bruno apparently refuses to be a party to suicide, however gradual, so I guess he kicked William out." And now Jenny actually did feel a little queasy. So this was what her boss had been going home to every night.

"Did he say where William went after that?"

"He keeps a studio in the Bronx. I've never been up there, but Bruno gave me an address on 161st Street."

"Better hand those over, then," she said, reaching for the keys.

"I can drive," he said.

"Are you kidding? This thing is Bruno's baby. You so much as scratch a fender, he'll never recover. Anyway"—she handed him the folder with Richard's manuscript—"this will give you time to do the reading."

The car was not some marvel of German engineering, but a neon-orange AMC Gremlin; Bruno's love for it, like his love for most things, had probably started out tempered with irony. But as she jockeyed it free of the gridlock on Houston and onto the West Side Highway, she could see how irony and sincerity might coexist. Out on the mottled brown Hudson, boats lay becalmed and innocent. Or as if becalmed. As if innocent.

It took them almost an hour to get out of Manhattan, and by that time the pages were back in their folder. Mercer ran a hand down his face. "This is unbelievable. You know I was the one who found her, right?" And, seeing Jenny's look: "The Cicciaro girl, the daughter. In the snow that night. I was leaving the Hamilton-Sweeneys' party."

"How would I know that, Mercer?"

"What if they think I'm the shooter?"

"The article makes it pretty clear it's Billy Three-Sticks they're after."

"I still don't see how you got ahold of this story, though."

"Richard, the reporter who wrote it—he lives next door. Or did.

He died in April," she heard herself say pointlessly. "What's driving me nuts is how he doesn't put together Billy Three-Sticks and William Hamilton-Sweeney."

Mercer picked it up. "It's not as rare an oversight as you might think. I mean, it wasn't until that dinner last summer . . . but hey, wait a second. That whole time he and Bruno were jawing about corporatocracy and bla bla bla, I could see you biting your tongue, like a self-hating capitalist was the worst kind. You're one of those power-to-the-people people, aren't you? And suddenly you're sticking out your neck for William Hamilton-Sweeney the Third?"

She sighed. They were now farther uptown than she'd been since her stint as a canvasser, having made their way off off-ramps and round roundabouts and back down in zigzag fashion among the crackerbox apartment towers of the Bronx. Containment units, was what they were, really. Warehouses. Prisons, with trapped air shimmering between. Horns and shouts and portable radios assailed the pavements. Then came blocks burned nearly to the ground. Yet still there were people, people with shopping bags, people with strollers, brown and black people, mostly, waiting for the buses that trundled up the long V of the street. And what if Jenny's longing was only a kind of homesickness for the place she couldn't see she was? What if that other world was already *in* this one, somehow?

Except a single, transcendent world wouldn't have three distinct East 161st Streets. The particular one they were looking for was impossible to locate. Every street ran one-way, going the wrong way. Half the signs were missing, and those that remained made no sense. At what point had 163rd Street turned into 162nd? How could 169th Street cross *itself*?

It took almost an hour to locate the freestanding tenement with *B.T. Sticks, Artist* under a piece of moldy laminate by the door. A demolition notice had been freshly wheat-pasted above. For a moment, Mercer seemed paralyzed, but when she reached out to mash the relevant buzzer, he stopped her and mashed the ones around it instead. The door buzzed, and they pushed through into the urinal light of a stairwell.

The smell got harder to ignore the higher you climbed: rotten food, animal fat souring in the heat. Behind and below, doors parted to the length of chains and snapped shut. Little paper envelopes crinkled underfoot. She could feel Mercer's ambivalence returning even before he knocked on the garret apartment's door. There was no answer. "I guess William's not here, either," he said.

"Shall we look inside and see?" She'd noticed a bent bobbypin hanging out of the lock. When she pushed, the door flew open, harder than she intended.

Mercer caught it on the rebound. "This is so wrong," he said, peering in. It was a single room, surprisingly big, crammed with old mirrors and broken furniture, newspaper twists clotted with paint. Nothing to suggest someone might be living here, though, unless you counted a half-empty pack of Necco wafers. No sleeping bag. No toiletries. And no visible drug paraphernalia.

Then Mercer flicked on a light, and she almost forgot what she was looking for. The walls, ten or twelve feet high, were covered in signs, the kind you saw on subway platforms, or taped to the bulletproof glass of bodegas. Something was slightly off about them, but it took Jenny a second to figure out what: the scale. A parking ordinance was a foot too wide. A stop-sign was skewed, its angles foreshortened. An Uncle Sam recruiting poster was taller than she was and missing an eye. A teenager might have ripped off a piece of poster to reveal the subway tile underneath, but this was trompe l'oeil; the whole thing, once you got up close, was oil paint. It was as if William Hamilton-Sweeney, despite to her knowledge never having sold so much as a painting, had been trying to re-create the face of the entire city, right here in this attic. She couldn't tell if it was good, exactly, but no one could say it wasn't ambitious.

"Help me lift this one." She indicated a canvas lying face-down under some mannequin limbs. It was a work in progress, an almost monolithic slab of blue, but when the dust was blown off, she could see other colors, blacks and oranges and greens rising like sparks from within. The paint wasn't quite dry to the touch. She was about to mention this when a voice from the doorway said, "I told y'all not to come back."

The elderly woman who stood there in her nightgown was as dark and squat as a fire hydrant, if a fire hydrant could carry a baseball bat.

"I done called the police, you better leave that poor boy's things alone."

Jenny, hands in the air, tried to reason with her—they were the poor boy's friends—but Mercer interrupted. "You're right. We shouldn't be here."

"All right, then." The old lady retreated behind her door.

Jenny could feel the whole building listening as they trudged back downstairs, and Mercer must have, too, because it wasn't until the vestibule that he let himself groan. Hadn't she heard? Someone else had already been here, probably the electricians. "So that's it," he concluded. "All's lost. The end."

Over the frantic course of the afternoon, she'd almost grown to like him, but this defeatism just annoyed her. And the annoyance was probably mutual, she thought, as she took from her pocket what she'd plucked from under the edge of that canvas. "This was on the floor." A prescription slip, edged in tacky blue. Stamped across the top was the dispensary logo. NEPTUNE AVENUE, it said.

76

THE SIGN-IN SHEET was a grid clipped to a binder on the counter of the nurse's station, with slots for your name, the time in, and all those Establishment hoops a real punk would sooner die than jump through. But the nurse on duty was looking at him funny, so Charlie stooped to leave a squiggle where his name should have been, and again in the space where you were supposed to say who you were here to see. Once the nurse was out of sight, Charlie hung a left onto the hall where he thought Sam was. He yanked out charts holstered next to doorframes to check the names. The door by *Cicciaro* was open an inch or two. Like the others, it was wide enough to fit a stretcher through, he thought. Or a coffin, before telling his brain to shut its face, because how many months had his brain just cost him?

The bed by the door was empty, so she must have been in the one closer to the window. He stood for maybe a minute, fingering the privacy curtain that had been drawn between them. Finally, he swept it back, but what he saw made him wish he hadn't. The fluorescent light bouncing off all the toothpasty green furnishings seemed to pool and deepen in the hollows of Sam's skin. Her neck, sticking out of the hospital gown, was just skin stretched over tendons, like paper over the wooden sticks of a Japanese lantern. Her hair had grown back to what it had been at New Year's, but there was this bald patch where they'd taken out the bullets. The saddest thing was the vase of cheap flowers, because they must have come from her dad. No, actually the saddest thing was the band-aid covering the place where the needle went into the back of her hand. The modesty of that. The hand, with all its nerve-endings, pierced. Oh, Sam. How could you have been naked in his bed?

Charlie thought he'd come here, finally, to ask. But the flesh-and-blood hurt of her made the answers meaningless. It no longer mattered.

He turned off the lights and climbed carefully onto the margin of bed her body left available. He'd ditched the smoke-smelling cover-alls in a trashcan outside. With his tee-shirt rolled up to his chest, he could feel how warm she still was under her gown and press his belly against her hip and remember how she'd lain once with her head on his lap. It wasn't dirty to do this, he felt, to show her how close he wanted to be. After a while, though, it got physically uncomfortable, so he retreated to the other bed, from which, if she'd been conscious, he could have held her hand. Her face, in profile against the bright window, was peaceful. But that was something you said about dead people, too.

A great weariness overtook him. He'd spent last night hunkered on some church steps with only a plywood awning to shield him from anyone on the street. Every time headlights rolled past, he'd found his grip tightening on the handle of the switchblade he'd remembered was in a pocket of his coveralls. And in between, he'd had the same argument with himself he was having now. On one hand, Nicky had been right; Charlie's faith in the cause was imperfect, there were spots on his raiment, or why was he so freaked out? On the other, these things happened. Ready to leave the house, you discovered last winter's snot on the sleeve of your sweater, and you couldn't be sure you hadn't worn it since then. Plus he recalled from the Bible that no prophet was perfect. Jeremiah was a notorious dawdler. Jonah basically turned tail and ran. And Post-Humanism turned out to be embarrassingly human. Look where he'd found himself: in a strange apartment, eyes burning, slopping water from the sink onto the bon-fire Nicky'd made on the floor. Soiled, worldly, the whole stinking business. At least he'd managed to save the dog.

Trees sighed outside and hazy clouds scudded past and the shadow of a flower vase swung from west to east on the plastic tray table. No one came in to feed Sam lunch, because she couldn't eat. Sometimes he imagined he was talking to her and she was talking back. Sometimes, without realizing it, he hummed. Sometimes he closed his eyes, but he didn't pray. Maybe he even drifted off for a little while, because when a man's voice spoke up in the hall, it took a second to really hear. *Just look in on her for a minute*, it said . . .

Oh, shit. How was he going to explain his being here? Charlie was an excellent sneak but a crappy liar. The voice, and another voice, that nurse or a lady doctor, were just outside the door. He had a few moments left to yank the privacy curtain closed around the bed he was on. Out of childish habit, he pulled the blanket over his head. Then came the footsteps. Then the complaint of metal on floor as a chair was dragged next to Sam's bed. Then the chair, mere feet away, creaking under someone's weight. Then nothing.

This couldn't be Mr. Cicciaro; he knew that voice from the phone, and the muttering that came now sounded more educated. No, Charlie understood suddenly—for *understanding was given in visions and in dreams*—that the person he was trapped here with had to be the one who had shot her. Returned to the scene of the crime. Or the body that amounted to the same thing. Beyond the closed door, machines beeped, wheels rattled, clocks were punched. Should he bolt for the nurse's station to raise the alarm? God, he was suffocating here. The light through the blanket's thin places was malevolent, green. He tried not to think of the afflictions of all the bed's previous occupants, snowing down on him in this underworld. He tried not to imagine this was how Sam had been feeling for the 192 days since this man had put her here, but he couldn't help it: it was like being buried alive. He groped in his pocket for his inhaler, but found the switchblade instead. Some coins slipped out and clattered against the bed and then the floor, and for good measure rolled around and around before rattling to a halt. The silence that followed was the kind where you can actually feel the weight of the listening: his listening, your own, the wispiness of the fabric that separates you. And the last conscious thought of the Prophet Charlie Weisbarger, before the killer swept back the curtain, was to hell with the inhaler. It was going to have to be the blade.

77

R EACHING CONEY ISLAND took several more centuries. The Triboro at rush hour was a catastrophe of millennial proportions, as was the Brooklyn-Queens Expressway, any time of day or night. (And didn't time always slow, anyway, the closer you came to what you wanted?) Somewhere around the Verrazano Bridge, the Gremlin's two-stroke engine began to whimper. From the passenger's seat, Mercer watched the gas needle flirt with E. Then a string of kitelike pennants in primary colors was snapping outside a line of dead storefronts, beyond which stretched seagulls and the sea.

They pulled into a near-empty parking lot. He heard the engine die. Across the street was the place they'd come looking for, a derelict pile of cinderblock with an impenetrable steel door and heavy mesh over the windows. A big-bellied man in camouflage pants dozed on the steps. In the heat beside him lay the spine of a dog with fur hanging off it. The clinic's sign was barely legible. *Methadone*, Mercer thought. A drug you take to stop using other drugs. William, who couldn't be bothered to give up heroin for him, had done it for Bruno. But why all the way out here?

He got out to sit on the hood of the car. It was a million degrees, but fuck it. He felt like a discarded marionette, or a building collapsing in on itself, floor by floor. Jenny plopped down next to him, too light to register with the car's suspension. "What now?"

"What do you mean, what now? The place is obviously closed."

"We could check if there's an open window."

"I'm sure we could, but what would be the point? He's not going to be in there. All we can do is wait for him to come get his dose."

"Do you really think there's time for that?"

Up until now, Mercer had been having trouble holding her gaze when he met it. "I read the article, too, Jenny. I saw the guy on the roof. But William's not at his studio, he's not in SoHo, he's not here. Anyway, what are you going to do if we get to him first? Lock him up safe in a tower somewhere?"

She thumbed the edge of the folder in her lap. "I just feel like we have to warn him."

"You're virtual strangers, Jenny, you said it yourself. No one's that altruistic."

"I'm trying to take responsibility. It's a choice I've made."

But this was ducking the question. "Sometimes you don't get to make a choice," he said.

"When have you ever not had a choice, Mercer? Okay, the man you love is an addict. Don't you still have to choose?"

Well, so much for subtext, Mercer thought. He laid his arms across his knees and lowered his head to them. There was a pause here, a silence, in which he could feel Jenny wrestling with something. "Mercer, it's not just that these people broke into my apartment. Do you understand how rare it is to get a real chance to save someone? You can't just blow it off—trust me. This might be our chance to redeem ourselves, but you have to stop second-guessing. You have to let yourself think."

What Mercer thought was that in the distorting chrome of the bumper, with his stupid beard, he looked like someone who'd been turned inside out—superficially soft, but with a hard shell where his tissues should be, holding the emptiness in. He could hear the pop of balls jumping off bats in cages and a bored voice through a megaphone, *They're here, they're weird, real live girls*, and a spectral organ recalling something from his youth, though he couldn't remember what. "You aren't a bad person," Jenny added gently, as if she could hear him.

"You know, people keep telling me that." When he lifted his head, the sun seemed impossibly close. Science-fictionally close. He wouldn't be surprised if up there behind the yellow haze there were two or three moons, and mutually exclusive evening stars. But even in this strange new cosmos, was there not still something of the old one left? "I suppose there is one other thing we could try," he said at last. "I'm just guessing you're not going to like it."

78

PULASKI HAD SUSTAINED NO SERIOUS INJURIES in last week's fall. Or *tumble*, as he'd put it in the car on the long homeward loop from a downtown ER. Just a deep-tissue bruise in his thigh and, he joked, some surface abrasions to his pride. Sherri was unamused. Back in Port Richmond, with the engine ticking down, she'd twisted her hands on the customized steering wheel and stared through the windshield at the garage's pegboard wall. Did he know what it felt like, to get that call? Did he have any idea what had gone through her mind, in the gap before the nurses put him on the line? She didn't have to tell him, of course. Nor did she have to remind him that, with his condition, he could have filed for disability years ago. That his overlords at 1PP had set him up to fail; that he had no probable cause to search the house on East Third, or even to assume the Feds weren't backward on this. There was no way they knew his city better than he did, and the carrot-topped kid he'd chased up Second Ave. could easily have been the lone member, or a product of Pulaski's own need to believe. . . . When a minute had passed without Sherri saying anything, he realized it was his turn to speak. He suggested they call and see if the New Paltz place was still on the market. Then she was crying. "For Pete's sake, Larry. I don't want you to do this because I want you to. I want you to want to do it."

He peeled her hands off the wheel, cradled them between his awful claws. "I do want to do it," he said.

Now that he'd submitted the paperwork, he even found that it was true. Pulaski hadn't realized how twenty-five years of work could tax a body, or how restorative it could be to start boxing up an office. At the bottom went anything from the mounds of files he'd be taking with him. Next came the velveteen cases to which his special pens returned, disassembled, and his hardwood pipe. Then the pictures. Other people kept photos of their kids; Pulaski had Sherri and Pope Paul VI and his late mother. The last dozen boxes were for books. He'd amassed a substantial library over the years, through a mail-order service he kept forgetting to cancel. The Time-Life History series. It had been the uniform and color-coded spines that had first caught his eye when he'd seen the special trial offer in the back of the *TV Guide*. He'd been meaning to repopulate the built-in book-cases he'd inherited from the previous Deputy Inspector. You needed books, if only to remind the subordinates who would be the only people to see the inside of your office that you knew more than they did. Over the years, though, he'd discovered that he liked to read them, too. To be a cop at this late date in history was to be, by defi-nition, a nostalgist; beyond the big window at his back, the streets were humming, anarchic, yet still every morning he'd taken up badge and revolver, pledged to defend laws laid down mostly before he was born. And even as he should have been bundling them into boxes, he found himself wanting to linger over the books one last time, as if saying goodbye to the friends of his youth. *The Mughal Empire. Pagans of the British Isles.* Probably he was just tired.

But now the hum from the open window started to seem more like chanting. He used the edge of his desk to swivel himself in his chair. The view was unchanged—water towers and the strutwork of the bridge—but when he craned to the right, a column of tiny people was flowing into the pedestrian plaza below. Heads seemed to lift toward Pulaski's window. Distance blurred their chants, so he couldn't quite hear their demands. For weeks now, he knew, "Dr." Zig Zigler had been hectoring his listeners to reclaim their city, but to no effect—until today. And reclaim it from what, from chaos? Pulaski wanted to laugh. The protest itself was chaos, and anyway, it couldn't reach him now. Or was all this just, as he'd once imagined, the mask worn by some deeper order? Because just at the moment when Larry Pulaski was about to shut the window and finish packing, the phone began to ring.

79

SHE WAS OLDER BY THREE YEARS, but around the time when William's patchy memories had fused into the single, continuous individual now before him—which is to say, in the afterburn of their mother's death—he'd decided that Regan was in need of his protection. In the Park, where Doonie took them afternoons, he'd fought the other boys off no matter the game: Cops and Robbers, Cowboys and Indians, Peter Pan. A shrink might have had interesting things to say about this. There was, e.g., the possibility that the woman up there at the front of the fortieth-floor press room, lit up for the cameras, had in fact been *his* protector. But William believed that psychoanalysis was at best a collection of insights you could figure out on your own, and at worst hippie-dippie bullshit. It had been one of the reasons he'd felt so threatened by Mercer's attempt to get him help there at the end, he was remembering, when a flashbulb in the vicinity of his elbow saved him from having to remember any more. They'd reached the Q&A portion of the press conference, and though Regan's prepared statement had been perfectly straightforward, etiquette demanded that the reporters pretend they'd just been made privy to some shocking new development. A blond Ken doll with shoulder-length hair (had Daddy's standards slipped?) pointed into the crowd and then the clamor died and one of the reporters repeated his question. Cameras turned. Turned back. William knew of pawnshops where a news camera could have fetched several hundred bucks. But no, what interested him, psychologically speaking, was the sense of continuity itself, the mind's insistence that this was the same Regan he'd known when he was eight; had anything befallen her, the Regan he lost would have been the one who'd perched on the black rocks of the park back then, with all her futures inside.

His arm had started to tingle from being held aloft so long, or maybe it was just the last spasm of withdrawal, when the guy finally called on him. "Yeah. Freddy Engels. *Daily Worker*," William said. He made no effort to consult an imaginary steno pad. Just crossed his arms and leaned against the wall. "My readers want to know, how much money has the parent company already wasted on the defense, and will it lead to sail-trimming at the various subsidiaries?"

Regan squinted against the light. He was sure she recognized his voice, despite the fact that it was scratchy from vomiting. Siblings knew these things. There had been months in the past when he'd felt her fretting about him from afar. Years when he'd known she was dying inside. She covered the mic with her hand and whispered something to the man, like a mobster at a RICO hearing. The man leaned forward. "I think that will be all for the question and answer period." There was another perfunctory clamor, and the bursting of flashbulbs, and under cover of brightness, William ducked out into the hallway to wait.

The Hamilton-Sweeney Building, despite its height, dated to the dark ages before air-conditioning, and updates to this part of the floor looked unfinished. His great-grandfather had evidently subscribed to the idea that marble had cooling properties, but on days like this one, the dog-slaying, hydrant-bursting, power-sucking July days, marble seemed instead to trap the heat, and all the fans could do was blow it around. On a window-washer's platform outside an open window, a pair of birds did their best to avoid unnecessary motion, but when William went over to see what kind they were, they took wing, as if they knew better than he did what was in his heart. Swooping out over the parks and streets, Madison, Park, Lex, they achieved an improbable beauty. But around them rose high-rises that hadn't been here when he was a kid, thousands more people crammed into boxes, and off beyond that two towers wavering in the haze. It seemed impossible that mortals had built all this. Men would be the size of fruit flies up there, battering themselves against the locked heavens. More likely, thought William, the towers had been quarried whole out of granite, and somewhere in Vermont twin holes plunged a thousand feet into the bedrock.

Then his sister said behind him, "You've got some nerve. And you can't smoke in here." She tried to snatch the cigarette from him but he fended her off. Reporters spilled from the press room, breached the quiet. She waited for them to pass. "Honestly, William, it's like you just learned to walk around on your hind legs," she continued, when they were gone. "And you look like death warmed over. But you know what?" She put up her hands. "I'm not getting sucked into this again, after your whole tantrum of renunciation. I'm a busy person."

"I embarrass you."

"Don't pretend that's not exactly what you were trying to do just now."

You love it, he wanted to remind her. *You love me.* But she was already halfway to the elevator, and he wondered again if there was something wrong with his memory. He looked at her and still saw Princess Tiger Lily grateful for her rescuer, but apparently his refusal to grow up was no longer an asset. "I'm sorry," he said now.

"Like hell you are. You've never been sorry. That's the whole problem."

"About everything."

She turned to scrutinize his face, wondering what "everything" might mean. He wondered himself. Sometimes things just came out. "What is it you want, William? You wouldn't be here if you didn't want something."

Touché, he thought, as the elevator doors rolled back to reveal a plump woman in plaid who held a rubber plant. William would just as soon have waited for the next car, but Regan was already squeezing in on one side of her, so he took the other. Scratched steel gave back his reflection. Regan was right, he was no Valentino. He'd lost weight, and there were little red slits where his lips were cracking. He needed a shave. He didn't smell fantastic, either.

The plaza at the foot of the building bulged with humanity, women one-handing food from vendors while packs of jacketless young men checked them out. "You grabbing a late lunch?" he said. "Because this is perfect. You can take me, we can talk."

"If you wanted to talk, William, the time was four months ago. Things have gotten a little hectic since then. Or did you not hear the press conference?"

"It doesn't have to be lunch." He scanned again to make sure he wasn't being followed. "We could get coffee instead. Your treat."

"I don't have time for this. I have a life, you know. I'm meeting someone for dinner."

"Good for you. I always had my doubts about what's-his-name." He knew Keith's name, of course; it was only that he couldn't help himself. But as she turned away, a belated shame broke over him. This was where he'd been supposed to be by thirty, one of these janissaries of the corporate state. Instead, he'd spent much of the spring on the nod in his studio, surrounded by what most people would have called trash. Even now, three and a half weeks clean, he kept collecting whatever municipal signage might fit under his cot at the halfway house, and then smuggling it up to the Bronx. To persist in a project you know seems crazy: Did this mean you were crazy, or the opposite?

Just then, the woman from the elevator trundled over to a trashcan already overtopped with junk and deposited her rubber plant at the center. "Hey!" William bounded across the plaza, jostling his way past secretaries and bankers. "Hey! What are you doing?"

"It's dying," she said.

"Well, that's no reason to throw it away."

The woman shot him a look of purest contempt. He was formulating something nasty to say to her when his sister caught up with him. "Have you lost your mind?"

It had been Mercer's question, too, but Regan had a way of making him second-guess himself. He might even have apologized to the fat lady, had she not already melted into the glassy heat. "It's money, isn't it?" Regan said. "If it's money, just ask for money. Don't put me through this." You assumed whatever was vivid to yourself was vivid to others, and vice versa, but she was going to make him spell it out, for the first time in either of their lives.

"If you must know, Regan, what I came for is your help." Then he plucked the rubber plant from the trash and, with a great and beleaguered dignity, headed west. He didn't stop to see if she'd followed. Didn't stop, in fact, until he reached a bench under the dried-out sycamores behind the Forty-Second Street library.

"Fifteen minutes," she said, taking off her watch and setting it between him and the rubber plant. "That's all you get."

"I don't understand why you're so angry."

"What do you want me to say? Oh, thank God, my brother's finally decided he's ready to receive me? Life doesn't work like that, William. You don't get to just disappear for however many years and then come click your ruby slippers and make it all go away."

"Now you know how I felt when you showed up at my place that night."

"I wasn't the one who ran away!"

She was being obtuse on purpose, he thought. She'd known every time he'd come to a family dinner drunk or stoned, and had known almost before he'd known it himself that he was queer. So how could she not now see the hell he was going through? "Listen. I didn't mean that about Keith. I'm sorry you're having problems." He worked the edge of a scab of paint under a fingernail and tugged at it, thinking of needles probing his toes. "Maybe we're just fundamentally destined for unhappiness."

"I don't see the point in looking at things that way, William. It's adolescent."

He could feel his tongue swelling in his mouth, his knucklebones aching for that sweet relief he would never feel again. "I'm saying, when you look at this family, you're getting divorced, I'm thirty-three and my life is basically defunct . . . Sort of makes you wonder, is all."

"If this is what we deserve?"

"That's not what I mean, Jesus. If anything, the reverse. I mean no matter what you deserve, how far you run, your fate stays stuck to your heels." Her eyes were glistening, but for some reason he couldn't reach out and touch her. It was like some gestures were so simple they were beyond him. "Hey, stop feeling sorry for me for a second, okay?"

"It's not you I feel sorry for, jerk. Have you ever thought about what it would do to Daddy if something happened to you? What it would do to me?"

Everybody had to die sooner or later, he said. And Daddy would be relieved.

Apparently William didn't understand anything. *Anything.*

"Well, I'm glad to hear you say that," he said. "Because, as it happens, this thing I need your help with is that somebody's trying to kill me."

She sniffed. Smiled a little despite herself. "You always did have that effect on people."

"No, I'm serious." And he proceeded to tell her as much as he knew.

AFTER THOSE LATE-NIGHT PSYCH-OUTS on the streets of deepest Brooklyn and the one verifiable run-in in Times Square, William's stalker had taken up position somewhere near the border between waking life and dreams, which, given the amount of dope William was into at the time, were hard enough to tell apart anyway. All it took was someone unusually tall in his peripheral vision, a sense of moving shadow, and he'd feel sure the Specter—he'd taken the name from a comic he used to read—had tracked him down again. He'd spin around to find only a rustling tree, or a splash of shade in the shape of a face on a parked car's windshield. But then some friend or neighbor (to the extent that he still had any) would mention that a guy flashing a press credential had come around, asking about him by name. Or rather, by his handle.

One evening at the end of April, after a week or two of this, he was riding a near-empty train back uptown from Union Square when he spotted the Specter peering through the doors between cars. Or possibly another Specter, dressed similarly in a sportcoat and hat. In any case, this time, he was real. How had William known? The height, for one thing: that head rising to block the light. And the messy salt-and-pepper beard hiding the mouth. Most frightening, through the smeary glass, were the eyes. They were somehow too intelligent for this Specter to be a narc, as William had thought. Yet somehow swimmy, damaged. Remote. As if they'd already bored through to the obverse side of the canvas. And then he understood that this man had come to send him there. To kill him. A bell dinged. The subway doors slid back, or one of them did, its twin being stuck in place. The junk he'd sampled downtown had turned to lead in his veins. He could have sat there, let it consume him, and was even in some ways so inclined, but there must have been beneath all the dead weight something still alive in him, and when it spoke, it was in Mercer's voice: *Run.* As the communicating door racketed back he lurched through the narrow gap that placed him on the platform. He knew better than to look back.

Along the soot-dark tracks, up some stairs, and then left, down a corridor lined with movie posters. It was one of those weird hours in the transit system when the normal crowds disappeared, leaving behind only black pocks of gum and passageways that seemed to stretch out forever. Impossible to say whether it was his echoing footfalls that sent rats up ahead scurrying to their holes, or the sight of his Specter like a bad moon behind. Turning to check would only slow him down. Then his fingers were closing on the metal of the exit gate, which groaned into motion . . . and stopped. Thick loops of chain held the gate shut. His steps echoed all around.

He turned to defend himself. The Specter, halfway back along the flickering tunnel, held out his long hands, as one might to a badger backed into its hole. Particularly if one intended to soothe the badger just long enough to throttle it to death. William saw off to the side another exit gate, this one blessedly unchained. A downtown train was gathering force in a nearby tunnel, preparing to platform. He tried like hell to recall the layout of this station, but his brain was a block of cheese the rats had gnawed holes in. Or the junk that had promised to fill the holes had. He bolted, pushed through the turning gate and took the steps three at a time. At street level, he didn't check for traffic before crossing; a car skidded, horns blared, someone called him an asshole, and then he reached the far side of Eighth Avenue. Down the downtown stairs, grasping in his pocket, please, let there be a token. And then he heard the gasp of an incoming train that had stopped one level down. He shot down the passageway, a cramp knifing between his ribs. He almost lost his footing on the steps, but made it onto the very last car of the train, where two black-hatted Satmars eyed him skeptically. He willed the doors to work. Oh please oh please oh please. And with a bing, they closed. Opened. Closed.

The Specter had made the platform, thinner now than in memory—William could see his shapeless fedora through the train's rear window—but he was shrinking even further, until the blackness of the tunnel swallowed him.

THAT HAD BEEN AN EXPRESS TRAIN, William said, and he'd ridden it to the end of the line, too terrified to get off. He'd spent the night in a diner in Ozone Park, Queens, drinking refill after refill of coffee, watching the sun come up over the old textile factories. Mercer had been right. He didn't know how to live. But how had he ever convinced himself that it was anything else he wanted? That he wasn't terrified to die?

He hadn't planned to go into such detail about all this with Regan, or about how hard it turned out to be to get into rehab—it would have felt too much like he was trying to impress her—but once he got going, he couldn't stop. "It's true. Demand exceeds supply. You need four straight positive piss tests to get into the methadone program on Fourteenth Street, like to prove you've got a problem or something. But by the third or fourth day, I wouldn't have wanted to quit anymore. So I ended up going all the way out to Coney Island. I handed over my wallet and keys, they locked me in a rubber room for a week while they tried to get my dosage right. I know I should have been glad afterward, but what I felt was absolute grief. The first time they let me out unsupervised, I walked out to the beach and just lay down in the sand and cried. I don't know if I ever really stopped."

When he looked up, the color had drained from Regan's face. She was twenty years old again. "But what about these people you say want to kill you, William?"

"That's the thing, though," he said. "I got off the methadone in June, and I've been staying at this halfway house in Sheepshead Bay. But I still go up to my studio in the Bronx sometimes to drop off stuff I might want to use, if I ever start painting again. Then last night, I find this demolition notice on the door there. And it smacks me that the whole time I was strung out, feeling hunted, the entire neighborhood was being razed around me. As a Blight Zone." Regan crinkled her brow, like a judge hearing an argument. "Can't you see it's connected? The Liberty Heights development, that big fire in April, Daddy getting indicted, the hitman. And I think I know how to make it all stop. But this is where I need your help."

Then her voice was doing the thing it always did: "William, I don't see how I *can* help."

"Sure you do," he said. "You can get me in to see Daddy."

80

S INCE THAT FIRST TIME IN JANUARY, unbeknownst to anyone, or even almost to himself, Keith Lamplighter had been returning at least once a month to the plastic chair next to the hospital bed. He'd slip in first thing in the morning, before work, anxious to avoid being spotted; his habit of signing in under a fake name indicated what a terrible idea this was. Not coming, though, was not an option. It wasn't that he still expected Samantha to wake up, or that he even felt close to her anymore, but she was his responsibility, somehow, and these lonely vigils reached something in him that church wasn't able to: the very thing the old kook with the shopping cart had pressed on with an ectoplasmic finger.

Now he hunched forward and clasped his hands together and tried to locate the transformation he'd felt dawning in himself after that encounter—like a back door opening in a dream. *Déjala ir:* Go to her? Go *from* her? Was he supposed to say goodbye to Samantha before he could get Regan back? *Just tell me what to do,* he thought. No, wait. Maybe that was the problem, right there. For as long as he could remember, his first thought had been only for himself. He would try putting someone else first and see what happened. He scrunched his eyes and bore down on the still-inchoate thing inside him. *Show me how to help,* he was thinking, or murmuring—*Make me an instrument of your will*—when he heard the rattle of loose change behind the privacy curtain, where the bed, every previous visit, had been empty.

He feared Samantha's new roommate was having some kind of episode back there, but the emergency that greeted him when he pulled aside the curtain was a zitty kid in street-clothes, kicking off the sheets with his combat boots, some kind of implement in hand.

"Hey," Keith said.

The kid didn't have a bad face; beneath those pimples and the home-cut hair were features that posted feelings like a billboard. In this case, panic. He rolled off the bed, waved the thing in his hand around as if fending off demons, and darted toward the door. Keith, whose blocking reflexes had never really faded, moved to cut him off. Somewhat less pronounced were his skills as a wrestler, and so when he caught hold of an arm, sending the implement skittering across the floor, it was all he could do to keep the kid from going for it. "Hey! Calm down! Where's the fire?"

"What fire?" The kid wouldn't look at him.

"I'm saying, what's the big rush?"

"If you don't let go of me, I'll scream for security."

The kid squirmed free, but Keith reached the thing on the floor first. It was a switchblade handle, not even out of its sheath, black with a silver button. "Why should I worry about security? I'm not the one with a knife."

The kid went a shade paler. "It's for self-defense. I'm a friend of the patient's."

"Yeah? Me, too."

"So how come I never heard of you?"

"Or acquaintance, is maybe the better word." Now it was Keith's turn to squirm a little. "You know what? I was just going to get food, so why don't you stay here and visit? I insist."

Hanging on to the kid's weapon made this an easier sell than it might otherwise have been. He barricaded the door with his body until the kid had slunk back to the plastic visitor's chair by Samantha's bed. But something wasn't right here—not least what happened when he tested the button on the blade. Keeping one eye on the room to make sure the kid didn't leave, Keith stole over to the nurse's station, temporarily vacant, and picked up the phone. There was no reason, really, for him to be carrying around the battered business card the reporter had pressed on him in February—to use it would be to acknowledge the role he'd played in Samantha's life. But maybe he'd just been waiting for the right moment to give himself up. For now he dialed the printed number and prayed someone would answer, so that he could inform DEPUTY INSPECTOR LAWRENCE J. PULASKI, whoever he was, that there was someone here he might be awfully interested to meet . . .

81

THE FELLOW ON THE PHONE insisted on giving his name, but it wasn't easy to hear, what with the cowbells and whistles, the tattoo of war drums outside. And though Pulaski could always have closed the window, the sound seemed to forbid it. He swiveled his chair into the slab of hot sun. Applied a thumb to one eyelid, an index finger to the other. Lamplighter. Lamplighter? "Do I know who that is?" Probably not, the caller admitted. But he was standing right now on the intensive care ward at Beth Israel Hospital, where he'd apprehended someone who might be of interest. And boom, there it was, Beth Israel. This wasn't going to be one of your catch-and-release-type herrings, the palm-reader's revelation, the suspicious van seen miles from any crime. Moreover: "Apprehended, did you say?"

Well, not exactly, the caller conceded, but he was standing *right outside* the Cicciaro girl's room, which is where he'd stumbled upon a youth in hiding.

There was an electric squeal below, like metal on slate. Pulaski recognized it (with some satisfaction at how this would sit with the Deputy Commish) as a megaphone. The marchers had brought a megaphone. Next they'd be issuing demands. The whole seething mass seemed to hold its breath. "A youth?"

"Like a teenager. A boy."

Pulaski squeezed again. "You want to describe him for me, please?"

The man on the phone saw like a man, with no real eye for detail, but each nudge—height? weight? complexion?—yielded more specifics, until the ellipses of unnamable color behind Pulaski's eyelids became a greasy face framed by wrought iron. A head of red hair he'd seen last week on Second Avenue. "There's really something fishy about this kid," the caller concluded. "He had what looks like a knife."

There's something fishy about you having my direct dial, Pulaski thought, but this was coming at him too fast to stand on a protocol that in a week or two would no longer apply anyway. "All right. I'll send someone over to bring the kid in for questioning. Meantime, try to make sure he stays put, would you? Buy him a Coke, call the guards, whatever. But Mr. Lamplighter—Lamplighter? Don't get yourself hurt."

Waves of percussion were swelling once more in the plaza below, and in the second before opening his eyes, Pulaski felt the strange serenity a fisherman must feel, sucked out to sea. He picked up the receiver again and ordered the girl on the switchboard to patch him through to the Thirteenth Precinct. From there, he scrambled a squad car to the hospital to bring in not only the boy, ASAP, but also the man who'd called. Then he lowered his face to the desk. *What are you doing?* Sherri would have asked. Letting himself slide back into some sort of mirror image, was what. Identical to his real life in every respect, only reversed, and minus a crucial dimension. Or maybe two, for hardly had his forehead touched the blotter when the intercom erupted at his ear. "Sir? You have visitors."

"You can send them on back."

Rallying, he watched the door for the first sign of the boy from the churchyard. What appeared instead was a Negro it took him a second to recognize. And, back in the shadows where the light had burned out, a small Oriental girl. Young woman, he was supposed to say. "It's madness out there," said Mercer Goodman. "I hope this isn't a bad time. But you said on New Year's, if anything should come to me . . ."

As at other moments of stupefaction, Pulaski's instincts were what saved him. "Don't worry about it," he said, motioning them in. "Or about the mess." It seemed unlike the Goodman kid to charge in first, but then, it had been months. The girl looked less sure of herself, picking her way through the maze of open-topped boxes. Attractive, though, in the casually androgynous way of women of her generation. Pageboy, bluejeans, a man's white Oxford shirt buttoned to the wrist, a folder under one arm—*she* was what had come to Goodman, it seemed. Once upon a time Pulaski would have welcomed any new leads. The question now was whether, already one deviation away from his plan for the day, he could afford them. "Please, sit." He'd have stood to help them move chairs but felt an urge to keep the girl from seeing his infirmity. "I'm in the middle of a few things, as you can see, but who's your friend here?"

"This is Jenny Nguyen. You have a mutual connection, we think." He waited. "Richard Groskoph?"

But that was the *last* name Pulaski wanted to hear! Give him Cicciaro, give him more on the boy . . . No, steady; keep control. "You were colleagues?" A guess, from her clothes.

"Neighbors," she said quietly. "I inherited his dog, and some papers."

Awful close for neighbors, then. Pulaski pulled an ancient cancerstick from his center drawer and tapped the filter against the desk. He'd switched to the pipe long ago, but found cigarettes handy for staying in character, or building rapport. Or pausing to strategize. "I first knew Richard back when he was a beat reporter, and even then it was plain he was going places. One minute, you'd be picking out songs on the juke, the next you'd be telling him about some goldfish that died on you when you were thirteen. He was a past master at opening people up." He addressed all this to Goodman mostly for the purpose of getting a better read on the girl. Once she'd softened a little, he turned to her. "I can't tell you how sorry I was to hear what happened."

Too soon, though; she was instantly back on guard. "This isn't a condolence call."

"We're here because we need your help," said Goodman. "He was writing something about the girl from the park New Year's Eve—"

Of course, Pulaski thought. *They* needed *his* help. "—and ended up collaborating with the aspiring novelist who found her there, I suppose? After swearing he'd leave the shooting alone?" What galled him most was the presumption of these writer types, as if there weren't actual people in the world, with jobs to do, appointments to keep, wives to appease, but only so much material. "I hope you're bringing me the name of the shooter, because if all you two are doing is carrying on the Groskoph torch, I'm afraid we're wasting each other's time. An open case isn't something I'm free to discuss. As Richard well knew."

"So you wouldn't want to see this draft of his article?" The girl brandished the folder she'd been holding. "And you must have already heard about Mercer's boyfriend."

"Roommate," Goodman corrected her, with a pained look.

She ignored him, setting the folder on the edge of Pulaski's desk, almost daring him not to reach for it. "Word on the street is, your victim was running with some bad people."

"That particular wild goose has been chased. The Post-Whosits. Tell me something I don't know."

"How about that the same people are now coming after Mercer's boyfriend? Sorry. Roommate. William. He moved out in March, after a fight, and has been missing ever since."

Now Goodman ignored the correction. "I know, it sounded nuts to me, too," he said, "but then I saw them. Men disguised as electricians, staking out our apartment. Or one man, at least."

"What makes you think these so-called bad men haven't caught up to your roommate already?"

"This was just this morning. I saw them with my own eyes."

The sheaf of pages before Pulaski seemed to tremble. A vision of underground connections flashed before him again, only inverted. A towering construction like a tree strung with lights, shimmering, changing, and in the middle, a darkness—the object or concept holding the visible together. But more likely that was the stomp of protesters in the plaza making the whole building shake. Anyway, these two sounded like druggies. What could the boyfriend, roommate, William Wilcox or whoever (his notes from the Goodman interview were in one of these boxes) possibly have to do with Samantha Cicciaro? In the street below, someone was exploring the megaphone's repertoire of built-in noises, its whoops and low groans. "Miss Nguyen, Mr. Goodman. Maybe if you'd brought this to me before the middle of July—"

And now inside and outside began to blur, as if the cacophony were not in the street, but in the hall outside his door. "It's not until the middle of July that someone breaks in and tries to torch my apartment! Did I mention that part? They had to be after the article, or maybe the 'zines."

"What's a 'zine? Look, I'm sorry you had to go through whatever it is you went through, but you're in Homicide, folks. If you feel better leaving this with me, I'll have someone from Burglary follow up . . ."

She was quicker than he was, though, and snatched the folder back. "Hell, no."

"This is how the system works. You take a number, you get on line."

"Seems like there are some pissed-off New Yorkers out there who are starting to doubt the system does work." A spine of steel, this one. On another day, he might have admired it. "You can find people, can't you?" she said. "So you're going to help us find William. We're going to make sure no one else gets killed."

But he had a spine of his own, however crooked. "Would you listen to yourselves? Disguises? Out to get people? And who's been killed? The Cicciaro girl is still alive."

"Can't you see it? Richard, is your answer. It's obvious he was . . ." She couldn't finish the sentence, but for a second Pulaski glimpsed under all her anger, her willfulness, the raw need to believe. And maybe could even relate. Did he have things backward himself?

"I suppose I might have a few minutes. I'll take a quick look at his article before my next appointment, how's that?" She loosened her grip on the folder. He sank back and opened it, trying to pretend there was no audience. The first thing to hit him was the absence of typos. He'd forgotten what a natural Richard had been, back when his column was coming out weekly. How lucid, how sure of himself. Though possibly too much so. Still, Pulaski felt vindicated, and also disappointed; for a dozen pages or more, "The Fireworkers" could have been one of his Time-Life books, rambling on about pyrotechnics, China, Marco Polo . . . Where were these two getting their homicidal conspiracy? And how had he nearly fallen for it, even for a second? Was that how badly he needed to escape?

A cough made him glance up. The noise had entered the building after all, for here at the door stood a uniformed officer, looking puzzled. "Sir? I've got these folks you asked for?" Just beyond was a man in a tailored jacket. And there to the left, looking glumly at his handcuffs, was the kid whose red hair, and whatever else, Pulaski had almost forgotten. "You want me to take them to the box?"

Pulaski closed the folder. "No, in here's fine for both."

The officer sat his charge down roughly in the one remaining chair. But before Pulaski could find a respectful way to tell the other two to take a hike, the boy looked up and blanched. "Hey! What the hell are *you* doing here?"

82

A ND SUDDENLY THEY WERE ALL AROUND HIM, crowding him, like kids at school, so he couldn't breathe, and he almost expected them to start pounding fists into palms, chanting, *Fight! Fight!* except he wasn't sure who'd do the fighting. There was the lying jock in the jacket, that asshole, whom Charlie would have welcomed a crack at, even if it would only earn him a shiner, and there was the beat cop who'd driven them both here from the hospital. There was the little hermit crab of a plainclothesman. There was Billy Three-Sticks's boyfriend and next to him the lady, looking somehow uncomfortable. Then the hermit crab found room to scuttle forward, and the leather-backed shield at his waist was right up in Charlie's face. "What is *who* doing here, kid?"

Crap. It had just slipped out. Charlie's blood was still up from the throng they'd passed through downstairs, and from trying to wriggle away in the reception area (hence the cuffs). But now it was a game of Think Fast. Explaining he meant the black guy—that would out him as a Peeping Tom. Then again, admitting he recognized the Asian lady from a picture in that apartment yesterday would expose his complicity in arson. Nope, if there was an answer that would keep him out of juvie, it was the crustacean himself, with whom he'd been eye-to-eye just last week, in the East Village. "You," Charlie said. "I meant you."

"It's my office. Of course I'm going to be here."

Before Charlie could respond to this, the man was rising to receive an object, the blade folded in its sheath. "That's courtesy of your informant," the beat cop told him. "Says he got it off the boy. You'll want to take a look, sir."

Charlie tried to appear unperturbed, but having his hands behind his back made it hard to sit up straight, forcing him into a parody of deformity. If this turned into a full-blown asthma attack, he'd really be screwed. He heard the underling clear his throat. "Uh, sir? Dispatch says for crowd control it's all uniforms on deck downstairs. Should I ask if they can spare a couple Homicide guys?"

His superior reached some decision. "I think under the circumstances I can handle things from here."

"Yes, sir." And there went one of the five. So why didn't Charlie feel 20 percent more at ease? Because the hermit crab was bending down again. His face, which had seemed merely weathered, now had gullies and canyons. "Look here, son. Do you know who I am?"

"Sure." Charlie's voice chose that moment to crack; it came out as puling. "You're a pig."

The cop's smile never wavered. "And what does that make you?"

"Scared stiff, obviously," the lady said, from somewhere behind him. "Why don't you give him breathing room, for crying out loud? And are the handcuffs really necessary?"

Charlie started to protest that he'd never been less scared in his life, but to his relief the three men were drawing back, insofar as there was any space to draw back into. The office, half-packed, was no bigger than a penalty box.

"He said in the car his name was Daniel," said the Asshole.

"No I didn't," Charlie lied, to spite him. "My name's Charlie."

"Okay, but who *are* you, Charlie? The name doesn't tell us much. For example, I'm Larry Pulaski, but I'm also a Deputy Inspector with the NYPD. Meaning I'm here to solve crimes."

"This is still America," Charlie said. "I don't have to tell you anything."

The Asshole had seemed agitated before, with an eye toward the window and the protest outside, but now he gathered himself. "Speaking of which, Inspector Pulaski, you forgot to mention on the phone that you were planning to drag me all the way down here."

"It's a formality. I'm sure this won't take long." Pulaski seemed to see the man as a diversion from his prime object. But wasn't it worth asking, just in terms of crime-solving, what had brought this Asshole to Sam's hospital room to begin with? Charlie would have asked it himself, but he didn't believe in ratting out even his enemies.

"It may be a formality, Inspector, but I was supposed to pick my kids up from day camp by three thirty. They'll think something happened to me."

"Something must have. It was past four when you rang me from the hospital."

The man reddened, but pressed on. "I lost track of time. Is that an arrestable offense?"

"No one's talking about arrest."

"Good. Because you have my name, I'm clearly more than happy to talk all you want later, but right now, I'm leaving to go get my kids. The little one's six years old."

Charlie tried to form a thought-beam. *Say no. Make him take some heat, too.* But Pulaski just asked how he could be reached. The man fumbled in his suitcoat, came up with a card. While the black guy and the Asian lady looked on, Pulaski studied it. "Expect to hear from someone tomorrow. Until then, I suppose I can't keep you."

Unbelievable! If Charlie had a business card, would he be sent waltzing out of here with no further questions? No, because he wouldn't be able to reach it; his fucking hands were still locked behind his back.

Pulaski tapped the card on the desk, considering. "I might as well make some introductions. Charlie, this is Miss Nguyen—"

"Can't you at least get him some water or something?"

"—and this is Mr. Goodman, who found the girl on New Year's Eve."

He *what?* Charlie couldn't help but jolt upright. But it was impossible to match the black guy, this weary post-teen, to the form hunched next to Sam in the snow, waiting for the cops to arrive. And when he turned back to the desk, Pulaski was braced against it, with a look like he knew everything that had happened to Charlie since. He put a hand on the folder beside him. Files on the PHP? Oddly, the thought was calming. What Nicky had been preparing all these months would be revealed to the Prophet Charlie at last. And no one would be able to blame him for anything.

"So now that you're up to speed," Pulaski said, "I do need to ask you some things, Charlie. Starting with Samantha Cicciaro. You knew her, didn't you?"

Being honest couldn't make Charlie look any worse, for once. "She was my best friend."

And did he know who shot her? Pulaski asked.

This was probably supposed to make him feel panicky again. Still, the answer was no.

"All right, changing gears then. Take a good look at these two." Was he sure he'd never seen Miss Nguyen or Mr. Goodman before? "And does the name Richard Groskoph mean anything to you?"

The black guy spoke up: "Are we ever going to get back to William?"

But these were the wrong questions! Nothing about Liberty Heights, nothing about two sevens clashing or Post-Humanism or the little house out back. Inspector Pulaski, so powerful five minutes ago, didn't even seem to be on the right case! "Look, like I told your guy, I was just visiting my friend at the hospital, and that's all I have to say. If you're going to keep me, I hear it has to be for something. So . . ."

"How about possession of a banned weapon? Would that work?" asked Pulaski, whose omniscience, it was now clear, was limited to ways of torturing Charlie.

"This is bogus. You wouldn't be doing this if I was some rich asshole. Don't I have the right to an attorney?"

Pulaski weighed the sheath in his palm. "Are you aware that concealing a blade longer than three inches is illegal in the State of New York?"

"You're bluffing."

"See, this is what I'm talking about"—the woman had jumped in again—"people running around with switchblades."

"Now where did I pack my measuring tape . . ."

But when Pulaski pressed the button on the blade, it might as well have lopped off a finger, is how surprised they all looked. What popped out was not a knife, but a black plastic comb too cheap to actually use. And at that moment, Charlie felt as far from understanding as he'd ever been in his life. It was right up there with finding Sam, or burying Dad. For what if he really had needed the blade to stop someone, not some jerk in a business suit, but someone actually capable of . . . But come on, how blind can you be? The person he'd needed to stop all along was Nicky. He'd been telling himself the PHP's violence was purely a means, but this comb, in its very uselessness, seemed to throw into final relief the question of *ends*. Like, what if Nicky's fantasies had been leading someplace so dangerous he didn't trust even his closest allies to follow him there? And what if, on the last point at least, he was right?

Charlie turned to the lady. "Can I just say that I'm sorry?"

"Sorry for what?"

"I know that was your apartment we were in yesterday. I saw your picture on the fridge."

"You little punk!" But then she turned to Pulaski. "See? I knew it wasn't an ordinary burglary."

"Right," Pulaski said. "Like you knew this was a knife."

Charlie pretended not to hear. "It wasn't my idea to set the fire or anything."

"—But in fact that's not entirely true," she went on. "You guys did take something."

"I didn't take anything, lady. I saved your dog. The fire was all Nicky."

She cocked her head. "Also known as Iggy, right? The manuscript uses both. 'NC' stands for Nicky?"

"Um, sure, I guess. Nicky Chaos."

"Whoa." She held up a hand. "Hang on. This is Captain Chaos, the wannabe artist?"

Another fatal blurt—was he officially a rodent yet?

"Jenny, you're talking about someone who played in William's band," the black guy said. "Why on earth would he be mixed up in a plot to kill his bandmate?"

Kill his bandmate? The lady now came over and grabbed an armrest. Squatted before Charlie. She wore a cheap black digital watch, and was really very pretty, though tired. "This is serious, Charlie. I understand you're devastated about your friend . . ." But it was a ploy; he'd read *Penthouse Forum*, he knew what went on. She would get him alone and she would tell him she was terribly sorry for him and attracted to him and offer to suck his penis if he would do the right thing. And the hell of it was he would probably tell her everything he knew. Which was still next to nothing. He got up and sort of limped to the window. No one stopped him. There were reactionaries teeming antlike below. The river beyond, dying as the sun did. A blaze of red on the bridge's wires, threatening to remind him of something, but the height had him too scared to think.

Pulaski, quizzical, was flipping through the folder on his desk, but the black guy interrupted him. "No, no, you've got to start after the pictures. The stuff about Billy Three-Sticks doesn't come until the end."

Pulaski flipped again, eyes racing ahead, and then, on one of the last pages, stopped. "Okay, at this point I'm really lost." As was Charlie— lost, sleep-deprived, angry, and ashamed. But Pulaski seemed to be referring to the passage beneath his index finger. "The initials 'NC' could certainly point in a lot of directions, Nervous Charlie comes to mind, Not Credible, but what about this Demon Brother character? He's a Hamilton-Sweeney?"

"*William* is a Hamilton-Sweeney," the black guy said.

The lights dimmed briefly, but no one noticed. Not even Charlie, tripping over all the crossing wires. He was thinking now of pictures. Of missing eyebrows and maimed fingertips, stolen clocks. Smelling a chemical smell that had been there all along. Holy shit, was he slow. "No," he heard himself say. "The Demon Brother is Nicky's weapon. The Demon Brother is a bomb."

There was a pause. Another flicker. From the black guy, a groan. Then Pulaski said, "Nice try, kid, but I'm buying exactly none of this. If you were out to kill Mr. Goodman's friend, you'd shoot him. Or stab him, as Miss Nguyen would have it."

It was unclear if the lady heard, or cared. "You're making yourself so hard to believe, Charlie, you have to see that. Captain Chaos has a bomb?"

He did his best. "The, uh, detonation must have been planned for 7/7, I think, except for some reason it got pushed back a week."

"Well, that's just peachy. A week like 'I'll call you next week,' or a week like seven days?"

"How should I know?"

"You see what I'm saying?" Pulaski said. "A murder plot, a bomb threat, and he can't even improvise a date."

The lady ignored him. "Because seven days from 7/7 would be 7/14. Which is tomorrow."

"Or a few hours from now," the black guy said.

"Okay, fine, midnight," said Jenny Nguyen. "We can still alert the cavalry, Charlie, if you just say where they're going to put it."

He looked from face to face. To Pulaski's doubtful face. And wondered at that moment if even his own face looked convinced. It was a curse, being stuck in here like this. Because honestly, he had no clue.

83

REGAN HAD PASSED THE HUGE COLOR-FIELD PAINTINGS here and in the Hamilton-Sweeney Building so many times they'd become simply a part of her mental furniture. But it said something about her brother (or about her understanding of him) that of all the things he'd had to renounce years ago, in that act of pride disguised as loyalty, the matched set of Rothkos had probably been the hardest for him to leave behind. She was halfway across the foyer when she saw he'd lagged behind to gape. "Are you coming?" she asked.

"Just give me a second."

She stopped by a small window with a western view. The sun was low and huge, as if it had come to engulf New Jersey. No wonder it was so hot. "William!"

"Right behind you."

As she turned to verify this, their voices dislodged a nut-brown woman from an adjacent hallway. Regan didn't recognize her, nor did she seem to recognize Regan. But this was nothing new; Felicia had trouble hanging on to help. Asked about Daddy, the woman looked puzzled. "Daddy?"

"My father."

"Mr. Ham?"

After some further negotiations, the woman led the way to the second floor and down a long corridor. It, too, seemed lifeless, but from the doorway at the far end leaked a trickle of voices. Regan was surprised to discover that one of them was her own. A large wooden television set had been dragged to the center of the defoliated library and connected to the wall by means of an extension cord. It was currently rebroadcasting the press conference from earlier today. Beyond it, in an armchair someone had pulled to the visitor's side of the desk, her father sat in Bermuda shorts. Violet varicosities chased one another down his bluewhite legs. On one foot was a canvas deck shoe. The other was bare. The smell was aftershave bordering on gin. But what time was it? Surely the news would be over by now. "Daddy, what is this?"

"Regan? I was just watching you." He patted the arm of his chair, as if she were still small enough to climb onto it. "You certainly know what you're about, dear. Kept those bastards on their heels."

She knelt on the rug in front of him and reached for his hands and tried to recall the last time she'd heard him curse. "Where is everybody? Where is your wife? You shouldn't be drinking on top of your medicine, you know that." Somewhere behind these concerns was an awareness that William hadn't caught up to her, and that there was still time to prep Daddy for his reappearance. Unless it was William who needed prepping. How much a person could change, even in a couple months. . . . "You understand what we did today, right?"

"Oh, yes," he said. "Amory was just explaining everything." His eyes hadn't left the television. Had he started hallucinating, on top of everything else?

"Amory isn't here, Daddy."

He blinked once or twice, as if roused from a dream, and turned and looked at the desk, the chair behind it, empty except for a video-tape machine Regan thought she'd seen once at the production office where Café El Bandito commercials were edited. There was a momentary stutter in the picture. "Perhaps he's gone to fetch my luggage. Felicia went down to open the summer place yesterday, after the latest envelope arrived from our lawyers. It's a good idea that I be there these next few weeks while the state comes up with a better offer, don't you think?"

"Where?"

"Block Island."

"Is that what they told you? That there would be a better offer?"

"But Regan, you could come, too! You and Cate and . . ."

"Will," she said, but he was lost again in TV. The French doors had been left open to let air in from outside. She moved toward the balcony half-expecting to see the tiny imago of her brother seventeen stories down, falling back to Columbus Avenue, having at the last minute changed his mind. Away and to the north, a few late planes or early stars glimmered inches off the horizon. The view would have been much the same from her living room in Brooklyn, where she should even now have been setting out the cheese plate, watching Andrew West peel the foil from a bottle of wine. A phone somewhere rang. Stopped. If this dragged on much longer, she'd have to call him to cancel. Then she listened, a deep listening that stretched to the farthest corners of the apartment, and down into the chasms of herself, where all was still. "Daddy?" How to break this to him. How to let a thing be broken. "I'm not here alone."

"You brought Keith? Now there's a young man I'd like to have a word with."

She wished the gin she smelled were actually at hand. "Daddy, please—"

But there was a commotion from the interior of the apartment, loud enough to be heard over the television. "You stay here," she said. "I'm going to see what it is." She stepped through the eastern doors and onto the interior balcony that ran three sides of the reception hall. Without the several hundred people the room was meant to hold, it looked barren. One of the wet bars from New Year's remained, however, and Amory Gould was standing behind it in an open-collared shirt. Or circling it, actually, highball glass in hand. Opposite him, also circling, was an unkempt figure brandishing a fireplace tool. Amory looked up at her. "My dear! Perfect timing! We were just about to have a drink!"

If he meant to create a diversion, it hadn't worked. "You are the motherfucking devil," the figure said, distinctly. But whatever came next was lost, because Daddy had appeared at her elbow to ask who that man was down there.

"It's Amory," she said, blushing. "You were right."

"No, the hobo," he said.

"That's what I've been trying to tell you," she said. "That's William, Daddy. That down there is your son."

84

FIRST THE BOY WAS BLURTING THAT THERE WAS A BOMB; next he was claiming not to know where it was. But how, Jenny thought, could he not know, when her entire life had been leading toward this moment? Was it even possible to make this stuff up on the fly? Then the detective, who must have seen the look on her face, spoke up Solomonically. While it would have been nice to get a location for this suspect device, he said—easier that way to show the whole thing was a sham—Charlie had screwed up; the moment you mentioned a bomb, you obliged police to run down every last lead you'd given them. And the kid had already given a lot. With the protest breaking up downstairs, there'd be plenty of extra manpower to redeploy to the East Village, where Charlie had been observed last week. "If there's something to turn up, we'll turn it up. I'll send a whole phalanx over to serve a warrant on his crash-pad, bring in anyone else we find."

"What makes you think they'd talk to you?" the boy said.

Pulaski seemed well-meaning, as cops went, but she thought she sensed some minute adjustment of persona. "Charlie, not all of my colleagues are as patient as I've been with you today."

"I'll drink to that," mumbled Mercer, dejected.

Well, if the poor guy wasn't going to keep pushing, Jenny would; her own patience was long since shot. "I'm glad you're taking some part of this seriously," she told the detective. "But what about William Hamilton-Sweeney?"

"Who's William Hamilton-Sweeney?" the boy asked.

"William Hamilton-Sweeney is Billy Three-Sticks."

"*Oy.*" His head hit his hands.

"Well, that explains your being at the gala," the detective said to Mercer. "But your friend's a separate issue. The kid's confabulating."

"I am not. There's a bomb out there. Why won't you listen?"

I'm trying, Jenny thought. *You're giving me nothing.* Yet around the boy remained a nebulous urgency only she seemed to feel. Out loud, she said: "Can we not walk and chew gum here? William's still at large."

"I'll put in a word with Missing Persons"—Pulaski pointedly continued to address Mercer—"but I can't say they're known for speed. It's a big city. That's if this William of yours isn't just on vacation. The bright side is, in the unlikely event someone did have it in for him, they wouldn't be able to find him either. Did you try the family, on Central Park West? I'm sure our switchboard could run down a number."

"William loathed his family," Mercer said. "With cause." The lights crapped out for a second.

"Reminds me of an old line they drummed into us at the academy, though. When you're investigating a woman, look for whoever loved her, when it's a man, hatred works just as well. And who'd be more worried if William Hamilton-Sweeney went missing? All drama aside, experience suggests anyone who was watching his old apartment would be working for the family. They may at least have some more recent whereabouts."

"So why don't *you* call the Hamilton-Sweeneys?" Jenny said. "You're the detective."

"Was the detective. My retirement comes through in the next couple weeks. Burning up resources on this other thing makes me look bad enough. I get tangled in the politics of the ultra-rich, they'll probably keep me here forever, as punishment. Here, I've got a phone." After a back-and-forth with the switchboard, he handed Mercer the receiver. Charlie had devolved into whimpers of frustration. Mercer waited to be connected.

"No one's picking up."

"Maybe you can try again later. But right now I've got to start in on my due diligence with Charlie here, so you folks are going to have to get out of my hair."

"We do have the car," Jenny found herself telling Mercer. "I guess I could drive you up there to talk to the Hamilton-Sweeneys."

"Perfect," Pulaski said, but it sounded to her ears like *whatever.* And as Mercer passed into the hall, she realized the folder was still on the desk.

"Don't you want us to stick around?"

"If I have questions after a more thorough read, I know where Mercer lives. But I must have been crazy in the first place to have you two in the same room with the kid. So unless there's something else on your mind . . ."

Jenny lingered in the doorway. The lonely boy looked up at her, then sank down even deeper into himself.

"Miss Nguyen?" the cop said.

"Oh, forget it," Jenny said, because as long as Pulaski was responding with the full force of his office, who cared whether he was convinced of the threat?

The reasoning held while she followed Mercer out to the elevator bank, and (on second thought) down the stairs, and really right up to the moment she and Mercer stepped out of the building. But then her misgivings returned, redoubled, coalesced: the demonstration. Far from breaking up, it had spread to fill all available space. It was like a Kafka thing she'd read in college, a lone courtier entrusted with a dying king's message, an empire too crowded to move through. The leading edge of the mass, pushing toward the line of cops at the doors, swept her forward and away. She thought guiltily about her own message, abandoned in that office, and the little seam between the two halves of the article—fuck, she should have remembered this earlier—but she was halfway across the plaza now, and it was getting harder and harder to go back. And that wasn't even really the problem. The problem was that without a receiver, no message existed. Pulaski wasn't stupid, he would see the overlaps with the boy's story even if she didn't point them out, but he would fit them to a reality that still came in discrete packages. Hell, who knew but that five stories up, those boxes still held. There had been a theft and then a shooting, that was clear. But what she'd seen in the folder, what had scared her so much in the first place, was what it couldn't quite contain: a disturbance to the universe so vast as to connect Samantha Cicciaro and William Hamilton-Sweeney. A rupture so large it had already swallowed three lives. And which of these pictures fit the reality surrounding her now, the awakening, the human mess, the sea of flesh that would still be keeping Pulaski's extra manpower busy at eleven p.m., or later? It had churned to a halt with half the plaza still before her, plus, beyond an archway through a building, the streets. These seemed to be the facts: out there somewhere was however much stolen gunpowder, ready to blow a hole commensurate with this madness. And she would be stuck here waiting. She could see people near the arch hoisting speakers onto stands, but what was left to want anymore? Then, as if in response, came a squeal, and an echo, and a voice she'd almost forgotten, looping obsessively back:

—but when are you going to get over yourself, New York? How can I make you see? I know I shouldn't be yelling in a crowded theater, but really, where's the fire? The hour's late, the odds are long, the patient's on life support . . . and if anyone's going to pull us through, it's going to have to be you. You longtime listeners, you first-time callers, you pussies—you need to come out by the thousands, by the tens of thousands, and go right to the source of the disease. You need to say, "This is my city. My city, goddammit." And you're going to have to act to take it back.

85

FIVE FLOORS UP, Pulaski steered the kid down a hall and across an open-plan bullpen. This proved tricky with the crutches, and with the file-folder rolled in his pocket, but the handcuffs cinched at the kid's back helped. His colleagues per usual seemed not to notice. They sat at cubicles, typing in shirtsleeves, or clumped at windows trying to dig the action in the plaza through the gathering dark. Well, that was fine. He'd be needing them shortly, when six or eight got sent over to East Third Street, laughing their keisters off at Pulaski's swan song, his last Overtime Special. They'd never understood you can't be too careful. But right now, he and Charlie were going to have a little heart-to-heart, and he needed to apply the kind of pressure no one, not even Pulaski himself, believed him capable of anymore. His instinct remained that this patter about villains and explosions was just an attempt to distract him. About the part that concerned Pulaski—about Samantha Cicciaro—he still felt jerked around. "Aren't you going to say something?" the kid asked, as the elevator doors closed. "Or I get it. You're giving me the silent treatment."

"I'm not giving the silent treatment," Pulaski said. "I'm thinking what to do with you."

"With me? I'm telling you, my friends have a bomb. Somebody could get hurt."

"There's nothing to be done right now that can't be done more efficiently when that crowd in front thins out." The doors peeled back to reveal the concrete basement called Temporary Holding. He frog-marched the kid past the phone another cop would ordinarily have been manning, and then the open-air pens where arrestees palavered. A couple of them obliged Pulaski by making smooching noises in the kid's direction. "You ever see the inside of a cell, Charlie?" Pulaski propelled him into an empty pen a ways off from the others and onto a concrete bench and went to shut the door. You could feel the pulse of the crowd up in the plaza, but only through cinderblock and who knew how many feet of schist. Pulaski had always found it comforting down here. Even the lights were in cages. "Now sit and soak in the ambiance, while I give this thing another look." The kid tried with his cuffed hands to work something free from a pocket, but it landed out of reach. An albuterol inhaler. Pulaski, ignoring it, lowered himself to another bench and took out the manuscript, opened to the page the pictures had been clipped to like a bookmark, halfway through. Okay, he could see here the bit that might have Miss Nguyen a little on edge, inclined at first to fall for the kid's shenanigans. Someone up there clearly didn't want him to finish, though, because the lights kept cutting out, so that reading was an instant headache. This whole day was an instant headache. And now he was late for dinner. But forget it. He knew what he was after. He stooped painfully to pick up the inhaler and then held it inches from the kid, like a carrot before a horse. "Charlie, who shot Samantha?"

"You asked me that already. You don't listen when I say there's a bomb, but when it comes to Sam I'm all-knowing?"

"You're the missing link. East Third Street, the girl—" He enumerated on cramped fingers. "If I could put you at the crime scene, I'd say you shot her yourself."

The boy's face was hot. "You take that back!"

"You ever hear of William of Occam, Charlie? He had only one tool in his kit, but it's a doozy. And I'm going to tell you what it says. It says you've been living in that house all by yourself. It says there's no such person as Captain Chaos. Or else you're Captain Chaos. You keep turning up, kid. You and you alone."

"Maybe someone wants me to keep turning up, did you ever think about that?"

And the lights in their cages began to flicker faster. On off on. Off for several seconds—on again. It was the darnedest thing.

"You really believe in this stuff, don't you, Charlie?"

"Hell, that's probably one of them now, coming to take me out."

86

TO BE HONEST, William had forgotten about the Rothkos. And even if he hadn't, he would have imagined (hoped?) their painful associations would have driven Daddy to sell them, or bury them under a dropcloth somewhere in the bowels of the Hamilton-Sweeney Building. Instead, the blue one was the first thing he saw when he stepped off the elevator. It alone might have been enough to send him running back downtown, had he not also forgotten another thing: how standing before this painting was like learning to see for the first time. Blue fields resolving into overlapping squares, identical in weight, distinct in hue. Stasis and motion, the purity of the thing simply seen—exactly what he'd been seeking, pressing his own wet brush to canvas, so long ago. He could have been back there still. Or further back, the day before Daddy's wedding, when the whole field of time lay open before him.

His mind continued reeling through these perceptual spaces as his body followed his sister's upstairs and down a long hall. Doors on the left were pools of inert gray, while those on the right let through rhomboids of light. In the bedroom where he'd slept one summer, the guest-beds were made tight as corsets. He stepped back into the hallway to find Regan had lost him again. He never had learned to navigate this place. He felt no alarm, though; he tried one door and then another and then descended a staircase, certain he'd find some other staircase back up to the other wing. And it was there, crossing an empty reception hall gone lunar with the fading light, that he spotted the suitcases, three of them, lined up by the bar. A child rummaged in the cabinet underneath, its back to him.

Except it was not a child. It was the Demon Brother. He hadn't changed in fifteen years, William saw, when he rose and turned. Not his clothes, not his face, not his prematurely white hair, which, William having sprouted a few grays himself lately, had the perverse effect of making Amory seem to be getting younger. "What are you doing here?" William said. There was a glint in the eye, but no larger sign of recognition.

"Why, I live here. What are *you* doing here?"

It was the solicitude of a person talking to a toddler: *What are oo doing here?* And William could feel his miraculous clarity collapsing. This had been a mistake. "Do you really not remember me?"

"William?" Amory took glasses from a breast pocket, put them on, leaned forward. "But you should always call ahead! Sadly, I'm about to depart for Block Island with your father. I'm already skipping a scheduled meeting, though I suppose the two of us might just have time to refresh ourselves. It really is thoughtful of you to drop by, after all these years." He retreated to the far side of the bar, stooped again, and suddenly bottles were appearing on the counter. "What's your pleasure? There's Scotch, gin of course, Haitian rum—"

The strangling muscles in William's arms had gone rigid. "I don't drink anymore. And I'm not here to see you."

"No, of course not. Though as regards your father, a few months ago a visit might have meant a great deal, but we're a bit concerned about agitating him just now." Amory paused, as if something were occurring to him. "But I don't suppose Regan will have told you about his condition? I assume she's here, too." He uncapped one of the whiskys. Was the bottle shaking? It was this slight tell, or counterfeit thereof, that led William to overplay his hand.

"What about the Specters, Amory? Did you fill Dad in on them?"

The other man looked up from his pour with genuine surprise. "The Specters?"

"Those spooks you sent to make sure I stayed out of the family business for good."

"Really, William. What kind of creature do you take me for?" Having returned the glasses to his pocket, Amory now reached with his free hand for the fireplace poker that had somehow replaced the rubber plant in William's. William could feel it slipping from his grip. For a second, the face before him began to change. Then the poker came free, and a noise made him look toward the balcony. William turned to find Regan standing one story up, and beside her, their father, lit by the last red lozenge of sun. Somehow, in the flood of projects, grievances, and delusions sweeping him forward, William had lost sight of the question of how it was going to feel to see Daddy again. But what did you expect to feel, damn it, besides this mingled fury and helplessness, your childhood all over again? Everything irrecoverable laid bare in a flash, as Amory Gould, the motherfucking devil himself, flew up the staircase to the balcony without spilling even a drop of his drink.

William could only follow, trailing the fireplace poker. Maybe he, too, looked more fearsome than he felt, because when he reached the top of the stairs, Regan asked what he was doing, and his father was saying, "Tell your brother this has to stop."

Amory was at Daddy's elbow, turning him toward the fading windows. "We really should make haste, Bill, if we want to catch the last ferry."

But Regan, turning him back, said, "No, Daddy. William needs to speak to you." So she was on his side again. Still.

Daddy must have felt it, too, because he hung, suspended. Amory changed tack. "Why don't we all step into the library, then, and talk things over like gentlemen?"

"I think William means one-on-one."

William nodded, giving himself over to her guidance, but Daddy was already following Amory through the French doors and toward the desk. "Anything your brother has to say to me, he can say in front of his uncle."

"Will you stop saying that?" William said. "He's not my uncle. Don't you see what this little fucker's done to our family?"

The tide of personality seemed to withdraw as Daddy's lined face floated above the desk, though maybe this was the condition Regan had alluded to in the car. Anyway, if Daddy wasn't going to sit, neither was William. But then, almost effortlessly, the tide came surging back. "This is nonsense, darling," Daddy said to Regan. "Amory has done nothing but good. It was your brother who abandoned us."

"I got cleared out, Dad. It's what the Goulds do. First Regan got put in her place—"

"He made his choice, Regan, and I have respected it." Daddy's voice had risen. People were always raising their voices at William.

Though possibly his father's breathing, his almost panting, was something to be worried about. Meanwhile, Amory remained by the window, looking out at the twilit city.

"—and now they're going to clear you out, Daddy. I was at that press conference today. You're going to be found guilty, and then you'll have to cede control of the company. Do you think this is accidental? Ask yourself, who's left to take the reins?"

"Your brother could have taken them, Regan. And his son, and his son's son."

Son. William was pretty sure Regan had mentioned her own son. Was this him, in the photo on the desk? A little boy and a littler girl, and himself an uncle—but momentum pulled him onward. "Daddy, did you ever stop to ask yourself if you've actually done anything wrong?" That he was certain his father hadn't was the difference between him and his sister. "Regan, have you asked? Well, *did* you, Daddy? Did you break the law?"

The great head shook slowly, fading again. Or pretending to fade. "I don't . . . I don't remember."

"But someone did, right? If you do any halfway competent investigation, it's going to lead back to a certain person, even you've got to see that. The same person who will have been working hardest to make sure an internal investigation like that never happens. I'm saying this just as a spectator who knows the players."

Amory, who had seemed to be contemplating nothing more serious than the moonlight in his drink, now turned. "Yes, a spectator. I couldn't have put it better myself. Now, if you're quite done with this childishness, William—except you never will be done, will you? You remain a perpetual seventeen. It sounds so pretty in pop songs, but is in the flesh merely embarrassing. Bill, I really can't abide these innuendoes any longer. I'm headed downstairs. Your car is waiting. But you know, I may just head to this prior appointment after all and catch up with you in the morning."

Daddy looked uncertain.

"No, listen, Dad. There are men out there trying to kill me. They're like six and a half feet tall. And right as a Hamilton-Sweeney project gets rolling in the Bronx and you're under indictment, one almost clips me. This can't be a coincidence, do you see what I'm saying? That man over there, your brother-in-law, he needs the once-and-future heir gone if he's to pull off his coup."

Amory snorted. "Piffle. No doubt drug-related. And hasn't he staged this scene once before? William, you've wasted enough of your father's time."

"A coup," Daddy said. He squinted, trying to recover his bearings. "These are serious charges."

"Fantastic, I'd say, Bill. Opium dreams."

"I'm not on drugs now, Daddy. I'm trying to understand my life as best I can." He heard his voice catching, hated himself for it; blew through it. "If I abandoned you to the Goulds, okay, I take responsibility for that. And maybe there's a reason I still can't get all the pieces to line up. But you shouldn't need me to tell you you're in danger. You've seen it yourself. I'm telling you I am, too. Your son. Send me away, and you're never going to see me again."

"Oh, come now," Amory said, though he seemed in a hurry to leave. "You can't really think me so monstrous as that."

"Or you can make him stop."

Daddy was all at once an old, old man, blinking against the lamplight. His blue eyes shifting like that painting, now muzzy, now crisp. As if anybody had a choice. They were William's eyes, too. How long had it been since the two of them had looked at each other like this? And William recalled, or his father did, or it arose somewhere between them, an Impressionist sky, blue, jostling with the perambulator, and in it the smell of Burma-Shave and a peach-colored smear with the same blue ellipses meeting him, as a rich, clear baritone intoned,

> *The King of Siam*
> *Is all that I am*
> *Is all that I am, and ever will be.*

Then the window where Amory stood thumped, as if hit by an errant softball. Daddy turned toward it, straining to become that man again, surging back toward him. Everything else went quiet. "Perhaps we should postpone our trip for a day or two, Amory, while we get this sorted out." And there was just enough time to register relief on Regan's face and shock on the Demon Brother's—surely some kind of first—before the room and the window and the lit buildings outside disappeared. A car screeched somewhere. Glass shattered. But all around, the city had dropped into darkness: the world they'd always known, just like that, blacked out.

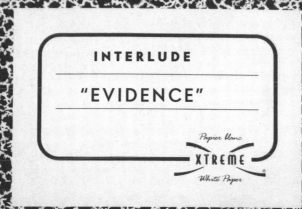

INTERLUDE

"EVIDENCE"

Papier Blanc
XTREME
White Paper

Sidewalk Closed Use Other Side. Purveyors of the Finest Quality Meats. No Parking or Standing. No Turns. Don't Walk. Buses Only. Off Duty. Off Duty. Walk. Use Crosswalk. Use Snow Route. Red Zone. Salt Zone Begins Here. Pour Popcorn Only Here. Now finally serving warmed food! Follow This Truck to New York's Most Delicious Chopped Liver. A Taste That's All It's Own. The Outside Service Are Needs Waitting Every 20 Minutes, With the Smile. Neither Snow Nor Rain Nor Heat Nor Gloom Of Night Stays These Couriers From The Swift Completion Of Their Appointed Rounds. Express Lube. Discreet Massage. Siamese Connection. Alive With Pleasure! Truly Aaaah-inspiring. No Unaccompanied Minors. We Are Happy to Serve You.... There Are Many More Flowers Inside. No Inappropriate Sexual Touching. Unpurchased Merchandise May Not Be Taken Into The Restroom Thank You. Read the Bible God's Word Daily. Chance of a Lifetime Jackpot Now 08 Million. Want to Know How to Prevent HEAD LICE???????? Come Inside and ASK. House of Orthodontia. House of Watch. The Bleach House. Last Wash 8 p.m. 3 Days Left! Last Chance! Be Wise and Repent. The Time is at Hand. The End is Fulfilled. Wise Men Still Seek Him. Uncle Sam Wants You... To Get CASH! CAN'T HOLD MONEY, WANT LUCK, WANT YOUR LOVED ONES BACK, WANT TO STOP NATURE PROBLEMS or WANT TO GET RID OF STRANGE SICKNESS? If you are seeking a surefire woman to do the things that are needed or WISH TO GAIN FINANCIAL AID or PEACE, LOVE, and

PROSPERITY, there is a WOMAN WHO WILL DO IT FOR YOU IN A HURRY. SHE TELLS YOU ALL BEFORE YOU UTTER A WORD. SHE brings the SPIRIT OF RELEASE and CONTROL to your every dealing. Don't Walk. Stand behind yellow line. Do Not Leave Your Trash in the Hallway, It Stinks, and Attracts Roaches. The Rats are Looking for their Winter Homes. No Feeding Pigeons. No Turns New. Post No Bills. Seriously: No Park Car. Walk Don't Walk. Risk of Shock, Do Not Cross Tracks. No Honking Except For Danger. Wait Until The Moving Platform Stops Moving. Violators of this Sign will be Persecuted. All Visitors Must Be Announced. Please the bathroom is ONLY for use of Customers and personel. It is NOT for doing ANYTHING ELSE in there. If we find something strange going on, we are going to ask the person to leave and not use the restroom again. Off Duty. Waste. No Radio. Out of Order. Out of Work. 12'6"... We Mean It! Your Dog Belongs To You, So Does What Comes Out of Your Dog. I Scream, You Scream, We All Scream For Ice Scream. Hotel Avantgarde. Guido Funeral Home. Cremation Consultants. Do To A Small Fire, We Will Be Closed. Don't Walk. To hot—to cold—to dry—to damp—or just plain uncomfortable? THIS IS THE DOOR TO NOWHERE. Warning: Look Out for the Stars.

BOOK VI

THREE KINDS OF DESPAIR

[1960–1977]

A student came to a Zen master and said, "In what state of mind should I train myself, so as to find the truth?"

Said the master, "There is no mind, so you cannot put it in any state. There is no truth, so you cannot train yourself for it."

"If there is no mind to train, and no truth to find," said the student, "why do these monks gather before you every day to study?"

"But I haven't an inch of room here," said the master, "so how could the monks gather? I have no tongue, so how could I teach them?"

"Oh, how can you lie like this?" asked the student.

"But if I have no tongue to talk to others, how can I lie to you?" asked the master.

The student said sadly, "I cannot follow you. I cannot understand you."

"I cannot understand myself," said the master.

—ZEN KOAN

87

THEY WAITED UNTIL FOUNDER'S DAY to tell William Hamilton-Sweeney he wasn't invited back for senior year. He was sitting in an office with his school tie wadded in his pocket, his packed bag already on the rug beside him. The rector, a gray eminence with a face like a tombstone, apparently expected a reaction, and, as it would have been impolite not to give him one, William struggled to look grave himself. *Not invited back* was, of course, a euphemism for *kicked out.* By that point, he'd heard them all: *academic hiatus, indefinite leave, not the right fit* . . . His surname, with its intimations of largesse, encouraged each new school in the delusion that it might succeed where the others had failed. A few months of missed mattress-checks and scuffles with other students and drunkenness at chapel, however, tended to alter the calculus. The latest last straw was an unauthorized absence. He'd been caught sneaking back onto campus before sunrise the night of Bruno Augenblick's going-away party. Having wobbled the last four miles from Boston on foot, he'd been too tired to offer any account of himself, or any explanation for how he came to be carrying a silver flask monogrammed with initials not his own. Nor did he intend to present a defense even now, notwithstanding the rector's hints that it might lead to a lighter sentence. At this very moment, Daddy's friend Arthur Trumbull was speeding north to collect William for what he thought was just summer vacation; were William to leave any wiggle-room at all, Trumbull would push for him to be readmitted. And the truth was, William had no intention of returning to New England in the fall. He observed what he thought was a seemly period of silence, as if weighing his options. Light from the varsity ballfields coaxed oaky fire from the bottles on the sideboard. Then he snatched up the flask that was Exhibit A and thrust a hand toward the baffled rector. "Well, Chuck, let no one say you didn't try your very best with me." Already gliding up the long drive outside was the chauffeured black towncar that was to carry him back to New York.

THUS BEGAN THE SUMMER OF 1960. Regan was still traipsing around Italy, and Daddy hardly seemed to notice that William had returned. The firm's recent absorption of its largest competitor had made all sorts of extra work, and after long days at the office, he often ate dinner at Felicia's new penthouse across the park. William got the feeling from certain silences among the domestic help that his father might even be sleeping there, but he couldn't prove it; when he came downstairs in the a.m., Daddy was always in his customary spot at the breakfast table. Which is not to say that this, their only real time together, was free from Felicia's encroachments. She would arrive halfway through the meal, not to eat (she never ate), but to natter at Daddy about wedding plans while he receded behind the *Times*. William tried to scare her off with dirty looks, but Felicia Gould was to all appearances unscareable.

His last stand came in mid-July. Regan was supposed to be returning from Italy that day, and William was determined to drive Felicia off for at least an afternoon. He came to breakfast in a loosely belted kimono he'd found at a secondhand shop downtown and a pair of bright white briefs. He sat back from the table, crossed and uncrossed his legs, let his thighs flash suggestively. This old routine had never failed when he wanted to outrage a schoolmate. (*Nancy?* He'd give them *nancy.*) But all he got now was Daddy glancing over the top of the business section, like an ornithologist at some mildly diverting bird. "What you need is a good suit."

William had heard this before—the virtues of formalwear being one of roughly six things Daddy could talk to him about—but what the subject recalled for them both was the child-sized black suit still hanging in the closet, the long-dead lilies he'd pocketed rather than toss, and Daddy had eventually let it drop. Now that it had become apparent that William's first big growth spurt, a year earlier, would also be his last—that he had topped out at five foot six—Daddy must have felt it was time to try again. Or was he just showing off for his intended? "I'll give you the number of my tailor. You could take care of it this afternoon."

"What do I need a suit for?" William asked. "I don't need a suit."

Daddy looked meaningfully at Felicia. "And we should get you a dinner jacket while we're at it. You're going to want one for the wedding." Ah. Here it was. William having completed fifth form, the World's Longest Engagement had become a finite quantity.

"I'm busy this afternoon."

"I can imagine," Daddy said, and began to refold his paper the way he always did—meticulously, so that there was no evidence of his having read it.

"Don't you remember? Regan gets into Idlewild at one."

"Is that right?" Felicia trilled. "Bill, darling, why didn't you tell me? You should take the afternoon off. We could all drive out to meet Regan—" And then, as if the mere mention of her name had magical properties, his sister's voice was out in the foyer. Before William could push back his chair, Daddy was hurrying toward the door.

Regan had always been his favorite, and William had long suspected Felicia of being jealous. If only she would confirm it now through some nervous adjustment to her silverware, or one of her unfunny jokes, it might compensate him, somehow, for the omnidirectional jealousy he was feeling himself. Instead, she leaned forward. Her only visible flaws were cracks in the foundation around the mouth. (This much he remembered about his mom's face: smiling had never caused a crisis there.) "What your father was trying to tell you, William, is that we've finally set a date. It'll be next June, as soon as you graduate." That was just the thing, he wanted to say; he wasn't going to graduate. But whatever he may have mumbled was quickly forgotten as Daddy led Regan in.

She glanced nervously around from behind dark glasses. "We landed early. I took a cab."

She looked at once thinner than William remembered and slacker, like a deflated balloon, though maybe that was her cardigan. Still, when he hugged her, she smelled pristine—bath salts and sweet white flowers and something else he couldn't place. He let his head rest in the hollow where her slightly damp hair met her shoulder, while Daddy fetched the camera. "Take off your sunglasses, honey, so we can see your eyes." They were bloodshot, but wasn't that why it was called a redeye?

After stopping the butler from taking her luggage upstairs, she brought out gifts. For Daddy, there was a briefcase, a little *à la mode* for his taste but made of leather soft as caramel. Felicia voiced actual *oohs* and *aahs* as it got passed around the table. For William, there was a Spanish guitar and a heavy, cloth-bound book on Michelangelo. He was disappointed the plates weren't in color (and noticed that the price-tag, weirdly, was in U.S. dollars) but he would keep it in his lap for the rest of breakfast, prompting Felicia to warn him about getting coffee on it. Finally, it was her turn.

"For me? You shouldn't have," Felicia said, as her hungry hands plucked a small package from the table. She was one of those people who actually unties the ribbon, slides her finger under the flaps to avoid tearing. From a narrow box came a tube that said *Italia* on the side. "A pen," she said. In other words, the crummiest gift imaginable, drained of the thought that counted. "It was duty-free," Regan said. And silently, William cheered: all was not lost! Then his sister excused herself; there was a lot of unpacking to do.

REGAN STRUCK ANOTHER BLOW FOR THE RESISTANCE that weekend, when she informed Daddy she wouldn't be joining him on Block Island, where he planned to repair with the Goulds for the month of August. "But when else would we see you, darling?" he said. "You hardly got back, and you'll be at school again after Labor Day."

"I thought I wrote you about this."

"Wrote me about what?"

"Did I not mention this? The internship I applied for starts Monday. It's at a little theater down in the Village."

Here Felicia, who'd been touching up her lipstick in the hall mirror, turned. "But what ever will you do there?"

"Whatever they ask me to do, Felicia, that's what 'internship' means." To Daddy, she said, "I can't back out now; people wrote me recommendations."

Daddy just repeated the word, *internship*. As an alibi, it was a thing of beauty: its overtones of responsibility, of upward aspiration, were perfectly calculated to jam his circuits. *Well, you know, we've already booked you a seat on the first manned spaceflight, but I suppose if you have an* internship . . .

On the other hand, it threatened to blow William's plans all to hell. Amory Gould had driven up a week ago to open the summer house, and waited there now. Which meant that, unless Regan reconsidered, it would be father, son, and the two Ghouls alone. He heard himself blurt, "I'll stay, too."

"And what, exactly, do you propose to do with yourself for the rest of the summer?"

"I don't know, Daddy. Walk. Think. Be a human being."

"This is absurd. I've given the staff vacation. Who would feed you two? Who would do your laundry?" But Regan had already annexed William's cause to her own.

"Daddy, he's seventeen years old. He can do his own laundry."

"Bill," Felicia said, with a hand on his arm. "If it would make you more comfortable, the kids could stay over on Central Park West. As a kind of test-run for next year, when we combine the households. The new place is too big to just abandon for the month, anyway."

Regan looked skeptical. "Who else is going to be there?"

"Just my maid, Lizaveta. I dare say she's as much of a cook as your Doonie ever was."

Daddy was doomed, and knew it, but made one last attempt; if you didn't know better, you'd have thought he *wanted* his son by his side. "Regan I understand, but if William's going to persist in doing nothing useful with himself, he might as well do it at the shore."

"Maybe I won't do nothing, though," William said. "Maybe I'll follow Big Sister's example. Look for some kind of . . ." What was that word again? "Internship."

IF IT ALREADY FELT ODD, moving across town for a month—why couldn't the maid just come over to Sutton Place?—the deal Regan reached with Lizaveta made it odder: she would take most days off, Regan would keep the refrigerator stocked, and they'd both keep it from getting back to Felicia. And so, for the duration of August, the younger Hamilton-Sweeneys were marooned in that enormous penthouse across the park, animals atop Mount Ararat.

That there were two of them did little to blunt the loneliness. In fact, William and Regan were together even less than he and Daddy had been. Her internship started promptly at nine, and by the time he rolled out of bed, she'd have left. She was often still gone at dinnertime, and was on some kind of weird diet anyway, which she must have picked up in Europe. And when she did get home she returned to the great library on the second floor, or to the adjoining guestroom, where she was staying. The one time she always managed to be around was Saturday afternoon, when Daddy telephoned. "Oh, we're fine," she said. Otherwise, her message was clear. She'd abetted William's escape from Block Island for his sake, not her own, and now she wanted to be left alone.

At first, William filled the empty hours with soap operas. He'd become a partisan of *As the World Turns*. But the sheer size of the apartment he was rattling around in (paid for, he was sure, with Daddy's money) made him feel decadent, and not in the good way. He'd always thought of his family as merely well-to-do, like their Sutton Place neighbors. Money was stupid, but it wasn't *wrong*. Here, by contrast, the denizens of the lower floors, affluent though they may have been, stayed hidden from view, as if they occupied a different plane of existence from the truly rich. And further cracks were appearing everywhere he looked. The newscasts that came on after *The Guiding Light* carried images of Communist upheavals in Indochina. Of black kids in neckties being cold-cocked at lunchcounters. Of busloads of protesters rolling toward the South. He thought of Doonie, forced into early retirement. Where was she now? Still in that tarbox neighborhood in the outer boroughs where she'd taught him how to drive? Certainly not in a place like this, with its acres of Persian rug.

He started going to public pools in the hot hours before dusk, just to feel connected to the lives of other people—to break free, somehow, of the prison of class. His favorite was 145th Street, where the Negroes went. At first, they stared skeptically at his baggy trunks and underdeveloped muscles and the thick novel he pretended to read to hide his nerves. But the attitude up here was live and let live, and by the third day, William was an accepted fact of life. He propped the book on his shock-white chest and, shielded by the cover, admired the gleaming bodies of the men stretched out on the concrete a few yards away.

One evening, after showering off the chlorine, he went up to the library to look for Regan. It was deserted, its windows muffling the dying noise of rush hour to the south. Sunlight gushed in, crimsoning the bindings on Mom's old books. They must have been moved over here recently, as everything would be someday. Libraries had never been William's thing. The vastness of their surroundings made the small clutch of books a person was capable of moving through in a lifetime seem puny, and the shelves themselves merely flimsy bulwarks thrown up against the slow fire of acid on paper, the great red H-bomb of mortality. He reached for the handle of a French door and stepped out onto a balcony. On the next balcony over, maybe five yards away, Regan sat in dungarees with her knees to her chest and one arm dangling a cigarette. She made him think of the *Pietà* from his Michelangelo book—an effigy of loss so bafflingly deep it made his own look like a birdbath. Worse: he didn't know why. "Hey."

"Hey yourself." The way she could become instantly casual irked him a little.

"Is that a Continental thing, the cigarette? *Un' affectazzione?*"

She let a boll of smoke hang before her open mouth. Sucked it swiftly into her nostrils. "If you're angling for one, forget it."

"You know damn well I've been smoking for years," he said. "I'm coming over."

When they were side-by-side on her balcony, though, silence again prevailed, not counting the traffic below. He wanted to assure her that whatever was eating her, she could tell him, but that felt suddenly impossible. All he could do was put an arm around her. Again, her hair had that smell he couldn't quite place. It must have been a new shampoo, he realized. Italian. "Hey. Can I ask you something? When you came back from the airport that day, your hair was still damp. How did you have time to wash it before you got here?"

"Do I seem in the mood to talk?" She must have heard how snappish she sounded, because after a minute, by way of apology, she offered him a drag of her cigarette.

But he saw as he took it that the summer would end without any deeper understanding between them. She would trek back to Poughkeepsie, and he'd be packed off to yet another school with the intercession of Uncle Artie. In short, other people were not to be relied on. If there was to be any growth here, any meaning, he would have to make it himself.

SNEAKING OUT AT NIGHT after Regan had gone to bed was a cakewalk: straight through the lobby, past the concierge who never said a word. William had been going to bars on and off since he was fifteen, but always under the banner of youthful high spirits. Now a kind of grim fury held sway. Where he'd once favored student dives and no-cover jazz clubs, or the iconic Cedar Tavern, hoping to catch a glimpse of de Kooning, he began to consult the atlas of cruising spots and fern bars he'd been compiling half-consciously for years. He'd known that whole time that he was a homosexual—had done little to hide it and had sometimes even reveled in it, as a weapon against people who wanted him to feel bad about himself. But the designation had remained largely theoretical until the school before last, where, with a handsome but confused senior from Westport, Connecticut, he'd had his first real physical encounter. The boy had been an eager enough collaborator as they spelunked each other there in a storage room behind the auditorium, but William's reputation was already atrocious, and afterward the boy had avoided him. William couldn't be sure, but he thought a complaint from the boy's parents might have been what led to that expulsion. At any rate, he'd been living for months like a sexual camel. Now he was ready to go further.

The art of the pickup happened mostly with the eyes. Usually all it took was one volley of glances. You felt someone looking at you, and the second you looked back he looked away . . . and then when he felt you still looking and looked back, you looked down at the surface of the Manhattan you'd ordered because somewhere you'd gotten the idea that's what grown-ups drank, and a claim had been staked. William would feel his legs jittering beneath the table; later, he and his subject would rendezvous outside, in cars with the engines already running. If he was being honest with himself, the danger was part of the rush. But his conquests mostly turned out to be dispiritingly courteous: shy, married men from New Jersey whose single greatest fantasy was to swap hand jobs with a teenager. He'd end up under the West Side Highway, staring out across the empty Hudson, and in the instant of his coming the pallid digits beneath him would dissolve and he would feel, paradoxically, a suspension of his loneliness, a widening of his life into something brighter, bigger. Then the damp and the cold would set in and he would feel lonelier than ever.

When the bars ceased to feel risky enough, he graduated to the Park. He bought Benzedrine strips from hopheads and dissolved them in cups of deli coffee and waited under his favorite streetlamp. Then, in the darkness under the trees, his repertoire expanded. There were young men in the Park as well as old ones, black men as well as white, and he found he wanted these particularly. He wanted them to be rough with him, to punish him for something. For wanting that, maybe. It would later seem a wonder that the worst he came away with was a little chafing. By September of 1960, when he arrived at his new and final school, he brought with him more experience, more awareness of how to get from other people what he was after, than he could have acquired in like a dozen internships.

THE DOWNSIDE was that, away from New York again, he no longer stood in the way of the wedding. He did indeed graduate, and the start of the following summer, a year after it had first been mooted, William found himself in the fitting room of a wizened Jewish tailor whose question-mark posture seemed designed to save him the trouble of bending to take inseams. Daddy had insisted on bringing William down here personally, as if it were some rite of passage, the fitting of the armor that would gird another Hamilton-Sweeney for the battlefields of the haute bourgeoisie. From the changing room, William could hear him out there on the sales floor. "We'll need a couple of suits, too, Mr. Moritz, in addition to the tuxedo. William has an interview at Yale." Which was ridiculous; he was a Hamilton-Sweeney. But if Mr. Moritz noticed, he didn't let on. His shop had a clubby air, at once polished and musty. No female had set foot there since the time of the Borgias. The front door, open to the unseasonal heat, wafted back a breeze of cigar-smoke and leather. "And the dinner jacket is for Friday, if you can do it. He's agreed to be my best man."

The William in the mirror had stripped down to boxer shorts and an undershirt discolored under the sleeves. He'd been wearing the shirt last night, in the bushes near the Ramble. A few leaf-crumbs still clung to it. There were cuts on his legs from the branches. He tried to remember if his dad had seen these legs in the years since they'd become hairy—wondered if he would even recognize this body as his son's, or how he would feel if he'd known what other men were doing with it in the Park, in the dark.

"Are you ready in there, William?"

He pulled on the tuxedo pants and the shirt to cover the offending body. His father, seeming not to perceive the roominess when William waddled out onto the sales floor, nodded approvingly. William almost slapped Mr. Moritz's hand as it palsied its tape measure up to his crotch. Outside, captains of industry passed, unmoved by the festival air. "My assistant will hand-deliver," the tailor said, rolling the tape measure back up with unthinking precision. "The girls can't resist a fellow in evening clothes."

"That's what I keep telling him," Daddy said, as William made a silent, fervent wish that the day of the wedding would be even hotter than this one.

THE TUX ARRIVED FRIDAY, as promised. He couldn't say it looked any different than the saggy travesty that had swallowed him in the shop, but when he tried it on, it fit. He adjusted the seal-gray vest, checked the mirror on the closet door. He looked good. Looked—he might as well admit it—sexy. Which was auspicious; Regan's fiancé, whom he'd met back in April, was coming down for tonight's rehearsal dinner, and though William didn't plan to seduce him, exactly (it was her own engagement that seemed to have pulled Regan out of the previous summer's funk), William did think Keith Lamplighter was about the handsomest man he'd ever laid eyes on. A single admiring look would be enough, and eliciting it was just the little project he needed to distract him from this matrimonial fiasco.

He'd turned all the way around to inspect the rear view when he heard a whimper from the closet. He went to investigate. Behind the hanging clothes was a waist-high crawlspace where he and Regan had played as kids. More recently, it had been a convenient spot to stash alcohol. It's where he found her now, in the same posture as last summer on that balcony: balled up, forehead pressed to knees. Wincing a bit for what it might do to his new pants, he crawled back until he was beside her. Was she hyperventilating? When he reached for her hands, she tucked them under her, pulling her legs tighter. She seemed to want to retract any extension of herself, to become a moveless white egg. He asked if she needed a drink. The only response was the laughter of guests somewhere in the house. "Because I sure do." He rummaged in the suitcase where he hid his booze and found the little silver flask he'd stolen from Bruno's party, as a keepsake. The bourbon stung. He left the cap unscrewed, extended it to Regan. The smell, at least, might jolt her back to the world. "Kind of late in the day to throw a rod over the wedding, if you ask me."

She turned away, as if afraid he would see her face. "Fuck you."

Well, this was a first. Not that he hadn't said the same thing dozens of times to her. "I know what you really mean is that you worship me, Regan, so I'll forget you said that. But are you going to tell me what's wrong, or are you just going to take it out on me?"

"How can I tell you," she said, possibly to herself, "when I haven't even told Keith?"

"Haven't told Keith what?"

She looked back, studied him in the dimness of the closet. Her cheeks were splotchy and red, but surprisingly dry. "You have to promise this stays between us. Promise." And then, huddled under the hanging clothes, she revealed that she hadn't really been to Italy.

"I knew it!" he said. "No wonder you wouldn't let me borrow the car."

"No, listen. Please. It's because of something that happened at the start of junior year. A misunderstanding, with a boy. I was . . . pregnant—"

"—Christ. What?"

"And I had to go away to take care of it."

"You had a baby?" This was bizarre. "Where is it?"

"William, please. There was no baby."

He slumped back against the wall. And now, she said, the boy responsible had shown up in the wedding party commandeering the guestrooms. The sole heir of the company Daddy's had swallowed. He'd been out to Block Island a couple times, that summer before the merger. Afterward, he'd joined the Board.

"*That* guy? He's notorious, Regan. He was a few years ahead when I was at Exeter. Or maybe Choate. I wish you'd checked with me before letting him into your bed."

In the end, she took the flask. "I just spotted him downstairs talking shop with Amory Gould. I can't bring myself to let him see me here, William."

"Why? The guy refused to help pay for it? Or was he a jerk to you after?" William took a mental inventory of nearby weapons: steak knives, paperweights, his great-grandfather's old safari piece that hung on the dining room wall. "I swear, if he was unkind in any way . . ."

"William, he was long gone by the time I even missed a period—"

"Oof, Regan. Phrase, please."

"He doesn't know a thing, I'm saying. And now, with Keith proposing, it has to be our secret." She was silent a long time. "But there's someone I worry does know. The person who introduced us."

He saw it instantly. "Amory. God damn him. Only wait: Knows how much?"

"It's hard to say. I've been thinking about it a lot since I've been back. The way he keeps looking at me. What if he found out I was pregnant? And then not. Illegally not." Another pause. "You don't think he'd tell anyone, do you? Or try to use it somehow?"

"Well I sure as hell wouldn't want him that close to *my* secrets. Ask yourself how he got that merger to go through. Not to mention the Daddy-Felicia merger, or that career mumbo-jumbo he tried to lay on your boyfriend. The man is a total manipulator." Regan looked as if something new and uncomfortable were dawning on her. But he'd worked himself up to a fit of righteousness, and couldn't stop to examine it. "Why do people like Amory hold on to secrets, if not to use them? He could be ratting you out to the guy right now, and together they make two seats on the Board. Think of what they'd have over Daddy. The only way to be sure it doesn't get used sooner or later is, you tell first."

"William, no! What would Keith think of me?" She pulled her hands out from under her, began to smooth her skirt. "Just give me a few minutes to collect myself."

They were siblings, though—they'd practically gone to war together—and so his job once again was to protect her. "You wouldn't be telling me all this if you weren't planning to do something about it."

"You promised," she reminded him.

"But do you really want to spend your whole life hiding the truth?"

"I don't know what I want anymore," she said.

"The impulse to keep it from Keith, I understand, but if you think Amory has found out, you need to take it to Daddy. Regan, look at me. You can trust him, he's our father. We should go to him."

"I guess you're right." She wiped her cheeks with the heel of her hand. "Okay. Okay. You're right."

GIVEN HOW STIFLING it had been earlier in the week, the day was incongruously beautiful, the sky high and mellow above the open top of Regan's car. And something else had broken with the heat, some sealed order they'd been under. William felt almost manic, on the edge of vision. It was not too late. Things could still change. On the fortieth floor of the Hamilton-Sweeney Building, they flew past the secretary only to find Daddy alone in his office, as if this were any other day and not the eve of his remarriage. The oxygen mask he was dictating into dropped as soon as he saw them. "This is a pleasant surprise."

"You have to call off the wedding."

"William—," Regan said. She hadn't realized he would go so far so fast. Maybe he hadn't either, completely. But no matter; it was all tumbling out of him, how they felt sure Amory had kept a damaging secret from Daddy, a potential scandal . . . except it wasn't striking the note William wanted, because he couldn't name the secret— could he?—and the one keeping mum about it now was his sister. Plus why in the first place hadn't she at least told the guy who'd knocked her up? A phone call would have done. The boarding-school circuit was full of similar stories, always made to go away quietly. She really wasn't helping explain this at all. "Come on, tell him what you told me, Regan. About Amory's little understudy on the Board. About the pregnancy."

When he turned, she was as red as he'd ever seen her—despite or because of which, his mind kept running back to lockerroom gossip about her lover. It was hard to recall, he was probably drunk when he heard it, but hadn't there been something about a townie girl from Nantucket whose family got paid off after he . . . oh.

Oh, Regan.

Was it possible the damage she was hiding, the violation Amory might use, went deeper?

Then would the right thing be to press on? Or retreat?

"Daddy, you have to listen to me now. Amory set your daughter up—"

"You've said quite enough for the time being, William," he said.

"The pregnancy thing, I'm sorry, you'll both have to get over. But Amory. Goddamn Amory—"

And then, only marginally less sharply: "It seems your sister and I need to have a talk." William tried to appeal to Regan, but when she looked at him he found he couldn't hold her gaze. "Alone," Daddy said. The next thing William knew, he was out in the waiting area.

What followed was the longest half-hour of his life. He sat there under the corrosive gaze of the secretary he'd blown past five minutes before. He tried to eavesdrop on what was being said behind the door, but could hear only the murmur of a Dictaphone playing back and the rapid chomp of typewriter keys, like a school of piranha skeletonizing a cow. On the far wall was the other Rothko: a giant field of color, rust brown and aortal red and the white of the white part of a candy cane. Its companion, blue on blue, had appeared on the wall of Felicia's penthouse at the start of Christmas vacation, as more boxes from Sutton Place had been making their way over. William hadn't understood why until they stepped off the elevator. *Holy shit,* he'd been powerless not to say. Then: *What's the catch?* "What catch? Regan tells me you're passionate about art, so I thought, something to make this feel more like a home when we move in. I got one for the office as well. Is this okay? I couldn't bring myself to buy one of the drippy ones." William wanted to say he hated it, but couldn't, just as he couldn't say now that he was backing out, that he'd been weak, that he'd never wanted to be Daddy's best man. All of which was secondary, he reminded himself, to whatever she was revealing in there. The paint seemed to throb under the pressure of his gaze, the red weeping at the edges, pouring over itself like a fountain. Then the door opened. Regan walked carefully back toward the desk where Daddy still sat. William was four years old again, summoned to answer for something he'd broken, a vase, a mirror.

"Son." What color there had been in Daddy's face was gone. His voice was shaking. "I know you oppose this wedding. I have tried in a number of ways to reach you. And I see I've failed. But using your sister's misfortune to try to smear Felicia's brother is simply wrong." The other part—that his mother would be ashamed—went unsaid, as it always did. Among all the many things William could no longer remember was why he'd ever wanted it that way.

Standing by the window, Regan couldn't turn to look at him. Now she was the one being a coward, still holding something back . . . he knew it. He fucking knew it. "I gather she told you how the pregnancy ended, at least. And Daddy, the Goulds must have seen all along how upset she was and kept it from you, so as not to sink the merger—"

Regan jumped in. "William, I never said Felicia—"

"Do the specifics even matter? I'm trying to tell you your daughter is scared of them. You're still pretending not to hear it. And she'll go right along with you, if you let her. It's what we Hamilton-Sweeneys always do."

"This is between me and Regan," his father told him.

"But I vouched for you. I thought you'd know how to set things right."

"You're obviously half-drunk, William, and in no position to tell me my business. And I've given up trying to tell you yours. You may come to the dinner tonight sober and presentable, or you can stay away. It's your choice."

"Regan?" If she had indeed held something in reserve, there was still a chance here for her to open up fully, to cast her lot with her family, and so to save them all. But Regan would be along later, Daddy said, with the car. They were not done talking.

AND THAT WAS THAT. By the time William saw her again, at the rehearsal dinner, the rival heir had been forced off the Board, and Regan asked to join in his place. Or so went the gossip at the restaurant they'd rented in Central Park, at which William would show up presentable, fine, but substantially less than sober, the flask nestled in his pocket. Weren't rehearsal dinners restricted to family? Half of New York seemed to be here, stepping from the backseats of cars, clogging the entrance, as if it were one of Felicia's awful beach retreats. He tried to spot Amory Gould, or to identify the protégé, but failed, and failed. He had no idea what he could do to either of them, anyway. And once his flask ran out, he sat at the bar, drunker and drunker, until the wrong they'd done his sister was a certainty. Unbelievable, that things were going to go on like this, just as before. Or not, because Regan had taken the payoff. Had become one of *them.*

When the meal started, he found he'd been seated in Siberia. He must have been stripped of his place in the wedding party. His sister, up at the head table, refused to turn his way. Her dumb, beautiful boyfriend kept rubbing her hands. But William was not about to be the one to go over there and apologize. If anyone had been betrayed, it now seemed to be him.

By the time dessert arrived, he felt doused in Burgundy, enclosed in a rubescent bubble. At least he'd decided what to do. Sounds seemed to swim all around, but he couldn't reach them from where he was, and nothing could reach him either, except the ringing of his fork-tines against his latest glass. And here it came again, urgent, insistent, like money, until the whole room had gone quiet. Daddy looked over. Regan did not. A microphone had been set up near the head table, back when he'd been supposed to give a toast, but William could be plenty loud unamplified.

"It's customary on these occasions to say a few words about the groom," he heard himself announce, impressed by his own eloquence. "But now that the time comes, I'm kind of at loose ends. This whole best-man bit goes against the natural order. I mean, what really is a son allowed to say about his father?" There was nervous laughter. If he tried to find its source, all would be lost. "His old man. Pater. The patriarch without whom nothing's possible." William caught the bewildered eye of Keith Lamplighter. Next to him, Regan was star-ing at her hands. He tried to focus on the glass in his own, refracting the red glow of an exit sign beyond the bar. "You think that's a fig-ure of speech, but you wouldn't if you'd been around when my mom died." His arm, held a hundred-odd degrees from plumb, had started to burn. "You'd seen us then, you would have thought it would ruin us. Or at the very least that our sense of self-respect would demand we not try to plug the hole she left. But nothing is impossible for my dad. A father's supposed to show his son what it means to be a man, and Daddy, whatever our differences, you've definitely done that." William's turn to laugh. His voice was slipping into an outsized sibi-lance he recalled from certain nights in the Village, his cocked wrist growing fluid. "I suppose that's why I appear to have shied from man-hood, as I'm sure you've all privately clucked over. I'd just warn you to remember that appearances aren't everything. I'm not only what you think, okay? And there are deeper things at work in my dad, too, and the Company, and in Felicia and Amory Gould. The most truthful thing I guess can be said by me or anyone is, all you folks deserve one another. So ladies, germs, what Goulds have put together, let no man put asunder. Don't be shy now. Bottoms up." And with that, William III, the last of the Hamilton-Sweeneys, moved his glass to his lips, knowing that once this wine's final swallow had vanished down his throat, he would break for the exits, and whatever might be waiting beyond.

88

MOM HAD BOLTED WITH THE YOGA INSTRUCTOR one bright Thursday morning in the spring of '71, when Sam was with the nuns and Dad over in Queens for that week's test firings, though the timing probably had more to do with opportunity than calculation. The documentary record either way was minimal. The note she'd left by the kitchen sink was only two lines long. Just enough so no one would think she'd been abducted, Dad said, when Sam asked what was in it. Later, checking the closets, she noticed Mom hadn't even taken a change of clothes. Dad seemed to construe this as a sign she might return. But Sam, who'd been paying closer attention, saw it the opposite way. Mom obviously wanted as little as possible to tie her to Long Island, to this wrong turn her life had taken. Confirmation came that August, in the form of a letter with an Idaho postmark. Mom had used a loopy Palmer script to write Sam's name on the envelope, so Dad wouldn't know who it was from. The letter's length was another surprise, but the gist was on the very first page. Knowing the pain she'd caused, Mom said, she had held off writing, but then she'd seen a Fourth of July spread in *Life* magazine, those happy crowds gaping at Dad's masterpiece from up on the Brooklyn Bridge, and she felt she had to explain to Sam that *everyone* deserved happiness—not just people you didn't know well enough to neglect. Cue the pianissimo: *can't tell you what to do . . . not saying you can't come with me . . .* And what? Hoe spuds in some field? Change her name to Saffron, get passed around like VD? It was no secret what went on at a commune. Even one that subscribed to *Life* magazine. What Sam never did find out was what pages two through five of the letter said, because before Dad could get home, she set the whole thing on fire. Gripped it with tongs from his workshop and turned it over a shallow metal bowl until the flames touched all edges, so that she wouldn't be tempted to reach in and save it.

It isn't quite so easy a thing to burn a mother out of your heart, but Sam eventually found the right equipment for that, too. Smokes, snaps, tunes. Mom had made her choice, had gone chasing after some frictionless ideal, and best of luck to her. Sam honestly felt by the time of the Bicentennial that she hardly thought about Mom one way or another.

But in the closing days of that year, she could suddenly think of little else. It was as if there *were* little else. As if the premise that any unit larger than the self could be held separate from any other—that the self *itself* wasn't corruptible—had crumbled. Her island life, her city life: it was all compounded now, and everything her eyes hands or lips touched could explode at any moment into a reminder.

Nothing was more prone to trigger that detonation than Dad, which was weird, because he was so rarely around. The day after the big Willets Point break-in, he didn't get home until nine at night. Then, over cold takeout, she was forced to listen to him seethe some more about the kilos of black powder, the phantom Ranger hustling toward Flushing. He'd convinced himself that this theft, like the one in November, was an act of industrial espionage. Yet remained dead-set against talking to the cops. "The sedatives they fed the dogs nearly killed one of them, Sammy," he said. "But I'll tell you what, I've still got a few tricks to show them." She almost blurted out that *them* included herself, but he wouldn't have been able to get his brain around it. So now she was the one changing into Mom. She used to wonder how someone so sentimental could have left her dad, but it turned out that truly unconditional love was suffocating, in that it took so little notice of who you actually were.

Then, in the morning, when he was gone, she was back to herself again. Back, almost, to twelve, to thirteen, trying to figure out how to put a life together. She got out her typewriter and her X-Acto and her glue pot and the various pieces of what was to be Issue 4 of *Land of a Thousand Dances.* But when she took down the pictures from that fall to edit them, the dozens of photos she'd pinned to the slack length of clothesline on her wall, they, too, were reminders. Their meaning was all tangled up somehow with a stack of family pictures she'd buried in the yard at fourteen, because there were some things—most things—she couldn't bear to burn. She didn't remember studying them beforehand, but how else had they seared themselves like this on her inner eye? Her mom in rolled khakis on a beach in a color-corrected dusk, holding a stick with a marshmallow on the end and laughing—was this possible?—at something her dad had said. Or in a two-piece near an open hydrant somewhere in Queens, not much older than the toddler splashing through puddles behind her had now grown up to be.

And then Flower Hill: she must have been the most incandescent thing ever to hit these streets. Sam wondered if incandescence was a heritable trait; if the weird way people in this town treated her didn't predate her delinquency, her funky new haircut, her tattoo. She'd go out to buy more cigarettes at midafternoon, and the blinds of neighbor women would twitch as she passed. Other times they pretended not to notice you at all. Once that fall, she'd seen the Weisbarger family station wagon slide past, driven by the woman she'd spoken to on the phone. It was impossible to know if Mrs. Weisbarger's refusal to turn her head was intentional or not. And how much easier things might have gone, Sam thought, if she could have just been in love with Charlie back, rather than merely loving him, in the way of an older sister or glamorous cousin. Maybe her mother had seen herself from this angle, too: a character stuck in the mechanistic hell of Greek mythology. To have this accidental power over every boy you met (Charlie, Keith, Sol, Brad Shapinsky) and, when you exercised it, to see them dissolve away to nothing.

AND THEN THERE WAS NICKY CHAOS. The first commandment of punk, Kryloned on the wall above *Loud fast rules* and *Die, hippie scum,* was *Don't rat out your friends.* Nicky was counting on her to remember this, she knew. It was possible that the theft of that mess of powder was just his latest test of whether she was loyal. But loyalty, like any other theoretical value—freedom, justice, beauty—cut against itself in practice. She was a punk, but also a Cicciaro. The difference was that the Post-Humanists were more vigilant than Dad. For all she knew, Sol's van was out of the shop again, idling in the cul-de-sac outside, monitoring the batik curtains of her room. If she was feeling torn here behind them, a dilemma's horns prodding her rebel ass, she had to keep her friends from finding out.

Christmas had been a Saturday. On Tuesday, she called the Phalanstery. Nicky had always avoided the phone, like someone was going to be listening in. Now she could hear him choosing words in shades of vanilla. "I thought you might get in touch sooner."

Why'd you really do it? she wanted to ask. *Why risk a second theft, a felony? Is this just to spite me for only bringing back three grams at Thanksgiving?* "Yeah, no," she said, equally cautious. "I've just had some family shit I've got to manage out here."

"I can imagine. But family shit isn't going to, like, change anything, is it?"

"Don't be a jackass. I'll probably be stopping by tomorrow, in fact. I think I left my camera in the basement the last time we were hanging out." Attention, wiretappers: that was code for fucking. "Or anyway, it wasn't in my bag, somehow. I'll need it if I'm still going to shoot Ex Post Facto on New Year's."

"It's Ex Nihilo now, Billy refuses to play along. But you are going to shoot it. And when the time comes, you'll shoot our Demon Brother, too." What that was code for she had no idea. "Should be a real spectacle. Meantime, we'll be here, if you want to, you know, hang out some more."

She thought of the glinty, mineral quality of his eyes lately, like the coke had whittled them down to pure pupil. In one sense, the scale of the damage Nicky aimed to do was an academic question. With as much bursting powder as was now doubtless sitting in that little house out back, you'd have to be an expert not to get someone killed. Plus just look what he'd done to *her*. "Seriously, don't be a stranger, Samantha."

"I won't," she promised, and rang off. But how straight she was being with him depended on how straight he'd been with her. Was everything he said a lie, or only half of it? The evidence now languished inside her camera, and could anyway, as with Mom's departure, probably be read several ways.

NICKY WASN'T ALL BAD, of course. He'd suffered growing up, and had been one of the first people she'd met who understood how *Brass Tactics* had changed her life. (The lyrics, he said, had heavily influenced his own thought.) But now, when she turned to that record for ideas, for hope, it seemed tainted by the association. All she could hear anymore, behind Billy Three-Sticks's rage and bravado, was the despair he was audibly trying to escape.

What she did still have—what never let you down, Charlie had once argued—was Patti. For *Horses*, even at its darkest, wasn't about escape, or not only. Yes, life was filled with pain, as Patti now sang from the record player. And life was full of holes: looking at the snippets jumbled on her pile carpet, Sam couldn't agree more. But there was also the warrior stuff, the priestess stuff, the Catholic stuff, *like some misplaced Joan of Arc.* Or like this: *And the angel looks down at him and says, Oh, pretty boy, can't you show me nothing but surrender?*

TWO DAYS BEFORE THE SHOOTING, Samantha dreamed of Patti Smith. She herself was in a pitch-black room somewhere. She could not see the walls or reach them—she was unable to move—but the room felt small. And there was a window nearby, she sensed, a vista of mountains and seas and tiny humans paddling around in canoes and just generally going about their business, if only she could see it. And then Patti appeared above her in a caul of low blue wattage and informed her that a time was coming when she would have to choose.

Choose what? Sam asked.

Choose for them to be saved, Patti explained—meaning all those little people, paddling and paddling—*or for you to.* That is, Sam could move upwards into the blackness, or down into the vista, but the moment was fast approaching when loitering in between would no longer be permitted.

Sam felt that this was totally bogus. Not to mention arbitrary. Plus what did that even mean, *loitering.* Or for that matter, *saved?*

Good point, Patti conceded, in a voice that now sounded suspiciously like Sam's mother. *But that's where we find ourselves. Having to choose, on the basis of imperfect information. If it comforts you at all, I can also tell you that time is only in your head.*

You're telling me either I go or they go? That's all you came back to say?

What I'm telling you, honey, is that you, personally, can only apply for an exemption for one or the other. And there will be a time, as it were, when you have to choose.

And this exemption you're saying I get—

—Apply for.

—Whatever. You're saying if I use it up on someone else, I don't get to stick around to see what happens?

If you go, Patti said, *all I can really tell you is that you will get to be very, very close to people. You try to be in life, and you can be, for a moment, but the moment has to pass. A better way of saying this is that time isn't in your head, exactly—I said that mostly because I wanted it to be true—but that it's a synonym for life. Beyond one, beyond the other. Beyond everything you'll be holding on to.*

Sam thought about this. *Wouldn't I miss it, though? Life?*

Oh, yes. This, quietly. *Most certainly.*

I don't understand. Why me?

Because shit happens, Samantha. Every once in a while, people get stuck in between, and they're either the lucky ones or the unlucky ones. That's why it's called a condition. Will be called, rather. You get to choose, one way or the other. But also, you have to.

Did you have a choice?

I wouldn't have been strong enough to let you go.

But you did let me go. Or was it a question? *Wait a second, aren't you supposed to be somewhere out west, Mom?*

Mom? Is that who you need me to be?

Sam either didn't quite follow or didn't quite want to. *So after you go, the people you love can still know how close you are to them?*

No, honey. Only you who are close can know. It's one of the Paradoxes.

But I know you're here right now.

This is a dream, Samantha.

Mom? (Patti?)

They feel us only rarely, mostly in dreams.

WHEN SAM WOKE, it was Wednesday, and her pillowcase was damp, and she was alone. Dad had gone back to work, if he'd ever come home, and beyond her window lay another gray day. Every day out here on the Island was dull and melty like this, a trough of drippy gray ice cream. But having pulled back the curtains, Sam felt weirdly elated, because she saw out there what she never could have before:

the ghost of her fierce self stalking these streets for all these years, refusing to give up or out or in. The moment she'd come closest was on Christmas, when she'd wandered into the front hall, still sick from news of the theft, and found, in the mail basket, the 'zine the post office had returned. That was the night she'd called Keith at home and he'd hung up on her, angry. But today she saw that, as with her father, he would be at work. Which is where, if she phoned right now, she would reach him: the closest thing to an actual adult in her life and also the single most persuasive person she knew. And *this* must be the choice Patti or whoever had meant, for *one who seizes possibilities, sees all possibilities*. Keith would feel too guilty not to agree to meet her at New Year's, if Sam applied the right pressure. (For he *was* guilty, in his own way, for delivering those envelopes, the ones he couldn't be bothered to look inside.) There, at the Vault, she would explain to him what had happened, and then bring him together with the PHP at last, and Keith, who could sell bifocals to a blind man, would speak for Sam. The powder would be returned anonymously to Willets Point, no questions asked, and the fires in the Bronx would stop. All fires, everywhere. There was only one piece missing, one more possibility, and her brain must have seized it, because when she picked up the phone, instead of dialing Lamplighter Capital Associates straight away, her fingers picked out a different number, and miraculously, it was not his mother but Charlie Weisbarger himself who picked up. Before she could even blurt out that it was urgent she see him, that she was going to need his help saving the city, he gave her that marvelously rude greeting she hadn't heard since the summer: "Another day in paradise, how may I direct your call?"

89

THE PLAN WAS SIMPLE. Especially after a drink or two to drown out any dissent. Open the freezer. Retrieve the plastic bucket from in back. Turn it over, flex its sides as if it were an ordinary ice tray. The foggy block within broke on contact with the floor, leaving a baggie half-protruding from the ragged ice. The next step was for Richard to get on the subway. Having finally finished his article, he would deliver the fanzines to his friend Larry Pulaski. Only here came that other friend, Complication. Pulaski wasn't at his office, where Pulaski always was, but at home on Staten Island, said his secretary. Richard could have just dropped a package in the mail, but the fanzines kept some hold on him, demanding to be entrusted to familiar hands. Besides, it always helped with the postpartum blues to get out and move. Slight adjustment to plan, then: pack the baggie in a satchel and affix to bike-rack. Maybe along with this bottle here.

Despite a late-April cold snap, Richard pedaled down to the ferry slip at Bowling Green, wincing against the wind. Even on the far side of the harbor, though, he wasn't quite ready to give up the 'zines. Sometimes you weren't yet the person you needed to be to do the work you needed to do. And at such times, he'd found, the best thing for it was to go to a nearby cemetery and spend an afternoon tramping among the graves. He wasn't far, in fact, from one he used to frequent before he'd left New York.

It was an old place, the earliest dates on the markers stretching back to the 1700s, the surrounding oaks not yet cleared to make way for malls. The burials had tapered off decades before he started coming here, so there was seldom anyone around save the dead. Evelyn Steward. Edward Woodmere. Hibernia Ott. These names, civilized, soothed his fear of having amounted to nothing. Amid them and amid the obdurate angels and the wildflowers pushing up through the earth, Richard could again be one among many.

This was what the work in Scotland had been about, too, he recalled as he wandered: the anonymity, the paring away. But trying to recover his discipline this last month since the leak had been like trying to nail together shelter in a hurricane. Candlelit vigils, updates at ten, a possible serial killer on the hypothetical loose, all this sturm and drang, this dreamwork, and only Richard had any sense of what was really at issue. Well, Richard and Zig Zigler. He'd been a dunce to write off the a.m. jeremiads Zig delivered with the same brio he'd brought to the poker table. But then again, what good had Zig done? His manic kibitzing about the dying girl and the Just City never ripened into specific demands. It was as if specific demands were a relic of a former age. Or as if, Richard thought, we had never moved on—as if the veil of the present had been cast off, and we were back in the desert fiefdoms of three thousand years ago, where the dead got honored with rent garments and a howl. Ivory St. James. Pierre Motell. He ran a hand along the rounded tops of headstones glazed with rain. It had begun to fall an hour earlier, light at first, then thickening. *Beloved wife. Delivered unto rest. All paths of glory.* Where a tendril of damp ivy had covered a phrase, he pried it loose. Then he took another belt of whisky.

No, he'd been suffering from a kind of blindness, dismissing Zig as obsessive, when really Zig had been right, that last time: Who was more obsessed than Richard? It could make you see more clearly than other people, or not at all. He still retained as a sense memory the excitement of spotting "SG" on that loading dock, back in March. His feeling, the moment he saw the flash of jersey between her lapels, that something was about to break, and how he'd wanted whatever it was all to himself. He wondered if this, and not his professional code, was why he'd failed to work her into the back half of what he'd decided to call "The Fireworkers." But the rain was really coming down now. The thermometer was plummeting. He reached again for the bottle.

What he felt guiltiest about was Carmine. The fireworker's final abjuration had mostly to do with the shooting itself, clearly, but still it couldn't have been wholly coincidental. Richard arrives on your doorstep one day, an emissary from the great world, and subsequently your orderly and secure life totally explodes. Father. Husband. Yet Richard had let himself believe the story he was pursuing could loft him clear of his own demons. *This writing is saving my life*, he'd been telling himself, right up until the last twist, the day before yesterday. Since then, everything had stopped. The fanzines yielded no more answers. SG was gone. Carmine wouldn't return calls. Richard was never going to find out who'd pulled the trigger on New Year's Eve, or what the Demon Brother had to do with anything. What was left in his head were the inklings he had or hadn't succeeded in turning into art; profound doubts about whether it mattered either way; and the last song he'd punched up on the Wurlitzer this morning before setting off. The water had found a seam in his shoe, and his left sock was wet. The rest of him would meet the same fate if he didn't soon take cover. Whistling to himself, he labored waveringly uphill.

The cemetery's mausoleum was less grand than it sounded, a kind of elongated archway. A folly, you would have called it, in a less terminal context. Through the center ran a passageway just tall enough for Richard to stand in. The sky had darkened to number 3 graphite, and as he neared the dregs of the whisky it let loose with wilder rain. Deeper in the passage he saw evidence of other souls on other days. Empty bottles, a Pringles can, the inevitable condom wrapper. He realized he had to pee. The bodies here were in the walls, not under the ground; still, it would have been a desecration to water this earth. But could he really make it all the way to that stand of oaks, in the rain? Remembering a touring rock band he'd profiled once, he picked up a bottle. When he'd finished pissing into it, he held his hands out into the rain to rinse. *Come on, Richard*, he thought. *Come back, good buddy.*

It was when he lowered his hands that he saw the punk. He was out there among the gravestones, maybe four hundred feet away, a muscly kid with tattoos and what looked like little Trotsky glasses. He was underdressed, too, his crewcut soaked wet, but he didn't seem to care about getting dry. Or avoiding being seen. Richard didn't recognize him, but he recognized Richard. His gaze was naked, ominous. (And was this not what Richard had wanted? To know how it felt inside the story?) When he started to back out of the far end of the folly, the punk moved, too, as if some signal had passed between them. And it almost didn't matter anymore who was the origin point of the signals, giving these various hoplites their orders. Of the last two people to draw their attention, one had been shot and one disappeared.

Richard turned, made to run, but found his feet heavy from liquor and the wet ground. He was out of shape. At the top of the next rise, he stopped to crouch behind a memorial, panting. Looked back. The boy was coming on, implacable, slipping from marker to marker without seeming at all hurried. Richard slid back down, leaned against the stone. The groundskeepers' carts had all disappeared. They must have gone when the rain came, meaning he was on his own here, surrounded by empty acres, no outside witness against whom to judge his sanity. Unless you counted the punk himself. And when Richard peeked again, he saw nothing but other graves. Someone could have been hiding behind any of them. Then a hand was on his shoulder.

A dark-skinned man about his own age held a shovel. Soil on his boots. He wore a transparent plastic slicker, a matching hood over his hat. "Everything all right, mister?"

"You didn't notice . . ." But Richard was struggling for breath, and saw how he might have looked. "Yes, I'm fine." He allowed the man's big hand to pull him to his feet. Ahead, directly downhill, was a muddy parking lot, a payphone box. Something occurred to him. "Bit wet for digging, though, isn't it?"

"Better wet than frozen. It's supposed to get down to thirty tonight."

"I'll leave you to it, then." Richard walked off, too embarrassed to look back. Down in the valley, he stayed tethered to the payphone. If the punk showed his face again, Richard would alert the cops, maybe even Pulaski, but for ten minutes or more, the only sign of movement was that little speck up on the ridge, rainproofed and solitary, bending and straightening over a hole. A gravedigger, digging a grave. Still, Richard wasn't going back for his bike, on the far side of the mausoleum. Not today. The safest thing was to call a cab.

By the time it arrived to collect him, he was shivering. He hadn't dressed heavily enough either, and had tapped out the warming potential of the booze. Nor could the car's dryness touch him. They inched back toward the ferry in the early rush. Donna Summer on the radio. Between warehouses and carwashes loomed the towers of the Battery, swallowed halfway up by bleary crowns of snow. He turned to check they weren't being followed. "You all right, buddy?" the cabbie said. Why did everyone keep asking him the same question? Then the cabbie cleared his throat. "You throw up in my cab, you pay to get it cleaned."

There was, thank God, a liquor store by the terminal, and it seemed only prudent to secure a couple of airplane bottles while watching out the window for that buzz-cut, those glasses. At twenty-nine minutes past the hour, he made a sprint for the gangway. The gate banged shut behind him, the engines rumbled below, and he went to put the spare bottle in his jacket's inner pocket, which reminded him: the 'zines, the fucking 'zines. He'd never taken them out of the satchel. It wasn't even a complete set—Issue 3 was still missing. And hadn't he known when he'd frozen the other two, really, that Pulaski, who might have made sense of them, wasn't aware they existed? Now they were no good to anyone, bungeed to a Schwinn on Staten Island. Or rather, in the hands of the punk who'd run him off—who'd obviously come to steal them. For fuck's sake, Richard. This one thing, this one simple concrete thing you could have done to protect Billy, to help Sam. And as with the writing, you'd failed.

With the boat in motion, the light around him had gone a sickly white. No one huddled on the other benches was going to meet his gaze, tell him it was all right. They were like one of those medieval crowd paintings. The White Death, everywhere. And here was another thing it was about time he admitted: Samantha Cicciaro was going to die. Maybe she would wake up first, maybe not, maybe it would be fifty years from now, but article or no article, she would at some point die, and so would Richard. Cosmically speaking, then, what had he even been running from? As an acolyte at Tulsa's First Episcopal Church, waiting for the moment to toll the consubstantiating bell, he'd thought of death as one of those revolving bookcases that led to secret corridors in comic books. You lay down, crossed arms over chest, closed your eyes, and when you opened them again, it was to new and unending life. Shazam! It wasn't really like that, of course, but if right-thinking people were right, and there was nothing at all after you died—*nothing*—well, how was he supposed to imagine that? As blackness? As emptiness? These were also metaphors, as fanciful in their way as a false-bottomed coffin. A true nothing had no precedent in this life. Yet he could feel it now, just behind his fellow passengers: the nothing that couldn't be put into words. And maybe this had been the flaw in his writing all along. He'd wanted it to be about losing, about the things we're born into loving and then lose. But if the things he'd written about were not called up out of nothing but willed up from the page, their loss was more like the loss of a well-tailored shirtsleeve than, say, of the arm inside it. Which was how real Richard, for better or worse, had always needed it to be. Had he honestly believed that, if he could make Samantha real enough on the page, he might trade one life for the other, ransom free the Sam captive in her metal bed?

Then he spotted the punk again, killing time behind a pillar. And Richard was indeed going to vomit. As the engines churned up the harbor, he fled out onto the deck. The freak April snow was now heavy enough to hang a porous screen a few yards to starboard, and had driven off anyone else who might have been out here. Yet he couldn't feel the cold. The door behind him took too long to shut. The punk had passed through, though he remained in shadow. Why didn't these Posthumans just come for him already? The notional little banister that had been welded here for safety was slick from snow. He made it over without incident, onto a lip two or three feet deep. It seemed reasonable this might give him an advantage. He was taller, after all. Once the struggle was joined, he'd only need to move his opponent that little distance. Or maybe he was trying to draw them out. Nothing happened. In windows, people stared at newspapers or the floor. The tattooed boy was no longer visible. Nor were the waterfowl that usually worked the wake at the back of the boat. There was only Samantha, watching from the safe side of the rail a few feet away. Any second, the punk would take her place; right now, though, she was as she'd been in that picture of his, the one she'd clipped inside the third issue, dark dye, porkpie, what had he done when he'd taken the photo out? Her face was drawn and sad and silent. Or was this his neighbor Jenny Nguyen, reproaching him for what it might do to her if Richard went down? He saw again the state he'd left his desk in that morning. At the center of the Groskoph mess sat a neat sheaf, thirty-three sheets of 28-lb. bond. Were this struggle to end with him being pushed off the boat, they might form an X-ray of the inside of his head. Jenny might read them and see why he was the way he was, and they might have a future. But this was a fallacy, another form of literary wishful thinking, and anyway, there was a paradox in there somewhere. She could almost have been his own kid.

Assuming it was a girl. He always had. *Leave me alone*, he thought. *Get out of the way of what has to happen.* As ever, though, there was hesitation. Never to face your own offspring. Never to touch the black silk of Jenny's hair. Never to feel again the heat rising off a woman, or off the summer pavement. The sidewalks he'd run along on his way home from church with his arms outstretched and a spitfire stutter he'd made with his mouth, like the one he made now when he'd had too much. Which he had, he was lurching pretty badly here with the movements of the boat and all the strife and indecision erupting in his head. The punk continued not to come, but now a voice like "Dr." Zig's was sounding under everything: fuck it. Fuck cabbies and neighbors and plutocrats and social engineers and Capote and the Pulitzer Committee and rent control like a Chinese fingertrap. Fuck fighting this so hard for so long. Fuck it, Richard. Fuck it fuck it fuck it. The boat hit another swell, and he felt an ancient tug—a promise of some final decision being taken from his hands. An answer or the lack of one. This is just the booze, something in him said. You should lie down and take a nap instead. There's no one out here with you. There isn't even any snow. But the hands hanging on to the rail could have been someone else's. The feet could have been someone else's. The strip of lit windows on the side of the boat was a ribbon threading through black water. He was standing now on the lip's very lip, unfolding himself, as if anyone could read the end of his own story. What had happened, what was happening? Was there really no one else besides himself who would come to hurt him, or help him? Was there even a difference anymore? But this was New York. All those tightly wrapped lives. And for a moment, just before the next wave hit and Richard Groskoph let go of the rail, this city he loved and hated spread before him on the horizon, all his again, so that contrary to what anyone might have thought, he was feeling nothing like alone at the instant he began to fall.

THE FIREWORKERS, PART 2

17

from t
of Car
to cre
conspi
corner
slower
on sh
that,
alrea
unkn
goin
from
that
jus
lif
orbs before me began to rise

BUT THEN, THERE WERE TWO OF EVERYTHING. TWO MIDNIGHTS,
two Cicciaros, two bullets, two workshops . . . two
charges for each shell bursting up in the sky, and
technically, two fuses. It was a mystery I'd confront
again and again in those months Carmine's daughter
lay in the hospital, and one that would complicate
considerably my attempts to understand how she'd got
there: every single thing that touched her seemed
entangled with some ecliptic other half.

Toward the end of that January, for example, I would
come into possession of a complete print run of the
fanzine Samantha's father had mentioned, Land of a
Thousand Dances. Far from alluding to the legends of
Southern soul, as I initially thought, the title turned
out to be a tribute to the rock singer Patti Smith.
And the essays and reviews and diaristic little
fragments within tracked an acolyte's search for a life
large enough to sustain her--a search only hinted at,

theretofore, by Samantha's edgy haircut and those pictures on her bedroom wall.

She'd begun work on the fanzine during her senior year at a private high school in the city. By Issue 2, she'd fallen in with a group of kids on the fringes of the new subculture emerging nearby. "Punk rock" offered a lens through which to examine both herself and the wider world. The view was complicated, as views tend to be, by sex and class and ideology and attitude, but slowly, haltingly, Samantha had given herself over to the tumult of "Downtown." While her father and I had sat on a patio in Flower Hill, speculating about her classes, the daughter was more likely smoking marijuana and listening to records somewhere in the East Village. In the period between Thanksgiving and Christmas of 1976, she seems even to have moved into a squat there.

The fanzine recorded no house number or street name; still, the first thing I did upon reading that winter of the squat's existence was set out to find it. I spent the day after her birthday walking the length of every block between Houston and 14th Street, from Lafayette to the housing projects along the river. Like the house she'd grown up in, the one I was looking for would have an outbuilding behind it. There was also, reportedly, a one-foot gap between it and the next house. This was the sort of thing Samantha had found beauty in-- guillotined parking meters, psoriatic postboxes, cars missing windows and wheels, the fact that behind the rhumb face New York turned to the world, nothing was quite in kilter--but it was hard to muster an aesthetic appreciation when the daytime high was 17 degrees Fahrenheit. I hoped instead to use the gap as an identifying mark, but it turned out such gaps were everywhere. Odd, that I'd never noticed this before. In the shops I stopped into for warmth, no one I mentioned the squat to seemed to speak English, or at any rate understand what I was asking. By nightfall, I gave up and headed back home.

Which isn't to say I wouldn't drift further in the weeks that followed. I began phoning anyone who might remember the fireworker's daughter. One day, a former math teacher was describing her as just another sullen girl in the back row; the next, a photo instructor at NYU was telling me how sad he'd been to see this "promising artist" drop his class. Out in Flower Hill, I made fruitless inquiries about "C," a boy she'd written about befriending the summer before she left for college. (I'd first heard of him in August, when I'd asked Cicciaro if she was dating anyone. "God, I hope not," he'd said. "There's one kid picked her up a couple times in a Buick wagon, but he looked like one of those weenies from the old Charles Atlas ads, getting sand kicked on them.") I then spent hours in the East Village, searching for her other "droogs," likewise identified mostly by initial. Samantha hadn't always gotten along with her friends on the scene; they had a destructive streak, if Issue 3 is accurate, that both repelled and attracted her. But as I observed their habitat, recalled what she'd written, accosted punks on St. Mark's Place who sloughed off all questions, I came to feel my own species of exasperated affection for these characters of hers, SG and DT and NC, sometimes called "Iggy." When people asked why I was looking for them, I finessed the truth; Samantha's name hadn't reached the papers, and I hated to cloud the objectivity of a source. Yet despite my scruples, or perhaps because of them, I'd begun to feel that I knew less than I had on New Year's Day. There had been two Samantha Cicciaros. And if there were to be answers--not about who had shot her, for that was a mugging gone wrong, I believed, but about what losing her might mean--then this other life, this second self, seemed to hold them.

OF COURSE, THE SIGNATURE EFFECT OF A GOOD FANZINE IS TO
make even the most out-of-touch reader feel invested in
the culture depicted therein. It's a lesson some writers
take a lifetime to learn: what makes us care about
things is other people caring, too. And what Samantha
cared about even more than school or friends or her
new punk-rock home in the city was the music. For her,
Patti Smith and Joey Ramone and Lou Reed weren't voices
from her stereo speaker; they were intercessory saints.
And hovering slightly above them all in the margins of
the fanzine, because more accessible (or more nakedly
vulnerable), was a man named Billy Three-Sticks, lead
singer for the early punk band Ex Post Facto.

About the band's history, I could find very little: the
punk rock of '74 was even three years later like a lost
colony, and Billy Three-Sticks a settler vanished into
the interior. I tracked down and listened to the one LP
he'd recorded, but despite an odd sense of having heard
it before, I found the music dissonant, and the lyrics,
for all their emotion, uninterpretable. "Kunneqtiqut /
What the fuck / Connect the dots / Jumbled up / On a
tilt / Around a bend / Alone, Atlantic / Antic end." Nor
could I crack that husk of a surname, Three-Sticks. From
the store where I'd bought the record, however, I did
manage to obtain an address. I went to pay a visit.

The old factory building I found in Hell's Kitchen
was so far from anything described in the 'zine that I
wondered what I even hoped to find there. I was weighing
what approach to take when, finally, I caught a break.
Or rather, two. Before I could cross the street to look
for a buzzer, a small, dark man in a motorcycle jacket
stepped from the vestibule. This was Billy Three-Sticks.
He moved, head down, toward the Eighth Avenue IND. Maybe
it was just the cold making him withdraw into himself,
but he looked so secretive I couldn't help but follow.

Then, a block shy of the subway entrance, I noticed
a second man, black and in some sort of repairman's
coveralls, keeping pace with Billy Three-Sticks across
the street. Intent on his quarry, he seemed not to
see me. By the time I turned back to Three-Sticks,
he had gone into the subway. The coveralled man was
descending, too, until there was only a stocking cap
slipping up in back to show a fugitive bit of green. He
was not a repairman at all, but a "punk"--perhaps even
a friend of Samantha's. And if so, then these "droogs"
of hers weren't simply the loveable fuckups of Land
of a Thousand Dances, but also some other thing that
accounted for his presence here: lurkers, watchers,
spies.

I MADE SEVERAL MORE TRIPS UP TO THE OLD FACTORY, BUT
each time I found the green man from the first day
there ahead of me, watching. Or a nasty-looking lunk
of a skinhead in matching coveralls. Or a girl in
grimy fur idling on a loading dock. Or just the glary
windshield of one of the graffiti'd white vans that
had lately become ubiquitous as pigeons. Three-Sticks
himself was a far rarer sight, keeping to a tight, even
compulsive circuit: vestibule to train to vestibule,
with occasional divagations toward an off-track betting
parlor or the Automat in Times Square.

As for me, I was now light-years from whatever piece
I'd set out to assemble. But I knew a story when I
saw one. Samantha's idol was obviously in some kind
of trouble; had she been too? I would come home at
night, have a drink with a neighbor, say nothing about
the drama I was watching transpire. Yet the next day,
when I rose from my desk for a constitutional, my
steps tended toward Hell's Kitchen. I had fantasies of
slipping into the building behind another resident and
going door to door. Or, failing that--because those

residents all appeared to be bikers who could have
snapped me in two--I would ring every buzzer. Once I'd
warned Billy Three-Sticks he was being followed, simple
gratitude would persuade him to talk. He could lead me
down, perhaps, to the house where Samantha had been
living before the shooting, or at least recall what
it had been like to be a young punk himself. But the
watchers were always there, and when they did finally
withdraw and let me get as far as the buzzers, one
Thursday morning in March, a biker's tattooed face
popped out of an upper window seconds after I rang. I
explained that I was looking for Billy Three-Sticks, and
got confirmation of what I already knew (if only from
the absence of an audience) must be true: I wasn't going
to find him here anymore.

"You're saying he's just disappeared?" I shouted.
Then, emboldened by the solidity of brick and fire
escape between us: "He's your neighbor. Doesn't it
concern you?"

The man suggested, not uncheerfully, that I mind my
own business. It was 7 a.m. People lived here.

IN HINDSIGHT, THIS WAS PROBABLY THE MOMENT TO INVOLVE
the actual police. But what did I have that I'd trust
them not to bungle? Not only did I never again see the
white van in Hell's Kitchen, but Billy Three-Sticks,
whom I'd taken for my passafuoco, my passageway into
Samantha, was gone, too. It was March. I'd spent a month
pursuing a dead end, when I should have been going out
to Long Island to keep Carmine company, or at least to
finish our interviews. And now I could do neither.

What I mean is this: after Billy Three-Sticks went
to ground, all the energy that had overtaken me that
winter evaporated. I descended into the worst writer's
block of a career that's had its share. I would rise

around lunchtime and instead of going out to report,
or sitting down to write, I would pour myself a drink.
It was remarkable, I was rediscovering, how much
more a person could drink if he was willing to start
during daylight hours, and how the character of his
intoxication changed. Once, I had felt the rightness
of the slang term "buzz": efflorescence, that bursting
of the shell of the self. Now, in the bleak white late-
winter light, my apartment was an Alaska. From beyond
the walls came the infinitude of sound, the beep
beep of trucks backing up, the rattle and whinny of a
garbage masher, and, nearer in, the elevator engine's
sigh, the ghost frequencies of the super's walkie-
talkie, the noise, real or imagined, of my neighbor, my
quondam drinking buddy, slamming cabinets next door.
Yet within me, where my own voice would have to come
from, was a silence so deep as to be pure potential.
And behind that, like the backing on the mirror: death.
It made even a phrase like "comatose in a hospital bed"
feel sentimental.

I left the apartment only to buy as many newspapers
as I could find--a habit, or vice, from my time at the
World-Telegram. Now, with just three dailies left in New
York, I suppose I could have taken out subscriptions,
but that would have missed the point. The point was not
to read, but to purchase. To feel, as you fumbled for
another nickel, that something big might have happened
since you last looked. In this way, you fought off the
anxious emptiness at the center of your head, the sense
that nothing under the sun was ever really new, and that
we were all of us therefore stuck with the lives we had.

Which is how, more than a month into my bender, I
discovered the photo of Sam Cicciaro on the front of
the New York Post. She looked nothing like she had in
real life. She wore an off-the-shoulder dress, for one
thing. Her hair was elaborately plaited and shellacked,

her head tilted, her smile slightly open-mouthed, as if the yearbook photographer had said something to make her laugh. I blinked and still she was there. Poured another drink. Still, she was there. Scooped, I kept thinking. I've been scooped.

An hour later, I was on the phone, dialing my old pal Larry Pulaski at the NYPD, who was now a deputy inspector. Behind the operator who answered, I remember, ringers trilled like slot machines. Every light on the switchboard must have been lighting up for comment.

"I wondered if I'd hear from you," Pulaski said, once I'd made it through. "But you should have used my office line."

"I'm looking at the _Post_ here," I told him. "You want the _Post_ or the _Daily News_? Because her name's in both."

"You sound like you've been drinking."

"How could you disclose it, Larry? Carmine's still out there all alone. If I were you, I'd be worried he makes some reporter for a prowler and you end up with another shooting on your hands."

"I'll tell you what worries me more, Richard, if you want to know. You're losing your objectivity."

But how much objectivity could I get? We were talking about page one of the f▓▓ing _Post_. Probably it was just static in the line, but I could have sworn I heard the snip of trimmers, the punctilious deity on the other end of the wire paring his nails. "Richard, do you think I like rubberneckers mooning around my crime scenes? Do you think I like your man on the radio howling for my personal blood?" A pause here almost made it seem he was waiting for an answer.

"You swear you had nothing to do with this?"

"There was a leak, is what I'm telling you, Richard. Several links up the food chain, probably."

"Why would anyone leak?"

"I'd love to know that myself, but bottom line, it's a big department, this stuff happens, and right now I've got multiple other fires to put out. I do the job they pay me to do. I suggest you put down the bottle and do the same."

I WOKE THE NEXT DAY WITH A VAGUE SENSE OF CRIMINALITY. I had been unfair to someone, but wasn't sure how. The miniblinds by the couch I'd passed out on were v-shaped in the middle, like something had struck them. On my coffeetable was a meniscus of dust. But there was my dog pacing incontinently by the door, his tail thwacking it on each pass. And when I reached the street, there were the trees breaking out into leaf. Springtime. Life. It shook loose a memory. Hadn't there been something about "no dead ends"? In any case, Pulaski was right: I had a job to do.

I'd uncovered, as near as I could tell, two avenues into the shooting. The first, though the connection remained obscure, was still Billy Three-Sticks. I'd had no luck at his place of residence, but had given up too easily. So I began looking for him at other local haunts. All I saw, from time to time, were the young men who were watching him. They were back. And when I observed the larger of them, disguised now in a preposterous sportcoat and beard, hunched up in a booth in the Automat, using a four-inch switchblade to saw a pus-soaked bandage off his hand, my search began to feel like an emergency. I widened it to other betting parlors and Automats, to Chelsea, to parts of the Upper West Side. I spent whole days walking, pausing, ducking behind newsstands, begging the city to put Billy and me into contact.

If I was home, I worked the phone. The name "Samantha Cicciaro" seemed to have leaked simultaneously to every paper and newsstation; it was impossible to say who'd had it first. But when the <u>World-Telegram</u> had closed, it had scattered my colleagues wide across the media firmament, and now I called them all, asking them to point me toward a source. Most refused--some vehemently--but in the end I reached one who obliged. He couldn't name names, he told me. But he had this funny idea the story of the shooting in the park had been timed to knock something else off the front pages. And he knew his friend who'd broken it had contacts high up in the Hamilton-Sweeney Building.

That name set bells clanging. For Carmine Cicciaro's chief competitor, I knew, was a wholly owned subsidiary of the Hamilton-Sweeney Company. When he'd suggested on New Year's Eve that these competitors were involved in the disappearance of three grams of polverone from his workshop, I hadn't taken him seriously: his theory imputed such personal animus to what he otherwise called "the money." (To the extent that I'd thought about it at all since, I'd decided that it was probably Samantha herself who nicked the three grams, in a moment of rebellion, or pique, or as some kind of offering for her firebug friends.) I knew, too, from paying just enough attention to the radio, that the Hamilton-Sweeney Company was in legal trouble, but I'd assumed--the dynastic merchant bank having mutated into a conglomerate in the '60s--that Carmine's competitor was a separate arm, and that superintending the whole would be some bureaucratic cabal too faceless to care about "sending a message" to a lone fireworker. But no, when I consulted the newspaper, there apparently was a Mr. Hamilton-Sweeney in the chairman's seat, and now under indictment. Was it so far-fetched to imagine that he might know something about this leak? This break-in?

A few days passed. I sat on my new lead, but kept researching the Hamilton-Sweeney case. Then two

nights ago when I was riding the subway back up
from the Village, the miracle occurred. Through the
communicating door between my car and the next, I
happened to spot a battered biker jacket. Billy Three-
Sticks. It was as if my ceasing to look for him had
summoned him forth. But he must have seen me, too, even
recognized me somehow, because when I passed through
the intervening doors, he bolted onto the platform and
up the stairs. I called out for him to wait, followed
him down a corridor. The gate at the end had been
locked for the night. Finally, we would connect; we
could still save each other. I reached for his shoulder,
almost fatherly, but when he turned, this skinny guy
who on his record sleeve didn't look a day over twenty,
he was so pale as to seem already dead. A side gate had
been left open, and he darted through it and upstairs,
and before I could catch him and explain the danger I
feared he was in, he was on a downtown train, the doors
closing behind him.

THERE WAS NO CHOICE LEFT BUT TO PURSUE THE HAMILTON-
Sweeney angle. The next morning, then, I gave the
picture in the paper a twice-over. Took a shower.
Grabbed a nearly clean shirt, figuring a few wrinkles
here and there would make me seem less of a threat.
Put on a tie. Folded a sheet of A4 into eighths, tucked
it into my breast pocket, took from its hook my old
fedora, and headed across town to the Hamilton-Sweeney
Building, where I would try to get a meeting with
William Hamilton-Sweeney II on the spot. It was better,
sometimes, not to give a potential subject too much
time to think. The first impulse of even the loftiest
chieftain, offered the bullhorn of mass media, is to
grab it.
    Rather than waving me up to the 30th floor, however,

the tubby elevator attendant at whom I flashed an old
credential told me to have a seat, his supervisor would
have to call up to the press office. A few minutes
later, an elevator expelled a small man who did not at
all resemble any press officer I'd ever seen, much less
the CEO depicted in the Times. His perfectly white hair
gave a false first impression; as he drew closer, I saw
that he couldn't have been older than early middle age.
At any rate, there were no wrinkles or superfluities.
The man himself was bespoke. "Mr. Groskoph, I presume."

Then a hand was at my back, steering me toward a busy
outdoor plaza. I had a few questions, I told him, once
we'd reached it. But he proposed to ask me one instead:
"Mr. Groskoph, what do you suppose you're worth?"

"Beg pardon?" I said, or words to that effect.

"I am asking you to imagine yourself forced to
liquidate everything you own, today. How much capital
might you come up with? What do you think you are
worth?"

He never turned from the street to look at me, but
I felt put back on my heels. Best, I decided, to be
direct--to admit I had no idea.

"Understand, I've had my eye on you for some time.
You've made inquiries concerning certain of our
contracts." There seemed to be around him a layer of
cold, but maybe I was just hung over. "The Company
has a pronounced interest in privacy. Time was, all
Americans did. Now I can pick up a magazine and see the
former Mrs. Kennedy in a bathing suit. Her affair, of
course, but the Hamilton-Sweeneys do not intend to join
her there."

"In the bathing suit?" I said. "And would you mind if
I got your name?"

"I see you haven't finished inquiring. But I have.
Since you called City Hall last summer, I've made it
my business to read most every word you've written,

Mr. Groskoph. Or rather, published. And may I tell
you I'm impressed? The piece about the Apollo program,
in particular. I said to myself, this is a man of
considerable intelligence, at some point he will
discover which end of the stick he's got. Frankly, I am
surprised it has come to this, but I am here to tell
you, face to face: this is that point."

"Sorry," I said. "Which point?"

"The point at which you cease and desist."

"It's a free country."

"Indeed. One whose civil code protects the legal
person against harassment, libel, and other incursions
against liberty. These matters are very hard to
adjudicate, of course, very costly. Like paternity
suits. Like calculations of palimony, child support."

He had somehow found out, he was saying, about the
child I'd fathered in Florida earlier in the '70s, with
an airline waitress whom I'd left on bad terms. She must
have been three years old. The child, I mean. I still
may not have believed this man would stoop to breaking
into Carmine's workshop for three measly grams of
powder, even to send a message; it was beneath him. But
there wasn't anything at that moment I would have put
beyond him.

"Financially, this family has long been prepared for
such eventualities. What I've been trying to ascertain
is whether you are, too."

"I'm afraid there's been some misunderstanding."

"On the contrary; things couldn't be clearer. Whatever
story has brought you to our doorstep, as it were, ends
this morning. Ends here. And now more pressing business
calls." He began to leave.

"But to whom should I attribute all this, for the
record?" I called out, loud enough that it caused other
people on the plaza to look over. But he didn't turn
around, and already the glare off the lobby's glass

was devouring him, a metal box arriving to whisk him
back into the sky. The attendant, sweating through
his uniform, must have seen something in my face as
I pushed back inside, approached the velvet rope by
the elevator bank, for he stopped me with a kind of
demoralized shrug. "It's not for nothing they call him
the Demon Brother." Then, when I pressed for an actual
name, he told me he was sure a good reporter could
figure it out. Besides, it was time I was on my way.

TO THE INNER LEAF OF THE THIRD AND FINAL ISSUE OF HER
fanzine, or at least my copy of it, Samantha Cicciaro
clipped a photograph of herself as a freshman, a new
arrival to the city. The issue itself has vanished
inconveniently among my papers, but the photograph must
have fallen out beforehand, for I found it in February
on the floor--and tonight, having sat for too long in
one place, grasping after a language not compromised
by time, I have it propped on the desk before me. There
on the median of Houston Street, the sun is so intense
that it's hard to make out details of her upturned
face. It will be even harder, I know from experience,
if I turn off the lights in my apartment. Then, in the
shifting glow of the jukebox across the room, she'll
become my colleague, co-conspirator, lost daughter,
best friend. But say I really could know her. Say I
could find the perfect wording for what flashes now on
my mind's eye: the rusted-out deckchair where she sat
on the last day of 1976, preparing herself for whatever
the new year would bring. The swallows blown off-
course over the yard where her mother used to hang the
clothesline. The secret cigarette stubbed out on the
bricks of the patio. The girl herself, hunkering down
deeper into her formless winter coat. Then where would
it stop? How many column-inches would it take to get her

from there to the little municipal train station, the
train, Central Park? I could fill a whole book with that
one day--I could find out who shot her--and it wouldn't
do justice to the quiddities of human life, much less
reveal what they mean. A miracle, a universe, I heard
a rabbi say once. Any of us, plucked out of the eight
million. The several billion.

No, that man, whoever he was, was right. I'll never
reach the end of her story. Never find out who wanted
to hurt her, or Billy Three-Sticks. Never be allowed
to get that close to either again, or to find that
second house, or the other, smaller house behind it, or
the awful truth or truths I now feel sure Samantha
or her phantom twin stumbled upon. There are too many
of everything. Too many of me, even. I set out here to
write a profile that would mirror the enigma it sought
to unravel: how, from canisters of inert material the
size of coffee urns, patterns of blazing color come
to fill the sky. I imagined myself engineering out
of discrete pieces a singular explosion. Instead, I
find now I've been trying to work backward from one,
to reconstruct from a random dispersal of elements a
single shell. An impossible shell, in fact, insofar as
there is no such thing as a perfect phrase, or a private
language, and insofar as time only runs the one way.

I'LL ADD ONLY THAT I DID MAKE IT OUT TO THAT HOUSE IN
Nassau County to see Carmine Cicciaro once more. This
was at the beginning of April, weeks into my slump. How
often in the previous months had I imagined returning
in triumph, with a typescript that would instantly
expunge my distraction and my disregard. Yes, yes,
I neglected you, but look what I found! Instead, I'd
brought only a pair of confessions: first, that I'd
stolen the fanzines from his daughter's bedroom back in

January; and second, that in my fog of this morning,
I'd forgotten to take from their place of safekeeping
the two remaining issues--that I'd noticed my own empty-
handedness only halfway out to Flower Hill.

I found Carmine Cicciaro sitting out on the back
patio, almost as if it were still August. He was no
longer the immovable object, though, who back then had
nearly forced me off his property. On the bricks between
his shoes was a beercan, and without a word for my long
absence, he reached into the cooler and fished me out
one. We clinked cans reflexively and then sat silent
on our matchingly grimed deck furniture, gazing down
toward the expressway, lost in our respective thoughts.
Out of nowhere, he said, "I ever tell you how the
Chinese name their shells?"

I shook my head, no.

"They look at the sky and just make up a story about
what they see when the bomb goes off. Pure bullshit,
but you get these beautiful names. Flower Scattering
Child, Golden Frog Bangs a Gong--I always loved that
one."

What would they have called us? I wondered. I didn't
know what to say.

When he spoke again, it was to tell me he was closing
up shop, putting the house on the market. The mortgage
was nearly paid off, and he was looking to sublet
a place in the city where he could be closer to the
hospital. And I decided then, if I hadn't already. What
good would it do to confess I had broken his trust? To
add a breach of faith to his sorrows?

So I finished my beer quickly and stood up, knowing
that if I stayed, I'd have to have another. Carmine
crumpled his own can and whipped it down the hill,
toward his workshop. A rusty chain, looped through
the place where the handle had been, held the door
impressively closed. The fans were off for good. Even

the workshop was to be abandoned. For what Carmine
Cicciaro had learned by then, and I suppose I had, too,
concerned not only the baffling multiplicity of all
things, but also their no less baffling integration.
No amount of art, even of the Great American variety,
can elevate you above, or insulate you from, the
divisions, the cataclysms, of ordinary life. Still, as
I turned to shake his hand and tell him I'd be seeing
him, I couldn't quite get free of how it used to feel,
waiting for the July 4th display, back on the humid town
common of the Tulsa where I was a kid. How, down on the
bandshell, a local vocal quartet would be warming up,
their candy-striped jackets a pink mess in the heat.
How I would lie on my back on the blanket, slightly
apart from my cousins, dreaming. At some point, the
Rutabaga Brothers and the Lemon Sisters would rouse
us to our feet and lead us in patriotic song, and then
it would begin: signal lights ascending the sky, two,
three, a dozen, a hundred. I had no other associations
then for the sound of mortar fire, for the cascades
of color swimming up to meet their counterparts in
the face of the swollen brown river. All I wanted was
more, more, more. I'd ask myself at each volley, in an
ecstasy of anticipation, was this the last one? Was
this? But maybe that is what, in the end, brings this
particular art closer to life than its more mimetic
siblings can ever manage--what I'd glimpsed in the
summer of 1976, watching the Bicentennial on a TV 3,000
miles away: each display of fireworks is utterly time-
bound. A singularity. No past and no future. Save for
the fireworker himself, no one ever knows the grand
finale is the grand finale until it's over. And at that
point, wherever one is, one won't ever really have been
anywhere else.

BOOK VII

IN THE DARK

[JULY 13, 1977-∞]

Wandering through the shadows, we listen to the breath
  That makes the darkness shudder;
And now and then, lost in unfathomable nights,
We see lit up by mighty lights
  The window of eternity.

—VICTOR HUGO
The Contemplations

In the dark,
It's just you and I.
Not a sound—
There's not one sigh.
Just the beat of my poor heart
In the dark.

—LIL GREEN
"In the Dark"

90

A T THE INSTANT THE BLACKOUT HITS, "Dr." Zig Zigler is staring at a pair of sandhill cranes that have found their way onto the CC local. Or maybe they're spoonbills. In any case, it's mesmerizing, this sort of beaky, wised-up look they have. And clearly a kind of intelligence, possibly the only kind there is, has been involved in negotiating turnstiles and platforms and boarding the rearmost car of an actual train. It happened at Thirty-Fourth Street, and ever since, they've been minding their business like proper New Yorkers, perched at the far end of a scuffed plastic bench, ruffling wings every so often as though shaking folds from a paper. The other passengers keep the same ten-yard buffer they would if these were panhandlers, so Zig's the only one noticing, but that's fine, he's used to it. He's been noticing stuff for weeks now it's probably saner not to see. Peacocks in crosswalks. A great blue heron, once, perched on the steeple of Grace Church on Broadway. It could just be the Dexedrine talking, but he *likes* this conceit of the walls between nature and culture breaking down, the animals taking over the zoo: this will be perfect, he thinks, for the show tomorrow. If there is a show tomorrow. If by that point the FCC hasn't yanked his card and the animals in question haven't torn apart the WLRC studios . . . which is when the world goes dark and the brakes start to screech and his ass goes sliding into the void.

Blackness persists even after the train has stopped. There are smells and sounds but nothing to stitch them together. The absence of engine noise is never a good sign. *Sheeyit*, a voice says, but it doesn't seem like anyone's hurt, or panicking—at least anyone save "Dr." Zig himself. When the birds rustle again, that little click of beak or claw, he wonders if they too are about to turn on him, because frankly it's been that kind of year: the shooting of the girl in the Park, this thing with his old adversary. And finally the uprising of his listener base, which turns out to be not some savvy cognoscenti, grooving on the ironies of his self-presentation, but the same Not-So-Silent Majority that jams up the Yackline each day. He can feel them massed out there now, agitating to take New York back to an imaginary 1954. Can't anyone hear past the spleen to his bleeding heart? 1954 was terrible! He has been misunderstood! Though probably this, too, is the drugs.

Gingerly, so as not to incite the birds, he gropes for the overhead bar and picks his way forward in the dark. He can feel the sheath of heat around each unseen straphanger. By the time he reaches the car's front end, he's swimming in amphetamine sweat. Around him conversations spark or resume, quiet at first, then louder, black and Spanish voices this part of town. Somebody wants to open the windows; like birdshit, is what it smells like.

Somebody else says no, they've got to hold in what little AC is left.

¿A quién le importa? This always happens, we'll be moving soon anyway.

Where are the conductors? Why aren't they fixing it?

Sheeyit. Motherfuckers couldn't fix a ham sandwich.

Time has its own way of moving down here. Still, it's got to be close to ten. In order to be up at the crack of three—one of the perquisites of pre-drive-time radio—Zigler should have been in bed hours ago, but he hasn't had a good night's sleep since May, since the news about Richard. Anyone who's spent so much as ten minutes listening to *Gestalt Therapy* (and even its producer, Nordlinger, who usually pops in earplugs after the opening theme and spends the remainder perusing porn) has to have figured out that "Dr." Zig's planning to punch his own ticket one of these days, to make a final point. And then the one-time National Magazine Award Nominee goes and one-ups him again. Diet pills have always been Zigler's secret for getting through four hours on air, but these days he lets them blast him right out of the broadcast booth at the end of the show and into the shift bars south of Times Square where you can be drunk before noon. Sometimes, early evenings, there comes a point where the speed wears off and he feels his meter running, but his sleep deficit is already so far beyond anything he'll ever be able to earn back that he figures he might as well pop another pill, have another drink, because what's another hour at the bar in the face of a million hours? What's a little hangover in the face of the infinite grave?

Someone lights a match, coaxing faces from the dark, and dimly, at the deserted end of the car, feathers. When the blackness is restored, Zigler smells tobacco. He should have checked his watch when he had a chance. There has to be a natural limit to how long anyone can spend like this, in a black aluminum suppository lodged in the asshole of the earth. Like: How much does body heat have to build before people start keeling over? And how long before someone starts to really freak?

He unbuttons a button, luffs shirt from chest. The air refuses to move. Then, through the window of the communicating door, he sees one of those deep, eyeless fish with the hypodermic teeth, a brighter light approaching. Zigler steps aside just as the door opens and a flashlight floats in, followed by a cool dank gust of tunnel air. Shapes play weirdly on walls and windows. One cuts around in front of the light. It's the Chinese man who came through earlier selling batteries from a trashbag. There were apparently cigarette lighters in there as well, or maybe this is a different bag he's offering side to side. Anyway, as soon as a lighter's been taken, he passes on to the next person. When Zigler reaches for his wallet, the Chinaman shakes his head. Meanwhile, from behind the flashlight, a booming, island-tinged voice announces that they can't be more than (*kyant* be more *dan*) a couple blocks from 110th Street. The stress falls oddly. "If we're care-FUL, we can exit through the front car, walk up the track to the sta-SHUN." The flashlight swings around to touch the door to the next car, the bodies in motion beyond. "Women first, unless there's babies." *I'm a baby*, Zigler wants to say—*Me first!*—but were anyone to recognize his voice, it would inevitably lead to blows over some bullshit he's said on air. Which is why every time he rides this train home now, he's afraid to speak a word. The shock jock's vow of silence. What if the power comes back on? someone says. "What if it doesn't?" booms the Jamaican. "You been down here forty minutes already." This seems to settle things. People flick their Bics, move toward the forward door. But "Dr." Zig Zigler, for reasons even he would have a hard time articulating, is fighting his way back to the cranes at the rear of the car. Maybe they'll attack him, tackle him, peck out his ravaged liver, but so what? It would at least be an exit Rich Groskoph couldn't steal. He supposes he means to prop open the aft door, in case what the birds want is to escape. But when he gets there and gets the new lighter working, they appear to have vanished completely.

1 POLICE PLAZA—9:27 P.M.

"SEE?"

"See what, Charlie? I can't see a blessed thing. Let me see if I've got some matches."

"This is like the oldest trick in the book. You put out the lights at the fuse box, or you unscrew all the lightbulbs before the person gets home—"

"This is Con Ed, kid. This is eight million people running air conditioners off an eighty-year-old grid."

"—and when they come in, wham! Or did you not see *Godfather II*?"

"Look around you, Charlie. Or I guess these don't put out enough light, but you're sitting in one of the most secure rooms in New York City. It's exactly where you'd want to be if someone was trying to bump you off. Which no one is. And if you would just cooperate with me a little about Samantha's shooting, I might be able to look out for you on some kind of longer-term basis. Ouch!"

"You don't give up, do you? It's like a fixation."

"Well, the lights are going to come back on sooner or later. Real life will resume."

"How many times do I have to tell you it wasn't me who shot her?"

"Okay. Have it your way. Let's say for the sake of argument your invisible friend, Mr. Chaos—"

"It wasn't Nicky either. He wouldn't. With anyone else, I know, a bomb points to that, but not with Sam."

"Again with the bomb, though, Charlie! You should know, the only thing I've seen that makes any sense with your story is a throwaway line in Richard's article, some gunpowder missing from Flower Hill." Another flame dies. The air is thick with sulfur. "I suppose if she knew about the theft, that could have put the girl at risk."

"Well, there you go."

"But only from your phantom perpetrator, kid, who you just ruled out. Anyway, three grams is barely a thimbleful. Certainly not enough to reliably kill this William fellow, even granting you the larger plot."

Nor was Billy Three-Sticks in danger so long as he steered clear of his uncle, D.T. had said. And inside Charlie now, a thimble begins to empty: a little anthill of black dust, a tiny, ineffectual anticlimax. But then why would Nicky spend months puzzling over circuits and timers? Something breaks from him. A sob-slash-manic-cough. "I'm not insane, okay?"

"No one said you were."

"And I'm not a criminal. I'm a loyal person. Be nice to me, and I'm loyal."

"Charlie, I'm trying to be nice. Do you not see me sitting here burning my blessed fingers so you can see no one's coming to get you?"

"But no, that's not true, I'm the worst thing. A rat. You hear that? It's footsteps—they're coming to give me what I deserve."

"That's just bodies in the other cells getting restless, and honestly, kid, better they beat on the cinderblock than each other. Here, can you see this?"

"No."

"I'm on my last match, so look close. That's St. Jude. He's been around my neck since long before you were born. In other words, I've had years to think about this. Justice doesn't mean stomping out a person just because he's done something wrong. Sometimes it means giving him a chance to set it right. I'm trying to give you—oh, for the love of . . ."

"Wait, say that again."

"I'm going to need a salve."

"No, the other. About justice. Oh, shit. Holy shit. I can see it now." Because forget D.T.; what Nicky had said last week, in that house cleared of even its meager valuables, was that *everybody* had it coming. Charlie had thought it must be another figure of speech—*Nobody escapes in the end*—but if it wasn't, that solved the timing problem right there: while the other Post-Humanists fled toward their fates, Nicky would *remain in light.* "That's why you'd use a bomb and not a knife. That's why you'd steal gunpowder . . . multiple victims, all at once."

"Boy. One of us is sure fixated, I'll give you that, Charlie. But all this pedaling is taking you farther away. Grams, is what the article says. It wouldn't blow up a kewpie doll."

Only Charlie's hardly here anymore; he's pushing down deeper in the darkness, thinking again of Mrs. Kotzwinkle on the importance of units. Hearing voices through the floor. "So how much powder would you need to kill three people at once, and maybe take out a house? Would kilograms do it?"

"Charlie, that's not funny. With a kilo of the stuff, you could take out a city block."

"But is that much enough to fill a duffelbag?"

For the first time, Pulaski sounds anxious. "Now you're talking a whole neighborhood."

"I saw the Rangers bag myself, going into the little house out back. Shit. I even helped prepare the way, dried out the floor, cleared the way for the fans. And when I left Nicky yesterday, he was on his way to deliver an invitation to Billy's uncle. For tomorrow. Or tonight. Operation Demon Brother. The duffel's full of black powder, kilograms of it."

"Motive again, though, Charlie. Give me a motive for any of this."

"Because he was in love with Sam. You said yourself that's the best motive. They were in love, and she got shot, and Nicky thinks it's the Hamilton-Sweeneys' fault somehow, but also his own for getting mixed up with them. He was fucking her, okay?"

"That's not the same thing."

Yet Charlie knows blowing himself up is what he would have done, too, if he'd really loved her enough, or ever been serious about atonement. "Maybe not, fuck if I know. But I'm telling you, that's his idea of justice now—to hell with everything. This Demon Brother guy's going to come to East Third Street, and he'll find a way to draw Billy Three-Sticks down there, too. As soon as all three of them are in the house, Nicky's going to blow them all to kingdom come. And you still haven't sent those cops."

"I don't have cops to send, Charlie. Not now that we're in a black-out. Not for a story like that, without a shred of evidence."

"I'm your shred. Why can't you listen to me? You've got to listen."

Again, there is the pounding noise. Like a giant at a fortress door. Then: "Geez, kid. I really wish you could have put all that together before the lights went out."

DOWNTOWN & POINTS NORTH—CA. 8:00 P.M.

THE FIRST THING KEITH DOES after leaving the cop shop is find a pay-phone. He knows no one at the day camp's going to pick up; the after-care program's start and end times, heretofore so hard to remember, are now emblazoned in neon across his frontal lobe. But after getting no answer, he takes a cab up to the school anyway, in case the kids are still waiting on the front steps . . . which they aren't, because when has anything ever been as simple as Keith needs it to be? He does manage, however, via persistent pounding, to get someone to unlock the door. The streetlamps have come on, and a glinty whistle dangles in the dusk. Attached to it is a manchild in gym shorts whose every sentence ends up a question. Maybe there's a simple explanation? Maybe Will and Cate decided just to walk home? Seeing Dad was two hours late? Or went over to their granddad's, like last time? The even temper Keith prides himself on is evaporating. Anger comes pouring out, as yet uncut by fear. There are intimations of liability. He may even use the phrase "educational malpractice." When it is proposed, though, that the manchild lead him back to the Assistant Head Counselor's office so they can try getting in touch with the mother, Keith sees he's in checkmate. No, yes, he is overreacting; they are indeed probably back home. Where he agrees now to betake himself, and no need to drag Regan into it again.

But that home—apartment, really—is as lifeless as a crypt. His message service has no messages. An impulsive call to her place goes unanswered, too. He has a sudden vision of an entire city of unused phones, receivers dangling from cords like hanged men in vacant houses. Of course, if the kids have tried to call here at any point in the last twelve hours, they will have gotten no answer, either. Where would *he* go, were he Will? What goes on behind that watchful face has always been a mystery. But Will is his mother's child, rational above all else, and since no one's at Regan's, the rational thing, Keith sees, would indeed be for them to go wait at their grandfather's, where there are sure at least to be servants to let them in, and which is infinitely closer, not a mile from the day camp if you cut across the Park. Yes, they'll be there waiting at Bill and Felicia's, or they'll be en route, in which case maybe he can overtake them before any of this gets back to his soon-to-be-ex-wife.

And so nightfall finds him on the Center Drive, moving at a decent clip considering he's in loafers, scanning for the kids. Baubles of electricity burn amid shadows. The sycamores have that green-gold quality where the leaves swallow the light. Other leaves, already dry at midsummer, explode underfoot. Joggers slide past in a gloom of sweat, smirking at the man clumsily run-walking in business attire. He's jogged around the Reservoir plenty of times himself over the years, but always for the sake of being the sort of person who jogs around the Reservoir. Not a few things about his life, come to think of it, have operated on this principle. Maybe it's why people think of him as shallow. Or if that's too strong, as somehow less . . . *dimensional* than themselves. Regan included. Will very much included. As if he hasn't fully developed whatever the third thing is besides ego and id, and so basically needs to be managed a little to keep from getting into trouble. And mightn't this sense of being treated like a teenager account for his history of acting like one? There was a time before the separation when he'd swum down to a place so deep inside himself it almost wasn't in contact with the adult world.

Then, as if to suggest he never came back up, the lit-up apartment towers he's been aiming for, the Dakota and San Remo, go dark, as does the roadway, and all those golden sycamores. Perfect. A power outage. He can't see a damn thing. Afraid that if he keeps going he'll break an ankle in a pothole, he stops and laces hands over head and breathes great, raggedy breaths, waiting for the lights to come back on.

Which they don't.

And don't.

And as the seconds pile up he feels a hole opening inside him, a black bulb searing through the bright film of life. His children are out there. Even say they are just ahead of him, crossing the Park. A person can get seriously hurt here in the dark. Has he warned them about this? Probably he hasn't, probably it's a subject he's been avoiding altogether. Probably he lost track of Will and Cate long ago, exchanging them for son- and daughter-sized symbols, like the pillows kids pile in their beds before they sneak out at night.

It's strange though how under the right circumstances a certain shallowness turns out to be an asset. Because instead of falling to his knees right here on the asphalt—*My daughter! My son!*—Keith makes a decision. He strips off his jacket and starts running again. Like *really* running this time, potholes be damned, shouting their names toward the pinprick lights of cars he can pick out on what he hopes is Central Park West. "Will! Cate!" He must sound like a lunatic; startled birds go leaping like fleas through the hoops of the headlights, whirl up against the moon. But who cares how he sounds? It's like, instead of deepening with his guilt, Keith Lamplighter has become even shallower than he suspected. No deeper than the pain in his trick knee. No thicker than the soles he's now burning through.

UPPER WEST SIDE—9:28 P.M.

THE FIRST RULE OF CRISIS MANAGEMENT is just to get through the first three seconds. On the other side—once you've got some kind of story into which to slot things—you'll forget what it felt like during these early moments when the future was whatever you feared most. And so, when the penthouse goes black, Regan begins to count. And by the time she reaches three, she knows the entire city must be powerless; otherwise light pollution would be silvering the library's curtains.

Her brother isn't, to put it mildly, the wait-and-see type. Whatever he's feeling at a given moment is what he's always been and always will be feeling. And so he's gone ahead and charged out onto the balcony, imagining the thump he heard out there and the subsequent darkness are further aspects of a worldwide conspiracy against him. Even when he calls an all-clear back through the open door, his voice is a little shaky, as if he doesn't quite believe what he's seeing. Or not seeing, as the case may be.

"What happened . . ."

This is Daddy, sounding somehow diminished, behind Regan and to her left. She turns, thrusting her arms into the nothing. She finds a body: a shoulder. A hand, cool in the heat. She takes it in her own, fumbles for a chair she might guide him to. "It's all right, Daddy. Just a blackout. You remember the one we had in '65? They'll have the lights on in a few hours, at most."

A lone siren. "There's no one out here," William calls again.

"We know there's no one out there, William, the universe does not revolve around you. Now could you come in and give me a hand?" To Daddy, seated, she says not to worry, she'll find some light. She's still effectively blind, but seems to remember a candelabrum over on the north wall. "Amory, I assume there are still candles up here?"

The moment she lets go of her father's hand, though, he starts in again with this mutter, as from a faulty transistor (*What is happening?*), so that she has to narrate. "Follow my voice, Daddy. I'm just feeling my way over, very carefully, so I don't run into anything . . ." In fact, the things she touches in the dark promptly thump to the floor. She must have hit a bookcase. But she gropes her way down until she feels the sturdy old credenza, salvaged from her great-grandfather's place in Greenwich at some point deep in the past. "Okay, it seems like the candleholders are empty, so now I'm feeling in the drawers for replacements. Amory, William, would one of you *please* go help Daddy?"

The center drawer is empty except for some papers, but in the one on the right are waxy sticks, intact wicks. She locates her clutch. She's still carrying around her hairdresser's lighter, for some reason. The wheel yields only sparks. One . . . two . . . She runs a finger along the lighter's tip, encounters a bit of fluff in the hole where the flame's supposed to be, tweezes it out, tries again. At last: fire. Touched to a candle-tip, it's bright enough to make her squint. She turns to see Daddy still in his chair and, just inside the French doors, making no move to go to him, William. She lights another candle off this one, pushes both into the candelabrum, holds it aloft, but there is no sign that anyone else was ever here.

"Where did he go, Regan?" William demands. "Where's Amory?"

The light barely reaches the far walls. "Looking for flashlights?"

"Halfway to Penn Station, more likely. The Demon fucking Brother."

"What would he be doing at Penn Station?"

"Snap out of it, Regan. Waiting for the power to come back on. Escaping, obviously."

"From whom? From us? And if he is, so what?"

"I'm going after him, is what."

"What are you going to do, make a citizen's arrest?"

"You're always enabling him, you ever notice that?" He's close enough now to pluck a candle from its holder—close enough for her to see he won't be reasoned with. "It's time someone stopped letting him get away with this shit."

She would ask him where he gets off, and also maybe where he came up with this word, "enable," which she thought was trademark Dr. Altschul, except he's already on his way out the door. "Daddy—," she says, as though her father were still a figure to appeal to, the grave-faced idol of her youth. But candlelight has eaten away the solidity; he is a confused old man. And William III, the brother she thought she'd restored to safety, is now just a glimmer in the dark beyond the jamb.

ON THE ROAD—9:58 P.M.

BY THE TIME the rendezvous went down, they'd be all the way to Chicago, Nicky promised. Or at least to South Bend. And before the NYPD could start looking for them—before the pigs had reassembled enough pieces to know there was even a "them" to look for—they'd be lying low in the land of the maple leaf, up in Manitoba. So far away from what they had done, thought D. Tremens, that it would be almost like it never happened. But the curse that's descended on them these last couple months isn't going to lift just on Nicky's say-so. If anything, Murphy or Gumperson or whoever's up there calling the galactic square dance tonight seems to be expending extra ingenuity just to fuck with the PHP.

There's the van, for instance. The first time D.T. ever saw it, he cracked a joke about baling wire and old rubbers, and Nicky said, Nope, what was holding it together was the single most important world-historical force, the human will. He must have cribbed it from a book somewhere; he had a ton, full of these impressive-sounding vocables that made you want to follow him, even if you weren't sure you knew what they meant. Counterhegemonic. Quaquaversal. Even if you weren't sure *he* knew what they meant. But those books are now only fifty-pound cartons that jounce around dangerously with every pothole and keep the van from attaining a top speed of more than forty-seven miles per hour. And then, just when it does seem about to break free, they have to pull over to let Sol puke. On the curb of Canal Street at rush hour. At a gas station on the far side of the Holland Tunnel. (Don't get D.T. started on the Holland Tunnel.) And an hour later, here they are in this strip-mall parking lot in— where the fuck are they again?

"Parsippany." The answer floats across vacant asphalt from the open window of the van. Then Nicky resumes whistling an off-key version of "Right Back Where We Started From." And of course he would whistle, with a joint in his hand and his map spread in street-light on the dash and his little battery-operated alarm clock he got from who knows where. D.T.'s the one who has to help Sol over to the grassy place where New Jersey's underfed bugs chirr all around like the thoughts in his brain. Because this is the other thing: the Prophet Charlie has flaked (true to form), and Sewer Girl, when it was finally time to leave, was nowhere to be found. At the end, it's just the three of them, the primary trio, the true Post-Humanists. Which would have sounded cool, in the beginning. Three's all you need to change the world. Look at the Bolsheviks, or the Jimi Hendrix Experience. But no, it's not cool to be sweating your balls off in Manhattan as the sun begins to drop, just because Nicky's got some last-minute errand to run with the van. And it's not cool to be smelling the dried pus on your infected friend's coveralls as you help him to his knees because he can't find them on his own. And it's really not cool to know that stretching all the way from here to Canada, if you ever reach it, will be a string of stops like forty miles apart where any witness might have seen him, a Negro with green hair dragging another boy, singly gloved and clutching his stomach, to right where you see that pink spatter, Officer.

Actually, that's bullshit. If D.T.'s honest with himself, the doubts now swarming within go back to last night when Nicky led him out to the cinderblock divider in the garage and gave him his first-ever look at what was behind. All you had to do was see the size of it, the pregnant bulge, to know what kind of suffering it was going to inflict. As he tried to look appreciative, he wondered if Sewer Girl had seen it, too—if it was the deciding factor. She'd been acting weird at least since May. D.T.'s perspective at the time was you did what you had to do, and they could hardly expect Nicky to be exempt. But this Demon Brother obsession was taking them far beyond the tactical, beyond culture and revolution and even revenge, and it was hard to say when Nicky had crossed that last line, or where it would stop. D.T. was awake past midnight replaying all the cloak-and-dagger they'd kept up after Billy went to ground. And early this morning, with Sol moaning in the parlor and Nicky out back soldering the batteries to the fail-safe, D.T. had taken the van on the pretense of an oil change and driven it up to the Bronx. He couldn't imagine what, aside from a mountain of smack, might be powerful enough to coax Billy Three-Sticks down to the Village again. Still, D.T. was going to warn him to stay as far uptown as he could get for the next twenty-four hours. And seeing the studio remained faded, abandoned, he swung back through Hell's Kitchen. Billy would probably never return there, either, but the memory of that tweedy soft homeboy, the boyfriend, seemed to speak to D.T.'s condition. You put more than one person together in a room, you got a monster of oppression, fine. But alone, almost everybody felt some kind of boot on the throat. Which maybe explained the boyfriend's reaction to D.T.'s admittedly poor choice to scout around with binoculars first, rather than going straight to the loft door to knock. And now there's no warning any of them, he's stuck here with the miasma of puke in his nose, the heavy body he's lifting into the van—to the degree that Sol's ever been liftable—and hey, when did the stars get so bright? He swings around toward the east, or what should be east, and the sky above the shuttered strip mall is exactly as dark and as light as every other patch of sky. It's like the whole bright side of the planet has been zeroed out. A universe equally empty in every direction.

He doesn't mention it to Nicky as they rattle back toward the highway. Instead, he announces that blood has started to mix with the vomit.

That's a good sign, Nicky says, medically speaking. "Like when you have a cold and start to clear the dark stuff. Productive."

"Unless what's eating away at your burnt hand is closer to gangrene," D.T. points out. "In which case, it's pretty troubling, in terms of signage."

By the light of a toll plaza, he peels back the glove Sol wouldn't have let him touch before. The tissue around the blasted fingers is nearly black, and the swelling has spread all the way to his shoulder. This should be Sewer Girl, doing the Flo Nightingale. But then, she was fucking Nicky for months there at the end. Maybe this was the betrayal she couldn't live with anymore. Or maybe she'd discovered that she, too, was just a substitution in some larger chain of substitutions. Sewer Girl wanted Nicky; Nicky wanted Sam; Sam wanted Loverboy, whom Nicky had never met but loathed anyway; and Sol, even after the advent of Sam, had never really stopped loving Sewer Girl. That had been *his* .32 kiped from the van that night—but the possibility had never occurred to Sol, and it was back under the passenger's seat before the last flashpot fizzled at the Vault. Love is everyone's blind spot. Or love and fear. It's like they've all underestimated the power of pure feeling to fuck up the most perfect system. And as they push deeper into America, even Nicky seems to sense his ability to hold together the PHP through sheer will waning. He's got two or three joints going now, to bring him down off the speed. "Hey, Nicky?" D.T. says, finally. "Should we still be able to see city lights out here?"

"How the fuck should I know?"

"You're the only one with a map."

Nicky turns the radio back on and starts skimming the ghost-channels for news. Of course, it's impossible to know anymore how much is for show. Maybe he's already heard the answers he seeks, and that's why he's so confident his operation will go off—or has gone off already. D.T.'s worst fear is that it is somehow even bigger than he's surmised, bigger than Billy and bigger than the uncle. Oh man it is fucking not cool to have that thing ticking down in the middle of your head, and to know there's nothing you can do about it anymore. Yet he's not sure he'd feel better if they were any closer to whatever might have been asked of them to stop it. And would it be so wrong at a time like this for D.T. to drop the wrist he's been holding and reach forward for a toke? To crack another beer, and then another? Even for the hardest of the hard-core, knowing you've just destroyed a bunch of lives is a lot to have on what an old-fashioned humanist would call the conscience.

Or really, even knowing you've destroyed just one.

DOWNTOWN—10:01 P.M.

IN HIS MIND Mercer is already miles to the north, dithering before a shadowy penthouse, when the realization that they've missed a turn pulls him back to the electric molasses of Centre Street. Jammed headlights play off street signs. "Wouldn't it have been a lot faster to cut left? From Hudson, it's a straight shot uptown."

Jenny seems to flinch, but maybe that's an illusion. "You picked a hell of a time to have a pissing contest about directions, Mercer." Then she apologizes. There's something she wishes she'd had the guts to tell him five blocks or fifteen minutes ago, whichever—when the power was still on. "Even if the blackout lifts, I can't take you all the way up to the Hamilton-Sweeneys. I've reached a decision. I've got a date with the East Village."

He waits for clarification, but none is forthcoming. "You're going to drag me to every godforsaken neighborhood in this city, aren't you?"

"I'm not dragging anyone. I'll drop you wherever you like. But I've had plenty of time to think about this. I know where to find Captain Chaos, I remember where I sent the check for that painting Bruno sold. And you heard what the boy said."

To be honest, Mercer's been trying to let the blackout blot it from his mind. He should have realized, though, that she wouldn't make this easy. "By that point Charlie would have said anything," he says. "He's in trouble with the cops, and he's clearly got some kind of problem with the truth." A blockage at Foley Square—a skirmish between two guys in white undershirts—is sending them left anyway, he's relieved to see.

"Did we not read the same article? 'NC'? The gunpowder?"

"The men in my family are all Army, Jenny. I can tell you, three grams of loose gunpowder is pretty useless, unless you've got an old blunderbuss lying around."

Though it comes out sounding more hypothetical than dismissive, she appears to relent. Really, she's just gathering force.

"You've never made a typo? Or had something misrepresented to you? We know the girl's dad makes fireworks, we know he's had security problems, and now we hear there's a bomb. Is it so hard to believe Nicky Chaos has whatever amount of explosive he'd need to hurt your boyfriend, excuse me, roommate?"

He brushes wrinkles from his shirt, strains for dignity. "Why don't you just pull over here at the corner. I'll see if the buses are running."

"I'm saying, why fumble around uptown in the dark, Mercer, when you can go straight to the source of the threat?"

"That's what cops are for," he says, as he opens the door and swings his feet to the curb. But the moment he stands, he sees that his reasoning has been off. For where earlier it was the protest clogging traffic around them, now it's the blue lights of the Furies shoving everything else aside. The whole police building back there is emptying itself into Lower Manhattan, fanning out to do God knows what. Defend the banks, stop murder in the tunnels, look busy enough to create plausible deniability. He's starting to sound like Jenny Nguyen. Still, it seems far-fetched that whatever the inspector said, a phalanx, is on its way right now to check out the boy's story. Which, if he really thinks about "The Fireworkers," is less improbable than he's hoped. "What are you doing?" he asks, hearing a beep behind him.

"It's a timer. Setting my watch for midnight."

"Jenny, they're not going to forget about this bomb stuff just because there's a blackout on. Pulaski will do the right thing. He'll be on the scene long before midnight."

"What makes you so sure?"

"You have to know him," he says, because the real reason, the kindness Pulaski showed him on New Year's Eve, is even shakier. Yet it feels like the person he's trying to convince is himself.

"Assuming you're right," Jenny says, "and the cops are there, we can park down the block and enjoy the perp-walk. Maybe they're not there, though. And if there's a bomb—"

"A bomb is why I'm telling you, please, this is a bad idea." Nicky Chaos can blow himself up, for all Mercer cares, and Jenny can probably still be talked out of going to stop him. Any other victim at this late juncture may simply be outside Mercer's brief. But what do you call someone who has second thoughts about even his second thoughts? Because, before he can get the words out, Mercer is pulling himself back into the car and shutting the door again. William is the one "NC" has pursued, which means that somehow William will have to end up there, too. And if that's the case, then what choice does Mercer have? If he loves William enough, he has to stop this from happening. Has to go.

Now, though, random groups of marchers, leftover traffic from rush hour, police cars, erratic pedestrians, and the blackout itself are forcing them west, west, until half the city lies between them and their destination. On the principle of steering into the skid, Jenny goes speeding toward the riverfront, where cars still zoom along.

The traffic signals are gone. Darkened streetlamps whip past the window. The water is flashes of moonlight. She'll cut across at Fourteenth and back down, she's telling him, as the cobbled streets of the old Meatpacking District start pummeling the Gremlin's suspension. They must be doing sixty in a twenty-five. Bent forward in silhouette, peering into the darkness, she herself is a little gremlin.

"Let me ask you something," he says. "Have you ever met Nicky Chaos?"

"Only on the phone. But I know the type."

"And we're going to charge in there with our awesome powers of persuasion and hope he has a change of heart? If things go wrong, do you even have a way to defend yourself?"

"Inspiration comes to prepared spirits," she says. And he is in the middle of voicing his warning that she's going to have to be the enforcer, he only cares about William, when he spots a huge puddle spread over the paving stones. It makes no sense, he's thinking, that someone should have opened a hydrant here in this forsaken part of town—and all at once he's aware of a curtain of water shearing up over the windshield and of a sort of floaty feeling, a loud blam halting his progress while something else comes and whumps him on the back of the head. His mind, still flying forward, just has time to emit a kind of clumsy lover's prayer. And then the blackout, for Mercer Goodman, turns an even deeper black.

UPPER WEST SIDE—10:10 P.M.

HE SPOTS THE STUNNED SHAPE behind the flares just before he'd otherwise flatten it: William Hamilton-Sweeney. In the years since Keith's seen him, he's gotten even thinner, but still with those noble features. His arm, when Keith grabs it, feels tacky. Hardening wax. Of all people. "Hey—you're coming from upstairs? Are my kids there?"

William is slow to respond, as if shaking off a vision. He seems even sweatier than Keith. Nearby, the doorman continues to lay out a line of safety flares along the sidewalk. Smoke billows like blood in a syringe. Shadows stand at hedged distances, everyone, it seems, obeying the same summons to come out into the night. But in the space beyond his shoulder at which William stares (*Where the hell did he go?*) there are only birds.

"Come on, it's Keith, your brother-in-law. Are they up there? Did you see them?"

Then William comes back to himself. "No kids, but Regan is." It's the worst of all possible answers. "But you weren't supposed to be here, Keith. She said you two split up."

Keith's running is catching up with him. A cramp stabs at his side, his breath coming in little gulps; still, he tries to keep his voice steady. All this time, Regan's longed for her brother's return. If he scares William off again, she'll never take him back. "It's a long story. I'd better tell her myself."

William leans in to look at him. It's hard to see much in the pink penumbra of the flares, but Keith feels uncomfortable. The last time their eyes met was in the middle of William's self-immolating best-man speech, when for a second Keith had sensed some attraction on the boy's side. On his own had been the force of Regan's feelings for the kid; everything she loved, Keith was helpless not to love. It was for her that he'd chased William back along a corridor after he'd fled the banquet hall. He'd almost managed to grab the shoulder of his dinner jacket. Then, with a juke move sideways, William had disappeared out a fire door and into the next two decades. Half a life ago, but only what, fifteen hundred feet away? As if even then they were racing toward this moment. Okay, William says at last; phones still work in a blackout, he'll go in and call up for her.

In the dim lobby, Keith collapses into one of those quasi-thrones probably no one's ever sat in, while William leans over the doorman's desk and dials. He seems to meet with some resistance on the other end of the line. "Tell her it's about the kids," Keith says. Then William hangs up and sits to wait, too, as the doorman, Miguel's his name, returns inside. The small-talk about baseball Keith used to make with him would be frivolous now. All anyone can do is watch the shadows beyond the big plate-glass windows. It's like being at the court of Louis XVI, waiting for the palace walls to collapse and someone to come drag them to the tumbrel. There is still time to reverse course, Keith reminds himself, but there isn't; a door has swung open. Regan's flashlight slides from William's face to his own. Just get it over with, he thinks, and finds himself explaining that the kids are missing.

Everything's silent for a second as the flashlight hits a wall-sized mirror, doubling the light. "You *lost* them, Keith?"

She makes it sound like he did it on purpose, when really he was only a little late to pick them up. A glance at William yields a sympathetic shrug.

"In this. You lost them." She turns to Miguel. "Is the towncar still waiting outside?"

"It's already gone, miss. Your uncle, he comes to take it while I'm looking for flares."

"That little fucker!" William explodes. "What did I tell you?"

But Regan has already collected herself. She orders her brother to go upstairs while she goes to hail a taxi. "This is important, William. One of us has to stay. Daddy's in no shape to be left alone."

The old William would have told her to go to hell, and in fact, there is a pause here, during which she screws the head of the flashlight tighter and clicks it off and on and extends it to him. "It's my kids. Your niece and nephew. Please." She has this total gravity, this total clarity of purpose calling her out of herself, and something must have changed in William, because he actually obeys, taking the flashlight and disappearing. She is halfway out the door when Keith realizes he's going to be left behind if he doesn't say something. The best he can come up with is, "How'll you find a taxi?" She doesn't answer, but also doesn't forbid him from following her out.

Sure enough, traffic is still bumper-to-bumper, not a single cab vacant. Then a roar is gathering blocks away, loud enough to shake buildings apart. It's hard to discern a direction; it seems to come from all sides. He tries to follow it, though, and after some seconds of pretending not to notice, she comes up behind him. Seeing dark shapes beetle by ahead, he hurries to the corner. It is motorcycles, rumbling down Columbus like an invading army. There must be hundreds. They've squeezed all other traffic over into one lane. Way up the darkened avenue he can see the lit signs of those taxis that have been swooft enough to fall in behind, the way they sometimes will with an ambulance. Illegal, of course, but the rules everyone's been living by seem to have been suspended. Which, despite everything, gives Keith a kind of hope. He steps right out into the gap between the dwindling bikers and the oncoming cabs, more or less daring the latter to hit him. The first one that stops he jumps into, and before Regan has a chance to say anything he tells the driver he's got two fifties in his pocket, and to take them wherever the lady wants to go—and step on it.

THE WEST SIDE ANGELS don't need the shadow of a Vincent Black Shadow flashing high against the clouds to summon them, or any Justice League junk like that. They just sort of figure when the lights go out some action's about to go down, and so, from all over Manhattan, they make for the pad of their Maximum Leader. Headlights like hard objects swerve around stalled cars, bear down on bottlenecks at speed, as in some colossal game of chicken. (Part of being in the Club is never letting on that you think about things like collision insurance. Helmets are an affectation. You sit your hog as if death doesn't exist.) And at the Maximum Leader's, as foretold, last night's party might as well have never ended. Bikes roost in rows outside, where riders pass bottles of Rheingold. To judge by the sound of things, two or more people are already getting it on on a loading dock. A bent spoon jams the lock of the downstairs door. The cage inside is, per usual, tied open with a chain, which you can see only by dint of the headlamp of the Harley somebody's driven straight through the entryway and idled at the foot of the stairs, facing out, as if, when the moment is right, the Leader will descend like the Last Mahdi to claim it. Its motor sends exhaust to every corner of the decrepit old breath-mint factory, but who's complaining? It isn't even clear who besides the Leader lives here—and again it isn't the Angels' way to think about this stuff.

The apartment on the sixth floor is wide open, a box of moonlight, but if the Maximum Leader is in here, in the dark, no one can find him. He's always been, despite that menacing jollity of his, sort of a cipher. For example: Is he white or is he black? (Or possibly half-Maori, with the face tattoos?) And: How has he managed to live for so long with no furniture, with no telephone, with (someone recalls, from back when the lights were on) a refrigerator missing its door? Under the giant shadows that lumber in and out crunches jetsam from last night. Bottles roll into the stairwell, go silent, and after a two-second delay, burst five stories down, where some chick keeps shouting, *Mother*fucker!

The real action, though, is up on the roof. Here, after the black slog of the stairwell, is enough light to party by—fat moon, improbable stars, a bonfire built in a wheelbarrow, and little bits of headlight swimming along the beaten tin gutterpipe—though poor visibility plus booze plus roof is an equation crying out for balance. Angels in various degrees of drunkenness play Spin the Knife, cradle lit cigarettes between knuckles in tests of endurance, argue about the blackout's origins, then cluster along the northern roofline to watch a warehouse burn ten blocks uptown. Two blond Rhinemaidens have stripped off their shirts to dance white-titted in the moonlight to a radio that plays this new band Chic on a continuous loop. Faggot music, someone mutters, but no one pays him any mind.

Atop an upturned trashcan near the bonfire, supplies of booze are soon depleted. A wobbly deputation gets sent down to ground level to scrounge for more. They make it no farther than the next corner, the desultory bodega whose plywood shelves always seem to contain exactly three of everything. Three rolls of one-ply toilet paper; three dusty cans of expired black beans; three vacuum-sealed bricks of Café El Bandito; three boxes of roach powder. These are pretty much a beard; for years, the store's real business has been to keep the Leader and his crew in beer. But now it sits silent behind the metal security gate the Angels slam their fists against. That's until somebody gets a brainwave.

Back at the mint factory, an engine revs. A bike bumbles down the street like some venom-swollen bee. It seems about to smash right through the security gate, but at the last second it stops, and the rider walks it back around until the rear tire nearly touches the bodega. Someone offers a chain from his regalia, and within a minute, the bike is lashed to the gate. How enterprising are these Angels! Set them up with brokerage licenses in place of bikes, and you'd have millionaires. There's a single rev, the throttle engages, and with a shriek that can be heard all up and down Tenth Avenue, the sheet metal is folding and tearing like the wings of a pinned moth, and then sparking on the street where the rider drags it along.

He has gone off to make a victory lap when a 'Rican with a familiar-seeming face bolts from the car that's just screeched to a stop. Angels scatter semicircularly, to a perimeter a shotgun barrel sweeps across. In high-pitched esoteric English, the man who wields it tells them they've just cost him a thousand dollars in repairs, and basically to fuck the fuck off.

There's a moment here when things could get grievous and/or bodily. The 'Rican has sealed his fate, or the Angels have, depending on who's responsible. Or maybe neither is responsible; it's this city, after all, that's smashed them together. But if there's one thing an Angel can respect, it's the individual standing up for hisself. They back away, trusting to the guy's shaky hold on the language to keep him from spreading word of their mercy. They rumble off in search of provender.

The bodega owner, meanwhile, enters his store, locks the door behind him, and sits on a stool in the dark, weeping. The shotgun he clings to like a lapdog—too late, but who knows? There may be other vandals. As for those Angels: Never again does he trust them. *Nunca jamás.* Across the street, they're still pouring in from the outer boroughs, Angels upon Angels converging like heat-seeking missiles on the flaming West Side. And on the rooftop, the bare-chested vestals haven't stopped shimmying—*Aaaah . . . Freak out!*—waiting for the Maximum L., their off-white Wotan, to ride out and rally the dead.

91

A S FOR JENNY, IT'S NOT AT ALL CLEAR what she's waiting for in the dark, with this liquid arrhythmia beating down on the cracked windshield before her. Or even clear, really, if she's waiting. That last collision must have been with the hydrant. The seatbelt saved her on the trip forward, but she hit pretty hard on the recoil, and it's done something to her sense of time. Ten minutes may have passed, or one. Then a voice comes, like a pirate signal jacking her frequency. *Wake up.* She turns, surprised to find her neck only slightly sore. A flicker at the mouth of a nearby street etches the shadow slumped in the passenger's seat. "You all right?" she asks. For a while, there's no answer.

Then Mercer reaches up to feel the back of his head, as if surprised to find it still there.

"I was out for a minute," he says slowly. Or what seems slowly. "No broken bones, if that's your question. But one hell of a knot. What do you have back there, tire irons?"

"Squash rackets," she admits. "Bruno's."

Maybe he's too stunned to assimilate. "How about you—are you okay?"

"You mean other than the fact that I've probably cost myself a job?"

"This is why they don't run drag races on cobblestones, in a black-out. Jenny, what were you thinking?"

"I was thinking, pretty reasonably, it seems to me, that maybe we should hurry. And then I don't know. With the water, I couldn't see. Now can we just get this over with?"

Mercer, unable to open his door, has to clamber out over the driver's seat. Still, it seems like her side has gotten the worst of the accident. From the hydrant the headlight's smashed against, water shoots straight up, a silver plume streaking into nothing and then hammering back down. A small flame over the front tire gutters and goes out. The cascade of droplets on the headlights makes the paint-job itself seem to burn. And beneath, the accordioned hood. Yep, Bruno's never going to speak to her again. Her shoes and clothes already half-soaked, she moves out of range of the water. And that's when she spots the form crumpled at the curb, like a sapling felled by the bumper. That first thud she'd felt. Oh.

Mercer, instantly at the body's side, is acting strange again—feeling for blood, she realizes. "Please tell me he's breathing."

The person she's struck is tall, trim, slender in an open-collared shirt. His face, inert in the half-light, seems drawn with worry. Or is that pain? Mercer's hand moves into the flashlight beam. Just water. "He seems intact physically, but he's totally unresponsive."

"We should call an ambulance."

"With what? The payphones down here are all missing their receivers."

She'll drive him to the ER herself, she says, if he'll fit in the Gremlin.

"The hell you will." The keys are still in the ignition, but before he pockets them, he discovers the engine won't start. It could be the sparkplugs are wet, he says, but the only way to know for sure would be to wait and see if they dry out. And what about the East Village? It's like an hour until midnight. Is there really enough time?

Just her luck, she thinks, to have landed doctorless in a deserted part of the city. Or nearly deserted, because there's that leap of fire again at the cross-street, and she keeps smelling kerosene. "Okay, fine. Fuck. You stay here for a second. I'll be back."

Triangulating between the headlights and the burning, she ducks down a tributary street that doglegs toward the river. This neighbor-hood was once an active port, but now feels, as she scours the dark, like a game preserve for muggers. Moist weeds, waist-high, spring through gaps in the pavement. There isn't a single pedestrian except the one whom, in her zeal to save lives, she's maybe just killed. What is she even looking for? An off-duty paramedic? Loose painkillers? A kindly old lady who'll invite her in to use the phone? Each idea seems stupider than the last, yet Jenny apparently still needs to believe some invisible hand's at work, balancing accounts. Any minute now, this fucked-up present will crack, and her real future will return to her, the one in which she redeems her life, or Richard Groskoph's. Or maybe she's supposed to be the one to crack it. To turn back. But here comes the kerosene again. Dogs barking. Smashed glass. More than righteousness, or charity, it is fear that spurs her on. Then another crash sends her ass-over-teakettle among the grasses. There's a bright mild ache where she's fallen, but that doesn't matter, because above her, backlit by the stars, looms the thing she's just tripped over: an abandoned grocery cart.

Of course, every solution bears the seeds of new problems. In this case, there's the noise the cart makes on the street. She'd rather not attract attention, but near the place she's left Mercer, paving stones push through patches of tonsured asphalt, and when the wheels hit these she might as well be whaling on sheet metal with a crowbar. But fuck it. She gathers her breath and sprints, pushing the cart ahead of her into the brightening intersection. "Quick, help me get him into this."

"A shopping cart?"

"It's what I could find."

"You're not supposed to move a body like this."

"Mercer, I've had a chance to scope the area. Power to the people aside, I would *really* like not to be here when those torches you're seeing down there arrive." She tips the cart on its flank. There's no gentle way to get an adult body inside, and it takes their combined strength—blocking the wheels in place with their feet and heaving at the handle—to get the thing upright again. She wishes there were some scrap of cardboard or old shirt she could use to cushion the guy's vertebrae, but if he's bleeding internally, he's not going to care. There ensues a brief argument about whether to head toward the hospital closest to here or continue to the East Side, and an even briefer argument about whether to take a couple of the squash rackets. Her position is, she'd feel safer with them; his is, having seen what she's capable of unarmed, he'd feel safer without. The torchlight is very close now, though, so she lets him win this one, too. "Come on. Push."

The added weight should make the damn cart quieter, but all it does is amplify the noise. She makes Mercer share the handle with her, and together, they find a speed somewhere between trot and sprint. "Quit groaning," she says. "You're giving us away." But he must not hear her over the approaching din, a clanking of chains, the sharp inhalation of more flames. He doesn't wait to find out if the sound is marauders, or revolutionaries, or citizens who just want to know where their power went. "Push!" she yells, and the handle surges forward, almost out of her grasp. She wouldn't have thought Mercer Goodman had it in him. At any rate, whoever is bringing this hellfire out into the street must be transfixed by the weird missile of the shopping cart, or the weirder duo trailing along behind, because just as another collision becomes inevitable, the noise softens, the flames draw apart, and Mercer and Jenny and the body before them are allowed, untouched, to pass.

UPPER EAST SIDE—10:49 P.M.

THEY ARE CAREFUL not to jostle each other as they move up stairs and down halls, past doors the neighbors have locked tight for fear of some disruption on the streets below—unless these same neighbors have gone out to join in. Either way, the vibe is of evacuation. The man fumbles for his keys, but the woman already has hers out. (What can it mean that she's held on to them?) Then her flashlight is sweeping through the open door and into a foyer he wishes he'd prepared for her coming. One thing he almost certainly would have done is try to make it look like he's capable of living without her. As it is, the critical beam seems to land on all the crap he's kept exactly the same since she left. The framed harlequin. The dish of New England pebbles. The row of shoes by the door, to which he now adds his loafers. On the other hand, not having changed anything means the emergency supplies are still where she always kept them, on the lower shelf of the hall closet. No sooner does he remember this than she's handing him a flashlight of his own. A flick of the button, and a second beam races out to lose itself in hers on the floor. "Will?" he calls. "Cate?" There's no answer. "I told you they weren't here."

"And now I know it's true."

The beams separate. Hers probes deeper into the apartment; his turns toward the kitchen. There's no sign that anyone has touched the room-temperature fridge since this morning, and no note on the door. When he doubles back to their—his—bedroom, it is aglow. Regan sits on the big horsehair bed, her back to him, an address book beside her. He's hesitant to intrude on whatever thoughts she might be having, but then he sees she's got the bedside phone to her ear. "Emergency services keeps giving a busy signal."

"Could the kids possibly have gone back to Brooklyn?"

"I just tried my place, and the Otanis'. No answer. And you already called, remember? You said you tried everywhere. They didn't have subway fare."

"They could have borrowed subway fare."

"And then gone anywhere. They could have gone to the game without you."

"The tickets are right here in my pocket."

"It's not like they're hard to get, Keith. It's the Mets." She doesn't turn, nor does her flashlight move from the mustard-colored bedspread where she's placed it, but things around them are becoming clearer. "Goddammit, where were you?"

"Hung up at work." It's the same shuck-and-jive he'd used about Samantha, but telling Regan he's already dealt with the cops once today would raise all kinds of questions he doesn't want to answer. Anyway, she doesn't seem to notice. She's unbuttoning her blouse.

"Well I'm not going back out in the dark in this suit, with a target more or less on my back. Where are those sweats I used to exercise in? And does Will have sneakers over here?" His flashlight stays on her as she plucks off her silver earrings and drops them on the bed and reaches back to remove heels barely worn. She has dressed to impress whoever she was supposed to spend the night with. Embarrassed to discover how much he's gleaned, he turns to the armoire and sends the sweats arcing through the dark. Then he finds his own jogging shorts. Puts his flashlight on the bed between them and removes his belt, his pants. When his shirt comes off, their eyes meet. Her navel is a slim caesura between her lacy slip and brassiere; he's down to his briefs. They're like kids playing truth or dare, he thinks—and then, given the gravity of the situation, feels ashamed again. "What?" he says. "It's going to slow you down if I change, too?"

She ignores him and pulls on the sweatpants.

"But what are you proposing to do, exactly?"

"If I can't get the cops on the phone, I'll get them on foot."

"And if you can't do that?"

"Turn the city upside down myself."

Doubtless she means it as a brush-off, but he sees a chance here to reassert himself as the husband he still technically is. "Then give me a minute to find my running shoes, too," he says, "'cause you're right, things could get a lot worse out there, and I'm damn sure not letting you wander around in it alone."

UPPER EAST SIDE—EARLIER

MOST EVERY OTHER AFTERNOON that summer, Will and Cate have been parked in aftercare, while Mom toils away at the office to save Grandpa, and Dad does whatever Dad does. This particular day, though, they're conducted at the end of regular camp to the cafeteria, from which the normals get dismissed. Absent the school-year complement of lunch ladies and clattering trays, certain things become clearer. That loneliness, for example, smells of barfed-into chocolate milk. It is extra-pronounced for Will, who is one of the oldest kids here and far too proud to fraternize with C-Formers. This leaves his sister to practice on her own the string game she learned in Arts & Crafts. "Quit it," he says each time her elbow quote-unquote accidentally jostles his. Then the Assistant Head Counselor comes in to retrieve another camper or cluster of campers whose punctual parent or nanny has arrived.

There are like forty kids to start with. Then there are twenty-eight. Then fifteen. Then five. Then it's just him and Cate, and they are led back out of the cafeteria, recidivists denied parole. At the threshold of the aftercare room, the A.H.C. asks if Will is sure their dad knows to pick them up today. Sure, Will's sure. Didn't he hear Mom say it on the kitchen phone last night, while he pretended not to listen? At least twice she'd asked Dad to repeat it—she had "plans for the evening," and not to be late. Then again, sometimes it takes more than repetition to remind Dad of his responsibilities.

At 6:30, the aftercare kids get brought out into the blast furnace of rush hour to wait for pickup on the school's front steps, so that the janitors can start cleaning inside. The sky, as usual, is perfervid.

Away and to the north, smog climbs the air. And still no Dad. Will can already see where this is headed: phone calls, embarrassment, the screwing-up of Mom's plans. (Maybe this is what Dad wants.) But can't they just leave on their own recognizance? He's almost thirteen, for God's sake. When the A.H.C. goes to use the john, Will approaches a Shaggy-haired Counselor-in-Training and points to a figure down at the end of the block. "I think I see him. That's our dad." And when Cate opens her mouth to contradict him, he pinches her, hard. Her shout seems to distract the C.I.T. enough that he doesn't look too long at the gentleman in question. Good thing, too, as Will can now make out a prayer shawl and yarmulke. He hustles his arm-rubbing sister down the steps.

It's only a fifteen-minute walk down to the old apartment, though the way Cate complains about her feet you'd think it was fifteen thousand. He's a bit nervous about going over like this unannounced, but you can tell even from the street that no one's home. The lights stay off, despite the fact that it's getting dark. Probably Dad's forgotten all about them and gone to the ballgame himself. And Will has left his extra keys at Mom's. He could always ask the super to let him in, but that would mean letting Dad off the hook, when the hook is what he deserves. He decides instead they'll walk back to Brooklyn. If they average a block a minute, they can be to the foot of the Bridge by eight. Or okay, maybe half past. How hard can it be?

What he's failed to account for here is Cate having to stop every five blocks to use the can, or drink from a fountain, or be bought a bagel with Will's last quarter. At Forty-Second Street, she makes them cut over to the library so she can sit out front for twenty minutes rubbing her sore feet. She's always loved knowing their grandpa's name is etched into a third-floor wall inside, like initials sewn into underwear. It occurs to him to turn the walk into a game for her, mapping out all the personal landmarks they'll pass. But as it gets darker out, he's getting worried he's made the wrong decision. He's never been on some of these streets before; people are watching from doorways, with what intentions he can't tell. He and Cate have come too far to turn back, but don't seem remotely close to Brooklyn, and he has no money left for even a phone call. It's only the thought of Dad pacing frantically outside the day camp's locked doors that keeps him going—of justice finally being done.

See, Will suspected what was going on even before he found out for certain. He wonders now if that was what had brought him back to the apartment that day he'd played hooky from school last fall, before the separation. He'd climbed into bed to read and had fallen asleep there. He woke to sounds coming from the living room as if someone were being hurt. But even kids know the difference between pleasure and pain; if it was the latter, why was Will getting hard? He'd padded to the door, hating himself for wanting to hear more, but maybe that was Mom out there with Dad, and everything was okay, if also gross. A floorboard creaked, though, and he froze. What came next was his father's voice. He sounded pissed at whoever the woman was. And what might he do if he caught his son spying on them? Will retreated to his closet and climbed into the laundry basket and pulled a pile of old sheets on top of him. He waited there, nearly suffocating, until he heard them leave. Then he waited another ten minutes, to make sure they weren't coming back.

Now buildings are coming on above them like bejeweled drunk ladies at parties. He leads Cate by the hand past lit-up nail salons and dry cleaners and Jewish bakeries, telling her every few blocks it's just another few blocks now. She's got to pee again, she says. And she's tired. He slings her overstuffed backpack over his own shoulder, where it bumps against his duffel. The street signs dwindle toward single digits, and it starts to seem they might make it to the Bridge. But somewhere below Fourteenth Street, there's a kind of whooshing feeling, and everything around them save the traffic falls dark.

It takes him a full minute, pinned to the middle of a downtown sidewalk, to figure out what's happened. To judge by the sudden quiet, cars stopped dead in the streets, Will isn't the only one afraid. He can feel people moving around and behind him, each of whom now registers as a potential threat. Sirens, undulant, paint distant sectors blue. "It's okay," he tells Cate shakily. "Just a blown fuse somewhere."

"I want to go back to the library."

"That was an hour and a half ago, Cate."

"But I've really got to *go*." He recalls having seen a parking lot up ahead and tells her she's going to have to pee between some cars. He stands guard and, when she's done, tells her she's a mensch and squeezes her hand and explains what it means. They start walking again. They must be heading south, because there are little lights flashing atop the Trade Center ahead. The farther they go, though, the higher the intervening buildings loom, until he can no longer see those flashes. They are east, too far east, in the Village. Down here, headlights prowl sharklike through unsignaled intersections, light up freakish swaths of streetscape: ashcans, knees, hydrants gushing senselessly. On one block, a man strides out of the dark with a TV on his shoulder. On another, music blasts. Behind a wrought-iron park fence black guys with sweaty chests writhe around to disco music. He makes Cate look away, but can't help staring back at the gate. When he does, a man wearing only a cowboy hat and a jockstrap is standing there, watching them closely.

Will is spooked. He takes a sharp right at the end of the fence, then another. He's navigating by feel, trying to veer neither into the mounting disorder nor into sockets of light where they'll look like gazelles dissevered from the herd. Fifteen minutes later, though, when he tries to straighten out their route with two additional lefts, the grid has broken down. He's starting to feel like one of his avatars in Eldritch Realms, the Gray Wizard, doomed to wander alone in the underlit maze of a once-great civilization. Or not even alone, actually. For when he looks back again, there is the man in the jock and the black hat, less than a block behind.

ANOTHER MOTHER

OUT ON LONG ISLAND, Ramona Weisbarger cranes toward her television set, where every few minutes the stalwart newsroom gives way to images from around the City. Battered storefronts, burnt-out cars, gangs of menacing ethnics perched on stoops in the dark. All the boroughs gone black, the anchorman repeats when he returns. *So how are your cameras still running?* Ramona wants to know, but Morris Gold has already decided there must be generators. Then he's gone a little huffily back into the kitchen to mix up another packet of iced tea, "for in case the ballgame ever comes back on." She's been doing her best, for an hour and a half now, not to compromise the illusion that she gives a damn about the Yankees. But she refuses to get up and help him, because here it comes again, the City flickering across the screen, and she knows, with maternal ESP, that her Charlie is out there in it.

Morris has lectured her on this, too, these last few months—how it's not her fault, how the boy has to learn his lesson. Though "lecture" probably isn't fair, his method is more what-do-you-call . . . the one where you ask the questions. *Wasn't it true that . . . Didn't she think . . .* Usually, she responds like a sensible woman, rather than the guilt-ridden creature she's become. And part of her knows he's right. Charlie's practically an adult, and it really is his fault for running away. To cover up the grief she therefore shouldn't feel, she's tried to adjust. Has, after those first few stunned and inconsolable weeks, spent many more trying to get used to the new order of things. Or just trying to distract herself (she sees now) from the absence at the heart of it. She has shown houses, gone twice as often for hair appointments, sat with a stiff smile through birthday parties the twins got invited to, renewed the Valium prescription her doctor first wrote back at the start of David's heart trouble. She has even begun, without either of them formally acknowledging it, letting Morris Gold stay over on certain nights when he comes to dinner. A family of squirrels died in his air-conditioning ducts over the long Fourth of July weekend, and with the humidity high every day since, there's apparently a waiting list for repairmen. The two of them sit on the davenport by the window unit and watch the late games beamed from other time zones, though she hardly knows an RBI from an APR.

This is not like that.

Morris comes back in, carrying a glass whose perspiration runs in clear tracks when he taps a spoon against it. He doesn't know how much sugar to put in, can never quite hit the saturation point, but she takes the tea and lets him gather her feet into his lap. The Channel 5 Newsplatoon is reporting that looting has spread to Brownsville, Harlem, Washington Heights, and the Lower East Side. Officials are cracking down, says the reporter on the ground, and hope to have the power on by morning. He is standing in an incongruous zone of bright white outside Con Ed headquarters, a nice-looking black man in a tie and windbreaker. Behind him, what look like protesters duck into waiting police cars. Careful of their heads! she thinks. Though who's to say that the reporter isn't standing on a soundstage somewhere, and that the rail-thin kids being paraded in handcuffs before the spotlight aren't just special effects?

"Where is Brownsville again, exactly?"

Her mental map of the City has, like the City itself, crumbled in the years since she and David moved out here, looking for an actual yard for the baby to run around in; still she's having trouble figuring out how something "spreads" from Hell's Kitchen to Harlem while bypassing the Upper West Side. Morris kneads her foot and says he believes it's in Brooklyn somewhere, and why? As if he doesn't know why. There are books in the library about these kids who turn on and drop out. She's learned how they collect in the poorest and most G-dforsaken stretches of the inner city; how they end up as addicts, or prostitutes, or both. It makes her think she's been too hard on Charlie, though here Morris would shift back to the interrogative mood: *Isn't it possible this is just the '70s talking?* She's never admitted to him that she voted for Jimmy Carter, whom he blames for abetting a *culture of permissiveness*, and now she wonders if he isn't right, if this President isn't too soft a touch. Still, Morris has no idea how to massage a foot, and sometimes she wishes he'd just rise to the bait and start yelling.

Update dissolves into anchor, and then quickly to commercial—even during a civic emergency, peanut butter must be sold—and when a leggy jar of Jif bumps and grinds onto the screen, she hears giggles from the foyer. She calls the twins' names, and two sets of feet go galloping up the front stairs. They stop at the top. She calls them again. "Abe, Izz. What have I said about sneaking out of bed?"

The peanut-butter music takes over as they confer in that unsettlingly wordless language of theirs. Then: "We can't sleep. Can Uncle Gold read us a story?"

No, Uncle Gold cannot, she's started to say, but Morris already has his hands on his knees to push himself up. "Don't worry. I'll get the little pikers down."

As he goes, she can feel the past going, too, when this would have been David, whom the boys merely pretend to remember now. Charlie was the only one of them who ever knew how to grieve. But what was she supposed to do: let him get drunk, wreck the wagon, come and go as he pleased? Just look at what happened to that girl in the newspaper! From right across the tracks. She still wants to believe that before Charlie gets into that kind of trouble, before he shoots himself up with drugs or sells the ungainly body she . . . she can't complete the thought. And she knows all at once that she can't be the only person holding her breath tonight for whoever it is she loves most. That it may be the only thing the darkness makes clearer: who really matters is whoever you're most desperate to see. Sometimes in the morning when the paper hits the front steps (easier to keep renewing David's subscription than to explain to *Newsday*'s phone reps why it is she wishes to discontinue) she rises from the heat of sleep convinced it will turn out to be him. She will come downstairs in her nightgown and unlock the door to find her son there on the flagstone porchlet, so tall even with his slouch, and he'll be shaking as she takes him into her arms. Every lover is a mother. Every parent is a home. And she has tried to be this for him from the moment the woman at the orphanage first offered her the bean-shaped bundle of swaddling. His shrieky red face, the scalp so furrowed under the fine copper hair she worried it might get stuck that way. She'd worn a crucifix, over David's objections, to convince the Mother Superior they were good Catholics. She'd started to wonder just what on earth she was doing when the woman let go. And now Ramona rises another level toward her daytime self, and the newspaper is only a memory of a newspaper. She won't repeat again the emptiness she felt the one morning she went so far as to go down and open the door upon that dewy empire of lawn after lawn, birds kiting down to peck at seed, no other human being in sight. She'll plant herself here on the davenport instead, she thinks, and keep watch, willing bad things not to happen to these dark young men raging in every motherless corner of the city. Or to her own son, her Charlie. Where is he?

UPPER EAST SIDE—11:11 P.M.

THE BLACKOUT MAY HAVE SOWN REBELLION EVERYWHERE ELSE, but as of a couple hours in, Lexington Avenue's adjusting seamlessly. Some of the cafés have even dragged candlelit tables to the sidewalk, boxed seats from which to take in the night's folly. When a Hispanic kid crashes his too-small bike into one of these tables, the couple there picks him up and brushes him off and sits him down for grappa. Keith stops to ask if any of them have seen a girl and a boy pass by; she's six, the boy is twelve but looks more like ten. But Regan doesn't wait for an answer, having already heard it a dozen different ways in as many blocks. (*Nope, Sorry, Nada.*) Far better to try to figure out where the next cop car's going to appear. They've been sweeping past every so often, but always a hundred yards ahead, on one of the cross-streets. When the next siren takes up its war-cry, though, she's miscalculated; the lights are passing east to west back behind her, on the other side of the brasserie. "Why didn't you try to wave it down?" she pleads, reaching Keith again.

"Did you not see me jumping around with my arms waving?" he says.

"How could I see anything?"

"The problem is, we're in the wrong part of town."

"I don't know where you're getting this."

"Think like a cop for a second, Regan. Your force has just eaten a fifteen percent budget cut, and suddenly the power's out and you've got to keep the whole city from going nuts. Where are you going to concentrate your strength? Not the Upper East Side."

"There's valuable property up here."

"Yeah, and people to protect it. Doormen, security guards, all these maître d's. . . . It's the dicier areas where the cops will feel they need to be."

"Since when are you the expert, Keith? But never mind. The person we need to think like is your son. And if you stop for a second you'll see he's going to want to be where the people are, because that's where he'll feel the safest."

"You think I'm not thinking about him? I'm telling you I'm ready to hurl myself into the combat zone. But we have to decide whether we're looking for the kids or the cops."

"Why don't we split up? One for each?"

"I already told you, no can do."

She should have put her foot down back at the apartment—he can't just decide these things *for* her anymore—but the truth is, her resolve is faltering. And now a police whistle shrills in the middle of the next intersection, and before her brain can unscramble her feelings, Will's sneakers are carrying her forward.

Only it's not a police whistle; it's a girl on roller skates, directing traffic. Headlights passing behind turn her filmy garment translucent. She's wearing nothing underneath, and Regan doesn't have to look to know Keith will be gawking. Come on, she thinks. This is a *child*. Of course, up in their old bedroom, changing just now, he'd looked like a child himself, yet hadn't she still longed for him to come and put his hands on her? You can hold people accountable for what they do, but not for what they are, and Keith is this: the call, the desire, the amoral tug toward the light. But wait—those parking lights a few spots down the avenue . . . is that an unmarked car?

As she approaches, the driver shifts deeper down in his seat. He's been ogling the roller girl, too, apparently: a big guy, in what her flashlight shows to be a Hawaiian shirt. But there is indeed a siren on the dash, a darkened snowglobe. She has to say "Excuse me" three times before he responds. "Ma'am, keep your light out of my car."

"Officer—"

"Detective."

"I need your help."

"Can you not see I'm working?"

Again, no, but by the time he climbs out of the car, Keith has caught up. "Our kids are missing," he blurts. "Two of them. We think they must be around here somewhere."

The detective takes a cigarette pack from his shirt's breast pocket, raps it on the car, extracts a cigarette. "You got a missing persons report?"

"Excuse me?"

"That's what you need, you need a missing persons report."

"What I need is to find my fucking kids," Keith says.

The detective lowers his lighter, not having gotten the flame to the tobacco, and sizes him up. Privately, Regan feels like cursing, too, but Keith's belated display of emotion is just making things worse. "Honey—"

"No, really. Who am I supposed to file a report with? You're the first cop we've seen in an hour, if you even are a cop. And when was I supposed to do it? They've only been gone a few hours."

"Then how do you know they're missing? They're probably grabbing a slice of pizza."

"In the middle of this mess?"

The world bobs queasily as three flashlights resettle.

"Please. You've got to have a radio. Can't you ask your colleagues if someone's seen them?"

The detective waves toward the intersection. "See that? See all those cars and all those drivers?" When Regan turns to look, it's partly so she won't have to witness Keith's comeuppance, and partly so neither man will see the size of the fear that now grips her. She's been operating on the assumption that this organism, her city, is essentially benevolent, but now it is revealing its deeper chaos, its drift toward unmeaning. "This is the trouble with your kind of people," the detective is saying.

"What's that supposed to mean?"

"With your pink wine and your special clothes to jog in. You think your problems are more real than anyone else's. But right now there's thousands of other New Yorkers needing to get home."

"So you're sitting in your car playing pocket-pool?"

"You looking to go downtown, buddy? Is that what you want?"

"Please, Officer. My husband doesn't know what he's saying."

The detective relents. The light of a passing car makes his eye-glasses look tinted, almost blue. "Look. The best I can do for you is, your kids don't show by morning, you go to your local precinct and ask for a form. But meantime, we've got our hands full. Now, if you'll excuse me . . ." And he climbs back into the otherwise featureless car and pops it into drive.

"Well, that didn't go as planned," Keith says tightly, as the car noses into the street.

"Not after you barged in and tried to take over!"

"You didn't tell me not to."

"What difference does it make what I tell you, Keith? You never listen anyway."

"That's not fair, and you know it."

"I said, let's split up the work. You ignored me."

"Out of concern for your safety," he says, with his maddening equanimity.

And to think she'd been ready to forgive him! "Everything is always so simple for you, isn't it? Everything that happens just happens. Who can be held to account?"

"What are we really fighting about here, Regan?"

"You can't apologize, can you? Why is it so hard just to admit you were wrong?"

"I've never understood where it was supposed to get us."

Rather than dignify this with an answer, she starts walking again, away from the intersection. She can feel Keith's gaze all across her back, between the shoulderblades, on the back of her neck. The phrase *eyes in the back of her head* doesn't do justice to the intense physicality of knowing a man like this—what he's thinking, how he's standing, how his heart is beating high in his chest. And of being known. She tries to tell herself this is only a trick of the shadows; he has no idea what's inside you! But then how does she already know he's not going to follow her here, into the darker places? And why does it hurt so much that he's giving up this easily, letting her just walk away?

ANOTHER FATHER

IT'S TRUE, things used to get jammed up sometimes when he'd go out to check on some municipal to-do, opening night at a bush-league ballpark, Casimir Pulaski Day in the Little Poland of New Jersey. Shows that small, he trusted Rizzo to manage. Still, Carmine Cicciaro, Jr., might drive out anyway right before the first ignition, see what kinds of effects he was getting. There were parts of the hinterland so starved for amusement that traffic would lock up for miles around—folks just pulling onto the shoulder and cutting their engines to gaze up at the wildness of the lights. And when Carmine couldn't drive anymore, he'd get out and keep going on foot, slip in among the spectators, studying faces, the only soul not looking at the sky.

This is not like that.

A scant two hours ago he was out at the shop, helping the youngest Zambelli, up from New Castle, fill a van with the two big Cicciaro boards, sign papers for the rest. He'd been locking up when everything went dark. His first reaction was relief that he'd already gotten done what needed doing. Then his mind went to Sammy. Her breathing machine. And though the phone was where it always was, in Shed 8, he couldn't get anyone at the damn hospital to pick up. So now here he is on an elevated approach to the Queensboro Bridge, where horns began honking at exactly the moment it became obvious it was pointless to honk, because there's nowhere for anybody to go. Other drivers lean out their windows to take in the mystery beyond the river, where the white heaps of Midtown always rose before. After ten more minutes of guilt opening back up, Carmine decides. Abandons the truck. Legs it down an exit ramp, following the blue sparks squad cars trace through the strutwork a mile off.

It's only after he reaches street level that he spares a thought for his own protection. These days, you drive under an overpass, you keep your doors locked even in daylight. And away from the cars up on the highway, the air now is filling with the smell of smoke, the dark spreading into a wide, paved plain. No payphones, just figures hunched around intervals of fire on the sidewalk. Hurrying between them. Two people sniffing something off the back of—is that an old horse cart?—look up to watch what this old fool is doing. Or maybe he just imagines it; these last months have been like he's back in the early days of his cuckolding, stared at wherever he goes. That's him. The husband. The father.

But *porca miseria*, the things night can do to time. In place of hardwired sequence, it's more like everything all mixed up. For now, even as he shakes his head and carries his reserve on toward the next clump of traffic, it's coming back from even deeper how his old man used to bring him to this very stretch of boulevard, needing more corrugated tin for the sheds, or thousand-yard spools of wire. Carmine's whole world up to that point had been the Lower East Side, three-room apartments stacked block after block and strung together with line-dried laundry. After his granddad had died, they'd taken in a boarder for the downstairs flat, hemming Carmine in, forcing him further inward. He figures his first imaginary shows, sketched in colored pencil on a secret bit of wall behind his bed, were a direct result. (And was this what Samantha had found with her magazine, the way out?) But then out of the blue his father would appear and reach down into his loneliness and drive him over to this far side of the river, and he'd hear the vendors say, Carmine Cicciaro! And this must be little Carmine. . . . They've since widened the roadway to eight lanes. Its frontage is altered not only by the blackout, but also by boxy silhouettes in places where there shouldn't be any and gaping vacancies where there should. Here stood Rafetto's Hardware, with its million little drawers of differential screws. And over there the by-the-hour hotel with windows full of unprepossessing girls it now occurs to him were hookers, so maybe things don't change so much after all. Darkness just loosens the mask. Sharpens the mind's eye. Makes the color of a remembered pencil, of a tick of waxy red on a cracked plaster wall, as vivid as that taillight a few feet away.

But it pulls the future closer, too, in the form of a bridge drawn a deeper black against the night. And as he follows its slope back up, a chasm inside returns him to what's brought him here—the sense that he must have done something to antagonize the powers he can't quite believe in, or let go of. This was why he'd never told the reporter about those nighttime walks along the shoulders of blue highways, communing with his art. It would have sounded like a violation. You weren't supposed to become your own audience, any more than you were supposed to attend your own funeral, or try to outshine God. And now Richard, poor bastard, is gone, and Sammy may be leaving, and God's never taken his calls, and here is Carmine on this bridge, stars he's forgotten he's forgotten falling down through the girders, making flickers on the lamped cars. His back's starting to hurt—the work isn't easy on it. The absence of a skyline makes him doubt he'll ever get where he's going, and behind him, where he's come from might as well not be there. He can't be sure that when he returns, if he returns, his truck won't be just a charred and hubcapless chassis. Or that on the far shore there isn't a line of mounted cops waiting to turn back all comers. That once every last car around him has reversed back down onto Long Island, they won't blow the bridges and sail Manhattan out for a Viking-style burial at sea. But behind the flames, Carmine reminds himself, everything will be dead already anyway. Everything besides his daughter. So he'll keep dragging himself up this bridge between possible worlds, this rickety ruin of light, trying to imagine it might matter if he makes it to the other side.

EAST VILLAGE—11:13 P.M.

BLESSED ARE THE POOR IN SPIRIT, Charlie recalls, as beyond the window a wino with a machete capers in the middle of Bowery. Over at the corner of East Third, a futon set burns down to its ribs. People huddle around, holding what look to be broken car antennas, meat spitted at the end. The inspector has to whoop his siren just to get them to move, and even then they mostly just glare over into the whirling blue light. And who can blame them? What cop cars exist for down here is to keep the masses in chains, and riding in one— even chained himself, sort of, in the backseat—marks Charlie as a class traitor. Then a fleshy something, a hot dog or possibly dildo, thunks into the glass by his head, and he feels a jolt of empathy for the cripple, with his special handle built into the steering wheel and his hand-operated brake. *Blessed are the peacemakers* . . . "What's that?" Nothing, says Charlie. It's nothing.

Out front of the Phalanstery, which wears its best poker face in the dark, the cuffs come off. "No hard feelings, okay?" the inspector says, pocketing the key. "Handcuffs are S.O.P., and I'm breaking a dozen regulations for you as it is. But I apologize for any discomfort."

Charlie hates to be a feeb, but can't help rubbing his wrists together as he trails Pulaski's wobbly flashlight. After pressing an ear to the front door for a minute, Pulaski stumps around to a basement window. He reaches for the plywood. "You feel that? It has some give." So does Charlie's resolve. What every sinew in him screams, at all the important moments, is *Run*. And if he were to bolt again this time, there'd be nothing this bent shape banked by bonfires could do to stop him.

Instead, he tugs on the plywood. The nails sing, then groan. These splinters are going to be a bitch tomorrow. He has to borrow the butt end of Pulaski's crutch to pry the wood the rest of the way off, making a hollow in the shadows. "Why can't I have the flashlight, too?"

But they've been over this, there's only one, and the inspector's not about to let Charlie handle it. "You understand this is all a courtesy, right? I'm still not saying I accept a word you've said." He runs his beam along the window ledge, like a jittery hand feeling for shards of glass or nails that have come out incompletely. "I assume you know your way around. You come straight up to the front door and let me in, and we'll go through together, see what we see."

Which isn't how it was supposed to go. The inspector was supposed to relay Charlie's allegations to the SWAT team, and they would converge here with M16s and helicopters, and the duffelbag would be brought out, and then Nicky and Sol, if Sol was still here, while Charlie watched from some safe distance where they couldn't see who'd finked on them, and then . . . And then Sam would live. He gets that the sheer implausibility of his story, coupled with the blackout, has required some divergence from plan, but he wasn't expecting to actually be the one to go in, alone, at what must be getting on toward T-minus zero. "What if someone's standing guard?" he asks.

"I hate to burst your bubble, but I can't see it happening. It's dead quiet in there."

Charlie has seen with his own eyes that the basement into which he's forced is bare of furniture, but as he lands on his hands, his memory seems unreliable, and that little square of moonlight awfully far away. He strains to hear voices, but the inspector's right: this blackout is silent as death. Which doesn't mean someone or something couldn't be lurking. In fact, a silent lurk is maybe exactly what you'd aim for. He wishes the fucking flashlight would shine down in here, but is scared even to whisper back over his shoulder. Plus who's to say the inspector's still up there. Who's to say Sol Grungy hasn't already lurched out from his hiding place and gagged Pulaski and stuffed him into the back of the van. People turn out to be capable of just about anything, which leaves only two reasonable positions: assume the worst of them, or take stuff on trust. At this point, it seems 99 percent likely that nothing worth trusting even exists. That Charlie's blown his one shot at belonging on some vaporous nonsense about the sanctity of life. Even these beatitudes he hums to calm himself are propaganda, like Nicky said all along. Propaganda with just enough holes to justify anything anybody wants. If there is any sin, it's Charlie's, too. But he can't just sit here like bait on a hook, so he takes a hit off his inhaler and finds the stairs, the foiled walls, the front hall. When he gets the door open—thank God—the inspector's on the far side, or his light is, swinging around to blind Charlie.

"This way, is where they'll be."

The back steps slow the inspector down, as does the irregular ground Charlie's shadow scythes across, tetanus-encrusted old bike frames ambuscading in the high grass. Feral cats yowl in ardor or rage. Someone calls down from an invisible building for them to stay the hell off her property or she'll call the City. "It's okay, ma'am," the inspector hisses up. "We are the City." But now his pistol's out all the same. It isn't exactly a stealth approach.

From outside the little carriage house, the light picks out only the tin in the windows, the layer of dust, the darkness. A shiny new padlock lies in the dirt near the door. Something else is different, too, or missing, but Charlie can't name it. Pulaski mates the flashlight to the gun, shoves through the door and yells "Freeze!" and the beam sweeps around to reveal . . . squat. The cinderblock partition's been dismantled and removed. Even the carpet is gone. There's just a pile of guitar strings and a kick drum with *Nihilo* on it.

Pulaski taps the drum. It's empty. "This is it? This is your big conspiracy?"

It never occurred to Charlie that Nicky wouldn't be here—that even these late epiphanies may be unreliable, he thinks, scanning frantically for anyplace you might stash a bomb. That Nicky's too much of a narcissist to off himself. Maybe instead of going down with the ship, he's planted his powder somewhere more secure and gotten the fuck out. Are enough minutes left on the clock to search the whole house? "No, no, just give me a little time."

He leads the way to the back steps, and then up, floor by floor, awaiting the painfully slow climb of the inspector, who still hogs the light. The interiors it skims seem distorted, as in a body reduced to its skeleton. Sooty floorboards, crumbling brick . . . it's like Charlie's dreamed everything he lived through here. As if he's the one stuck in bed, with the morphine drip. There's nowhere for a bag to hide. He'd like at least to have that packet of photographs, to show the inspector he's not crazy, there really is a PHP, but only in the attic do they find anything at all, and then it's just crap he left yesterday, thinking to be gone only an hour, the bedroll, his piled clothes, and Sam's filmless camera. He watches his hands reach for the strap. Loops it over his neck and shoulder, resists a gathering tightness. With the windows closed, it's a sweat lodge in here. The chimney is bricked up. Still, it reminds him there's a level above.

He's halfway up the ladder to the roof when the inspector says, "Where do you think you're going? I can't climb that."

"So wait here. But I'm going to need the flashlight."

"Charlie, I've seen enough for one night. I was curious. I gambled. I lost."

"Please—you said you'd give me a chance. I trusted you."

Some more time may pass. Then, to Charlie's surprise, Pulaski hands over the light.

Charlie's already stepped off the ladder's top rung when the sense of height catches up with him. He has to get down on his hands and knees, like a baby. From there, the flashlight finds nothing more solid than a wrecked pigeon coop. Through the slats and wire comes the human light of the street—cars and fires and other flashlights—and beyond that, Nicky's wet dream: the entire financial district, blotted out. Or almost entire; red lights flash atop two ghostly towers, since even in a blackout, you've got to warn the planes. Scrabbling around toward Midtown, he can just make out the Empire State, a black bar against the stars, and the needle of the Chrysler. Then something glimmers between them. A gilded rhombus flaring redly into view.

"Tell me what you're seeing up there," calls a voice from the trapdoor behind him.

"Nothing," he has to admit. "I'm seeing nothing."

"There's no such thing as nothing, kid. Tell me what you see."

Charlie levels his faint beam as if it could reach all the way uptown. It reminds him of an exhibit his dad took him to once at the Museum of Natural History. You pressed a button, a light shot from the building top; eight seconds later, it reached the moon. Around the far-off skyscraper with the gilt roof, there seems to be smoke—that's what's causing the glimmer, gray over gold—only it doesn't behave the way smoke should. Instead of hanging, or rising, it sweeps back and forth like a veil. Shit. What's missing from the garage out back, and now the roof, are Sol's birds. And there they are, circling that tower a mile away, like the flying monkeys of Oz, or the fowls of heaven, desperate to tell him something. "I'm seeing this one building with its warning lights still on," he says. "The one with the golden pagoda on top."

"The Hamilton-Sweeney Building, you mean."

And for a second, Charlie has a new sense of just what's on the line tonight. What was the thing they used to say, back when there were no skyscrapers? The higher the building, the closer . . . Oh, God.

92

A FTER THE LAST BLACKOUT, in '65, eight of Manhattan's nine major medical centers invested heavily in generator modernization. Guess which one didn't. That's right: Beth Israel, at present, still relies on a single, ancient, diesel-powered afterthought that dwells in an annex to the boiler room. The emergency plan on file with the city includes a courtesy call from Con Ed in the event of an outage, so that the main circuit can be switched over, but tonight no call comes, and the whole towering superstructure is struck momentarily blind. Then some janitor must take it upon himself to brave the infernal circles that are the subbasements of any urban hospital and find the manual bypass—for light is returning to the upper floors, along with a rumble that wasn't there before. Windows tremble in their frames. Personal-sized tins of syrupy fruit cocktail jig across oblique eating trays. Albeit attenuated by layers of floor and thick-soled shoes, the rumble reaches even the nurses as they squeak along the surgical pink halls.

Wednesday night is generally the week's slowest, and right now most of the physicians are finishing up dinner in Westchester. As with the cops, many will be called back to the city in the course of the next few hours. They'll form little agonistic clots in the waiting areas, arguing about who's responsible for what, but it's the nurses, really, who are the pacemakers of this short-circuited heart. Their first order of business is to visit each of the 937 inpatient beds to check that its equipment has come back online. It's a daunting task, but these same thickset Eastern European and West Indian women who can make your life hell if you're perceived to take a tone with them have got protocols down cold. They check vital signs and change glucose drips and "bag" patients whose respirators went haywire when the power came back on. They move down the hallways with a briskness that to anyone watching would appear majestic, like firemen at the sound of a bell.

It's doubly hard, then, to account for the hours it takes before anyone looks in on room 817B. Or trebly hard, as the eighth-floor nurses—Magdalena and Fantine and Mary and Mary Pat—have taken a near-maternal interest in its occupant, who at 193 days has been here the longest. They've closed the window on cool evenings when her father's left it open, and cranked it open mornings when there's something she would theoretically like to see. They've soaped her with golden sponges, the kind husbands use on the family wagon on weekends. They've changed her and wiped her and in a technical sense fed her, too. Fantine and Mary Pat have sung to her; the others are not the singing type. But all have touched her hand or cheek to say *Hello in there* and *So long for now* and *Get some rest, Sleeping Beauty*. It was Fantine who came up with the nickname. And maybe, on second thought, this was why it took her so long: the nearer a thing is to us—the more a part of us—the easier it is to lose sight of.

It is after midnight when Fantine finally wheels the new IV stand in, and she hasn't made it three squeaks inside the door when a knife goes into her heart. It's hard to say which she sees first: the respirator gone dead in the corner, or the mountain of golden flesh looming over the bed. A hospital gown is coming apart at the back, revealing inky claws or wings that ascend the vertebrae to the neck and skull. This must be the man who shot her, Fantine realizes—the Kneesocks Killer, come back to finish the job. His hands continue their strangling motions as he turns to take in the source of the gasp. The tattoos extend halfway onto his face; she's never seen anything like it. From his ear hangs a tiny dagger. Then, like some predator too powerful to take notice of a morsel like her, he returns to his labors.

Back in January, that crooked little man from the police force had gathered the nursing staff together at the shift change and told them to keep special watch on Sleeping Beauty. It was like just because her skin was white they valued her more than other patients. Though the newspapers didn't name her, they were already turning her into a kind of story about what was wrong with the city, when in East Flatbush walking home from the train late you heard gunfire more often than not and no one cared. Some anonymous philanthropist would soon step forward to cover the girl's hospital bills. But that was back before the girl meant anything to her personally, and now Fantine sees the size of her own failure. Someone said there was some commotion here earlier in the day; she should have known to watch closer. She tightens her grip on the IV stand as if it was a harpoon. She tries not to think of what the man's hands could do to her. Then they move again, and there is a sound she recognizes, like the crumpling of an empty milk carton. She glimpses the blue bag of a hand-operated breathing pump. And the man says, for all the world as if they know each other, "You going to take over, or what? My arms are killing me."

His easy manner frees her to fly across the room as she wasn't able to a moment ago. Who on earth does he think he is? What is he doing here? This isn't his . . . she reaches for a powerful word. "This isn't your jurisdiction!"

"Well, one of us better work this thing, sister, 'cause your breathing machine there's been on the fritz for hours." But as he offers her the bag, a reflex makes her slap his hand away, and the blue, life-giving bellows falls to the floor. Every other care in her mind clears before the horror of the pulse monitor starting to wail. She scrabbles on her hands and knees. Then she is up again, fitting the clear-plastic mask over the girl's nose and mouth, pumping the bag furiously. After a few breaths, she orders the intruder to put a thumb on the girl's wrist.

"Now count, damn you," she says, bearing down again. "Don't stop until I say."

Her bosom is only six inches from his huge shoulders, his arms bursting like prize hams from the sleeves of a too-small gown. Among the tattoos is a swastika she pretends not to see. After fifteen seconds, she calculates a heart rate of forty-four beats per minute, which is what the electrocardiogram says, too. It stops beeping. Air flows in, out, fogs the plastic. In the glassy jar of the breathing machine, she can see her own scowl. "Visiting hours are over, you know. O-V-er."

"I'm not a visitor. I'm a patient."

"That so?"

"I reckon this dashiki you people put me in means I can walk the halls if I want to. And Samantha here happens to be an old friend. You're lucky I came up for a visit, or I wouldn't have heard that pulse-taker there beeping blue murder when the lights came back on."

She cannot look at his face. "You should have called a nurse."

"You see a phone up here?"

"There's a call button. We've got special training. Do you have special training?"

"Hell, it don't take a diploma to see Sammy wasn't breathing. I spot this thing by the sink and I've been sitting here ever since, pumping away at her pretty face." Fantine looks to see what kind of sauciness is in this devil, but the black ink curled crablike around the mouth and one of the eyes makes it hard to say he's anything but sincere.

"These tattoos, they're bad for you, you know."

"That's what Ma always said, God rest her."

"The ink gets in your blood, it can give you hepatitis."

"I'm not long for this world anyway, darlin'. Cancer of the nut." He gives the front of his gown a gratuitous squeeze, but winces. "Got the old snip snip tomorrow. Maybe they'll do the left one, too, just in case. But you wouldn't tell anyone, would you? 'Cause I'd have to kill you. Or leave town, one or the other."

She studies him.

"Then again, what do you care, right? That ain't your jurisdiction, just like this ain't mine. I'd better get back downstairs like a good boy and gargle my barium."

"No," she's surprised to hear herself say. "You stay. You need to stay." Here in 817B, this flaw of light above a dark city, she feels like a mollusk unhoused from its shell. A quivering gray life. One more meeting of the eyes or collision of skin and skin and this rude and twinkling man will know all the things she goes around trying to hide from the world, and from herself. How she felt when she'd stuck the butcher knife in her first husband that night he'd beaten her so bad. How she felt every day after that, knowing what she'd done. *Wake up*, a voice says somewhere, quite clearly. And she is trying. She is trying. "We need to see if there's any damage. Someone's got to work the pump while I go get the doctor."

Of course, Bullet could be the one to go, but she shows him proper technique on the bag, where to put your thumbs so you won't strain the muscles of your wrist. Only from the doorway does she allow herself a full glance at this big octoroonish biker-type with his tattoos and his long chain of an earring. She wants to warn him to remove it before he submits to any scans, but the words are stolen from her by the metamorphosis she's witnessing. With what impossible daintiness does he check again the seal on the mouthpiece. With what seriousness does he watch the wall clock's lagging second hand, waiting for the next squeeze.

MIDTOWN—NOT ACTUALLY 9:27

"TWENTY MINUTES, THEN I'M CALLING IT," the inspector says, shutting Charlie's door behind him, but it's hard to know anymore what "twenty minutes" means. The clock on the bank across the way is stuck at 9:27. Inside the car, whose radio has once again died, the siren spins mutely. Bands of blue sweep uncollected garbage on the curb. Otherwise the dark is undisturbed until, a few feet shy of the lobby, Charlie sees a red flash above. And there they are, three football fields up: those birds last glimpsed from the townhouse miles away. It's like time itself has been suspended. And this isn't how a mystery is supposed to end, he thinks. But what if he's right? How many tons of rock crashing down, leaving a stadium-sized crater in Midtown? How many people in surrounding apartment buildings taken out by the rubble, or the flame? He can almost hear the air ringing up there in alarm. At ground level, the inspector's having no luck with the building's revolving door, which any idiot could have told him would be locked. He flips open his badge, raps metal against glass. His flashlight barely penetrates. "Police!" Charlie fidgets, glancing around, another slurp of inhaler. These blocks are creepily quiet, without buses or motorized loading gates or a single plane overhead. Then there are feet, hard soles on a hard floor, and the answering eye of a light inside.

The light-bearer, when the door opens, is a fat guy with a crappy moustache. Lint on his velvet monkey-suit. These uniforms used to seem so sharp back when Charlie would come here for his annual tooth-cleaning. He can remember standing by the elevator bank, trying not to panic, Mom squeezing his arm. It's Pulaski squeezing now, muttering for Charlie to keep his mouth shut. Then something cracks as the little inspector draws himself up to his full height. "We need to inspect the premises." No way they'd get away with this by daylight.

"What are you, reporters?"

"NYPD."

The inspector pulls the badge back as a hand reaches for it.

"So what's with the camera?" Indicating Charlie.

"My partner here is undercover—"

"We need to see the fortieth floor," Charlie says. It takes nerve, in the face of Pulaski's dirty look, but he's recalled something else: the brass directory board, and, a few spots above Dr. DeMoto, *The Hamilton-Sweeney Company, Suite 4000.* It's as if, he thinks, nothing's ever really gone—as if the shards just hide somewhere inside, waiting to be put back together. He might find this comforting, given time to linger on it, but the fat attendant's still blocking the way.

"I'll have to go get the building manager."

"I'm afraid there's no time for that," Pulaski says.

"Then *I'm* afraid you're going to have to show me a warrant."

The deal with this city's functionaries is, you want to keep them from establishing position, because once they do, they'll defend it to the death. But the inspector is unsnapping something up near his armpit, flashing his beam there. His words stay courtly, but their timbre is tougher. "It seems to me there are extenuating circumstances. Our typewriters downtown are all electric. Not to speak of how hard it is to reach a judge at, what is it now, quarter to twelve? So let's say in the spirit of civic cooperation you show me and my partner the fastest way up to the top floor. No, I mean physically guide us. And don't fret about your boss. When the time comes, I'll tell him what a stand-up guy you were."

A skyscraper turns out to be a lot like a person. There is the outward face, with all its impressive ornament, and then suddenly vulnerability: in this case, a hinged maple panel behind the security desk. It swings open at the attendant's touch. The two flashlights loop and dart over patches of unpainted concrete, ashtrays and scattered playing cards, a bucket of custodial orts. A stairwell leads up into a dark that might be infinite. Charlie's lungs tighten again. "You mean your elevator's not hooked to a generator?"

"Pal, if there was a generator, would I be dicking around with a flashlight?"

It's a solid point, but then how to explain that warning light up top? That is, unless it really is the signal Charlie's been waiting for all these months, summoning him in to begin his climb.

BETH ISRAEL HOSPITAL—CA. 11:50 P.M.

BUT MAYBE THEY SHOULD HAVE GONE TO ST. VINCENT'S. The man in the cart is so much heavier than she's assumed, and the crosstown blocks so much longer. They've just come through one of the city's two Lighting Districts; she'd thought it wonderful, once, that there should be enough of anything to constitute a district (enough flowers, enough fashion, enough diamonds). But tonight there was no light in the Lighting District, only dark, vaguely hominid shapes moving singly or in pairs, and then, drawing close behind, sirens, smashing, the odor of flame. The faster she and Mercer pushed, the more the sidewalk jolted the cart, until it almost seemed the body inside was stirring. There have been periodic pauses, too, to bicker. But now there is relief, trees, rustlings of leaf no longer quite invisible in their boxes—and above, the massive hospital, windows stacked and fully lit, the only real light in sight.

What she wasn't expecting was the line. It seems to stretch all the way back to Second Avenue. Men in uniform flank the doors by the ambulance bay. Paramedics, with clipboards. "I'll be back," she tells Mercer, and goes to talk to them. She passes wheelchairs, splinted arms, clutched stomachs, a person leaning over to retch into a bush, another with what appears to be a club-wound to the head. The medics, by contrast, are crisp and untroubled. They could be twins. *Where were you an hour ago*, she wants to ask. *And now, with all these people . . . ?* She figures the ER must be understaffed—a supposition the medics confirm. Every exam room, every stretcher, every seat is full. Unless you've got something high up on the triage list, you could be out here till dawn. "It's not me," she says. "It's one of the guys with me. A car hit him. He's been unconscious since."

"You saw the collision?"

How to put this. "In a manner of speaking."

"He bleeding?"

"Not that I can tell, but—"

"As long as he's breathing, he's doing better than anyone inside.

We'll send someone over to do an assessment, but most likely he's going to have to wait."

Walking back toward the corner, she imagines a campaign to swap out the city's entire disaster-response apparatus with conscripts, like jury duty. Well, not the fire department. Show her a firefighter, and Jenny will reach for her heart and sing you "The Star-Spangled Banner." But just as she's trying to explain to Mercer why they'll have to stick around for a while, there's a small electronic beep.

"What's that?" Beeep. "It's your watch, isn't it?"

An indictment. She hands it to him. Her tongue feels stuck to the roof of her mouth. "It's the little button on the side. But midnight doesn't necessarily mean anything, Mercer. Don't you think we'd hear it if a bomb went off in the East Village?"

"I don't know anymore. I don't know what we would have heard."

"The timing was a guess, remember, and someone could have gotten there first to stop it. Didn't you say—"

"But not the target, that wasn't a guess! We've known all along William was in danger. Yet here we are, with this other guy."

"Wait, listen—are those sirens?" Again, if she hadn't known better, she would have said the figure in the cart had stirred. "No, sorry. Same one. As long as there's not some big exodus of ambulances from the line up there . . ."

Another siren keens. Another pause. Five seconds. Ten.

"This has been a farce," he says, "this whole expedition. I have to go."

"Mercer, we can't just leave this guy to suffer. At least not until a doctor comes."

"Don't you dare act like I'm indifferent to suffering. I'm telling you, I have to find William. I have to know, one way or another."

"I didn't ask for any of this," she says, already hearing he's right. How selfish it sounds. "But I guess that's not your problem. I know you need to find out. Just be careful, okay?"

Mercer is almost to the corner when she notices that the white guy in the shopping cart is sitting up, watching him go. "You're awake!" But by the time she looks back to Mercer for a reaction, he has passed beyond the light.

"Who are you?" the guy asks. "Do I know you?"

"Damn . . . You can talk, too! You're at the hospital." Maybe it's for the best that he doesn't seem to remember why. "There was an accident, a car. Look. How many fingers am I holding up?"

"I can't see for shit. What did you do to the light?"

"It's a blackout. Wait, stop moving, you're not supposed to move." But he is already standing, so tall in the cart that others on line turn and gape. He looks nothing so much as surprised at their sheer number—the way a ghost might on discovering there's an afterlife after all. Which in a sense is the case, Jenny just has time to think, before he leaps to the ground, falls. Rises and begins to lope off down the street. He is graceful in the air, but less so on the hoof. When he collapses again, a half-block south, she is only a few yards behind. Deeper back, people watch, mystified. "Hey. Hey." She takes his arm. "Are you familiar with the phrase 'the triumph of hope over experience'? Somebody practically drove over you. We've got to get you checked out."

In the light of a passing car, he looks younger than before, his mouth as sensitive as a child's. It pinches in concentration. She can hear the machinery of his brain ratcheting into gear, until that turns into someone trying to start another car stalled down the block. Ayuh yuh yuh. "I've got to get home." He has a little twang, like Mercer. *Git.* If I can't physically compel his return to the ER, she thinks, I can at least out-talk him, but then a further voice speaks up again—or not actually a voice so much as an idea, implanted in her head. How does she know it isn't her own? Because it is to *Let it drop,* and Jenny's never done any such thing in her life.

"Well, how is that going to happen? You can't walk unsupported, obviously."

He tries to demonstrate he'll do just that, but his knee crumples again after a few more yards. "Damn it!"

She waits for him to ask for help, lets him hang there a minute. Does she have to do everything herself? Then she sighs and pulls his arm over her shoulder. It will be much later in the night, or at least seem to be, before it even occurs to her to ask where they're going.

UPPER WEST SIDE—EARLIER

DEEP DOWN, WILLIAM HAMILTON-SWEENEY has always believed that were he ever to give his father an honest accounting of his feelings, the world would spontaneously combust. What happens instead is precisely nothing. The library's walls do not collapse, nor is there even any change in Daddy's audible breathing. He presses on. "It's true. I'm sure Regan's come up with a million reasons why I stayed away, she's the champion rationalizer, but the reality, Daddy, is just that simple: you're an asshole. And if I've got to sit up here—which I only agreed to do as a favor to her, by the way—I don't want there to be any temptation for either of us to pretend not to know what's in the other's heart."

A dozen little beads of flame glimmer behind the divan where his father perches. Unless the word is settee. The domestics seem to have jumped ship before Amory did (assuming he didn't have them whacked as well), so Daddy must have been the one to settle himself like this, propping expensive cushions under his elbows in the manner of some Old Testament judge. No candles having been lit on his side of the room, though, his grimace at William's impropriety remains barely perceptible. "Although that would be the Hamilton-Sweeney way, wouldn't it? I should have known you'd just sit here and not say a word."

And in a sense, silent disapproval is worse than any explosion. William moves toward the chest of drawers on the north wall, ostensibly looking for more light, but actually awaiting another infusion of courage, or candor, or whatever this is. It's as if a great inscrutable force, the higher power to whom he's been addressing himself these last few weeks, has steered him back to where everything started, and now he badly needs it to tell him what to do. He cocks his head, tries to lose himself in the spines of books. *Amends*, is the word Bill W. uses in the Big Book. Maybe he's supposed to use his own silence to wrench from Daddy the amends he wants, but all he gets is Daddy's cleared throat, this cartilaginous tic that was always annoying as hell.

"The irony is, I was only a couple miles away all these years. Amory didn't mention that either, did he? But trust me, I'm sure he kept abreast. The drugs, all of it. You could have found me easily enough, but why do that? I was doing you a favor by not being around to remind you of things we both knew. It's like we've been living in two different cities. You up here in all this marbled comfort, and me down there, killing myself in slow motion."

It is one of Bill W.'s precepts that talking about your most shameful behaviors, exposing their undersides to the air, will make you feel better. In practice, though, as long as he won't do more than harrumph at the possibility that they're worth listening to, it's Bill H-S who has the upper hand. And he knows it, they both know it.

"One of those things being that I'm a homosexual, Daddy. Or what was it you used to say when Liberace was on TV? A queer duck. I know this comes as no surprise, but for the record: I am attracted to men. I have sex with them," William hears himself say. "And since I'm laying my cards on the table, I did end up finding someone I could fall in love with. Do you want to guess what happened next? I fucked it up, is what. I lied. I withheld. I was cold and prideful and within myself. All this shit I've been carrying around because of you, I couldn't let go of, because I no longer knew where it stopped and the rest of me started. I clung to it like a guy who's shipwrecked and doesn't trust he can swim."

There's a rush of heat now on the back of his neck, like someone else has brought a torch into the room, but when he turns, he finds only more darkness. It's just him and the inscrutable face before him, a contest of wills. Of Wills, he thinks. He lapses into silence, which he manages to keep up for an impressive time, whole minutes, maybe. But every impulse becomes unbearable sooner or later.

"Did you notice how you never touched me, Daddy, after Mom died? It was like I had contracted some disease. You had plenty of chances to like tousle my hair, or hug me, or punch me, even, but the best I ever got was a handshake. I used to think I remembered my shoulder being squeezed at the burial, but that was Uncle Artie. I'm sure this sounds like more childishness, but back then, I still looked at you like a god whose big hands could rescue me, if only I could get them to touch me."

There's a single candle left in the rightmost drawer, and a book of matches he uses to light a cigarette. He squints against the smoke.

"One of the things recovery has helped me see is how I was always trying to put myself in a position to be rescued. Regan was usually the one who rode in on her white charger, but one day, I thought, if I could just make it so the trouble was too big for her, you would have to step in. But you couldn't even do that for Regan, could you."

What he himself can't do, having crossed again to within a half-dozen feet, is meet Daddy's gaze. There's a sour-sweet smell like ammonia, but he ignores it.

"I think you know I was right that day, by the way, no matter what Regan decided to hold back. The day we came to you, before the rehearsal dinner. You always did have feelings, where she was concerned. And you're not a stupid man. Your daughter was left pregnant, without good options, and entirely on her own." He's had half a lifetime to circle around what a just resolution might really have looked like. "You should have called off the merger, at least, if not your marriage. You should have had the guy's head on a pike, and Amory's. Don't tell yourself that keeping Regan close, making her a Director or however you say it, was the same as giving her what she needed. She was suffering so much with what happened that she used to make herself throw up. Did you know that? I hadn't seen her for fifteen years, and I pretty much knew. You like to think of yourself as a man of duty, but when you've got one kid with a finger down her throat and another shooting his inheritance into his veins . . . you kind of have to wonder. And now Amory's got you poised for the fall, from what I can see. Not to mention trying to have me taken out. And what's your first instinct when I come to tell you? You stick up for him."

Somehow, though, the closer William gets to justice, the worse he feels. There's that "condition" people keep alluding to; maybe Daddy doesn't remember any of this. Maybe, in fact, it was grief over William's running away that began his decline. In which case who, really, owes amends to whom? And who is that enormous impersonal consciousness he senses out there beyond the edges, watching, expecting, disapproving? Maybe it's none other than himself. Maybe *out there* is in here.

"I'll tell you something else. I keep having this fantasy about some wide river or channel I'm on the bank of. I can look up, and on the far side is another, better self, holding hands with Mercer—that's his name, my ex—and both of them are watching me flail over here, watching me from the life I'm supposed to have had. When did it become impossible to get there from here? When did that bridge get burned? Until tonight, I would have said it was the day before your wedding, with Regan and the toast and all that, but right now I'm thinking it's right now. I mean, here we are for the first time in years, I'm talking about you never having touched me, and meanwhile your hand is right there, three feet away, and you still can't reach across whatever separates us and just touch you. Me."

He sits there for a while feeling the implications of this error, like a man running his tongue over a loose molar. Time is doing this funny thing where he can't tell how much of it is passing. Also space: the darkened walls seem to have slid back on tracks, like scenery into the wings, leaving the two of them alone in this flickering circumference. There has to be *some* way to wound Daddy. To make him feel the cruelty Amory Gould had presided over. But it had taken William years to riddle out its intricacies himself, and then only after he'd been able to put aside the belief that Amory had marshaled resources beyond his grasp of human nature. Years Daddy wouldn't spend. Or didn't have. Meaning Amory hadn't had to preside, not really. And somewhere, William must still be seventeen, the boy rushing to throw himself athwart the tracks of his fate, because he feels that at last he's reached it, the part that matters, the thing that must be seen. (As somewhere else, he turns away, because he cannot bear to look.) Try again, William. Make it all connect. Grip the knife and twist.

"It was rape, Daddy. Rape that got her pregnant. The son of the man you merged with. Rape that I brought to you in your office that day, when all I could think about was wrecking a fucking wedding. Wrong after all, both of us—and if I managed to set the usurpation back a decade or two, so what? However it went between Regan and his protégé, Amory was always going to end up with strings to pull. But he wasn't pulling my strings when I stood there in front of you, unfeeling, using Regan's suffering for my own selfish purposes. I convinced myself that if you refused to see a problem, maybe it would go away. Daddy, I know you understand. I know you understand me."

In truth, though, he knows no such thing. Because when, at last, on an impulse, he reaches out to touch his father's hand, what shakes free is not an apology, or a condemnation, but a snore. Daddy has been asleep for some time now, to say nothing of that smell. Which means (William thinks—and it kills him) he's going to get away with everything.

EAST VILLAGE—12:12 A.M.

CRUMMY ORPHEUS THAT HE IS, Mercer has resisted a last look back at the hospital. Even if the shopping cart weighs more than you'd think, even if the man inside it is paralyzed, Jenny will be okay, he knows; this side of his own Mama, he's never met a more stubborn girl. Anyway, what has today taught him if not that all he can do for other people essentially amounts to very little? If William is dead, he is dead.

Yet a strange thing happens as he drifts south and east: nothing. Or rather, everything. There is more than one way to be out of time, it seems, and now he is stranded between two worlds, one in which a bomb has gone off and one in which it hasn't, at least not here. To judge by what stands around him, William still lives. But to the extent that it only means less finality and more heartache, Mercer is no longer even sure if this is the world he wants to be in. If he's ever loved William enough.

In the breast pocket of his shirt is the last joint from his mother-lode. He's never quite adjusted to the fact that in New York you can walk down the street smoking this stuff openly, but now he thinks what the hell, he's invisible anyway. He lights it. Coughs. Inhales again. It doesn't fail him. Where usually a high creates thought-connections that lead elaborately away from the moment he's in, this one pulls him back from the brink of the future. A façade on Four-teenth Street has sprung a hole, through which other holes shuttle in and out, laden with free groceries. Alarms and sirens wail in clashing keys, but no one notices until the cops are upon them.

He walks on, past flashlights and floating cigarettes, sticking as close to the street as possible. He hardly recognizes these as the same sidewalks he wandered back when he lived with Carlos, not only because of the blackout, but because so much of what he'd seen then he'd refused to admit to seeing. The denim boys on roller skates, the hustlers in twos and threes with their come-hither glances. All of them, like William, were willing to endure a certain quantum of danger in pursuit of pleasure, or vice versa. A solitary moped whiz-zes past, its headlamp streaking the bars of a wrought-iron fence. The word that occurs, *spectral*, is probably not the right one for how Mercer feels. How he feels is: like a human pinball. Then a voice out of the darkness rasps, "Hey, you." Meaning me, he thinks. Meaning him.

He has made his way, as best he can determine, to the northern entrance of Tompkins Square Park, where he once heard Ex Post Facto play. It's a wonder he hasn't thought to look here for William before tonight; the place is notorious (he'd subsequently pretended not to have learned) as a spot for cruising and drugs and worse. From the dense shadows beyond the gate comes the smack of skin on skin, followed by laughter and swift steps ebbing among the trees. Music somewhere. The voice speaks up again. "Yeah, you. You got any more of that?"

"Any more of what?"

"'Any more of what,' he says." Mercer's unsure whether this is meant for him or for some third party, also invisible. "Of what you're smoking, Your Majesty."

He hesitates. "How do I know you're not a cop?"

At this, the laughter ramifies into what's definitely more than one voice. They sound half-stoned already. Mercer's roach makes a neon arc as he extends it, less out of a sense of camaraderie than in hopes of satisfying them and thus ending the interaction. The joint flares, crackling, and he can just make out liquid eyes in a face his mother would have called "high yellow." Then, like the Cheshire Cat's, they're gone. Instead of returning to him, the joint drifts farther back, to be inhaled by another man, or boy, it sounds like. Mercer's face is heating up, but why be embarrassed? Mama's not around to see him, nor could she, were she. "Just so you know, I don't have any money," his mouth says, because some rational part of him still thinks it's worth getting this out there. But his interlocutors apparently don't give a shit. "The end is nigh, brother. We're just trying to have a good time."

Uh-oh. Walk away now, Mercer thinks. Trouble is, he's grown attached to this joint. And so, as if some more powerful narcotic has been mixed in with the dope, he's following the voices and the dwindling orange bloom of it back along the path. There's a bend, which as he rounds it gives way to more light, a thousand feathers curling through the leaves. Then the vegetation clears, and he can make out bodies, beefy, hairy, some of them sans shirt. Music thumps from a ghetto blaster wedged into the crotch of a tree. An exfoliated disco ball dangles among the branches, and a man in leather chaps and a train conductor's cap plays a flashlight across it, which is where the light comes from. Well, that and a trashcan someone has set unfragrantly ablaze. Where the flicker barely reaches, men hold each other and sway. Mercer blinks to see if they'll go away. "You want a beer or something?" says the boy holding the joint. His shirt's open at the chest, which glows like molded brass.

"I guess." Mercer hopes the diversion will allow him to turn and go. But he finds he can't, even after the boy has disappeared into the dark behind a bench.

Waiting, he tries not to look out of place, to make too much eye contact or too little—tries, that is, not to see the melding of bodies in the underbrush, most of them dark like his own, the shocking pink flashes of tongue and palm. At not seeing, he's had lots of practice. There used to be a path made of flagstones between Mama's kitchen and the vegetable garden. One spring, heavy rains had loosened them in their footings, so that you could see around each one a little black gap just perfect for a penknife. He'd gotten the idea to pry one up, and when it came free—a wet, sucking sound—he'd found the verso teeming with shiny-backed creepy-crawlies asquirm in the blacker mud. One of the things he fears most is that beneath the masonry of his own consciousness lies some similarly primeval carnival of appetite, and so, from the moment he first passed through Port Authority, he's been patrolling the borders of his thoughts, tamping down the flooring, keeping things cool and dry and orderly. And perhaps (it occurs to him) cutting himself off from what's available for his art. Or does it explode?

"I brung you this." The boy is back. A beer bottle, its label damp and peeling, insinuates itself into Mercer's hand.

"Brought."

"Huh?"

"The participle." The boy stares puzzled at his flame-licked profile. Mercer wonders if William used to think of him this way: as a boy. *I don't drink*, he wants to say now, as he said then, but what would Walt Whitman do? Obviously, Old Walt would take up the burden, bear the brunt. Bringing the bottle to his lips, he nearly chips a tooth.

"You've got to . . . here, let me . . ."

The boy does a thing where he uses his own bottle to dislodge the cap of Mercer's. Mercer repeats the swigging motion more cautiously. What's inside might as well be beechwood-aged horse piss, but in the last twenty-four hours, he's been chased, cross-examined, and nearly sent through a windshield, all without eating; he can be forgiven if his mouth is dry. "How old are you?"

"How old are *you*?" the boy asks.

"I asked you first. Twenty-five."

"Nineteen," the boy says, which, Mercer not having been born yesterday, probably means the same age as his students, fifteen, sixteen. Former students, rather.

"And this is where you spend your time, at nineteen?"

"You mean with my friends? Why wouldn't it be? I'm not some window-shopper who has to hustle back to my closet every night."

"I'm sorry. I just don't have much experience of how this is supposed to go."

"We could dance, for starters. You like to dance?"

Not anymore, Mercer is thinking, when the boy shoves him out into the churn of bodies. Between two tenements beyond the treeline, the moon should be luminous and precise, except oily smoke from the trashcan keeps interfering. *You can dance* . . . , the radio insists, but the best he can manage is a sort of shuffle from foot to foot in time to the boy's more expressive gyrations. The closer they get to the flames, the hotter it is, and the boy undoes yet another button of his shirt. The Dionysian torso moves closer. Mercer takes several more swigs of beer, trying to use his bottle-arm's elbow as a baffle, but the boy, a dab hand at seduction, finds his way through, and even as Mercer's heart clenches, his lower body brings him close enough for wrists to rest on shoulders, for a finger to loosely trace the nap at the back of his head. He closes his eyes in what might be perceived as surrender. Maybe the point here is that he does *not* see clearly. That he never saw clearly.

Then a blue light throbs inside his eyelids. He has a feeling its source is something he doesn't want to know about, but as the outer world grows noisier, he can't help opening his eyes. Beyond the shoulders of this stranger, high beams are zooming along a path into the park, rendering it not nearly so tangled or secret as Mercer's been imagining. Another flash of blue. *The park is closed,* says a voice over a loudspeaker. And then what sounds like: *Don't eat 'shrooms.* At the circle's edges, some men dive for underbrush, but most stand their ground, stunned in the lights of the Finest. And among them, a dozen yards away, he notices for the first time a lone woman: Is she some kind of cop, too? It seems at any rate improbable that he should cross paths with the law multiple times in a single day. But then, what if this isn't the law, and his search for William has just been one more projection? What if it's really *him* they've been after all along, these powers in their various disguises?

ON THE ROAD—?

AS FAR AS THE DEMON BROTHER WENT—or Ghoul, or whatever he was to himself in his secret life—that part had been simple enough. The man came on like some master of the black arts, but really extortion was just a function of the strength of your material. And the material he had on Amory Gould would make even an angel cry. He'd kept a careful archive of their entanglement from the start; what he'd sent along yesterday had been, as he'd put it in the attached letter, "just a taste." But he could no longer be sure how he'd ever hoped to lure Billy Three-Sticks, too, to a high floor of the family building. Or quite remember why. From certain angles, it looked downright ungrateful. In the wasteland of metro Boston, at thirteen, fourteen, his big dream had been of a gun to his own head, putting him out of his misery—a misery that by sophomore year of college was indistinguishable from everybody else's. *Brass Tactics* had pointed the way out of all that. Out of college, but also out of formlessness, powerlessness, the brute facticity he'd been beating his head against. Can't make it better? Make art. So yeah, there had been a time when, to protect Billy, he'd have thrown himself on the blast. But his education must be ongoing, because now he's on the run, and he can't even say for how long; his clock's stolen battery died somewhere back near the Delaware Water Gap. He was searching for the time on the radio, in fact, when he'd picked up that little blip about a blackout. It explained the snuffing of the city lights—and seemed to cement his triumph. Then more foothills turned the signal to crap. He'd pre-rolled a dozen joints to take the edge off the pills, but has since been burning through them to mark time until the zero hour. Only now there's just one left, and he's getting this vibe of insurrection from the back of the van. Maybe what's needed is a breather, at least until morning, when they can get themselves organized again, the unruly phalanges closing into a fist. And look: right up here's a rest stop.

He pulls off the highway and onto a ramp that cuts back among some trees. Sees an empty gravel lot, picnic tables under a lone streetlight. The little lavatory kiosk is locked for the night, but the vending machine out front's still lit, just waiting for someone with a disregard for property and a bad case of the munchies to come along and smash the glass. First, though, he can't help turning the radio back on and flipping around for further word from Manhattan. Out here you get evangelical preachers and album-oriented rock and ad after ad—and as the analgesia of the pot wears off, he discovers a pit in his stomach. Or a pit in the pit he'd carried out of that building. He's sure it will go away once he confirms he's finally accomplished something—an explosion at the heart of civilization. No gimmes, no takebacks, the kids used to say. Antacid tablets coat as they soothe. Crystal Blue Persuasion, hey hey. We will make buying a new or used car truck or van so easy. But he's too jacked up to stay with anything anymore, the dial keeps turning. Then amid the contextless barrage of information the sense of the roach singeing his fingers awakens him to the fact that he is alone. He opens the door. Leaves it open, so the blown speakers can keep filling his head with crap in which maybe the nugget he waits for waits. The thing he's done: revenge for the Blight Zone, for Sam, for the general fuckedness of this life. He climbs down to join his friends.

It's cool out here, a smell like a lilac bush or something. Enough starlight to see D.T.'s got Sol laid out flat on the ground. And the stars, they've always creeped Nicky out, made him feel like a nothing. "I say we make camp. We can push on in a few hours, once we see how the land lays back there." He's aware of some shakiness in the formulation, but can't identify what it is. It's like when he was a little kid that year in Guatemala and Dad broke his jaw because he'd come back from the PX with *jamón* instead of *jabón*.

D. Tremens looks up from where Sol's puking. "Get a grip," he says, so gently it's like he's been practicing. "I know you heard that thing about the blackout."

So the signal hadn't died fast enough, after all. Maybe that accounts for the whispering. D.T. feels it too: the sense of destiny achieved. "Yeah, but who cares, D.T.? If the city's in an uproar, that just gets us closer to where we want to go."

"It doesn't make you wonder if something's gone wrong back there?"

"I'm telling you, something's gone right—*Weltgeist* in action."

"The newslady didn't say anything about a bomb. We're way past midnight now."

And it's true there are a couple of loose ends he couldn't bring himself to clip so neatly. (What had Sewer Girl taken him for, some kind of monster?) But this was why you compartmentalized in the first place. D.T., for example, had been kept in the dark not only about the location, but also about the real time everything was to go down. Midnight would have been more symbolic, ideally the stroke of 7/7, if he'd managed to track down Billy, but every system, if it's not to collapse under its own contradictions, needs some randomness built in. A clinamen. Sometimes a system will even generate its own.

"D.T., you genius. You're still carrying a watch? I could kiss you. Have we hit 2:30 yet?"

"Nicky, I'm just going by the fact that we're in the middle of Penn-sylvania. You guys trashed every timepiece we had getting the thing to work, remember?"

Fuck.

"But sure, say it's 2:30, it's 2:45, it's four in the morning, what difference does that make? Can't you see we've got to get Sol to a doctor?"

Sol himself doesn't speak, but his eyes supplicate upward, like a puppy's who thinks you must be its master just 'cause you've given it a kick or two. Maybe D.T.'s been right all this time, maybe they should belay three thousand years of Western thought and make room for the comrade to lie down properly on the ratty carpet back there. But he's got a few choice volumes to share with anyone who thinks His-tory is made of a thousand little kindnesses.

"Yep, get some shut-eye and keep trucking. What say, Sol—you up for it?"

It takes Sol only a few seconds to hoist his undamaged thumb in a feeble thumbs-up.

"See? Sol understands the magnitude of what we've achieved. We've got to keep moving, this is part of what you—wait. Quiet."

"Nobody's talking but you, Nicky. Nobody's been talking."

Except he is already crouched by the driver's-side door, the bet-ter to hear a news flash. The bomb? No, what he hears again is just: power failure. Eastern seaboard in midst of largest blackout in his-tory. Only this time with a cause, lightning strikes in Westchester, a pair, a freak coincidence. And now it's coming back to him, that other flash of pure stochasm. The orange of that boat. The white. Those little bottles. Not that you shouldn't act to eliminate a threat, but he'd known from watching the reporter sit and brood behind a pillar that he'd never really been one. Just another drunk, like D.T. Another loser, like S.G. A failed artist, a poor dreamer, and far too easily scared. He didn't mean for the guy to die—who hadn't even had the third 'zine. But then out on the deck, there was the lanky body going over the side. And as he looked down into the fast black water, it seemed once again that there was no outside, no end to the emptiness. The world was the world, perpendicular to any attempt to make or do anything but damage. And fuck Billy, he'd thought, for dreaming otherwise. For the way he could just stare at his shoes and fill any space he was in. That had been the moment he knew why he had to hunt Billy down again, to inveigle him onto the scene, too. Which means, simultaneously, the instant the wheels had begun to come off. As they are coming off his attention now, because right as a voice is saying, *At the tone, the time will be*—Sol begins to yack again, loudly, on the gravel. And as quickly as it came, the signal goes back to static. *Fuck*. It was a single syllable they'd said, right? *Two* o'clock? Or is it already three?

"Did either of you catch that?" He waits for someone to refocus on the real problem here, but now D.T. and Sol just crouch and vomit, respectively, and this is all he needs to remember there may indeed be something binding them together. D.T.'s not as dumb as he acts, or possibly even as high. Maybe he's convinced Sol they've been sold out, proposed a hasty plan B. Maybe to go join back up with Sewer Girl, wherever she ran off to. Sol will be too ill to go on, and they'll make a play for the van, leaving him here like an animal, in the dark. "You know, the pigs aren't going to go any easier on you for jumping ship after the fact."

"Who said anything about jumping ship?" says D.T. "That's what I'm telling you, man. We're in this together. We've got to get Sol help."

"Sol's coming with me. Isn't that right, Sol?" But Sol pretends to have passed out. What is even happening here? Why is everything always falling apart?

"You can go on, Nicky, if that's what you need. But leave us the van, at least."

Here it is, if he still cared: proof of their conspiracy. He looks across the clearing. There, between the kiosk and the little creek burbling in its defile, is a payphone on a stand, its lightbulb burned out, busted, or otherwise nonexistent. He now perceives with his higher faculties that D.T. lied at that last puke stop about not having a dime. The very first thing they'll do after ditching him is call the cops. How long could he survive out here, in the woods, were it to come to a manhunt? Not long, is the answer, because he can't get the city out of his blood. "Fuck you. It's my van."

He realizes he means it. If Operation Demon Brother has indeed foundered, then the Econoline and the books inside are all he has to show for his own existence, and he's not about to give them up, even if the van is by most lights Sol's. And before the thought can be finalized, he is moving to cut off lines of approach.

"Come on, Nicky. You're in no shape to drive anyway. Why don't you give me the keys?"

"You can't have them," he repeats. "They're mine."

"Will you listen to yourself?"

He almost falls for it. But consistency is as somebody said a hob-goblin, one you can't let trip you up, not if you aim to get a single thing done in this world. And for how long has Nicky Chaos been trying to teach them not to be so credulous? They are even in their mutiny basically asking permission. When all there is, he's been tell-ing them, is the power to will. Quickly, before they can adjust, he's back in the driver's seat closing the door, fumbling with the key, that deeper darkness in the dark. Palms swat zombielike at windows, flat-ten pale against the glass. Someone yells over the static. Then the speed overpowers the pot, the engine catches, and he is fishtailing over the gravel, leaving behind his former vassals, D.T. and poor Sol Grungy of the doleful countenance. And finally just a long plume of dust to fatten in the moonlight.

LITTLE ITALY—??

IT'S NOT EXACTLY GOING TO SET THE WORLD ON FIRE, their hobbled pace, but in fits and starts, it's quickened, as has the guy's recall. Mike, is his name. Age? Twenty-seven. No, twenty-eight. From West Vir-ginia, originally. And for the last few years, Bay Ridge. Asked why then they were headed toward Chinatown, he seems to sputter. He had to find a new place on short notice, he explains, and he was on a budget. His job—he reads government reports for a living, con-denses them into slightly smaller reports—hardly pays. He'd been walking home tonight to save a subway token. But it could be worse; he had cousins who were carnies. Anyway, he's fine to go it alone, he's not in pain . . . though there is, Jenny thinks, something a little pained about Mike, or at least hangdog. And every so often he stops to kind of squint into the darkness where her face should be.

They're just descending into the oldest and narrowest part of the city when they meet a more serious block. A knot of several dozen young men has gathered on the corner, muscle-shirted, sort of Knights of Columbus, lit by idling cars. Her instinct is to cut east, leave a wide berth, but already the chaos has begun to form itself into lines. There's a strange New York compulsion, in moments of bewilderment or fury or fear, to queue, which must be hers now, too. As she steps closer, she sees something being passed hand to hand out of a storefront. Are these the orderly early stages of a riot? Or have the owners of this bakery, their refrigerator cases disabled by the power cut, decided to treat it as a promotional opportunity? At any rate, within a minute, some jayvee mafioso has handed her a paper plate. Then another. On them sweat heavy wedges of pale yellow cheesecake. Little groans of pleasure rise above the horns. "I'll be damned." She turns back to Mike, who's propped himself on a parking meter. "Here. Eat. The calories will do us both good."

The cheesecake is the Italian kind, made with ricotta or maybe mascarpone, and as good as Jenny remembers from other times, but also more complicated, as the present so often is, with a sweetness that recedes deeper into richness the more she tries to savor it. With no fork, she has to use fingers. And as the lushly textured filling coats her palate, the stranger at her side seems to be remembering, too. "My girlfriend used to make something that tasted like this. Only Uzbek," he adds, as if the taste were drawing him back. He takes a last bite. Looks for a trashcan. "Little blintzes, with the sweet cheese. After a night of dancing at the Odyssey, two in the morning, we'd come home and eat them straight from the fridge."

He resumes their walk, fully under his own steam. "Now, bam, this is my life, on my own again. I never saw myself living solo in a basement in Manhattan, but I guess everything in this city is different than I imagined it would be." He turns to her. "Sorry if I'm boring you. Same old story."

No, she wants to say, keep going. But from up ahead comes a high whine, a crack, a conflagration of blue and red. "More light!" a child is crying on the far side of what should be either Broome or Grand. An old man bends to touch a long match to the mound of darkness before him. Out of its top erupt ten thousand sparks, like a waterfall in reverse, lighting the lower landings of fire escapes before succumbing to entropy and night. Reductive but true: at any given hour, the hawkers of Chinatown will be hawking, the mah-jongg players mah-jongging, indolent fish lazing in the tanks that front the seafood restaurants. And special occasions, all the way back to the Tang, call for fireworks. A pang of memory. Or is that the recollection of this other man studying her again, trying to pierce the dark? "What."

"Nothing," he says. "Just, this is my block." As the light fizzles back down, he points to a sign for a street she didn't know existed. Or an alley—asphalt running right up to the building fronts.

He limps into the closing shadows, and she falls into step behind. To people like her dad, watching from afar, overpopulation seems like the big problem of urban existence, but really, it's desertion you have to look out for. Crowds teem under blazing sparklers a couple blocks away, but here all lights are off, all stores locked down. She should make sure he's safe. Keys jingle, then stop in a doorway. "I guess we part ways here."

"I'd at least like to see you get in okay," she says, after a moment.

"But you can't stand here waiting. Any lunatic could happen along."

She knows they barely know each other, but if recent history is any guide, it's Mike who should be nervous. "Looks like I'll have to come with you, then."

"My place is unimpressive."

"Points for honesty," she says, following him into a foyer ten degrees hotter than the street. It smells like someone's been raising cattle in here. From two or three flights up comes the sound of an old person singing in Chinese, but without moon or stars she can see nothing. This is evidently not a problem for Mike, who finds her hand and places it on a railing angled down. Careful. The steps are narrow.

After a dozen or so of these they emerge into a room lit only by the pilot light under a water heater. As far as she can tell, it's a cookie-cutter bachelor's den. There is a small shelf of books, a minifridge. Along one wall, a kitchenette. "Let me get you some water," she offers. But Mike has already lowered himself to his mattress, with a groan that might have been building for years. Unable to find where he keeps the glasses, she settles for a rag. She wets it in the sink and brings it over and kneels to place it on his forehead. He catches her wrist. His hand is steadier now. For a second, she is afraid. He says, "You don't have to keep this up, Jenny."

"Oh, stop."

"I'm saying, with the shopping cart, that was already above and beyond."

"I owed you that much." Then she bites her lip. He is still holding on to her free hand, but where, she wonders, will she go if he releases it? Is she supposed to walk forty-odd blocks home in the dark? And why does she care? It can't be any less risky than what she's doing now. "Seeing as how I was responsible in the first place. Mike, I was the one who ran you over."

The hand drops. "What? You said it was an accident—"

"It was."

"I could have died. Shit. I knew there was something."

"You're fine, you said so yourself. Just a little banged up. And if you think back you'll see I didn't lie. I just . . . elided."

"Talked your way in here on false pretenses, is what you did. Where do you get off?"

She stifles a huff. Refolds the rag to tuck the sweaty side away, but he's propped himself up again, and won't let her return it to his forehead. "Look. You were telling me how it's a long way from Appalachia," she says. "Well, imagine growing up outside L.A. with your dad designing airplanes and your mom barely speaking English. My whole life, I've been trying to get off the map that was laid out for me. You know the concept of utopia?"

"You're changing the subject."

"I'm not, I'm trying to explain. I spent my pothead teens and my early twenties committed to this idea of a better world. After that I had to scale it down to the size of a city. Then even further, to almost nothing. But I guess I've stayed so wrapped up in the idea of like *doing* something for the people in my head that I ended up not paying attention to the people right in front of me. One of which ended up being you."

"Jenny, did you have anyone check your vital signs? Because what you're saying makes no sense."

Well, obviously, because making sense would require further unpacking: Mercer and William, Pulaski and Charlie, and beneath that, those nights when she'd go over to Richard's apartment and he'd move stacks of paper off the couch to give her room to stretch out. Always more to unpack. Out goes the breath. "I don't suppose you've ever read the Upanishads."

"I'm not some kind of Asia fetishist, if that's how you have me pegged. I see that you're—"

"American. My parents are Vietnamese."

"I was going to say a would-be intellectual, or righter of wrongs. But I don't understand what that's got to do with you hitting me with a car and then jawing your way into my apartment."

Something turns over in her brain. "Maybe I don't understand myself."

For another moment, he stays silent on the mattress. "You're stuck with your version of the night, and I'm going to have to be stuck with mine, you're saying."

"No, that's not what I'm saying. I'm saying, no matter where I start, or how I spin it, it's not going to help either of us settle the question of guilt. So maybe sometimes it's better just to follow your intuition that you're no more or less real and free and fucked up than anyone else. I mean, we're here in this apartment, you with your bruises and me with your impression that I must have some kind of cranial trauma, but at least you're alive. Am I making sense now?" She reaches out to touch his face, his sad, wan, confused face. And then, perhaps confused herself, leans down to kiss him, full on the mouth.

MIDTOWN—2:19 A.M.

THIS IS JUST THE KIND of best-foot-forward shtick his orthopedist has warned about. The kid in front, the attendant in between, and himself, Pulaski, wincing along behind, in an endless black column getting hotter with his huffing. In fact, his foot keeps not making it all the way up to the next stair, knocking stupidly against the edge. If he'd been thinking more carefully, he would have brought some peanuts for energy. Also water. And another flashlight; at the start of their climb, Charlie had asked to requisition the elevator attendant's, but Pulaski, feeling bad about having bullied the guy, had said no, that would be wrong. Now, if the kid should glance back, all he's going to see are two white beams, and not the way Pulaski's putting his poor body on the line.

Which is not even to speak of his pension. In the car on the way up here, the two-way kept crackling with calls for anyone off duty to report to the nearest precinct. Up to that point, Pulaski might have pled guilty only to some procedural liberties, but now he was crossing into outright dereliction of duty. Or, with the flash of his gun downstairs, Class D felony. And for what? A scenario so screwy it wouldn't pass muster at a movie house, much less with Internal Affairs. How real can this bomb be, after all, if Charlie keeps stopping every few flights to suck on that inhaler? And here it comes again, a goony echo. Some partnership they make, the cripple, the asthmatic. And as they resume their climb, Charlie hews to the wall, away from the railing—acrophobic, to boot.

In his defense, though: you have to weigh probabilities against consequences. Even a single kilogram of gunpowder on an upper floor could bring the whole pile down on the surrounding blocks, overbuilt with residences in the boom years. Ash, dust, falling rock, fire. Not that he'd imagined it would be placed this high. Even so, the first thing Pulaski had done upon leading the kid out of lockup was call Sherri to warn her it might be a while. No, he couldn't explain, honey, not right now—only there was no answer. As the line rang and rang, he knew that she'd finally done it. Gone to her sister's in Philly. Left him. So add her, his only family, to the stack of chips teetering on this sorry table.

And now his hands are tightening their grip on the railing, hauling him up with muscles years of backyard laps have hardened. The elevator attendant lingers on a landing, panting, but Pulaski prods him along. And when Charlie takes advantage of another pause a half-dozen flights up to snatch away the attendant's weakening flashlight, Pulaski lets him. Who gives a poop anymore about Internal Affairs? This overworked muscle, his mind or heart, feels freer than it has in years. And of this, at least, the Sherri who used to know him might approve. He reaches out now through the solid walls of the stairshaft and over the eight million stories and the harbor and the landfills to where she'd be by now, a pair of headlights zooming south on the Jersey Turnpike. *Come back*, he thinks. *I'll be better.* That is, if he doesn't end up in jail. Or dead. By the time Charlie's ill-gotten flashlight starts to peter out ahead, even the dark has ceased to matter. Larry Pulaski carries his own light. It streams through his pores, he feels, lets him read the number on the door the attendant leans against, wheezing: **40**. "Stay back," he says, and draws his weapon, and pushes through.

He isn't sure what he's expected, but not this: a bulletin board with a few announcements, a dead electric fan, and a strange whirring sound, as of an engine. He can't find the source anywhere, and otherwise, the hall appears empty. "Where are we?"

"Dunno," the attendant manages between breaths. "I brought some reporters up here earlier today. But aside from press conferences, I don't think anybody's really used this floor since '75. The executives all moved down to 30 so they could start the renovations."

"You couldn't have mentioned this ten flights ago?"

"You had a gun."

The whirring grows louder, and when Pulaski turns, his flashlight finds a window that should be shut but is canted open like a door. A shape breaks away from the streaks of light on the glass and comes winging low across the hallway. It is huge and black, as if dipped in tar. And as the three of them duck, a new voice, female, pipes up from the shadows. "Oh!" The light swings around, back and forth. When it settles, it is on a girl in a Rangers home jersey, crouched behind the stairhead door.

EAST VILLAGE—CA. 2:00 A.M.

. . . AND WHAT YOU'RE FEELING THEN IS—

Despair. Absolute despair.

Which you're suggesting is connected to the tragic sense, which up to that point you've said you felt deficient in.

Is that what we're talking about?

It is.

I'm sorry, Mercer thinks, but I seem to have lost the thread.

It is years later, and it isn't. He is backed up against a transformer box in an East Village park, shielding his eyes against the blue waves of the police lights. He is also, simultaneously, in a crimson-carpeted room somewhere, in a folding chair placed opposite the folding chair of the man asking the questions. In his time away, the imaginary interviewer has changed again—he is now a slight, dark-haired man, graying at the temples, with a closed-off posture and some kind of radio in his breast pocket. Only the face (and of course the ontological status of any of this, of Mercer's feeling of great compassion for and wisdom about himself, looking back) remains obscure.

You said—

And here a white beam from the police cruiser makes a wound in the night. It rolls across strangers in varying degrees of dishabille who stand around waiting to see what will happen, as bits of charred paper drift through from somewhere, paraffin-thin. Meanwhile, the imaginary interviewer flips back through his notes. He apparently has a record of every stray thought Mercer's ever had. There must be two dozen legal pads stacked in his corduroy lap. An amplified voice from behind the light says something that includes the word "disperse." Mercer can't quite hear it over the interviewer. Who has chosen, admittedly, a strange time to return.

You said that for you, the poet's job, "preeminently" was the word you used, was to find things to praise, but that the praise had to have a background, a canvas to exist upon. And here you say that this background has to be, quote, "a sense first-hand of the overwhelming probability of there being nothing at all." A.k.a. the tragic sense. Whereas what you had was merely "adolescent self-pity." End quote.

I said that?

I can give you a date, if you like. This was late October of 1977.

But it's only July.

Hmm . . .

The interviewer withdraws into an archival fog. Still, Mercer wonders, does he have it now, this tragic sense? When he looks at the crowd dispersing here, is the loneliness he feels really an aberration, or is it the norm? Except the crowd has stopped dispersing. In fact, one of the onlookers is marching toward the police cruiser: the lone woman, the one he thought was in disguise. Her posture is grim, resolute, like a celluloid cowboy's, and if there remains something covert about her, he can't place it; that beer has gone straight to his head. "Hands up! Hands up!" the squad car says. And now in its polished hood her reflection can be discerned, backed by liquid flames from the trashcan. Tall in life, she looks impossibly small when doubled in light, the blue, the orange. She reaches down to hike up her miniskirt. Or rather, he does. Mercer sees what's next a beat ahead of its actual happening.

Then the first splash of urine hits the cruiser's hood, and with all due respect to the engine, the ABBA, and the murmur of the men around him, it is the only sound. It positively thunders. Mercer can see the precise look on his mother's face when the vice squad calls to say her son has been picked up in a dragnet. Public lewdness, possession of a controlled substance, resisting arrest . . . No, not that son; the good one. Still, he cannot help admiring what's happening. The transvestite is patiently waggling off the last drops in full view of the faceless black windshield. Then, from somewhere under the trees, someone wings a bottle at the cop car. It goes wide of the mark and shatters on the path, but the next one hits square-on, knocking out a light. And you have to hand it to the man in the miniskirt. Even when the siren bloops, even when the megaphone sizzles to life again, s/he stands his/her ground. A fusillade of further bottles makes effervescent bursts all around.

Whereupon the cop car reverses in a hurry, engine whining, misery lights still a whirl. People salute with middle fingers, and when they are gone break into cheers. And as the vacuum the cops have left draws people in, the applause does not die, but becomes general, rhythmic, gathering strength as those who have fled into the bushes return. Someone climbs on top of a bench and clasps hands like Muhammad Ali, and a roar goes up that can probably be heard for blocks.

"They thought the old rules still applied, but they fucked up, didn't they?" Voices shout unintelligibly in response. Mercer can't quite tell which is his own—only that the one now exhorting the crowd is not the transvestite, whom he's lost track of. There's something about power. Something about belonging. And ultimately: "Tonight, we're taking this city back."

Already a formation is flowing toward the park gates, as though there might be other cops out there to confront. Or formation is the wrong word, it's more like a force of nature, pressure bursting from an underground spring. The guy is right: the streets out here belong to them now, if they didn't already. And it's not just the queens of the East Village; when Mercer looks he sees punk rockers, shorn of head, and some Latinas from around the way, and even a couple of insalubrious old hobos falling into line, howling at the moon.

But then at the corner of Houston, they encounter a howl equal and opposite to their own, and headed in the other direction. It's that law-and-order demonstration from earlier today, and it's ten times as large. Candles and flashlights and torches, tee-shirts soaked in kerosene and tied around broomhandles, bob like little boats on a sea of darkness. Or one big boat, a Flying Dutchman, aimlessly haunting downtown for the last however many hours, waiting for something to collide with. Here, in the middle of backed-up Houston, they've found it. From one side of the boulevard or the other, a chant arises. *TAKE IT BACK!* Which half of the crowd it's coming from is hard to say, because the other half picks it up, more echo than answer. *TAKE IT BACK! TAKE IT BACK!* Mercer is not so intoxicated as not to notice the ambiguity around just who is supposed to do the taking, and from whom. But maybe this is a virtue, because by the fifth or sixth iteration, *mirabile dictu*, the opposing crowds have merged. It's hard in the darkness to tell anymore the boho hobos from the petit-bourgeoisie—or to know which camp he might fall into himself. It's as if the two halves are aligned at last, and oriented, as most hive-minds are, toward restoration.

93

THE THING IS, SHE NEVER MEANT TO DO ANY OF IT. She is a good person you have to believe her—this is all stuff she'd wanted to tell the reporter guy that day. She remembers the words filling up her mouth like gumballs she couldn't bite down on fast enough: *You take a good person, stir in childhood, then puberty* . . . Okay, she gets it now, this is the classic play for sympathy, you could say the same about ax murderers, but as late as that first winter after hitching to New York, when she'd met Sol and they were living out of the back of the van, she literally wouldn't hurt a fly. Even the dumb little ants she'd find lumbering over his shoulders in the morning she used to scoop up and drop out the back window instead of squashing, because life is life; her mom taught her that. Later, she and Sam would bond over the flakiness of hippie moms. Camped out at Lenora's, nursing coffees until the waitresses shooed them away, they played Top This. Sewer Girl always won, sure, but who was keeping score? Every Post-Humanist had at least one crazy parent—at least until the Prophet Charlie came along, who had a dead dad. A crazy parent in Sewer Girl's experience provoked one of two reactions, rebellion or identification. Her own mom had had a burning desire to get right with the universe, whatever that meant any given week, and she handed it right on down. So Sewer Girl was a good person, basically.

And honestly, for all his grouchiness, Sol had been, too. Though God, were they poor that winter, the winter of '74. They had to sneak into the Vault through a bathroom window, or sometimes the Angel who guarded the door would let them work off the cover charge by filling in as bouncers for a half-hour or so. They'd stay until the lights went on and the push-brooms came out and Bullet yelled his line about how you didn't have to go home but you couldn't stay here. (It pretty much saved everyone who heard it a semester's worth of *Being and Time*, Nicky later said.) Aside from the music giving them something to get through the day for, the club was sweaty and alive and the alternative was the van, where they had to put on all the clothes they owned and huddle together under a pile of dropcloths for warmth. Sometimes she would hear people poking around outside, despite the sheet of paper taped to the window clearly reading **no dough, no radio**. Sol would lie awake for hours cradling her protectively, with his Saturday Night Special at his side. No one ever went so far as to break in, which was lucky, she thought, because Sol definitely had it in him to pull the trigger. (She didn't know then that everyone has that in them.) And in the morning they had to clean everything up, because Sol's boss would fire him if he found out they were sleeping in the van. Business was slow then, the whole city falling apart on the front pages of newspapers, freezing as if the sun were burning out. Even if Sol had been getting paid per hour instead of per window, it wouldn't have been enough to get an apartment of their own, and he refused to go back and live with his mom in the projects. Mrs. Greenberg was horrible. Polish, originally, and jealous, and a nasty drunk. No one knew where Mr. Greenberg had gone. So there was all that, for extenuation. The churchmouse poverty and the struggle and the science-fictional cold of that time before Post-Humanism—whose aftertaste now seems almost sweet.

And there was this, too: Nicky Chaos, and the debt she owed him. He alone had noticed how pale she and Sol were, and how they needed about twenty minutes after entering the club to stop shivering, and he had taken them into his home. Okay, maybe it wasn't quite a home, or even his—he was squatting, right?—but at least he'd arranged for the heat to stay on, or someone had. Nicky never said a word about a patron back then. He would spin these stories instead about the already-legendary Ex Post Facto, and his eyes would flash, and his perfectly imperfect white teeth, and all the misery S.G. had endured would just fade away. It was as if a bit of the legend had already worn off, dusting Nicky's spiked hair with gold. And when he began to talk about trying to join the band, and grokked all the shop-class stuff Sol had picked up at P.S. 130 (Sewer Girl herself had dropped out at fifteen, when her mom became convinced she was being brainwashed) and parked him behind the soundboard in the garage out back, Sol started to stand a little straighter, as if he'd been given back his pride.

For one or all of these reasons, anything Nicky said automatically carried weight with Sewer Girl, and he took a pretty hard line that the hippies' quasi-Kantian imperative to do and be good without nailing down any definition thereof led to a kind of moral paralysis. Like, what if a train was speeding down a track threatening to kill two people, and if you yanked a lever it would go onto another track and kill only one? Or, like, what if the numbers were bigger? A million, say, versus a couple hundred thousand? What if the train was the system underwritten by liberal humanism? What if the lever was? What if moral paralysis was its whole end and *raison*, a bait-and-switch, a three-card monte? The system kept all threats to itself in sealed compartments. Hide away the possibility of action, and you could be guilty without ever having been responsible, or responsible without ever having been free, or free only in the sense of not copping to your own guilt. Over months, these terms—guilt, responsibility, freedom—became part of the air Sewer Girl breathed. But it didn't occur to her then that action meant anything other than starting a few fires. She liked just to hear Nicky talk. She would have listened to whatever he had to say.

Only after the link was made between Nicky and Sam did she start to wonder if she was in fact such a good person after all. Because frankly, she was livid. Watching him pull her friend aside for private debates on the theory and praxis of Post-Humanism, she had the thought that *Sam was not actually her friend*, which was how her deeper feelings about Nicky came to light. Not that she shouldn't have seen this coming. It was like her decision to run away to New York, even though Mom, crazy as she was, kept a roof over their heads and food on the table, and even though Sewer Girl's prospects on her own were manifestly dire. Did putting the doomed thing ahead of the dependable count as rebellion, or identification? Tough to say, because her mom was not one person. Half the time she was going around with her little whisk-broom; the other half she was waiting for the Martians. In any case Sewer Girl wanted Nicky's dark eyes to burn in her direction once in a while. That first big explosion in the Bronx last fall, the fact that people might actually get hurt . . . this didn't deter her. If anything, her physical longing quickened with her sense that something real was at risk. She wanted Nicky's hedge-hog hair prickling the insides of her thighs all the time. She wanted to rub his come into her skin like a transfiguring lotion. When she woke, and the glaze cracked, she would be powerful and unitary and pure. But whenever they did fuck now he always seemed to be some-where else. And when she found out, once Loverboy had gone away, that Nicky was also fucking Sam, it cored her, essentially, gored and quartered, jammed the blade down into the soft white flesh and ran it around in there until almost nothing of the person she'd thought she was was left. As it had done for Sol, she knew (though, as Nicky would say, *mutatis mutandis*. Sol had had like cartoon wolf-eyes for Sam ever since they first started seeing her at shows). That didn't mean there wasn't still love between the two S.G.s. There is a bond that forms between people who have had to depend on each other to survive, and Sol was nothing if not loyal, in the sense of never let ting go. In fact, she'd come to see this as the heart of his attachment to Nicky, a loyalty not ideological but instinctive. And in his own brute way, Sol sensed she was suffering. He asked her a few times in the dark, in bed—or, more precisely, on floor—if she was okay, to which she said of course, obviously, what was he talking about? But the atmosphere in the house now felt unstable, as if everyone already had a weapon aimed at everyone else.

It was into this atmosphere that Sol had returned on Christmas Day with the Rangers jersey and the bulging gear-bag. It was his habit to steal anything not chained to something else, but even minus his shoddy disguise, she would have known from the way Nicky grilled him that this particular theft was premeditated. And in a similar way, she figured out the secret inside the bag long before Sol spilled the facts. As a tool for reversing what had happened with the Blight Zone, it was brilliant, but also predicated on Sam's not snitching—on a loyalty Nicky should have known from the fanzines didn't exist. Sure enough, Sam then fell out of pocket. Granted, it was the holi-days, but this felt like a confirmation, and Sewer Girl couldn't com-plain to Nicky, because when it came to Sam he couldn't be trusted either. Among the Post-Humanists, D.T. had always seemed the most ambivalent—when he said "revolution," you could almost hear the scare quotes—but he was the one she ended up confiding her fears to, and to her surprise, he shared them. They'd both seen Sam photographing their early-December bombing runs. Between what was in her camera and what they'd just liberated from her dad, she probably had enough to send them all away for a long time. Or at least Nicky and Sol.

And so on New Year's Eve, when the Prophet Charlie let slip that he was supposed to meet his best friend Sam Cicciaro uptown, she'd caught D.T.'s eye across the dingy basement of the Vault. He'd pretended to be too drunk to go back out and play the second set, which meant there would only be drums, bass, and a handful of malfunctioning flashpots to cover Ex Nihilo's awful secret—the fact that Nicky was clinically tone-deaf—but the band was already almost an afterthought.

She remembers passing a Hamilton-Sweeney soiree on the far side of an Upper West street. Nearer the corner, pressed into the unshoveled snow, was a lacework of footprints, as of many people crossing each other's paths. Or of a single person reversing course over and over, unable to decide whether to go in. Then it was S.G. and D.T. backtracking, looping around through the park, just in case, and when they neared the street again, the Prophet's first prophesy proved accurate. There was Sam on a bench. Waiting for someone who'd be at that party—there was no other reason to be so far uptown. And who knew what Sam might disclose? Who knew what anyone might do anymore?

It had been D.T.'s idea to take the pistol from the van, in case Sam needed convincing they were serious. But there in the Park, the punks ended up passing the gun back and forth as in a silent movie while Sam told them to knock it off, they were being silly. "I mean, we've all made our choices already, have we not?" You could hear here an echo of Nicky, of their whispered colloquies in the basement, only changed into the opposite of whatever he meant. And something changed in that second for Sewer Girl, too. The gun happened to land in her hands, while Sam's own hands flew up in front of her like birds in the moonlight. "Easy," she said. "I'm still your friend."

It seemed to go off on its own, she thought the safety was on, these were things Sewer Girl would tell herself later, but really, Sam was always a threat. She claimed everything, when S.G. had practically nothing—except, contrary to what everybody seemed to think, volition. In spades. So had she known what would happen when she pulled the trigger? Maybe what she'd wanted all along was to find out. And there her friend was, on the snow, blood pumping out of her, a rasp like she was dying. There was just enough light to see D.T. take the gun and bring it close to Sam's ear and, turning his head away, fire the second round. This was because the first one had done such a crappy job, he would say, and sometimes you had to be cruel to be kind. It turned out D.T. had done a crappy job himself, but they didn't know that then, as they took off toward the subway, counting on the snow to fill in their tracks. As it would, provided all that lay between it and the tunnels below was grass, concrete, a little dirt. But Sewer Girl was already coming to understand the true substance she'd left her mark on. Or wasn't this city really the sum of every little selfishness, every ignorance, every act of laziness and mistrust and unkindness ever committed by anybody who lived there, as well as of everything she personally had loved?

And all this she had come within a whisker of blabbing to the reporter guy on the loading dock. Something about the face beneath the beard said he knew a thing or two about survival. She'd looked down at the piece of greasy wax paper turning around and around in her hands. Wanted to tell him about that instant of almost joy, feeling the gun jump, knowing it was too late to undo. It was possible even now she didn't totally believe that . . . but when her mouth opened, it was to find a reason to go.

Her confessional urge would swell throughout what followed. When the reporter turned up dead, she knew in her bones it was Nicky who whacked him. Which made two lives she was responsible for, two not very happy lives, it seemed, but still. And his black powder was going to destroy what was left, when nothing that could have driven him to it was worth the cost. But the night the two sevens clashed, something had changed again. The Prophet Charlie had seen, she thought, what she'd been going through. She'd gone up to the attic meaning to take his virginity, as a kind of apology, and then she would rob him of his cluelessness, too, and maybe together they could do something to stop the Demon Brother. Or Brothers.

Maybe she still could stop it, even on her own. It was what had brought her this afternoon to the Hamilton-Sweeney Building. Only there were no offices on 40, as the blueprint said there should be; just this big press room. Once the cameramen had cleared out, she'd locked herself in and looked high and low for the bomb. She kept imagining a ticking sound, but couldn't find where Nicky had hid it. Eventually, it dawned on her that this was to be her fate—to die up here alone. So she shut off the lights and lay down in darkness to wait for what she had so amply earned. Responsibility, guilt, and freedom, hurtling back together. Disaster and shame and renewal. She hadn't realized that the rest of the world had gone dark, too, until the sound of voices roused her and brought her out into the hall. And now, as the flashlight beam swings away from her again, she sees Charlie Weisbarger standing on an open window's ledge, his hands braced on the frame. The cripple with the flashlight is charging toward him, or staggering, yelling *Don't*. But it's doubtful Charlie can hear him amid the churn of what must be ten thousand gulls or pigeons whirling outside. Nor will he see any of this, because his eyes are squinched shut, as if he's on a direct line to the cosmos. As if he really is an honest-to-god prophet, about to take the step that will change all their lives forever.

"HERE"—2:30 A.M.

DETONATIONS CRASH IN FROM NEARBY like walls she's a void at the center of. Or waves crashing down on the change she has tried to be, in the city she has longed to become. It is the concussion of other people, of ten thousand spires now crumbling to the sea. As if a radio went suddenly untuneable. Or as if something in the heart were breaking. Then again, everything is always breaking, and crashes can also celebrate: glasses stomped or tossed into hearths, concentric ringings of spoons on glassy tabletops, with jags of laughter after. So take a breath, Jenny. Gather these leaves into the cupboard of the self and attempt some arrangement. What do you believe now? You believe this boiling blackness to be a basement. You believe the body below you to know things you do not. Feel your way back through the black for whichever damp face and pull it to your own again. She is too tired at this ungodly hour to make any more sense than she does, but a tongue is a language, too, even one that tastes of not having eaten, of gum about to lose its flavor. *You were gone*, she says, coming up for air, *I swear* . . .

And can he know for certain she isn't right? It's possible he was never even here. There was that very first day he spent in this room, unwilling to move any further. Unmoving to will himself to the temperature of the empty minifridge, of vodka that burns when it is after all only doing its job. But how to explain this other person now finding her way inside? Ribcage to ribcage, soft small breasts, mouth on his mouth. How can you ache like this all over but still not stop her reaching for your belt? He feels as a cage, opening, feels. As a gaunt and captive tiger, however much it costs the tiger each time he is seen. And wanting rushes in as a pressure, as a hunger to press her painlessly to any handy wall. The trained tiger would carry a dove in its jaws without breaking a single feather. Or is he still the one being carried? Hard to know anything for certain save her body in the dark, her smell, small tongue, hot breath finding the inner ear. He is scared of being still on the floor but to find the button of her jeans is to be down and under to the slick heat that fits just under the hand it is made for, proximal to that deeper fire. To be back in the wiry black ununderstanding of woods he used to wander in, in the fog where you lose and find yourself. Her breath like the sea in a shell, find it. Find what's hidden. Find the crux where outer disappears in secret and in secret disappear there.

I mean I thought you were dead. I thought, I am watching him die.

For a second, her white underpants burn like a candle in the dark. Her head aims toward the ceiling where headlights swim through the squat window, triangular whiteness at the throat. She is simultaneously below, a second person. Then they merge again. She is aware of the friction of the mattress on her knees, but also, strangely, on her back, as one of them moves the other across the bedding. They are like the ladder that climbs itself. Like kids crossways on a swing, pushing higher and higher. There is a power inside you that has never been expressed. That is not perhaps expressible. And this must be why sometimes fucked is the most beautiful word in the language. A white flare pains as a shoulder bitten into and a flock of bright dots upwelling blots out what they've seen there can be no end to . . . and then once again, she is only herself. Free to make all the noise in the world.

EAST VILLAGE—2:30 A.M.

A POP LIKE A BURST BULB jerks Mercer back out of his lucubrations. A parking meter off to his right has been beheaded. At the corner of Avenue A, some men with penlights shout: "No! Not that way! This way!" He can barely hear them over the chanting *(Take It Back! Take It Back!)* but as the whole crowd surges west, it overtakes him.

Fires are erupting from the crumpled trashcans along Houston. Farther on he spots a phone booth tipped across the entrance to a sidestreet, presumably to block the cops, and then a barricade of sawhorses. The rending of metal can be heard every now and then amid the chants. At the corner of Broadway is a Modell's whose big security gate won't hold out for long against the contingent of teens now climbing it. A roar goes up as it comes crashing down, and again as plate-glass drops like a heavy curtain to the ground. A tall man rushes into the firelight in a tee-shirt covered with white dots. He runs along on tiptoe, like a panther darting from one tree to the next, carrying a Louisville Slugger. Then come croquet mallets and tennis rackets. Someone presses something into Mercer's hand, and when he raises it to his face he sees a fungo bat.

Next to him, a man his own age argues with a woman with kerchiefed hair. "Please!" she's saying. "What if someone breaks into the apartment?"

"Leave me alone," the man replies. "I've waited years for this. You know where the gun is, you can hold down the fort."

A bearded white guy beside them lectures anyone who'll listen on Hegel's theory of history, all the while swinging a golf club, knocking out the windows of parked cars as methodically as a jeweler with his little hammer. A boy's voice asks if there are any extra golf clubs. "Get lost, kid," the guy says. "It's a revolution, not a shopping spree."

Fire breeds fire, and escalation escalation. As the mass surges up LaGuardia Place, delis and newsstands are targeted. Some particles break off to avenge themselves on mailboxes. A faction has somehow gotten the high beams to work on a taxi and hoisted it into the air like the world's largest flashlight. Brightness sweeps across Washington Square, which is full of people. Great rolls of toilet paper arc like ejaculate through the black sycamores. Spraypaint—*Fascists Out! My City Right Or Wrong!*—blossoms incoherently on the triumphal arch. As to actual fascists, which is to say the fuzz, they appear here and there on the periphery, but only with rollers off, under orders to stand down.

Earlier, Mercer had watched them try to cordon off that shadowed grocery up on Fourteenth Street. While supervisors called for backup, while higher-ups waffled about strategy, women kept emerging with carriages full of Similac and Pampers. Some people laughed or whistled from doorways. Others sold batteries for three dollars apiece. Still others attacked these profiteers, jabbing fingers in faces. The night watchman, surveying the wreckage, cried, "Oh, those scum, those animals, those rotten bastards!" To and fro the squad cars went, but Mercer had felt even then the futility of attempts to restore order; there was something wrong deep within that order itself.

Now he gives the fungo bat an experimental swing—its swish sounds brutal. Alarms clang on University Place, and drums begin to beat, unless that is his heart. The crowd surges into administrative offices, carrying out typewriters and sheaves of scattering files. Mercer finds himself bearing an ergonomic deskchair like some kind of trophy until, after a block or two, his arms get tired. Up ahead is Union Square. A needle park, they call it; maybe William is *there*? But no. None of that, now. By way of punctuation, he takes the fungo bat and smacks it into a parking meter. The head stays on, but the little kidney-shaped glass cracks, strewing change on the street. A cheer goes up from the men around him. They have all turned white—skinheads, it seems—but maybe he has, too. The physical world keeps dissolving into darkness, and the very last scraps of Mercer's sense of who he is appear to have disintegrated along with it. There is no imaginary interviewer left to ask him how this feels, but were there still a Mercer to answer, he might call it a relief, the way it must have been a relief for C.L. at boot camp the first time he threw himself out of a plane. As if he were at once looking down from a transcendent height and giving himself up to gravity.

But is giving up the self really possible? For here, ahead of the little vanguard he finds himself in, looms a something in the nothing: a pile of lapsed-high-Anglican limestone glowing in the moonlight. He doesn't need to look at the inscription chiseled into the lintel to know what it says. For he can feel the building returning him to his body, pinning him to the past, passing judgment; it is the Wenceslas-Mockingbird School for Girls.

UPPER WEST SIDE—EARLIER

BY THE LIGHT of the branchy candle-thing William's taken up, his father's closed eyelids are like glass in an old window, thin near the top and gradually thickening downward with gravity. The heavy body, always so correct, looks uncomfortable, its kneecap way out to one side. Feigned sleep is an excellent defense against the slings and arrows of responsibility. Like a four-year-old who covers his ears and says *I can't hear you* over and over. Only how feigned is it? Daddy's pants are darker at the crotch, and the velvet of the divan is damp to the touch. William brings his fingers to his nose. Yep. That's piss. Well, fuck him. Fuck *him*. Let the servants deal with this. But again, there are no servants. Bringing the candles closer gets no response from the sleeping father. It is sweltering up here. He tries snapping his fingers near one ear, then the other. Only when he grips Daddy's withered biceps do the old windows flutter up. "William? Is that you?" It's as if the last hour and a half—the last decade and a half, for fuck's sake—never happened. He's heard nothing.

The phones are working; he could call the doctor, if he could find a number, but part of him clings to the belief that Daddy's faking. Still, he has to actively tug to get Daddy to his feet, and then the eyelids are wavering again, the blue eyes panicking in the gloom.

"William?"

He sighs. "Come on, old man. Let's get you to your room."

Of course, he has no idea where said room might be, but at certain junctures Daddy's gait grows fluid, and William feels himself being led, down some stairs and up some others and down another corridor to a bedroom that has all the charm of a convention center. The bed looks unslept-in; maybe he and Felicia move to a new room each night, like affluent bedouins. He positions Daddy in front of a bureau's mirror, orders him to undress, turns away. Blades of light angle up between the white curtains from the cars that again pass below. Youthful hoots carom off the street. This opulent shell is as thin as an egg's—he's learned that much, if nothing else. Still, when you're inside, it is so fucking persuasive. And he feels so powerless. Powerless, e.g., not to glance back at the Bermudas bunched around the ankles, the palsy in the arms, the way his father gets hung up on a shirtbutton, even when it seems no one's looking. He used to imagine Daddy's head would fall off like one of Bluebeard's wives' if he so much as loosened his necktie. Now he's just a pathetic old man, with a tuft of wiry hair sprouting from the neck of his undershirt and that wet patch down near the hem. William puts the candle-thing down and goes to help him balance. "No, Daddy, no, don't sit on the bed, you're going to—"

"Is that you, William?"

Using towels from the bathroom, he does his best to blot the urine from the coverlet. He spreads some more towels and has Daddy sit on those instead. It's terrible, what happens to a man's body. It will happen to William one day, too, except, at the rate he's going, he probably won't live that long, so let no one say there's no silver lining. He kneels to unlace the shoes, to pull the bunched pants over the feet, helps with the undershirt. He drapes a towel over Daddy's shoulder and sends him into the bathroom with a clean pair of briefs from the dresser. The door he leaves open, hoping the candle will throw enough light for Daddy to finish undressing without falling and breaking his hip. At any rate, William's not going to change his father's pissed undershorts. He has undressed men before, scores of them, but there are lows below which even he will not go.

As the splashy noises of the toothbrush commence, he lights a cigarette off a candle. These death-tubes, these little crutches or fuses: useful for getting through all sorts of things you don't want to get through. It's why they're so popular at the halfway house. Each time he inhales, a balloon of heat inflates in the immaculate room. But it's already a million degrees in here. He flicks some ash on the carpet, screw Felicia, and moves over to the curtains for air.

Why she would covet such a place is obvious. The height means you can see everything. There's no balcony off this room, but when he leans out the window he can see all the way up to the reddish northern fringes of the park, Harlem and the Bronx burning in the night. That's where he should be: in his studio, behind three dead-bolts, with a great flame coming and no radio and no phone under his actual name, and so no way for anyone to warn him he's about to be incinerated.

Then he turns to find Daddy standing in clean underwear by the bed, looking unsure what it's for. "Oh, for Pete's sake." William goes and helps him slip between sheets of recklessly high thread count. Some further ceremony seems called for, but what's he going to do: lean down and peck him on the forehead, as if Daddy really were a child? He can't even see the face anymore. In his dreams, this is always a deathbed. "I don't hate you, you know," is what he says. Daddy's line is supposed to be, "I'm so sorry." But for a second now, William sees himself as his father must see him, backlit by candles and curtains, and he understands that what Daddy's thinking would probably be closer to "Hate me for what?" The same old father-son bullshit, as if nothing else in the world existed—no sisters, no lovers, no mothers. And in fact what comes next is the snorting noise again. Make that snoring.

Only later, when William has blown out all the candles save one, to light his way back to the library, does a voice croak from the shadows. "There's something for you on the dresser."

Has he imagined it? William listens for more, but the snore has resumed, the world gone back to what it was, and all he can find on the dresser is the little rosewood lock-box Daddy used to keep his cufflinks and shirt-studs in. It is unlocked, though, and inside is an envelope, his own full name written across the front in schoolhouse cursive. The paper looks positively ancient, yellow with age, but it's just possible to glimpse a shadow inside. There's a shadow inside everything, he's starting to feel. Maybe it's best not to look too close. Then again, he already knows that, whatever this document is, he's likely to sit up until dawn poring over it by candlelight. That's assuming dawn ever comes.

BETH ISRAEL—2:35 A.M.

BY THE TIME THE STRANGER APPEARS, the respirator's been repaired, albeit with an anxious squeak midway through each stroke where the bellows chafes the glass. Or conceivably it's Bullet who's anxious. Still stationed in a chair by the door, he feels the hour's lateness with a keenness reserved for the dying. As does this unshaved dude in the doorway, it seems. Bullet has an unwonted sensation of not being sure he could take the guy in a fight, if it came to that. But then some recognition passes between them—that is, Bullet recognizes this must be Sammy's father, and the father decides to assume nothing funny is going on. Bullet hauls himself to his feet with a grunt. "She's all yours, chief."

It would be physically impossible, even with the extra-wide doorway, for the tattooed man to squeeze past Carmine Cicciaro without forcing him to move. He can't weigh less than three hundred pounds, and Carmine, no beanpole himself, has put on an extra fifteen or twenty this last half-year, from all the junk food. But he's already spent hours fighting his way here, and he's not about to retreat.

Nor, having planted himself in the still-warm chair, will Carmine get up even once to visit the vending machines that hum in an alcove off the waiting room. This is a place he can sit for long periods of time without thinking much of anything. Some of the things he's not thinking about now: his own body flying between his daughter and the gun, instead of weighing down a fireworks barge in bumblefuck New Jersey. The empty cans of Schlitz surrounding him a few hours later, when the ringer forced him from his bed. The man who'd whisked his wife away, and how that face, as Satanically youthful as Dick Clark's, had returned to him just before he'd answered the phone, at four a.m. on day one of the new year. Her yogurt constructor, he'd thought she'd said, that first airy mention. But then, he'd been only half-hearing her for years. He'd been too busy clamoring for space . . . and even after she left couldn't get it. Baby-fat fallen away, Sammy was the image of her mother, right down to the secretive way her lips pursed at rest. *You've done your best for her,* the reporter had said. *Sacrificed a lot for her education.* But what had Richard known, in the end? Not shit. Carmine was never more than halfway present to his daughter, either, and sees this is all his fault—or would, were he to think about it, which he doesn't. And does she? Not if the doctors are to be believed.

Here comes one now, looking like a young Jawaharlal Nehru. "Let's take a look," he says, consulting the chart he carries. "Ah. Cicciaro." The clipped efficiency with which he pronounces every syllable exposes his warmth as a pretense. Carmine has a vivid fantasy of shoving the paperwork down the man's throat. Instead, he asks the same question he does every time he meets a new doctor, as if it might change the answer. How long will this last?

The ve-ge-ta-tive state? asks Nehru. There's an absence of gesture here, of the head-scratching and turning away Carmine's gotten used to. There are cases, mi-ra-cu-lous cases, where a patient wakes up, but the data are very much against this. And Carmine isn't a re-li-gi-ous man, is he? No, he hadn't thought so. She might go on like this for years, in body, but without these machines, she would already be dead. "I am sorry," the man then says, as if a different and deeply pained person has commandeered his larynx, but when he tries to touch Carmine's arm, all Carmine can think of is getting him down on the floor among the wheeled bases of the equipment and horsewhipping him with his stethoscope until he needs a machine to help *him* breathe.

Sammy's in no pain, of course—of that Nehru is certain. The

grimace Carmine sometimes thinks he sees is just a combination of muscular reflex and his mind's own drive to make meaning. The doctors are constantly reassuring him of this: she is neither warm nor cold, neither angry nor forgiving, and certainly not in pain. And for months now, instead of grieving for the soul, he's been trying simply to see her as this, a vessel, a shell. The shiny petroleum jelly the nurses apply around the nostrils, the chapstick he puts on the lips, the cracking it can't quite prevent. Dehydration is a danger. Bedsores a danger. Weight loss: a constant danger. He untucks the sheet at least once per visit to inspect her legs, which is where you'd really expect to see it. Each time he imagines she'll have held steady thanks to the doctors (who now come to check on her every ten minutes, you could set your watch, because apparently there's been some trouble earlier with her breathing apparatus). And each time, instead, there's a little less of her. He looks again. With their down grown back, the legs could be a skinny boy's. The ankles like pencils. No matter what they say, she's suffering, and it's the sins of the father, his sins against the very idea of fatherhood, she is paying for.

All he would have to do would be to ask them to unplug the machines, and no one could blame him; this, he sees at last, is what Nehru was too green not to imply. Is what they've been implying one way or another since January. She is never going to recover. But Carmine knows he would blame himself. Would live the rest of his life as if he'd been dipped in polverone and white arsenic and lit on fire, tossing off sparks.

Nehru, returning with a colleague, pretends no longer to see Carmine. The colleague frowns as he examines the connections on the respirator. Nehru makes tiny marks on the chart and says something about how long the machine was off, the potential for further brain damage. Carmine can't quite make it out, because a chant has arisen outside the window. Three beats: *Da da DAH*. It's that protest march he heard about on "Dr." Zig this morning. It must still be going strong, but when he gets up to look, all is dark out there, save for a blip on an office tower a half-mile away, like an eye that sees him—that sees what's in his heart. It would see even if everyone else was eager to accept that somehow, in the power failure, the technology keeping her alive had failed too. Mechanical error, one of those things, her time, the Lord's will, not in pain anymore. For the best. Is he man enough, is the real question. Is he man enough to sit here and watch his own daughter gasp like a fish on a line and not turn back? Because if he does it, he isn't going to leave the room till it's over.

Don't, the crowd outside is shouting, as the doctors retreat again. *Don't do that*, or maybe *Don't turn back*. He used to think sacrifice meant giving up his own life. Nope. It means giving up hers. And he wants it to hurt more than anything has ever hurt, more than she's hurt, if she's hurt, and to annihilate him with hurting. He wants the black powder all over, consuming him from the outside, but never quite finishing off the core, which will stay screaming inside for all eternity. Those other fathers were man enough. Abraham. Jehovah. And now here is Carmine Cicciaro, reaching for the mask.

THE FOUR VISIONS OF CHARLIE WEISBARGER

THE FIRST VISION, PROLOGUE TO THE OTHERS, is of the narrowness of all previous visions—the way they never reached much beyond the limits of Charlie's skull. Meaning they must not have been visions at all. Or anyway, not like this. For it is the outside world that transforms itself now. What seemed to be a window becoming a door.

THE SECOND IS A NOISE. A voice. You have to decide whether to step through, it says. To awake. But there's a problem: the birds are blocking the doorway, so he can't see what's beyond with any clarity. The others distracted by the presence of Sewer Girl (as he too might have been, under different conditions), he closes his eyes and pulls himself up onto the window ledge. The strap of the camera forces breath from his lungs. An iron fist squeezes his heart. He doesn't have to look to know how far it is down to the street, and these birds seem pissed. They thrum just beyond the window like a vengeance machine, the tight wind they churn up blowing his hair all around. But he cannot bring himself to open his eyes. Or maybe he doesn't need to. Maybe it would just detract from the next vision, the one now unfurling inside.

THIS ONE INVOLVES A FUTURE, OR FUTURES. He is floating above Midtown, the office tower below him an ancient ruin, along with everything in a several-block radius. Farther off, beyond the intact wall of the Financial District, is the harbor. The waters are placid at first, glinting, but then they stir under the pressure of something coming from the north and west. What Charlie witnesses when he turns, from the top of what was once the Hamilton-Sweeney Building, is incredibly fast and bright, even twenty miles off, a pair of little suns, gold flaws in the blue. They leave too little time for anything to be done to stop them—just enough for him to understand that July 14 was only the leading edge, that the KGB or the PLO or some other letters will be blamed, and struck, and strike back, and be struck back, until ultimately everything he's ever known is consumed. What does the end of time look like? His mom, in her kitchen window, watching the sky go white like a flashbulb. His brothers, sleeping, turned to ash or air. Everything he has not loved as he should, everything he has forgotten to be choosing at every second, because this is evidently the only life one gets: the skyline and the bridges and the grasses of Long Island, and the granite slab that was to bear his dad's name into the future, all dead. In this future, Sam is dead, too. And these last seconds he spends utterly alone with what he knows. And in the other one—the one he chooses if he goes through?

THE LAST OF THE FOUR VISIONS OF CHARLIE WEISBARGER is just a glimmer of where his error was. He's been looking for a way to change what is, but it is never going to arrive from outside. This was in the Gramsci Nicky gave him, and the Marx, and even in his Bible somewhere. "No man hath seen God at any time." The only available change has been inside him all along, where the lines between indication and invocation get hopelessly unclean. He's been waiting for a finger to point, but God is more like the meaning of the pointing—a thing whose existence depends on the observer. Act like there's nothing larger than yourself, no justice or mercy or community or whatever, and there won't be. Or you can try somehow to call it into being. There are Paradoxes here you could disappear right up the butt of, and he does for a second, but then he's feeling again the flashlight making that pink cave on the backs of his eyelids, and he can hear the rubber tip of the inspector's crutch striking the floor, once, twice, coming to rescue him, and when he opens his eyes he can just make out beyond the light's white spot the fat attendant and

Sewer Girl. *Don't do that! Now's not the time!* But time is just the language of God. Or so he'd tell them, only he doesn't want his last words to be bullshit, and there's no time to decide if this is. There is no time, even, really, to be afraid anymore, as Charlie turns to face the outer world and the feathers caress his face and he gathers his last breath and hurls himself into them, the wings, the arms that are also the void.

MIDTOWN—2:20 A.M.

FOR A WHILE, Keith keeps slowing to talk to passersby just loud enough for Regan to hear that he's still behind her, that she hasn't succeeded in making him give up. Eventually, though, he stops bothering. He's known all along that no one will have noticed two little kids in this outer dark. It is probably no less effective, all things considered, to go back to what he was doing forever ago, before the lights went out: cupping hands to mouth and shouting their names. "Will! Cate!" A half-block ahead, near a cataract of brakelight, Regan stiffens. He is drawing attention. But that's exactly the point, and soon she's doing it, too. "Will! Cate!"

They're a peculiar team, her ahead, him behind, separated by the street between them. They could be strangers, were it not for the way their voices cross and part in the garbage-smelling heat. (*Will, Cate. Willcate. Late. Kill. Wait!*) Cars crawl by but do not honk, and sometimes offer a little bit of visibility. He can see, for example, that they're now less than a block from the Lickety Splitz Gentleman's Club at Fifty-Third and Third. If she turns left, she'll lead them past the very spot where he stood in the snow on New Year's Eve and decided not to go meet his mistress downtown. Time was he would have wanted to pause here, to genuflect, but when Regan heads straight he merely sends the names of his children clattering back among the fire escapes and trashcans.

For an hour, they zag north and south, east and west, past increasingly unlikely places. Past the Plaza's eponymous plaza, the entryways of S.R.O.s, the whited sepulchers of the U.N. He's never thought of these as having any commerce with each other, but in the dark it's all surprisingly close together. Maybe the vastness of Manhattan is just a kind of accounting fiction you use to justify your own insignificance, your own helplessness, the fact that when you call, no one answers. A sense of constraint is already creeping in when Regan plunges into the cavern of Grand Central, darker even than the night outside. "Will! Cate!" He's never heard a silence like the one that comes back. The ceiling is gone, but starlight dimming through the vaulted windows at either end of the concourse reveals shapes like vultures huddled under the departure boards. Or possibly these are highwaymen, alert to their presence. They rustle, ready to bar the exits, but he takes it up, "Will! Cate!" He is finding there is no hell into which he would not follow her—

And they are out again into the warm open air. They pass a slab of shadow he recognizes as the library, and the park behind it, where scholars score heroin. There's a car crash on Sixth Ave.; someone has rammed into a storefront. Cops scuttle through the disco whirl of red and blue, but they seem preoccupied with the car hanging half-out of the smashed glass, and Regan ignores them. The next block, if memory serves, should be a gauntlet of electric come-ons, peepshows and X-rated theaters, but the blackout has obliterated it, and without the promise of live flesh, foot traffic is thin. Farther on, though, it thickens. He is able to make out faces. And then suddenly, between the black shoals of office buildings: the light.

There is always light in Times Square, true, but it should be an incandescent custard coming from the marquees above. Instead, this light is white and mineral in its intensity, and as Forty-Second debouches into Broadway he can see it's streaming from two king-sized discs that hang from cranes several stories above the ground. Below mill certifiable masses of people, tens of thousands, filling the streets where cars normally go. Traffic islands puncture the crowds at intervals, and on each is a raised platform, draped in red, with an old-fashioned circus cage on top. One houses a lit-up panther. Another, a bald eagle on a branch. Nearest him and Regan, a few dozen yards away, is a ruffed black bear who must be ten feet tall, even slumped on his little stool. In his years in the city, Keith has stumbled upon enough movie shoots to know this must be one, but the scale here is like Cecil B. DeMille, or that Soviet version of *War and Peace*. Plus where are the cameras? And are the people around him people, or actors hired to play people? Have any of *them* seen his son?

He's about to ask when a long chord sounds from atop the army recruiting center. He hasn't noticed, but there's a whole choir up there, ranked in gray robes he can just see the shoulders of. A tuxed conductor gesticulates with his back turned. As if at his command, the rest of the square goes silent and still, all except a shopping bag aflap on an updraft. Keith could yell out, and probably the whole square would hear, but he feels under some tremendous pressure to stay silent. Regan must, too, for even she has stopped shouting.

The song that now begins is slow and mournful and in a language not their own. Russian, he'd guess, from the deep double basses. The buildings loft the sound toward the sky and smear it, blurring the edges. Keith wonders if somewhere back in the Lamplighter family tree are some Slavs, because it calls to him, this elegy, if that's what it is. Requiem. He wants, suddenly, to be standing on some great precipice, overlooking something huge—the way he used to put on his *Best of Scottish Pipes and Drums* LP to buy a few minutes to think at the end of the day, to send the kids running for the far corners of the apartment with hands over ears while he stood by the window, the light in his heart the color of the light through the Scotch in the glass. Below, on the street, rush-hour people hurried home. His own individual life had felt like a shirt shrunk in the wash . . . but now he would welcome such straitening. Why must he always be running from some place he never was to some place he'll never be? What would it take for him to just be where he is? He wants, almost, to be his own ghost, casting his shadow on the little world these other people move in. And he wants Regan beside him—where she is, only a few feet away. She makes no attempt to hide the tears rolling down her spotlit face. She is frozen there, in a note that places them outside of time. And the honey so long withheld from him is given: Keith can hear, he thinks, what's inside her. *Honey*, she's thinking. *I'm afraid.*

He wants to tell her not to be, but it's only fair that he not be able to hide from her his own fear.

Where can they have gone? What's going to happen here?

I don't know, he thinks. *Who knows? But I have to believe, Regan, they'll be okay. We're going to find them.*

I wish I was strong enough to believe, she thinks.

It is baffling, and he can't quite say why, until he can. *But you are*, he thinks. *You're the strongest person I've ever known. You're the only one who could have been strong enough to bring me through.*

To bring you through to what?

It forces him to think harder. She needs him to think harder. And if he can think this hard without her hearing, can he reach her at all? *To this, Regan. To a life without protection.*

Then, abruptly, the held note ends, and someone yells "Cut!" The song is over, the planetary discs of light clicking off overhead and shadows moving over their faces. The bear growls once, dejectedly, in the gathering dark, as if to say, *I knew it all along.* And then Times Square, that insane monument, has vanished around them, which really is almost enough to break Keith's heart. He can't find her hand. "I'm sorry," is what he's left with. "I am so, so sorry."

"No, I'm the one who dragged you into this," Regan says, somewhere.

"I mean for all of this. Always." But out loud, it sounds like more self-regard.

Then her hands are clamping around his. "We can talk about that later, Keith, but it's not going to help us find the kids." It is the old Regan and the new one together, honest, responsible, long-suffering—the real self she'll only let you see under the direst of circumstances. Which may be true of everyone. He really wishes he could see her face. "The best we can do now is go back to Daddy's and stay there. Give them a stationary target. Get a couple hours of rest, clear our heads, and if they still haven't turned up by dawn, we start working the phones again. But no more magical thinking, okay?" She squeezes his hand once, with what proportions of the maternal and the connubial it's hard to tell. And she begins to pull him through the extras, who are stirring now, as from a dream. The whole city seems to stretch, to sigh. He hears for a moment the beat of wings, a flock of birds passing overhead like incompetent demiurges, no longer able to stitch this world together. It's as if the pagan order is crumbling, making way for whatever's next. But probably this is what she means by magical thinking.

GREENWICH VILLAGE—3:22 A.M.

ONCE UPON A TIME, MERCER GOODMAN HAD A VISION OF HIS OWN. This was back in those early months after moving in with William, when the sex so intoxicated him that he couldn't get to sleep for hours after. He'd lie awake thinking about a city where people might actually be able to communicate their longings and disappointments and dreams, and so move beyond the illusion of being unknown and unknowable, as in the lights of passing buses, the half-finished self-portrait flared up and died. But later, Mercer had begun to wonder if the sense of illusion was itself an illusion. Because there were so many things he'd never understand about William. And there was his own work, the manuscript he never talked about. One of the reasons he started avoiding it in the first place was the swelling contradiction between the world and the novel as he imagined it. In his head, the book kept growing and growing in length and complexity, almost as if it had taken on the burden of supplanting real life, rather than evoking it. But how was it possible for a book to be as big as life? Such a book would have to allocate 30-odd pages for each hour spent living (because this was how much Mercer could read in an hour, before the marijuana)—which was like 800 pages a day. Times 365 equaled roughly 280,000 pages each year: call it 3 million per decade, or 24 million in an average human lifespan. A 24-million-page book, when it had taken Mercer four months to draft his 40 pages—wildly imperfect ones! At this rate, it would take him 2.4 million months to finish. 2,500 lifetimes, all consumed by writing. Or the lifetimes of 2,500 writers. That was probably—2,500—as many good writers as had ever existed, from Homer on. And clearly, he was no Homer. Was not even an Erica Jong. He had been writing for all the wrong reasons, for the future, for *The Paris Review*, for the cover of *Time* (the peak of cultural attainment, so far as the other Goodmans were concerned)—for anything but the freedom he'd once discovered in ink and paper.

This had led to the first of several resolutions to set aside his dream-city and the wild ambitions that had led him north.

But it all keeps coming back, doesn't it? The old desires, the old fears and delusions, like a maze you'll never find your way out of—not because of how it's built, but because of who you are. All this time he's believed himself free, he's really been tethered to fate, or whatever is its opposite, the force that's returned him to his Waterloo. A light flickers in one of the school's high windows. Someone who has a life of his own, about which Mercer can know no more than anyone else does of him. Or he does of himself. Or of the quartet of skinheads now catching up behind him. It's possible, even, that they're not skinheads at all, but off-duty Marines, or alopeciacs—in the moonlight it's hard to see much beyond the cropped scalps. He braces himself as they come right up to the base of the steps. One flicks a lighter, which sparks but does not catch. Then Mercer's sense of return is turned inside out, as is his sense of opacity. As are those scalps, it seems, and for a minute, they are naked consciousness, trembling in each other's presence. Fag, they're thinking. Hick. Jigaboo. But again this is an illusion; it's not him they're after. One asks, "What is that, a fungo bat?"

Another one laughs. "Out of the way, friend. We've got business to attend to."

The person who speaks is holding a cinderblock. No, a gasoline can. Oh. They mean to . . . And they must think he's . . . But the condescension, the disregard, shake something loose in him that open hatred would only have reinforced. "What's this place ever done to you?" he hears himself ask. "It's just a school."

"Are you kidding? Where do you think the ruling class gets the idea they're better than us in the first place?"

"I mean done to you personally."

"It's nothing personal. Though it should be for you. You think they admit your kind?"

"Well, actually, the administration has made serious efforts in that regard. I worked here for a while—"

"Remove head from ass, bro. Look around. This whole fucking city's like an injustice factory. Maybe they buy you off with a little something you're afraid to lose, a paycheck or a color TV, but you'll never get where they are. Meanwhile, your brother's rotting in a cell somewhere. Your sister's pouring water on the kids' cereal 'cause she can't afford milk. Do you really need me to do the whole bit, in the middle of a riot? The short version is, you're hung up on something that's never going to love you back."

It's an oddly educated diagnosis, but that's not the main problem. The main problem is that it is in most points correct. For what is Wenceslas-Mockingbird, if not an armory for the existing order? An order both unjust and untrue. And as long as the world is stuck being this particular world, he is stuck being hapless old Mercer. So he stands aside, and the mob in the background refocuses itself to batter down the doors. Total pandemonium. Rioters from all corners surge through halls and classrooms, splashing gasoline, burning walnut paneling and oil paintings and the leather-bound volumes of the library. And then it is on to City Hall, to Wall Street, to the Empire

State and Hamilton-Sweeney Buildings. When the sun rises a few hours from now, it is on a city where no trace of the past is legible.

Except that's not what happens. Mercer doesn't in fact stand aside, but looks up again at the one lit window above. It could be Dr. Runcible, that old closet case, communing with Matthew Arnold by candlelight. It could just be a janitor. Still, amid all the fucked-up ossifications of the whole concept of liberal Enlightenment, there is the human person. A soul you may not be able to save if you don't destroy its body first, but that you almost certainly can't save if you do. This is ridiculous, he thinks—is he really defending prep school? Still, Mercer has wasted months on the bird in the bush, and when the man tries to push him aside, he pushes back.

And is shoved. Then he is sprawling on hard concrete, while the skinheads pin him down. His fist shoots out and he feels it connect— not as it does in movies, with a crack, but with the fleshlessness of dreams. It feels good. As it feels good, in some weird way, to take one right in the nose.

As he gives and receives these punches, again and again, it is almost as if he is the other man, at war with himself, enjoying the taste of his own blood. All around him now, blows are being exchanged, as violence feeds on the crowd. Here is one to the jaw for all that is noble and valuable and conducive to dreams, and here comes one on the ear for all the suffering those dreams underwrite. He knows he's getting woozy, drifting away from the copper in his mouth and the pain all over his face. Premonitions of paving stones whoosh near his head, but the guy's companions must likewise be having a hard time figuring out who's on top. Still, any minute . . . The stars that peek between the bodies are dimming.

And then a noise rips the night in half and it's as if a bowling ball has barreled into pins. A can smashes against the asphalt, a bat is rolling, footsteps are scattering, and a voice, dreamily familiar, is commanding the skinheads to come back and retrieve their friend, who lies moaning some feet away on the sidewalk. When Mercer turns his head, that body's being dragged away. At first, he thinks someone's finally been shot tonight—but the gun that made the noise is aimed straight up into the air like a starter pistol. No, what has damaged the skinhead is Mercer's own fists. The little pistol, a mere shadow, descends to a waiting purse. The purse itself descends. The rioters in the street's broad center have resumed their march, if indeed they ever stopped it, and seem not to have noticed anything's happening here at all. Hard to say, what future he's ended up in.

Then a flame stutters to life far above his head, and above that, in smoke, floats the head of Venus de Nylon. She's sitting now on the front steps of the school, legs crossed elegantly at the knee, and peering down at him with a kind of mild interest. Not a hair of her wig is out of place. "You look like you've seen a ghost."

Mercer pulls himself into a sitting position, hugs his knees. He hurts all over. Especially his nose, which feels broken. His voice when he speaks is adenoidal. "Geez. Was that you? You were amazing."

"If I had a nickel for every man who told me that, I'd retire to Aruba."

Something occurs to him. "No, wait. You were back there in the park, too, weren't you?"

"Now you're just hypothesizing."

"I had no idea you had it in you." Is she some kind of goddess? A devil? A hallucination? The face that appears when the ember flares up again is sad, and somehow, beneath the lipstick and the rouge, infinitely old.

"No one ever does, Mercer, until they get pushed too far."

He spits some blood onto the sidewalk beside him. "I guess tonight pushed me too far."

"That's funny," she says. "Because I would have said you were just a baby. I hope they didn't beat that out of you, by the way. Though it looks like they got everything else."

"Is it that bad?"

This gets no answer, and he supposes she can't see him any more clearly than he can see her, now that the flame is gone. He stands up.

"But if you're here, where's William?"

"Was I supposed to be looking? Big groups were never his scene, anyway, if you remember." Of course he remembers, Mercer thinks, as he bends to retrieve his trampled glasses, and to feel for the rock that nearly bashed in his head. This must not be Venus's scene, either, because once he straightens up, she is standing—towering really—and brushing off the seat of her micromini. "I should be getting home. Shoshonna's not been well."

"Wait," he says. "I still have to find him. There's something I needed to say."

"See? Just a baby. It's really not an unattractive quality, if you know how to wear it."

"But you were his friend. Where else can I look?"

"Just ask yourself where you'd go, if you thought it was your last night on earth." Without looking back over her shoulder she gives her fingers a little wave, *Ta*. Those long legs are tap-tapping away toward Union Square, and then she is just a faint smell of tobacco. It may perhaps be getting light now, because the rock in his hands is actually a brick. He sets it on end in the center of the limestone steps—Dr. Runcible can stumble over it in the morning, and at least know or wonder how close it came to the glass—and then returns to street level. And as the multitude hisses in a million tongues around him, as if a pan had been placed under cold water, Mercer Goodman hobbles off north, in the direction of what is now, or once was, his home.

BROOKLYN HEIGHTS—2:35 A.M.

BY THE TIME THE TAXI DROPS THEM OFF, the air in the apartment is black and soupy and about a million degrees because there's no electricity to cool it down. Will lights some candles and starts opening windows. Brooklyn is passed out below. Cate, too, is sleepy. Her pigs especially are so tired she doesn't know how she would have made it if the man in the undies and black hat hadn't finally caught up to them and asked where they were trying to get to. Or on the other hand how he would have caught up at all if she hadn't been so tired. Will had been grunting at her to *hustle*, but she was ready to lie down right in the middle of the sidewalk. Now she's on the big new leather sofa that sticks to her arms and legs. She can hear from the kitchen her brother rattling open the fridge, pinging something made of glass against something else made of glass. Then he's standing over her in the dimness with a beverage in his hand. It's like her favorite word. Bev er ej. "Come on, kiddo. Time to brush."

"You're not brushing."

"Someone's got to stay up and wait for Mom."

"You promise she'll come home?"

"Of course she'll come home at some point. She just didn't plan on us being here, is all." His voice has something funny in it. His breath smells like Mrs. Santos's. "It's her one night free of the rug rats."

"You're going to be in trouble."

"What, this?" He looks at the beverage like someone else put it in his hand. "Everything in the fridge is going bad, anyway. Somebody might as well make use of it. Now come on. I'll let you sleep in the big bed."

Everybody knows that, since the move, Mom's bed has been Cate's preferred sleeping place. The best thing about it is actually not its bigness, but the windows on two sides of the room. They make pale gold angular shapes on the other two walls, streetlights and car lights from down below and lights from other buildings and the buildings across the water, and when Cate wakes up in the middle of the night they throw off enough light for her to see her arm by and know that she is real. Her favorite is when it rains and drops cling like stick-on jewels. Not tonight, though. Tonight there is no Mom, and no light. And you know how hard it can be to get to sleep sometimes if somebody startles you right when you are about to do it, to fall? Well, she has that. Will has left the door open only a crack. She lies there listening to his waiting. It's the sound—just when she thinks maybe he's fallen asleep like Mrs. S. and she can get up and wander—of more beverage splashing into glass, of little ice-cube air pockets popping.

There are a lot of shouldn't-ofs Will has and does. He likes to save them up, and then when everybody has forgotten, to reveal one, like an uncle who does things with his arms and his voice to make you forget the quarter you gave him is not in his left hand but in the other one, the one slipping into his pocket. Vwa la! No quarter. Will's favorite audience is Mommy. *Vwa la!* he will say. *Dad lets us ride the subway by ourselves!* Or *Vwa la! Dad gave us each our own TV, for our rooms!* That's okay, Cate has her own secrets. For example, that Mommy is still in love with Daddy. Which is why Mommy can get so mad at him about stuff like this. Or for example, that there are all the shouldn't-ofs she knows the benefits of pretending not to know.

The bad part is, with the lights out, there's nothing to look at. That's why she gets up and goes to the corner where the two windows meet. At first all she sees are two pink blinks on top of the towers across the water. Gradually, though, stars come out, and there are other towers of different heights and shapes huddled around below like kids around the legs of grown-ups, and the faint flush turns the water into water, moving. Is the sky getting lighter? Have they been gone that long? Or is this just her eyes adjusting to the dark?

Then she sees that the ledge outside the window is not stone but a lot of stone-colored birds. It jolts her so she might never get back to sleep. And down below in the little park where they wait for Daddy, the two trees: those aren't leaves, they're birds. There must be a thousand of them out there. Even as she withdraws a step into the dark, she knows that if they've come for her, it's pointless to resist.

When she works up the courage to look again, there are even more than she thought. And now reinforcements course down out of the sky, as if on wires, falling into spaces on the fronts and roofs of apartment houses, finding room where none existed. The buildings look like faces, mobile, alive, and there are all kinds of kinds, pigeons but also sparrows starlings falcons and here, outside this very window, what she recognizes by moonlight as a blue parakeet. Some owls dive toward the playground equipment, and great colonies of gulls settle like foam on the harbor, and tiny dotlike crows blow up through the pulse of pink light way over there. There are too many for just her, she understands now. She feels they do not wish her ill or well, except maybe that parakeet, which with its rotating neck looks back at her as if warning her to keep quiet. Which she does. Is anyone else awake to see? Is she? There must be as many birds out there as there are people in her city, and they are all *assembled*, waiting for someone or something to appear on that playground, which is the center somehow. Then a great big old bald eagle with sooty feathers and one eye missing and wings sixteen feet across alights at the top of the slide, turns his head 270 degrees. She imagines him issuing marching orders: *Brothers and sisters!* Or else telling them that they are dismissed, their work here is done.

Only now does she remember the bird they found there last winter, her and Mommy and Will and Will's friend Ken. Oh, she thinks. Oh. It has taken the others this long to find where he fell. Are they mad at her for taking the body? No, she decides. They have just come to—what is it Mommy said, when they went to that funeral for Daddy's Mommy, and Daddy yelled at Cate and some cousins for grabassery at the VFW hall where the meal was? To pay their respects. By morning, when the light comes and wakes her up, the birds will have scattered, so that no one will believe her if she tells them. And anyway, being half Hamilton-Sweeney, she won't.

94

A S THE YEARS PASSED, then parceled themselves into decades, William's feelings about the great blackout of 1977 would recede into fuzz. His sister speaking sharply to him when the lights went out—this he remembered. He remembered, too, that whatever she'd said had stung. But the words themselves would remain inaccessible, like the past more generally, upon which he'd learned not to brood.

Then one morning he found himself in the offices of a bond-trading firm at 7 World Trade, supervising the hanging of some portraits shot back during the plague years. Anything '80s, anything downtown, had lately acquired a kind of millennial cachet—particularly among the people responsible for downtown's ruin. Clients, was the technical term. His motto had been *Non serviam*, but darkroom supplies weren't cheap these days, nor (various liabilities having cannibalized Daddy's estate) was rent. Besides, anyone who might have accused him of selling out had either beaten him to it or died. And didn't the Medicis underwrite Raphael? Hadn't his own father subsidized the Rothko kids' therapy bills? "A little lower," he told the art hanger, a blue-eyed ectomorph who, two years out of Bennington, was clocking sixty-five dollars an hour. William popped another bitter square of Nicorette from its foil-backed sarcophagus. Then, catching himself watching for the strip of lower back that showed whenever the kid's shirt rode up, he knelt to pry open the last crate.

You reach a certain age, you can encounter old work without feeling much of anything. He must have seen these images a thousand times, in tearsheets and blowups and magazine layouts: old friends and lovers, most no longer living, staring balefully up from the silver gelatin. Or okay, maybe it was inaccurate to suggest that he didn't feel *some*thing, but whatever it was glimmered behind layers of numbness, like the sensations of dental work. You felt the pressure, but not the pain. And of course he'd been holding something of himself aloof even then from the faces on the far side of the lens.

It was exactly this quality of abstention, or "maturity," that had finally won him the esteem of the art world at the end of the long string of personal and professional disasters that had been the 1970s. Even before *Artforum* declared him a born photographer, he'd set up a darkroom and dumped all his stiff-bristled brushes into plastic bags and put them out on the curb for Tuesday garbage collection. Mercer would have objected, but Mercer was by that point in Europe somewhere. And maybe this was why that last, unfinished painting had never worked: without Mercer, there was no one left in New York who believed in capital-A Art. William himself was already losing his ability to think like a painter, but he gave it one last shot—this would have been the summer of '81—working from memory, passing up the chance he usually relished to hire a model to stand in front of him and disrobe or more, depending on what signals passed back and forth. He started this time with newspaper bound to canvas. He painted it black, but not so black you couldn't make out the ads. He stapled a triangular scrap of white shirt to it, off-center, with big, visible staples. He'd always liked the Rauschenbergy effect of an actual thing approximating a representation, rather than vice versa. Let this fabric stand for the body, the torso it was shaped like, racing out of negative space. But when it came to the painterly part, the face, he couldn't quite get it to resolve, because the dark had been so dark that night, despite the ferocity with which he'd tried to see. He felt like Whistler laboring over the proto-Ab-Ex fireworks in *Nocturne in Black and Gold*, which John Ruskin, his supposed buddy, had likened to "a pot of paint thrown in the public's face." Who needed the aggravation? Still, it now seemed to William, stranded amid the whisper and click of fictitious capital, that something had gotten lost back there. His addiction, to be sure, but also something else, something possibly of value. "You happy with that?" the art hanger asked, as the name for it trembled near the root of his gum-numbed tongue.

Actual cigarettes had gone the way of red meat and anonymous sex in early '87, just before his first major West Coast solo show. Well, he'd been more careful about the sex for several years prior, even as he'd put off getting tested; he didn't want to spread anything, but also didn't want confirmation that it was in him. William's political platform, to the extent that he had one, could pretty much be called anti-Deathism, because the other available option, socialism, was hard, and required sharing, whereas death was so obviously stupid that the opposition was open to anyone. Increasingly, friends were joining up. And getting flattened. And William, between his reckless second heroin binge and the great bathhouse wallow of '79, was due to be flattened, too, only a funny thing happened post-diagnosis. They put him on drugs, things went up and down, but he lived. He lived. It was like a waiting room where they kept not calling your name. Until this morning, when he'd looked down in the shower and seen the lesion on his chest that meant the current drugs had stopped working. Other drugs had stopped working before, but he knew already this was different. It would be another week before he went to the doctor, but more out of fecklessness than fear. Whether one placed the *fin* of the *siècle* in 1999 or 2000 or was still on the Julian calendar, William had survived it. He'd never expected to see the spring of 2001. "You happy?" the kid repeated. With what? he was about to say, when he realized that what was meant was the alignment.

"Yeah," he said. "I can live with that."

And time, far from running out, was crumbling into powder. Part of him was high-fiving the art handler, leading him to the elevator, offering to take him and his boyfriend to Balthazar for breakfast. Part of him was thirty thousand feet over America, flying back from the show in L.A., having told no one there what the test had finally revealed. But a significant part, he saw, was still back on Central Park West, a half-hour into the '77 blackout, squinting at the figure rushing desperately out of the night. Seconds from now, he would discover that he knew it well, but at that moment, Keith's face seemed like one you saw only in dreams. And say Regan had been right—say group meetings four nights a week still hadn't drummed into him that he, William Hamilton-Sweeney III, was not the center of the universe—he might have imagined for an instant that this white scrap of Brooks Brothers cotton was a messenger meant for him alone. A terrible ghost or angel come to bring more life.

MIDTOWN—3:25 A.M.

IT IS ONLY AS THE ADRENALINE BEGINS TO WEAR OFF that Pulaski discovers that's what it was all along: adrenaline driving his crooked body up the thirty-nine flights, adrenaline launching his last doomed sprint toward the window, and adrenaline—well, that and the elevator attendant, and the girl in the Rangers jersey—helping him back down to his car when it was all over. That this night has *not* miraculously healed him is clear even before the keys are in the ignition. The spasms in his legs are worsening by the second. As is an inner tension. From the attendant's desk, he's called his old pal from the U.S. Attorney's office and asked him to alert the Bureau to the scene up on the fortieth floor. It seemed sanest, though against the grain of years of jurisdictional intransigence, not to bring his own Department barging in, asking the kinds of procedural questions that get you fired without benefits. And if that's how he's going to play this, B. has warned (none too pleased to be roused by a three a.m. phone call), it's important to get as far away from his current location as humanly possible. Yet just scrabbling in his pocket for some aspirin takes all of Pulaski's resources.

Luckily, he has plenty of practice with childproof lids. The half-dozen tablets that tumble into his palm are dusty, possibly expired, but he knocks them back dry and shuts his eyes and does his best to tune out the lint on his tongue. If he's done permanent damage to his legs, Sherri will never forgive him. Heck, she may never forgive him anyway. He tries rubbing them, but can't do it the way she used to. The pain has gone glacial, an ice-cream headache thudding deep inside each thigh.

Gradually, though, the aspirin thaws the edges a bit, and he becomes aware of a choked sound coming from the passenger's seat. Any other night a perp could belt "Tiptoe Through the Tulips" four Cs above middle C in here and it wouldn't faze Pulaski, but this specific sound is the kind that can really make the little hairs above your collar stand up. For one thing, he's almost forgotten he's got two extra bodies to figure out what to do with. For another, one of them—the boy—is crying. And here's a secret about Larry Pulaski: a clutch situation, late innings, lives on the line, he's Mr. October, but at the more intimate scale at which life mostly gets lived he has no idea what he's doing. Nor does the girl in the jersey, apparently, who stays silent in the backseat. All he can think of is to offer the kid a smoke.

There's an intake of saliva, snot, tears; "Huh?"

Pulaski focuses on the red beacon still pulsing atop the Hamilton-Sweeney Building, just beyond the upper edge of the windshield. It is not his pain. "I keep a pack in the glovebox for emergencies. This would seem to qualify, if you want to dig around in there."

The boy mumbles something about his asthma, but what else is Pulaski supposed to do for him? Reach across the space separating them, this Naugahyde vastness reeking of Christmas-tree air fresheners, and hold his hand? He'd probably get sued. That's if he's not getting sued already. "Well, I'll take one," he says. "I'm a pipe man, ordinarily. The wife puts up with it because she likes the smell. Reminds her of her grandfather. But I come home smelling like cigarettes, I sleep on the couch. These are mostly for witnesses. You'd be amazed how people can open up."

The pack dates to New Year's Eve, and maybe old age has strengthened it, or maybe it's just been too long since he's had one, because the last time a smoke hit him this hard he was a kid himself, sneaking them out beyond the garage in Passaic. It's doing everything the aspirin can't. His legs are drifting away. His head is swimming like a lobster trap back up to the fortieth floor, where he sees again how at the critical moment he had failed. How his body had failed him. How the boy had thrown himself from the window. How having dragged himself to his feet again, he, Pulaski, had beaten back those birds (or had they already been clearing?) until he was staring at the flicker of far-below cars. He'd smacked his flashlight to get it working again. And—sweet Jesus—that flicker turned out to be the rickety slats of a window-washer's platform, not a dozen feet under the sill. There was the boy on his back like a chalk outline, eyes closed. He couldn't have known the platform would be there to catch him, could he? It had been far too dark, not to mention the birds. But in each hand was an alarm clock. And next to him, maybe a foot from where he'd made impact, was a duffelbag with loose wires poking between the zippers.

The beacon stains the upper edge of the windshield again. A texture of beseechment. "I know what this is like, Charlie, trying to keep everything inside."

The girl in the backseat breaks in. "Does it seem like he wants to talk about it? I don't think he wants to talk about it."

Pulaski no longer has the touch, it seems, to cajole anything out of anyone. He has a brief image of being relieved by superiors, who have been relieved by their superiors, on up the chain. Yet something fixes him in place. And when he senses other vehicles moving in the dark, he can't help reaching back into the side pocket for his binoculars.

Phoning B., he was expecting federal agents in cheap suits and black cars. What instead emerge from the sidestreets now are plain white vans, a half-dozen of them, no sirens, no rollers—just overdriven engines at high speed. They halt in front of the Hamilton-Sweeney Building in perfect formation, nose to curb, so that their high beams aim across the plaza. A blond fellow jumps out of the second van and seems, for a second, to look Pulaski's way. He bends to his walkie-talkie. Then jumpsuits are crisscrossing the headlights. They pull on balaclavas—all but the one with the walkie. With baton lights, with utility belts flashing, they disappear behind glass, leaving only the vans and some orange safety cones. If you were an onlooker, you might imagine a maintenance exigency was being addressed.

"Who is *that*?" says the girl in the backseat.

"I don't think we're meant to ask."

"It's not like it matters anyway," says Charlie, finally. A caul of red expands around him. Goes dark. "She didn't make it."

Who didn't? Pulaski wants to ask. Then he remembers how the boy had looked as they pulled him back in. They'd looped an extension cord under his armpits to hoist him up and through the window, keeping up a pep talk all the while—*don't look down now, you're doing fine*—but the point was moot; he didn't open his eyes until he was back inside. It was like something he'd seen out there had changed him. Something he was afraid to blink away.

Pulaski is still tracing out ramifications when there's a knock on the roof. A white light bursts into existence on the other side of the half-open window, though he's seen no one approach. "Can I ask what you folks are doing?"

"NYPD." Pulaski reaches for his shield only to find he's stowed it in the wrong pocket. Here it is. "You mind aiming that thing somewhere other than my eyeballs?"

The white orb hovers for a moment before flitting to the roadway. An athletic-looking man crouches to look through the window. He is young—too young, in the way of some people who are scarily good at their jobs—and reeks of Speed Stick. His jumpsuit, unzipped to the navel, shows a necktie, as if after this he's going to head back to punch a clock in some second life. Even in poor light, the blond hair spilling over the shirt's arrow collar has exceptional luster. Why this should surprise Pulaski is hard to say. "I see your badge, fine, maybe sitting in a car counts as work for you. But what's their excuse?"

Pulaski cringes as the girl in the backseat speaks up again. "Who do you think called in the threat, pig? If it wasn't for *him*, you wouldn't be here."

"Ah. So you're the famous Deputy Inspector Larry Pulaski."

"And I'm taking these two into custody," he says. "But my name wasn't supposed to get dragged into this."

"Information has a way of reaching us. Like, for example, that you'd taken early retirement. I thought I'd come down here and offer congratulations while my team wraps up. But then I find you aren't retired after all. Why is that, Larry?"

Good question.

"So retire already. It's four in the morning. Forget this ever happened, and you never have to see my face again. Which, trust me, would be very bad for your future plans."

Surely the jumpsuits can't be emerging again—hasn't Pulaski only just finished his cigarette?—but here they are, more of them than should fit in three vans, moving with the dispatch of paramedics, though maybe it's the lump they carry between them, the size of a child, that makes him think that. The duffel. A church choir has begun to keen out there in the night, unless he is imagining that, too.

"That goes double for you two hoodlums. I'm not supposed to say this, but Uncle Sam has a little offsite deal with certain overseas governments. You know what those guys do to prisoners? Unless you aim to spend the rest of your natural lives finding out, remember: nothing happened here. Understand? You'll make sure they understand, Detective? This is all a bad dream." He doesn't wait for a response. Another knock on the roof, and he is gone, this young man Pulaski is now certain operates orders of magnitude beyond his own pay-grade. Which must mean—he tries to make contact with the spectral chorus, the distant ground of his pain—which must mean that it really almost came to pass. He can still see the two identical alarm clocks, hands stopped at 2:26, where the one on the bank over there says 9:27. The hours in between he may never get his head around.

But he doesn't need to, he sees, as the first of the vans departs. He is done with imagining there are answers. He will go away and forget any of this ever happened. It never happened.

"Like I was saying, Charlie"—he fumbles around for where he left off—"I know what this is like. What you need to do is take things one step at a time. Start with sleep. Go home and take a hot shower and just sleep."

"You're not going to take us in?" The girl sounds disappointed.

"Anything you have to confess, sugar, I frankly don't want to hear. The fellow was right. It's best no one knows you were involved."

"Best no one knows *you* were involved, you mean," Charlie mutters. "You're the one who pulled a weapon on the elevator guy."

"This is your get out of jail card, kid. Don't look it in the mouth." The choir is fading away. He is startled by the actuality of the engine when he turns the key.

"You want me to drive?" the girl asks. Then: "Your legs."

"They're fine." He moves the transmission into D, grits his teeth as he gives it gas. "Just tell me where I can drop you two. Surely you've got homes somewhere."

"Matter of fact—," she is saying, when the boy interrupts: Yes, he says. As a matter of fact, there is somewhere he wants to be left.

UPPER WEST SIDE—4:27 A.M.

AT FIRST, IN THE DIM BLEAR of what could be dawn or just more humidity, the thing on the bench across from Daddy's building looks like a bag of garbage, or a heap of schmattes, or some other of the million sorts of refuse this city specializes in. Keep walking, Regan tells herself, because helping anyone else is a story for the faint of heart. There's only expedience, the pursuit of one's own desires. Witness her husband, already halfway across Central Park West. But this is almost exactly where those ambulances were on New Year's Eve. And maybe at this very moment, someone on the other side of the island is walking past two lost-looking kids, wondering whether to intervene. Anyway, it has enough of the human about it, this thing on the bench, that she's already stepped back onto the curb.

"Regan, what the hell?" Keith says behind her, but she tells him to go ahead upstairs and check on William and Daddy. "I'll catch up in a minute." He pauses. "Please." She's been looking all night for any sign that he accepts her independence . . . and now, to her surprise, he gives her one. Goes. She squats by the bench. The thing is indeed human, hunched in the chin-to-chest posture of a subway drunk, but she smells only tobacco and sweat. She has an urge to touch him, but isn't brave enough. "Hey." And when he looks up, her heart stutters. He's just a kid himself: rough-cut hair, fair skin, the hollows of a face. A camera-strap across his chest. "Hey," she says, softer now. "Are you lost?"

"Do you mind?" he says. "I'm trying to concentrate here."

But this is karma. Has to be. "My father lives right across the street. Why don't you come inside where it's safe, at least until the lights are back on?"

Without another word, the boy gets up and stalks off toward the shadows of the park entrance; she is only making things worse. "Anything you need, we've got," she calls after him. "There's food, a shower . . ."

He stops. "How about a radio? One that takes batteries."

"I'm sure we could find you a radio. The important thing is that you not stay out here in the dark, where it's dangerous. Come on. Let me help you."

She lets him precede her into the lobby. A haggard-looking Miguel rises to his feet, but she nods to him; it's okay. The boy reaches the stairwell first and starts climbing with the weariness of someone much older. She's been holding out some hope that Will and Cate will have found their way to the penthouse, but when she reaches it, all is still. A far-off tugboat is the loneliest sound in the world. The men must be upstairs. The boy, meanwhile, has stopped to study the Rothko. For Regan, it's just part of the world's furniture, another thing to pass by, but as she stands next to him, trying to show she's not going to push him beyond where he wants to go, it becomes an entirely different painting. The blue at its heart is actually a bruised violet, though maybe this is an effect of the million candles William has lit. Anyway, this heat can't be good for it. Or for the boy, whose breathing is ragged. "That sounds bad. Let's get you some water."

"It's just asthma," he says. "I must have dropped my inhaler somewhere."

"Water never hurt anyone. The kitchen's this way."

She can't recall the last time no servants were here. She has to go all around the perimeter opening cabinets just to find glasses, and when she turns on the faucet, nothing comes. They're on the seventeenth floor, and there's no power to draw the water up. She can feel the boy's eyes on her back. In the unlit fridge she finds a pitcher, dips a finger in to taste. "Is lemonade okay? It's lukewarm."

"It's fine," he says. His face is flushed. Then: "Why are you doing this?"

"I don't know," she admits, but she has this feeling of knowing him from somewhere. She should ask his name. Instead, she pours herself a dram of the Grand Marnier she's discovered in her tour de cabinet. It's nauseatingly sweet, but on the plus side goes straight to her head. The boy sets his camera on the counter. They sit in complicated quiet for a minute or two. Then she asks what he thought he was doing down there on the street—"if you don't mind my prying." When he doesn't answer, she takes another sip. "I mean, I'm sure you have your reasons. Most people do. But you're not sleeping out there, right? Because people get mugged. The streets are wild."

His gaze is unsettling, so she turns and starts shutting the doors of the cabinets she's opened. "I speak from experience here. Our kids got lost on the way home from day camp tonight, and we must have walked ten miles looking for them, my husband and I. But I keep thinking they must have gone somewhere safe." There's a little desk where the cook can sit down and write out menus, and on the hutch above are picture frames, including another of the million prints of that photo from Lake Winnipesaukee. She hands it to the boy. "This is them." He has the kind of fair skin that goes pink with the slightest stirring of blood.

"Wait. *This* is your husband?"

"Ex-husband. Or almost. We're separated. He was supposed to pick them up." Then the oddest thing happens: the boy reaches for her glass, and for a second, their fingers are in contact. When she lets go, he dumps what's left of the Grand Marnier into his lemonade. Bolts it. Closes his eyes and doesn't speak for a minute. "We should all just go home," he says at last.

"Beg pardon?"

"You said this isn't your place, right? A kid will always want to go home."

"Are you okay? You're a little pale."

They look at each other for a minute. Of course she knows him, she thinks. He has lost someone, too. They are the same, he and she. "Can you show me the phone?"

The telephone cupboard is a little velvet-cushioned room under the stairs. The boy shuts the folding glass doors carefully behind him, and she retreats to a far doorway for discretion's sake. Through the galaxies of flame on the glass, she can see his slouched shoulders, his face turned toward the wall. *I'm in this rich guy's house*, he might be saying into the receiver. *Bring the duct tape and the guns.* But she feels certain he's talking to a parent. Asking, she thinks, to be picked up.

"Your turn," he says a minute later, emerging even more rumpled than before.

"What?"

"Your kids," he says. "Call home. Keep calling."

She catches herself about to explain to this boy all the reasons calling an empty apartment again defies logic. But what is there to do, really, besides take the receiver and squeeze past him into the cupboard? Its interior now smells like Will's gym socks. She's just pulling the door shut when he reminds her about the radio. "With batteries. You promised."

"There's an exercise room a few doors down that hall. I think there's one there." And then the boy is gone, and Regan's sending herself through the little holes in the earpiece. Each ring is a rock dropped in dark water. Leaden circles, nine or ten, spreading outward without striking anything solid. But then, incredibly, there Will is, and the thing he says is not hello but "Mom? Is that you?"

His voice sounds blurry somehow, as if explosions inside have fogged her hearing. Still, he is oxygen; the air could not be full enough of him. "Will, baby, where are you? Jesus."

"Uh . . . you called me, remember?" But she's called so many places tonight that she's already forgotten which one this is. "The new apartment? Tall building? Big water? Ringing any bells?"

"I mean, where have you been all night? Is your sister all right? I'm just ill about this, we've been looking—"

"Cate's asleep in your bed." *Aschleep.* "We're fine. Geez, if you want to be pissed at someone, be pissed at the person whose fault this is."

"I want you to stay put," she says, surprised at her own firmness.

"It's like four in the morning, Mom, where would we go?"

"Stop that. No more of that. I'm leaving Grandpa's as we speak."

"What are you doing at Grandpa's? Is he okay?"

"Everything's fine, but I can't say how long it'll take your father to find us a cab."

"Dad's there?"

"Of course Dad's here." She once heard someone describe space orbit as a continuous freefall. His silence now is a little like that, she's falling through the universe in her little glass capsule. Then she strikes something solid: Keith. It's Keith he's been mad at all this time. "Honey?"

"I don't see why he has to come. He's the one who stood us up in the first place."

"Will. Your dad loves you more than anything." Again that pause, as she realizes it is true. "We both do. Be a little human here."

"Fine. But if I'm asleep when you get in, don't wake me. It's been a hell of a night." He hangs up, and for once, she is thankful for Felicia Gould's excess, for the fantasy of elegance she forced on everyone around her, for now the door can be kept shut as long as Regan needs. She doesn't know why she's still so afraid to let other people hear her cry, except that presumably the sun is going to rise here at some point, and the world of the past, which has not looked kindly on displays of naked emotion, will reach out to touch the world of the future, like an aerialist finding the next trapeze, or a sleeper remembering herself as she awakes.

When she tracks down Keith, he is on one of those spiral staircases in the great hall, coming down from the second floor. He's started to report that her father's sawing logs, and William reading, when she calls out across the open space that she's finally reached them.

"In Brooklyn," she says. "At the new place."

He sits down right there, a few steps above the parquet.

"I told Will we're both on our way. I figured you'd want to see them," she says.

His eyes are at exactly the same level as hers, separated only by the openwork of the staircase. He does want to see them, he says. Very much.

This means leaving Regan's runaway to wait for his ride. William can look after him, make sure he doesn't steal any of the silver, but she feels she should at least tell him they're leaving. Which is something she has to do on her own, she says, determined for some reason to keep him and Keith from crossing. If her husband has objections, he doesn't raise them. (Is this how things are going to be now? And is that bad or good?)

Earlier, she thought William was putting her on, pretending not to remember his way around the penthouse, but dimness has re-arranged the side-passages, and for a minute she gets lost herself. Then a radio is chirping up ahead, and after two closets and a cigar room, she finds the fitness center. The candlelight hits a nautilus machine and a treadmill and not one but two scales. Their shadows on the walls look like tools for the mortification of the flesh. There's a moment when she almost feels sad for Felicia. Then she spots the boy. He's on a wrestling mat on the floor, his legs tucked up under his chest and his head down next to the radio, like one of those Muslim cabbies you see hauling flattened cardboard out of the trunk at prayer time. It's what he was doing on the bench outside, she realizes: beam-ing his requests toward Mecca or wherever.

Now he is either lost to the chatter of talk radio—needing it to tell him something—or asleep. Little ridges of vertebrae push against his tee-shirt along his back. It is warm and damp, but not feverish. Her hand, resting there, looks like another person's. Like the memory of a hand.

And then it is twenty years later, and all of this is irrelevant. She is waking from a nap, in the mid-to-late afternoon, in the spring, bits and pieces of her flitting down from the corners of a sunny room and assembling themselves into the person she is now. That cramp in her left hand is arthritis. The drone she's dreamed was a plane is actually the maid's vacuum in the hall. Beyond an open window birds twitter and buses sigh, but even after she can tell herself these things with some authority, she remains recumbent, a sweaty pillow over her head. Not that there will be anyone trying to get her up. Cate works long hours at a firm downtown, and Regan experiences her these days mostly as a visitor for Sunday brunch. Keith is up in Rye for the afternoon; retired, he's taken up golf and Republican politics (which amount to the same thing). And Will . . . Will is an answer-ing machine on another coast—and every once in a while, when she can catch him at an odd enough hour that he has to pick up, a voice, reticent, pixellated by satellites. Still, Regan wouldn't trade the life she's made. She's got her brother back, and it seems like he might be around for a while yet. And Act 2 of her marriage has been much better than Act 1. The company's eventual implosion has not only put her and Keith on more equal footing, but also freed her to figure out what to do with herself. At his urging, she sent out résumés, and the next year was hired as head of community relations at St. Mary's Hospital for Children in Bayside, Queens. The creation of money from money wasn't ever something that fulfilled her; this is. More importantly, she's learned to live with herself, which she now knows is a precursor to learning to live with other people. Sometimes in the early evening, she will look up from a magazine to find Keith in the chair cattycorner to her, just looking. "What?" she'll ask, and he will say, "Nothing," but with a kind of wonder. You can build a life on this: two people who know each other's failings electing nonetheless to sit together, in socks, in lamplight, reading magazines, trying not to look too far beyond the day just passed, or the one coming up. Only at the borders of sleep, really, will she ever find herself rooting back along overgrown passageways for a place where her current life split off. And what she comes to, more often than not, is this fantasy she'd once had of having recovered the son or daughter she'd lost, as if that whole night had been a vast Rube Goldberg contraption for showing her that what she wants is not what she's thought.

Under her hand, the boy doesn't move. For a few seconds, things could go either way. As long as her eyes stay closed, it's not impossible she does say something, and whatever happens after that will have become her future, and her current one the dream. But she has come to believe or remembers believing that she has to choose: either the path not taken seventeen years earlier, or the path that leads to her actual children, as opposed to imaginary ones. And this boy has his own life, as does she. It was a mistake to think she ever didn't.

Still, she keeps her hand on his back a few seconds longer. Tries to memorize the pale lines of scalp branching through his hair. She holds on to the feeling until it is exactly the size of her body, and then she lets go. She's been awake for twenty-three hours. Her eyes are dry. The sky outside brightens, or doesn't. The daytime maids will be arriving soon. Under one of the boy's inert hands she places a note. *Make yourself at home. William (brother) upstairs, can help with food. I'm at this number if you need anything.* But already she knows he won't call. She is never going to see him again. And after a last look, she prepares to return to reality, pursued by the babble of the madman on the radio, like a voice out of a dream.

LAST TRANSMISSION

"—ANYWAY, THERE WE ALL WERE, hands on shoulders. Yours truly ends up in line between a woman in an Arab hair thing and a Hasid who seems nervous I'm going to cop a feel. The tunnel? Hotter than I ever thought a tunnel could be. Flames barely reaching the graffiti and that weird brown residue the trains leave, like inside the barrel of a gun. Turns out to have its own smell, by the way, mushroomy and sweaty and metallic all at once. You've smelled it before and thought it was something else. I'm just starting to ask myself are we being led into an ambush when the wall on the left becomes an echoey black vacuum. The platform. The guy behind takes his hand off my shoulder. All these little lights drifting apart. We're just folks coming home from work again. Then I'm up and through an open exit, screwing on the old face. Because there above, everything is in limbo. Whole apartment blocks as dark as the train. And at ground level, obviously, shades of the Last Judgment. I'll spare you my man-on-the-street; you just lived through a version of this yourselves. But suffice it to say, many hours and blocks later, when I spot a light in the WLRC windows—don't let anyone tell you Zig doesn't put your needs first, New York—I'm instantly thinking, burglary. Then it comes to me that the station has a generator. And at quarter to five a.m., the blocks below Canal are such a ghost town I can already hear music through the window: thump thump thump. And again at the top of the stairs.

"Go look at a disco record some time when the lights come back on. Each side looks like a single song, only stretched out to fill twelve inches, because God forbid when there are wars on and kids starving in Eritrea anything should stop you from shake shake shaking your booty. This particular side is about halfway through, and there's another record cued on the turntable beside it, so the switchover can be made seamlessly. The broadcast booth's deserted, but there's a cigarette burning in an ashtray. I figure Wolfman Jerry, our midnight-to-four guy, must be around somewhere. Me, I'm going to sit and wait for Nordlinger to come, tell me if I'm blacklisted for stirring up trouble or still clear to hit the air.

"To kill time, I pick through some of this mail that's always piling up in the station. Promo platters, yes, but also publicity shots and autographs, the endless self-promotion. Maybe one of you nutjobs out there has sent in topless pics, I'm thinking, or at least a death threat—*some*thing. But every time I glance to see how much time's left on the record, the swath of grooves between the needle and the spinning label has gotten smaller. Two inches, an inch. You'll be shocked to learn, boys and girls, that it's making 'Dr.' Zig tense up. This station's been broadcasting without interruption since like 1923, but someone's going to have to come switch the record soon or there will just be silence, that irksome pertussion of needle on groove. And we're getting down to the nitty-gritty here, like a half-inch from the center, a quarter inch, someone's scrawled 'Fast Fades' on the sleeve, any second now the pulse is going to stop, so at the very last possible instant I lean forward and switch the fader. Any idiot could do it, by the way, bloop, push a button, bleep, throw the switch, and you've meted out another seven minutes forty of life. Which doesn't mean disco doesn't still suck. Let me just wash these down.

"Ah. Better. What was I talking about? Accomplishment, is what I was talking about. My sense of it lasted about as long as the buzz of a smoke does after you stub it out. About as long as the afterglow of intercourse, before the voices start to froth again in the brainpan. Good for her? Good for me? Who leaves first? How soon's too soon? Because my assumption of what's been going on has just shifted: there's no one in the station at all. No Wolfman Jerry, no Nordlinger. Which means no one but me at the controls. It's a lot of pressure, I'm saying, and there are few places creepier than an empty radio station with the mic this hot and the monitors up loud, because you can't hear a thing over your own voice. Like if the Kneesocks Killer or the Son of Sam were sneaking up behind me at this instant, I wouldn't hear. You can talk yourself into being too scared to turn around . . .

"But wait. Who put this record on in the first place? Whose cigarette butt is this? I start to wonder—don't laugh now, you city of palmistry and dashboard Jesuses—but to wonder if the place is haunted. I've mentioned my buddy who took a dive a few months back, right? And how he came to see me? Four years of silence, and there he was at the door, drunk, with a photograph and some questions about a leak. Maybe it even gave me a little pleasure to say: You're over the line, pal, I got nothing for you. I can't believe I never mentioned this. These pills must be eating away my mind. Anyway, I now get the strangest feeling he's here in the studio with me. Or someone is. Any second now he's going to swim up before me, or flicker, or however ghosts do, I don't know, because I've always been certain they're just a way of not having to face ourselves—only why, boys and girls, am I then so scared? Maybe because I've just walked six miles in the dark in a city that wants me dead?

"Or maybe because, when you get right down to brass, it's 'Dr.' Zig who's been the fraidy-cat all along. Yes, I hate to disabuse you aspiring jocks in the audience, but this broadcast booth is nothing but a hedge, a layer of glass protecting you from the horror show that is other people. Screwing around with which is what got this friend of mine in trouble. And I feel like he's only inches away now, about to lay a hand on me, to start whispering in my ear, like, if things are verily as hopeless as you say they are, Zig, why not go ahead and have the courage of your convictions, pull the trigger—and you know what? I'm no longer ready to hear it. So I flee back out to the WLRC lounge, which is really just a closet with a couch in it. I've still got a few minutes before showtime to recollect myself, pull together whatever my message is going to be to you this morning, New York, when suddenly: a crash from the john. Oh, Zig, I'm thinking. You neurotic pardon my French fuck. This whole time you thought it was just you, there's been a colleague here using the can. Or else some miscreant off the street.

"What—you were expecting an actual ghost story? I may be a coward, but I'm also an empiricist. I go knock on the door, hollow-core steel, I'm not sure why, though come to think of it, the can's got one of only two windows in the entire studio, so maybe someone else is worried about break-ins, too. Which would explain the padlockable latch on my side of the door. Remember, I've just walked through fifteen of my own riots and found myself too appalled to join. But I'm not going to be a coward anymore. The record's going to have to be changed again in what my finely honed instincts are telling me is three point five minutes, and one way or another, this is going to have to be settled before I go back in that booth, i.e., the one you're hearing me from now. So I take a deep breath.

"Take one with me now, New York, if you're still out there. Shoulder to shoulder. Shoulder to the steel. Listen once more for that racket. Now push.

"I need a few seconds to grasp what's on the other side. The window, the one I saw from outside, is open. Toilet paper everywhere, soaking up water. And there, thrashing around on the floor, is a frayed pigeon. It's gotten stuck on one of those glue traps you use to catch rats. For years now, they've been scattered around the station, because we've been having a rat problem. Or what we assumed was a rat problem. And loyal listeners will be aware of the Zigler axiom that beneath the feathers, pigeons and rats are the same animal. Now there's dirty down and fuzz flying off everywhere; all that remains is to give the thing a good stomp and be done with it. Barbaric, you say, to which I reply, no, this is the very essence of civilization. A willingness to do the stomping, before the vermin bite your children and contaminate your grain.

"But as I raise my shoe, the bird darts toward the toilet like it knows the end is near. It can't quite fly because one wing's still glued to the trap, and it's making this cooing, this mourning dove sound, but with an undertone of absolute emergency. What am I supposed to do? There can't be more than a couple minutes left on the record now, I've got to get back to the booth, and I don't want to leave the thing like suffering.

"Have you ever tried to pick up a pigeon? This one basically panics and shits my hand, so I flip the glueboard upside down, remembering this as a falconry trick, only no dice. The bird is surprisingly lightweight, but those wings can generate a hell of a lot of force, and I'm pretty rattled, my instinct is to hold the board gingerly, but that would just lead to dropping it. So I've got it out and away from my body, trying to avoid getting pecked to death, and I climb up on the wobbly toilet seat and very slowly when the wingbeat subsides put bird and board and then my head out through the transom, where the sun is just coming up, praise be to the dashboard Jesi, red morning, streets beginning to articulate again, but there's no time to commune with you, New York, I disengage the wing from the glue, and then I've got to do the legs, too, but soft, so as not to rip anything, which occasions another flurry, and all of a sudden I'm furious at the position I find myself in, I don't know if I mean in the bathroom or in this city or as a human being or what, but I'm yelling, 'Hold still, goddammit'—and everything I ever told you is a lie if the thing doesn't go completely still, pluck pluck, the legs come unstuck, and without thinking I open my hand and it just . . . plummets. My shoe goes into the crapper, my sock is wet as I speak, but what do I care, because I've just cost a living thing its life. Only: four stories down, a few feet from the sidewalk, the damn thing remembers its wings, and with a few flaps it's escaped into the sky. I've got no time to process, as they say, the record is dying, *Slow Fades*, this one, so I lollop with my one wet shoe back into the booth and lean toward the mic, breathless, which is where you came in, whoever you are, and why I've been here now for the better part of two hours, doing all this processing on air.

"Or okay, fine, you got me, maybe it didn't all happen this way. Or is a fantasia on other stuff that did—doesn't matter. What matters is the signal this story delivers as we near the top of the hour, which is this: 'Dr.' Zig has misdiagnosed you, *Damen und Herren*. I've had most of my facts right, mind you, but still somehow the picture I've been drawing is full of holes, because I never really believed you capable of change. And even now they're writing over history, finding ways to tell you what you just saw doesn't exist. The big, bad anarchic city, people looting, ooga-booga. Better to trust the developers and the cops. But let no one tell you you didn't change into something else last night, New York, if only briefly. It's been enough to make me think maybe I can change, too. So I want you to do me a favor. It's 5:58 a.m. I want you to turn your radio off. I know I'm supposed to be here 'til seven, but if every last one of you would just turn me off, right now, I could shut the fuck up and no one would know it. Like *Peter Pan*, only upside-down: if you just stop clapping, I can walk out the door. Maybe we'll even run into each other out there, you and I. We won't have to recognize each other, so long as we don't speak. It'll be like starting from scratch. So get up off your collective ass now, New York, and please, just *please*—"

WEST SIDE—5:58 A.M.

THIS TIME OF MORNING, trucks from Manhattan's last remaining factories should be stacked at the Battery Tunnel, diverting traffic onto surface streets, but the backup is paltry; anyone looking to get out of the city is already gone. What diverts Pulaski instead is the thought of having to descend into darkness again, with the sun finally having started to rise. Instead, after killing the radio, he cuts across Chambers to the bridge, and is soon soaring up over the harbor, and thence onto an expressway that for once merits the name. Pedestrian overpasses fly by. Signs for the Verrazano are grimed but legible. In the car there's only the hum of asphalt punctuated by expansion joints. Everywhere else, on the water, on the windows, on the rusted chain-link, is light, is light, is light.

Then, just as he reaches Port Richmond, the cobra-lamps over the highway snap on. The sky behind them is the color of a gum eraser—it tends to get that way in summer, something to do with landfill gases—so the brightness is nothing to write home about. Still, it puts a lump in the throat. The neon ninepin out front of BowlRight Lanes flicks through its angles of collapse. Bulbs flash on one of those wheeled letterboards, *NOW OPEN WEE DAYS AT 10*, referring either to Shenanigans Irish pub or the Greek Orthodox church next door. In the bays of the carwash just before the subdivision entrance, two sponges whirl like dingy sheepdogs, their dreadlocks reaching out for a car that is not there.

Some kind of circuit must have blown on his garage-door opener, too, for as he pulls into the drive the door is going up, then down, then up again. He can see Sherri's Thunderbird inside, which is odd, unless Patty came last night from Philadelphia to pick her up? He parks in the driveway. The slam of his door sounds overloud, even to him, and startles a few wrens from the neighbors' privacy hedge. It's possible he himself is a little frightened. You remember that saying, "Today is the first day of the rest of your life"? There's something awful about that saying. "Stay here," he mouths through the window, to the still-silent form in the passenger's seat. He stands and watches the garage door go up and down, up and down, a few more times before heading inside.

"Sherri?" He makes, by habit, to put his service revolver in the lockable drawer of the table by the front door, but then reconsiders and checks the safety. In the kitchen, the heating element on the coffeemaker has come on with the power, coaxing a curdled deli smell out of yesterday's coffee, but no one's there. Their bedroom, too, is empty, the bed with its motel corners. He heads upstairs, leaning heavily on the railing, hardly noticing another door-slam outside. Their bedroom used to be up here until about five years ago, when Sherri complained it was too big—a way of sparing his feelings— and they had movers come in and take everything downstairs to the smaller room where a son or daughter would have slept. Now she calls the old bedroom "a room of Sherri's own." She likes to sit on her papasan chair with an afghan in the winter months when the pool is covered over and have her tea and read her book. The curtains that are never drawn are drawn, and the room smells of candlewax, and it is here on the round chair that Pulaski finds his wife, curled up asleep with the earpiece of her little transistor radio in her ear.

He limps toward her, the shag of the carpet swallowing all sound, and when he's close enough takes out the earpiece. There is no noise. Either the battery died or she turned it off. "Sherr?" He pulls back one of the curtains. Light from the pool redoubles itself on the ceiling, building in wavery white lines, waves of light buffeting this little room. He wants to get closer to her, but to kneel now is basically impossible. He's stuck looking down, though it feels like she's the one above.

She opens her eyes. Their blue still startles. "Have you been up all night?" she says. It's not an angry question, but maybe she's beyond anger.

"I called. I thought maybe you went to Patricia's."

"Why don't you go to bed, Larry? We'll talk things over in the morning."

But he can't just go to bed. She's been right here the whole time, not ten miles from the Hamilton-Sweeney Building. "It is the morning," he says. "What things?"

"You know what things."

"Look at me, sweetheart." He grasps after the words. "They're going to be different from here on out. I'm going to be different."

"Larry, how can I trust you?" There follows a long period of looking at each other. Still, he can't quite read her face. Because this, too, takes work; when did he forget? Then she reaches up for the sleeve of his sportcoat. "I can't believe you're still wearing this, with this heat," she says. "You know you lost a button."

He wants her to keep on holding his arm, but it's too late to say anything. He limps back to the window, pulls his shield from his pocket. The sun seems hungry for it. How you identify yourself: with flashing metal. He pulls up the screen and side-arms the badge with an ease that surprises him. It arcs up, flapping its leather cover like a busted wing until he loses it for a minute in the light, and then it plops, perfect sound, in the shallows of the pool. "Hey!" a girl's voice says out there. "That was almost my head!"

She is under a flowering catalpa; the most he can see through the scrim of green is the shimmer of a Rangers jersey. "Old man?" she calls. "That you? Is it time for my entrance?"

He turns to look at Sherri. "Honey, you remember how you talked about needing projects to fill the time, if we were going to move upstate? I've got someone I think you should meet."

ANOTHER COAST—THREE WEEKS LATER

HE'D ALWAYS FOUND AIRPORTS SOOTHING SOMEHOW. The in-between-ness. So many bodies, superficially distinct, rushing along the terminals. After his previous misstep, during a decade of semi-exile, he'd spent months in these places, almost as much time as he'd spent in the air. ATL. TGU. MIA. Remarkable, even at the dreaded Paris-Orly, to feel oneself precipitate out of ten thousand other people, merely by refusing the rush. And, wasted time being the hand-maid of pointless hurry, he would use this suspension not to loaf, but to prepare for his return. His features were unmemorable. Lenses diluted his eyes. A hat hid his blank head. His luggage was plain and functional as only luggage can be and did not bear his name. He might sit at a gate not his own and assume the affect of a sales-man bound for Cleveland, his briefcase full of carpet samples. Or a Kentish auctioneer. A baker from Spokane. Or at a bar in one of the lounges strike up a conversation with whoever looked loneliest, and not a word from his mouth would have weight, nor would it matter. What mattered was setting a goal, however arbitrary, just at the outer limit of the attainable: the target would buy him a drink, say, or carry his bags to the gate. And how did he calibrate these goals, achieve the maximum available yet avoid the steep penalty for non-attainment he'd laid out for himself years ago? Through a patient estimation of his fellow travelers' secrets. It was secrets that bound people, he believed. Secrets always ready to hand. So many different secrets, and underneath—by virtue of their secrecy—the scandal of their same-ness. This one sex, this one drink, or some other, dreary shame.

And did this sameness still cover everything, in light of his own more recent failure? Arriving at LAX for the next leg of his flight, Amory Gould was beginning to wonder.

As he stepped from the cab to the bright sidewalk outside the concourse, a consternation of passengers, shirttails flapping, board-ing passes in hand, was flocked around a service counter. There had to be dozens of them, enough to fill a plane. He gathered, in short order, that there had been further setbacks, in this season of systemic malfunction. A mainframe down yesterday in the Rockies, delaying some connections, knocking out others. A cascade effect through all the nodes. And as he was habitually hours early for check-in, and as this irruption offered by its very difference a species of interest, he resolved to pause here at the edge of the edge, as it were, and to study what had lately puzzled him more than any individual: the psychology of a crowd. Yet when he moved to sit upon a nearby bollard, he found someone else already there, taking in the fray. A short woman of Asian extraction. Her baggage rested near her feet. Her sneakers did not quite touch the ground. And what brought him up short was less this than an intimation of affinity, as if she existed right here with him, outside. Above. Where most people wouldn't have noticed his approach she glanced over, watchful. Well, of course. From her perspective, it would seem as if he were the one seeking company. He struck a match. Bent to puff at his cigarette. "Quite a show, isn't it?"

"Is it?" Her alertness now revealed itself as partly exhaustion. "Sure, I guess it is."

When she declined his offer of a smoke, he returned matches to pack and pack to vest pocket. Had a long, melting drag. And evaluated her again. No, she seemed a promising guinea pig, if he could figure out what she might be made to do. "Business or pleasure?"

She seemed perplexed. "Beg pardon?"

"You'll indulge me. A little diversion I invented to pass the time, with all the travel I have to do for work. I look at a fellow passenger, and I try to guess: is it business or pleasure that brings him here. Then I find out if I'm right."

"Oh. I'm just out visiting family for a weekend. I'm not sure it counts as either anymore."

"Family does tend to take it out of one."

She looked a little embarrassed. "All of us here were scheduled to fly back to New York yesterday on a DC-10 that as far as I know is still refueling in Wichita. This is the second all-nighter I've pulled in a month."

He puffed again. The tremor of a raw nerve. What could it be? Aside from encounters with maids and at breezeway ice machines, it had been a while since he'd spoken to a flesh-and-blood human. Possibly his reflexes had slowed. But this was why it was good to practice. Anyway, her regrets themselves didn't matter; it was how they could be turned to account. "As it happens," he said, "I'm coming from

New York myself. Well, came some weeks ago now. Just after the blackout. You must have been in it, too."

She looked at him.

"See, I knew there was something about you," he continued. "But I do wonder that someone your age, your whole life ahead, would even bother to go back. In fact, it's what convinced me to pull up stakes. A whole city, effectively irredeemable."

"That's funny, because there was a moment not too long ago when I had this idea the good guys might be returning to take the joint over. A little colony of light . . ." She caught herself. Though was that still wistfulness in her voice? "Anyway, I don't have much choice but to go back. I start graduate school at the end of the month. But what about you? On to bigger and better things?"

"Hong Kong," he said, which was true, if provisional. As this had been provisional, this long layover in a city he detested, holed up in his wretched airport hotel, waiting for the knock that would mean federal agents, and meanwhile working the phone. He'd assumed his new life would wend south, into the shade of the Subcomandante. But it had become widely known that Amory Gould had had a falling-out with his sponsors. The merchant bank to which an old associate had matched his hastily forged résumé was in Asia. Asia, about which he was trying to be optimistic. And perhaps this was more optimism, more striving, but he realized now what he might convince her of, and in so doing prove himself to himself. "I don't suppose you've been?"

"I've never been west of Mendocino. Not since I was three." Her expression had hardened a little. Perhaps he'd been wrong about women after all. She was obviously bright. And was that an announcement, sounding behind this ungovernable mob? He made his tone soft, confiding.

"You know, your bag is already packed, if you would prefer to spend your last weeks of freedom on a real adventure, rather than return so soon to that difficult city." No turning back now; careful. "There are trans-Pacific flights boarding, even at present . . ."

"You ever tried to change a ticket on this short a notice?"

"Call it a whim, but perhaps I could help."

"You're right, that's a hell of a whim." There it was again, wistfulness. Hesitation. The pressure of the withheld.

"Let's just say I've been fortunate in life," he says. "Fortunate and driven. Nothing makes me happier than helping a young person of similar drive. You could return to school this fall with at least a bit more of the world under your belt. And we've lived through something together, you and I. There is a certain confraternity. In any case, it wouldn't be a gift so much as a loan."

"I wouldn't know where to send the repayment. You haven't even told me your name."

"Or I'm sure an open return could be arranged. Isn't an open ticket what people like us are looking for, really?" Beyond the immediate assurance that he was still the man he'd been, he was seeing already a future where in five or ten or fifteen years it would work its way back to him, this favor, through the grid of connections he would throw across the jungles and the plains. He was being forced to reinvent himself—unless of course one was only ever always inventing oneself—and he would need to seed favors in this new quadrant of the world, people who could help him translate his ambitions into actualities. Or what was this all for? Still he was mindful to hold on to his Exigente, the dizzy ember. The edge of the edge of the edge . . .

"It's a generous offer, really, mister, for being so fucking impulsive," she said. She worried a clasp on her carry-on. Then she shrugged. "But we're just not the same. Even if it might take me a long hard time to know what they are, I've still got things to find out back there. So thanks again, but I should go buy a danish, and a magazine. It looks like I might have a while yet to wait."

And she was gone from the bollard before he could respond, plunging herself into the mass of Manhattoes and tourists all jostling the beleaguered skycap who had no planes under his control. It was as if she'd never really been here. Amory concentrated. Tried to send himself into the skycap. Or past the crowd, into that girl. There may have been something wrong with him after all. Along his arm now he could feel the firm circles under the soft white cloth, the little map they made of his corrections, the freshest not a month old. He would not have thought he'd be adding to it so soon. But Amory Gould was nothing if not hard-nosed, and was already turning slightly away from the crowd, and without looking down beginning to remove the cufflink from his rumpled but still beautiful sleeve. You can get away with anything right out in the open, so long as you don't look down.

HELL'S KITCHEN—FOREVER

BUT RIGHT NOW it's still some time before dawn. William Hamilton-Sweeney sits on a futon he can barely see, fondling the Nikkormat the kid left in the kitchen back on Central Park West. It's been years since he touched a camera, but he knows the button won't work unless you first push this lever thing. It makes a ratcheting sound when he thumbs it. Snick, goes the shutter. Ratchet. Snick. He probably should have checked to see if he's wasting actual film, but sometimes when he gets going like this, it's almost impossible to stop. It's mostly to distract himself from the fascination of the button, then, that he raises the viewfinder to his eye. The window of the loft has lightened enough since his return that he can pick out the cat perched on the sill, but when he calls her name, she won't look at him. She's not his anymore, if she ever was. He pans to the futon's black cushion, where the letter from his father lies creased into thirds. He has half a mind to take a match to it, but what good would that do? Certain lines are already lodged too deeply in his brain to burn them out without also destroying part of himself. Which he's discovering he's loath to do. Snick.

One risks less . . . that entire world inside . . . Really, the problem these phrases point to is one of foreshortening. It isn't that he's been wrong about what was in his father's heart, so much as that the universe of his own feelings keeps crowding everyone else's out. It is a constant struggle to see other people as people, rather than as denizens of a dimension one level below the one in which he's doomed to wander, imperially alone. That someone close to him might right now be awake in a different part of the city, feeling a pain every bit as real as his own . . . he can *think* it, but cannot seem to remember it. And is "remember" even the right word for something for which you have zero empirical evidence? Postulate, maybe. Imagine. He sweeps the lens back toward the window, where the cat hasn't stirred. Her tail twitches. An idea threatens to form, but doesn't.

Then there's a commotion out in the stairwell. Probably some straggling Angel. There were several of them passed out on the landings when he came in, and you could just tell from the liquid squelch beneath the feet and the spiritual reek of their snores that there had been many, many more here in the course of the night, doing what Angels do. But when something starts to rattle the lock on the far side of the pebble-glass, he is suddenly afraid. Light from the skylight frames a huge-headed man. He realizes just as the door swings open that the head is hair—that the man is Mercer—and has only a microsecond to make himself seem normal. And what could be more normal, in New York City, than a person with a camera to his eye? The little focal circle floats over cracked eyeglasses. A black eye. A beard. A split lip. It's like William's got the lens backward somehow; he should be the one standing there, beheld and wondered at. Not that he can say this. "Well, it looks like someone had a night to remember."

There is an impossible pause. Then, as if William isn't even there, Mercer lumbers toward the window to greet Eartha. Through the viewfinder, the room with all its shadows seems too large to cross, but William is up and crossing it. He can smell Mercer's sweat, and the spice of . . . is that pot? He reaches for a shoulder, trying not to feel excited.

"No, really. What happened, Merce?"

Mercer slips out of range of the hand. "You have no right to be here."

"But I wanted to see you," William says, which has the virtue of being true. This would be easier if they could see each other's faces. Easier or harder—one or the other.

"Oh, for once, William, can we please drop the pretense that you have any idea what you want? You go purely on impulse, is what you do. And as soon as you get an impulse to run back out of here, you'll leave again." Mercer keeps shifting to the left and the right, trying to get to the door. Finally, he slips free. "I'm going out again. When I come back, I want you gone."

He slams the door so hard it seems the glass might break. But the feet in the stairwell, instead of descending, head up to the roof. And William is left standing here like an idiot. There is water, somehow, between the windowpanes. It has beaded up in one corner and elsewhere left ghostly tiger-stripes on the glass. Beyond it, Mercer's cinderblock planter is a graveyard. The sky is the dark purple-gray of a bruise. Again, the idea threatens to come. Something about showing versus saying. But how to gesture at the thing doing the gesturing? Coffee—is that the idea?

Five minutes later, the damp stairs are again squelching beneath his Chucks. The door at the top is half-open, the bottles massed on the uppermost step burning with the imminence of morning. This used to be where he came to savor his isolation. Like all large canvases, his city required that: a place far enough away to step back and view it. He would run into Bullet up here, might even plunk down next to him and have a beer or three, and still, a certain inwardness obtained. He was a connoisseur of that inwardness. Still is. But his city is changing now. There will be waves of new pioneers, like the Angels stretched out here and there on the tarpaper, sleeping off the blackout. Or unlike them, who knows? And where has Mercer gone? To the top of the giant "O" of the Knickerbocker Mints sign. He sits there Indian-style, eight or nine feet up, like a thumbtack pinning this present to the past. There's enough light now to make him look broody, solitary. Adult.

William stands below. "Hey, look at us. Breaking night." That local idiom has always rung heroic in his ears, but Mercer has never before—even in their earliest dating—managed to make it all the way till dawn. And he says nothing now.

"Anyway, I brought you something." On tiptoe, William reaches up to place the mug of coffee from downstairs beside Mercer. Then, hunching forward for balance, he scurries up the sloped girder that supports the *O*. He settles at the letter's opposite end, maybe an arm's length away, with the coffee between them. It's El Bandito Instant, but smells so good he's tempted to try it. N.A. has habituated him to the lowliest swill, from the biggest, most burnt-smelling urns. It occurs to him to tell his unresponsive lover about the meetings, so he does. Since kicking methadone, he's been going almost daily, hanging in. "It's sort of the substitution of one set of addictions for another. But I did just get my first chip. Clean and sober thirty days. I thought you should know before you read me the riot act."

Mercer looks away. The light is rising steadily around him, as though operated by sliders on some cosmic mixing board. Objects acquire shadows. Away to the south are the trade towers, the farther hiding behind the nearer like a child behind its mother. William raises the camera. Lowers it.

"Another thing is, I saw my dad. I mean I didn't just see him. I sat with him through most of last night. He's kind of losing his marbles."

At this, Mercer finally turns to look at him. One eye is nearly swollen shut. The other's so brown as to look black.

"It actually makes things easier, it turns out. The loss of marbles, I mean, not the sobriety. Although I suppose it's made Daddy vulnerable to people who don't have his best interests at heart. A category that possibly includes me. Anyway, it looks like we might be seeing more of each other, so that's something, right?" A blaze of red has appeared at the tip of the gray north tower. "It's a good thing I speak silence so fluently, Mercer."

"What's left to say, William? I don't know what it feels like to be whacked-out on drugs, and you obviously have no idea what it feels like to wait around for half a year for your lover to call."

William wonders if there is an exposure long enough to capture the range of looks Mercer is giving him. "So help me understand."

"Understand what? How every time the phone rang, my heart would catch? How I almost wanted you to be dead in a gutter somewhere? Because I must have known even then this was what would happen instead. You'd come back knocking and knocking and working on me like this to let you in. But when were you ever going to let *me* in, William?"

Ah. So there it is: Mercer is no longer unaware of the essential predicament. He has discovered its exact dimensions—that his body is a dwelling built for one. But William feels now, in his longing to reach Mercer, that he's stumbling upon a door. One that, all this time, has been locked from inside. Snick.

"I wasn't telling you that stuff because I expected you to take me back, Merce. I just wanted you to see what you gave me. I was probably too slow to see it. I know there was something I was too slow to see."

The red blur, tinged with distance, is racing down the east edge of the trade center at the rate of the earth's turning. It is as if the building is on fire. *Photographic*, he thinks. *Written in light.* And then, nonsensically: *Pornography. Written in porn.*

"You're going to make me say it, aren't you?"

"Say what?"

"No, you're right, probably it makes no difference." He reaches for the warm brown hand resting on the verge of the aught, but it's already slipping out from underneath as Mercer drops down to the roof proper, leaving the coffee behind. He's moving with such purpose that William is scared he might just speed right off the rooftop, like the roadrunner from the cartoons. Or (the image comes with Magritteish lucidity) spread his arms and flap up into another life. In this one, of course, neither is possible—Mercer will stop at the parapet, as close as he can get to his first New York sunrise—but William still is not ready to be limited to mere possibility. He wants to freeze Mercer Goodman like this, the way he looks through the viewfinder, against the vanishing city. Behind the bones of its buildings, a red line is rising out there, the leading edge of a curve that might keep arcing outward forever. The tiny specks of black poised against it may be the first birds of morning or the last ones of night . . . or the ashes of a thousand incinerators, or incipient blindness, he doesn't know which yet, but surely there's a message here, if he can just look hard enough. A sign. A sight. An end or a beginning. He holds off on pushing the button another second, another second. And one more after that. Because if he plays his cards right, William feels, if he can just stop trying to race out ahead of himself, one of these moments is going to prove decisive.

POSTSCRIPT

THIS CITY, WHICH NOT TO LOOK UPON

WOULD BE LIKE DEATH

Nothing dies; all is transformed.

—BALZAC
Pensées, sujets, fragments

TO: reganlamplighter@hotmail.com
SUBJECT: Re: Disposition of Estate/Evidence III
8/27/03, 4:52 a.m.
ATTACHMENT: TCWNTLUWBLD.doc

First, Mom, let me say I owe you an apology, not least for the lateness
in replying to your email of 7/14. If it helps, you were right about almost
everything, including how much longer all this would take than I
estimated. I seem to need to believe a piece of work will be easier than
it is in order to begin it. Which is at least doubly true here, in that we're
talking about more than one kind of work. These last weeks, I've been
at the laptop all day and half the night just to get my notebooks typed
up. The good news, though, is that as of the close of this email, it's
done, I think. And I finally settled on a way of presenting the third part of
the triptych that feels true to what Uncle William was after. Augenblick
introduced me to a computer programmer he knows up in Murray Hill.
Now there's a little piece of software logging every keystroke. Including
these.

You'll notice that all traces of the U.S.S.R. not collapsing in '89 and
John Travolta becoming leader of the free world have been weeded
out of the attached document; you were right about that, too, and I'm
sorry for blowing up at you for reacting as you did to that first, more
fantastical schema. I was in a bad way at the time. I felt like your
resistance on principle to posthumous exhibitions was overriding your
ability to see what I needed. In my defense, artistically speaking, I think
I really was trying to demonstrate the possibility of things being other
than they are. But of course what I've learned is that you can't prove
most of the things that matter; it seems to be a violation of the rules,
which require you rather to dream. Besides, the nature of life on earth
is so breathtakingly unschematic. It ended up being both cleaner and
more honest, somehow, to leave open the whole question of ontology,
preserve some freedom of play. I mean, you and I both know that
all this really happened—I've got the documentation here—but I've
found that even in a courtroom, documents are increasingly unlikely
to persuade the unpersuadable. And thinking about issues of legal
indemnity, not to mention the larger implications, maybe it's better to
leave room for people who still need to imagine "Evidence III" as some

sort of fairy tale. Certainly, for me, it's been that, among other things: a path to somewhere other than the awful place I was last winter.

I'm aware that I'm falling back into it even now, the habit you pointed out to me. Cleverness as a defense mechanism. "Intellectualizing." Or should I say temporizing? The bald fact I'm avoiding writing about is that after our long summer apart, Julia is due in tomorrow night, which is now tonight. (You can see from the timestamp above how well I'm sleeping, but I'm happy to report no bad dreams.) And when I think of her plane touching down, her voice, the fact that maybe since we last spoke she's changed her mind about being willing to do whatever it takes—to surrender me for three months to this mitzvah—I get nervous. Though sometimes nervous can be good. I hope this is one of those times. The truth is, I missed her awfully, Mom. Miss her.

But anyway, as regards the first part of your email, the plan is: vitrines. Those plexiglass containers like in the D. Hearst (Hurst?) installation with the shark. Augenblick is having sixteen of them made to my specifications, long low things with frames of reclaimed wood. The "Evidence III" material will be distributed among them and sealed permanently inside—all those archives from '77, the fanzines and Groskoph's manuscripts and so on, but also Uncle William's correspondence and interview transcripts from the fall of 2001, when he was getting back in touch with what his diary calls (with a level of sarcasm not ascertainable on the page) "the old gang." In keeping with the idea of leaving room for other people's New Yorks, you'll be able to see in these vitrines the paper trail I followed here, though not all of it. They'll line the front room of the gallery, the one you enter through.

In the other, larger room, the walls will remain big white blanks. In the center will be rows of chairs facing four ways, and likewise four projectors. The night of the opening, Augenblick will press "play" on his computer and the little piece of software I mentioned above will run like a player piano. Over the course of the next ten days, the walls will fill up with projected pages from this attachment, 220-odd sheets per wall, as though a ghost were writing. And then, at the midpoint of the exhibition, which is to say when the entire document has been "typed" onto the wall, the program starts to run backward, and over the final ten days, letter by letter, page by page, the whole thing disappears.

Augenblick's arranged to keep the gallery open day and night during that time: people can come and go at all hours. Afterward, I guess he'll sell the vitrines, assuming the Feds don't swoop in and impound them in Area 51 or wherever they bury the cases they just want to go away. Any proceeds, minus his commission, will be added to Uncle William's estate, and thus pass to you. But I've already told Augenblick he can't have my end of the piece, attached here. (Into which, hoping you don't mind, I will also paste this email as a postscript.) As of September 30, your inbox will hold the sole copy. What happens after that I leave to your executorial judgment. The important thing for me, I want to believe, is to put all the ghosts to rest. To feel like it is done.

As for our itinerary, Julia has us flying back to LAX the 12th, the day after opening night. I know she's right. It's time. In a way, though, as much as I'm feeling now an incredible and totally unexpected gratitude for the life I do have—and as much as I mean never again to let her go—I wish we could stay in New York for the full run of "Evidence III " I find myself curious, especially, to see who fills the chairs. Mostly Augenblick's black-jeaned disciples, probably, and a few members of the press. But, crazy as it is, I'm imagining Mercer Goodman might come, too. I only ever met him that one time at Thanksgiving, obviously, but found him amazingly understanding and helpful on the phone, and (though perhaps you already know this) he and his husband Rafe apparently flew over from Paris there at the end to help Uncle William with cooking and cleaning and getting down to the new park along the Hudson every so often to see the sunset. And I've invited the Pulaskis, for whom I insisted there be space for a wheelchair. And maybe Charlie Weisbarger got my email after all and will take a few days off from his work with juvenile offenders in Boston. I'd like to meet him in person. I'd like nothing better, Mom, than to have a chance to reintroduce you.

And this brings me to the most unexpected thing of all: the people whose faces I'd most like to see watching the thing unfold (not counting Julia's) are yours and Dad's. Maybe you sensed all along what the outcome of this summer would be—maybe it's why you helped arrange for this apartment—but I find I'm not mad at either of you anymore. Can't stop trying to think my way into you, in fact.

I find myself recalling, in particular, how the morning after the blackout, the two of you came back to Brooklyn Heights together. Do you remember? Cate was snoring on the new master bed, doing that cocooning she always did with the covers. I was stretched across the foot, pretending to sleep. The light was everywhere. Dad was the one who spotted on the windowsill the wine-bottle I'd half-emptied in the night (and which—let's be honest—I probably left there to be found). Through slitted eyes, I saw him turn to you, swirling it around by the neck. And you were the one who shrugged. Please, Keith, let them just sleep. You were wearing my sneakers. You used to have this certain way of taking off your shoes, kicking up each leg behind you and reaching back. I watched you swap out the sweatshirt you'd been wearing for a white V-neck tee Dad seemed surprised to recognize was his own. And then you climbed into bed and folded yourself into the space between me and Cate and closed your eyes. I wonder now if you meant for him to feel tested. Stay or go? Either way, the knowledge of what he'd done was going to follow him. Either way, there would be constraint. It occurs to me that what adulthood actually is is the problem of what one wants to constrain oneself to.

There was still a narrow strip of real estate along the bed's edge, I'm remembering, on the far side of Cate. He squatted to untie his own shoes and then stretched out on his side there, gingerly, as if we were about to wake up at any minute and tell him he had to go. And just then I thought of a story he'd told me when I was nine or ten, when I asked if he actually believed in God. The story was about Cate's birth; at first I couldn't see the connection. But everything had slowed down in the final stages before the crowning, he said, and the doctors who came periodically into the waiting room seemed concerned. One mentioned a surgical option, if something didn't change in the next minutes. You were exhausted, I think, and they were concerned a labor this long could put the baby into distress. "I wasn't sure if I did or didn't believe," Dad said, "but when that doctor left, I went into the bathroom and bolted myself into a stall and got down on my knees on the floor anyway." Did he ever tell you this? The prayer was, characteristically, a kind of trade. "Let this baby be okay, and let Regan be okay, and I will give up caring about anything else."

God, questions of existence aside, apparently held up His end of the contract, but I think now that Dad, for years afterward, had been feeling himself to be more or less in breach. I'm not making excuses, understand. Just saying I can sympathize. But then, would God really be a God who asked him to give up caring—who wanted everything? Maybe what Dad had learned the night of the blackout was that in fact he didn't care about anything else, at least not in the same way he cared about me and Cate. And you. The way I think he still does care. I know, at least, that as I pretended to sleep that morning, I could feel him lying stiffly on his side, trying to feel his way back to the people who were right there, breathing.

And now here I am myself in much the same position, in this too-nice apartment on West Sixteenth Street. Groping. Feeling, as the sun comes up over the pavement outside. I'm imagining myself in the Galerie Bruno Augenblick, in some third space, watching through a slit in the wall as Dad reads these words, and you do. I'm trying to figure out what I want them to say here, where the tide of type has washed farthest up the walls, before the white starts to eat away at it again and the whole fucking thing dwindles away to a nothing that's either meaningless or not. Or no; I'm imagining all of us here, in this third place, together. It's a private space, or private-ish, but one finally big enough to leave room for other people. Dad's there, and Julia, and Cate and Mercer and Samantha and the Prophet Charlie. And you're there in the dark right next to me, Mom, your hand in my hand. Waiting for the end. Knowing each other as we do, we probably wouldn't need to say anything out loud. But I guess what I would want to leave each of you with finally—tender some Evidence of, against a life's worth of signs to the contrary—comes down simply to this: You are infinite. I see you. You are not alone.

ACKNOWLEDGMENTS

A book is a shared labor. Grateful acknowledgment for this one goes first to Diana Tejerina Miller, its editor, and to Chris Parris-Lamb, its agent.

Huge thanks also to their colleagues: Andy Kifer, Rebecca Gardner, Will Roberts, and all at the Gernert Company; Maggie Hinders, Chip Kidd, Paul Bogaards, Nicholas Latimer, Maggie Southard, Amy Ryan, Lydia Buechler, Andrew Miller, Carol Carson, Andy Hughes, Roméo Enriquez, Oliver Munday, Loriel Oliver, Betsy Sallee, Robin Desser, LuAnn Walther, Sonny Mehta, and all at Knopf; U.K. editor Alex Bowler, Joe Pickering, and the team at Cape.

Further support and inspiration came from: Naomi Lebowitz, the Insight Lady of St. Louis; the faculty of Washington University; Brian Morton; all at NYU/CWP; the New York Foundation for the Arts; Matthew Elblonk; Scott Rudin, Eli Bush, Sylvie Rabineau; C. Max Magee and *The Millions*; early readers Buzz Poole, Janice Clark, Jordan Alport, Fridolin Schley, and Jürgen Christian Kill; Gary Sernovitz, Ron Hibshoosh, and the New York Public Library (especially David Smith and Jay Barksdale) for a measure of factual footing; Patti Smith, Lou Reed, the Clash, Springsteen, the Who, Talking Heads, Fugazi; Woodley Road '96 (D.T., M.M., Walker Lambert, Chris Eichler, Barton Seaver, Nuria Ferrer, Daron Carreiro, Kevin Mullin, the Sports); MDG; NYC; Vicki and Claude Kennedy; Bill and Christy Hallberg; Rachel Coley; Amos and Walter Hallberg.

Finally, and always, the deepest debt is to Elise White.

ON SOURCES

Paige Harbert and Derek Teslik graciously gave permission for the remixing of elements (images, editorial choices, two guest columns, and a trip to the diner) from their respective 'zines, *Firefly Cupboard* and *Helter Skelter*, themselves works of folk art whose tributaries reach back as far as the Yippies. Though misapprehensions and outright fantasies are attributable to Richard Groskoph and his author, "The Fireworkers, Part 1" is studded with bits of pyrotechnic detail, lore, taxonomy, mise-en-scène, and bibliana taken from *Fireworks*, George Plimpton's beautiful book on the subject. In particular, Richard's three paragraphs on the manufacture of a "bomb" lean heavily on Plimpton's reporting. The images on pages 295 and 751 appeared in *Fireworks*, too. Several background incidents and a line of dialogue in Book VII were reported in *Blackout*, by James Goodman. Though the text of the novel draws on too many books, songs, films, and people to name here, Ken Auletta's *The Streets Were Paved with Gold*, Jonathan Mahler's *Ladies and Gentlemen, the Bronx Is Burning*, Legs McNeil's and Gillian McCain's *Please Kill Me*, Philip Gourevitch's *A Cold Case*, Joan Didion's "Sentimental Journeys," and the anthologies *New York Calling* (Marshall Berman and Brian Berger, eds.), and *Up Is Up, but So Is Down* (Brandon Stosuy, ed.) were among the key resources—as were, in a different vein, Douglas R. Hofstadter's *Gödel, Escher, Bach* and Gregory Bateson's *Steps to an Ecology of Mind*. The zen koan is a condensation of one quoted in Hofstadter. Some slight mishearing or forgetting may inflect the quotations of song lyrics in this novel; certain Scriptural passages depart subtly from extant translations; and the title of the third interlude (give or take a word) comes from an artwork by Damien Hirst. Finally, it should be noted that those seeking the ur-text for Nina Simone's iconic performance, "In the Dark," can seek Lil Green's song under its original title: "Romance in the Dark."

Garth Risk Hallberg was born in Louisiana and grew up in North Carolina. His writing has appeared in *Prairie Schooner*, *The New York Times*, *Best New American Voices 2008*, and, most frequently, *The Millions*; a novella, *A Field Guide to the North American Family*, was published in 2007. He lives in New York with his wife and children.

A NOTE ON THE TYPE

This book was set in Janson, a typeface named after Anton Janson, who was a practicing typefounder in Leipzig during the years 1668–87 The type is actually the work of Nicholas Kis (1650–1702), a Hungarian, who most probably learned his trade from the master Dutch typefounder Dirk Voskens.

Composed by North Market Street Graphics, Lancaster, Pennsylvania

Printed and bound by RR Donnelley, Crawfordsville, Indiana

Designed by Maggie Hinders